ORIGINAL SIN

Also by Tasmina Perry

Daddy's Girls
Gold Diggers
Guilty Pleasures

TASMINA PERRY

Original Sin

HarperCollins*Publishers*

HarperCollins*Publishers*
77–85 Fulham Palace Road,
Hammersmith, London W6 8JB

www.harpercollins.co.uk

Published by HarperCollins*Publishers* 2009
1

A catalogue record for this book
is available from the British Library

ISBN: 978 0 00 726554 1 (hbk)
ISBN: 978 0 00 726556 5 (tbk)

This novel is entirely a work of fiction.
The names, characters and incidents portrayed in it are
the work of the author's imagination. Any resemblance to
actual persons, living or dead, events or localities is
entirely coincidental.

Set in Sabon by Palimpsest Book Production Ltd,
Grangemouth, Stirlingshire

Printed and bound in Great Britain by
Clays Ltd, St Ives plc

Mixed Sources
Product group from well-managed
forests and other controlled sources
www.fsc.org Cert no. SW-COC-1806
© 1996 Forest Stewardship Council
FSC

FSC is a non-profit international organization established
to promote the responsible management of the world's forests.
Products carrying the FSC label are independently certified
to assure consumers that they come from forests that are managed
to meet the social, economic and ecological needs
of present and future generations.

Find out more about HarperCollins and the environment at
www.harpercollins.co.uk/green

Acknowledgments

I would like to thank the following people: my parents, Farrah, Damian, Daniel and Fin who are always there for me and provide continuous support, ideas and encouragement. Mum especially, you're a complete star. Also John Kelly, Quentin Humberstone, Sam Baker, Margi Conklin, Niki Browes, Camilla Kay, Lisa Oxenham, Victoria Moss, Louise Roe, Kerry Potter, Jacqui Swift, Natasha Hunter. I am also hugely grateful to Jonathan – I couldn't think of a better lunch companion to steer me through the waters of publicity and crisis management. And to George in Maui and the Riley's in Ventura County – thank you for your rooms with a view!

I am fortunate to have such a dedicated agent Sheila Crowley and a wise and wonderful editor Wayne Brookes, who always knows what's right for my books and has made the last four years of my working life such a pleasure. Thank you, thank you, thank you.

Continued thanks to the terrific team at Harper Collins: Amanda Ridout, Lee Motley, Wendy Neale, Clive Kintoff and the rest of the sales, publicity and marketing team – I'll always be grateful for your hard work, help and support. And a special mention to the production department, including Penny Isaac, for making my deadline stretch when this book got longer and longer – and later and later.

And finally, to my beloved John – captain of the Pez Gang, obtainer of rare antiquities, sound-board and editor par excellence and all-round hero – I couldn't do it without you.

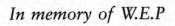

In memory of W.E.P

Prologue

Confidential magazine
September 18, 1964

Pill-popping starlet feared dead after wedding vanishing act
Friends of the Hollywood actress, Olivia Martin, who mysteriously disappeared after the Louisiana wedding of cosmetics mogul Howard Asgill at the family's Riverview Estate, now fear she might have taken her own life by means of a fatal late-night walk into the Mississippi River after consuming a cocktail of barbiturates. Martin was last seen leaving the $50,000 nuptials of Asgill and New Orleans socialite Meredith Carter just before midnight last Saturday. When Mr Asgill noticed her absence at the lavish brunch the next day, the newlyweds assumed that Olivia, known for her colourful love life, had left the celebrations with another guest.

But when she had not appeared forty-eight hours later, Martin's sister Valerie filed a missing persons report, and Louisiana police began their inquiries.

River of death
Friends of the *After the Sunset* actress began assuming the worst when Louisiana State Police found prescription drugs in the guest cottage where Miss Martin was staying on the Carter family estate. So far police have not trawled the Mississippi, which runs just one hundred feet past the guest cottage and is almost one mile wide at this point. If the theory of a death plunge is true, investigators fear the body of the actress might never be found.

Haunted by Hollywood rejection

Insiders say the twenty-seven-year-old redhead had been sliding into depression after her contract with MGM Studios was cancelled in 1961 and a highly anticipated television career flopped. However, last year Martin signed a five-figure contract to be the face of Asgill Long-last Lipstick. She had proved so successful for the brand that the company had her lips insured for $1 million. But her modelling success was no substitute for her acting career, and a slide into drink and prescription-drug addiction was well known to those around her.

Dark cloud over wedding

Although the search for Miss Martin continues, her disappearance has cast a dark cloud over one of the most stellar society events of the season. Ava Gardner, Gregory Peck and Anita Ekberg were just some of the guests at the Asgill wedding. The CEO of Asgill Cosmetics was the butcher's son from Brooklyn who turned a home-brewed face cream into a multimillion-dollar cosmetics company. Meredith and Howard Asgill, currently on honeymoon in Capri, Italy, issued a statement yesterday expressing their concern. 'Olivia is a dear friend and wonderful ambassador for Asgill Cosmetics. We pray for her swift and safe return home.'

1

Present day, London

'Wake up. I've got something for you.'

Tess Garrett forced her eyes open and peered over the top of her duvet to see her flatmate Jemma Davies sitting on the bed.

'You gave me a fright. What time is it?' sighed Tess, casting her glance to the bedside clock next to her. *Five thirty*! As deputy editor of one of the UK's Sunday tabloids she was used to early starts, but the birds weren't even singing yet. As her eyes adjusted to the light, she saw that her friend was dressed head to toe in black.

'What are you wearing?' asked Tess warily. 'You look like a cat burglar.'

'Come on, shake a leg,' said Jemma, bouncing on the mattress impatiently, 'this is important!'

'So is my sleep,' mumbled Tess, pulling the covers back over her head.

Seeing that Tess was going to take some shifting, Jemma stood up again.

'Okay, I'll go and make some tea. Then we can talk. Five minutes, okay?'

As soon as Jemma had left the bedroom, Tess heard a muffled groan coming from under the pillow next to her.

'You know I can't hear you through six inches of goose down,' said Tess.

A hand flung back the pillow and the handsome face of her boyfriend Dom Barton popped up, squinting into the light.

'I said, "Remind me when Jemma said she was moving out?"'

'Shhh! Keep your voice down,' said Tess, peering through the

3

open bedroom door where she could see Jemma filling the kettle in the galley kitchen across the hall. 'Cut her a bit of slack, eh? She's been through a rough time.'

'She finished with Chris three months ago, Tess,' hissed Dom, leaning back on his elbows. 'Plus, the flat is a tip, and how can I use the study to write my book when all of Jemma's belongings are in it?'

Tess glanced around and had to admit that things were a tight squeeze in their two-bedroomed Battersea flat, but Jemma was her best friend's sister, she had known her since school; and besides, Jemma's line of work sometimes came in handy.

'Honey, you are never going to write that novel, with or without anyone living in our spare room. You've been talking about it for as long as I've known you. Come on. It's time to get up anyway. Your flight leaves at eight thirty – shouldn't you be at Heathrow in an hour?'

Dom was the deputy travel editor of the broadsheet, the *Sunday Chronicle*, which meant he was on some exotic press trip at least once a month. Groaning, he slid out of bed, scratching his tousled hair. Tess rubbed her eyes as she watched his gym-honed bum cheeks vanish into their en-suite bathroom. Jemma returned with two mugs of tea and thrust one towards Tess.

'So, what's worth a five thirty summit meeting?' Tess smiled.

Jemma took a slurp of tea. 'I've been to a Venus party,' she said with a grin.

Tess's eyes opened wide and she sat cross-legged on the bed, feeling suddenly energized. Jemma was a paparazzo photographer who usually sold her work into one of the big picture agencies, but sometimes Tess asked her to work on solo projects for her. Tess had been hearing rumours of organized 'membership only' sex parties in London for years but, despite the best efforts of Fleet Street's finest, no one had ever been able to track them down. She had begun to suspect they were one of those wishful-thinking urban myths, like Diana's love child, but, around three months ago, Jemma had got the scent of a new underground scene called 'Venus parties' and the whisper was that they took decadence to a whole new level. Understandably, access to them was near impossible – entry was via personal recommendation and the vetting process rigorous – but the guest list was said to be dynamite: senior politicians, Hollywood stars and players, high-ranking police, Premiership footballers – and that was just for starters. Tess had put Jemma on a retainer to work on tracking them down.

'There was a Venus party last night at a big house in Wycombe Square out in St John's Wood,' said Jemma gleefully. 'I got in.'

'That's fantastic,' said Tess, barely able to hide her excitement. 'How on earth did you get past the checks?'

Jemma glanced behind her, making sure that Dom was still in the shower. Tess understood; Dom might have been her boyfriend, but he still worked for a rival publication.

'I was a security guard,' she whispered.

Tess laughed. 'You? A bouncer?'

Although she was dressed completely in black, the pocket-sized busty blonde looked more like a glamour model than a security guard.

'Don't laugh,' said Jemma huffily. 'These parties need women at the door. Ironically they're to frisk the female guests to make sure nobody's taking in cameras. It took me two months to get the gig. I had to moonlight on the door of a club in Chelsea first.'

'Was it worth it?'

Jemma smiled. 'Oh yes.'

Tess was practically salivating; this would be an excellent story at any time, but Jemma's timing was perfect. All week she had been acting editor of the *Sunday Globe*. Her boss Andy Davidson was on holiday and she had picked up the reins. This could be her big chance to make her mark.

'So, come on,' she said impatiently, 'who was there?'

Jemma rattled off a list of household names. 'There were a few Hollywood names as well. I had the misfortunate of seeing that foul producer Larry Goldman in the buff. He has man-breasts the size of space-hoppers.'

'What about photos? We need photos.'

In her twelve years in newspapers, the unwritten law had always been 'assume they won't sue', and Tess had always found that it was an accurate enough yardstick. She had a little black book of litigious stars and those who rarely took legal action, but when anybody did seek to challenge a story they had printed, the onus was on the newspaper to prove what they had written was true. That was why photographs were essential for a story like this.

'The quality isn't great,' said Jemma, opening her laptop to flick through the digital images she had taken. 'I used a spy camera that I'd hidden in the house during the afternoon.'

Tess leaned over her shoulder and pointed at an image of a flaxen-haired blonde. 'Who's *this*?' she asked. The woman was wearing nothing but a strap-on and a Venetian mask and stood astride a naked fat man on his hands and knees.

'That's Larry.'

'But who's the woman?' said Tess hopefully.

Jemma shrugged. 'Some hooker, I think.'

Tess's excitement was starting to wane. So far, this wasn't the big-noise story she was hoping for. Ten years ago, a cheating MP had been front-page news; but today hookers and studio heads did not shift newspapers like footballers and soap stars.

'Do we have anything clearer of a bigger name?' she asked hopefully. 'What about a soap actress?'

'How about this?' said Jemma, enlarging an image with a triumphant look.

The picture was grainy. The man in the shot was naked and bent over what appeared to be a line of cocaine. Tess frowned and squinted.

'Don't you recognize him?'

Tess shook her head. 'Who is it?'

'Well, maybe you'll see better in this one.'

Jemma clicked onto an image of a black van. You could clearly make out that somebody was being carried into the back of it on a stretcher.

'Shit,' said Tess, her eyes widening. 'What's going on here?'

'The same guy being stretchered into a private ambulance,' said Jemma with a smile. 'He's at a private hospital in North London now.'

'So who is it?' asked Tess.

'Sean Asgill.'

It took Tess a second to recognize the name. Sean Asgill was a New York playboy. Heir to a cosmetics family fortune. Handsome and wealthy, he was a fixture in the society pages with a string of model and actress girlfriends. It was a headline all right: 'Tragedy at A-list Sex Party.'

'Christ,' said Tess. 'Did he . . . die?'

Tess felt bad asking, but it was an occupational hazard for someone in her job, wishing the worst on people because it made a better headline.

'I followed the ambulance on my scooter and I told the nurse I was family. She told me it was a suspected ketamine overdose. Asgill probably thought it was a line of coke. Apparently he's in a coma. I hung around for a bit and, after half an hour, this guy of about fifty turned up. His dad maybe? I scarpered pretty quickly.'

Jemma looked at Tess hopefully. 'So what do you think? Is it the splash?'

Tess shook her head. The irony was that, in the States, this would not only be front-page news, it would also lead the TV news and would probably even make waves in Washington. Sean Asgill's sister had just become engaged to the son of one of America's richest and most powerful men, which made her brother's drugs overdose at a sex party very hot gossip indeed. But over here, Sean Asgill was virtually unknown outside society columns.

'We'll talk about this later,' whispered Tess, snapping the laptop closed as Dom walked back into the room, naked except for a small towel wrapped around his waist, his tanned skin glistening with droplets of shower-water.

'What are you two gossiping about?' he smiled, clearly enjoying the two women's eyes on him. 'And where's my tea?'

The *Sunday Globe* was a newspaper whose glory days were long gone. Tess sat back in her chair and looked at the chipped paint-work and tired carpet: the state of the office reflected the paper's decline. After twenty years as a *Daily Mail* wannabe with a dwindling circulation, it had been bought by ruthless media mogul Matthew Jenkins, who had turned it into a red-top tabloid, but the change of direction had failed to boost sales; Jenkins had drastically cut costs and jobs to keep afloat. He certainly hadn't spent any money on improving the working conditions, thought Tess, shutting down her temperamental and near-obsolete computer. When the *Globe*'s much-loved editor, the jolly, corpulent, fifty-something Derek Bradford had had a heart attack and died, Tess had been considered a shoo-in for the top job. Even though she was only twenty-nine, she had paid her dues: three years in local papers doing hard news, women's editor at the *Mirror*, features editor at the *Sunday Globe*, and finally deputy editor. Quite a CV for someone her age. She'd been disappointed but not entirely surprised when, six weeks ago, the vacant editorship had been given to Andy Davidson, number three on the daily paper and Wentworth golfing buddy of the proprietor. Jenkins had long been labelled a misogynist; she'd even heard that he'd once laughed that, as far as the editorship of one of his flagship titles was concerned, he 'wanted to fuck Tess Garrett, not give her the top job'. Well, he could go and fuck *himself*, thought Tess angrily, taking a quick swig of coffee. It was why she was determined to use this week in the editor's chair to prove her boss had made the wrong decision.

Tess stood up, smoothed down her Armani skirt and slipped on her sharply tailored jacket; it was time to show them who was boss. Every morning at ten a.m. the *Sunday Globe* had a news conference for the editorial team and, as today was Friday, the urgent item on the agenda was the splash for the Sunday front page, the first edition of which was sent down to the printers at six p.m. on Saturday night. Friday was therefore the most hectic time of the week, with the staff often working right through the weekend until the early hours of Sunday morning, ready to change the splash if a better story came in. In newspapers, the front page was everything.

'So. Nothing obvious for the splash yet,' began news editor Ben Leith boldly, when the key editorial staff were gathered around the oval conference table. Tess narrowed her eyes. She knew Ben was after her job, but there was no need to blatantly undermine her at the first opportunity.

'Well, what *do* you have?' asked Tess pointedly. 'Speaking as news editor.'

Leith sighed. 'There's still the air hostess/prostitutes story hanging around. But the lawyers think the airline might sue.'

Tess grimaced. That particular story had been filed three weeks earlier and so far Andy had passed it over, leaving it for a dire week when there was nothing to splash with. Tess certainly didn't want to run the lame-duck story in her week as editor.

'We have Serena Balcon's hen-night shots,' said Jon Green, the *Globe*'s photo director eagerly. 'She's in Miami topless.'

Tess shook her head. 'Great for inside, Jon, but we can't run a nipple shot on the cover.'

'Yes, the nips are out in every shot,' replied Jon, looking a little deflated. 'Although we could always put globes over her tits for the cover-shot. Readers might think it's funny,' he said, gaining a few sniggers from the younger members of staff.

'I think people want to see Serena's nips,' said Ben Leith, seizing another opportunity to put pressure on Tess. She reminded herself that the news editor was best friends with the editor, Andy, and would no doubt be reporting everything back to their boss.

'Maybe we can run something next to the logo,' said Tess, firmly, 'but it's not the big story.'

Leith looked sulky and muttered something about feminist bull-shit under his breath, but Tess ignored him.

'Let's take a view at four o'clock conference. Ben, can we meet after lunch? I have a stringer working on a story which we might be able to turn into the splash.'

She stalked back to her office, sat in her chair, and swivelled it to stare out of the window. Her reflection stared back at her. Dark green eyes, a strong brow, creamy skin with good bone structure; a face to be reckoned with. *A glamorous newspaper editor's face*, she smiled grimly. That meeting was exactly the reason she was struggling to enjoy this week as editor. There had been none of the empowering buzz she always thought she would feel in the editor's chair, and she had been tense and crotchety all week. It was not that she didn't think she was up to the job – she had spent her whole adult life wanting to be a newspaper editor, from the first time she'd seen *The Front Page* and *His Girl Friday* as a little girl, to the day when she had got her first paying job as news assistant at her local rag in Suffolk, where she'd covered village fetes and bicycle thefts, and she knew she could do it better than anyone. What bothered her was the acknowledgement that she was just wasting her time. That the new editor and the CEO were just biding their time until they could get rid of her in the most inexpensive way possible.

Just then, the phone rang. It was Andy's assistant Tracey.

'I have a Mark Wilson in reception for you.'

Tess didn't recognize the name, but had an instant intuition that whatever Mark Wilson wanted it was going to be trouble.

'He says he's acting for the Asgills, if that makes any sense to you?' said Tracey.

'Oh shit,' groaned Tess under her breath. This was exactly why she hadn't broken the Asgill story in the meeting: she wanted to be sure of it; she didn't want word to get back to Andy of the story that never was. She walked over to the small window of her office and snapped the blinds shut just as there was a sharp rap on her door.

Mark Wilson was in his mid-forties, dressed in a conservative tailored suit and carrying a silver briefcase. He held out a card, but Tess simply slipped it into her pocket. She didn't need Mark Wilson to tell her he was an expensive lawyer, because he looked exactly like every other expensive lawyer she had ever met.

'Tea? Coffee? Water?' Tess asked, motioning towards a seat in front of her desk.

'Straight to business I think, Ms Garrett,' he said as he settled down. 'Some illegal photographs were taken of my client at a party in St John's Wood last night.'

'I know,' said Tess, refusing to be intimidated. 'Sean Asgill was partying so hard he ended up in a high-dependency unit at a North London hospital.'

Wilson looked slightly taken aback by the blunt, attractive woman seated across from him, but quickly rallied.

'Well, Ms Garrett, you're an experienced journalist, *one assumes*,' he said. 'So I don't need to remind you of the privacy laws at issue here. Sean Asgill was enjoying a night out in a private place and that privacy has been invaded. Run these pictures and the legal ramifications could be punitive for your newspaper.'

Tess looked at him, determined to stand her ground, particularly after Wilson's snipe about her experience. In fact, Tess had been in this situation many times before. Andy Davidson didn't do much hands-on editing and was more often to be found schmoozing politicians and publicists; he certainly never dealt with Rottweiler lawyers. It was Tess who was sent to deal with them, and, as barely a week went by without some celebrity publicist or media lawyer threatening the *Globe* with injunctions, Tess knew the law backwards.

'I'm well aware of the law, Mr Wilson,' said Tess, counting the points off on her slim fingers. 'Number one, and correct me if I'm wrong, but didn't this incident involve heavyweight drug usage? Heavyweight *illegal* drugs, I might add. Number two, it didn't happen at Mr Asgill's private residence; in fact it was at a public event, and a morally controversial public event at that.'

Wilson smiled thinly. 'That's rich. Your newspaper talking about morals.'

Tess took a sip from the glass of water in front of her. 'This is a drug overdose at a sex party, Mr Wilson. It's not as if we stormed into the Pope's bedroom. You and I both know that no judge in England will grant an injunction on those photos based on privacy.

Besides, as your client is very high profile, I believe we could argue public interest, given the circumstances.'

'Please, this is a young, vulnerable man who ingested ketamine mistakenly,' said Wilson in a more conciliatory voice.

'Vulnerable?' snorted Tess. 'Well, I don't know Sean Asgill, but from what I read he's hardly Tiny Tim. He's a playboy whose fast living has finally caught up with him.'

Mark Wilson's face was impassive but Tess knew she had got him. He stared at her for a few moments, then shrugged slightly.

'I take it you haven't written your splash story yet?'

'Not yet.'

'Who owns the photographs?'

She paused for a moment. 'We do,' she said. Actually, this was technically true, even if the paper was unaware of it. Tess was paying cash-strapped Jemma a one-hundred-pounds-a-day free-lancer rate and hiding the fee in her office expenses. That meant the *Globe* could claim copyright to Jemma's photographs, although no one except Tess and Jemma – and Sean Asgill's people – even knew of their existence. Mark Wilson nodded slowly.

'Well, I'm sure we can work something out,' he said, reaching into his pocket and pulling out a cheque, placing it carefully on the desk in front of Tess.

'One hundred thousand pounds,' he said simply. 'It's yours if you kill the story, give the photographs to us, and forget any of this ever happened.'

Tess stared down at the table, feeling her heartbeat increase. She knew deals like this had been done before: celebrities paying to have photographs taken off the market. Some of the most amazing, career-shaking exposés and inflammatory pap shots were fated to lie forever unseen, tightly locked in the vaults of newspapers. But this was different; this cheque was made out to her. None of her colleagues knew about the sex party photographs, no one knew that the paper technically owned the copyright, and Jemma had already been paid for a week's work. Although her friend could potentially get tens of thousands for them if she realized the inter-national impact this story could have, Tess knew she could fob Jemma off by saying there were legal problems with the story. But *could* she? Almost involuntarily, her hand moved forward, her fingertips resting on the cheque. What she could do with a hundred grand! Pay off the mortgage. Buy a sports car and a brand-new designer wardrobe. Go on a fantastic two-week break to somewhere incredible: Le Touessrok, the Amanpuri, somewhere hot and luxurious where she could have a beach butler and personal masseuse. Or she could simply refuse the bribe, run the story, and take the glory. *What should she do? What would her father have told her to do?* She tried to lift her fingers, but found her hand didn't want to move. Finally, reluctantly, she breathed out.

'I can't help you,' said Tess, pushing the cheque across the desk towards him.

Wilson raised an eyebrow. 'Are you sure?' he asked.

Tess nodded.

'Then make sure your mobile is turned on over the weekend,' he said briskly as he got up to leave. 'And you'd better warn your lawyer.'

Tess walked home. It took over an hour to stroll from the *Globe* office, close to Lambeth Bridge, to Battersea, and on balmy summer nights she did it regularly. But tonight, feeling so unsettled, so confused, she just wanted to clear her head. She set off along the river, the cold wind pinching at her cheeks.

A hundred grand, she thought. *Today I turned down a hundred grand.* No matter how hard she tried to tell herself she had done the right thing, a small voice inside Tess's head kept nagging away at her: 'You bloody idiot! You coward! You just weren't ruthless enough to take the bribe.'

An even more depressing thought had also occurred to her: what if Mark Wilson had some sort of sway with a judge and did manage to get his injunction to stop the photographs being published? Then there'd be no big fat cheque in her bank account, no story, and a humiliatingly blank front page on Sunday. Tess Garrett would have failed. She had brought herself up to be tough, spending her entire twenties surrounding herself with a hard protective shell, so that sentimentality would not get in the way of her ambition. But did she really have half the mettle she thought she had?

The worst thing was that she couldn't even talk it through with anyone. She certainly couldn't discuss it with Jemma, and Dom would have gone through the roof. For years, they had dreamed of buying a smart flat over the water in Chelsea, the sort of place Dom's posy public-school friends were now living in. A hundred thousand pounds wouldn't buy them that, of course, but paying off the mortgage and having full equity on their current home would put them in a strong position to finally trade up to the apartments that twinkled on the other side of the Thames.

Tess was now walking past the New Covent Garden Market where she loved buying armfuls of beautiful flowers on weekend mornings. Suddenly she could hear the soft purr of a car engine behind her. Glancing over her shoulder, she saw a shiny black car hugging the pavement. *What the hell . . .?* Tess began walking a little faster, her heart beating a little quicker than usual, but the car overtook her and stopped thirty yards ahead. Tess didn't scare easily, but she was still unnerved. The street was dark and, on a cold night like this, she was the only person walking. As she drew level, the rear window of the Mercedes purred down.

'Tess Garrett?' called a voice.

Tess stopped and warily looked into the car. Leaning towards the window was an elegant sixty-something woman with fine-boned features and a cloud of champagne-blonde hair that fell to the sable mink collar of her coat. She looked familiar, but for the moment Tess could not place her.

'Meredith Asgill,' said the woman with a faint nod. 'I'd very much like to talk to you. It's a cold night, isn't it? Perhaps you'd like to step inside the car.'

Tess exhaled, her breath making a small white cloud in the night air. Meredith Asgill, Mark Wilson's employer; she didn't know whether to be anxious or relieved. Before her was the matriarch of the Asgill family, head of the cosmetics dynasty and, of course, Sean Asgill's mother. Tess opened the car door and stepped inside, sinking into the black leather seat as Meredith leant forward to instruct the driver to head for Mayfair.

'I didn't think I'd find you walking home,' said Meredith with quiet amusement. 'I thought British newspaper proprietors might provide drivers for senior members of staff, but when I called at your office your PA tipped me off that you were walking home this way.'

Tess smiled politely. 'How can I help you, Mrs Asgill?'

Meredith nodded, as if to signify that she too preferred to get down to business. 'Mark Wilson tells me you intend to run with the story in Sunday's edition,' she said, folding her hands on the lap of her blue silk dress.

'No disrespect to you or your family, Mrs Asgill,' said Tess, trying to keep her cool. 'But I am simply doing my job. I'm the acting editor of the *Sunday Globe* and obviously I have to pick the best stories for our readers.'

'Of course,' said Meredith with a faint smile. 'And of course it will be a boost to your career. I know you were passed over for the editor's job. I know you have a point to prove with Mr Davidson being away; you want the most salacious stories for a big-selling issue.'

'And is there anything wrong with that?' asked Tess.

'Not at all. It's what I would expect from someone of your capabilities and ambition. In fact, I was not surprised at all that you turned down Mr Wilson's generous offer. You have a reputation of making it on your own merits.'

Tess tried not to betray her surprise. It was unsettling how much this woman knew about her, but she supposed a quick Internet search and some join-the-dots suppositions would do the rest. Out of the window, Vauxhall came into view.

'This is all very flattering, Mrs Asgill, but is there anything else I can help you with? You'll appreciate this is a very busy time for me.'

Meredith paused, scanning Tess's face. 'Actually, the point of this conversation is how I can help you,' she said.

Tess gave a quiet, low laugh.

'Really?' she asked.

'Indeed. In fact, I like to think of the proposal I have as a win-win situation.'

Tess held her breath. Was she going to up the offer of a hundred grand? And more importantly, would she be able to turn it down? Meredith looked out of the window.

'I expect you know a little about my family,' she began. 'I expect you know that last week my daughter Brooke became engaged to David Billington?'

'Yes, "Manhattan's new John Kennedy Junior",' nodded Tess. 'I think that's how *People* described him. And I assume that's why you've been particularly keen to keep your son's adventures out of the tabloids. I imagine sex scandals don't go down too well with rich, powerful families like the Billingtons.'

Meredith nodded slightly. 'David's family is very rich, very powerful and, as you would expect of one of New York's oldest families, very conservative. They are more established than the Kennedys, as rich as the Rockefellers. They are also very politically active. Over the last four generations, the Billingtons have provided America with two secretaries of state, four governors, a vice-president and half a dozen senators, but in David they see the potential to finally add a president to the tally.'

'Really?' said Tess, intrigued now. 'I didn't know David was in politics. Isn't he a news reporter?'

Meredith laughed. 'For the moment, yes. He's due to run for Congress next year and, naturally, he will be elected.'

All at once, Tess felt the pieces fall into place. She looked across at this elegant woman and realized the look on Meredith Asgill's face was not composure, but controlled fear. She knew that if Jemma's photos were ever seen, the whole Asgill family would be damned and the Billingtons would not risk being tarred by the same brush. Given those circumstances, one hundred thousand pounds seemed a small sum to keep everyone's reputations squeaky clean.

'Mrs Asgill, I wish your daughter and David Billington well,' said Tess carefully, 'but it's my professional responsibility to run the story on your son.'

Meredith looked at her. 'Your responsibility as acting editor?'

'Yes.'

'And what if you weren't acting editor of the *Globe*?' asked Meredith.

Tess felt a flutter of panic. Even without the marriage to David Billington, the Asgills were a rich and powerful family in their own right, and Tess wondered how far Meredith's influence reached. Cosmetics companies certainly had a lot of power in the publishing industry and, although the *Globe* didn't run any beauty advertising, it was still very possible that Meredith had the connections to have Tess removed from her job.

'Are you threatening to have me fired?' asked Tess, her face flushing.

'Fired?' laughed Meredith, gently tapping Tess's knee. 'No, darling, I want to offer you a job.'

'A job?'

Meredith leaned forward. 'I want you to come and be my family's personal publicist, to promote the Asgills' image and to keep scandal – should there be any – out of the media.'

Tess gaped, completely taken by surprise. 'But I'm a hack,

not a flack,' she stammered, using the industry slang expression for PR.

Meredith nodded. 'And many top publicists are ex-journalists.'

Tess began to say something, then stopped. She didn't really know what to say. She gazed out of the window, watching the lights of London, trying to think it through, surprised at her own interest in the idea.

'But surely a New York journalist would suit you better?' said Tess. 'My contacts are largely UK-based.'

Meredith smiled. 'You have friends working at the *Post*, the *Times*, and the *Daily News*.'

Tess conceded the point, again a little surprised by the depth of the woman's knowledge of her.

'You've done your homework.'

'Of course,' said Meredith. 'We can offer a good six-figure salary, one I feel sure is more generous than the one you are currently on, plus a rent-free apartment in the West Village.'

'I already have a well-paid job on one of the biggest papers in the country,' said Tess, playing for time.

'Yes, but you're unhappy, unmotivated and . . .' Meredith paused. '. . . You're about to get the sack.'

'I am not!' said Tess indignantly. 'What on earth—'

Meredith held up a dainty hand. 'It's a matter of public record that the *Globe* Group are streamlining, making redundancies, and pushing people out. I read the *Wall Street Journal* and the *Financial Times*, Miss Garrett. I also keep my ear to the ground, and I hear that your editor is bringing someone in to be co-deputy editor. I'm sorry, I don't wish to be rude, but it does appear your days at the *Globe* are numbered.'

Tess could only stare in front of her. Meredith Asgill might have been playing hardball, but her words had the ring of truth to them. It stung her to hear them from a stranger.

'I've got a good reputation,' said Tess, with more bravado than she was feeling. 'I don't think I'll have any problems walking into a new job.'

Meredith smiled politely. 'I'm sure you're correct,' she said. 'But please be aware that my offer comes with a bonus. A two-hundred-and-fifty-thousand-dollar bonus when the bride and groom marry.'

'A quarter of a million dollars?' said Tess slowly. She'd definitely be able to afford that Chelsea flat with that cash injection. Dom would do cartwheels. But Tess's head was doing its own back flips – she too had heard rumours about the recruitment of a co-deputy editor being brought in to work beside her. More importantly, Tess had always wanted to work in New York, and this might be just the opportunity to get a visa, and look for a proper job at the *New York Post* or *Daily News*.

'This is an opportunity to make some real money, Tess, not to mention contacts and friends *at the highest level*,' said Meredith, seeming to have read her thoughts. 'The secret of all successful people is an ability to think outside the box. Think of Howard Rubenstein or Max Clifford in London; they make far more than any newspaper editor and have far more real influence. Besides, PR is more civilized than tabloid journalism, don't you think?'

'This wedding has to happen, doesn't it?' said Tess, and again, behind the cool patrician façade, she saw a flutter of anxiety.

'Yes. I will not let anything stop it,' said Meredith firmly. 'Now, have you eaten?'

Tess shook her head. Behind them, they could just hear Big Ben striking nine p.m.

'How about you join me for a late supper? I'm at the Connaught. I can tell you all about Brooke's fabulous engagement party that's going to be held at the Billington compound. I assume you've never been?'

'Not yet,' smiled Tess.

'Well, I think that you might like it there. In fact, it's tomorrow night; you can hop on the jet with me back to New York. How's that sound?'

2

'Brooke? David's here.'

The pretty Chinese girl squeezed into Brooke Asgill's tiny, cluttered office and swiftly removed a cup of cold coffee from her superior's desk. Brooke looked up and nodded. Strictly speaking, Kim Yi-Noon wasn't Brooke's assistant. As a lowly commissioning editor in the children's division at the Yellow Door publishing house, Brooke wasn't entitled to such privileges, but then lots of things had begun to change since her engagement to David Billington. Working conditions had mysteriously improved; she now had an office of her own – tiny though it was – for instance, and a star-struck intern willing to moonlight as her assistant. Then there was the unasked-for pay rise and the parking space she didn't need. It was as if the management could smell power on the breeze.

'Great, thanks Kim,' said Brooke, smiling. 'Send him up.'

'I suggested that,' said Kim apologetically. 'But apparently the paparazzi are hanging around the office again. He thinks it's better if he stays in the car.'

Brooke winced and glanced down at the manuscript in front of her. Every Friday afternoon she set aside an hour to read submissions from the 'slush pile'. Most publishers didn't bother, leaving unsolicited manuscripts to the most junior members of the publishing team, and Brooke had to admit that, most weeks, it was an hour wasted. Vanity projects, poor copies of whatever was hot last year; most of it was mediocre at best. But the book she had picked out today, well, this was something else: it had that indefinable *something* that made her want to keep reading.

Kim coughed politely. 'Sorry, Brooke, but should you even be here?'

18

she asked. 'It's in my diary that you've booked half a day's holiday today.'

'No, you're right,' said Brooke, putting down her Montblanc pen. 'We've got another wedding venue to see and we should have left two hours ago. Although I think the novelty of venue-hunting has worn off for David already. He goes pale every time I mention another one. Just wait till it's your turn.' Brooke stopped, realizing that might sound patronizing, especially since Kim could only be three or four years younger than she was. It was funny how dating David and mixing with his highbrow politico friends had made her feel much older, *think* much older. She wasn't even married herself yet.

'Brooke? Can I ask you a favour?' said Kim slowly, a look of embarrassment on her face.

'Shoot.'

'Don't take it the wrong way, but could you please not talk to me about this stuff?'

'Oh,' said Brooke, surprised. 'I'm sorry, I didn't mean to . . .' Brooke could feel her face flushing. She had always felt awkward even asking Kim to get her coffee; she certainly didn't want to be one of those editors who treated her assistants like crap – she'd seen plenty of that. Even here in the children's publishing division, generally considered a genteel working environment, they still had their fair share of bitches.

'Oh, it's not that I don't like hearing about it,' said Kim quickly. 'It sounds lovely, all the wedding preparations and dates with David and such, but it's just that some journalist called me up yesterday and offered me two thousand bucks if I would tell her where the wedding is. It's sort of tempting when you're on fifteen thousand dollars a year and most of that gets gobbled up by your rent.'

Brooke stared at the girl, open-mouthed. Of course, it made perfect sense, given the media furore over the wedding; she could almost admire the journalist's initiative. She could also understand how tempting it would be for someone like Kim Yi-Noon. For her twenty-first birthday, Brooke had been given a fully furnished 'classic six' apartment on Sixty-Fifth Street. As a member of the Asgill family, she really had no idea what it was like to struggle to make rent. She had no idea what it was like to struggle for anything.

'What did you say to him?' asked Brooke finally.

'I said I can't tell them anything if I don't know anything,' shrugged Kim. 'And if we can keep it that way, we won't have a problem. Is that okay?'

'Of course, of course. And I'm grateful, Kim. Thank you,' said Brooke, making a mental note to try and get Kim a pay rise. Keen to change the subject, Brooke tapped the paper in front of her.

'By the way, this is the covering letter from a slush-pile manuscript I've been reading. There's only a few chapters of it, so can you phone the author for me and get her to send the rest if there is any more? If there is a completed manuscript, maybe we should suggest she gets an agent while she's at it.'

Kim nodded in a brisk, efficient manner. 'I'll do it now.'

Glancing at her watch – David would definitely be getting cross now – Brooke stuffed the manuscript into her orange Goyard tote and pulled a compact out of her top drawer. *Not bad*, she thought, flipping open the mirror. The day had faded her make-up, but with her grape-green almond eyes and high cheekbones, Brooke Asgill was still one of the most beautiful girls in Manhattan. She swept some gloss over her lips, then suddenly felt guilty, recalling a snarky little news story in *Star* magazine about how 'Brooke Asgill puts on a full face of make-up before she meets the paparazzi.' It had annoyed Brooke more than it should, mainly because she knew the words one showbiz writer had tossed off in ten minutes would now pop into her head every time she looked in a mirror. The truth was that Brooke Asgill was not vain, if she put a spot of blush on her cheeks, or some gloss on her lips when she stepped outside, it was because she just figured that if people were determined to plaster her face all over every newspaper and magazine in America, she might as well try and look half decent.

She rode down in the lift and rushed through the Yellow Door lobby, bracing herself as she pushed through the doors onto East Forty-Second Street and heard the familiar click-whirr, click-whirr of the camera shutters. Since her engagement, that had been the soundtrack to her life. *You should be used to this by now*, she thought, unconsciously pulling her bag closer for protection. Brooke had always been a private person and she found the attention difficult to get used to; she'd actually had a panic attack the first time she had been followed.

'Brooke! Brooke! Over here!' called the voices, but she did her best to ignore them as her long legs carried her across the sidewalk to David's waiting silver Lexus. Sitting on the back seat, tapping at his BlackBerry, was David Billington, the man formerly known as America's Most Eligible Bachelor; until two weeks ago, when their engagement had been announced and thousands of hearts were broken. He looked so handsome, thought Brooke – some might say unfairly handsome for someone whose family was worth fifteen billion dollars. Even in just a pair of grey trousers, open-necked blue shirt and a Paul Smith pea coat, he still looked fantastic. His dark hair was slightly wavy, his eyes such a dark blue that they made his face look serious – until he unzipped his smile. He was confident, not aggressive, charming, not smarmy. *People* maga-zine regularly called him Mr Perfect. Sometimes Brooke thought they were right.

'So, what have you been doing up there?' asked David, finally pulling back from their embrace. 'I thought we wanted to try and beat the traffic.'

'I've just been reading a manuscript.'

'Must have been good.'

'You didn't give me the chance to find out,' she smiled, wanting to keep the excitement of her discovery under wraps at least until she had read more. 'How was your day, anyway?'

'Fifth consecutive day I've been studio-bound,' sighed David. 'I'm sure it must be some kind of record.'

David was a co-anchor for CTV's *World Today*, a lunchtime news programme that broadcast from eleven a.m. to one p.m. each day, often broadcasting live from the scene of breaking news. In any given month he could be in Afghanistan or Somalia, Paris or Moscow.

'Good news for the world, I suppose,' she smiled. 'No hurri-canes, no *coups d'états*. And definitely good news for me.' She squeezed his knee. Sometimes she enjoyed David's busy schedule, but it was nice to have him home once in a while, especially now when there was so much to be done.

'Not such good news for CTV, though,' said David. 'The ratings have been down and one of our big interviews fell through, went to Anderson Cooper.'

'Ah honey, that's a bummer,' she said, genuinely disappointed for him.

'But . . .' He paused and looked at her. '. . . It looks like I've got twenty minutes with the Palestinian PM on Sunday.'

'You're going to Palestine?'

'It's gone crazy over there again.'

Brooke began to protest, then bit her tongue. She knew it was futile reminding David that they had three possible wedding venues to go look at in Connecticut and, anyway, she had to agree that the pressing details of their seating plan seemed slightly petty compared to discussing the finer points of the Middle East crisis with a world leader. Still, it was a blow. She had been looking forward to them spending a little time together for once, getting wrapped up in the romance and excitement of the wedding.

'I guess I'll go and look at those venues on my own then.'

'Come on, honey,' said David, stroking her cheek, 'I thought girls loved this stuff. Don't tell me your DNA skipped the bride gene?'

She laughed, despite herself.

'Well, maybe you should take your mother?' suggested David.

'I'm not a masochist,' she smiled. Ever since the engagement, they had quickly found that both sides of the family had very strong ideas about where and how they should be married. David's mother, a *grande dame* of New York society, had very decided and conservative views about venues that were considered 'proper' by 'the right people'. It needed to be large enough to host all her influential friends, and grand enough for her family. Only a church ceremony would be considered, preferably with a bishop – at the very least – presiding. Meredith, meanwhile, had vetoed every possible reception venue they had been able to find in New York. The Ritz Carlton was 'too dingy', the New York Library 'too public', and even the many gorgeous venues that Alessandro Franchetti, Manhattan's premier wedding planner, had tracked down were similarly rejected. Brooke was beginning to think nothing would ever please her mother. It was a feeling she was familiar with.

'Well, you never know,' said David. 'Alessandro might have come up trumps with the place we're going to see today.'

Brooke gave a wry smile. 'Don't hold your breath; he did call it a "wild card".'

'We're going all the way to Duchess County for a wild card?' asked David, annoyance in his voice. 'It's a long way to travel to say no. Anyway, I thought we were picking him up?'

'We are.' She leaned forward and tapped Miguel, David's driver, on the shoulder. 'We have to detour to Sutton Place.'

David pulled a face. 'Couldn't we have met him there?'

Brooke laughed. 'He's not that bad.'

'Oh he is,' grinned David.

Outside a smart brownstone on Sutton Place South, a short, overly groomed man was standing on the roadside looking at his watch. Alessandro Franchetti was a former bit-part TV actor turned society wedding planner, who had recently made it onto *New York* magazine's Hot 100 List. Although there were thirty couples in the city delighted to have Alessandro planning their nuptials at vast expense, the truth was that most of their weddings were arranged by Alessandro's team. He took on only two weddings a year himself, and this was by far his biggest, possibly the biggest of his career. No wonder he was looking anxious. Brooke and David wanted an early fall wedding and they still didn't have a venue. Screw this up and he'd never work in New York again.

'Nice building,' said David, peering through the car's tinted windows.

'The average New York bride spends one hundred thousand dollars on her wedding,' smiled Brooke. 'He has money.'

'At last! My two favourite people in New York,' gushed Alessandro as he clambered into the passenger seat next to the driver. 'And I'm so glad to finally have you both together. There is such a lot to talk about.'

Snapping open his briefcase, Alessandro pulled out a spreadsheet and put on a pair of black horn-rim reading glasses. 'I can only look at this for a second because reading and travelling makes me feel sick,' he said in an aside.

David's lips twitched with amusement.

'I had an early start at the studio,' he whispered to Brooke, settling back in his seat. 'I might just grab a little shut-eye.'

Brooke jabbed him in the ribs. 'No, you don't!'

Alessandro looked up, oblivious to their whispering.

'Now, I know everyone is keen to set a date as quickly as possible, but you've said no to The Pierre. No to the Four Seasons Pool Room. No to the Plaza, St Regis, the Yale Club and the Frick.' He turned round and eyed Brooke and David carefully. 'Do you know how many strings I had to pull to even put the Frick as an option?'

'The problem is we all want somewhere new,' said David, turning on the charm. 'Somewhere we haven't been before.'

Alessandro peered over the top of his glasses. 'Between the two of you, you must have been to every wedding, funeral, benefit, and bar mitzvah in the Tri-State area. *New* is presenting something of a challenge.' He sighed, pushing out his tanned cheeks.

'Are you sure you don't want it at Belcourt or Cliffpoint?'

Belcourt was the Billingtons' magnificent family estate in Westchester County, and Cliffpoint was their forty-five-roomed summer house in Newport. There were, of course, other properties the family owned: a villa in Palm Beach, a ranch in the Santa Ynez Valley, and a palazzo in Venice, but the reason for not hosting the wedding at one of the Billington-owned properties was the same.

'Ahem, how shall I put this?' said Brooke. 'It's important to my mother to have the hosting responsibilities.'

'And you've definitely ruled out Parklands?'

Parklands was the Asgill family home. Three years ago it had been the venue for a large and rather overblown wedding for her sister Liz, who was divorced from her husband twelve months later.

'Mother doesn't like the omens.'

Alessandro took off his glasses and sighed. 'Lord save me from the mother of the bride. Well, never fear, Toots, I've got a good feeling about this one.'

The car slipped out of Manhattan, crossing the George Washington Bridge and heading up into New York State, the metropolis quickly thinning out into towns and then fields. Brooke was glad to escape the city. She had always loved New York, she was born and bred there, but lately the Big Apple had started to shrink. It wasn't that she disliked the attention, but the constant intrusions – people she didn't know calling out her name in the deli, teenage girls pointing and giggling; she'd even had a death threat – it was all starting to wear her down. It had been nine months to the day since she had met David Billington; despite also being a native of Manhattan, Brooke had had to go all the way to Europe to meet him. She had been in the Alsace region on a nostalgic trip to France to visit a family with whom she had done a summer exchange in her junior year at Spence. Three days into the trip, her host Mrs Dubois had discovered her husband was having an affair. Brooke supposed this might not be a problem for the chic Frenchwoman, but Mrs Dubois kicked him out. Politely withdrawing, Brooke hadn't wanted to go home, so on a whim she'd headed down to Biarritz. A Park Avenue girl, she had always been athletic and outdoorsy, and she wanted to go surfing on the legendary beaches down there.

When she first saw David, she was standing on the shore in her wet-suit.

He had come over to the shore to check she was okay; she remembered thinking he looked vaguely familiar, but she had not been expecting to meet New York's most eligible bachelor in a wetsuit on a cloudy, blowy day on the Atlantic coast. The attraction between them was instant, although Brooke suspected that David's interest in her went up a notch when he discovered she was also from a very wealthy New York family. If she was honest, some of that was true for her too. Like most little girls, growing up, Brooke had always dreamt of marrying a handsome prince, but in her case it had almost come true.

Not that it had been exactly a fairy tale; back in New York, the first three months of their relationship had been conducted in secret. Dates were either dinner at unfashionable restaurants in Brooklyn, or ridiculously luxurious hotels in remote locations like the Hudson Valley – sometimes it felt like having an affair with a rich married man. David didn't explicitly say that he was testing her out before he went public with their relationship, but Brooke knew the rules of dating were just not the same for men like David Billington. Last month, on Valentine's Day, he had whisked her off to Paris. Well, it wasn't exactly the fourteenth of February. It had been ten days later, thanks to work commitments in Beirut and Uzbekistan, but it was wonderful nevertheless. The penthouse suite at the Bristol, shopping in St-Germain, where David had treated her to armfuls of gifts from Saint Laurent, then dinner at Le Voltaire. Back at the hotel, he had popped open vintage champagne on their terrace overlooking the city, which had been studded with hundreds of glowing tea-lights. Even so, Brooke hadn't expected it when he had pulled a ring out of his pocket and dropped down on one knee. They'd been dating less than a year, but the night had been so perfect, it had been impossible to resist.

It was almost seven by the time they arrived in Duchess County. Light was falling out of the sky, the dipping sun casting an orange glow over the lake. Brooke had been there before to visit the Rhinebeck Antiques Fair for its lovely old chests and gilt mirrors, and loved the area's raw natural beauty.

'This place certainly smells good,' laughed Brooke, breathing in a cool fresh scent of mist and freshly mown grass through the open window. They came off the road and through a pair of white gates, down a long gravel drive curling around the lake, framed by horse chestnut trees bursting with their long ivory flowers. At the end of the drive was a short pier where a small motor launch was moored.

'Is it across the lake?' asked Brooke, excitement in her voice. They all climbed out of the car and up onto the pier, David taking Brooke's hand to help her on. It smelt of linseed oil. The boat took ten minutes to chug across the lake, finally turning into a bay dominated by a huge white colonial house. Brooke gasped.

'Isn't it spectacular?' grinned Alessandro, spreading his arms dramatically. 'Now, when we get there you'll see it's a little run-down, so I want you to use your imagination.'

'I quite like the fact it's not too perfect,' said David as they swung into the dock.

Brooke gave a small laugh. 'Is that how your mother will see it?'

'She'll like it if we do,' he said, not sounding entirely convinced by his statement. 'Anyway, I love the location. It's private.'

Alessandro clapped his hands together. 'My thoughts exactly, darling. The paparazzi are going to be all over this wedding, so we have to do what we can to keep everything *secure*. This is the ideal solution. I've even had a word with the local sheriff, who has kindly agreed to enforce a no-fly zone over the lake for the wedding, so paparazzi helicopters can forget it. Now, David, I know your mother wanted a church wedding . . .'

'Cathedral,' smiled Brooke.

'*But*, I've already spoken to Reverend James, the pastor from your family's local church. He baptized two generations of your family, I believe? Well, he's happy to officiate here, which should please your mother.'

Alessandro turned to Brooke and touched her arm. 'And you, my darling, I know you wanted something intimate, but—'

'But it's beautiful,' interrupted Brooke. 'Big, but beautiful.'

They walked up through the gardens from the jetty and into the house. The building was even more impressive close to, and the entrance hall was huge, with vaulted ceilings soaring forty feet above them.

'Wow,' said David simply.

Alessandro held Brooke's shoulders and turned her around towards the lake. It was glowing a rippling orange as the sun sank.

'Look over to the west side of the lake,' said Alessandro, pointing to the lawns next to the formal gardens. 'See how it slopes down? It's a natural amphitheatre. I was thinking very simple cherry-wood pews, a carpet of petals as an aisle, and the vows being exchanged looking out over the water.'

Brooke was silent for a moment, picturing the scene.

'What do you think, Brooke?' asked David. When she turned towards him, there were tears in her eyes.

'It's just incredible.'

David pulled her close. 'The bride gene surfaces,' he whispered.

Alessandro walked a little way off, continuing his commentary like a tour guide. 'The house used to belong to a very wealthy Manhattan family, in mining or something, I think. Now it belongs to an educational trust, but it's been used for films in the past, one featuring Johnny Depp, can't remember which. Anyway, don't worry about the slightly tired exterior. My ex-boyfriend is a Hollywood set designer and we still speak. I think he can do something very special.'

David and Brooke exchanged a small smile at his rapid-fire monologue.

'We don't want to go too high concept, Alessandro,' said Brooke. 'No *Gone with the Wind* fantasy, okay?'

'Well, if we're thinking left-field with all this, I was wondering about a dusk wedding? We could line the path around the lake with torches and ferry you over to the ceremony in a little boat covered in iceberg rose petals.'

'Alessandro,' said Brooke, gently admonishing. 'No drama, remember? Although, I do like the idea of getting married at this time of day. When is it available?'

'Pretty much whenever,' said Alessandro, flapping his hands vaguely. 'A fall wedding *would* be magnificent. Can you imagine those trees over there glistening with scarlet leaves? Oh, but realistically a September wedding is way too tight. I mean, your dress is going to take three, four months minimum, more if we're thinking lots of Lesage beading. I know one bride who had to put her wedding *back* because the embroidery was taking so long.'

'Which leaves us with next spring or summer,' said Brooke thoughtfully. 'Winters will be vicious up here and I don't want to make it too difficult for people to travel.'

'We definitely wanted the wedding within the year,' said David, looking at Brooke. 'I don't want this one to get away from me.'

Alessandro coughed politely. 'Maybe I'll leave you two alone for a few minutes,' he said.

'So what do you think?' asked Brooke when Alessandro was out of earshot.

'I love it.'

'Oh honey, I'm so glad you said that,' she gushed, her face lit up like a little girl's. 'It's the perfect spring venue, isn't it? I mean, smell that air. New beginnings.'

She could see David stifle a wry smile. He was too polite to laugh. He wrapped his arms around Brooke's waist. 'It's perfect.'

'It's big though, isn't it?' said Brooke, biting her lip. 'All that talk about amphitheatres.'

'We have a lot of guests.'

'Your parents have got a lot of guests,' she said.

Brooke was a Pisces, a romantic; perhaps that's what drew her to books. In her mind her wedding would have all the trappings of the fairy tale – the beautiful white dress, the huge cake – but she'd always thought of it as a private ceremony, conducted in front of people she knew and loved. The last thing she wanted was a circus.

'Should we run off to City Hall and just do it?' said Brooke impulsively.

David shook his head slowly. 'You know we can't do that.'

She looked at him and saw sadness in his eyes; it was the weight of expectation, and most of the time he wore it well. David might be a television reporter right now, but that was not where his future lay. Already he was being touted in serious magazines as a White House hopeful, despite having not a jot of political experience to his name. Their wedding would be talked about and written about for years to come; in many ways, it *needed* to be a circus, even if it was not a three-ring circus.

'Honey, are you sure you're ready for this?' he asked softly.

She looked at his dark-blue eyes and couldn't believe that out of all the women in the world he had chosen her.

'Do you mean have I passed the point of no return?' she asked.

'No, I mean are you ready to be a Billington wife?'

Brooke felt a shiver run through her and wondered if it was the chill in the air.

'Is anyone ever ready to be a Billington wife?' she sighed. 'I don't know if I am. Who could? But what I do know is that I'm ready to marry you.'

David's face lit up in a broad grin.

'That's good enough for me,' he laughed, and pulled her down into the grass.

3

Standing inside the glass elevator that ran along the west-facing wall of midtown's magnificent Somerset Tower, Liz Asgill pushed the brushed-chrome button labelled 'penthouse'. She turned to Enrique Gelati, Manhattan's most in-demand hair colourist, as the lift began its swift ascent.

'It takes thirty seconds to go forty-three floors,' she purred as night-time Manhattan disappeared beneath them, revealing the blackness of Central Park, the taxis buzzing around it like yellow wasps. 'It's the Ferrari of elevators, nought to sixty in two point five seconds.'

'I hope the spa is also as good,' said Enrique in a syrupy Spanish Cuban accent. 'Asgill's is not such a good name, no? Asgill's is not La Prairie, I think.'

Liz turned and smiled thinly. Enrique had a reputation for being difficult, but he got away with it as he was regarded as a genius in his field. Great with brunettes, even better with blondes, half the Park Avenue Princesses owed their glorious honey-coloured manes to Enrique Gelati. Liz even knew of one household name who came to him to get her muff colour-corrected every six weeks. No wonder the waiting list at his Madison Avenue salon was three months long. As *Allure* magazine had said many times, 'It's easy to spot an Enrique Gelati blonde, but it's impossible to get an appointment.'

'I think you'll be surprised at the spa,' said Liz confidently. 'The Skin Plus brand is a completely separate brand to Asgill's. We're just backed by the company money.' She smiled warmly. Inside she was fuming, but she had to keep him on side. The Skin Plus Spa launch was only a month away and having Enrique as the salon's creative director would be a huge coup.

Unlike many great businesses, Liz Asgill's latest brainchild had not begun with a small idea but a very big, very ambitious one. She had decided to create Skin Plus as Asgill's new up-market 'cosmeceutical range', a line as removed from the frumpy dead-duck family brand as a Rolls-Royce from a cart and horse. Liz's plan was to start, not with the range of beauty products, but with a spa so sensational, so exclusive, it would have all of America talking. So far it was looking good. The spa's interiors had been designed by Kelly Wearstler, she had poached spa therapists from Chiva-Som in Thailand, and colourists and cutters were decamping from John Barrett and Frédéric Fekkai to join her. There was just one problem. Liz needed a star, a big-name creative director for the hair salon, preferably someone who could bring a long list of celebrity clients with them. In this town, it was vital to have a name because New Yorkers were the most status-conscious women in the world. She could name a dozen Upper East Side socialites who had their hair cut by ninety-dollar local stylists but told their friends that their blonde buttery shags were the work of Sally Hershberger.

The lift door pinged open and they stepped out into the 25,000-square-foot space that occupied the top floor of Somerset Tower, a space that had taken Liz six months of ruthless negotiating to secure. Enrique's eyes opened wide as he saw it and, although he was trying to play it cool, she could tell he was impressed.

'Welcome to heaven,' she said, sweeping an arm out.

They walked into a domed roof atrium of Venetian glass, with silver and ivory silk wallpaper and a long white leather reception desk. Liz led Enrique into a large room to the left.

'This will be the waiting room for the salon,' she explained. It had been repainted five times until Liz was satisfied with exactly the right shade of white.

'The spa and hair salon areas are to your left and right. The organic restaurant is through there,' she said, pointing down a long ivory corridor. 'There's a champagne and juice bar and VIP spaces in all zones. The colour studio is over here,' she continued, gesturing up to the glass ceiling. 'Obviously in the daytime, it has fantastic light, which I think is crucial for you.'

Enrique nodded.

Liz felt a crackle of excitement as she showed off the rest of the premises to Enrique. For the first time in her career, she had been able to see an idea through from concept to launch, consuming so much of her time and energy over the past five years that it had cost Liz her marriage; but, as far as Liz was concerned, with success came sacrifice. She had a six per cent shareholding in Asgill Cosmetics, conservatively estimated at being worth about twenty million dollars, but it was a shareholding that was falling in value all the time. Since the death of her father, Asgill Cosmetics had been pitched into a downward spiral. Her brother William was now CEO, and nothing he did seemed to be able to stop the rot. Liz knew she was the only one who could save it, and this spa was the vehicle by which she would do it. She spun round on her five-inch heels to face Enrique. Before the guided tour, she had spent two hours buttering him up with pleasantries and compliments over dinner. Now it was time for business.

'The deal is that I would like you to come and headline the salon, working three days a week here,' she said.

Enrique pulled his long black ponytail out of its band and shook his hair onto his shoulders.

'Liz, I tell you at dinner that I am very busy. As you can imagine, my phone is ringing all the time with proposals from people like you.'

Liz pursed her lips thoughtfully. 'Well, that's funny, because in the light of everything that's going on at your salon, I think the offer I'm making is a very attractive one indeed. A lifeboat, as it were.'

Enrique frowned. 'I don't understand you.'

'I hear things aren't too great with Gary,' she said flatly. Gary Eisen was Enrique's long-time business manager and backer.

'He's fine,' said Enrique, tossing back his black hair. 'He's on the West Coast right now, checking out real estate for an LA salon.'

'Really? I heard he was on the West Coast to check into Promises rehab clinic.'

'Bullshit,' he replied defensively, but his eyes betrayed his panic. Liz smiled, enjoying the moment: knowledge was power and she intended to use what she knew to her advantage. For the last month she'd had a corporate investigations team look into Enrique's business and had found that, despite Enrique's profile, his salon was being woefully mismanaged. Their plans to launch an Enrique hair-care range had not come off, and minuscule profits suggested that Gary was siphoning off money for his expensive coke habit and love of Brazilian rent boys.

'Enrique,' said Liz, 'you need to face facts. You're never going to make any serious money with just one salon, no matter how many celebrities you've got on your client list, especially when that salon is badly run. The money is in product ranges, selling twenty-dollar colour shampoo to secretaries in Cleveland. But . . .' Liz took a deep breath. '. . . We both know that no one wants to work with you to produce those products because you and Gary are too unpredictable.'

'Bitch. How dare you?' he hissed. 'It's taken me fifteen years to have my own salon. I worked for everything I got. No rich daddy gave me mine.'

Little Latino prick trying to play hardball, she thought, but then Liz was not in the business of trading niceties. She was glad she towered above him in her Giuseppe Zanotti heels. Hands on hips, bright-red lips, complete intimidation.

'Listen to me,' she said evenly. 'I'm trying to help you. Your business is going to go to the wall, no question. In two, three years' time, you'll be back in Miami, some colourist that once used to be big in New York, just another industry casualty. And then all that hard work will have been for nothing.'

For a few seconds he didn't speak, clearly torn between rage at having been spoken to in such a way and needing Liz's help. Finally he flapped his arms in surrender.

'What do you suggest?' he pouted.

'My proposal is that I buy out Gary Eisen's stake. You work two days at your salon, three days here at Skin Plus. Meanwhile, one of my team will manage the Enrique salon, increasing its profitability, and Asgill's will license your name to produce an Enrique product range that we can get into drugstores by fall.'

Of course, that was only part of Liz's plan. She was so proud of her full agenda that she almost wanted to blurt the rest out: that in twelve months' time she would close down the Madison Avenue salon, integrating the entire Enrique salon into the Skin Plus Spa. She already had an idea who would buy the lease on the prime Madison Avenue real estate occupied by Enrique's salon – and then she could screw him over the licensing deal and send the arrogant little jerk back to Miami with his balls in a sack.

'I need to think about it,' said Enrique, trying to hold his head high.

'How about I give you till Monday?'

Down on the street, Liz watched Enrique disappear into a waiting car. She looked up to the top of Somerset Tower, a shard of illuminated glass stretching into the night sky. Adrenaline was still coursing through her blood; the thrill of a deal always did that to her; there was no way she could go home to sleep. She knew exactly what she needed.

She flagged down a yellow cab, its light spilling a glow onto the puddles on the road. Inside, she told the driver to take her to Clinton. Relaxing into the seat, she pulled a cosmetic wipe from her bag and carefully cleaned make-up from her face. She flipped open a compact and stared at the blank canvas of her features. Her blonde hair was cut into a short bob. Her eyes were small, her nose too narrow from bad rhinoplasty in the mid-Nineties, but she had a wide, sensual mouth and full lips and the overall picture was striking, handsome, and strong. People often compared Liz to her mother when she was younger, which Liz knew wasn't exactly a compliment, especially as her father Howard was a ridiculously good-looking man. Meredith was several notches down the attractiveness scale, but her family had money. That was just the way it was in their world.

She took out a lipstick and painted a slash of deep maroon across her lips; instantly she looked different, more sexual. Liz smiled at the power of cosmetics to change your face, your identity. She pulled another pot out of her bag. Asgill's hair wax, which she ran over her hands and through her hair, combing it down severely along the contours of her skull.

She glanced up and could see the taxi driver looking at her, his eyes opening wider at her transformation. In thirty seconds, the smart woman with the smoky eyes and glossed lips – the typical groomed Manhattan businesswoman – had morphed into a futuristic sex kitten. Arriving at her destination, she exited the cab and wordlessly handed the driver a twenty-dollar bill.

Liz stood on the sidewalk and smiled at the neon sign for the Red Legs bar. It really belonged in the old Clinton, she thought. For years Clinton had been one of New York's most notorious areas: poor Irish gangs and white trash living in comparative squalor. Hell's Kitchen: that's what it had been called before Giuliani had cleaned up the city. Now it was becoming gentrified, but the musicians, artists, and students were taking their time moving on and, if you knew where to look, you could still find a taste of down-and-dirty New York, a city that never ceased to excite her. She had spent time in London and Paris for the company, but nowhere had her as entranced as her hometown.

The entrance to the club was a metal door. There were people outside smoking, a transvestite blowing smoke rings into the night air, a couple having an argument, all the usual sights and sounds of the Big Apple. Liz descended the stairway and put her coat in the cloakroom, pausing at the entrance to the main room to check her reflection and compose herself. She knew what to expect; she had been to the club a couple of months before. It was one of her golden rules not to frequent the same place regularly, but she liked this place. A doorman pulled open a soundproofed door and Liz was engulfed by sound. The club was one huge underground space, crammed with sweating, writhing bodies moving to the deafening music as spotlights criss-crossed and whirled. The room was bathed in deep red light and, with the pulsing and shaking of the walls, Liz felt as if she was walking inside a giant beast. Pushing her way through the crowd, she took a seat at the end of the black glass bar, sitting at right angles to the room, where she could observe the action without attracting attention. Nodding at the model-grade barman, she ordered a single-malt Scotch, wishing for the days when you could light up a cigarette.

She savoured the heat of the liquor in her throat and watched. She only vaguely listened to the music; that wasn't why she was here. It was ten minutes before she saw him. Tall, handsome, a little dishevelled, a painter perhaps. But when their gaze met, he had a look in his eye that Liz recognized.

'Can I buy you a drink?' he said over the music.

She gave a small smile, shook her head. 'I'm not staying.'

He took a seat next to her and propped his elbow on the bar, just looking at her. Liz didn't mind such a brazen approach; in fact she enjoyed it. She uncoiled slowly, watching his reaction as she crossed her long legs. Liz might not be beautiful in the way her sister Brooke was, but she had always been sexy. Her hardness, her cleverness, her sexual experience – who knew what drew men towards her? But Liz had an aura, a scent that only the right – or the wrong – kind of man could pick up.

'I'm Russ. Russ Ford.'

'Hello Russ,' she said, staring off across the room, feigning indifference, even mild irritation. It was all an act, a game. She knew men well; she had been in this situation many times before and experience had taught her that men as good-looking as Russ liked to be treated like this. She waited, savouring the moment. *He will speak,* she thought, *any moment . . . now.*

'Are you ignoring me?'

Exactly, thought Liz.

'What are you looking at?' she asked, still not looking at him.

'The cleft on your chin,' said Russ, 'I have one too. I wonder where they come from?'

'It's where the right and left side of your jawbone hasn't fused completely. It's a Mendelian trait.' She took a drink and watched his reaction.

'A what?'

Liz touched the small dimple at the base of her face. 'Genetics. It's a dominant gene. I was unlucky. My sister escaped it.'

'Mendelian trait, you say?' he laughed slowly. 'You're a smart girl.'

Choate Rosemary Hall. Princeton. Wharton Business School, thought Liz. He didn't know the half of it.

'Sorry, I missed your name,' said Russ.

'I didn't tell you it.'

Now she turned the full power of her eyes on him, looking at his face in detail, feeling a growing dampness between her legs. He was good looking, really good looking, like a greeter at Abercrombie & Fitch. No more than twenty-five, twenty-six. Tanned skin, a smudge of stubble over his chin. He seemed self-assured, arrogant even. Keen to challenge her, banter with her. She knew she had chosen well; this was exactly the sort of man to respond to her.

'So what should I call you?'

She paused, a hint of a smile. 'Lisa.'

'Okay, smart, lovely Lisa,' he said. 'Forgive the corny question, but what are you doing in a place like this?'

'A place like this?'

'A place full of hookers and transvestites?'

'Is that right? And which category do you fall into?'

He chuckled.

'Neither, I'm afraid,' he smiled. 'I live round the corner. It's cheap and I'm broke. Bars like this suit me. What about you?'

'I work nearby,' she lied.

'What do you do?'

She stifled a smile, wondering what he would say if she told him she had just come from the twenty-five-million-dollar spa she was about to launch; wondering whether it would make her more or less desirable to him.

'Things I like to forget about by drinking Scotch.'

He laughed. 'I like mysterious women. So can I buy you that drink now?'

What was the point of stringing this out any longer, thought Liz. More games, more Scotch? Why not move in for the kill?

She looked at him directly. 'Only if you'll fuck me.'

His eyes seemed to shine a little brighter in the dark redness, his face showed no surprise except for a slight pull of the right corner of his lip. Liz stood up and, as she moved, she ran the tip of her finger across his jeans. She simply turned and began to walk towards the exit. She didn't need to turn round to know he was following her. Since her divorce from Walter Baker, a hotelier she had known since her teens, Liz found that she had no need for relationships. She had no interest in the complications, cluttering her life with thin emotion. But she wanted, she *needed* sex. It charged her.

He caught up with her as they left the booming main room of the club.

'Keep walking,' he whispered into her neck. 'I know somewhere downstairs.'

He steered her into a corridor and down a short flight of steps ending in a door marked 'Staff'. Inside was a dark six-foot-square room lined with black. In one corner was a Formica stall and a white ceramic sink. She heard the click of the door being locked behind her and then felt his hands snaking round her waist. His lips sinking into the warm skin of her neck. She spun around to face him and his lips brushed her ear lobes before they came crashing down on her mouth. His tongue slid into hers and she could taste her own lipstick. He was a fantastic kisser, his touch almost as expert as her own. He rucked up her dress and peeled down her hose and thong in one movement. His lips heavy and urgent on hers, he pushed Liz up against the edge of the sink, raising her feet off the floor, and then spread her thighs with his hands.

Liz groaned as she unzipped his jeans. He pushed his hand under her top and bra until her breast sprang free. Desperate, Liz pulled the fabric over her head. Russ had unhooked her bra so it fell to her waist. He circled one breast in his hand and lowered his lips onto her brown nipple, which grew bigger and harder in his mouth. After pulling a condom out of his pocket, he pushed his own jeans down to the floor, as if they were white-hot against his skin.

Wrapping his hands under her buttocks he pulled her closer. She could feel the roughness of his fingertips on her skin. Blue-collar hands she had felt many times before. She moaned as she felt his thick hard cock enter her, his hands holding her steady as he deepened his quick thrusts.

Biting into his shoulder, she responded by pulling her knee up and back so he completely filled her.

She cried out, barely registering that his urgent hands had turned on the taps behind her. Feeling the water pouring on her back, she reached behind her to grab at the cold liquid. She stroked the water across his face, letting him suck her fingers.

'Faster,' she groaned, tipping her head back until it knocked against the mirror. Her breathing quickened as she was about to come. As she grabbed his thick, coarse hair she felt spasms swell from her core to every nerve ending in her body.

'Shit,' he winced, his body shivering as he exploded inside her.

As he slid slowly out of her, Liz inhaled deeply to regulate her breathing. She shut her eyes to enjoy the sensation of his thickness retreating, until the tip of his cock just tickled out of her cunt.

Slipping off the vanity unit, she picked up her discarded tights and thong and slipped on her shoes. She looked at him, all excitement gone, like air from a deflated balloon, the electricity in the room unplugged. All that was left was a panting twenty-something with his pants down and a rolled condom still on his cock. She almost laughed. So he was good-looking. Usually it didn't matter. She wasn't after someone she had to look at for the rest of her life.

'I've got to go,' she said, rolling down her dress.

He touched her arm as she tried to walk past. 'You're kidding, right?'

'Not tonight.'

'But, but where do you live?' he asked. 'Let me come with you.'

She smiled slowly and shook her head. As she opened the door she turned to look at him one last time. Her third nameless, faceless fuck this month. He had been good, very good. What a shame she would never see him again.

4

Paula Asgill smiled to herself as she lay back in the soapy water, gazing through the open bathroom doorway at the luxurious guest cottage on the Billingtons' exquisite country estate, Belcourt. At first she had been disappointed not to be staying in the main house, which she could just glimpse in the distance through the cottage's pretty leaded windows, but now she was here, she knew she'd hit social gold. For years she'd been forced to listen to her connected Upper East Side friends boast about the legendary parties they'd attended at Belcourt: how they'd marvelled at the seventeenth-century chandelier in the ballroom, swayed on the polished dance floor suspended over the Olympic-sized swimming pool, or visited the 50,000-bottle wine cellar, from which endless glasses of Château Pétrus, Mouton Rothschild or d'Yquem flowed. For years, she'd had to stand there and take it, but now it was time for revenge.

Paula stepped out of the roll top bath and wrapped a fluffy white towel around her pale, lithe body. Tomorrow she could talk about all those things and more. Yes, her friends were familiar with Belcourt's interiors and furnishings, but how many of them were au fait with the grand estate's guest cottages, the twelve sumptuous mini-mansions dotted around the thousand-acre grounds, all exclusively reserved for Billington family members. How many of her tormentors could describe the exquisite Stubbs paintings over the fireplaces? The Cornish pottery in the petite, handmade French kitchen, the lavender-scented Porthault linens on the sleigh beds or the view of the cherry-blossom trees from the east window? Not one. It was priceless social ammunition, and Paula could barely wait to use it back in New York. She would almost pass up tonight's party to see their faces. Almost.

Walking into the pastel-peach bedroom she let the towel drop to the floor and slid into her black lace Dior lingerie and silk robe, then reclined on the crisp sheets, luxuriating in her good fortune. It was very nearly a perfect moment; the only niggling annoyance was a small fly buzzing around the room. She flapped her hands at it and shuddered. The thought of insects or germs of any kind made Paula feel physically sick. She pulled her robe around her tightly and hurried to open the window, but recoiled when she touched the metal handle. What was that? Rust? Not wanting to take a risk, she ran to the dresser and pulled a bottle of hand-sanitizer from her wash bag, scrubbing her hands thoroughly. By now the fly was gone, but it had ruined her mood.

Walking back to the living room, she took a sip of camomile tea to settle herself, wondering why she felt so jumpy at the moment, so nervous. It couldn't just be the prospect of Brooke and David's engagement party tonight; after all, it was only a night out, wasn't it? At least she had the dress, *the killer dress*, she smiled, glancing back at the long pale-violet gown hanging by the door. The moment the Belcourt party had been announced, Paula had dispatched her personal shoppers at Bendel's and Bergdorf Goodman to find something wonderful, something elegant, something absolutely nobody else was going to be wearing. It was Cheryl, a friend from her modelling days who had reinvented herself as a celebrity stylist, who had finally come up trumps with a McQueen sample that had not gone into production. Cheryl had warned her that violet was a difficult shade to wear, making brunettes look too sallow and blondes too garish. But against the alabaster paleness of Paula's skin and the rich red of her long, straight hair, it looked magnificent. A small size eight, Paula was slim enough to squeeze into the sample size, although the cut made no concessions for bumps of any kind. Paula had therefore spent the past week on a rigorous diet and had let nothing but the tea past her lips in the last twenty-four hours.

Looking good meant hard work, thought Paula, but converting those looks into success was even harder. She had learnt that hard lesson from her mother, Helena. A sunny blonde with perfect features, Paula's mother had once been an incredible Southern beauty, but she had sold herself short by falling head over heels in love with Samuel, a trucker and dedicated alcoholic who had been killed drink-driving on a long-distance job when Paula was nine. With a grieving heart and a young daughter to support, Helena had taken on three jobs, in a launderette, the general store, and the local bar to pay the bills. She had been trying to break up a brawl at the bar one night when an enraged hooker had smashed her glass into Helena's face. With an ugly six-inch scar across her cheek, all work except the launderette shift had quickly dried up. It had broken Helena. She worked hard, and where had it got her? When the MS had kicked in, it had ravaged Helena's body quickly; she simply seemed unwilling to fight it. By the time Paula was nineteen, her mother was dead, but she hadn't missed the point of the life lesson.

Paula worked damn hard to make her own beauty count. When she moved to New York to model, she was not the most beautiful or even the most interesting girl on the circuit; otherworldly-looking girls like Karen Elson and Erin O'Connor were making their mark. But Paula was not disheartened, even when a booker at Ford had told Paula that Julianne Moore had cornered the market in pale, interesting redheads. Paula simply put in twice as much effort. She never arrived late for a job, never had sex with a photographer or a client, never took drugs or drank too much. Instead of partying, she perfected a regal bearing that made her stand out in a city awash with young exotic beauties. Even so, Paula was never quite flavour of the month, but shoots for St John and Escada kept her in work until she met William when she was twenty-three. That was when all the hard work had paid off.

Just then, husband William walked in and dropped his overnight bag on the floor with a grunt. A tall, athletic-looking man with a full head of sandy hair and an open face, he looked tired and slightly world-weary; inevitable, thought Paula, considering his job as CEO of Asgill Cosmetics. It seemed a thankless task.

William moved behind her and nuzzled his lips into her neck. She giggled, genuinely pleased to have him there, holding her. It was getting dark and it felt a little isolating to be on her own on the estate.

'What kept you?' she asked, turning to kiss him.

William sighed. 'I would have been here an hour ago, but I was waiting for Liz. Then she decided she was going to make her own way here.'

'Typical Liz,' snorted Paula; her sister-in-law's selfishness was one of those things that made William's job that much more difficult than it had to be.

'Well, David's mother called two hours ago wanting to know if we want to take a couple of horses out,' she continued, gesturing towards the window. 'Apparently from the ridge over there you can see the whole Manhattan skyline. Do you think it's too late?'

'We can go tomorrow morning,' smiled William in his easy-going, almost placid way. 'Besides, I think it would be wise to check with security. There were already extra guards on the gates when I came through, and I've heard a couple of choppers already. I'm not sure whether it's paparazzi or party guests arriving.'

Paula sat down in front of an antique dressing table and began to pad the underside of her eyes with foundation. She had always been skilled with cosmetics; she could do it better than any make-up artist.

'Great place, isn't it?' said William appreciatively as he looked around the cottage. 'We should do this more often: get away for the night without the twins.'

Paula shook her head. 'I hate leaving them,' she sighed.

'Honey, it's just for the night.'

She gazed at her reflection in the mirror.

'I think it would do wonders for the twins if we had a place in the country. Somewhere with stables where they could keep their own ponies,' she said finally.

'We've got our own place,' said William, referring to Parklands, the Asgills' country place in Bedford, New York.

'Oh, that doesn't count,' she pouted. 'Parklands is your mother's.'

William stood behind her, gently running his fingers though her hair. Irritated at the way he had ducked the issue of the country retreat once again, she pulled away.

'Please, honey. It was blow-dried this morning.'

William held up his hands. 'Hey, I'm sorry. I like my wife's hair. Sue me.'

She pulled her stool forwards. 'Can you just pass me my bristle brush? It's in the cream suitcase. No, not the paddle brush. The round one.'

As she watched him in reflection, she felt a little pang of affection. For all his faults – *I mean, how many CEOs with a multimillion-dollar shareholding would think twice about buying a weekend retreat?* – William Asgill was loving, loyal, and decent, all of which were rare attributes this high up in society and, for Paula, they were the glue that held their marriage together. It was, however, an unfashionable point of view among Paula's circle of friends, most of whom had one eye on their current marriage and another eye on someone else's more successful husband. Five years ago, such trading up had been rampant. In fact, it had been one such adventuress named Lynette who had married and divorced William when he was in his early twenties. His first wife now lived in Scotland, the consort of a handsome fifty-something duke.

However, the world had changed rapidly since then. With the implosion of the hedge funds, there was a comparative paucity of genuinely wealthy men in New York, whereas each passing day seemed to unleash more and more beautiful girls into fashionable Manhattan; the competition had become cut-throat. These gold-diggers were no longer just the usual Park Avenue Princesses, but models, celebrities, and ambitious suburbanites seeking their fortune in the Big Apple. This was all very bad news for Paula's friends, meaning slim pickings on the next rung of the ladder and danger from below. After all, any self-respecting thirty- or forty-something Wall Street player would be looking to upgrade too, and those buxom, smooth-skinned, pre-child bitches would look mighty appealing.

For herself, Paula had always been pragmatic about her love life; if relationships were a game of poker, she was not going to cash in her chips now when there was a strong chance of losing everything. So William and Paula's sex life limped along, getting the odd boost when her diets allowed her to feel good enough about herself to put on the Dior lingerie, and their relationship chugged along in what could be best described as remote companionship. However, Paula did not fear the predatory females she knew William encountered in the city; she knew he wouldn't stray. Perhaps it was the sting from his first marriage that had made him less demanding, much happier with his lot. In her gut, Paula felt that their marriage was not a question of resignation but expectation: expectation that the other would not stray. It was why she trusted her husband to be faithful and stand by her side. She walked over to the door and unwrapped her dress, slipping it over her lithe body. She didn't need to look in the mirror; she could tell she looked stunning from the expression on William's face.

'I think we have some time to kill before the party starts,' he smiled, nodding towards the antique sleigh bed. For all her affectionate thoughts about William and their marriage, Paula still felt her stomach clench.

'Honey, no,' she said, 'I've just showered.'

'And I thought the idea of conceiving at Belcourt might appeal to you,' he laughed, stroking her neck with his fingertips.

She reached up and held his hand.

'Don't bring this up again. Not tonight.'

William frowned. 'Bring what up?'

'Darling, I'm not a baby machine,' she said, turning away and scooping her hair into a chignon.

William gave a hollow laugh. 'We've got two kids, Paula, not ten.'

And that's enough, she thought as she busied herself pinning up her hair. Unlike William, who had declared a desire to produce 'a brood', Paula had no intention of having any more children. On the surface she was elegant and confident, but underneath she was anxious and prone to depression. Something to do with her upbringing, perhaps, but, whatever the reason, pregnancy was certainly not a condition that suited her. Two years into their marriage she had conceived while on the pill, only to miscarry ten weeks later. William had been wonderful throughout the entire ordeal, sending her to recuperate at his uncle's waterside house in the Florida Keys, but he was obviously devastated by the tragedy. Paula was more sanguine.

'Something was wrong with our baby,' she had told him matter-of factly. 'The miscarriage was a sign. A gift.'

William had hugged her and told her that she was in shock or post-traumatic stress and that she would feel better about it very soon. Paula knew that he was wrong. Two years later, under pressure from William, they had actively tried to get pregnant again, and to Paula's relief it had been swift. The twins were born healthy and pretty and she felt she could now relax, having paid her dues.

'Paula. The twins are nearly six,' said William. 'You're thirty-two now, but you know how difficult things get after thirty-five.'

'I know the biology,' she said with a little more force than she'd intended.

'Hey now, don't be like that,' he whispered, pulling her towards the bed. 'You never know, it might be fun.'

As he kissed her bare shoulder beyond the strap of her dress, she smiled. If William thought the smile was in anticipation of the patter of tiny feet, he was dead wrong. Paula adored her children, and she had to admit that the idea of conceiving a child at Belcourt did appeal to her. But she was not going through the ordeal of pregnancy again under any circumstances. Her wolfish grin covered the thought that if they had sex tonight, she could forget about it for another month at least. As for the contraceptive injections that she had administered by a discreet gynaecologist on a regular basis, well, that would remain her little secret. In the meantime, it was back to her wifely duty. And, as he said, it might even be fun.

'Are you ready yet?'

Tess tapped her nails impatiently on the doorframe of the bathroom. Brooke Asgill's engagement party was beginning at seven-thirty p.m. It was now six forty-five and the venue was over an hour away. It was somewhere upstate – 'Belcourt, Westchester', it stated simply on the stiff white invitation, as if everybody was expected to know where it was – and Tess was anxious enough about going without her appearance-conscious boyfriend making them late too.

Dom was standing by the sink, rummaging through the complimentary toiletries.

'They haven't got shoeshine,' he grumbled, flinging a shower cap back in the basket.

'Since when do you ever use shoeshine?' asked Tess with surprise.

'They have shoeshine at the Plaza.'

Tess took a deep breath and counted to ten. They were staying in a luxurious suite at The Pierre, one of, if not *the* most fabulous and luxurious hotels in New York and therefore the world, and here he was bitching about the tiniest detail. It was especially annoying as this beautiful room had been booked and paid for by Meredith Asgill. Tess turned him round and began to fasten the black silk bow tie hanging around his neck.

'Just chill out,' she said as calmly as she could. Her nerves were frayed. She was excited about the party but edgy over what was expected of her, not to mention tired from the flight, even if they had flown on a Lear Jet into a convenient private airport in New Jersey.

'Come on, honey, we are in New York at a fabulous hotel and about to go to an even more fabulous party. And, let's face it, you look fabulous too.'

Dom looked at his reflection in the mirror and tugged at his shirt cuffs, adjusting the jacket of his smart one-button suit and smoothing out his bow tie. Finally he grunted with satisfaction.

'Exactly how posh do you think it's going to be tonight?'

'Posh enough for a shoeshine,' she smiled. Seeing his anxious face she squeezed his arm reassuringly. 'Hey, I'm joking. I really don't know how posh it's going to be, but I do know you'll fit in fine.'

She glanced at her own reflection behind him and thought how great they looked together. So rarely did they have an opportunity to dress up like this, and she had made a special effort to look as sensational as possible. Her shoulder-length black hair was too short to do anything exotic with, but she had swept it up, framing her strong face. A dash of bronzer sharpened her cheekbones and her green eyes dazzled with the help of pearlized cream over her lids. In her favourite cocktail dress, a cream Ossie Clark shift that made her look and feel like a glamorous Twenties flapper girl, she had to admit she felt wonderful. Now if she could just resist the urge to chew her nails . . .

'I also know that Belcourt is supposed to be one of the finest private residences in North America,' she continued. 'I mean, the Billingtons are worth fifteen billion dollars. They can afford to throw a good party.'

'Which is why I'm a bit concerned,' said Dom as she walked back into the bedroom to pick up her clutch bag. 'Isn't this job offer for the Asgill family and not the Billingtons?'

'Yes. What? I don't follow.'

Dom opened the minibar and took a swig from a miniature vodka bottle.

'I mean that if this job was for the Billingtons, I'd say fine, fantastic. They're rich, connected, politically influential, *useful*. But who are the Asgills? They've got some mid-market cosmetics company and they aren't even on the Forbes List. That private jet we flew over on was all well and nice, although I bet it's not theirs, and here we are in a junior suite. I thought they were trying to impress you.'

'I think that's a little ungrateful.'

'I'm just not sure this is the best career move for us, Tess,' said Dom, draining the rest of the vodka. 'Granted, the money is fantastic, but whatever happened to "I want to be editor of the *Sun*"? Who wants to be some nouveau-riche nobody's hired help?'

She looked at him, wondering if he had noticed how unhappy she had been at the *Globe* over the past two months, her ability constantly questioned by her new boss. Perhaps it didn't matter to Dom, so long as her salary meant they could live life high on the hog.

'This isn't about how rich this family is,' said Tess firmly. 'And it's certainly not about how big our suite is. The point is that Meredith Asgill might be right, and in a month's time I might not even have a job at the *Globe*. We both know how tough it is on the papers at the moment. Who's to say I'm going to get another job any time soon? And after the week I had last week, I'm not entirely sure I want to be an editor any more.'

He blinked at her, clearly taken aback by her response. 'You've changed your tune,' he said sulkily.

'Think of the money with this Asgill offer, Dom. Think of that two hundred and fifty thousand dollar bonus,' she said, her eyes glittering. 'Plus it's New York, rent-free. I've always wanted to work here.'

'But what about me?' he asked, his lips in a thin, unhappy line.

'I know this transatlantic thing is going to be hard,' she said, stroking his cheek. 'But if you come out to New York once a month and I come to London once a month, we'll see each other every two weeks. It's probably more than we see each other at the moment.'

'That's a bit of an exaggeration . . .'

'Okay, a little. But remember that it will be temporary – it's a fixed-term contract until the wedding, then we'll play it by ear.'

'At which point they'd get me a visa?'

She looked away, feeling a pang of guilt. Only last week Dom had told her how his old friend Mungo had bagged some fancy editorial position on the *Wall Street Journal*. His handsome face had been etched with envy. At twenty-one Dom had been part of an elite band of graduates destined for the very top of the newspaper tree, starting his career on *The Times* training scheme. Although his peer group was only just touching thirty, they had begun to start scoring columns with *The Spectator*, jobs in Manhattan or senior positions on the big, prestigious broadsheets, making Dom's deputy travel editor's job seem not as impressive as he'd once thought. Perhaps Dom was unlucky; perhaps he was too fond of press trips and free lunches – Tess knew he was rarely in the office these days – but, either way, no fancy New York job offers had come his way and she knew how desperately he wanted the status he thought he deserved, especially when Tess's own career, the recent wobble notwithstanding, had taken off like a rocket.

'Well, we didn't get round to the small print,' Tess said cautiously. 'But Meredith did invite you to the party this weekend, so she obviously wants to seduce you with New York too.'

'That's not the same as getting me a visa,' grumbled Dom.

'Well, if you want a visa that badly –' she began, running her fingers across his crotch and being gratified by an instant response – 'then I guess you're just going to have to marry me,' she smiled mischievously.

He pulled her in close and grinned. 'If I thought for one second that either of us was the marrying kind, I might just do that.'

Tess smiled back. It was one of their shared jokes, a pact almost. After nine years together they had no intention of taking the plunge. It wasn't that they disagreed with marriage; they just wondered what was the point? Marriage was, after all, just a piece of paper, a shackle that made a break-up, should it ever happen, more difficult and expensive. Tess had seen her own parents' marriage dissolve with such animosity and rancour that she had not spoken to her mother since she was nineteen. Besides, she had seen too many friends disappear into marriage, children, and that whole cloying suburban routine. She had no desire to follow them.

'How do I look?' asked Dom, taking one last glance in the mirror.

'Like James Bond,' she said, ushering him towards the door.

'Now come on, the car is waiting. We've got the world's greatest party to get to.'

When Brooke had first agreed to the idea of an engagement party, she had assumed that it would be a small affair for friends and family. Looking down into the crowded, buzzing entrance hall of Belcourt, she almost laughed at her naivety. From her vantage point on the mezzanine terrace, it was obvious that tonight's party would be more lavish than a state dinner. There were huge arrangements of rare orchids on every surface, silk draped everywhere, and a medieval feast was being arranged in the Great Hall. Such excess was inevitable, really, since they had left the arrangements to David's mother Rose, but it was incredible what she'd been able to pull together in two weeks. I mean, where *did* you get so many orchids at this time of year? Waiters in white tails milled around in almost choreographed movement, their trays piled high with canapés. Vintage champagne was served in Baccarat crystal and the flowers perfumed the air like bespoke scent. Couture-clad women danced with captains of industry to the sounds of a big band jazz orchestra led, she could have sworn, by Harry Connick Jr on the grand piano.

There were hundreds, no, maybe even a thousand people here at Belcourt tonight, and they were all here for her. How ironic she didn't even know most of them! Brooke's first hour of the party was spent in a whirl, being introduced to scores of people she had never even heard of, let alone met, in nine months of dating David Billington. There were David's Yale friends, CTV newsroom friends, Andover friends, celebrity friends (yes, that *was* George Clooney at the bar!). Friends from the think-tanks he belonged to, friends from across the political divide. David, it seemed, had friends everywhere. By contrast, when David's mother Rose had her assistant call her future daughter-in-law for her list of invitees, Brooke had provided her with sixty or so names.

'What are you doing hiding away up there?'

David met Brooke at the bottom of the steps and took her hand. Dressed in a midnight-blue suit that complemented the darkness of his hair and the pale olive of his skin, he looked devastatingly handsome.

'I'm not hiding,' she said, tapping him playfully. 'Just taking a little time-out. I'm still in a state of shock that George Clooney is at my engagement party. If he's at the wedding, I might pass out at the altar.'

'I'd better hope he's filming then,' grinned David, handing her a stemmed glass.

'Try that. My mom's butler has come out of retirement just for tonight to mix his special martinis. They'll keep you awake until sunrise.'

Brooke gaped as Colin Powell walked past and clapped David on the arm in a familiar way.

'Are all these people coming to the wedding?' she asked.

David laughed. 'My mother maintains this is a gathering of close friends.'

'Meaning they'll be more people on the wedding guest list?' she said.

'The venue can handle it,' he said obliquely. 'Besides, it's good for the charities. We don't need gifts, do we? So we'll get the guests to give donations to charity. The more people, the more money we can raise.'

He took her hand and led her through the room. 'Come on, there's someone I want you to meet.'

'Not another friend of the family?' she said suspiciously.

He laughed. 'Not this time. My cousin Lily, she lives in London so you haven't met her before.'

'Nice of her to come all this way.'

'In her own words, she's come to audition.'

Brooke looked at him. 'Audition. What for?'

For a second, David's confident demeanour deserted him. 'To be a bridesmaid,' he said, pulling an embarrassed face.

She laughed at the idea. 'Really? You're serious?'

'It's one of those family things, honey. Twenty-something years ago I was a pageboy at Lily's eldest sister's wedding. My mother wants to return the favour.'

'Wasn't it enough that you were an angelic ring-bearer?'

'Let's call it a family tradition. It would mean a lot to my parents.'

Brooke had tried to avoid thinking about the issue of her brides-maids because frankly, none of her friends was suitable. Her good friends from Spence and Brown had split off into two increas-ingly distant groups: career girls and socialites. Predictably, she rarely saw the career girls as they were far too busy moving and shaking in finance, media, and PR, while the friends who had married into money or spent their lives on the party and charity circuit, well, she found them a little too . . . shallow? Competitive? She had never been able to put her finger on it, but these days she enjoyed their company less and less. A few years ago Brooke had embraced that whole Park Avenue Princess scene – being rich and beautiful it was almost expected – but she had found it exhausting. As legendary socialite Nan Kempner had once said, you had to 'entertain constantly', you were constantly locked in a battle of one-upmanship, jockeying for position on the most prestigious junior committees, making sure you were dressed head to toe in the hottest designs.

In some ways it had been fun, especially the big events such as the Costume Institute Gala and the summer parties in the Hamptons, but the constant pressure to get a manicure and blow-dry every time she set foot out of the house quickly became tedious. Slowly Brooke realized she preferred to socialize in a more low-key way:

dinner at her favourite restaurants Sfoglia or Raoul's with friends, for example, or old movies in little art-house theatres downtown. Such individuality was not something that was approved of in the socialite clique, and Brooke had found them drifting away. It had frankly been a relief, when she had started seeing David, that she could step away from all that endless competition, but it did rather leave her without a natural choice for a bridesmaid. The irony of course was that as soon as the engagement was announced, she was swamped with invitations to lunch and parties from the in-crowd; any one of them would have given their entire Manolo collection to be Brooke's bridesmaid now. So this might actually be the ideal solution: a sweet little cousin might be a way to avoid snubbing her old circle.

'I quite like the idea of having a pretty little flower girl,' said Brooke, thinking it over. 'How old is she?'

'Not sure. Twenty-nine, thirty, I think.'

'*Thirty?* You're kidding!' said Brooke.

David shrugged. 'Come on, baby, you haven't exactly asked anyone else, have you?'

She looked at him in shock. 'That's hardly the point, honey. I'm not going around suggesting a best man for you.'

'It's Robert, it was always going to be my brother, it's tradition in our family,' he sighed. 'Come on, honey, it's no big deal . . .'

'It's a very big deal,' said Brooke, her face flushing. 'For a family so fixed on observing all the correct traditions, you're very quick to ignore them when it comes to me. I suppose you're going to choose the dress for me next.'

David put his hands on her shoulders and gave her his best smile. 'Don't get so worked up,' he said. 'You don't have to say yes, just come and meet her.'

Brooke took a deep breath. *This was all meant to be fun.*

'Why is she so desperate to be a bridesmaid anyway?'

'Nice dress, great party, eligible best man . . .'

Brooke smiled a little. 'There's a very cynical side to you, David Billington.'

In the flesh, Lily Salter couldn't have been further from Brooke's idea of a 'sweet little cousin'. She was tall and pretty, with long dark bouncy hair and beautiful posture, although her eyes looked a little glassy from too many late nights. Lily had gone to London to work in the Marc Jacobs London press office, and now had her own up-market PR agency. She was a mainstay on the Notting Hill American ex-pat party circuit, and it showed.

'Brooke,' said Lily as David introduced her. 'You look amazing. Very Helen of Troy.'

Brooke smiled, grateful for the compliment. Brooke had always loved clothes; she enjoyed putting outfits together, playing with styles, but in the days since her relationship with David had gone public, she had lost a bit of confidence in her own dress sense. Every time she left the house she was scrutinized by the press; every dress and shoe examined, her outfits declared 'Hit' or 'Miss' in the weekly tabloid rags. Before David, a night like tonight would have been great fun, playfully imagining herself as Lauren Hutton at Studio 54, Mia Farrow's Daisy in *The Great Gatsby*, or Veronica Lake in some Forties film noir. The endless public scrutiny crushed that pleasure and ate away at her faith in her own judgement. Tonight, however, had been different. Tonight Brooke felt beautiful in a putty grey Grecian gown that fell in gentle waves to the floor; comfortable because of the relaxed structure, yet sexy as the fine silk brushed against her skin. It had a sweeping neck that showed off a rose-gold choker – an engagement present from David – and a low back perfect for showing off her buttery blonde hair.

'Thank you,' said Brooke, flushing slightly. 'David bought it for me for the party.'

He grinned. 'I've been assured there are only two in existence. Apparently Kate Moss has the other one. I'm sure Brooke wears it even better than she does.'

'It's beautiful,' said Lily appreciatively. 'Who styles you?'

'My fiancé,' laughed Brooke.

David gave Brooke's arm a squeeze. 'I'll leave you two girls to it,' he smiled.

'Do you ever wake up and pinch yourself?' said Lily, as she watched David move through the crowd shaking hands and exchanging jokes.

'Pinch myself? About the engagement?'

Lily nodded. 'About David. Every girlfriend of mine has been in love with him since school. I know he's my cousin and everything, but I do think he's sexy – is that wrong?' she giggled. 'Anyway, I'm so happy for you. Tell me about the proposal, I bet it was romantic.'

'We were standing on a terrace overlooking Paris and when we looked up we saw a shooting star sweep across the sky. How could I say no with an omen like that?'

Lily's mouth formed an 'O'.

'And where's the wedding going to be?'

Brooke pulled a face. 'We're keeping it under wraps for the moment.'

'Well, let me know the second you want me to do something. I know it's a bit trickier with me in London, but we can work all that out. It's *totally* an honour to be invited to be your bridesmaid.'

Brooke looked at her, puzzled. 'I'm sorry?'

Lily just laughed. 'Oh, I know it's silly, but you know how everyone says David is going to be president one day? I have this little fantasy where sometime in the future everyone is going to be interested in every detail of this wedding; the dress, the venue, even the bridesmaids,' she giggled. 'There might even be a little guided tour where the guide says, ". . . and this is where Lily Salter caught the bouquet".'

Brooke didn't know whether to be furious or grateful that at least the bridesmaid issue was settled – even if she hadn't actually made the decision herself. Had Lily somehow got the wrong end of the stick, she wondered, or had Rose, David's mother, simply offered her the job? Worse still, had *David* gone ahead and recruited her without asking? He had looked rather shamefaced when he mentioned the 'family tradition'. Whatever the source of this mix-up, Brooke began to feel a worrying loss of control. If she didn't have a free choice of her bridesmaids, then what else could she rely on?

Oblivious to Brooke's discomfort, Lily hooked her arm through Brooke's and took another glass of champagne from a waiter.

'Rose thought it would be a good idea if we fixed up a lunch before I went back to London, what do you think?' she gushed. 'There's so much to talk about, isn't there? I mean, is it going to be a church ceremony? If it is, I think bare shoulders might upset some of the older family, but if it's not, I was thinking strapless, cut away low at the back. Backs are so important. After all, that's what the congregation are going to be looking at . . .'

Tess and Dom had spent the first hour of the party wandering around Belcourt, their mouths open. Away from the Grand Ballroom, where hundreds of glamorous people laughed and danced, the house was even more impressive, corridor upon corridor lined with fine art and tapestries.

'It's like visiting the Louvre at night,' whispered Dom.

'It's amazing. But a bit eerie. It really would be like living in a museum.'

'So you're telling me you wouldn't like to live here.'

'I never said that at all,' she said with a little hiccup.

Tess was a little worried that she had drunk too much. Belcourt had been so intimidating she'd needed a couple of martinis just to loosen up. Dom's negativity at the hotel hadn't helped, although his mood had improved considerably since the town car had swung into the tree-fringed driveway and they'd got their first glimpse of the house. It was magnificent. The drive was lined with flickering torches, while Klieg lights turned the limestone façade of the house a blinding white. In the fading light, Tess could see that Belcourt's grounds were as magnificent as Richmond Park, Tess's favourite spot in London, but it was the interior that really dazzled. It was wall-to-wall marble, with huge gilt mirrors and polished oak panelling, but it wasn't only the decor they were looking at. If Tess hadn't known how influential the hosts were, she might have believed her eyes were playing tricks on her. After all, how many 'intimate gatherings' could get die-hard Democrat George Clooney and Republican ex-president George W. Bush in the same place at the same time? She had honestly never seen so many famous faces in one place before. For a second, Tess considered phoning through the story to the *Globe* offices, before remembering that her loyalties might soon lie elsewhere.

In an attempt to get a grip on herself, Tess found a quiet spot in the conservatory at the side of the house and sent Dom to the bar to see if they could rustle up some coffee.

Outside in the blackness, a fountain sprayed silver ribbons into the sky; as she stared at it, Tess reflected that she really hadn't been prepared for this trip. She wasn't at all sure what she had expected, but Belcourt was certainly more grand and imposing than she had imagined. She supposed the trouble was that she wasn't particularly experienced in society parties. She had been to a few swish press launches in her time, she had even been to 10 Downing Street for a briefing on women's issues, but the only real party of this calibre she had attended was when she had browbeaten the *Globe*'s showbiz desk into getting her an invitation to Elton's White Tie and Tiara ball.

Pull yourself together, Tess, she scolded herself. *They're only human.* It really wasn't like her to be so nervous in a social situation. Newspaper reporting didn't allow for such delicate personalities. Doorstepping enraged politicians, interviewing bereaved families, witnessing murder scenes and accident sites; it all toughened you up. But this was something else. Inside this house, she had felt invisible.

'Ossie Clark Nineteen Sixty-three,' said an upper-class English voice behind her. 'Which means you are British, making me wonder why we haven't ever met before. I thought I knew all the interesting English people in New York.'

Tess turned to see a slim man of around seventy regarding her with amusement. His voice and appearance were in perfect harmony; he sounded like a Raj-era colonial viceroy and was dressed accordingly in a cream three-piece suit with a scarlet spotted cravat. He had two-tone spectator shoes on his feet and a gold pocket watch sticking out of his waistcoat. To complete the look, he carried an ivory-handled cane hooked over his arm.

'Wow, yes. This is Ossie Clark,' said Tess, smoothing down her dress. 'How on earth did you know?'

'The designer of your dress or that you're a Brit?' he asked, one eyebrow raised.

'Both,' smiled Tess.

'The former because I knew Ossie and Celia intimately. The latter because New York girls generally don't do vintage. Certainly not so tastefully if they do.'

'Well, not all of us can afford couture,' said Tess, blushing slightly.

'No one with your legs needs couture, my dear.'

Tess knew she had only just met this man, but she liked him immediately. He was charming, open, and a little mischievous, a combination of qualities she felt was in short supply in New York society. More than that, with her journalist instincts, Tess immediately sized him up as being someone worth knowing.

'Sorry, I'm Charles Devine.' He extended a frail hand. 'Interior designer. An old friend of the Billingtons, the Asgills, and well, everyone worth knowing.'

Tess shook his hand warmly. 'Tess Garrett. Journalist. Friend of nobody in this room.'

'Good Lord, a journalist?' cried Charles with mock alarm. 'Are you a gate-crasher? I thought the security was as tight as Fort Knox out there.'

Tess laughed and shook her head. 'More of a last-minute invitee. I only arrived in New York this morning.'

'How extraordinary,' said Charles appreciatively. 'I can see we're going to be friends. It takes some people a lifetime of social mountaineering to score an invite to Belcourt, and here you are, straight off the boat. Now, you simply must let me show you around.' He offered Tess his arm and led her back into the main house where the party was in full swing.

'It is a fantastic party, isn't it?' said Tess, still wide-eyed at the spectacle.

'Indeed,' nodded Charles. 'One of the best I've ever been to – and let me tell you, my dear, I have been to a lot of parties. In fact this one might even make my memoirs. I'm only sketching them out at this stage, of course; the problem is not what to put in but what to leave out.'

Tess was intrigued. Charles Devine was clearly a character; perhaps he could give her more insight into the family. She had a hunch that if Charles didn't know about it, it wasn't worth knowing. They sat down on two Louis XV chairs facing each other.

'Brooke and David are a lovely couple, aren't they?' said Tess, fishing for gossip.

'Indeed,' he smiled. 'Everyone has very high hopes for them, although personally I'd prefer New York's premier power couple to be a little more interesting.'

'Oh dear. So what's David like?'

Charles laughed playfully. 'Too good-looking to be dull, too ambitious to be fun.'

'And what about her?'

'She's sweet. So sweet I wonder if she can handle all this attention,' said Charles. 'Fair enough if she's in it for the money, but one suspects Brooke is marrying America's most eligible bachelor because she is in love with America's most eligible bachelor. I'm always a little suspicious about those sorts of girls.'

'I got the impression that Meredith is the ambitious one.'

Charles smiled coyly. 'Darling, I'd love to give you more information, but first you must give me a little juice in return. Do tell: how did a *journalist* manage to get under the wire? I doubt it's simply beginner's luck.'

'Actually, I'm being wooed for a job with the Asgills.'

He raised his eyebrows again. 'As . . . ?'

'I'm not sure I can say any more,' smiled Tess playfully, knowing it would be unbearable for him not to know.

'Darling, just tell me. I'll find out somehow.'

She shrugged. 'They want me to be the family's publicist.'

Charles laughed, a delighted, tinkling laugh. 'Well, I suppose everyone in Manhattan has their own publicist now, don't they – present company excluded, of course – I've really never felt the need given the reliability of the grapevine . . . I'm only surprised it's taken the Asgills so long.'

'I think it's pragmatism in this case,' smiled Tess. 'They can't have Brooke involved in any scandal that would stop them marrying into all this.'

'Yes, I can see that . . .' said Charles thoughtfully. 'The hypocrisy of the rich at work once again, of course.'

Tess frowned, sensing a story. 'What do you mean?'

'Well, of course you're right; David has a big political future and so Brooke won't be able to put a foot wrong – that's why they need someone like you. But it's a little rich to say it's all about Brooke's behaviour. David dated someone five, six years ago, you see. Actress, beautiful girl. Photographed taking cocaine in some nightclub in LA. Terrible business. Six weeks later she moved to France to film some "art-house movie".' Charles framed the phrase in quotation marks. 'She was never heard of in this country again. Then of course there's Wendell,' he said, pointing the handle of his cane in the direction of an older man with pewter hair, brushed white at the temples. Tess recognized him as Wendell Billington, David's father, who had been pointed out to her earlier.

'In my direct line of vision I see at least four women Wendell has had sex with, one a long-term mistress. Can't keep his regal cock in his trousers, but of course that's fine. Joe Kennedy was a terrible philanderer and it didn't hurt his son's presidential ambitions one jot. It's a question of class, you see. The Billingtons are in a different class to the Asgills. They are more . . . how shall I put it? More bullet-proof.'

'Class?' said Tess. 'I didn't think that existed in America.'

Charles chuckled. He swept his hand across the room dramatically, only pausing to take a glass of champagne from a passing waiter in one fluid movement.

'This city is full of money, but what everyone wants is class. Obviously you can acquire class much quicker over here; you only have to look at the Lauders to see that. Old Estée Lauder was a Hungarian immigrant, but she builds a cosmetics dynasty and now they are one of the grand families of New York. But no, the Asgills aren't the Lauders: they're not rich enough and their business is not as prestigious. In fact, people still refer to Howard, Meredith's late husband, as 'the butcher's son'. And then there was all that business at his wedding,' he added, leaning in and dropping his voice. 'The missing actress,' he whispered.

'What missing actress?'

Charles smiled a wicked smile. 'Oh my dear, I thought you were their publicist? Surely a keeper of secrets has to know what they are.'

'Hey, I haven't taken the job yet, remember,' she smiled. 'Maybe you can persuade me.'

Charles stood up and gestured for Tess to follow. Glancing around like a stage villain, he led her into a quiet alcove and they sat down in a window seat upholstered in purple velvet.

'Howard and Meredith got married at Meredith's parents' home in Louisiana,' began Charles with relish. 'In 1964, I think. Her family had money – new money, mind you. Father had bought one of those antebellum plantation houses from an old sugar-caning family that had lost everything, and that was where they got married. Think *Gone with the Wind*, only right down by the river. Anyway, on the night of the nuptials, one of their wedding guests went missing. An actress called Olivia Martin. A beautiful, vivacious girl. The best ankles in Hollywood,' he added without a hint of irony.

'How awful,' said Tess.

'It certainly was for poor Meredith and her lovely new husband, Howard, especially with all the allegations that were flying about.'

'What allegations?' asked Tess, hoping desperately that Dom would stay searching for coffee. She didn't want anything to interrupt this story.

'Olivia was last seen at the party after the ceremony. She was staying in a guest cottage on the estate. When they realized she was missing, the police were called and her cottage was found unlocked and empty.'

'What do they suppose happened to her?'

Charles shrugged. 'Suicide, perhaps. She was addicted to dolls, what we called barbiturates in those days. Every starlet was on dolls; it was part of the scene. And she was known to be depressed about something. Theory was she walked into the Mississippi – it was yards from the cottage.'

'That's horrible, but it's hardly a scandal, is it?' said Tess. 'I mean, no one could blame the Asgills, could they?'

Charles smiled knowingly.

'There were whispers – and they were only whispers once people had been paid off – that Olivia was murdered, and some people were pointing the finger at Howard Asgill. Apparently he and Olivia had been having an affair.'

'From what you were saying about Wendell, that doesn't surprise me,' said Tess, feeling a sense of intrigue. 'But it doesn't mean to say he killed her, does it?'

Charles shook his head. 'Of course not, and that was why the story went away. There was no body, no proof. No evidence of any kind, in fact. Stories appeared everywhere about the extent of Olivia's drink and drug problem and how depressed she was. People believed that she had wanted to die.'

Tess let out a long breath. 'Well, I had no idea.'

'No, most people haven't,' said Charles. 'After all, it was decades ago. Forgotten. *But,* bringing us back to the present day and to you, my dear . . . one dead starlet is enough scandal for the Asgills for one lifetime, especially when their daughter is marrying America's bright new political hope. No wonder Meredith wants to hire a troubleshooter.'

'Nothing to do with my abilities, of course,' smiled Tess.

'Oh, I'm sure you'll do a marvellous job,' said Charles thoughtfully. 'Trouble is, the appointment might well be forty years too late.'

'Darling, how are you enjoying yourself?'

Brooke turned to her mother and embraced her. She smiled, knowing that Meredith had spent the evening having the time of her life, mingling like a statesperson. Brooke had to admit she looked the part too. Her hair was styled back into a champagne bun. She had on a long blue dress that Brooke recognized from the cowl neck as Oscar de la Renta and a large sapphire sat regally on a string of fat pearls around her neck.

'It's been a lovely night,' said Brooke, 'despite the fact it's full

of "close friends" I've never seen before in my life,' she added playfully. 'So who was that I saw you talking to earlier? The pretty girl
in the sparkly dress? Good-looking man with her.'

Meredith looked over to the other side of the ballroom where
she could see Tess sipping coffee while her boyfriend drank his
champagne rather too quickly.

'That's Tess Garrett. She may be doing some public relations for
the family in the run-up to the wedding. I must introduce you.'

'Oh, Mom! What do we need a publicist for? I've told you, I
want to keep things as normal as possible. For my sanity, *please?*'

'Did I hear the words "public relations"?' said a deep voice
behind them. 'Do you really think this lovely young lady needs any
more publicity?' laughed Wendell Billington, putting his arms around
the two women. David's father was an impressive-looking man,
with dark, narrow eyes and a strong chin. He wasn't tall, but he
had a presence that seemed to overfill his space. 'You needn't worry,
my dear,' he continued in his gravelly baritone. 'My office will be
overseeing the communications side of the wedding, keeping a lid
on it all. I'm sure we've all started thinking about the guest list,
and there will obviously be security issues with some of the people
attending.'

'Of course, Wendell,' smiled Meredith, putting a hand on his
forearm. 'We were just talking about someone working for the
Asgill group. Hello, is that Alessandro Franchetti?' she said suddenly,
looking over Wendell's shoulder. 'Where on earth has he been all
evening? I thought he might be a bit more noticeable, the amount
we're paying him.'

As Alessandro approached, Brooke kissed him lightly on both
cheeks, but his expression remained grim.

'I haven't seen you all evening,' she whispered in his ear. 'Where
have you been?'

'I haven't been here all evening,' he hissed back, leading her
away from Meredith and Wendell. 'I've been firefighting.'

'What's the matter?' she asked as soon as they were out of
earshot.

'Everything's the matter,' said Alessandro. 'This afternoon I
phoned the owner of the Hudson Lodge in Duchess County to tell
him we definitely wanted it for the wedding. He said I should
contact someone else about it – someone in Dubai.'

'*Dubai?*' said Brooke, a sinking feeling in her stomach.

'Last week he agreed to sell it to some sheikh.'

'Then why did we drive seventy miles to look at it yesterday?' said Brooke, her cheeks burning and tears welling in her eyes. Alessandro looked at the floor.

'I'd been dealing with his sister,' he said. 'She obviously wasn't in the loop.'

'Darling, what's the matter?' said Meredith, seeing Brooke's distress.

'There's a problem with Hudson Lodge,' said Alessandro. 'The good news is that the new owner wants to renovate it to the standard of The Point in the Adirondacks.'

'And the bad news . . . ?' asked Meredith.

'Work on it won't be starting for three months and renovation will take over a year. That means we're looking at next fall at the earliest.'

Brooke took a deep breath through her nose and willed herself not to get upset. *It's only a venue*, she reminded herself. *It doesn't mean anything.* But suddenly she thought of the shooting star in Paris, only this time the glittering orb was obscured by a big grey cloud.

Wendell took a step forward and rubbed Brooke's arm kindly. 'Perhaps you should reconsider our place in Newport?' he said.

Brooke had a sudden flutter of panic, feeling the wedding getting further and further from the vision she had always had of her perfect day: a relaxed, happy, perfect occasion with the barefoot bride saying her vows next to lapping water. Yes, Cliffpoint, the Billingtons' summer 'cottage', as David liked to call it, was majestic, but it was like a museum, so manicured and painstakingly tended. Brooke wanted wildness, rawness, the romance of nature. She didn't want Cliffpoint, or Lily Salter as her bridesmaid. Wasn't planning your wedding supposed to be fun?

'Surely Cliffpoint would be perfect for a spring wedding, don't you agree, Meredith?' continued Wendell. 'We have to make sure we're sending out the right signals. Family values are important to us.'

Meredith looked conflicted, although she was disguising it well.

'Thank you for your suggestion, Wendell,' said a deep voice, 'but it's all under control.'

Just then Brooke felt two warm hands on her shoulders and turned to see a handsome older man smiling down at her. It was her Uncle Leonard. Leonard was Meredith's brother, younger by a

couple of years, and he had taken on a fatherly role since the death
of Brooke's own father. Brooke smiled back at him gratefully; his
was just the friendly face she needed when she was feeling under
such pressure.

'I've offered Brooke and David Jewel Cay,' said Leonard smoothly.
'We think it will be perfect. Keeps it in the family too. Didn't you
tell them Brooke? David and I have just been discussing it.'

Brooke caught Leonard's lightning-fast wink, then took a slow,
deliberate sip of champagne to cover her grin. David walked over
and gave her a reassuring nod.

'Jewel Cay? What's that?' said Alessandro, clearly searching his
mental database for a mention of the venue.

'It's my house in the Florida Keys,' replied Leonard. 'I didn't
want to offer it before; didn't want to butt in on the bride's big
day.'

'Oh but it's gorgeous,' gushed Brooke, wondering why she hadn't
thought of it before. 'It's a beautiful big white conch house on its
own little island, a few miles from Islamorada. We used to go every
winter. It would be ideal, Uncle Leonard!'

David nodded. 'And the weather is perfect from late November,'
he said, smiling at Brooke's delight. 'The hurricane season will be
over. It won't be too hot.'

'A winter wedding,' smiled Brooke, grabbing David's arm and
squeezing.

'What about New Year's Eve?' he asked.

Alessandro raised an eyebrow and gestured towards the party.
'Impossible. Half this crowd will be in St Barts or Palm Beach.'

'Well, if they've got better things to do, then we'll uninvite them,'
said Brooke happily.

'Thinking about security,' said Wendell, stroking his chin, 'it
might be a good thing if the world thinks it's going to be at Hudson
Lodge sometime next summer. I'll speak to my contacts in Dubai.
Get in touch with the new owner. See if they'll be in on it.'

'It couldn't have worked out better,' said Brooke, throwing her
arms around Leonard's neck. 'Thank you, thank you, thank you!'

Leonard picked her up and laughed. 'I take it that's a yes, then?'

All her life, Tess had wanted money. Not in the way Dom liked
money: to keep up with or show off to his coterie of privileged
public-school friends. Tess wanted money because she had never

had it growing up. The bankruptcy of her father's business had not only destroyed the family, it had destroyed his self-worth because the bank – and your fellow men – judged you on your ability to pay your bills. Her father had died unhappy because he felt he had failed his family, failed as a man. Tess never wanted anybody to make her feel inferior, and it had fed her ambition like petrol on a bonfire. The red soles on her Louboutin shoes were a statement that she could afford nice things, but also that she could take care of herself. She loved ticking the 'Over seventy-five thousand pounds' income bracket on magazine questionnaires, and was one of the few people who actually enjoyed getting accosted by the charity muggers on the high street, as when she signed the direct debit form, she felt she was in control. So, if she was honest, when Meredith Asgill had offered her the job of family publicist, the only thing that had really stopped Tess taking the job immediately was that niggling feeling that the job was a mirage. After all, this was a clever, influential family who had no qualms about offering Tess a large bribe to make a story disappear. QED, there was a strong chance that the high-paying job in New York – a city that every ambitious twenty-something wanted to work in – was simply a more acceptable bribe.

During dinner at the Connaught the previous evening, Meredith had certainly spun some wonderful tales about life in Manhattan that were clearly designed to whet a young girl's appetite for the glamorous excesses of living in New York. But Tess was still concerned that the 'job' was the equivalent of the 'project development' room at the *Globe*, the sideways promotion given to troublesome or failing executives. It was not a proper job, just a well-paid purgatory to keep the marked person busy until the CEO and their team of lawyers had worked out an inexpensive way to fire them.

But now, after Charles Devine's revelations, it looked as if Tess had been mistaken about Meredith's offer. There really *was* a job to be done protecting the Asgills. There were secrets. Plenty of secrets. And Tess's gut feeling – a reliable instinct honed on the tabloid frontlines – was that there were plenty more skeletons still rattling away in the cupboard.

Tess looked out over the crowd and spotted Meredith on the other side of the ballroom. Catching her eye, Meredith began to walk across the dance floor towards her, gliding like a peacock, her chin lifted, her back straight, the silk skirt of her gown rustling as she walked. She looked like a czarina, the most refined sixty-something Tess had ever seen.

'Tess. Are you having a good time?'

Meredith looked composed as she played with the stem of her martini glass, but her eyes had the jubilant look of a lottery winner.

'Incredible party,' nodded Tess. 'I heard someone say that David's mum pulled this all together in a fortnight?'

'She's very experienced at get-togethers,' said Meredith gracefully. 'I only wish she could have persuaded David to say a few words. He's such a wonderful speaker. But the pair of them wanted to keep things as informal as possible.'

Tess smiled crookedly. 'If they wanted informal, they shouldn't have had it at Belcourt. Buckingham Palace would have been more low-key.'

Meredith just nodded.

'So is Sean here?' asked Tess.

'He's in Minnesota,' said Meredith evenly, holding Tess's gaze. 'Rehabilitating.'

'Good. I'm glad to hear he's getting better.'

Meredith nodded over towards Dom, who was laughing with a group of young girls and waving a bottle of champagne about in illustration of some story he was telling. 'Is your boyfriend enjoying himself?'

'He likes it here,' said Tess, carefully covering her annoyance at the jibe. 'He was wondering – if I took the job – whether a visa could be sorted out for him too?'

'It's not impossible,' said Meredith. '*If* you took the job. *If* things work out.' She straightened the pearls around her neck. 'But I can't hold the job offer open indefinitely.'

'Well, on that subject, I've just had an interesting insight into the family. It's given me a greater idea of the challenges of the role.'

'Really? Who from?'

'Charles Devine.'

Meredith laughed gaily. 'Dear old Charles. How on earth did he get an invitation? He's not terribly fashionable these days, contrary to what he thinks. What nonsense has he been telling you?'

'He told me about Olivia Martin,' said Tess, looking straight at Meredith.

There was a minute's pause as Meredith blinked and swallowed. 'What about her?' she asked.

'About her death.'

Meredith's expression clouded over.

'Charles Devine is just a silly busybody,' she said with force. 'He's Manhattan's biggest gossip. Half of what he says is a figment of his imagination. He . . .'

Then Meredith seemed to stop herself, closing her eyes in an effort of self-control.

'Whatever he has said to you . . .'

'I have to know everything, Meredith,' interrupted Tess. 'I can't help you if you don't tell me everything. And I mean everything.'

Meredith took a sip of corner, and touched her arm to escort her into a quiet corner. 'Forgive me, but I was not keen to tell you about private matters affecting my family when you haven't even taken the job,' she said, looking around to make sure no one was listening.

'Why were there rumours about Olivia and Howard?'

Meredith laughed coldly. 'When a beautiful starlet and a rich businessman are friends, there will always be rumours.'

'And what do you think happened the night of your wedding?' Tess felt stronger now she was on familiar ground – probing, getting to the bottom of the story. She was even beginning to enjoy herself.

Meredith looked at her and saw she wouldn't let it drop. She sighed.

'I honestly don't know what happened. I believe that Olivia was depressed, but I barely knew her; I had only met her a couple of times before the wedding. She was only there because she was an ambassador of the Asgill lipstick range. If she is dead – and that was never proved – of course it's a tragedy. It was certainly a black cloud over our entire wedding, so you can understand me wanting Brooke's big day to be perfect.'

Tess looked at her thoughtfully. 'I thought this job was just to get me off the *Globe* and out of London,' she said honestly.

'No, I can see why you might think that, but there is a job to be done here, Tess. My family needs protecting and I think you could be good at it.'

She looked across the crowd. Brooke and David were standing on the staircase, having their picture taken and laughing.

'Look at how happy Brooke and David are. A perfect president and first lady, don't you think? That's what's at stake here, Tess, not just the reputation of the family. It's bigger than that.'

Tess took a sip of champagne and carefully plated the flute on the table beside her. Dom was nowhere to be seen. Not that he would affect her decision anyway.

'I'll take it,' she said simply.

Meredith's face broke into a warm smile. She took Tess's hand in both of hers.

'I knew you'd come to the right decision,' she said. 'Resign from the *Globe* on Monday and you can start as soon as you can get here. There's plenty of work to be done. And Tess? Welcome to the family.'

5

The Asgill Cosmetics conference room was an impressive place. The silk wallpaper, the shelves full of industry awards, and the Chippendale chairs lined up along the long walnut table all reeked of corporate success. Should anyone be in any doubt as to the company's place in the world, the floor-to-ceiling windows looked out onto the bustle of Manhattan, a city full of grateful customers. But, despite the grandeur of the surroundings, anyone attending an actual meeting in the conference room could detect that all was not well. Only a decade ago, Asgill's had been one of the top ten cosmetics companies in America. Not as big as the giants such as L'Oréal or Maybelline, but within striking distance of Max Factor and Cover Girl. Today, though, Asgill Cosmetics was in trouble, a situation that had developed not suddenly but over a protracted period of time; a state of affairs that at least one member of the board found totally unacceptable. Liz Asgill was already seated at the far end of the table as the rest of the executive board filed into the room, and she watched the general managers of the individual brands shuffle to their seats with barely concealed contempt. From their grey faces and dour expressions, Liz felt sure that their reports would be filled with nothing but bad news.

'Perhaps we should make a start,' said Liz officiously, once everyone was in the room.

William, nominally the head of the company, seemed distracted, fiddling with his laptop at the head of the table, the prestigious slot that Meredith – as company chairman – had occupied during board meetings until about six months ago. Now she sat to his

68

right, Liz opposite her. Finally William looked up and nodded deferentially to Liz before addressing the room.

'I know you've all prepared your report for the individual divisions,' he said apologetically. 'But I think today we just need to concentrate on the first quarter's results and look at where we're heading in the light of those.'

There were unsettled grumblings around the room as William introduced Quentin, their chief financial officer, and asked him to run through the figures. Liz could tell within a minute that they were the worst results the company had ever posted.

Liz watched William closely, waiting to see what spin her brother would attempt to put on the latest downwards turn, which had been caused by the recent launch of Vital Radiance, a low-priced organics range that – in theory – dispensed fresh beauty products from pumps placed in stores.

'As you can see, we're quite a way off where we'd like to be at this point,' said William. 'The launch costs of Natural Glow have obviously been fairly heavy, ditto the forthcoming Skin Plus.'

'Presumably we're going to have to reforecast the end-of-year results?' asked Meredith. William shook his head.

'We should wait until the second quarter for that. Obviously we're all hoping that Natural Glow is going to be a big hit.'

Liz watched as the rest of the board followed William's cue and started smiling and nodding at this slim chance of rescue. Clearly nobody else had detected the slight waver in her brother's voice that betrayed panic.

'Quentin, have we got a breakdown of the Natural Glow sales figures?' she asked, interrupting William's flow. Quentin nodded and handed out his First Quarter Financial Report. Liz didn't miss the uncomfortable glance he directed at Eleanor Cohen, general manager of the Natural Glow line, as he passed her a copy. Eleanor was an experienced cosmetics industry executive who'd been recently drafted in for her knowledge of marketing in department stores.

'The first few weeks after the November launch were admittedly slow,' she said, clearing her throat. 'But retail conditions for everyone this Christmas were difficult.'

'Not for everyone,' said Liz.

Eleanor tried to avoid Liz's stare, instead directing her comments to William and Meredith.

'However, the press coverage we've had is excellent. *Allure* gave us half a page for the avocado cleansing oil, which is showing all the signs of becoming a cult classic.'

Liz almost laughed. Already there had been rumours that the drugstores were going to cut back on the retail space they had allocated for Natural Glow because of poor initial sales. If that happened, it was a certain death warrant for the brand.

'Eleanor, let's face facts,' said Liz irritably. 'We are dead in the water if we don't do something radical immediately to start shifting units.'

'Liz, now is not the time for scaremongering,' said Eleanor.

'Scaremongering? Natural Glow is haemorrhaging money. It won't last until fall at this rate.'

Liz looked over at her brother. Only eighteen months older than her, William looked at least a decade her senior: old and tired, worn out by the responsibility. He had none of Liz's flair and none of the natural authority of their father; he was just a worker bee, a drone reluctantly forced into the queen's seat. Liz, on the other hand, had been profiled in the *Wall Street Journal* as 'that rare executive, one who combines creative brilliance with astute business sense'. They both knew who should be sitting in William's chair.

William cleared his throat. 'Let's not forget that the product we have here is good.'

Liz laughed. 'Of *course* it's good.'

Before Eleanor Cohen had been brought in to launch Natural Glow, the product had been Liz's baby. The fresh organics concept had been her idea, and she had spent fifteen hours a day working with industrial designers to perfect the dispensing pumps that mixed the fresh ingredients in-store.

'The problem is not the product,' said Liz, looking pointedly at Eleanor, 'the problem is the marketing.'

'Well, it would have been nice to have received this insight before we launched,' replied Eleanor tartly.

'I assumed marketing was your area of expertise,' retorted Liz. 'Wasn't that why we hired you?'

'Okay, everyone, let's keep things constructive,' said William. 'Liz, you clearly have some ideas.'

A faint smile played on Liz's lips. She had been anticipating another difficult board meeting and relished the opportunity to place herself in the sun.

'Okay,' she said, 'First of all, we're not using our core brand effectively. Nobody knows that Natural Glow is part of the Asgill brand.'

'You are quite happy for Skin Plus not to have brand association to the company,' scoffed Eleanor.

Liz shook her head vigorously. 'That's different. Skin Plus is being positioned as a premium, luxury product, so we need to distance ourselves from Asgill's. Natural Glow, on the other hand, is very mass market. When you've only got fifty dollars disposable income a week and you're spending a chunk of that on a face cream, the customers want the reassurance that it's good. They like the validation that a major cosmetics player is behind it, so we should have branded it Natural Glow by Asgill on all the retail units.'

'I disagree—' said Eleanor, before Liz cut her off mid-sentence.

'Point two. We've created these fantastic pumps that allow us to deliver fresh product, with fresh ingredients blended and dispensed in front of them, but does the consumer really understand that? Have they been told about the benefits of this unique product? I don't think so.'

'We had the idea of putting the star bursts on the retail units,' offered Caroline Peterson, the marketing director.

'Nice idea, shame it didn't happen,' said Liz witheringly. At this point, Liz reached behind her and picked up a Natural Glow advertising board.

'Three,' continued Liz, now in full flow. 'Advertising.'

The image she held up was of a sliced avocado sitting next to a tumbler of water, a drip of water on the rim of the glass. It was an image that made Liz angry just to look at it, an affront to all the hard work she had put into research and development to bring the product to life.

'Look at it,' she said, tapping the board. 'How is an *avocado* going to make Natural Glow the market leader in mass-market skincare?'

Caroline Peterson looked embarrassed as she opened her mouth to speak.

'We worked with O&M for twelve months on this campaign. We felt that the avocado summed up in one image everything that the brand stood for. Exotic yet accessible. Fresh and natural. The soft lime green of the fruit . . . it says healthy and aspirational.'

Liz rolled her eyes. 'This line is aimed at the under-thirty-fives. They don't respond to a fucking avocado.'

Now she pulled out another board with a pasted-up image torn from magazines. It was a photograph of a beautiful woman running along a beach.

'This is what they respond to. Straightforward, aspirational lifestyle images. They want to be fit and beautiful, and this product will give them that.'

'Are you now proposing we ditch an advertising campaign that has been running for less than ten weeks?' asked Eleanor with alarm.

Liz nodded. 'Absolutely. I also propose that we recall our retail units to rebrand them "Natural Glow by Asgill". I also think we need a celebrity face, shot in a lifestyle context rather than in the bland studio shoot everybody else does. In fact, I was thinking we could use Brooke.'

There was another murmur from the board, this time one of approval and interest. Liz knew she had their attention.

'Brooke?' asked Meredith cautiously. 'Are you sure?'

'Remember Aerin Lauder fronting Lauder's Private Collection fragrances? Everyone thought it was the perfect fit. I think this will be a perfect fit too. Who better represents what the young woman of today wants than Brooke Asgill?'

Liz held up her photo of the girl on the beach. 'Imagine this girl is Brooke. Now, imagine the headline: "Fresh, fun, fabulous – Natural Glow by Asgill". In fact, having Brooke as our front woman might even save us rebranding the in-store pumps. After all, everyone in the country knows who she is.'

William shifted uncomfortably in his chair. 'These are great ideas, Liz, but it would be such an embarrassing U-turn in the industry.'

Liz spun to face him, anger prickling her cheeks. 'Either we save face and we discontinue the line, or we take decisive action now,' she said fiercely, her frustration at William's ineffectual leadership spilling over.

Things had been so different since her father died. Howard and Liz would have huge debates in board meetings, constantly challenging each other, bouncing ideas off each other, so that they produced better results than anyone had originally hoped. Liz and Howard had been so similar, so close. Liz knew he had wanted her to be CEO of the company when he stepped down, but his death from a stroke four years previously had been swift, and formal provision for Liz had never been made. Meredith inherited Howard's shareholding and she had allowed William to take over the company.

Still, she had some allies. Leonard Carter was nodding his head. Younger than Meredith but still in his sixties, he too no longer worked five days a week, but he was still a respected member of the board. After all, he'd spent twenty years as vice president in charge of international development.

'We could certainly use Liz's ideas to roll out the Natural Glow launch in Europe. We're only just liaising with the media planners now. The avocados were going to be the global brand image, but we could change that.'

'Hmm, I'm not sure the Billingtons will approve of this,' said Meredith thoughtfully.

William pointedly ignored Liz's glare and glanced down at his watch.

'We should push on. Let's save this for the Natural Glow brand meeting.'

Meredith had a glorious corner office from which she could see the Empire State Building. She mixed herself a drink from the cabinet by the window, watching the yellow cabs and pedestrians below. Moving behind her desk, she picked up Quentin's financial report and began to read. It didn't look good, not at all. They needed this wedding more than ever, it seemed. Just then there was a crash, and Meredith looked up in alarm as Liz strode in, and slammed the door.

'Liz, what on earth is the matter?'

'We need to talk, Mother,' said Liz, leaning on the desk.

'Yes we do, Liz,' replied Meredith, taking her glasses off. 'You are senior management. *Management*,' she emphasized. 'You cannot behave as you just did in there. The way just talked to Eleanor, I'd be surprised if we didn't have her resignation letter on my desk by tomorrow morning.'

'Well, that would be a start,' said Liz, more coolly, sitting down in the Eames chair in front of Meredith's desk, crossing her long legs. 'Mother, this company is about to go under and you seem content to let that happen.'

Liz studied Meredith's reaction carefully. For all her skill at reading people, Liz was never entirely sure where her mother's loyalties lay. Clearly Meredith did not share Liz's vision for the business, but she wasn't sure whether that was a head-in-the-sand refusal to acknowledge the decline of Asgill's, or whether she was simply so blind to William's shortcomings that she was prepared to let the company suffer under his weak direction.

'Don't be ridiculous, Elizabeth,' snapped Meredith. 'No one wants to see this company in difficulties, least of all me.'

'So are you happy about what you've just heard in there?'

'Everyone is disappointed by the figures,' said Meredith patiently. 'But you know as well as I do that the industry is facing some tough challenges. Need I remind you that we are still an independent, family-owned company, and not under the wings of a multinational? In hard times, it's harder for the little guy.'

Liz shook her head in disagreement. 'Now you're being ridiculous, Mother. So what if we're not in the L'Oréal stable? Smaller companies can still thrive in the beauty industry if they innovate and market themselves properly, but there's no margin for error. We can't afford to make any more mistakes.'

Liz took a deep breath, knowing that, for once, she had to be completely honest. She had never been convinced by her brother's leadership but had stopped short of saying so to her mother because Meredith had the power to appoint his successor.

'The weak link is William,' said Liz, pressing on. 'We know it, the industry knows it, but we can still restore confidence if we remove him.'

Meredith looked unmoved. She sat silently, regarding her daughter.

'The key attribute for running a company successfully is not necessarily the ability to shout the loudest, Liz,' she said finally.

'Perhaps not, but I always assumed an ability to turn a profit might also be required.'

Meredith shook her head. 'Rome wasn't built in a day, Liz. When William took over as CEO, we all agreed that we needed to innovate more. He's doing that.'

'*He's* doing that?' laughed Liz. 'When has William ever done anything innovative? Natural Glow was green-lighted in Dad's time. All William feels comfortable doing is cost-cutting.'

'He's overseen two major launches, Liz: Glow and Skin Plus. Not to mention the successful re-launch of The Balm.'

Liz shrugged. She had to concede that one: a simple repackaging of the cleansing pomade that had made her father's name when he had launched the company in the late 1950s. They'd replaced The Balm's dated black plastic pot with a sleek brushed-glass one and increased sales by twenty per cent.

'That was three years ago,' said Liz, shaking her head.

'Well, I believe in your brother,' said Meredith and, with those words, Liz knew she was wasting her breath; she knew her mother would never hear her objections. Not for the first time, Liz felt a sinking sense of disappointment and rejection. *Why do I even bother trying?* she thought miserably. Yes, she had been born into wealth and privilege, but Liz had never taken it for granted, working twice as hard as anyone else. But what good was all that effort? All those summers she had spent in the Research and Development lab as a student when all her college friends were having fun in Mexico, Australia, or the South of France, or the MBA she had earned at Wharton in order to understand the business side better. It was all a waste as far as her mother was concerned. Meredith's attitude seemed to be 'keep quiet, the boys know best'. The problem was, Liz had been born first and she had been born a girl.

Liz stood up and silently walked out of the room. She was sick of her brother, sick of her mother. She was sick of trying to save the company with her creativity and the hard work she got no credit for. *Screw them*, she thought to herself as she quietly closed the door behind her. *Screw them all.* It was time to look after herself.

6

'Welcome to Asgill's,' beamed a tanned blonde as Tess walked nervously into the company's reception area. If she hadn't already been anxious on this, her first visit to the offices on the thirty-second floor of a midtown skyscraper, the receptionist was enough to unnerve her. She looked like a super-charged *Cosmopolitan* cover girl; all bouncy, tawny hair, perfect skin and feline eyes. Tess wondered how anyone could look so perfect and perky at seven o'clock in the morning. Then again, all of New York seemed to bristle with an energy she had never witnessed in London, certainly not this early. For her first day at work she had wanted to be the first in, but it seemed as if the rest of Manhattan had had the same idea. The streets below her were already full of people, cars, and noise, and Starbucks had been so busy she had walked straight past it – no one needed a latte *that* much.

'I'm Sally,' said the blonde, handing Tess a security pass and leading her down a long cream corridor. 'When did you get into town?'

'Last night,' replied Tess. Everything had happened so quickly that it was easy to forget she was in a completely new city on a new continent. The Asgill offices seemed like a different world, too, especially compared to life at the *Globe*, which had been one huge airless room full of ringing phones, old Formica desks, and the smell of stale tea. Here, on the thirty-second floor, everything was tasteful and calm, with pale-ivory walls, chrome cantilever furniture and huge photographs of the company's advertising campaigns. It even smelt delicious, thanks to vast arrangements of fresh lilies everywhere. *We're not in Kansas any more, Toto,* she thought as she tried to keep up with Sally's brisk pace.

'Office hours are eight to five, although some of us get in earlier, others a little later,' said Sally, nodding over to some smaller offices off the main open-plan block.

'Mrs Asgill has the corner office and she gets in at nine a.m. She'll drop by and see you this morning. In the meantime, Patty Shackleton, our legal counsel is going to show you around and get you up to speed.'

Sally stopped outside a small, sunny office and motioned for Tess to step inside.

'Home,' she said with a grin.

When Sally had gone, Tess took her jacket off and hung it on the coat stand next to the door, then went to sit behind the glass desk, closing her eyes for a moment as she felt the morning sun pour through the windows and warm her back. *My new life,* she thought, feeling excited, on edge, and just a little bit sad about how easy it had been to leave London, the city she had called home for almost ten years. She had flown back to England the day after Brooke Asgill's engagement party and given her notice letter to a smug, suntanned Andy Davidson first thing on the Monday morning. Unsurprisingly, he'd been more than happy to accept her resignation. 'Leave at the end of the week, yeah?' he had said. 'No sense hanging about, is there?'

Tess was inclined to agree, and her plane ticket to JFK was booked for the day after that. Her farewell drinks in the upstairs of the pub next to the *Globe* offices prompted a good turnout, but only confirmed to Tess that she was making the right move. There were so many new faces in the crowd. Tess knew she was part of the old guard at the *Globe,* and that wasn't a good place to be at twenty-nine. Even when her girlfriends turned up to say goodbye, Tess realized how infrequently she saw them, and how distant they had grown. Seeing them once or twice every six months: no wonder all they had to talk about was celebrity gossip and memories of nights out that had happened years ago. Tess knew she had fallen into a rut; it was time to get new stories and have new adventures. That's what Dom had told her on the drive to Heathrow, and it was what she had kept telling herself as she walked through Departures, willing herself not to get upset. After all, it wasn't as if she was *emigrating,* it was more like a very long press trip from which she would return richer, hipper, and infinitely more connected than if she had stayed in London.

Just as she was firing up the computer in front of her, she heard someone enter the room. Looking up, she saw a tall black woman wearing an expensive trouser suit, her hair worn like the singer Sade's, scraped back off her head.

'Patty Shackleton,' the woman said, briskly offering a long, manicured hand.

Hell, even the lawyers look like models here, thought Tess, rising out of her seat to introduce herself.

'Pleased to meet you, Patty, I'm Tess,' she said, smiling.

Patty didn't move, her face wearing a taut, concerned expression. 'Have you read Danny Krantz?' she asked quickly, pulling out a paper from under her arm and opening it with a rustle.

Tess felt a flutter of panic as she instantly fell onto the back foot on her first day, feeling both incompetent and unprofessional. Danny Krantz penned the gossip column in New York's *Daily Oracle*. Together with Page Six in the *New York Post* and Rush and Molloy in the *Daily News* it was one of the juiciest, best-read newspaper columns in the country.

Shit, she silently cursed herself, *of course* she should have read all the papers, but there seemed to have been so many other things to do that morning.

'Not yet,' she replied quickly. 'I've organized for all the papers to be delivered to my apartment, but that won't happen until tomorrow,' she said, blushing.

'It came online at five a.m.' Patty did not say it in an unkind or accusatory way; it was a simple relaying of fact. She tapped the page. 'Read that.'

Tess took a swig of coffee as she read the story, wincing both at the strength of the coffee and the gossip item.

Brooke Asgill, fiancée of New York's most eligible man, David Billington, may look like perfect wife material, but this morning news emerged that Brooke is a home-wrecker.

Tess glanced up at Patty, her expression grave.

Brown University professor Dr Jeff Daniels left his wife of ten years to be with Brooke Asgill when she was a student at the institution. Although the relationship between Daniels and Asgill didn't last . . .' Tess quickly skimmed the rest of the story, reading the last line out loud.

'*Old flame Matthew Palmer, now a doctor at the Columbia-Presbyterian Medical Center says: "Brooke was always hot. I'd be surprised if any man could resist her."*'

Tess shook her head, then looked at Patty. 'I guess this means our guided tour is off?'

'I guess so,' smiled Patty. 'Instead you've got a baptism of fire. Nothing we can't handle, though.'

Tess didn't doubt it. She had done all her homework on her contacts at Asgill's and she could still recall Patty's impressive CV: Duke University, Harvard Law School, five years at a Wall Street commercial firm, three years here at Asgill's. She was exactly the sort of person you'd want on your side in a crisis. Tess was glad *someone* knew what they were doing.

She looked back at the newspaper in front of her and began to feel her old journalistic curiosity creeping back. *Interesting*, she thought. *So Brooke Asgill does have a dark side after all.* She almost smiled, before remembering which side of the fence she was on now. At the *Globe* it was all about exposing people's misdemeanours; now she was being paid a great deal of money to cover them up.

'Have you contacted the paper?' she asked.

Patty shook her head. 'I called Brooke as soon as I read it. She's denying it all, of course, but I wanted to get the full facts from her in person. She's due in the office any minute. In the meantime the story has run too late for the other papers to pick up until tomorrow, although I guess some could go online with it.'

'Can we get an injunction? Stop it from appearing anywhere else?' asked Tess, hoping she sounded more confident than she felt. Her knowledge of American law was sketchy at best. At work she was used to feeling in control, but here, with efficient Patty in this clean, sweet-smelling office, she felt displaced, out of her depth, and unsure of herself. She didn't like the feeling, not one bit. Patty was thoughtful for a moment.

'Well, it's certainly more difficult for celebrities to sue the media than it is in London,' she replied. 'The beauty of the First Amendment,' she smiled, her icy demeanour softening.

They both heard Brooke before they saw her: a click-clack of heels followed by a sniffle and a sob in the corridor before she appeared in the doorway. Even though she was wearing wide black sunglasses, you could tell she'd been crying from the puffiness of her cheeks.

'Hi Brooke,' said Patty, her head cocked sympathetically. 'I don't know if you've met Tess Garrett before?'

Brooke nodded as she sat down. 'Briefly, at my party. Sorry about the sunglasses. I look like Gollum this morning.'

Yeah, right, thought Tess. With her long butter-blonde hair, quivering lip, and Tom Ford shades, she looked like a young Jane Birkin on holiday.

'So. Is any of it true?' Patty asked earnestly.

Brooke looked desperately miserable and fragile as she looked down at her hands.

'Yes and no. Jeff Daniels and I dated for about six months when I was twenty-one. Yes, he was one of my tutors at Brown, but we didn't start dating until a few months after I'd left college and by then he was separated.'

'Or he *told* you he was separated,' said Tess.

Brooke looked up, her green eyes flashing.

'It wasn't like that at all,' she said firmly. 'He had been separated from his wife for about twelve months before we went on our first date and his divorce came through a couple of months later. There was no overlap at all, none. I'm not a home-wrecker.'

Brooke rubbed her eyes with the heels of her hands. 'David's family are going to go crazy,' she whispered.

Patty and Tess exchanged a look. They couldn't really deny it.

'What's David got to say about it?' asked Tess. 'He's the important one.'

'He's not very happy, as you can imagine,' said Brooke, wiping her nose. 'But he says he believes me.'

'And have you heard from the Billingtons?' asked Patty.

Brooke shrugged. 'My phone is probably jammed with messages, but I haven't been able to face it.' She turned to Tess, her eyes pleading.

'How did this happen? I thought the Billingtons were like the CIA; how come they didn't stop it?'

Tess shook her head. 'The first they will have heard about it was when someone read a first-edition paper this morning. I suppose you have to know about something to stop it.'

Tess squirmed, hoping that would not seem like a dig. It was obvious Brooke was suffering enough over this without Tess reading her the riot act about keeping her past to herself.

Patty glanced at her watch and then rose to her feet. 'I want to talk to Meredith and then I'd better go and make some calls.'

At the mention of her mother, Brooke's face paled. Tess could sympathize; she barely knew Meredith Asgill, but she didn't imagine this would play out well with her either. There was of course a chance Meredith would try to blame this on Tess, although – according to Sally the receptionist – office hours were eight until five, so strictly speaking Tess hadn't even started work when the *Oracle* website ran the story.

'So what's the plan?' asked Tess.

Patty folded her arms in front of her. 'I can get it taken down from the website but it's obviously too late for the paper. Good news is that the *Oracle* publishes a European edition, so I can threaten to sue them in the British courts. That should be enough leverage to make them print a retraction in tomorrow's paper.'

She looked at Tess meaningfully. 'Then I'm afraid it's up to you to do the damage control.'

She spun around on her high heels and walked out of the room. When Tess looked back, she saw that Brooke had picked up the paper and was reading the story again.

'I can't believe Jeff would do this,' she said dejectedly. 'I guess he needed the money.'

'Why do you think it was Jeff who went to the papers?' asked Tess.

Brooke looked up sharply. 'It must be Jeff,' she said, her eyes widening. 'They've run pictures of his wife and kids. How else did the paper get hold of those?'

'Newspapers have their ways,' said Tess, feeling a slight sense of guilt for having committed similar crimes at the *Globe*. It was different when you were on the other side of the fence.

She examined Brooke carefully. Tess's last week at the *Globe* had been spent using its substantial resources to dig up everything she could about the girl she had been hired to protect. In fact, Brooke had led a very low-key life for a girl from such a wealthy background, which was no doubt part of her appeal for a politically ambitious family like the Billingtons. The big surprise for Tess was that Brooke Asgill appeared to be everything she was supposed to be: beautiful, clean-cut, honest. Certainly, none of the features or photographs did justice to Brooke's natural beauty and grace. From her years in the media, Tess knew that average people with good PR and clever marketing could become household names, but with Brooke's raw material – her looks, marriage, and sweetness, she really could become more iconic than Jackie O. More importantly, if Tess succeeded in helping her do that, it would put her in a very strong position indeed. If the rumours about David's political future were true, she could even follow Brooke to the White House.

Tess smiled to herself. Before she could start indulging in any fantasies as a glamorous Chanel-clad aide climbing aboard Air Force One, she had to deal with the matter in hand. Scandal might do a B-list soap actress some good, but to establishment families it was dangerous, even fatal. Society could forgive anything except embarrassment.

'And who is this Matthew Palmer?' said Tess, rereading Danny Krantz's column more carefully.

'An old friend,' said Brooke, looking irritated once more.

'Says old flame here.'

'Another lie!' said Brooke, her voice raised and trembling.

Tess raised an eyebrow.

'Honestly,' repeated Brooke. 'I haven't seen or spoken to Matt since I left Brown. I've no idea why he'd say such a thing.'

Tess snorted. 'I'll give you two good reasons. Money and fame. Brooke, I worked at a national tabloid and, trust me, there's always someone you think is on your side who is really selling stories. In London there was one star, part of a very fashionable London clique, who sold stories about her famous friends to fuel a drug habit. But it could just as easily be a hairdresser, a stylist, a cleaner, even a relative. There's always someone wanting to make a quick buck. Which is why I'd love to know who leaked this story. This is going to happen again if you don't find out who it is.'

'And how do we let people know I'm not a home-wrecker?'

'Well, if Patty can swing an apology in tomorrow's paper that will be a start, but it won't be big or prominent so we need to set up an interview with you, somewhere like the *New York Times* 'Style' supplement . . . I'm also going to sort you out some media training.'

Brooke looked up. 'Which is what exactly?'

'The art of being vague and uncontroversial,' smiled Tess.

'And to think I told my mom I didn't need you,' said Brooke sheepishly.

Tess reached out and touched Brooke's arm. 'People are snakes Brooke,' she said kindly. 'The second you have something that everybody else wants, people will be out to get you. You are going to be the target for stings, whispering campaigns, and jealous and disgruntled people who just want to mouth off about you. You're going to have to be on guard twenty-four/seven and you're going to have to develop a thick skin. Added to which, you'll have to think about everything you do and perhaps modify your behaviour.'

'My behaviour?'

'For example, you'll have to be generous and kind to everyone. I'm sure you are that way naturally, but now being a stingy tipper or walking past a beggar is a news story. From now on you have to be a saint.'

'A saint?' said Brooke sceptically.

'I think you'll do fine,' smiled Tess as Brooke stood up.

'Thank you, Tess,' said Brooke, offering a slim hand. 'I'm glad you're on my side.'

'Think of it as a penance for past crimes,' said Tess. 'I've been a bit of a bitch to people like you in my past life, but at least you know you've got a bitch in your corner.'

As Brooke left the office and closed the door, Tess let out a long breath.

To do this job, I'm going to have to be the biggest bitch New York has ever seen.

7

'So, how was everyone's weekend?'

At table seven in La Revue restaurant, Paula Asgill unfolded her starched white napkin, stabbed her fork into her thirty-dollar Caesar salad and flashed her friends an uncommonly full smile. Twice a month, Paula, Gigi Miller, and Samantha Donahue gathered in whichever restaurant was currently white-hot for the Upper East Side's ladies-who-lunch crowd. This month it was La Revue. The East Sixty-First street eaterie had mediocre food and appalling service, but it was irresistible to the fashionable lunch crowd due to its unpublished impossible-to-get-hold-of reservations hotline.

Eating here was just one of the reasons Paula was feeling particularly buoyant. In her myriad of acquaintances in the city, Gigi and Sam were the nearest thing she had to close friends, all having children in the same class at prestigious coed prep, the Eton Manor School. Sam was a nice middle-class girl from Oregon with an art major college degree who had married well and liked pretty dresses. Her husband, Gregor, was a fallen Lehman's high-flyer who had downgraded to a smaller bank but still commanded a low seven-figure salary that allowed the Donahues a small household staff and a summer Hamptons rental in one of the less prestigious streets in Quogue. Gigi, a former modern-ballet dancer who now populated the party pages of W magazine and Style.com, was married to Bruce, another investment banker. Bruce was often found at the Beatrice Inn, invariably the oldest man at the fashionable downtown night-spot, and had once suggested to Paula that they 'fuck sometime' while standing in line at the Lincoln Center coat check. Paula had been uncomfortable going to their house for supper ever since.

Gigi was currently distracted, watching as Wendi Murdoch and Nicole Kidman were seated at table number eight, the most coveted spot in the restaurant. Paula silently cursed. She had only ever scored table eight once, and that had been one Monday lunch last August when half of Manhattan were at the beach. She'd hoped, after news leaked out about Brooke's engagement, that she would be promoted to table eight, but no. *Perhaps Nicole had got in first*, she thought.

Sideshow over, Gigi signalled to the wine waiter to bring more San Pellegrino and turned her attention back to Paula. 'Oh, not much this weekend,' she said, tossing back her bouncy, blow-dried hair. 'We went to Jenny Groves's daughter's christening.'

'Was it nice?' asked Sam, absently playing with the silk bow tie on her Chloe shirt. 'Greg's in Europe so we didn't go.'

'Oh honey, you missed all the drama.'

Paula listened with interest. Jenny Groves and her husband Oliver had kept a low profile on the social scene in the last year; the official word was that Oliver had temporarily relocated to Chicago on business and Jenny had gone out to be with him. But everyone knew the truth. Jenny had used a surrogate mother in Florida to have the baby and had kept out of sight to pretend she had carried the baby herself.

'You'll never believe this,' continued Gigi with relish, 'Sienna Spencer was godmother and got too near one of the candles at the pulpit. Her hair was set on fire.'

'Ohmigosh!' said Paula and Sam in unison. Sienna was a well-known Upper East Side handbag designer, married to one of the wealthiest hedge-funders around.

'I know!' cackled Gigi. 'Two thousand dollars' worth of John Barrett extensions ruined!'

'Was she okay?' asked Sam.

'*Sienna* was. Jenny's nanny, the Australian girl? She was standing close by, tried to smother the flames and her nail extensions caught fire. She had to be rushed to Cedar Sinai.'

Gigi pushed a lonely lima bean around her plate. 'It's all very inconvenient,' she continued, lowering her voice to a whisper. 'The nanny's out of action for six weeks with burnt fingers. Jenny and Oliver are thinking of suing the church, but it's such a good social scene down there that Jenny didn't want to make a fuss.'

All three women nodded in agreement.

'So how was Belcourt?' said Sam finally.

Paula smiled sweetly. How typical of them to wait so long to ask. She had been in such a good mood when she had arrived at lunch, but now she felt irritated at their feigned lack of interest in the party of the year. Of course they had both hoped Paula would be able to wangle them an invitation, but Paula had claimed the guest list was strictly restricted to close friends and family. The truth was that Paula simply hadn't wanted them there diluting her moment of high social exclusivity.

'Oh, it was good fun,' said Paula casually, stirring a straw around in her mineral water. 'Although I almost sliced my finger off on a window in the guest cottage. I couldn't say anything, though. After all, the Billingtons are family now.'

Gigi's smile was fixed like plaster. 'Well, I wouldn't speak too soon. Did you read that *Oracle* home-wrecker story the other day? That can't have gone down too well with David's family. Anyway, have you heard? Princess Katrina has just enrolled her daughter into Eton Manor.'

Paula bit her tongue, furious at not being given the opportunity to elaborate on the grandeur of Belcourt, yet secretly satisfied at the speed with which Gigi had steered the conversation back into her comfort zone. She knew she had scored a direct hit with the guest cottage detail.

'Princess Katrina?' said Sam. Paula could tell she had no idea who Princess Katrina was, but was afraid to say the words out loud for fear of committing a social faux pas.

'She's just fabulous, isn't she?' declared Gigi, flapping a hand. 'She's Italy's Marie-Chantal. Her husband's family would be Italian royalty if they hadn't been deposed.'

'Legendary wardrobe,' nodded Sam. 'She has a Birkin for every day of the year.'

'And she's enrolled her child at Eton?' asked Paula.

'Carlotta, a five year old, the same as our babies,' said Gigi, using her fork to draw patterns with the drizzle of balsamic vinegar on her plate.

It was Paula's turn to pretend a lack of interest. 'Do we know which class she's going in?'

All their girls were in Transition class, but there was another class of twenty-two pupils for children of their age, which made only a fifty/fifty chance that Carlotta would be in their class.

'Not yet. A girl in Bruce's office knows the sister of the admissions' secretary. All we know is that she's been accepted by Eton Manor, and starts after the Easter break.'

'Well, those parents' coffee mornings need some fresh blood.'

Gigi looked at Paula, each knowing what the other was thinking – what they were all thinking. The parents of Eton Manor pupils were some of Manhattan's most wealthy, successful people, and consequently the school's packed events calendar was one of the best networking opportunities in the city. Deals were quietly brokered on the father-son camp-out, lucrative friendship bonds nurtured at the Christmas fair. This, however, was on a different level. Princess Katrina would be new to the city and looking for social contacts. This was a solid-gold opportunity to make a new friend who moved in the very highest circles.

Paula dabbed her glossed lips with her napkin and felt a charge of determination surge through her. Attending Brooke and David's engagement party had stirred conflicting emotions. The exhilaration she'd felt when she had first arrived at Belcourt had been quickly replaced with an unsettling sense of dissatisfaction with her own life. Okay, so she had been granted entry to an even more exclusive circle of Manhattan society, but it was one in which she felt uncomfortably small and insignificant. Belcourt's ballroom had crackled with star quality that night; every single guest seemed to radiate some potent force that had made Paula seem to wither. But Paula was a fighter. Every setback was an opportunity. She knew she needed to improve her position. When she had first met William, Asgill's was talked about in the same breath as Revlon, and everyone expected it to be snapped up in a billion-dollar take-over. But it hadn't happened, and Paula knew from William's moods after a day at the office that business wasn't good. She couldn't rely on him to improve their lot. But she had two things on her side. New social leverage thanks to Brooke's engagement, and steely practicality that had brought her from Greenboro, North Carolina to Manhattan's Upper East Side, a force which she knew could propel her to even greater heights.

Her eyes flickered over to table eight, where Nicole and Wendi giggled over their poached pears. It was a snapshot of everything she had ever wanted: wealth, celebrity and power. It will be envied and admired. To get the best table in the house, no matter who else was in the room. Then her gaze trailed back to Gigi and Sam.

They were nice girls, of course. Fun and harmless. But Paula was beginning to feel as if she had outgrown them. It was time to move up a gear. And she already had a few ideas about how she was going to do it.

8

Patty Shackleton had worked her legal magic. The *Oracle* agreed to print a retraction on their website and an apology in the main paper the following day, but Tess wasn't taking any chances. She knew that newspapers didn't take too kindly to being pushed around by lawyers, and the last thing she wanted to do was spark a tabloid vendetta against the Asgills. A charm offensive was called for, so two days later she had arranged to meet Rebecca Sharp from the *Oracle* for lunch. Sitting under the yellow awning outside Da Silvano, watching the traffic thunder down Seventh Avenue, Tess smiled broadly as she watched her old friend climb from a taxi and glide over to her table.

'You look fantastic,' said Tess, quite taken aback at her glamour. Becky had been at the *Colchester Observer* with Tess over a decade earlier, and they had moved to London at around the same time, Tess on the women's pages of the *Daily Mirror*, Becky on the Bizarre showbiz desk of the *Sun*. Back then she was known as Bonkers Becks, tall and chunky, a great laugh, obsessed with music, and for the first year in the Big Smoke they had cut quite a swathe around town, going to any premiere, party, or gig to which Becky could get a plus one.

Tess had not seen Becks since her transfer to the New York *Oracle*'s entertainment and celebrity news desk three years earlier, and her transformation was incredible. Her long hair, once the colour of marmalade, was now a honey blonde, falling in soft curls onto her tanned shoulders. She had lost at least three stone and her Amazonian physique had become slender and graceful in her thin cashmere vest and skinny jeans.

'I cannot believe you're finally here,' squealed Becky, causing a couple on the next table to look at them with alarm. 'And as a publicist of all things! How's it going on the dark side?'

Becky's accent had picked up a transatlantic burr and she had always been loud, but her time in the Big Apple seemed to have increased the volume another 10 per cent.

Tess laughed. 'My first day at work I got into the office at seven a.m. and I was almost the last person to arrive. How do you fit sleep in here?'

Becky waved her hand casually in front of her. 'Sleep's for wimps, darling. The second everyone heard how Anna Wintour gets up at five for a game of tennis and a blow-dry, everyone wanted to be in the office before dawn. You'll soon learn that in Manhattan: it's all about *competition*.'

'So where are you living?'

'Brooklyn,' said Becky, pulling a face. 'Mind you, *everyone* is there right now, the rental on a shoebox on the island is insane. How about you?'

'Just a few minutes away actually,' said Tess casually. 'On Perry Street in the Village.'

Becky almost choked on her Perrier. 'You bitch!' she screamed. 'I hate you! Someone's paying you far too much money. Shit, I *dream* of the West Village, that's why I love coming here for lunch, so I can play "Let's pretend".'

'Let's pretend?' asked Tess.

'Pretend that I'm someone like that,' she whispered, nodding towards a super-glamorous blonde at a nearby table. The woman was stunning, with a flawless up-do and two-thousand-dollar dress that Tess recognized as Marni. She was sitting opposite a forty-something man wearing chinos, a navy sweater, and a scarf wrapped around his neck. He was overweight and, frankly, ugly.

'You want to be a woman like that?'

Becky looked surprised. 'Who doesn't?'

'But have you seen who she's with? He's wearing a pashmina!'

'Darling, every woman in this city wants to land a rich husband. Some women, most of my friends in fact, devote their whole life to finding one. And these days you can't be too picky.' Becky let out a dramatic sigh. 'Ah, the joy of not having to work.'

Tess smiled. 'You love work.'

'Completely beside the point,' said Becky flatly. 'It's the option of not *having* to work.'

She leant forward conspiratorially.

'Speaking of women with very rich men, how's your new friend Brooke Asgill? You *are* going to get me an interview with her, aren't you?'

Tess pulled a mock-outraged face. 'After the stunt your newspaper has just pulled?' she cried. 'Seriously though, you do realize you have royally pissed off two of the most influential families in New York – and what for? A two-column pot-shot story that has to run an apology the next day?'

'Actually, my editor loved the story,' said Becky. 'Anything to do with the Billingtons is big news, and David and Brooke are the sexiest New York couple since JFK Jr and Carolyn Bessette. It's not like a tabloid is going to be best friends with them anyway.'

The waiter arrived with their ravioli and the girls started eating.

'I need a favour,' said Tess. 'Two actually.'

Becky looked up. 'Shoot.'

'I need an introduction to all the media high-rollers you know. Newspaper editors, society column writers, editors-in-chief, and features editors on all the big glossies. I know a few people out here but I need to know everyone worth knowing very quickly.'

'No offence, but I *was* surprised when I heard the Asgills had got you in. PR gigs are all about contacts, aren't they?'

Tess pulled a sarcastic face. 'Thanks for reminding me.'

'What else did you want?'

'Tell me who gave you the story about Brooke.'

Becky gave a long slow laugh and wagged her finger. 'Come on, Tess. You worked in papers; you know we never reveal a source. We have journalists on the paper who have been to jail rather than give up the name of their contact.'

'Since when did you become Miss Integrity!' laughed Tess. 'I clearly remember you giving endless column inches to no-hoper bands on your music page in the *Sun* in return for a press trip – or even a glass of Cava!'

Becky smiled at the memory of their shared time on the loose in London.

'So what can you do for me?' she asked.

So much for friendship, smiled Tess. Becky hadn't got this far simply by being a good laugh. Beneath the fluffy, party-girl exterior she was as hard as nails.

'Help me now and I'll see if I can get you a story exclusive on Brooke and David's wedding.'

'Honeymoon shots?'

Tess shook her head. 'Can't promise that, but certainly something exclusive, something that will earn you big brownie points.'

Becky took a big orange leather diary from her expensive-looking tote and began flicking through its pages. She scribbled down an address on a fluorescent pink Post-it note and handed it to Tess.

'There's a bunch of us going down to Soho House tonight. There's a Cinema Society screening of the new Coen Brothers' film. *Very cool crowd,*' she said. 'Everyone from Glenda Bailey to Col Allen should be there, and there will be drinks afterwards. That should start you off.'

'Sounds good,' said Tess, folding up the paper. 'Now what about the source?'

Becky laughed. 'Tess, you're like a dog with a bone!'

'Tell me,' said Tess, but Becky held up her hands.

'I don't know, honestly. It wasn't my story.'

'Come on, Becks, you know everything.'

Becky looked at Tess for a long moment, then leant forward. 'I think it was an ex-girlfriend of David's,' she said. 'You know what they say about a woman scorned? Well, in New York, that fury is multiplied. Never underestimate the damage a vengeful social climber can cause.'

'I'll bear it in mind,' grinned Tess.

Becky put her hand on Tess's. 'Honey, it's so good to have you over here. Honestly.'

'It's good to see you too. Especially as you're doing so well. I mean, just look at you. Where did Bonkers Becks go?'

Becky laughed out loud, again causing heads to turn. 'You know, I used to think that New Yorkers have no time for love because they throw themselves into their careers,' she said thoughtfully. 'Now I think it's the other way around – they become workaholics because it's so hard to find love.'

'So I take it you haven't found your pashmina-wearing Prince Charming yet?' smiled Tess.

She laughed again, casting a glance towards the couple at the next table. 'No. The problem is, I think those banker types are pricks,' she whispered.

Tess giggled.

'Not that I've given up, of course. I even went to this "Fashion and Finance" speed-dating thing the other week,' continued Becky. 'Very popular right now, full of pretty girls and rich guys all looking for love, but I have to say I was absolutely bored to tears. I ended up going home with a woman.'

Tess's eyes opened like saucers.

'Her name was Dita,' smiled Becky. 'A freelance fashion PR. We had much more in common than any of those boring farts in their sensible shoes.'

'Wow,' gasped Tess. 'So what happened?'

'Nothing,' laughed Becky. 'Mother Nature kicked in; I couldn't do it. But that's New York, baby. That's how desperate it is out there. I think it was God's way of telling me I am destined to be alone. Anyway, how's the very sexy Dom?' she asked, sipping her water. 'I think he always wanted to work in New York more than both of us.'

Tess's smile faded at the mention of her boyfriend. 'Dom's still in London.'

'You guys haven't finished, have you?' said Becky, her expression softening.

'No, no, nothing like that. He hasn't got a visa, so we're having a transatlantic affair.'

'Very chic,' said Becky. 'Are you missing him?'

'Working fourteen-hour days I've not had a chance to miss him.'

'Hmm. Or maybe you just don't,' said Becky, raising a brow.

Tess looked thoughtful. 'No, I think it's more that I had to come here to get out of my comfort zone.'

Becky laughed. 'You two are hardly in a rut, are you? Whenever I hear from you, you're always flying off to some exotic location.'

'Maybe not, but we've been together for nearly nine years. Sometimes distance can bring you closer together.'

Becky hesitated, playing with her fork.

'Do you trust him, Tess?' she asked softly. 'No disrespect to Dom, but I don't think I would leave a man that fine alone two minutes in big, bad London. More to the point, do you trust yourself to be let loose in this big city?'

'The answer is yes,' said Tess firmly. 'Yes and yes.'

Although she couldn't help thinking back to the one time she'd been unfaithful. It had been eighteen months into their relationship when she began struggling with the idea of commitment.

She was only halfway though being twenty. Should she not be young, free, and single, and enjoying all London had to offer? One weekend, Dom had been away on a snowboarding trip with his friends, and Tess had been invited to a party by an associate editor on the *Globe*. It had been at a big Victorian villa in Barnes, stuffed to the gills with media types she recognized from the TV or from their photo by-lines in the papers. The moment she saw Charlie, she knew something was going to happen. He was thirty, an advertising director and the son of the old chief executive of the *Globe* group. He was also engaged, but that hadn't stopped him stroking Tess's neck. She'd been flattered by the attention of someone five years older and infinitely more successful, so they'd gone back to her flat in Clapham and the sex had been explosive. Charlie had left at seven the next morning, but not before telling her about a features editor position he knew was coming up at the *Globe*. 'Keep what happened last night between us,' he'd told her and she had kept her word. Three months later she was the youngest senior journalist at the *Globe*.

She looked up and had the uncomfortable feeling that Becky had been reading her thoughts.

'Don't get too comfortable without him, honey,' she said seriously. 'Let Dom go and you might be single for the next five years. Some people call New York a jungle. Well, let me tell you, when it comes to love, it's a fricking desert.'

9

David grabbed Brooke's hand and led her past the doorman into the lobby of 740 Park Avenue, one of Manhattan's most prestigious apartment blocks.

'It's going to be fine,' he whispered, his voice almost lost against the tip-tapping of Brooke's heels on the black-and-white chequered marble.

Brooke smiled weakly, feeling her anxiety grow. The last thing she felt was fine. She had spent the last three days torturing herself over the revelations in the *Oracle* about her relationship with Jeff Daniels, swinging back and forth between disgust, disappointment, and anger. Her first instinct was to run away and hide, but she knew deep down that the only thing to do was put on a brave face and 'step up to the plate' – wasn't that what they said? She had been able to keep up a façade of calm at work, where she knew and trusted most of her colleagues, but it was quite another thing to face people on David's extensive social circuit. Brooke didn't understand David's insistence about coming tonight – Graydon and Estella Winston were not particularly good friends of his – but she had not felt in a strong enough position to argue. David had been a rock since the scandal had broken. He'd been in Boston on a CTV conference and had rushed back to Brooke's apartment to be with her. Although Brooke was sure he'd had to endure a severe tongue-lashing from his father, David had been calm and relaxed, running her a bath and giving her a heavenly foot massage while he had said lots of reassuring things about how none of it mattered and how much he trusted her.

Brooke pressed the button for the elevator and turned to her fiancé. 'If people are whispering about me, we're staying twenty minutes and then we're going home.'

David chuckled. 'Honey, these people are not *Oracle* or Page Six readers – most of them consider the *Wall Street Journal* light reading. Anyway, they fancy themselves as having more important things to talk about than your college adventures.'

Just then the lift doors pinged open and a smartly dressed couple stepped out. They walked past, and Brooke heard the woman give a low laugh that echoed around the lobby.

David read her thoughts and shot her a crooked smile. 'Don't be paranoid, darling,' he said. Brooke knew he was right, but this crisis had only confirmed Brooke's love-hate relationship with the Upper East Side. She had called this, the wealthiest pocket of Manhattan, home for over twenty years, and in many ways it felt safe and familiar, but it could be a cold place, its inhabitants mocking and judgemental. The truth was, whether David's friends were Page Six readers or not, they thrived on gossip as much as any celeb-obsessed housewife. Gossip was the lifeblood of polite society.

The elevator doors slid open and the sounds of smooth jazz and lively conversation met them from the open door of Graydon and Estella Winston's sixth-floor apartment. There were already about fifty people in the room as a waiter took their coats; most were in their thirties and forties, although their conservative clothes and stiff bearing made them seem about ten years older. Women were in trouser suits or little black dresses, sporting short, serious hair-cuts and few accessories except for the aura of self-confidence. Graydon was the editor of a glossy political magazine; his wife the daughter of one of New York's biggest Republican donors. According to David, the rest of the guests were a mix of media players, academics, and politicos.

'Don't leave me,' she whispered as she accepted a flute of champagne with a smile.

Before he had time to reply, a slim man in a black polo-neck jumper and grey sports coat came over to shake David's hand. She recognized him as Niall Donald, a right-wing columnist, TV commentator and author of *Power and Prestige: America's political future on the world stage.*

'David, Brooke. How are you both? You look lovely, Brooke,' he smiled, although Brooke noticed how he had directed all of his pleasantries to David, never even glancing at her.

'We enjoyed your report on China the other week,' said Niall, taking a thoughtful sip of Krug: Brooke had been dismissed. Niall Donald was the sort of society bigwig that Brooke loathed most of all. Pompous, smug, arrogant. She remembered another interminable dinner party when she had been forced to listen to Niall boast that he had not only attended Harvard, but had been a Rhodes scholar at Oxford, then later had heard him quip how David had only 'scraped' into Yale. Brooke wanted to hit him.

Instead she touched David on the arm and whispered, 'Excuse me.' She drifted off, looking for sanctuary. She'd been to dozens of parties with David, and while most of them were fun, she found these gatherings of New York's intelligentsia self-important and boring.

But while she didn't enjoy them, she at least learned how to survive them. Small talk with the host about bland, uncontroversial topics, letting other people ramble on about themselves (there was nothing a New Yorker liked better than talking about themselves), or spending long periods 'touching up her make-up' in the powder room, Brooke was an expert at making herself invisible.

But one thing she always loved was having a discreet snoop around other people's homes, and Graydon and Estella's duplex was a spectacular space. Lofty ceilings, virgin cream carpet, original art – including, she recognized, Dufy and Chagall – sleek, expensive, bespoke furniture. It was the sort of place that demanded you wear something beautiful to complement its sophistication, but Brooke was glad she had dressed down in a black sleeveless Alice Roi dress worn with a simple gold choker. She had even dispensed with her favourite black Louboutin heels, fearing them a little too racy; she knew how suspiciously she would be viewed tonight. New York society women were notoriously icy at the best of times, but encountering someone with a newly minted reputation as a home-wrecker might drive them to freeze her on sight.

'What's your view on the trade deficit?' asked a smooth female voice behind her.

Brooke's throat felt thick with anxiety. She felt as if she was about to go into an exam.

She turned to face an elegant brunette in a wasp-waisted dress that was the reddy-gold colour of a Japanese maple leaf. She had an outrageously pretty face, and she was not much older than Brooke.

'Yes, er, the trade deficit . . .' stuttered Brooke, before the woman's wide mouth broke out into a smile. Brooke laughed.

'Sorry,' whispered the woman. 'It can get a little tedious at these things, so I like to have a little joke.'

Brooke smiled, grateful that she had found at least one kindred spirit.

'I thought the whole point of a party was to enjoy yourself,' agreed Brooke. 'Although no one exactly looks as if they're having a good time tonight.'

'Well, parties like this are all about alignment. David always used to say, "We can't socialize with who we want to all of the time." He's right, of course. The people in that room will be advising government in five years' time. Some already are.'

She took a sip of champagne and held out a pale hand. 'Alicia Wintrop,' she said. 'I'm sorry I couldn't come to the engagement party. I hear it was fantastic.'

It took a second for Brooke to make the connection, then her heart lurched. David had once dated a girl called Ally Wintrop.

'You're *Ally* Wintrop?'

Alicia laughed. 'Oh I know, old names die hard, don't they? David and I dated when we were kids. Our families had cottages in Newport just by one another. Everyone knew me as Ally back then.'

'Oh, I thought you dated more recently than that,' said Brooke as casually as she could.

Alicia nodded. 'I worked in Rome after college . . . I was at Brown two or three years ahead of you, I think.

'You were at Brown?' replied Brooke curiously.

She nodded. 'Anyway, David and I started dating again when I came back to New York, but when David got the foreign news job at CTV I just couldn't handle all that travel. It felt like I was dating a nomad. I think we were just both *too busy* to be together.'

'Oh really. Too busy?' said Brooke with as much politeness as she could muster.

'Um-hmm,' said Alicia. 'I curate a gallery downtown. The Halcyon on Spring Street. Fabulous exhibition on at the moment of Masai warrior painters. They paint with spears; it's so *conceptual*. You must come down. I do some art consulting too, in Europe. I spend an awful lot of Russian money.'

Brooke started planning her escape strategy. She knew, of course, that David had a past with plenty of ex-girlfriends, but she didn't particularly want to stand there talking to one. She realized that she was squeezing her champagne flute a little too tightly.

'I'm sorry about that business with the *Oracle*,' said Alicia. She sounded sympathetic, but Brooke wasn't convinced.

Brooke shrugged. 'I guess it goes with the turf.'

'Luckily I didn't have it so much,' said Alicia lightly. 'Perhaps it would have been different if we had become engaged. Or perhaps we were too *obvious* a couple to be interesting.'

Brooke smiled thinly. Before she could feign a headache to get away, David came over and handed her a glass of champagne. He looked buoyed up and happy.

'So you too have finally met?' he said.

'Don't worry, I'm not telling her any of our secrets,' said Alicia, nudging David playfully, tilting her face up to smile at him.

'I don't want to know,' said Brooke, forcing a smile.

'Well, I'll leave you two lovebirds to it,' said Alicia. 'I simply must go and compliment Graydon and Estella on their new Lucian Freud.'

As they spent the next half-hour drifting from group to group, Brooke floated at the fringes, keeping a close eye on both David and Alicia. David's ex had now returned to the man she had come with, a sombre-looking man in a dark suit and heavy-framed glasses – an architect, according to David. To a disinterested observer, Brooke was simply standing by the window, enjoying the view, soaking up the rarefied atmosphere, whereas in actual fact she was looking for any telltale signs that David was still interested in Alicia – a sly glance or an ever-so-casual touch, perhaps. There was nothing; they barely even spoke. Slowly Brooke's irritation at having been ambushed by David's ex turned to fascination as she watched them both expertly working the room. David was magnetic, and not just because of the good looks she had fallen in love with; he had a natural composure and a good-natured confidence. He spoke with conviction and authority and he had an indefinable presence that seemed to fill the space he was in. Alicia had another tactic entirely. When Brooke was close to her, she eavesdropped on Alicia's conversation, and it was soon clear that she had nothing particularly clever or interesting to say, but she had something more powerful than intelligence or wit. Alicia was a world-class flirt. She flirted not with sexual invitation, but in a way that the person she was talking to felt like the most important person in the room. Consequently, they responded to her as if she were spouting Descartes.

Brooke glanced at her watch. It was almost eleven.

'I know that look,' whispered David into her ear. 'You want to go, don't you?'

She smiled at him gratefully. 'Is it that obvious?'

They had only been at the party two hours, but to Brooke it had felt like an eternity. She didn't miss all the surreptitious glances sent her way, or the whispered comments when she was just out of range. Her mouth was aching from the permanent smile etched on it. She felt like the village idiot.

They rode down in the elevator and, when they stepped outside onto Fifth Avenue, Brooke felt her shoulders relax. A cone of moonlight shone down on them and he turned to her and kissed her, his tongue licking the inside of her mouth. It was delicious and quite unexpected – spontaneous kisses, especially those in public places, were becoming thinner on the ground as they were constantly watched. His driver was parked across on the far corner and they walked to the car with his arm around her shoulders.

'I'm sorry we were there so long,' he said, opening the door of the Lexus for her. 'But it wasn't that bad, was it?'

'Oh honey it was,' she laughed.

'I didn't hear one person mention Jeff Daniels.'

'They would hardly discuss the ins and outs of some scurrilous tabloid story with you,' she said. 'But believe me, they all knew the details.'

He was silent for a moment as the car engine started. 'You seemed to be getting on well with Ally.'

'She's nice . . .' said Brooke obtusely.

'You're not jealous?' he said, laughing softly.

'I don't trust her,' she blurted out.

'Trust her? What do you mean?'

'Call me crazy,' said Brooke, 'but I've just got this *feeling*.'

'A feeling about what?' asked David. His words were measured, clipped. She could tell he was annoyed at the 'trust' jibe. Brooke supposed he had a point, considering how understanding he'd been about the Jeff Daniels accusations.

'I just wondered if it was Alicia who leaked the *Oracle* gossip story,' said Brooke.

'*What?*'

'Look, I spoke to Tess Garrett today and she said the story came from one of your ex-girlfriends.'

'It sounds to me as if Tess Garrett is trying to justify her existence.'

'She sounded pretty sure.'

'On what basis?'

'A source at the *Oracle*.'

He pursed his lips together.

Brooke paused before saying anything more. She never liked bringing up the subject of past girlfriends. In her experience it only made you look jealous or needy or both.

'Aren't you going to say anything?' she asked.

'How am I supposed to react?' he said, anger in his voice.

'Well, don't you think it was Alicia? It had to come from somewhere.'

'On what grounds?'

'Well, she did go to Brown . . .'

'Brooke, you're being ridiculous.'

'Am I?' she said, challenging him.

David was a serial monogamist: through his twenties there had been at least five girlfriends who had all lasted between six months and two years, and the Jeff Daniels leak could have come from any of them. They all had the same potential motivations: sour grapes, mean-spiritedness; some sense of thwarted entitlement, perhaps.

But it had been Alicia's bright-eyed friendliness and a feeling of gleeful pleasure when she mentioned the *Oracle* story: it all made her suspicious of Alicia. Call it female intuition, but she was sure she was behind it.

'Yes you are being ridiculous! After all, it was your friend, that Matt Palmer, who was quoted.'

She frowned. 'It wasn't him. I told you what he said. A journalist tracked him down and misquoted him.'

'And you believe that?' he asked.

'Yes I do. He's got less motivation for doing it than Alicia.'

He turned on the seat to face her.

'Alicia's parents and my parents have known each other forever,' said David tightly. 'She is a lot of things, but she is not deliberately evil.'

'It sounds to me like you're defending her.'

David rarely sounded angry. He always dealt with problems in his usual cool, composed way, but now his voice was raised. 'I am *not* defending her. I just wonder what motivation *she'd* have for doing something like that.'

'Oh, grow up, David,' shouted Brooke. 'Maybe, just maybe, she still loves you, did you ever think of that? Maybe she'll do anything to stop you from being happy with anyone else.'

David turned to look at her. His face was stony.

'Brooke, *she* finished our relationship.'

It stung Brooke like a slap in the face. She had always had the romantic notion of David Billington, America's most eligible bachelor, rejecting each of his previous girlfriends because he was still searching, like Prince Charming, for the one girl who was perfect in every way. Childishly, she had allowed herself to believe that she had been that girl, that she was his one true love. Not for moment did she imagine she was second choice, that all along he had been pining for the one he could not have. She wondered momentarily if David and Alicia would still be together if Alicia had not called it a day, and the image of David and Alicia glad-handing the party in natural symmetry jumped into her head. But she knew she was right about Alicia, she just knew it.

'Just because she finished with you doesn't mean she wants anyone else to have you, David,' she said. 'It's naive to think Alicia is somehow incapable of being spiteful and underhand just because you were once in love with her.'

'Well thanks for the vote of confidence.'

It did not escape Brooke's notice that he had failed to deny he had been in love with Alicia, but despite her hurt and anger she still felt a pang of protectiveness. She hadn't been striking out, she had been telling the truth: David was strong in so many ways, but he had one Achilles heel. He always saw the best in people. There was nothing naturally suspicious or cynical in his make-up, and she knew that if he were one day to run for office, it could be a fatal flaw. Her voice softened and she put a hand on his arm.

'Oh honey, let's not fight about this,' she said softly. 'You know I'm only saying it for your own good.'

'No, you're saying it because you're pissed,' he replied flatly. 'You've had a crappy night and you're feeling sorry for yourself. I'd just cool it, if I were you, Brooke. Okay, so you had one lapse of judgement with that Jeff Daniels character, but that doesn't mean you have to assassinate everyone else's character. It's not very attractive.'

His words scalded her. 'A lapse of judgement? So all that stuff about how you believed my story and how you trusted me was just crap, was it? Do you even care about how I felt back there tonight?' She felt hot tears pricking at the back of her eyes.

He puffed out his cheeks. 'Of course I care,' he said in a low voice. 'It's just that if you're going to be my wife, you're going to have to get used to these parties, these people. It's my life, Brooke.'

They were just a couple of minutes away from her apartment and she couldn't think of anywhere she would rather be. She tapped the driver on the shoulder. 'Miguel, can you drop me home please?'

David tutted loudly. 'Honey, don't overreact.'

'I'm not overreacting. I just want to go home,' she said quietly.

David nodded at Miguel. 'Take her home.'

10

'We have a major problem,' announced Mimi Hall, publisher of Yellow Door's children's division. They were only two minutes into the weekly executive editorial meeting and already Brooke was on edge. Mimi Hall could be a very frightening woman, particularly when there were *problems*, when she always seemed to cleverly shift the blame onto other people. Brooke's privilege and celebrity were no protection here; in fact it was something that seemed to annoy Mimi Hall. Everyone in the room knew Mimi did not belong in the gentle, good-natured world of children's publishing, Five years earlier she had been a hotshot in the adult fiction division at Doubleday, but a string of high-profile flops and their consequent financial losses had got her fired. She'd taken the publisher's job at Yellow Door, not because she thought a move into children's publishing was exciting – far from it, Mimi Hall didn't even *like* children. But it was a job, and sitting out her purgatory, awaiting a plum MD job somewhere, Mimi Hall seemed hellbent on taking out her professional frustrations on everyone else. Particularly Brooke.

'This morning I had a long conversation with Jennifer Kelly and at this point it seems unlikely that she's going to deliver in time for an October launch.'

She delivered the news casually but, sitting next to her, Edward Walker, the division's affable English-born managing director, went pale. Jennifer was currently Yellow Door's biggest author. Rumour had it she accounted for 15 per cent of the company's annual profits with her whimsical love stories based in rural Ireland. A huge hit with Midwest teenagers, her first three books had topped the

New York Times best-seller list for weeks. She had been one of Mimi's discoveries; she'd bought world rights for a five-book deal for fifty thousand dollars, which was precisely why her present reign of fear was tolerated.

'But, Mimi, a couple of weeks ago you told me she had *delivered*,' spluttered Edward. 'It's April, Mimi. April! The book should be in.' Even from the other end of the table, Brooke could see the panic in his eyes. Mimi turned her head and looked at Edward contemptuously. It was no secret that Mimi was waiting for Edward to retire, move on, or *be* moved on.

'You clearly misunderstood me, Edward. I said Jennifer was *about* to deliver, but unfortunately she's pregnant and so she can't meet the deadline.'

'She's pregnant?' said Edward disbelievingly. 'When I last met a pregnant woman I think she was still capable of sitting at her laptop.' Edward was by nature a polite and calm man, and this was the first time that Brooke had ever seen him rattled. 'And if she was *about* to deliver, then she can't be that far off finishing the manuscript.'

'I need not remind you that we have to keep her on side,' said Mimi, still casual. 'Once Jennifer delivers this book, she's out of contract. We both know that every publishing company in town has got their chequebook out ready to win her over. Even though she owes her entire career to me, loyalty means crap in this town. In other words, the kid gloves have to go on whether we like it or not.'

Everyone around the table knew what was really going on with Jennifer Kelly. Her latest book, *Chocolate Kisses*, was only one hundred and fifty pages long – and what there was of it was bloated and poorly written. It had still sold to the loyal fans, but it was obvious that their star writer's heart wasn't in it any more. She had earned millions of dollars in royalties from the books alone, and last Christmas the Disney adaptation of her second book, *Butterfly Heart,* had broken all box-office records. Just thirty years old, she had a villa in Provence, an apartment in Manhattan, and a small manor house in Ireland. The truth was, Jennifer just couldn't be bothered. 'Can't we get a ghost to churn something out?' asked commissioning editor Debs Asquith, Brooke's best friend at Yellow Door and one of the few people with enough balls to speak out in front of Mimi.

'We don't *churn* out any books on my list,' said Mimi wither-ingly. 'But yes, I have gently discussed the possibility of Jennifer working with a ghostwriter to get it done, but – understandably – she was a little upset. And anyway, the trade press would have a field day if they found out. Jennifer is a big star. We want to keep her that way, not jeopardize her career and reputation.'

Edward raised a hand.

'Mimi. We can take up this issue separately. In the meantime, I don't need to tell anyone that Jennifer's potential failure to deliver leaves a gaping hole in the October schedule, one that might well be financially punitive for the company,' he added, looking directly at Mimi. 'So. Has anyone got any ideas about how we can fill it? Joel, how about getting Pete Coles to write something?'

Joel Hamilton was a well-regarded publishing director who edited Pete Coles, a former US Army Marine who wrote *Bourne Identity*-style thrillers aimed at teenage boys.

Joel pulled a face. 'Sorry, no. He's training for a North Pole expe-dition and doesn't think he has to deliver anything until Christmas. Anyway, it's April, so we can forget about anything that isn't completely done. It would be touch and go even to turn a re-release around at the moment. For an October launch we should really have sold into the retailers already.'

'Debs?' said Edward hopefully. 'You were out with William Morris and Trident last week. Anyone got anything interesting?'

Debs shook her head sadly, her long red curls swishing behind her. 'Nothing guaranteed to fill a two-million-dollar hole in the P&L, boss.'

'Brooke,' said Mimi, smiling thinly. 'You must have a young celebrity girlfriend we can work with. Miley Cyrus? What about that Bush twin who teaches kindergarten?'

'I don't know Miley actually,' said Brooke, feeling her cheeks flush. Brooke knew she had the most unimpressive roster of authors of anyone in the room, certainly in terms of financial return. Brooke's speciality was commissioning beautifully illustrated books and sweet stories aimed at the 7–11 age group. To even her own surprise, one of her books had just won the Carnegie Medal at the Bologna Fair, but, in terms of sales, which was all that counted in this cut-throat climate, they were all strictly mid-list. The really big hitters of children's publishing – J. K. Rowling, Stephanie Meyer – were the ones that had crossover appeal with the adult market.

Then suddenly Brooke thought of a female magician. *Of course* – the amazing manuscript she had rescued from the slush pile. She had taken what she had Belcourt and read it on the afternoon of the party to distract herself from the circus that was going on around her. It had been even better than she had hoped.

'Actually,' she said, tapping her pencil against her lip, 'I have seen a manuscript that I think has real potential.'

'Really?' said Mimi sarcastically. It was no secret that Mimi didn't think Brooke should be attending these meetings. 'So give me the elevator pitch.'

Brooke always felt as if she was being interviewed whenever she spoke to Mimi. 'It's about a teenage female magician.'

'Uggh,' groaned Mimi, rolling her eyes. 'Not another Harry Potter wannabe.'

'Not at all,' replied Brooke. 'It's more of a mystery novel. She solves an assortment of crimes over a trilogy of books.'

'Who's the author?' asked Edward more graciously.

'Eileen Dunne.'

'Never heard of her,' snapped Mimi.

'No, she's a first-time author,' said Brooke hesitantly.

'So who's representing her?'

'No one yet. Actually, it's a slush-pile script.'

'Enough said,' said Mimi, holding up one manicured hand. 'Now has anybody got anything else that might be of *genuine* interest?'

You are such an old witch, thought Brooke, feeling suddenly protective of the magician book.

'It's actually really very good,' she said, interrupting Mimi. 'Dark and funny, a young adult book that adults will buy as well.'

She turned and met Mimi's glare. 'I think we should give it a chance. The manuscript is completed; even better, it's a trilogy, and the author has the second book almost finished too.'

'We like trilogies,' smiled Edward. He turned to his left. 'Mimi, I think you should take a look at it.'

Her sigh was audible.

'Very well. I suppose if it's bearable we can pick it up for peanuts. She'll think all her Christmases have come at once.'

Let's hope mine have too, thought Brooke.

11

The Eton Manor School, on a quiet corner of East Ninety-Third Street, was a beautiful mansion with a quaint courtyard and functioning bell tower that had once been a Greek Orthodox church. Although the school was only twenty-five years, old, it had quietly become one of the most exclusive schools in Manhattan, challenging the old guard like Brearley, Chapin and Collegiate. Eton Manor did not pretend to have links to the great British boarding school, but with an austere British head teacher, it was *the* school of choice for the rich and fashionable who wanted a coed school where they could channel their inner Englishness.

As Paula pulled up in her Porsche, it was exactly eight fifteen a.m., right in the middle of the prime fifteen-minute window for the school drop-off. Paula ignored the bickering in the back seat of her two children, Casey and Amelia, for a moment, pausing to scout out the area, checking for anyone else in the school zone. Across the street she recognized the black Escalade belonging to Nicole Nixon, the wife of one of New York's most successful record producers. A plume of exhaust fumes showed its engine was still running, and three giggling children were ejected onto the pavement. Noticing it was the Nixons' nanny, not Nicole Nixon herself driving, Paula's gaze moved on. Just to the side, Robyn Steel, who had a son in Casey and Amelia's class, was parking her convertible Mercedes, the boy squashed in the back, her miniature schnauzer on the front seat, but otherwise it was fairly uneventful people-watching. It seemed today, more than ever, was a day for nannies to do the drop-offs: a harassed-looking Australian, English, and Filipino girls pushing Silver Cross buggies. Paula unloaded the

108

children from the car and strode into the school's courtyard, clutching the girls' hands tightly.

'It's so great you're taking us to school today, Mummy,' said Casey, her eldest twin, looking up at her mother and smiling.

'You know how busy Mummy gets in the morning,' she said, squeezing her daughter's fingers.

'Why are you going to see Miss Beaumont?' asked Amelia, always the more suspicious, guarded child. 'Are you sure we're not in trouble?'

'Absolutely sure,' smiled Paula.

Paula paused in the courtyard, positioning herself just below the head teacher's office window so that anyone inside could see. Then she crouched down eye to eye with her girls and embraced them tightly. She watched them go, their blonde ponytails swinging from side to side under their felt berets, then straightened her Chanel jacket. She was ready to go to war.

'Mrs Asgill, so good to see you again.'

Miss Fenella Beaumont, Eton Manor's headmistress, extended a plump hand across the large walnut desk that dominated her office and settled back into her chair, smoothing down the heavy black robe she always wore over her blouse and skirt. She was a formidable-looking woman: tall with ash-blonde hair set on her head like a helmet, and a powerful speaking voice honed at the Oxford Union, Miss Beaumont having studied Classics at the university in the early 1970s. Paula was well aware that the school's pupils and many of their parents wilted under her fierce gaze, but she had no intention of letting a pompous English spinster get in her way.

'Thank you for making the time to see me,' said Paula, giving the headmistress her sweetest smile. She was careful to conceal her true feelings here, but Paula had been absolutely furious when it had taken her a week to get an appointment with Miss Beaumont. They were paying ten thousand dollars a term each Casey and Amelia to attend Eton Manor. That was sixty thousand dollars a year, not including the hiked-up lunch fees, ballet classes, French tutorials, music lessons, and sundry 'donations' they paid on top. For that money, Paula had expected to see Miss Beaumont immediately. The teacher nodded graciously.

'What can I do for you today?' she asked.

'It's the girls,' said Paula plainly, waving away the offer of tea.

Miss Beaumont glanced down at a sheet of paper in front of them.

'I understand Casey and Amelia are both doing quite well.' Paula did her best to look troubled.

'Yes, that's true, but . . . it's not easy being a twin.'

Miss Beaumont's forehead creased slightly, perhaps perceiving a slight against the school.

'Generally speaking, of course, my husband and I are very happy with the school,' continued Paula carefully. 'But lately we are getting a little concerned that your teachers seem to be – how shall I put this? – seeing the girls as one.'

Miss Beaumont poured milk into her tea from a tiny china jug and nodded thoughtfully. 'Please. Expand.'

'Well, the girls say their teachers have addressed them both by the wrong names on numerous occasions. Casey, Amelia. Amelia, Casey. Amelia particularly has been getting very upset about it, as she is the more sensitive of the girls, as I'm sure you know. I could almost understand it if they were identical twins, but, well, that's not the case.'

Miss Beaumont was not a woman to get flustered by fussy parents. She fixed Paula with a baleful gaze. 'Well, naturally I'm sorry for any distress,' she said. 'I'll talk to all the teachers concerned.'

Paula released a disappointed sigh. She had been rehearsing the sigh for two days.

'Well, that would certainly be a start,' she said. 'But, really, I fear this is impacting on the girls' personal development. My husband and I would be much more reassured if we could work out a way to try and stop this happening again.'

'What did you have in mind?'

Paula took a breath. 'Casey and Amelia should be separated, put in different classes,' she said. 'As soon as possible.'

Miss Beaumont's brow creased. 'Really? I understood that you wanted them to be together in class?'

Paula met her gaze without flinching. This was actually true. William had made a big deal about it when they had originally been accepted for the kindergarten class eighteen months earlier.

'Secondly, I'm generally against moving a pupil into another class away from the friends she's cultivated over the last year. Especially mid-way through the academic year.'

Paula examined Miss Beaumont's face, looking for any trace of suspicion. Had any other parents heard of Princess Katrina's arrival at the school and tried to get their child in the same class? But no, that was impossible. Word might have got out on the grapevine of Carlotta's enrolment, but not even the admissions secretary's sister knew which of the two Transition classes the royal child was going to be in. The beauty of twins, thought Paula with the smallest of smiles. With one of her beautiful daughters in each class, she would have all bases covered. Play-dates at the Princess's palatial Seventy-Second Street town house were surely just a matter of weeks away.

'Are you saying you can't help us, Miss Beaumont?' said Paula, introducing a note of challenge.

The headmistress shook her head.

'Not at all, I'm simply saying I should talk to the teachers concerned and review the situation in a few weeks.'

She was as tough as old boots, thought Paula grimly. Fenella Beaumont had the inscrutable earnestness of someone that could not be bought; rather foolish of her, given the position of power she was in, thought Paula. Still, she had an ace up her sleeve.

'A few *weeks*?' she cried, adding a quaver of hysteria for effect. 'Who knows what psychological problems might have set in by then? These are sensitive girls at a critical juncture in their development.'

Paula had, of course, anticipated Miss Beaumont's objections and had spent many hours thinking of a way to combat them. She had thought of reporting that Amelia, the younger, quieter twin was being bullied, but that would involve accusation, *names*, and Paula had no intention of making unnecessary enemies of influential parents.

'Miss Beaumont,' she said, adopting the intonation of a political chat-show host, 'you should know that we have already seen a child psychotherapist about these identity issues.'

She'd practised saying the words so many times that she now almost believed that Casey and Amelia *had* been to see a shrink. 'Dr Hill is worried, very worried. In his professional opinion, the girls being in the same class, the name mix-ups; it's all causing *damage*.'

She emphasized the word 'damage' and the implication was not lost on the headmistress. She might be British, but she still understood the litigious culture of America.

Fenella Beaumont exhaled slightly, her plump cheeks expanding like a goldfish's.

She flipped open a class register and seemed thoughtful for a moment.

'We do have one new pupil joining Transition B next term, but that's cancelling out Lucy Kwong's departure from the school.' She looked up quickly. 'Her father has been posted to Dubai.'

'Well, if someone new is starting, perhaps another new pupil joining the class would make it easier for both of them,' said Paula.

Miss Beaumont nodded. 'I suppose that makes sense.'

She snapped the register shut and stood up, her gown billowing behind her as she rose. 'I will see what I can do. For the welfare of the girls, you understand,' she added with emphasis.

'Thank you, Miss Beaumont. We believe Casey should be the one to move into Transition B,' added Paula casually. 'More buoyant, more confident. I think she will adapt to new classmates quicker than Amelia would.'

'Yes, quite,' said Miss Beaumont. 'I certainly agree.'

Paula smiled. Beautiful, popular Casey. Her golden girl. The sort of child that everyone would want to befriend. Yes, she thought, with a soaring sense of triumph. Casey would be her entrée into the very highest society.

12

Brooke Asgill snatched up the phone and speed-dialled Kim Yi-Noon's extension.

'Kim, can you come through? We've got a crisis.'

It was eight thirty in the morning. Brooke hadn't even taken her jacket off when she noticed the manuscript of her magical slush-pile discovery *Portico* sitting in the middle of her desk. It had a coffee ring on the cover plus a bright yellow Post-it that read: 'Buy this. Cheap. Mimi.'

Kim came running into Brooke's office. Ever since the editorial meeting, Brooke had been trying, unsuccessfully, to reach Eileen Dunne, *Portico*'s author. She seemed to have disappeared in a puff of green smoke.

'Hi Kim, where are we on tracking down Eileen Dunne?' She waved the Post-it at her assistant. 'Just got this from Mimi; looks like it's getting serious all of a sudden.'

Kim nodded. 'Yes, I was trying the author all last night and this morning, but I finally spoke to her a few minutes ago. She's been out of town. Seems very nice.'

'Especially since we probably got her out of bed,' smiled Brooke, plumping up the vase of roses that David had sent her the day before to finally put Saturday night's spat behind them. Neither Alicia nor Matthew had been mentioned since and she thought it best to keep it that way.

'Well, that's good news, can you get her on the phone for me . . .' she began, but the look on Kim's face made her stop.

'Oh,' said Kim, looking slightly embarrassed. 'Eileen told me she's being represented by Vanessa Friedmann, so it's probably best if you speak to her in the first instance.'

The news was like a body blow to Brooke. The smile dropped off her face and she sat down in her chair.

'Vanessa Friedmann,' she gasped. 'How? When did that happen?' Her eyes strayed back to Mimi's note and a feeling of panic rose in her stomach.

Kim flipped open the diary she had tucked under her arm. 'On Friday the fifteenth you asked me to phone Eileen and suggest she get an agent. I recommended Vanessa, Jane Grubman at IAA and Larry at Authors Inc.'

Brooke stared at Kim, hoping it was a nasty joke. '*Ohmigod.* You recommended three of the toughest negotiators in New York?'

Kim nodded earnestly. 'You said Eileen needed an agent, so I thought it would be better for you if your authors had prestigious ones.'

Brooke took a deep breath. Kim was efficient and super-keen, but she had an awful lot to learn about the publishing business. She wanted to shout at her, but Brooke knew that Kim had no idea what she had just done.

'We'll talk later,' she mumbled, shooing Kim out of the office and putting her head in her hands. Vanessa Friedmann was fierce, the master of the deal. She took on very few clients and was famous for getting six-figure deals for all of them. *Breathe, breathe,* she willed herself. She flicked through her Rolodex and dialled Vanessa's number with a sense of dread. This was the part of her job that she hated.

'Vanessa, *hi.* It's Brooke Asgill. How are you?'

'Brooke Asgill,' said Vanessa. 'This is a nice surprise. Didn't think you'd still be working.'

'Really? Why?'

'Brooke, you are America's most famous bride-to-be. That sounds like a full-time job in itself.'

'Well, remind me to take a long holiday when it's all over.'

Vanessa laughed a little too enthusiastically. 'Well, congratulations on your wedding. I hope your favourite agent is going to get an invite, and if you ever want to publish your memoirs, I'd be happy for us to talk.'

'Actually, that's why I'm calling.'

'Fantastic!' said Vanessa, her enthusiasm real this time.

'No, not about me. About a slush-pile script that came into me a couple of weeks ago. I believe you're looking after the author.'

There was a pause and a rustling of papers.

'Ah yes, Eileen Dunne. I was going to call you this week. Incredible book, the hairs on the back of my neck stood up when I read it. In my thirty years in the business that hasn't happened very often but with *Portico* – phew! This is the real deal.'

Brooke was experienced enough to know she was being set up. It was just agent's hyperbole; in fact Brooke seriously doubted that Vanessa had read more than the first few pages. Eileen Dunne already had serious interest from a publisher; for an agent it was a no-brainer. Who cared what the book was like?

'When a book is this good, obviously I want to go straight to auction with it,' continued Vanessa briskly. 'But the author insisted I give you first look.'

'I'm glad,' said Brooke, trying to sound bright although her heart was pounding. 'I did rescue it from Yellow Door's slush pile after all. And I think one of our assistants recommended you to Eileen.'

There was a long pause which suggested that what she had just said cut no ice.

'So you are interested?' said Vanessa finally.

'Well, I've only seen the first few chapters. I also gave it to Mimi Hall who liked it as well,' Brooke replied, trying to keep her voice casual. It was a game: agent bigging up the manuscript as if it was literary gold, editor down-playing their excitement. It was like a lover's dance.

'How about I give you twenty-four hours to come up with a pre-empt?' said Vanessa smoothly.

'Did you have a figure in mind?' asked Brooke, the words sticking in her throat.

She was not a tough negotiator like Mimi, who could eat even the fiercest agent alive. For someone who had been brought up in a very wealthy family, she was uncomfortable talking about money, and haggling over advances with agents actually made her feel physically ill. It was certainly not what she'd signed up for when she first started at Yellow Door as an editorial assistant with the dreamy notion that life in a publishing house would be spent leisurely reading books. Vanessa gave a low laugh down the phone.

'It's a trilogy with enormous crossover appeal. If it went to auction it could go to seven figures for a three-book deal.'

Seven figures. A million dollars, *minimum*. Brooke swallowed as quietly as she could.

'I'll need to talk to Mimi about this one.'

'Fine. How about we put in a call for five p.m.? I want to drop the manuscript to other editors by tomorrow lunchtime.'

Brooke put the phone gently back into its cradle. She felt nauseous. She was not confrontational by nature and wondered what would happen if she offered Vanessa the maximum advance she could. Seventy-five thousand was her limit as a commissioning editor. Vanessa would probably break a rib laughing. Steeling herself, she picked up the manuscript and walked down the hall to Mimi's office. The corner room was by far the best office on the floor. Bright morning sun was streaming in through the floor-to-ceiling windows, along with the unmistakable sounds of a normal New York morning: road-drills, beeping taxi-cab horns. The bustle and energy of the city served as a welcome juxtaposition to the hush of the Yellow Door workplace.

'Come in,' said Mimi at Brooke's timid knock on her open door. For a moment, Mimi didn't even look up from her notebook. She tucked her dyed black bob behind her ears and placed both palms on the table before she favoured Brooke with eye contact.

'Brooke. Good,' she said. 'Have you spoken to the Dunne woman yet?'

Brooke held the manuscript in front of her like a shield. 'I've just spoken to her agent.'

'Agent?' said Mimi, looking up with alarm. 'I thought you said this one was slush.'

'It was, but it looks like she's got an agent in the meantime.'

'That's unlucky,' snapped Mimi, her voice accusatory. 'Who is it?'

'Vanessa Friedmann.'

'Fuck,' said Mimi, her expression concerned. 'So how much is that bitch trying to squeeze out of us?'

'She's putting it out to auction tomorrow, but we have first refusal.'

'What did you say? You do know we can't go any higher than forty thousand dollars?'

'Each?' asked Brooke hopefully.

Mimi looked at the ceiling. 'For the whole trilogy,' she snapped.

'Well, it seems that Vanessa is looking at something considerably higher. She mentioned seven figures.'

116

'*What?*'

Mimi stood up and started pacing behind her desk. Against the bright light she looked silhouetted.

'If you'd acted as soon as I said I was interested in the fucking script, we wouldn't be in this position,' she muttered. Brooke could read between the lines of Mimi's angry frustration; she had seen this before. Mimi believed in the book, she could see its potential, but she didn't want to pay a penny more than she had to for it.

'Did you call Vanessa?'

'No.'

'Good. Call the author, ask if she's signed a contract with the Friedmann Agency. If she hasn't, make her an offer directly.'

Brooke shook her head. It was hugely unethical to say the least, possibly even actionable should Vanessa choose to claim – not unreasonably – that she had already begun negotiations on the deal.

'We can't do that,' protested Brooke.

'Oh yes you can,' said Mimi brusquely. 'Do it now and let's get this wrapped up by the end of the day.'

When Brooke left the office, her heart was thumping. To stitch Vanessa up would blacken her name with one of the most respected agents in New York. Mimi might have the arrogance to do it, but could she? And anyway, it wasn't Mimi who had to suffer the consequences. Sitting back down behind her desk she took a few moments to do some breathing she had learnt at yoga class. It did nothing to calm her down. She was trapped. If she defied Mimi, she risked being frozen out in the department, and if she went straight to the author, Vanessa Friedmann might well use her influence to put an end to her career in publishing. She longed to phone David to ask his advice, but he was on his way to Darfur to film a documentary for the network. Feeling the beginnings of tension headache, she tapped out an email to Edward Walker.

Hi Edward,

Mimi and I both love the slush-pile manuscript. Remember we discussed it – New Harry Potter? Author now with Vanessa Friedmann so advance may go high. Authorization to pay up to four hundred thousand dollars?'

She pressed send and took a long swig of water from the bottle on her table, her hands trembling as she twisted the top off. She hadn't felt like this in a long time. Perhaps never.

She jolted when she heard the ping of her message inbox.

If you think it's that good, yes. Edward.

She snatched up the phone. 'Vanessa, it's Brooke.'

'Glad you don't hang about. What's your offer?'

'Two hundred and fifty thousand dollars.' Brooke pressed her hand onto the table as she said it. As she lifted it up she could see an imprint of her fingers.

Vanessa snorted. 'Come on, Brooke, don't insult me. You know what I said earlier.'

'Two hundred and fifty in today's climate is a great offer, Vanessa. You know how difficult young adult books are to call. For every J. K. Rowling or Stephanie Meyer there's a thousand others in the remainder bin.'

'I have my client to think about.'

What would Tess Garrett do? thought Brooke, picturing her steely, slightly frightening new publicist.

Brooke cleared her throat. 'Your client sent her manuscript to Yellow Door and we'd already made contact, in fact we were going to make an offer directly to Eileen today. Unless you have actually signed a contract with Eileen, I think our lawyers can argue that we have precedent. You don't want to lose your commission, do you? Fifteen per cent of two hundred and fifty thousand dollars is a lot of money, Vanessa.'

There was a long pause, so long that Brooke was beginning to think Vanessa had already hung up.

'I can't consider anything below four hundred thousand dollars,' she said finally. Brooke could imagine her sitting in her midtown office in her Armani trouser suit, her mouth pursed into nothingness.

'Three hundred thousand,' said Brooke. 'We'll allocate a six-figure marketing spend to make sure it hits retail with a splash.'

'And three hundred thousand would just be US rights?'

Brooke wondered how far she could push it. 'Three hundred thousand. Three-book deal. US rights only,' she said firmly.

'I'll need to talk to my client.'

'I have our legal department calling me in an hour. My superiors want me to go direct to Eileen.'

'I don't want to sour our relationship, Brooke,' said Vanessa, her voice cold.

'Neither do I.'

She put down the phone and exhaled. Every nerve ending in her body seemed to be tingling. What have I done, what have I done? she thought to herself. It was far, far beyond anything she had ever dared do before. But she had a sneaking suspicion that maybe, just maybe, she had outgunned the mighty Vanessa Friedmann.

'Who'd have thought it?' she murmured, feeling a little giddy. She sat there watching the phone, fearing to take her eyes from it. When it rang after five long, painful minutes, Brooke jumped an inch off her chair.

'It's Vanessa. You have a deal.'

Brooke sank back into her chair, whizzed it round and suddenly shouted, Yippee! She'd just joined the big boys. And it felt fantastic.

13

Tess slipped the chunky wooden ring onto her middle finger and held her hand up to admire it. The polished walnut nub was the size of a pingpong ball and shone in the sunshine, its size and shape making her hand look dainty and elegant. The Broadway street vendor was busy putting silver earrings into tiny plastic bags, so she tapped him on the shoulder.

'How much?' she asked, her hand already rummaging for her purse.

'Forty dollars,' he said, shaking a long brown ponytail over his shoulder.

She knew he would take thirty dollars, but what the hell? She had a sudden romantic notion that he was a struggling artisan jewellery maker by day, but a gifted modernist artist by night, and she felt almost altruistic handing over her four crisp ten-dollar bills. *Supporting the arts*, she thought with a smile. True or not, the ring went beautifully with her Seven jeans. *Very downtown.* Crossing Broadway onto Spring Street she spotted a lovely old yellow ice-cream van parked on one of SoHo's cobbled side streets. She bought a red currant waffle cone and took a big satisfied lick. Overnight the weather seemed to have turned and today was Manhattan's first warm spring day. *How could you be down on a day like this?*

Not even her disappointment over Dom could ruin her mood today.

This weekend was supposed to be Dom's first visit to New York to see her, as part of their transatlantic pact to each spend one weekend a month in their respective cities, but the arrangement had fallen at the first hurdle when Dom had called to say he had to be in the office all day Monday – the editor had called a conference about redesigning the travel pages. At first Tess had felt upset and let down, *jilted* even. She had spent her first two weekends in New York rushing around trying to get everything organized for his visit. Finally her new apartment in the West Village was straight and ordered, her clothes all out of suitcases, her possessions removed from the FedEx cardboard boxes. It didn't quite feel like home yet, but at least it was a solid, familiar base from which to properly explore the city.

But maybe, she thought with a pang of guilt, *maybe it is for the best*. As a travel editor, Dom was extremely familiar with most major cities, plus he had a tendency to show off about his knowledge. It might actually be more fun to discover New York herself, finding her own hidden little corners, uncovering her own secrets, which she could share at a later date. And she had to admit she had loved the selfish indulgence of her day so far, with no one to please but herself. She had woken up late and taken a solitary brunch in Pastis in the Meatpacking District, a short walk away from her apartment. She had sat there nursing a latte, watching with fascination the glamorous women dressed in skinny jeans and Chanel sitting in huddles, laughing, drinking coffee, and picking at food.

She had then wandered back into the Village, meandering up and down as if on a snakes and ladders board: up busy Seventh Avenue, back down quiet residential streets lined with smart town houses with brown stoops and shiny front doors. There had been a long leisurely window-shopping session down Bleeker Street, past the long lines outside the Magnolia bakery, queuing for cup cakes and delicious slabs of red velvet cake, the warm, syrupy scent drifting out onto the street. Then past shops selling antiques or guitars, second-hand books, designer clothes or fifty different types of bread, then up into SoHo, which had a different vibe entirely, with its narrow cobbled back streets and multimillion-dollar lofts, street stalls selling finger puppets – five dollars for three – right outside galleries displaying African art without a price tag.

It was a different New York from the one she had first sampled almost a decade ago when she and Dom, in their first summer as a couple, had got two cheap bucket flights to Newark, New Jersey and caught the Amtrak into Penn Station, right next to Madison Square Garden. It had been July, which she now knew was the worst time to visit New York, but back then the stifling heat made it even more exotic. They had stayed in a hostel on One Hundred and Fourth Street, bought hot dogs in Central Park and pizza slices at Sbarro. 'One day, we will work in Manhattan,' they had decided as they stared out at the view from the top of the World Trade Center. Nine years later, Tess had made it: she was finally living the dream.

Glancing at her watch, she was shocked to see it was already four p.m. The day was going too quickly; it was always the way when she was alone, she thought. She was enjoying being outdoors, feeling the sun and lazy spring breeze on her face, but passing the Angelika Film Center on West Houston Street she was tempted to go inside. After walking for so many hours her feet were aching – and anyway, *how long* had it been since she had been to the cinema? She read the screening timetable behind the ticket booths. There was a Woody Allen film she'd read about – terrible reviews – then there were a couple of films that were part of the Macedonian Film Festival and a Brazilian foreign-language film that she was sure was excellent . . . but not today. But then her eyes stopped on *The Pact*, a low-budget horror film that had picked up a buzz at the Sundance Film Festival. *Looks like fun,* she grinned.

She joined the long line snaking up the steps, which seemed to comprise mainly intelligent-looking twenty-somethings, killing time by scrolling through her BlackBerry, hoping for a message from Dom. At the pay-booth, she put down a twenty-dollar bill distract-edly, her eyes still on the BlackBerry.

'Excuse me, ma'am. Are you the parent or guardian of this boy?'

At first she ignored the voice, assuming it was directed at someone else.

'Ma'am?' a cinema attendant said more forcefully, and she looked up to see a tall boy in jeans and a stripy T-shirt standing next to her.

'Come on, Aunt Liz,' he said, looking straight at Tess. 'Can we get some popcorn?'

Confused, Tess looked back to the attendant in the booth. 'Is he with you?' she asked Tess again, with a perfectly balanced mixture of disinterest and impatience.

'Aunt Liz!' said the boy. 'Come *on*.'

He was about twelve or thirteen and she had certainly never seen him before, but there was something about the pleading look on his face that made the words tumble out of her mouth without thinking.

'Hmm. Yes. Yes, he's with me,' she said, pushing more money into the slot.

'Fine,' sighed the attendant, sliding two tickets across and looking around Tess. 'Next in line?'

Tess and the boy walked further into the lobby.

'Pleased to meet you,' she said archly, handing him his ticket. 'I take it you're my long-lost nephew? Which is a neat trick considering I don't have brothers or sisters.'

'Look, I'm sorry,' said the boy. 'They're real age-Nazis here, but I really need to see *The Pact*. Some kids from my school came last night and paid for the Woody Allen movie, then slipped into the horror. I tried it for the one thirty showing but they caught me.'

'Ah, so you thought you'd use some poor mug?' said Tess, attempting a stern voice.

'Come on, you must remember what school's like?' said the boy. 'There's an in crowd and an out crowd. I'm pretty new at my school, I need all the help I can get.'

She couldn't resist a smile; she knew exactly how that desire for social acceptance felt. She'd moved to Suffolk from Edgware when she'd been sixteen, and her first month at her sixth-form college had been awful. Everyone was already in their tight little friendship groups from their respective schools. Tess had been what her mother kindly called a 'late developer': awkward, introverted, and a little mousy. Even her exotic background – coming from sophisticated 'London town' – didn't cut much ice with the country set. Out of desperation, she had signed on with the college magazine and, to her surprise, it had been her salvation. Shielded by her notebook and Dictaphone, Tess found she could talk to people, even boys, even good-looking ones. In fact, she found she was actually rather good at it and, quickly, her confidence grew. As if to reward her courage, Mother Nature gave her an overdue makeover, giving her shiny raven hair, clear skin, wide green eyes – and admiring glances from all angles. And to think she owed it all to journalism.

'Popcorn?' said the boy, falling into step with her. 'It's the least I can do,' he said, handing her a huge bucket.

She wanted to tell him to just bugger off.

'I'm Jack by the way,' he added. 'Can you just stick around until we get into the theatre? That woman in the booth keeps looking at us. Do something, maybe ruffle my hair?'

'Do what?'

'Or give me a dollar to get some gum. You know, something aunt-like.'

She rolled her eyes as Jack kept chattering. Finally they filed into the dark theatre. Tess wondered whether it was nerves or whether he was like this all the time. He certainly had a lot more to say for himself than she'd had at his age.

The film quickly started and it was exactly what Tess had been looking for – pure escapist fun, the sheer luxury of letting two hours slip by without thinking about anything much. Still, during the more gruesome bits, she found herself glancing over at Jack with concern. She had almost zero experience with children and had no idea whether this was irreversibly damaging his young psyche, or whether this was actually quite tame to a modern thirteen-year-old with access to a PlayStation and the Internet. By the time the credits rolled, Tess was starting to feel a niggling sense of guilt.

'I can't believe I let you watch that!' she whispered as they walked out together. 'All that violence and swearing. I hope you closed your eyes when, you know, the man and the lady were kissing.' Tess was surprised at how protective she felt.

'Kissing? I think they were doing a bit more than that,' smirked Jack. 'Thanks for bringing me anyway, Aunt Liz,' he added. 'I thought it rocked.'

'Yes, it was pretty good actually,' she admitted. 'Worth us almost getting thrown in jail, in fact.'

They filed out into the street, both screwing their eyes up in the bright sunlight. After a couple of seconds she realized he was following her.

'So where is your mum this afternoon?' said Tess, rummaging around in her bag for her sunglasses.

'In Greenwich.'

'London?' said Tess, surprised.

'Connecticut,' said Jack casually. 'She lives there now with her new boyfriend. Is that where you're from? London?'

'London? Yes, I moved here three weeks ago.'

'And does your husband live there?'

Tess winced at the assumption that she'd be married. She thought she was so hip with her new ring and her bags full of Marc Jacobs shopping, but in Jack's eyes she was probably ancient. She shook her head.

'No, I'm not married.'

'Oh,' said Jack, tagging along with Tess as she walked off along West Houston Street. 'But don't you miss your friends?'

Tess felt another sudden flush of guilt. The truth was she hadn't really missed anything about London. Packing for the move, she had felt bogged down with anxiety and nostalgia; she had expected to feel terribly homesick being stranded thousands of miles from home, but, as it had turned out, she really hadn't missed any of it: not the buzz of the newsroom, nor even her old flat opposite Battersea Park.

'A little, I suppose,' she shrugged.

'What's England like?'

'Rainy.'

'So was Buffalo,' said Jack enthusiastically. 'I used to live there with my mum and dad. My dad was in the army and got stationed in Iraq. When he came back my mum left him for someone else.'

'I'm sorry to hear that.'

Jack shrugged. 'I like New York and, anyway, I think my mum is happier where she is. I go up to Greenwich every coupla weeks; she comes down here, but today she cancelled on me.'

'There's a lot of it about,' said Tess with an ironic smile. They were passing a park and she sat down on a bench, turning her face up to the sunshine. Jack sat next to her and peered at her sideways.

'So your mum and dad are split up too? Is that what you mean?'

'No, my dad is dead, I was actually talking about my boyfriend. He was supposed to be out here this weekend.'

'What about your mum? I bet she's sad you live all the way out here now.'

'She doesn't know.'

'Why not?' asked Jack, amazed.

Tess puffed out her cheeks, exhausted by his relentless questioning.

'Don't you have somewhere else to be?' she asked.

Jack just blinked at her. 'Nope.'

'Well, I do and I've got to be heading home, so it's been nice meeting you, but—'

'You gotta let me walk you home,' interrupted Jack quickly. 'It's a tough city on your own, all kinds of lowlifes everywhere. Where do you live?'

There was just no shaking this kid.

'Perry Street in the Village.'

'Hey, that's just by me,' said Jack, delighted. 'I'm on Charles Street, we're neighbours. Perry Street, huh? One of those fancy red houses, I bet.'

Tess smiled, thinking about her top-floor apartment. Jack was right; it was one of the smartest buildings in the area. It was only small but it was picture perfect.

'*Nice*,' said Jack appreciatively. 'Our place is kinda a rat-hole. My dad has three jobs but we're not rich. You like pizza?' he added, shooting off on a tangent. 'Let's go to Joe's on Carmine Street. Best pizza in New York . . . Oh no.'

Tess looked up, following his gaze. Across Bleeker Street she could see a tall, stocky man in jeans walking purposefully towards them.

'What's wrong?' frowned Tess.

'My dad.'

He looked like a soldier, thought Tess. Sandy hair cropped close to his head. A crisply ironed khaki shirt and a nose that looked as if it might well have been broken a few times. He wasn't particularly good-looking but there was something strong and solid about him and right now something a little frightening.

'Where the hell have you been?' demanded the man.

'The movies,' muttered Jack, suddenly much quieter now.

'And what did you see that couldn't wait until tomorrow? You know we said we were going to go together tomorrow.'

Jack's cheeks flushed and he looked down at his feet.

'*The Pact*,' said Tess, her voice trailing off as if she was also about to be punished.

'Sorry, who are you?'

'Tess Garrett,' she replied, feeling very naughty. 'We just met today.'

Jack's dad raised a brow. 'And what did he do, tag behind you in the line?'

She gave a slight shrug, not wanting to get the kid into too much trouble.

126

'For an eleven-year-old he's sure gotta lot of guile,' Jack's dad said flatly.

Tess glared at Jack. 'Eleven! You said you were thirteen!'

'Sorry,' said Jack sheepishly.

'He is eleven years old and shouldn't be watching *any* R-rated movies,' said Jack's dad sternly.

Tess winced. 'I didn't know. I'm so sorry. As you might have guessed, I'm not used to kids.'

The big man sighed and shook his head. 'Listen, Miss Garrett was it? I'm Kevin Donovan, Jack's dad, and I'm sorry if I sounded rude. It's not just the movie thing. Jack was supposed to be with his mom, but she cancelled and I managed to get a babysitter at the last minute.'

'I don't need a babysitter,' said Jack sulkily.

'Obviously, he gave the 'sitter the slip,' said Kevin, ignoring his son. 'She didn't even notice for an hour. By the time I got a call at work, he'd been missing for nearly three hours. I was about to call the cops.'

Tess looked at Jack disapprovingly. 'Your dad is just worried about you.'

Jack nodded, his head down. 'I didn't like that babysitter.'

'I didn't have much choice,' said his father wearily.

Tess felt a sudden pang of sadness for this little family unit. A poor single dad overstretched with his three jobs and a clever, easily bored son looking for fun. As an only child she knew exactly what it was like to be lonely and in need of things to do.

'Listen, I'm just around the corner, if you're ever stuck again,' she found herself blurting out.

Jack looked up, a broad smile on his face. 'That's great,' he said brightly.

What have I just said? thought Tess. Panicking slightly, she back-pedalled. 'Of course, I'm not home all that much and I work crazy hours . . .'

'Well, thanks,' said Kevin, clearly not overexcited by the idea. *You can hardly blame the guy*, thought Tess. *I haven't come across as the most responsible adult in Manhattan.* Kevin put his hand on the back of his son's head and pushed him gently along the street. 'Come on, pal. Time to go.'

'Bye Tess.'

She watched as they walked away, Jack's back bowed, Kevin's erect.

She didn't doubt that he was reading Jack the riot act. When they turned the corner, Jack glanced back and gave a little wave. Tess slid her shades back on and smiled. *The glamour, the glamour.* Her first new friend in New York was a child.

14

Employees of the Yellow Door publishing company had become used to seeing paparazzi loitering outside their East Forty-Second Street offices. Many would mutter under their breath or complain about the inconvenience that it brought to their calm, genteel world, but just as many secretly enjoyed the reflected glamour, the excitement of imagining themselves on the red carpet for a few seconds every day. That evening, however, the sidewalk outside the office was clear. Brooke let out a sigh of relief as she pushed out of the revolving doors and onto the dark street. Ever since the 'home-wrecker' story had broken almost two weeks earlier, not a day had gone by when she hadn't been snapped either on her way in or coming out of work. Perhaps the press had lost interest in her, she thought hopefully. More realistically, it was probably down to the late hour – it was now almost nine p.m. and the photographers and reporters plaguing her would expect a glamorous woman like her to be at some party or opening rather than still in the Yellow Door offices. *At least a twelve-hour working day has some benefits*, she thought, feeling a fog of tiredness roll over her.

She looked around for her driver – it was funny how fast you became used to luxuries. She'd always resisted having a car on call; somehow it had seemed far too ostentatious and arrogant for a junior editor at a publishing company, as if she was saying 'I'm an important person', when she was just the same as everyone else. But when the paps had started to trail her, Meredith and David had pressured her to take what they called 'sensible measures', to which Tess Garrett had added certain 'rules'. Brooke now had to change her cell-phone number every fortnight. Friends and family were discouraged from leaving messages on her answer-phone; Tess had told her how easy it was for reporters to hack into her phone and access sensitive information. The idea of a bodyguard had also been mentioned with increasing regularity, but she shuddered at that idea. That was all a bit too diva-esque for her. It was for the same reason that Brooke had always asked her driver to park a little way from the building, which was why she now found herself standing in the cold street, looking around for the car. It was then that she noticed a man looking at her from the other side of the street. *Damn*, she thought, turning to walk towards the corner, putting her sunglasses on quickly, *the paparazzi are here, after all.* The man kept pace with her on the opposite sidewalk, one hand raised as if hailing her. The usual routine, trying to get a reaction, a more interesting shot. They were shameless.

'Brooke! Hey, Brooke!' he shouted over the traffic. She glanced across again as he began to cross the street towards her, his jacket flapping behind him as he dodged speeding yellow taxis.

'Brooke. Wait. It's me!'

He was better-looking than the usual hack, she noticed that much; and there was something vaguely familiar about him.

'Brooke, it's Matt!'

The name made her stop. At first, she wasn't sure if it was him or if it was some well-informed pap trying to trick her, but as he leapt away from a blaring truck, she could see it was him.

'Matthew Palmer,' she said slowly, shaking her head before beginning to walk on. In many ways she would have preferred it to have been a tabloid photographer. At least they responded to threats.

'Why haven't you returned my calls?'

'Because I don't want to speak to you,' she said crisply. Brooke always tried to be scrupulously polite, but when Matt had phoned her office, *twice*, in the three days after Danny Krantz's column, she had instructed Kim to field his calls. She was too angry; she felt too betrayed.

'Please, Brooke, just give me a minute.'

He followed her along the pavement and grabbed her elbow. She averted her eyes, wanting to be anywhere but here.

'Listen, Brooke, I read the piece in the *Oracle*. I know how it must look.'

She rounded on him angrily. 'How it *looks*? Matt, do you know how much trouble that story's caused? How much did they pay you? I hope it was worth it.'

'Pay me for what?'

'Leaking the Jeff Daniels story to the *Oracle*. I assume you're who told them.'

She looked at him. His college-boy hair had been cropped closely around his head.

'Why the hell would I do something like that?'

Brooke frowned in puzzlement and Matt nodded towards the Helmsley Hotel across the road. 'I think we'd better sit down and talk about this. What about a drink?'

She shook her head. She suddenly wanted to hear what he had to say for himself, but she certainly wasn't going to go into a public bar with him, not when the press had labelled him her 'old flame'. Paparazzi aside, everyone in New York had a camera phone these days. She glared at him for a moment, then let out a long breath.

'All right, two minutes. This way.'

There was a small Italian restaurant on the next block. Brooke was a regular there and could always count on their discretion. Luigi, the owner, greeted her warmly and led her to a quiet booth at the back, out of the view of other diners. Luigi hovered and Matt ordered a beer. Brooke asked for still water, but pointedly did not unbutton her coat.

For a second, she imagined they were back in college, in dingy bars and student parties. It had been at one such party, at a big house on Prospect Street in Providence, that she and Matt had met for the first time. Brooke had drunk rather too much of a potent cocktail someone had branded 'Love Punch' and Matt had found her having a power-nap on a pile of coats, where someone had sprinkled her with rose petals.

'Rise and shine, Ophelia,' he had said, dragging her into the kitchen to give her his 'patent hangover cure': force-feeding her a banana for potassium, adding a couple of Tylenol and making her drink a large glass of water. Then he'd walked her slowly home, promising her that, despite the cold, a long walk would make her feel ten times better. He'd been right, of course. He was a doctor, or was going to be, a third-year med student at the Brown Alpert Medical School. As he'd helped her weave back to campus, it had begun to snow, and she remembered her tiredness and drunkenness

131

dissolving as they'd ambled along talking about everything and nothing, her feet slipping in the slush.

From that day on, they'd become unlikely friends, all the way through her time at Brown. He was completely different from her other friends at college – popular, wealthy New Yorkers and Bostonians, fresh from schools like Chapin, Nightingale-Bamford and Dana Hall – and that had been part of his curious appeal. Matt was from a small town in Illinois. He liked Guns N' Roses, ice hockey and motorbikes, Black Russian cocktails, and John Fante novels. He worked shifts in a coffee shop to help pay his way through college and he always looked tired. He fixed her car. Took her drinking, introduced her to the excitement of live music in dingy bars, and always had a reassuring diagnosis for Brooke's many imagined ailments (handbag elbow, stress headaches, broken heart). For a girl from the Upper East Side, it was all an unthreatening walk on the wild side for her carefree days at college. But now, in New York all those pleasant memories had melted away. This man had betrayed her – and for what? Some pathetic flash of fame in a tabloid?

She crossed her arms and stared at him. 'So, are you going to explain yourself?'

He gave a slow half-smile. 'Maybe if you take your sunglasses off. I'm not convinced anyone's looking.'

She pulled them off and placed them on the table between them. Matt took his beer from the waitress and took a long drink.

'I don't know what makes you think I tipped off the papers. I didn't. I swear to you. For a start, I barely knew about you and Jeff Daniels. Didn't all that happen after you left Brown?'

She nodded begrudgingly. 'So you swear you didn't tip off the papers?'

He looked angry at the suggestion. 'I didn't do it, Brooke. You were my friend. Besides, I wouldn't stand on a cold street waiting for you for two hours if I was guilty.'

'That means nothing, I can tell you.'

'Cynic.'

'Realist. So how *did* your name end up in Danny Krantz's column?'

'A journalist called me up a few weeks ago,' he said, wiping his mouth. 'Said they were doing a profile piece on you. Actually, I think they described it as a *celebration* of you.'

Brooke raised her eyebrows.

'I don't know how they got my name but it all sounded kosher. I just said something really innocuous about you.'

'Like what?'

'They asked me how I'd describe you. I said kind, beautiful, and smart. Everyone loved you. And I never said I was your boyfriend, or ever was. I was mad as hell when I saw that "old flame" thing.'

She put her head down to hide a little flutter of embarrassment.

'So you didn't say: "She's gorgeous. Men just love her. Any man would go crazy for her", or whatever it was?'

Matthew put his beer down. 'Have I ever been that sleazy?'

Brooke finally allowed him a smile.

'I'm sorry, Brooke. I'm so sorry.'

Brooke shrugged. She knew very well how the media would twist things, even fabricate them to make something salacious out of nothing. And, despite her anger and frustration over everything that had happened with the column, she did believe him. Out of all the people she knew, Matt was the least interested in fame and money. She just couldn't see his motivation for doing it.

'No, I'm sorry,' she said slowly. 'It's good to see you again, Matt.'

'Dr Palmer to you, Asgill.'

She laughed. They'd always had that sort of relationship. He'd never seemed impressed by her rich, fashionable friends, never let her get away with any pomposity.

'Sorry, *Doc.*'

She took a sip of her water, wishing now that she had ordered the beer.

'So how is it?' he asked.

'How's what?'

'Life as a real-life American princess?'

'Hey, come on . . .' she said, flushing.

'Okay, future first lady.'

'David is a news reporter, not a politician.'

'Give him time,' said Matthew. 'How old is he? Thirty-two, thirty-three? I read the papers, Brooke. People are already talking about him as a senator or governor. We both know David Billington was born to be president.'

Brooke smiled. 'He'll probably run for Congress in the next few years, but president? Here's an exclusive for your New York *Oracle* friends: he's honestly never mentioned it.'

'Well, I do know that Wendell Billington is one of the most ruthless, powerful men in the city. He's like Joe Kennedy but with more class and even more money and, to give them their due, I think the Billingtons are positioning David brilliantly. They've recognized the power of the media and he's already a big star. People trust him. I'm not a Republican by a long shot, but even I might be tempted to vote for him. Even though I bet *I'm* not his favourite person at the minute.'

While he was talking, Brooke examined her old friend with detached curiosity. On the outside, Matthew looked virtually the same. A little rougher, a little older, but the same face, the same smile. It was funny how seven or eight years could change you inside. Now her rocking college boy was serious, grown up.

'Since when have you been so interested in politics?' she teased. 'You would have struggled to tell me the name of the president in college.'

'Politics is the new rock and roll, baby,' he smiled, knocking back his beer and nodding to the waitress to bring him another.

'So you know where life's taken me. What about you? I take it you never made it as a rock star?' She smiled in memory of his student band, Ded Squid.

He shrugged playfully. 'Coffee shop boy, med student . . . something had to give. I'm refusing to believe it was lack of talent.'

'So where do you work? Columbia-Presbyterian, wasn't it?'

He nodded. 'Yeah, in ER. I guess I should have gone into cosmetic surgery, then I'd have been mixing in your social circles uptown.'

'I'll tell you a secret. You really wouldn't want to.'

She found herself glancing down to his left hand. His ring finger was bare.

'What about any lovely ladies for you . . . ?'

'I was married.'

'Was?' asked Brooke without thinking.

'Katie. A nutritionist.'

'Are you divorced?' she asked, surprised.

'She died. It was a little over a year ago now.'

'Oh, I'm so sorry. I had no idea. Me and my big mouth. How?' she asked quietly.

'It's called Sudden Adult Death Syndrome. A congenital heart defect. You don't stand a chance.'

'How awful.'

He nodded and stared down at his beer.

'We were on holiday in France,' he said finally. 'We didn't have a honeymoon, both too busy, so we were sort of taking it two years later. We went to bed one night in our hotel and when I woke up she was dead.'

She put her hand on his, without thinking if anyone was looking. He paused and took a deep breath.

'You know what drew me to ER?' he asked. 'It just seemed like the most pure form of medicine. In minutes, seconds, you can save a life. Every day you can help dozens of people from something frightening or life-threatening: gunshot wounds, heart attacks, whatever it is. Every day I did it, saved hundreds of lives, but I couldn't do a thing to save the woman I loved.'

He drained his glass and gave her a small smile. 'We'd better go. Before someone sees you and the Billingtons make me disappear,' he grinned.

'They're not that bad,' smiled Brooke, getting out her purse and putting twenty dollars on the table.

He got up to follow her.

'I'd better leave alone,' she said quickly. 'Crazy, I know.'

Matthew reached into his pocket and gave her a card. It was small and grey with the words Matthew Palmer MD and a mobile number stamped in tiny black letters.

'If you're ever on the West Side . . .'

For a second she thought about giving him her card, but really what was the point? It had been a relief to get the Danny Krantz gossip column business cleared up, and she'd enjoyed catching up, but that was all. There was a reason they had drifted apart since she had left Brown. Their lives had gone in completely different directions. And right now the last thing she needed was more complications.

'Well, so long, Matt,' she said with an awkward wave. And she turned and walked out of the restaurant back into the street.

15

It was an extraordinary night at Somerset Tower, the iconic new skyscraper at Columbus Circle. Outside, military-grade searchlights swung back and forth across the building, making the party visible anywhere in the city. At street level, paparazzi yelled and jostled, their flashlights popping like gunfire, as New York's most beautiful people walked down the red carpet and through the lobby to the doors of the high-speed elevator. Already there was a queue forming of people clamouring to be whisked up to the Skin Plus launch on the sixtieth floor, though no one appeared to mind the wait as they were plied with Riedel flutes of Cristal and delicate canapés from drop-dead-gorgeous waiters. Liz Asgill swept through the centre of her creation towards the executive elevator, listening to the snippets of conversation as she passed by.

'It's sensational.'

'Have you seen the light-therapy booths?'

'*Apparently* they are booked up for the next three months already.'

The words made Liz giddy with pride and excitement, although she didn't need the congratulations of the three hundred guests to know she had created magic. As the lift doors opened onto the top floor, she could see the excitement crackling across the room like electricity. Skin Plus was a hit. In a city saturated with luxury spas, the Skin Plus Day Spa was the most cutting-edge, the most desirable, the most *now*. In every corner of the 25,000-square-foot space were technological advancements to make NASA blush: skin imaging banks that helped diagnose skin problems, light-therapy pods that helped reverse the signs of ageing, and the patent-pending nervo-dermis machine, a contraption that used light pulses to stimulate the elasticity of skin, eliminating lines and wrinkles. Alongside the space-age gadgetry were rows of products, their boxes proud and pristine, lined up on the gleaming glass counters. The nutritional centre, home of the spa's cuisine, would tonight also offer tastes of their tantalizing dietary supplements, which promised to keep a complexion's brightness, and 'Skinny Smoothies', fruit drinks packed with properties to keep your skin looking good from the inside. New Yorkers were a breed that liked to look and feel young, and everything they needed to do that was here.

The only thing missing from the scene, the one thing that would have made the night perfect for Liz was her father. Eight years ago, just a few weeks after her thirtieth birthday, Liz had floated the idea of a high-end cosmeceutical range to Howard Asgill over lunch at the Rainbow Room. The restaurant, on the sixty-fourth floor of the Rockefeller Center, was her favourite place to lunch in the city; a place where she felt in charge, successful, and almost literally on top of the world, and she'd felt buoyed further by her recent appointment to the post of Vice President of New Product Development. At the time, cosmeceuticals, a term coined for a combination of cosmetics and pharmaceutical expertise, meant sterile serums dispensed by doctors and dermatologists, or expensive creams created by the most up-market brands in the industry; brands that could afford to spend huge amounts on research and development into such scientific advances.

Liz's idea to enter the cosmeceutical sector was a bold departure for Asgill Cosmetics, who had until that point concentrated on mid to low price points for their products. The profit margins on cosmeceuticals were lower than in other sectors of the beauty industry, due to the vast amount of research involved, but Howard Asgill recognized that cosmeceuticals were going to be one of the fastest-growing and most important sectors of the skincare market, one they could not afford to miss out on. So he had given Liz the go-ahead and approved her idea to launch the new Skin Plus range via a luxury spa. She knew this venture would succeed or fail on image alone; consumers had to believe that the Skin Plus range was absolutely the best available and they had to believe it worked. What better way to convince them than by showing them the products in action? And a huge dose of A-list exclusivity never did any harm either, especially in Manhattan.

The Skin Plus range certainly had that, thought Liz, watching the faces of the party-goers, glowing with the knowledge that tonight they were at the very centre of things. If only Father could have been here to see it, to see *me*, thought Liz.

Meredith swept to her daughter's side looking imperial, flushed with a happiness Liz had not seen since Brooke's engagement party.

'This is just *fabulous*, darling. Absolutely everyone is here.'

Liz smiled thinly at her mother's enthusiasm. She had spent weeks arguing about the budget for the party with Meredith and William, who both thought a launch event costing a million dollars was excessive and unnecessary. William particularly had thought it better to take a select band of journalists to the Turks and Caicos to gently persuade them to give favourable and extensive coverage to the Skin Plus range in their publications. But that was cheap talk, thought Liz – quite the opposite of the Skin Plus ethos. Beauty editors were exhausted from trips and they would cover the Skin Plus range anyway because of the amount of advertising Asgill Cosmetics gave their magazines.

'Not quite everyone,' said Liz, craning her elegant neck. 'I can't see Brooke and David anywhere. Patrick McMullen is here and is desperate to get a photo of them.' McMullen was the famous party photographer who sold his work into all the prestigious media outlets. If the golden couple did not appear, the chance of blanket coverage in the papers and magazines was not so assured.

'It's okay, Brooke has just arrived,' said Tess Garrett, drawing up beside them. 'It took us twenty minutes to get through the lobby downstairs. I don't think I've ever seen so many paparazzi.'

Liz looked at Tess sharply. The meaning of her words had only just sunk in.

'What do you mean *Brooke* has just arrived? Where is David?'

Tess looked surprised. 'I thought you knew. He's out of town.'

'Out of town?' snapped Liz. She could barely believe the selfishness of her sister. For weeks Liz had been impressing upon her the importance of the photo opportunity.

She saw Tess glance at her mother. Since when had those two been in such cahoots? Liz wondered. The Brit, however, did not look ruffled.

'Don't worry, Liz, the papers want pictures of gorgeous women on the front of their newspapers, not good-looking men, however important they are. And if the feeding frenzy downstairs is anything to go by, we don't really need David. Brooke will be front page of the *Post* and the *Daily News* tomorrow without him.'

How dare she? thought Liz, narrowing her eyes. The pushy hack had been here two minutes, didn't even have anything to do with Asgill Cosmetics, and here she was giving her a lecture on PR and marketing strategy!

'I think it's for me and my corporate communications director to decide what we do and don't need,' she said coolly. Meredith touched her daughter gently on the arm.

'Tess is only here to help, Elizabeth. We're all on the same side.'

Liz took a breath. She had been talking to Dr Derkowitz, one of the Skin Plus dermatologists a only an hour ago. What was it he had said? Stress is one of the worst things for the skin.

She forced a smile towards her mother. 'You'd look very lovely this evening if you didn't look so angry,' smiled Meredith in return.

Liz felt disarmed by the compliment. It was rare that her mother even seemed to notice her at all, let alone comment on her appearance. Her slate-grey silk Balenciaga cocktail dress, skimming her lithe body, and five-inch satin heels, had meant she had attracted almost as many compliments as her spa. Enrique had blow-dried her hair, collagen regeneration, road-tested at the therapy rooms, made her skin look plump, and her custom-blended scent ensured she looked, smelt, and felt sensational. For as long as Liz could remember, Meredith's parental joy and pride seemed to be only directed at William, Sean, and Brooke. It had stopped mattering to her many years ago, the second she realized her anger and sadness were simply futile. Instead, Liz had buried those unwanted emotions of rejection, of feeling overlooked and underappreciated. But perhaps tonight, finally, after all these years, she had done something right.

'I'm not angry,' said Liz, relaxing a little. 'Just anxious.'

'With such an adoring crowd around you?'

They both looked around and smiled. It was incredible how many people had come. Madonna. Demi Moore, Lindsay Lohan. She was glad the younger crowd had come too. And of course, they had the full complement of editors and beauty directors from all the publications that mattered. Knowing that an up-market beauty range from a company like Asgill's might not be taken seriously, Liz had sent the important journalists' invitations to the Skin

Plus launch in a Globe-Trotter vanity case stuffed with products, together with a VIP black card allowing them a free treatment every month. And all the heavy-hitter management from the Condé Nast, Time Inc., and Hearst publishing companies were here too. *Good*, thought Liz. It was the least they could do, considering the hundreds of thousands of dollars in advertising she had given them: ten double-page-spread Skin Plus adverts in *Vogue*, *Harper's*, and *Town and Country* alone. Liz's marketing director had doubted the wisdom of this advertising blitz, especially as the stand-alone Skin Plus boutique would not open until September. That meant that Skin Plus products could only be bought through the spa, which could only accommodate a few dozen clients a day, but Liz understood the value and power of exclusivity. People wanted nothing more than something they couldn't have.

Liz stepped away from her mother and towards a podium at the end of the room. She took a sip of lemon water to steady herself. Liz was not gregarious by nature, but knowing the value of salesmanship, she had taken acting classes at the Lee Strasberg Institute to make her both more outgoing in social situations and a better public speaker.

The noise of the room hushed as Liz pinged a spoon against a glass and began to speak into a microphone.

'I'd like to welcome everyone to the Skin Plus Spa,' she said in a steady voice. 'We have the greatest team of beauty professionals working with us and tonight I'd like to welcome another important member to the Skin Plus team. Ladies and gentlemen, please welcome Enrique Gelati.'

Gasps and murmurs of approval went around the room as the hairstylist graciously stepped forward and took a bow.

'We have spent many years getting to this point,' she continued, 'creating a comprehensive skin health system that will have you looking better, longer. We offer personalized treatments and skin diagnoses and nonsurgical procedures. When our store opens later in the year, we will be selling salon-quality products for you to take home . . .'

She kept the speech short. She understood what parties were like in New York – people came and people left to hop onto the next one, no matter how good you were. No one came to hear an executive read out a press release. Even so, when Liz finished, three hundred pairs of hands burst into loud applause. Her heart was beating wildly. If only she could bottle this feeling and sell it through the spa she'd be a billionaire for sure.

Descending the podium she was swamped with well-wishers; important and influential people clamouring to tell her that her baby was beautiful. It was almost overwhelming. Needing a little space, she walked up the steps to the mezzanine area where the spa's treatment rooms were located. It was officially out of bounds, although a few people had wandered past the velvet ropes. Liz sat on an elegant chair, took a sip of her cocktail, and tried to relax. She had spent the last few nights running on nervous energy and had barely had any sleep. Still, when she looked down at the spa, the sum total of eight years of hard work, she knew every minute had been worth it. The collapse of her marriage, the stress, even the erosion of her position within the company – she knew her single-mindedness on this risky project had won her few supporters on an already jumpy board; but they were all sacrifices she had been prepared to make and, given the enormous success of tonight's launch, they had clearly been sacrifices worth making. Skin Plus was a hit, and already her mind was whirling with expansion plans. She wanted a Skin Plus Spa in every major capital of the world, plus a diffusion line in every big city from Pittsburgh to Prague. More importantly, her standing in the company would be unassailable. With Natural Glow failing, and Skin Plus the talk of the town, she was sure her mother would finally be forced to acknowledge William's short-comings and make her CEO. And then Liz could really get to work. *Watch out, Estée Lauder*, she smiled to herself. She envied their rival's breadth in the market; from the most premium products like Crème de la Mer to the lower-end made-for-TV beauty brands they quietly owned, the Lauder family name was synonymous with the entire cosmetics industry. It was the way she wanted to take Asgill Cosmetics. So lost was she in her thoughts and plans, it was a few moments before Liz realized there was someone standing next to her.

'Hello Lisa.'

For a split second she did not recognize him, but as she saw past the smart one-buttoned suit and the clean-shaven face, she remembered with rising panic that it was the guy from the Red Legs bar. She couldn't remember his name; was he an actor, perhaps? She certainly remembered that dark bathroom, however. Urgent hands, teasing fingers, hot kisses. His thick cock inside her.

'Lisa?' she said casually, summoning up everything she had learnt at the Lee Strasberg Institute. 'My name is Liz.'

He lifted his finger to her face. 'That cleft in your chin. It's a Mendelian trait.'

Her heart was beating so hard she was sure he could hear it.

'I'm sorry, but this area is private,' she said as evenly as she could. 'I think you'd better go back downstairs.'

'You can't turn me away,' he whispered. 'Not after the effort it took to get me in here tonight. I owe my agent a big favour.'

She began to walk away, but he caught her arm and spun her round, pulling her so close his mouth was by her ear.

'How about another fuck?' he whispered. She angrily jerked away and she saw he was smiling, only this time the sexy curve of his lips, the dangerous twinkle in his eyes, was menacing, not seductive.

'You know, I couldn't believe it when I found out my lovely Lisa was really Liz Asgill, multimillionaire director of Asgill Cosmetics. I saw you in some paper, the business pages, actually; quite a pleasant surprise, I have to say.'

'I'm calling security,' said Liz, but he just chuckled.

'I think they're just down there.' He pointed down the stairs. 'Next to the journalist from Page Six who I think might be interested in talking to me. I can give them a new spin on their coverage, spice up another boring product launch. I'm sure they'd love to hear how the president of this smart, chic new cosmetics company likes to fuck strange men in basements.'

Liz looked at him sharply. She could see he wasn't bluffing. After all, what did he have to lose? *Russ*, that was his name, she thought randomly. Russ Ford. Not that knowing anything about *him* would do her any good now. He held all the cards, and he knew it.

'Okay, so we had sex,' she said carefully. 'Once. It's no big deal.' Her voice was low and controlled although her stomach was churning. Of course, Liz had considered the consequences of getting caught doing what she did, but like a compulsive gambler with a house riding on each hand, she couldn't resist the risk. And the more times she had met men in bars for sex and then never seen or heard from them again, the more her actions felt detached from real life.

'Once, you say?' asked Russ, a note of triumph in his voice. 'That's funny, because after I saw you in the paper, I saw you at the sports bar on Tenth Avenue. It was as if me and you have some sort of *destiny.*'

Liz was now starting to feel physically sick.

'You were with some blond guy, kind of a rugged, redneck type. You left with him after about ten minutes.'

'I'm sorry if this is about a broken heart,' she hissed.

Russ shook his head, laughing slowly. 'Seriously, honey, I don't think so.' He took the martini glass from her hand and took a slow sip of her cocktail. Liz caught her breath. She hated this man, feared him and what he could do to her. She wanted to kill him, erase him from existence. Yet she was surprised to find how much that one haughty, arrogant action of snatching her drink had affected her. It had turned her on.

'So I went back to the sports bar the next day, spoke to Blondy,' continued Russ, draining Liz's drink. 'We swapped notes about what a great fuck you are. Except he knew you as Julie. And that's when I knew for sure.'

She turned on him. 'You knew what?' she spat.

'How you forget about your fancy Upper East Side life and just play the whore with faceless fucks you never have to see again.'

He grinned and held up his hands. 'Well, honey, I'm home.'

'All right. You've gloated enough,' said Liz fiercely. 'What do you want?'

'Keep it up, Lisa. You're making me hard.'

He trailed his finger down her tanned, toned arm so she felt the familiar roughness of his fingertips.

'Don't worry, you can afford it. I just want some incentive to keep our little secret. Because I kinda doubt the Billington family are going to like this either.'

'There are laws against blackmail,' she snarled. 'My lawyer is here tonight and by the time the cops are finished with you, you'll wish you'd never seen my face.'

He snorted, brushing the threat away like an irritation. 'Blackmail?' he said with a note of surprise. 'Oh no, I was thinking of it more like patronage of the arts. Me, struggling actor. You, hotshot businesswoman.'

'Don't fuck with me,' she growled.

'I think we're past that point already.'

Russ put the martini glass on a chair and fastened the button on his suit. 'Why don't I give you a couple of days to think

143

about it? But don't take too long . . . Just to give you a little hint, I was thinking somewhere in the region of two hundred thousand dollars.'

As he walked away he smiled. 'Well, I know where you are now,' he said, gesturing at the Skin Plus logos on the doors of the treatment rooms. 'Maybe I'll book an appointment. I've got a feeling I'll be able to afford it real soon.'

Liz opened her mouth to speak, then closed it again. For the first time in a long time, she just didn't know what to say.

Tess wasn't sure how long she'd been asleep when her mobile started ringing. She groped across her bedside table, grabbed the phone, and squinted at the time on the glowing screen. Two thirty a.m. *What the hell?* Calls at this time were never good news, unless it was from London, in which case some selfish sod hadn't factored in the time difference. She sighed. Which probably meant it was Dom.

'Do you know what time—?' she began to croak, but she was quickly cut off.

'Can you come round?' The voice was female.

'Who is this?' asked Tess suspiciously.

'Liz,' came the testy reply, as if it were perfectly natural for Liz Asgill to call in the middle of the night.

'Oh. Er, hi,' said Tess. Her brain felt foggy and she felt slightly sick. One too many Manhattans, perhaps. She struggled to sit up in bed.

'Is everything okay?' Tess had only left Liz a few hours earlier at the launch. She had not said goodbye before she'd left – Tess hadn't been there to handle the launch PR; her job was to keep an eye on Brooke and ensure her photographs got in all the right magazines and newspapers. When Brooke had left just after eleven, Tess had quickly followed. She badly needed the sleep; the two weeks since she had landed in New York had been a blur.

'I need to see you,' said Liz urgently. 'Right away.'

'Well, I'll be in the office at seven,' said Tess blearily. 'Let's grab a coffee as soon as we both get in.'

'No, I need to see you *now*.'

There was an agitated, desperate edge to Liz's voice that made Tess reach over and switch on her bedside light.

'Liz, it's two thirty,' she said, immediately regretting the words the second they were out of her mouth.

'This is not a nine-to-five job, Tess,' snapped Liz. 'I wouldn't be calling you unless it was urgent.'

So far, Tess had had very few dealings with Liz and she had been rather relieved that their paths hadn't crossed. Tess had met many formidable women in her time, but Liz was something else. There was a chilliness about her that made Tess feel as though she was treading on eggshells whenever they met. She was certainly not a woman to piss off before the day had even begun.

'*Okaaay,*' sighed Tess. 'Give me your address.'

Unable to find a pen, she wrote it down with lipstick on the front of a magazine.

'I'll see you in thirty minutes.'

Liz lived in a two-bedroomed apartment in one of the most luxurious condominiums in the city. Fifteen Central Park West, a huge wedding cake of a building overlooking the park, was home to some of the most powerful people in New York: celebrities, CEOs, and money-men; people who could afford to pay up to one hundred million dollars for the privilege of living there. At three a.m., the building's lobby was silent and stately with its oak panelling and marble pillars, the only noise the occasional crackle of the huge log fire. Tess took the elevator to the twenty-fifth floor where she found the door to Liz's apartment slightly ajar. After two tentative knocks, she walked in. Her first thought was that Liz's home was not as stark or minimalist as she was expecting. Sophisticated and tasteful, yes, but Tess had expected an ice queen like Liz to go for chrome and exposed brick. In the dim light, however, the living room actually felt quite warm and comforting, although she supposed the spotlessness of the big white sofas and cream carpet, along with the complete absence of clutter, did reflect the perfectionism of its owner.

'Thanks for coming,' said a voice, and Tess jumped. Liz was standing by the windows overlooking the park, half hidden in the shadow. She was still wearing her slate-grey cocktail dress from the party, her arms wrapped tightly in front of her as she nursed a tumbler of amber liquid and gazed out at the city lights twinkling in the dark. *What a view*, thought Tess. New York looked so majestic and peaceful, she could see why people were prepared to spend so much to live here. Liz, however, looked anything but at peace. As she stepped into the light, her face was as pale and expressionless as a corpse's.

'This is uncomfortable for me,' she began, 'so I only want to say it once.'

Tess nodded. 'I'm listening,' she said quietly.

Liz took a deep breath and let it out. 'I am being blackmailed.'

Tess simply stood and listened. Years spent interviewing a whole range of people, from aggrieved neighbours to political protestors to celebrities, had taught Tess not to interrupt her subjects; to let them simply talk until they had nothing left to say.

'A few weeks ago, I had sex with someone, an actor called Russ Ford,' continued Liz. 'I didn't use my real name and I didn't see him again afterwards, but tonight he showed up at the party and now he is asking for money.'

Tess frowned. She had been expecting a much bigger revelation given Liz's grey-faced demeanour. It wasn't good, of course, but neither was it a disaster. Liz having a one-night stand was hardly going to derail the Asgills' social standing.

'Okay,' she said, trying to sound both sympathetic and businesslike. 'What's Russ Ford threatening you with exactly? I don't mean to be rude, but the newspapers aren't going to be too interested in a single woman having a one-night stand.'

Liz paused again. 'He saw me again a few nights later in another bar with another man.'

'And he was jealous?' asked Tess, still confused.

Liz remained silent.

'Liz, I can't help you if you don't tell me everything,' said Tess with a little irritation. 'I really don't see how a one-night stand—'

'I like casual sex, okay?' Liz interrupted. '*Very* casual sex. This guy Russ says he is going to the papers with details. "Sex Addict Liz Asgill screws men in bathrooms of seedy clubs": do you think that's the sort of headline the tabloids might be interested in?'

Tess nodded. She understood better than Liz knew – after all, covering up the story of her brother Sean's overdose at an orgy was what had brought her to work for the Asgills in the first place. *It's a funny old family*, she thought, almost smiling at the understatement. Ten years ago, Tess would hardly have believed that a successful, elegant woman like Liz Asgill would have such a sordid sex life, but years on Fleet Street had opened her eyes to what went on behind closed doors. And, of course, some of the most hair-raising stories – the breakfast TV presenter who let her Alsatian lick dog food off her naked body, the cosy soap actress who could only have sex after her boyfriend blew cocaine up her arse, the supermodel who was a thirty thousand-pound-a-throw hooker – they never saw the light of day thanks to the prompt behind-the-scenes intervention of lawyers and publicists, who made deals and threats to keep it all quiet.

'Listen, Liz, having a couple of one-night stands doesn't make you a sex addict,' said Tess soothingly.

Liz shook her head. 'It's more than just a couple,' she said, a slight catch in her voice.

'How many?'

She shrugged. 'Once, twice a week.'

'A *week?*'

Tess hadn't meant to sound so surprised, but it was crazy – and amazing that she hadn't been caught before. What was Liz playing at? Russian roulette with men she hardly knew? Tess had a sudden sinking feeling.

'Do you ever pay them?' she asked.

'*No!*'

Liz glared at Tess for a second, then closed her eyes, trying to gain control. She sat down on the corner of the white sofa and lit a cigarette, crossing her long legs in front of her.

'I don't want to get Patty Shackleton involved,' she said, blowing the smoke out in a long stream. 'And I certainly don't want my mother to know. Can I trust you?'

'Yes, of course.'

Liz looked down at the sofa, brushing imaginary crumbs from the material. 'Good. I haven't got time to give you a lesson on Asgill family politics. But let's just say my mother won't like it. She'll make me suffer.'

Tess had a sneaking suspicion that *she* was the one Meredith would make suffer if she ever found out that Tess had been colluding with Liz to keep secrets, but she knew that she didn't really have a choice. She had enough problems with the Asgill family already, without making an enemy of Liz.

'So tell me what you know about this guy,' said Tess, sitting on the opposite sofa.

'Hardly anything,' said Liz. 'As I said, we didn't exactly talk the first time I met him.'

'And do we know what he wants?'

'He says he can get two hundred thousand dollars for his story.'
As Liz spoke, Tess was calling up the Internet on her BlackBerry.
She typed 'Russ Ford' into imdb.com. He had a very short list of
credits in some minor made-for-TV productions; he was hardly
Tom Cruise. It figured.

'Do you know if he's spoken to anyone yet?' she asked.

'He could have spoken to everyone for all I know,' snapped Liz.
'Forgive me for not going into too much detail with him at my
company's launch party. What are we going to do?'

'Don't worry,' said Tess confidently, 'I'll take care of it.'

As she said the words, she felt a real surge of adrenaline. She had
spent the last two weeks constantly on the phone or taking meetings in fancy watering holes around the city like Per Se, Michael's
and Tao, simultaneously buttering people up and playing hardball.
It had paid off, of course – she had managed to swing a cover for
Brooke in *Vanity Fair*, without allowing her to be interviewed, which
was no mean feat. But this sort of publicity work wasn't rocket
science, especially given Brooke's white-hot social standing. This, on
the other hand, felt like real drama, a real challenge.

'My instinct says we shouldn't pay Russ,' said Tess, thinking on
her feet. 'But if he does force our hand, would you be able to raise
the funds?'

'This time, yes. But I don't want to have to keep on paying.'

Tess walked to the window and gazed out at the park as she
thought. Then she picked up her BlackBerry and made a call,
checking her watch. It wouldn't even be eleven o'clock in London
yet. She saw Liz watching her and walked back towards the entrance.

'Hi Jem. It's me,' she whispered. 'Just a quick one. Which big-
time movie producer did you say was at that sex party again?'

16

For as long as Brooke could remember, she had always loved fashion. As a little girl she had a big dressing-up box full of her mother's flamboyant Seventies cast-offs and she had spent most of her teen years flitting from one iconic style to another. From the age of fifteen, when she had grown tall enough to pull it off, she had played with Left Bank beatnik, Gatsby preppie and Pre-Raphaelite boho, each change inspired by the art and literature she was encountering at school. She even had a brief, albeit cutting-edge, flirtation with Goth when she had teamed her sister's Comme des Garçons and Yohji Yamamoto hand-me-downs with thick black leggings. But as a woman, Brooke had settled into her style, which could be described as 'chic with a twist', especially as she liked supporting up-and-coming designers like Phillip Lim or Proenza Schouler, not that she was averse to mixing Chanel with American Apparel.

Even before her relationship with David was made public, it was her fashion sense that had got her noticed on the New York society circuit, where she was recognized as one of the city's most beautiful and stylish girls. But for all her fashion knowledge and experience, when it came to her wedding dress, Brooke was completely floored. It didn't help that hers was one of the most high-profile weddings in years, so she had been approached by some of the biggest names in fashion; the choices were almost limitless, an embarrassment of riches. And while she had done her best to ignore her mother's melodramatic statement that 'this dress is going to be remembered by generations to come', Brooke knew it still had to be special, the most special dress she would ever wear in her life.

'Darling, I think he's here.'

Meredith bustled out onto the terrace of their eighth-floor suite. They were staying at the Plaza Athénée, the opulent Left Bank hotel which had one of the best views of Paris's skyline; Brooke could barely tear herself away. Dusk was settling over the city, the sky was streaked charcoal and gold behind the silhouette of the Eiffel Tower, while the lights in the buildings below shone like a galaxy of stars.

'Just coming,' sighed Brooke, feeling both apprehensive and giddy. Guillaume Riche was one of the most flamboyant designers in the world, a master of showmanship. Over the past three decades he had created dresses for some of the most famous women on earth and his glorious evening dresses, seen many times on the red carpet at the Oscars, were nothing short of pure theatre. Preferring to work with vivid colours, Guillaume did not usually do wedding dresses, even as a tradition at the end of his couture show, but he had declared with typical modesty, 'For this beautiful flower, I will create something of genius.' At first Brooke hadn't been convinced that she wanted to use him, as her all-time favourite wedding dress was Carolyn Bessette's stunningly minimal column dress; surely that would be too simple for Guillaume's tastes, she thought. Brooke had finally bowed to the pressure, however, as simply *everyone* had said that Guillaume was the best and, as the wedding dress was going to be Brooke's first *haute* piece, it made sense to see the king of couture. It had also made sense to meet Guillaume in her hotel suite, despite the fact Brooke had been desperate to visit his atelier. One of her favourite childhood memories was visiting Yves Saint Laurent's Avenue Marceau atelier with her mother. She could still vividly remember the rolls of exquisite fabric and the long wooden tables where the seamstresses worked, surrounded by swatches, pins, scissors and, to Brooke's young eyes, magic. But although the problems with paparazzi were less severe in Paris, Brooke still had to be discreet while in the city. She couldn't stand the general public knowing about the designer of her wedding dress before her husband-to-be.

'I hope he doesn't mind coming to the hotel this late,' smiled Brooke, her excitement showing in her voice. 'After all, we haven't officially commissioned him yet, or whatever you do to order couture.'

'Of course he doesn't mind,' said an irritated voice to her left.

She looked over at Liz who was sitting upright in an armchair, flicking through a copy of French *Vogue*. 'This will be a very high-profile commission for him; he'll bend over backwards to secure it.'

Brooke hated it when her sister's mouth took on that thin, disapproving line; it reminded her too much of their mother. Liz had been in a particularly foul mood ever since they had boarded the flight at JFK. Meredith had thought it a good idea that the two sisters have a bonding weekend in Paris, combining the meeting with Guillaume with shopping on the Rue du Faubourg Saint-Honoré and a spa day at Carita, but now Brooke wasn't so sure. When Liz was in a mood like this, she could make life unpleasant for everyone. Really unpleasant. The doorbell buzzed and Liz went to answer the door, her cold, stiff demeanour instantly changing to warmth and graciousness as she welcomed Guillaume.

The designer kissed Liz, swept into the suite, and then kissed Brooke and Meredith on both cheeks. He flung off his black cashmere cape and settled into a duck-egg blue armchair.

Brooke sat opposite him and instantly felt his eyes on her, already appraising her and sizing her up as she moved.

'*Ma chérie*, I am blessed,' he said finally. 'You have a model figure and a complexion that will suit all shades of white.'

'So white is not white?' smiled Brooke.

'*Mais, non!*' he laughed, waving away the offer of champagne. 'There is pure white – what artists call Chinese white, ivory, ice blue, oyster, blush, and a dozen shades in between.'

Meredith picked up a document folder and spread its contents on the table between them.

'As discussed, I've brought some photographs of the venue,' she said, her voice crisp and polite. 'The wedding is being held on a small cay off the Florida Keys. Sadly there is no church big enough to accommodate all our guests in the immediate area, so the ceremony will be held at the venue, with a small blessing the following day for close friends and family.'

Guillaume began examining the photographs of Leonard Carter's white colonial-style mansion house. Every now and then he made notes in his leather notebook in long sloping handwriting.

'It will be warm in the Keys in December, *non?*'

'Hot, yes,' replied Brooke. 'Although the ceremony will be at six p.m. when it has cooled a little.'

'This is not a beach wedding?' he said with distaste.

'No.'

'This is good,' said Guillaume, staring down at his notes. After seeming to gather his thoughts, he began sketching. Brooke craned her neck to see, too excited to speak.

'Evening weddings can be dramatic,' said Guillaume quietly, almost as if talking to himself. 'So our fabrics can be sumptuous. Glorious tulle or silk jacquard, I think.'

'I was thinking of perhaps a long silk column,' said Brooke nervously. 'Something elegant and timeless.'

Guillaume chuckled good-naturedly. 'How many times have you worn a tasteful little evening dress?' he asked. 'Something long and silk, slim-fitting? I suspect many times.'

Brooke found herself nodding in agreement. Increasingly she had to attend all sorts of dinners and benefits with David, and she was always drawn to the dresses he had described, whether it was a Grecian style or a long silk bias cut. It was an obvious choice as they suited her tall, lean body; they did not shout too loudly for attention and they always looked fantastic. Guillaume now began asking Brooke all sorts of questions about seemingly banal details of the day: the proposed music for the ceremony, the aspect of Leonard's house, even the tone of David's skin.

'This is your wedding and you are fabulous,' he explained. 'You must therefore wear a fabulous creation, a dress you have never worn before or will ever wear again.'

The thick black pencil lines of his sketch were already beginning to take shape. It had a voluminous ruffled skirt and a slim, fitted bodice with tiny cap sleeves. It was a Cinderella gown, a truly romantic confection, but somehow Brooke felt disappointed. *It's just an idea*, she told herself firmly. *This doesn't have to be the one.*

'Remember, I want Brooke to look unforgettable,' said Meredith, sipping at a flute of champagne as she paced around the art-deco suite.

'You want me to create your dress, I will go away and draw. We will make you the dress of the century.'

'How many fittings will I need?'

'Couture takes time,' he mused. 'A dress like this will take the atelier maybe six or seven hundred hours. Many hundreds more for the embroidery work.'

Brooke gasped.

Guillaume continued. 'First we make the pattern, a *toile*, then maybe we see you two more times. Finally I will come to the wedding and we can do the last adjustments on the day.'

'Wow. *Four fittings?*' said Brooke slowly.

'Perhaps more for something this special.' He shrugged.

'Does that mean I will have to come to Paris for every fitting?'

'*Oui, oui.* I like it for you to come to the atelier,' he nodded. 'Other couturiers work in different ways, their dresses get sent out to China, even Saudi; but for me, couture is Paris.'

'It's what we expected,' smiled Liz, touching Guillaume lightly on the hand. 'We know that art takes time, but we're all so very, very excited.'

Guillaume beamed, then kissed all three women lightly on both cheeks before swinging his cape around his shoulders like a villain in a silent movie.

'I will go downstairs for supper now,' he announced. 'The chef Alain Ducasse is a friend, we do not need a reservation. Would you care to join me?'

'And undo all the work we've done to keep this so secret?' grinned Brooke.

'Ah, but of course,' he laughed. 'I will get them to send you up a little chocolate pot.' He held up one finger. 'But only a little one. We must maintain this wonderful figure, no?'

For a few seconds after he left the room, the three women were silent.

'Well?' asked Meredith, looking at her daughters. 'What did you think?'

'I thought he was fabulous,' said Liz, striding towards the window and looking out in the darkness. 'What are we waiting for? Guillaume is the best at what he does.'

Brooke gave a nervous laugh. 'But one thousand five hundred man-hours to make my dress? I'll have to put back the date of the wedding.'

'But darling, it will be worth it,' said Meredith.

Brooke held up one hand.

'Hold on, Mother, I thought this was just a conversation with Guillaume. We can talk to other people, right?' She looked over to Liz for support, but she was staring out of the window, her arms folded. 'David's mother thinks we should go for an American designer like Vera Wang or Oscar de la Renta.'

Meredith laughed tartly. 'Speaks she who is dressed head to toe in Chanel Couture.'

'But an American couturier would be easier from a time point of view.' She had already done a quick mental calculation, the thrill of her first couture gown giving way to drab practicalities. Four fittings, each one taking two or three days, not to mention the travel there and back: how was she supposed to fit in her working life at Yellow Door? They had two weeks' holiday a year, and that had already been stretched like elastic. She had a vision of Mimi Hall having a full-on hissy fit and winced. 'Just go with Guillaume, for goodness' sake,' said Liz, one hand distractedly playing with her short blonde hair in the window's reflection.

Brooke looked at her sister with irritation. They had never been particularly close; growing up, Liz had always made Brooke feel that she was at best an annoyance, at worst a complete irrelevance. Brooke wanted to point out that it was her wedding dress, but Liz had that 'do not mess with me or I will bite your head off' expression.

'And why are you so sure?' she said tactfully instead.

Liz went over to the drinks cabinet and began to pour herself a shot of vodka. She looked up and Brooke noticed Liz and her mother exchange a look.

'Because commissioning Guillaume isn't necessarily just about your wedding dress.'

'Now then Elizabeth,' said Meredith warily, 'this isn't the time or place.'

'What else can it be about?' asked Brooke with surprise.

Liz took a sip of her drink and looked over at Brooke.

'Don't be so naive, Brooke,' she said. 'If Guillaume makes your dress it's good news for the company. Asgill's have been negotiating with Pierre Follet, Guillaume's business manager, for months about getting the licence to manufacture a fragrance for them. Riche pour Femme, Riche pour Homme. Frankly it's amazing he hasn't done a fragrance already. You could put Guillaume's name on a bottle of cat-piss and it would sell through the roof, especially in Europe. So commissioning Guillaume to design your dress is Asgill's chance to secure the licence. Perhaps make it a *condition*.'

'Is this what my wedding is for you?' said Brooke incredulously. 'A business deal?'

Liz looked unmoved and her coldness just upset Brooke all the more.

'It's not just about you all the time, Brooke,' she said. 'You have to think about the family. We can't let business opportunities pass us by, not in this climate. Guillaume Riche is big news in Europe, but designing your dress will make him a huge name in the States too. He knows that, and that's why I want to go back to Pierre Follet and try and hammer out some initial agreement before we officially commission him to do the dress.'

Brooke looked at her mother. 'Mom, help me out here . . .'

'Brooke,' she said soothingly. 'It's only a dress.'

Her skin burned hot. 'Only a dress! This is my *wedding dress*!'

'Now you know I didn't mean it like that,' said Meredith, coming over to hold Brooke's shoulders. 'What I mean is that Guillaume is one of the best designers in the world: why not have him design your dress? I saw how excited you were to come and meet him and, if you like what he does, then Liz's idea is just a bonus. The dress is still the important thing.'

She looked at her mother, feeling betrayed. She wasn't a fool. Her mother had barely stopped smiling since her engagement to David. Brooke was aware that the alliance between the two families was a fantastic social and financial opportunity for both her mother and the Asgill Cosmetics brand, but she had hoped that what would matter most to Meredith was that her child was happy. It was her wedding day; Brooke wanted to feel like a princess, not a pawn.

She thought of the afternoon she'd imagined at the Carita spa and felt foolish. 'So I suppose this girls' weekend was just a ruse for Liz to meet Guillaume and position herself?' she said, her eyes filling up with tears.

'Now don't be silly, Brooke,' Meredith said, stroking her daughter's arms. 'This is your special time, but you can't blame Liz for wanting to take advantage of the situation. It's all for the family, after all.'

'Just think of it as your turn to do something for the family business,' said Liz with a small triumphant smile.

Brooke walked over to the table and snatched up a glass of champagne, drinking it down. She glanced across at her mother and sister, who were still staring at her with a mixture of annoyance and pity. *Was she being selfish?* Perhaps, but she was still furious at the way they had planned all this without having the courtesy, the respect for her intelligence, to consult her, to explain the business situation. That was what hurt. They still saw her as some flighty, soft-brained socialite who couldn't be trusted with such sensitive information.

'Brooke, honey. At least think about it,' said Meredith. 'This is a win-win situation for everyone.'

Not quite everyone, thought Brooke, striding over to her bedroom and closing the door shut.

Larry Goldman, the eleventh most powerful man in Hollywood according to the latest Hot List in *Variety*, was a difficult man to track down. The fourth time Tess had phoned his New York office without response, she told his secretary she was calling about a movie entitled *Wycombe Square*, the name of the Venus party's location. Tess added that she was sure he would want to talk to her. Within the hour, Tess and Larry had scheduled a meeting at the bar of the Four Seasons Grill Room. He was already there by the time she arrived and she recognized him immediately: short, rotund, salt-and-pepper hair, dark, hooded eyes and the round, worn face of a retired boxer. He certainly didn't look like one of LA's biggest players, but then neither did he look like the kind of man who would routinely attend orgies. The restaurant had closed a couple of hours earlier and, although still open for drinks, the room was almost empty apart from two cocktail waiters polishing glasses and a couple of businessmen propping up the bar. Under the circumstances it was wise to be discreet.

'Why do I suspect this conversation isn't going to be good news?' said Larry as he looked up from his drink – still water. Tess had heard that he'd been on a liquid-only diet for the last month in an attempt to take him from obese to merely overweight in readiness for his wedding – his fourth – to a glamorous Venezuelan set designer he had met on his last film.

Tess straightened her Dolce&Gabbana suit as she sat down. 'Actually, it might not be as bad as you think.'

He looked at her suspiciously.

'So you work for the Billingtons? I know Wendell very well,' he said, his eyes wandering away. Force of habit, thought Tess with a slight smile. In Hollywood, you were always scanning the room for someone more important, even if the room was empty.

'Actually, I deal more with David and his fiancée Brooke.'

'Personal publicist?'

'Something like that.'

She ordered a white wine; she felt like she needed it. Despite her outward calm, her heart was pounding. Larry Goldman was a poor kid from Nevada who had become one of LA's biggest players, his films were big budget and netted huge receipts – his last five films alone had taken over one billion dollars at the box office. The annual party he held at his home in Bel Air was one of the hottest tickets on the LA social calendar. Tess knew that you didn't get to be that guy without being incredibly tough and utterly ruthless. For a second, Tess wondered how she could bargain with him and come out on top. She took a deep breath; she was about to find out.

'So how do you know about Wycombe Square?' he said before she could speak. His voice had lowered a couple of tones and his black eyes were now fully focused on her. She was taken aback at how nervous he was acting. For one moment, Tess wondered if she'd missed something, whether there was something bigger Larry was hiding. After all, it would surprise no one that a big-time super-rich Hollywood producer got his rocks off at a sex party. The coke-and-hooker antics of Tinseltown big shots like the late Don Simpson made Larry's nocturnal activities seem like teenage fumblings by comparison. She shook off the feeling and ploughed on. She had to focus on what she knew.

'Before I worked for the Asgill family,' she began, 'I used to work for a British tabloid. A photographer of ours was doing a story on the Venus parties. She managed to infiltrate the Wycombe Square party.'

Larry looked at her blankly, giving nothing away. 'I assume the story never ran,' he said, 'I'd have heard about it.'

'You're right. It never got published. I came to New York to work for the Asgills, and the story came with me. The details of that night and who was there won't be public. For now, anyway.'

She took a sip of her spritzer. Her fingers left a clammy smudge on the stem of the glass, but Larry's eyes never left hers.

'What do you want from me, Miss Garrett? Money?' he said in a cold voice. She had to tread carefully.

'No, I don't want your money, Mr Goldman. I need your help.' She noticed the tight line of his mouth soften ever so slightly.

'I've protected your privacy; I hope I now have your confidence. What I'm about to tell you is fairly sensitive.'

Larry looked at her, more interested now, and then nodded begrudgingly.

'I have been hired to protect Brooke Asgill and David Billington's interests,' continued Tess slowly. 'A member of the Asgill family is being blackmailed by an actor called Russ Ford and the information he has could be damaging.'

'Russ Ford? Never heard of him.' He swilled his water around in the bottom of his glass so that the ice cubes chinked against the side.

'You won't have. He's small time.'

'So what did they do? This member of the Asgill family. Kill someone?'

Tess hesitated before she told him. 'They had a one-night stand. With Russ Ford.'

Larry was nodding sagely. 'I get it. So this Asgill is gay. Is it Sean Asgill?'

Tess didn't want him getting ahead of himself. She shook her head, careful not to tell him anything more than she had to.

She noticed that Larry was already looking at his watch and his drink had been finished. 'So what's this got to do with me?'

Tess folded her arms and leant forward on the table. 'This Russ Ford guy is a creep,' she said. 'We can pay him off, of course, but the problem with people like Russ is that you have to keep paying them. When the time comes that he needs more money, he'll be back. I need something that is more persuasive.'

She told him her plan. It was as underhand as anything she'd ever attempted as a Fleet Street hack, and she actually felt quite proud of it.

'This guy had better not be the new Brad fucking Pitt.'

Tess shook her head. 'I doubt it.'

Larry stared at her, his eyes narrowing. For a moment, Tess was sure he was going to tell her to go screw herself, maybe threaten to have her arrested, maybe even worse. Then, slowly, the lines around his eyes began to crinkle, and for the first time in their meeting, Larry smiled.

'Fuck, you're tough for a limey,' he said admiringly, offering her his hand. 'And I thought only New York chicks had balls.'

The Old Tap, on a side street on the Lower East Side, looked like every other bar Tess had ever seen on *CSI* and *Law & Order*. It was the sort of place where deals were done, secrets and information passed on. Long and thin, its bar running down the right-hand side, the wall lined with bottle spirits and illuminated signs advertising beer, The Old Tap was already busy, the padded bar propped up by tired-looking men wishing they could still smoke. Tess glanced around and took a vacant booth still cluttered with beer bottles. Russ had said he'd be wearing a leather jacket, but practically every man in the place had one on. A pretty waitress in bum-hugging jeans came over.

'What are you having?'

'Do you do tea?'

'No. Can getcha a coffee?' Tess nodded. She didn't like the drink, but she figured she wouldn't be around long enough to enjoy it. Tess saw the handsome twenty-something man pushing in from the street several seconds before he saw her.

'Tess?'

She nodded.

Russ unzipped his jacket and threw it onto the seat opposite Tess with a James Dean swagger. *Shit, he really was good-looking*, thought Tess, for a second almost envying Liz's wild encounter at Red Legs. *Maybe we should have met in a McDonald's*, she thought. Bars were always more covert and sexy – more dangerous, too. The waitress put a cup of black coffee in front of Tess, and Russ shook his head to say he didn't want anything.

'I hope you're not going to sit there and judge me,' said Russ with a smile. Despite the even teeth and sharp cheekbones, Tess could detect a nastiness to Russ Ford. Maybe that's why he'd never got anywhere. No one wants to work with an asshole, especially not a nobody asshole.

'No, Russ, I'm not here to judge,' said Tess.

'Because a woman like Liz Asgill shouldn't do the things she does,' he said loftily.

'And you want to profit from her mistakes?'

'As I told Liz, we're considering it as patronage of the arts.'

She could see his eyes stray down towards her tote bag.

'Is that for me?' His head nodded towards a brown manila envelope that was poking out of her bag.

'Yes, it is.'

She put it on the table and pushed it towards him.

'A cheque?' he smiled, inching his fingers towards the brown paper.

Tess shook her head. 'A letter from Larry Goldman. I'm sure you've heard of him.'

Russ's expression was caught halfway between confusion and greed. Tess had to suppress a smile; she was surprised at just how much she was enjoying this.

She could see him try to relax and be more casual. Ah, *that's* why he's never taken off, she thought. He's a terrible actor.

'What does Goldman want?' asked Russ. 'Is this some sort of payment in kind? We didn't talk about this but I could be open to it.'

Tess remained expressionless. 'I think you'd better read it.'

She watched him open the letter, allowing him to read just a few lines before she spoke again.

'You see, Larry is a friend of mine,' said Tess slowly. 'He's also one of the most powerful men in Hollywood. He can make careers and he can also break them in a heartbeat,' she said, clicking her fingers.

Russ looked up and their eyes locked. In a matter of seconds, every hint of smugness had been snuffed out and she could almost feel his fear across the table.

'Larry will have you blackballed from the entire entertainment industry if you breathe a word about Liz Asgill. You think times are tough for you now? You think acting jobs are a little thin on the ground? Believe me, you won't be able to get a job shovelling shit off the Chinese Theater walkway if you say one word against Liz or any of the Asgills.'

Tess thought back to her drink with Larry. The producer hadn't been too impressed by the 'deal'. He was the sort of man used to having all the bargaining control and had not taken too kindly to being manipulated by some twenty-something British broad. But he had admired her chutzpah and was also relieved that Tess's form of blackmail didn't actually involve the exchange of money. The richer they were, the meaner they were; that was something she'd noticed around many very wealthy people. Something she doubted Russ Ford would ever find out.

'But I had a deal with Liz Asgill,' he blustered.

Tess shook her head. She was playing the hardest of hardball and she knew full well that this strategy carried a high degree of risk. She was gambling on him wanting a career in the movies very badly, but she'd done her homework. Russ had a decent agent and had landed a few bit-parts in the soaps and sitcoms. He'd even had a lead in a pilot for a series that was never made. Russ Ford had tasted success on the tip of his tongue and she was gambling on him being hooked on the taste, hoping he was desperate to keep his acting dream alive.

'No, Russ, you had a *conversation* with Liz Asgill. She spoke to me and I spoke to Larry. If you ask me, you're getting off lightly after a stunt like that. Blackmail is a felony. The Asgills could end your career right now.'

The look on his face, panic, disappointment, disgust, told her she'd called the right way.

He let out a long breath. 'So what happens now?'

'What happens is that if you keep your mouth shut we can pretend none of this ever happened.'

Russ simply nodded.

'Oh, and Russ?'

She put ten dollars down on the table to cover the bill and stood up to leave.

'See you in Hollywood.'

17

Brooke was taking Eileen Dunne to lunch. As the author was coming all the way from her hometown of Baltimore, Brooke had booked a table at Gordon Ramsay at The London to make an event of it. She wasn't sure how she was going to justify such extravagance to Mimi when she signed off her expenses, in fact it was probably safer to pay for the lunch out of her own pocket, but, as far as Brooke was concerned, it was worth it. Already Eileen's magician book *Portico* was creating a buzz around the Yellow Door offices, and not just in the children's division. A senior publishing director in adult fiction was already making noises about rejacketing it for an adult edition and getting it shelf space in Wal-Mart, which was the holy grail for a children's book. Hell, for *any* book.

To her surprise, Brooke found that she was uncommonly nervous about this meeting. She preferred to meet an author before acquiring a book to assess their marketability and whether she would enjoy working with them, but in the scramble to sign Eileen, that just hadn't been possible. She'd spoken to her on the phone, of course, but that never really gave you an idea of who the person was. So, for all Brooke knew, Eileen Dunne was a Ku Kux Klan sympathizer with a series of dead bodies in her deep freeze. *You're just being silly now*, she scolded herself, but Brooke was still edgy. Eileen's book was fantastic, but in today's market, that wasn't enough – they needed a story, preferably a weepie. Brooke was well aware that J. K. Rowling's back story as a single mum writing stories in an Edinburgh coffee shop had been perfect for developing her image as the ordinary person rising above the odds. Similarly, Stephanie Meyer's image as a straight-laced Mormon mother, who thought of the plot for vampire love story *Twilight* in a dream, had worked wonders in interviews. They needed something equally PR-friendly with Eileen or there was still a chance her brilliant book would sink without trace.

Brooke tried to settle down at her round corner table and watched the opaque glass doors anxiously. Was that her? No, the woman entering was wearing a DVF wrap dress – this season's – and Jimmy Choos. Her heart jumped again – no, just the maitre d'. Calm down, Brooke, she told herself, taking a sip of her fresh orange juice. And then there she was – Brooke was sure of it. A red-haired woman about her age, dressed in black trousers, a sparkly top and a strange nylon windcheater. She looked as if she'd been unable to decide whether she was going for a walk in the rain or for a night on the town.

Brooke felt a little deflated, but stood up and smiled as Eileen walked timidly to the table.

'Nice place,' said Eileen weakly, looking around. She looked as though she expected someone to eject her at any moment.

'I love it here. They have a great bon-bon trolley,' smiled Brooke.

Eileen sat down, carefully removing her coat.

'Let someone take that for you,' offered Brooke, waving to the waiter.

Eileen looked up with alarm. 'I'd better keep hold of it; it's my mother's. *Ralph Lauren.*'

The woman flushed and for one moment Brooke wondered if she should have picked another restaurant. Eileen looked awkward, sitting bolt upright with her precious nylon coat draped over the arm of her chair. Was this all too intimidating for her? Brooke stopped herself. She was being patronizing. Still, when the waiter approached, she made sure she gave Eileen a little time to settle herself as they read the menus.

'I'll have the pork with apricots,' said Brooke.

'I'll have the same,' said Eileen quickly. Brooke poured their water and glanced at her new author. She wasn't bad-looking, quite pretty in fact, but she had terrible blue eye shadow and too-red lipstick. She badly needed a makeover to bring out her best. Yes – Brooke felt sure she could help her in that department, thinking of all the designer clothes, bags, and cosmetics she got sent daily.

Eileen caught her appraising look and her hand flew nervously to her face.

'What's the matter?' she asked.

'Oh nothing, I just expected you to be older,' smiled Brooke.

'Is it the name?' Eileen winced. 'It's a family tradition, you see. The oldest girl gets the same name as her grandmother. Anyway, I was expecting you to be more scary.'

Brooke giggled, thinking of the paparazzi photos that got printed in the tabloid magazines. Shots when she'd be sneezing or rubbing something from her eye or just changing expression and which always seemed to make her look in pain or miserable. 'I get that a lot.'

She took a sip of orange juice. 'Well, I have to tell you that we are all so excited about *Portico*,' said Brooke, 'although we will have to turn it around very, very quickly. Still, we're getting there. The manuscript should be going into proof next week.'

'What's a proof exactly?'

'An uncorrected manuscript bound up like a book. It goes out to retailers who decide if they want to order it. Then it goes out to the press so they can decide if they want to review it.'

'Wow, that's a lot of hoops,' said Eileen, wide-eyed.

'Don't worry, the whole company is getting behind it,' said Brooke.

Eileen nodded and looked down at her lap, fiddling with the cuff of her mother's jacket.

Brooke's mouth opened as she saw that Eileen's eyes were filling with tears.

'Hey, hey, what's wrong?' she asked.

Eileen shook her head, still staring down. 'I'm sorry, I'm just so grateful.'

Brooke felt her heart swell. She was so sweet. '*You're* grateful?' laughed Brooke. 'Eileen, I'm the one who should be grateful. This is the book I've been waiting my whole career for.'

'But for you, Brooke, publishing books is just a job, isn't it?' she replied not unkindly. Catching Brooke's expression, she added: 'I read *US Weekly*. You're rich. You're marrying into a family even richer.'

She blew her nose on the tissue Brooke offered her.

'The difference is that you've changed my life,' continued Eileen. 'Six weeks ago I was working three jobs. That's not easy when you have three kids as well.'

'You have *three kids*?' said Brooke, wondering if Eileen just looked very good for her age.

'Oldest is eight. Youngest is three,' she grinned. 'And, before you ask, yes, I *am* twenty-six.'

'That's incredible,' said Brooke, taking a slow sip of orange juice. 'Not the fact you have three kids, of course, just that you manage to do everything. You must have a very supportive husband.'

Eileen looked down again. 'He left me last year.'

'Oh, I'm sorry. I have a habit of putting my foot in it.'

Eileen shook her head. 'Don't be. Danny – that's my husband – he worked at the local garage. I went down there one night and found him in the office with the boss's PA, pants round his ankles. My friends said "forgive him", said "you need him" – and they were right, seeing as I'm only making twenty thousand bucks a year.'

'But you kicked him out?' said Brooke eagerly, wanting to hear more.

'Sure I did! You don't stay with a man who doesn't respect you.' She shrugged. 'I thought it would be scary, being left with three kids, but I guess it's better to be on your own than with someone who doesn't really love you. Truth is, it was never right. I married Danny when I was eighteen because I got pregnant and I used to look at him and think, "Do I want to grow old with you?" "Do I want to share life's adventure with you?" "Do you make me happy just by being there?" And the answer was no, so things happened for the best.'

'It was still brave,' said Brooke, marvelling at Eileen's story.

'Not really, but I guess it's paid off now. See, the week after I threw his bags on the street, I started writing the book. I used to love writing stories at school, but when I left high school and got married I just didn't have the time. But this time, I made time. Part of the reason was to keep me busy, to stop me thinking about how he . . . how he disappointed me. The other reason was to try and make some money. My friends were right about that much. Even three jobs doesn't stretch very far when you've got three kids.'

Brooke felt a sudden stab of shame. Since she could remember she'd always had everything she wanted: a pony, a car, fabulous clothes. She'd even miraculously got into an Ivy League college, despite her standing in the family as the 'pretty one' to Liz's 'smart one'. Eileen was right, she enjoyed her job at Yellow Door, but it was still just a job, something she did because she wanted to, not because she had to. And she realized with a terrible jolt that her wedding dress alone was going to cost ten times more than Eileen made in a year. Looking across at Eileen, she felt a rush of resolve.

'Eileen,' she said, 'I'm going to make you a star.'

'You sound like Simon Cowell,' said Eileen more cheerfully.

'I mean it!'

'Really? Well, thanks,' blushed the author. 'But why?'

Brooke smiled. She wasn't exactly sure herself, but she just had an urge to do her very best for Eileen Dunne.

'Let's just say I feel it's something I have to do.'

18

'You're early.'

Paula greeted William in the long hall of their Park Avenue apartment building with a kiss on the cheek, but her tone was less than warm. William tried to hide his annoyance as he glanced at the decorative striking clock behind him. It was five fifteen. He had made a special effort to get home before six and felt hurt that his wife had not appreciated the gesture.

'Am I not allowed to come home early every now and then to spend time with my girls?' he began, but was instantly interrupted.

'Daddy!'

Casey and Amelia ran to their father, their white Dior socks skidding on the highly polished walnut floors. They grabbed his legs while he kissed them on the top of their heads; then he scooped them up into his arms.

'Come and tell Daddy all about your new class,' he laughed.

'It's nice,' said Casey, wriggling free and skipping back down the hall.

'*Nice?*'

Paula rolled her eyes. She made the girls read two items in the *New York Times* every morning and discuss them. Amelia always seemed out of her depth, much preferring the pretty pictures in the fashion reports, but she expected more of Casey than to describe her new class as *nice*.

'No play-date this afternoon?' William asked, setting Amelia down and walking through into the living room. It was a beautiful space, recently redesigned in the style of a boutique English country hotel. Antlers on the wall hung alongside Diane Arbus pictures on the Colefax and Fowler wallpaper. David Linley had designed the two bookcases that flanked the limestone fireplace and the whole space was softly lit and smelt of Diptyque figuier candles that Paula had shipped over in bulk from the company's Left Bank store.

'Mrs Wong is coming round for Mandarin class,' said Paula, fluttering her hand in the air to summon Louise, their Australian nanny.

'Louise, can you take the girls? They are still in their uniforms.'

'How's Casey been? She seems quieter than usual,' asked William, sitting down on the velvet George Smith sofa and slipping off his brogues, rubbing his tired feet with his fingers.

'She's exhausted, poor thing,' said Paula, perching on the very edge of the chair opposite her husband.

'I guess having to make a whole new set of friends is going to be taxing when you are six.'

'Well, there is another new girl just starting too,' said Paula. 'So hopefully they'll bond. You know that Casey is very sociable.'

William crumpled his brow. 'I just don't see what was wrong with the girls being in the same class?'

Paula stood up and began smoothing fluff from the back of her chair.

'Darling, Mrs Wong is due round any minute,' she said, looking with disapproval at William's bare feet. 'If you want to lounge around, why don't you go into the den?'

'So we're doing this Mandarin business,' said William, ignoring her. '*Mandarin.*'

Paula lowered her voice. 'I'm not sure Amelia is up to it, but Casey has such a way with languages that I thought the sooner the better.'

'My question is whether they should be doing it at all,' said William. 'The homework load from Eton is already quite large.'

Paula opened her eyes in outrage. 'Are you saying you don't want to stretch your children?'

'Paula, I'm saying that the girls are six.'

She looked away from him, angry at his questioning. The girls attending Eton Manor was already a compromise. For some reason, William had got it into his head that the girls might be *happier* attending Steiner schools. And how was *that* going to get them into an Ivy League college, playing with wood and knitting blankets

until they were fifteen? She couldn't understand her husband sometimes. What did happiness have to do with an education? Okay,
so she loved Amelia, for all her faults, and she felt that one day
she would model and marry well. But Casey, she had the potential to be brilliant. You only had to look at Ivanka Trump. A model,
a socialite, and a Wharton Business School graduate to boot. Surely
William could see the parallels in his own family? Brooke, of course,
was beautiful. People fawned over her for her astonishing doe-eyed
looks, yet it was Liz who seemed to generate a quieter, more genuine
respect in the *serious* media outlets. You only had to talk to Liz
for a few seconds to see her fierce intelligence, her knowledge of
books, of literature, of wine. Of course, the ideal was to be both
smart and beautiful, and Casey had that promise. One day, she
might even take over Asgill Cosmetics, make something of it, then
marry into the highest circles – possibly royalty. Why not, when
Paula was doing her utmost to give her the tools for the job? For
a second she felt annoyed that her efforts weren't appreciated.
Unlike most mothers on the circuit, Paula put in time with her children. She only had one nanny for the two girls. She took them to
swimming lessons and ballet and art class at the Ninety-Second
Street Y herself. Mrs Fortescue, a Juilliard-trained piano instructor,
came by the house and Paula supervised the lesson, and when Paula
didn't have her one-on-one Pilates instruction, she took the girls
to school. Once, when she had found Louise their nanny in the
kitchen, crying over some boy, she had sat down with her, and
Louise had told her that she was the most hands-on mother in all
the Upper East Side. As if reading her thoughts, William stood up
and came over to his wife, wrapping her in his big arms.

'I know how much you do for the family, for the girls,' he said.
'I just don't think we have to try quite so hard. If Amelia isn't
fluent in Mandarin by the time she's ten, what does it matter? If
she doesn't turn out to be academic, what does it matter?'

'I just want the best for them.'

She looked down at a photograph of the twins on the coffee
table. It was beautiful. Shot at Christmas by a photographer who
worked for *Vogue Bambini*. She *did*, she only ever thought of them.
William felt her tension and held her tighter. At that moment, Paula
sensed that he *did* understand and it almost made her shiver. She
had never told William the whole truth of her past. He would never
know how a ten-year-old Paula, in bed at night, would cover her

ears to the sound of her mother having sex with men from the bar and later . . . well, she had tried to shut that out completely. But William still knew enough. He knew about her childhood in a trailer park. He knew how her mother had died of MS when Paula was barely nineteen and how she had turned to modelling as her way out of poverty. He knew all these things, and yet he still loved her, not less, probably more. It was just one of the reasons she had never left him, never tried to work her way up the social ladder by judicious marriages. Breathing deeply, she allowed herself to settle into his arms, smelling the crispness of the cotton and reminding herself, how, in her own way, she loved him too.

'Look. I've got something to tell you,' said William finally.

She pulled away from the embrace and looked at him nervously. 'What is it?'

'I've made an appointment with Dr Flasco. Right now he's the best fertility specialist in America.'

'Oh William, we don't need a fertility specialist,' she said flatly.

'Honey, we've been trying for nearly eighteen months and nothing.'

Paula looked away. 'We haven't exactly been trying that hard.'

'Well, that wasn't for lack of me trying,' he said with a laugh.

She glanced back at him, wondering if he was making a point, telling her that he knew. No, that was not William's style, although, should he choose to complain, she really couldn't have blamed him; their sex life had dwindled to almost nothing and, when they did have sex, Paula wasn't exactly enthusiastic. She didn't want to encourage him. Of course, there was little chance of her falling pregnant because of her hormone injections, but her doctor had warned her that she should not take them for longer than eighteen months – a period that was drawing to a close. What would she do then? She took a breath to compose herself.

'We've had this conversation time and time again, darling. I wanted a gap between the twins and the next one.'

'The twins are six, Paula. Do you want them to be starting college before we try again?'

She flashed a look at him. 'Don't push it, William.'

The smile fell from his face and she felt a stab of guilt. The poor guy didn't know the full story, how could he?

'It's fine for you,' she said quietly. 'You don't have to go through the pregnancy, the nine months of worry, terrified that there will be something wrong, worrying when they kick, worrying when they don't. And it only gets worse when they are born.'

'But honey—' he began, but she cut him off, snatching the photograph up from the table and showing it to him.

'Look at them!' she interrupted. 'The twins are beautiful, precious; we have two beautiful girls. You hear so many horrible stories. *Birth defects*. What if something awful happened . . .'

She felt sick just thinking about it. She knew she fretted more than she should about her girls and that her concerns were bordering on neuroses. How many times when they were small did she creep into the nursery to check they were breathing, putting her fingers underneath their nostril to feel their reassuring warm breath? She did not want to go through it all again. She *couldn't*.

'Honey, I know you are just being a good mother, but you are being a little dramatic.'

Her husband put his hand in his jacket pocket and pulled out an envelope, throwing it onto the table between them.

'What's that?' asked Paula.

'A weekend at The Point. This weekend.'

She gave a weak smile. The beautiful Adirondacks resort, one of the most exclusive hotels in America, was where he had taken Paula for their first weekend together. She thought back to how she had reeled him in: she had played it perfectly, using all the tricks in a woman's arsenal. Not answering his phone calls, being elusive when it came to pinning down dates, not having sex for the first three months. William was an uncomplicated man, but he was a man, and she knew that he had loved the chase.

'I've arranged for the girls to stay with my mother,' said William with a soft smile. 'Louise will go too of course.'

Drawing close to her husband, she kissed him lightly on the cheek.

'Thank you, darling, it will be wonderful,' she whispered, thinking – no, *swearing* – that there was not a chance in hell that she would become pregnant again, however many romantic mini-breaks William arranged. If she had to keep taking the contraceptive injections beyond the recommended limit, then so be it. Whatever it took, she was never going back there. *Never.*

19

At eight thirty a.m., Tess was on her way to an appointment with Meredith at her home on East Ninety-Third Street, a wide grey town house, not dissimilar to the ones Tess used to dream about owning in Kensington. A uniformed maid opened the door and led her into a large high-ceilinged living room. Although Tess could not identify Biedermeier furniture, Meissen porcelain, or Aubusson rugs when she saw them, she knew enough to tell that this was one of the most expensively and tastefully decorated homes she had ever been in. Meredith entered looking refreshed and glowing, her blonde hair set like pale gold candyfloss around her face. She was wearing an elegant powder-pink dress, grey lizard-skin court shoes and a long sapphire necklace. Perhaps a little overdone for so early in the morning, thought Tess, but then elegance doesn't happen by mistake, does it?

'Have you had breakfast?' asked Meredith. 'I can ask Marlene to do pancakes.'

Tess held up her hand. 'No thank you, I'm fine.'

She had put on four pounds since she had arrived in New York and was now desperately trying to get them off. How was anyone expected to keep trim in New York, when every corner sold bagels and pretzels and every deli had long counters of noodles, pizza, and creamy potato salad? Still, everyone she met was so slim and well groomed. The secret, she supposed, was complete self-control, something she'd never been that good at when it came to food. In the Asgill office, she had never seen the girls eat anything more than a couple of pieces of sushi the size of a postage stamp. To eat in New York was obviously a sign of weakness.

'Well, at least have some juice,' said Meredith, indicating she should sit on a fragile-looking cream tapestry chair. 'Marlene has just pressed passion fruit, lemon, and apple. It's quite delicious, and an excellent detoxifier.'

Tess sat down carefully as the maid brought over her drink.

'Sean is dating a lovely young woman in London,' said Meredith, sitting down opposite Tess.

'Really? Who is she?'

'Annabel Calthorpe, someone he met in the clinic,' said Meredith, without a flicker of embarrassment over her son's latest fall from grace. 'She's an actress, I think, but from a very good English family. She knows William and Harry, the princes.'

'So when did he get back to London?'

'Last week.'

'Well, that's good,' said Tess. 'I haven't heard any rumours coming from London about him going to rehab. No one seems to know.'

Meredith nodded. 'We told the London office he had been seconded back to New York for a few weeks. If people have been suspicious, then I haven't heard about it.'

Tess thought for a moment. 'Even so, I think we should get some pictures of him out to the US and British press,' she said. 'Maybe at some high-profile charity event. I know there's a big Prince's Trust event coming up soon. I've looked through the photo agency files and all they have are pictures of Sean in nightclubs or at the polo. I think now is as good a time as any to start getting rid of his playboy image.'

The older woman smiled and Tess wondered how her face was so free of wrinkles or lines; how many face-lifts she'd had, how regularly she had Botox, what expensive creams she must use. If it was the latter, they weren't Asgill products, Tess felt sure of it.

'So, how are you enjoying it?' asked Meredith after a pause.

'Well, it's busy,' said Tess with a smile. She told Meredith about all the recent lunches she had been on with the biggest players on the Manhattan media scene. With the help of her friend Rebecca from the *Oracle*, she had managed to secure time with everyone, from the social editor of the *New York Times* to the publisher of the *Daily News*. Meredith nodded her approval.

'Well, we could have done without the Jeff Daniels situation,' she added. 'But I think you handled it well.'

'Patty has been terrific as well,' said Tess modestly.

'Is everything else all right?' asked Meredith. 'All seems quiet on the western front.'

Tess tried to hide her frustration. The biggest problem with her job was that the better she was at it, the less it looked as if she was doing anything. She was like a conjurer who had to make the rabbits disappear before anyone even thought to look in the hat.

'Well, there was a minor situation with Liz,' said Tess hesitantly. She knew Meredith wouldn't like the fact she had been kept out of the loop, but at the same time a voice inside her was screaming, *Tell her how good you are!*

'A situation?' asked Meredith.

'Just a one-night stand. The man involved was threatening to go to the press.'

Meredith gave a little tinkly laugh. 'Hardly Watergate, my dear.'

Tess bit her tongue. As much as she wanted to tell Meredith about her brilliant coup involving Larry, Liz, and Russ, she knew it was wise to be economical with the truth. Hers was a difficult position to be in; Meredith was her boss, but she had promised Liz that she would keep the Russ Ford episode completely under wraps. Were the situation reversed, Tess felt sure that Liz would welch on such a gentleman's agreement in the blink of an eye, but for now Tess knew it was best to keep Liz on side.

'Has everything been resolved?' Meredith asked, sipping her detoxifying juice.

Tess nodded.

'And how much did it cost us?'

'Actually, that's the good news. I pulled a few strings; it didn't cost us anything.'

'Good. Although I thought Elizabeth was cleverer than that.'

Meredith looked at Tess expectantly. After all, she had been the one to request the meeting. 'Well, what else can I do for you?'

Tess steeled herself. For the last few weeks, Tess had been feeling very alone. Navigating the lives and loves of the Asgill offspring had been more difficult than she had imagined. In the past month, only William Asgill had escaped from any sort of trouble – and who knew what problems might be lurking under that particular rock? Tess had met William with his wife Paula, and some instinct told her that there was trouble brewing there. As much as she was enjoying her new job, it had nothing like the camaraderie of the *Globe* offices, and Tess was feeling very much in need of assistance

with the research and a sounding board when she ran into problems – which seemed to be daily. Patty was far too busy with her
legal work to be able to talk to her very much, and Lucy Cummins,
Asgill Cosmetics' communications director, felt so threatened by
Tess that she only contacted her via email.

'I need some backup, Meredith. The workload is much heavier
than I ever expected, so I'd like a former colleague to come over
and help us.'

Tess held her breath. Throughout her professional life, she had
never been one to ask for help, instead preferring to soldier on and
do everything herself, usually because she could do things better
than everyone else. But the problem with that tactic was that if
you told people everything was fine, they assumed you were in
control and therefore no one noticed your Herculean efforts to fix
everything single-handed. So far she'd not encountered a situation
where things had grown so big and unmanageable that she'd not
been able to handle them alone, but she didn't want to play the
odds. Meredith's face barely registered any surprise at the request.
Either Tess had been correct about her boss's addiction to discreet
cosmetic procedures, or she was unmoved by Tess's plight.

'Who is this colleague?' asked Meredith blandly.

'Her name is Jemma Davies. She is a paparazzo friend of mine,
very good, very discreet.'

Meredith began to play with the sapphire around her neck.
'Discreet is not a word I would normally associate with those
people,' she said disapprovingly. 'Tess. You know the protection of
my family means everything me, which is why I am paying you to
protect them.'

The implication was clear: I am paying *you* a six-figure salary
to crisis-manage the Asgills. I don't want to pay anyone else, least
of all someone who is effectively the enemy. Tess could almost see
her point.

'I understand that you might think that I should be able to handle
everything,' said Tess. 'But there is an enormous amount of legwork
involved in this job. In the past few weeks, I have had to deal with
a potential crisis involving three of your four children. In an ideal
world, I need to be there to advise and assist them all, but what
with managing the press, doing research on potential problems,
and dealing with sudden emergencies, I don't have time. I can't be
everywhere at once, Meredith.'

Tess swallowed hard. At this rate she was going to talk herself out of a job.

'But Tess, you do have the full use of our family lawyer and our corporate communications director. I could almost understand if you were asking for a simple assistant, but still don't see why we need a paparazzo. Aren't we trying to protect ourselves from them?'

'Celebrities use paparazzi all the time for their own purposes,' said Tess. 'Many of those long-lens pictures you see in the gossip magazines are actually setups arranged by the celebs. Rather than have a rogue paparazzo take unflattering pictures of them, they will work with a friendly snapper to get the pictures that put them in the best light and give them an added career boost – and the papers are happy because the pictures are clear and well framed.'

'But couldn't we simply do a deal with a photographer for one of these setups?'

Tess shook her head. 'People have to believe that these photos are real, and we can't afford to have anyone leak the story. This photographer I'm proposing is extremely trustworthy. She is also very good at the other side of the job – keeping her ear to the ground with the papers and magazines, as well as other paps; finding out who knows what and feeding us the information back before it becomes damaging to the family.'

Meredith thought it through. 'Brooke won't like it,' she said finally.

Tess smiled. 'Brooke doesn't have to know for the moment.'

Jemma had once told her that she often liaised with a celebrity's manager or PR; sometimes the star didn't even know they were being followed, although all the while their manager would be feeding her information about the star's location.

A crease appeared between Meredith's brows. 'This won't have any implications with the Billingtons?'

'Number one, we are *protecting* David and Brooke. Number two, David is every bit as media savvy as we are. Every positive piece of press for him is a step nearer to Congress. All I am talking about here is getting pictures of them visiting soup kitchens and libraries, strolling hand in hand through Central Park. We will portray them as two young people in love, not arrogant rich kids out of touch with the electorate. David might be popular, but he's still a Republican. In a liberal city like New York, he needs all the help he can get.'

Meredith smiled thoughtfully. 'You know, there are a lot of people out there who think Brooke can be iconic.'

'Absolutely,' agreed Tess. 'But that doesn't happen by accident, Meredith. Brooke is by nature rather low-key. We need to get pictures of her with the right people, going to the right parties.'

Tess thought back to her meeting with Brooke the day before. They had run through her weekly schedule and the only thing that Brooke had planned was the annual Costume Institute Gala. For a woman with potential to be an American icon, she was keeping a very low profile.

'You know, I had a good feeling about you, Tess,' smiled Meredith. 'From the moment we met, in fact. You had a purposeful stride; you can tell a lot about someone by the way they walk.' She glanced at her watch. 'Well, she will have to stay in the West Village apartment.'

'Who?' asked Tess quickly, her mind still thinking about her walk.

'This paparazzo woman. Jemma?'

'So she can come?'

'Yes, of course. Speak to Leonard about remuneration and Patty about contracts. I want those watertight: we must own the copyright to any Brooke and David photographs she takes.'

Tess stood up and gathered her bag. 'Thank you, Meredith,' she said formally.

'Not at all,' said Meredith, gracefully guiding her towards the door. 'And Tess? I'm glad we had this conversation.'

Me too, thought Tess, trying not to punch the air with excitement. *Me too*.

20

At seven fifteen in the morning, Brooke was already halfway through her run. She was a little earlier than usual, after being woken by David at five a.m., who had to get to the airport. She had crossed East Meadow, circled the running track by the reservoir, and was now heading down towards Strawberry Fields, her breath hard but steady. She felt good. Even before the announcement of her wedding, Brooke had liked to keep in shape and tried to stick to a regime of a run every other day. It was time to herself, time to block out the rest of the world and, with her low baseball cap, old jogging pants, and tinted yellow wraparound cyclist glasses, it was a time to be anonymous. It was not a best-dressed-list look by anyone's measure, but it was enough to stop most people from recognizing her and, for that sole reason, it was one of her favourite looks in her closet.

Not breaking stride, Brooke glanced down at her watch, thinking it would take her another twenty minutes to make her way back across the park and be home in time to shower, change, and meet Vanessa Friedmann for their nine a.m. breakfast meeting at the Ritz-Carlton. Tap, tap, tap. The sound of her battered running shoes hitting the road was almost hypnotic. She veered off the main pathway down a slope and under a tunnel. As she came out the other side, she could hear heavy footsteps echo from the tunnel's bricks. *Dammit!* she thought angrily, *they've found me.*

'Hey, Brooke! Brooke! Over here!'

Still running, she looked over her shoulder and saw a man, not with a camera, as she had expected, but with a small DVD recorder. He was one of the new breed, a videographer. A few weeks ago,

178

Tess Garrett had given her a set of 'press-fighting' rules to learn. She remembered reading the point headed 'paparazzi', which said something like: 'When confronted by a photographer, stop and let them take one quick photograph.'

Brooke was amazed. 'Why should I make things easier for them?' she had asked with distaste. 'They make my life hell!'

'They're going to take the picture anyway,' Tess had replied. 'It's better you're smiling.'

So how was she supposed to deal with this? thought Brooke. *What should she do when someone was taping her?*

Unsure of the protocol, she picked up pace. Surely she could outrun a man carrying a big camera, she reasoned. She pumped her knees as she crested the slope then made for the flat road, one of the tarmac arteries that ran through the park, but as she jumped the path, her foot hit a loose rock on the path. She skittered sideways, holding her hands out to break her fall. Her wrists jerked back painfully and her knees stung as they scraped along the gravel. Her ankle felt as if it was on fire.

The videographer had caught up with her and simply stood filming her as she lay on the ground panting for breath. 'Please. Leave me alone,' she pleaded between gasps. 'I've hurt myself.'

She looked around desperately and saw a yellow cab was coming around the bend towards her. With one big effort, Brooke lifted herself up and waved her arms. The cab stopped with a screech. Barely upright, she hobbled to the vehicle like a wounded foal. The videographer was still following her, moving on his haunches, keeping low to focus on the blood running from Brooke's grazed knee. Desperate to escape, Brooke yanked open the cab door and, a split second later, heard a thud and a crash of splintering plastic. She turned to see the man crumple to the floor clutching his head.

'Oh shit,' she cried. 'Oh my God, I'm so sorry.'

The man hurriedly picked up his camera, rubbing his head with one hand and pointing the lens back towards her. 'Fucking bitch!' he shouted. 'You fucking whore!'

Brooke stood there motionless, her mouth opening and closing uselessly.

'Hey, get in!' shouted the cab driver. Without thinking, Brooke did as she was told, sinking into the faux leather seat of the cab, her body shaking. She glanced behind and saw the videographer still pointing his camera at her as the cab zoomed away.

'He deserved that, Miss Asgill,' said the cab driver. 'Those people, they make me sick to my stomach.'

She looked up. It still surprised her to be recognized by complete strangers.

'So where you wanna go? The hospital? I think you better get that looked at.'

Her entire leg was throbbing now.

'Hospital? Yes. I think . . . no, hold on.'

She stopped herself, suddenly visualizing the aggravation of turning up at ER. She quickly unzipped the money belt around her waist and pulled out a slim mobile phone. She always took a cell phone on a run, along with her house keys, twenty dollars, and a mace spray. This was New York, after all. She scrolled through her contacts book, stopping at Dr Powell, the Asgills' family practitioner on the Upper East Side. She was just about to call, when she noticed the name next to it: 'Matthew Palmer'. For a second she sat staring at his number on the LCD display. She wasn't sure why she had transferred the number from his business card into her phone, but then maybe everything happened for a reason. Right now she needed an ER doctor without the aggro of hospital. She clicked to his number and pressed 'call'.

Matt's apartment was in a modern block on West Eighty-Ninth Street, a short walk from Riverside Park. The lobby was bland and a little run-down, its main feature a long row of mailboxes. It reminded Brooke of an old suburban library she had visited with David as part of a National Literary Awareness event. Well, until she slipped a little on the tiles and jarred her foot, letting out a gasp of pain. Then she couldn't think of anything much.

'Come on,' said Matt simply, offering her his arm to lean on. Dressed in jeans and a ragged T-shirt, he looked rough and tired, but his arm still felt solid in her grasp.

They rode the elevator in silence. Was he annoyed at being disturbed or did he simply not have anything to say? Whatever, Brooke couldn't concentrate on anything except the pain in her foot which was now searing all the way up her leg. The slightest pressure made her feel as though her entire foot had been locked in a vice.

He led her into the apartment, an open-plan space painted in a soft dark green, with two sofas, a table by the window and a long bookcase along one wall stuffed with books and magazines and random objects – a baseball, a pen pot, and a boomerang. Amazing the details your mind picked up when it was trying not to concentrate on something else, thought Brooke, as Matt semi-carried her to one of the sofas and gently eased off her running shoes. She tried hard not to yell.

'Just cut it off,' she said with a forced laugh.

'It's only a sprain,' he said, flatly peeling off her sock and examining her ankle.

'Only!' she said. 'I'm in agony.'

'Brooke, a twisted ankle is not agony,' he said, not unkindly. 'Not when you've seen what I've seen in ER today.'

'I guess not,' she said softly, feeling a little guilty. That must be why he looked so drawn. She could only imagine what he'd had to deal with in the last few hours.

Matt got up and walked through into another room, returning with some tablets and a glass of water. 'Take these. They're strong, but they'll do the trick.'

'Professional strength. Wonderful,' she smiled. 'The beauty of having a friend in the medical profession.'

'So we're friends now?' he said with a smile.

'The least I can do is forgive you, particularly when I've disturbed your breakfast.'

She nodded over to the table where there was a large pizza, still in its cardboard box.

'Still warm,' he said. 'Want some?'

'Pizza for breakfast?'

'Breakfast or an extremely late supper,' he nodded, rubbing his face wearily. 'I'm not entirely sure which. Hours mean nothing after a fifteen-hour shift.'

He bent down and gently lifted her leg, then popped a cushion under her injured foot.

'How come you called me?' he said, not looking up as he put a dressing on her grazed knee.

'You said if I was ever on the West Side . . .' she joked. 'Seriously, I was running in the park and a pap guy chased me. I fell and pow, my ankle went. I thought I'd broken it.'

He lifted his head and smiled. 'I'm just surprised you came to me. Shouldn't you be being attended to by your personal physician?'

She raised an eyebrow. 'Matt, I'm not the Queen of England.'

'But I bet you have staff,' he said with a smirk.

'No. Well, yes. Kind of.'

'Do you have a driver?'

'Sometimes. Well, actually he's David's, I get him when he's not busy.'

'What about a maid?'

'Yes . . .' she said, starting to feel embarrassed. 'I have someone who cleans for me, but that's not unusual, is it?'

'A personal trainer?'

'Come on, this is New York,' she grinned with a wince, and Matt laughed, stretching across to get a slice of pizza. He folded it into three before he wedged it in his mouth. Just then a thought hit her.

'Oh damn, I'd better phone my publicist,' she said distractedly.

Matt burst out laughing, strings of cheese falling onto his chin. It slightly irritated her, knowing he found her lifestyle so amusing, but she still liked it when he smiled. Most of the time he was so intense, almost sombre, but when his face broke into a smile, it lightened his features. Turning away from him, she dialled Tess's number. Tess answered immediately.

'There's been an incident,' she said.

'Go on.'

She quickly told Tess about her run, the paparazzo with the video camera, and her fall. 'When I jumped in a cab, the guy was still trying to film my leg. I, well, I think I hit him with the door.'

Brooke heard Tess take a sharp intake of breath. 'How badly was he hurt?' she asked.

'Not so badly hurt that he didn't carry on filming. And shouting gross things at me.'

'Oh Brooke,' sighed Tess. There was a disappointed, distracted pause. 'When did this happen?'

'Maybe forty-five minutes ago? Look, I got the cab driver's cell number. He saw that it was a total accident. He said he would tell the police that the pap was harassing me.'

'Well, that's good,' said Tess, a little mollified. 'Are you hurt? Where are you?'

'At a friend's place. He's a doctor.'

'Which friend?' said Tess suspiciously. Brooke suddenly had the strongest sense that it probably wasn't too wise to have come here.

'Matt Palmer,' she said quickly, hoping it wouldn't register with Tess.

'Matthew Palmer?' cried Tess so loudly that Brooke had to jerk the phone away from her ear. 'Matthew Palmer the *old flame*? The Matthew Palmer from the Danny Krantz stitch-up?' Tess was almost yelling now.

Brooke glanced over to Matt who took the hint and left the room.

'Tess. I told you,' she hissed into the phone. 'He's just a friend. More importantly, he's an ER doctor and I was ten blocks from his apartment.'

Brooke could hear Tess take a deep breath. 'We'll discuss this later,' she said. 'In the meantime, I think we should put out a preemptive statement about the pap incident.'

'To whom?'

'To one of the news wires. I don't want this videographer guy jumping the gun and putting a story out that you assaulted him. I think we can be pretty certain he'll try.'

Brooke felt a flutter of panic. Until that moment, the only thing she had been concerned about was her aching foot. 'But I didn't assault anyone!'

Tess's voice was reassuringly calm and efficient. 'I know, Brooke, but paparazzi want to make money and the more sensational the story the better. You can bet he's going to spin it as a vicious unprovoked attack on an innocent bystander who just happened to be there filming the squirrels. So what we should do is beat him to the punch with our story: how you were followed and harassed by a professional lowlife and sustained an injury during that pursuit. I've no doubt Patty can threaten legal action too, and hopefully that should be enough to scare him off. Failing that, maybe we can buy those photographs.'

'It was a videographer.'

'Whatever. We don't want it getting on Extra! Or HollywoodTV.'

Brooke let out a deep breath. 'Thanks, Tess.'

'Give me Palmer's address and I'll get a driver to collect you. Then I'll make an appointment with your doctor. We might need someone to say how badly you were hurt.'

'Surely that's not necessary?' Brooke added nervously.

'We'll see.'

As Brooke hung up, she noticed Matt was standing in the doorway watching her.

'From the outside things always look better,' he said quietly. She looked at him puzzled.

'Your life,' he said with a frankness that made her uncomfortable. Brooke waved a hand. 'Don't feel sorry for me.'

'It's me you're talking to, Brooke,' he said. 'All this crap must get you down.'

Brooke looked at him, then shrugged. 'You know the weird thing is that I liked it at first. Okay, not the getting followed by the pap bit, but getting bags and dresses sent by designers, every invitation to every hot party in the city, a reservation at any restaurant. I felt like *someone*. Does that make sense?'

'I guess. Come on, let's strap you up.' He produced a roll of bandage and pulled some scissors from his pen pot. He rested her foot gently in his lap and began wrapping the crêpe fabric around her skin.

'Ouucchhh,' she cried again.

'A sprain is just damage to the ligament surrounding the ankle,' he said as he worked. 'You should be back on your feet in a week, probably completely recovered in maybe three weeks.'

She looked at him with alarm. 'But it's the Costume Institute Gala in two weeks. I have to go.'

'Have to?' he smiled, finishing the bandaging.

'Well, kind of *want* to go,' she shrugged with a smile. 'It's the one thing I've been excited about.'

'Well, for the minute you're not going anywhere, young Miss. Doctor's orders.' He stood up and threw her the TV remote control. 'I'm going to get some sleep. Do you mind?'

'No, no, of course not, you go.'

Just then, Brooke's mobile started ringing and she glanced at the screen.

'The cavalry?' asked Matt.

'Something like that.'

He helped her get off the sofa. 'I'll come downstairs with you,' he said wearily.

'No. I'd better go alone.'

'In which case, wait there.'

She hobbled towards his bedroom door, where he was rooting around his closet noisily.

'I bet this has seen a lot of action,' she laughed as he handed it to her.

'The hockey stick or my bedroom?' he asked.

184

She flushed and tucked the hockey stick under her arm as she put on her cyclist goggles.

'What the hell are those!' he exclaimed.

'My disguise,' she said, arching her brow as playfully as she could when her foot was so sore. 'I don't want to be recognized leaving a man's apartment at eight in the morning, even if it is only you.'

'Only me,' he scoffed. 'You'd better remember whose hockey stick it is, Asgill.'

'Listen, Matt, you've been great. I don't know how to thank you.'

'Maybe a beer when you're back on your feet, hopalong?'

'I'll make it a magnum of champagne if I'm back in Manolos by the weekend.'

'Does that mean you'll let your assistant put through my calls now?'

'Okay, give me a pen and paper.' She scribbled down her number. 'No giving that to your friends at the *Oracle*, okay?'

'Ouch. So cynical.'

'Maybe . . .' she smiled, waving the hockey stick. 'I'm still watching you, Palmer.'

As she hobbled to the lift, she found she was looking forward to that drink.

21

Liz couldn't believe she was back at the shrink. More to the point she couldn't believe she was being forced to go by that jumped-up publicist Tess, who was threatening to tell Meredith the details of the Russ Ford fiasco if she didn't make an appointment. She shifted in her seat in the psychologist's waiting room and tried to calm down. Deep breathing, wasn't that what the last headshrinker had told her? She closed her eyes and tried to think of cool wet grass, or a deserted beach or something. It wasn't as if she hadn't been to see a therapist before. There had been a six-month stint after the death of her father, and another spell in her senior year at school, when she was so concerned about getting perfect exam marks that she had lost a stone in weight. Liz snorted. She still didn't see how that could be a bad thing.

Anyway, she was here now and she was mollified by the thought that this particular doctor might actually be of some use to her, even if she failed to remove every hang-up and mental tic. Dr Dana Shapiro was considered *the* shrink of the moment. She had heard the name whispered around the more powerful members of her circle for years. An expert in relationship issues, she was rumoured to have treated several A-list stars for sex addiction. It never hurt to make useful connections, thought Liz.

'Elizabeth? I'm Dana Shapiro. Come on through, please.'

The doctor was a petite woman wearing gold-framed spectacles and a helmet of iron-grey hair. She led Liz through into a wood-panelled office that reminded Liz of a professor's study at Princeton. Liz sat on a plum-leather chesterfield sofa while Dana took a seat in a red button-back chair opposite her.

'Just relax,' said Dana. 'Tell me about yourself.'

Liz silently cursed Tess Garrett for putting her in this position. Still, as she was here, she was determined to deal with Dana Shapiro in the same way she dealt with everything: with brisk efficiency.

'Well, Doctor—'

'Dana, please.'

'Okay, Dana. The reason I am here is that I like sex,' said Liz, meeting Shapiro's gaze. 'Personally, I don't think it's a problem, but a friend of mine wanted me to speak to somebody about it.'

'Well, you're right of course,' said Dana. 'An enjoyment of sex isn't a problem; in many ways it's essential. But something about your behaviour has obviously made your friend concerned.'

Liz shrugged. 'I enjoy one-night stands. I have one or two sexual encounters a week.'

Dana made a steeple in front of her face with her fingers. 'And who are these men? I assume they are men.'

Liz gave a nod of the head. 'Usually I meet them in bars. Occasionally through the Internet.'

'So you enjoy anonymous sex?'

'I prefer to use the expression "uncomplicated sex",' said Liz tersely. 'I am a very busy working woman. I run the best spa in the city and I have no time for a relationship. I have a healthy sex drive and I have found an outlet for it. If I was a man I'd be patted on the back, but because I'm a woman I'm a nymphomaniac.'

Liz had always enjoyed sex. She had always enjoyed the things she was good at: tennis, schoolwork, business. She had been sexually active since she had lost her virginity to the pool boy at Parklands when she was seventeen. Before her marriage to Walter three years earlier, she had taken around thirty lovers, which, spread over sixteen years, barely worked out at two lovers every year. Was that excessive? Abnormal? Liz genuinely didn't know the answer; it was something no one talked about.

'Well, let's not jump to any conclusions just yet,' said Dr Shapiro. 'But from what you have described to me, your behaviour shows an addiction to sex as well as to risk.

Liz laughed. 'I am not addicted.'

The doctor paused for a moment. 'Sex of this nature can be highly addictive, Elizabeth. Do you drink?'

'A little,' shrugged Liz. 'Why do you ask?'

'Often people come to me with more than one addiction: drink, drugs, gambling.'

'I've told you I am not addicted,' said Liz, a little irritated.

'Okay,' smiled Dana. 'Well, what we need to discover is why you indulge in this behaviour. Can you remember when it began?'

She looked towards the window beyond Dana. Liz could actually pinpoint the exact night. It had been three months after the death of her father and she had been feeling . . . not depressed, exactly, but melancholic. That had been the day of the Asgill's board meeting; the day her mother had appointed William as chief executive. That evening Meredith had thrown a private dinner in the Orchid Room upstairs at 21 Club. Liz had been so angry she had barely spoken throughout the entire meal, and had left straight after dessert. Walter had been out of town on business so she had no reason to go home. She had simply walked and walked, straight down Fifty-Second Street until she found herself in Hell's Kitchen. She knew better than to walk around those streets late at night, but she didn't care. She had needed a drink. She sought out a bar and a good-looking musician had hit on her almost immediately. What had begun as a terrible, hateful night instantly turned into a thrilling, uncharted night of adventure and possibility. He lived in a walk-up a block away and all her anger and frustration had been channelled into the most fantastic sex of her life.

'So that first casual sexual encounter was retaliation?' said Dr Shapiro. 'You believe that you and not your brother should have been given the job.'

Liz frowned and kept silent.

'How long was it before your second sexual encounter of this nature?'

'Two months into my marriage. My relationship with my husband was faltering; we both worked too hard. Sex was perfunctory.'

Now that was an understatement, thought Liz with a private smile. Liz had never really felt attracted to Walter and, now she could admit it, she had never really loved him either; but she'd seen something in him, a business brain as sharp as her own, a work ethic to rival hers. They were matched in many ways, but certainly not in the bedroom.

'You might call my behaviour risky or addictive, Doctor,' said Liz. 'But to me, it's a very considered way of fulfilling a need.'

'And does it fulfil your emotional needs too?'

For a second she remembered the day she had finally separated from Walter. One night he simply did not come home. The memory of waking at dawn, light struggling through a crack in the blinds onto the empty space beside her in the bed, it was still raw. They had drifted so far apart it had been no surprise, but the pain she had felt . . . well, that had truly caught her by surprise. Even more so when he'd told her he was moving in with a junior executive from the hotel. In fact, her hurt had swiftly turned to fury when Walter had followed their quickie divorce with the announcement that he was going to marry the slut. She was a Dartmouth-educated blonde who immediately gave up her career and dedicated herself entirely to making Walter's life more comfortable and squeezing out babies. Liz's fury had turned to shock and dismay. How could you respect a woman like that? She had no desire to devote her life to another person; she had no desire for children. You were brought into this world alone and you left it alone. Emotional needs? Where did they get you? She could see Dr Shapiro watching her closely.

'Forgive me, Dana, but my major was economics not psychology. Am I to take it that you think I was rejected by my dead father, rejected by my mother, and then dropped by my husband, so I need to go out and find sex to fill the hole? Is that what you think? That I equate sex with love? Sex is my way of making up for a lack of emotional support in my life?'

Dr Shapiro cocked her head. 'What do you think, Elizabeth?'

'I think it's a lot of horseshit, Dana.'

'Well, I think we've achieved a great deal today,' said Dr Shapiro, standing up and smoothing her skirt. 'Let's both have a think about what we've discussed and meet back here in a week?'

Liz closed the door behind her. *'We've achieved a great deal today,'* she mocked. What exactly had it achieved? It was a waste of her precious time and money. But at least she'd fulfilled her obligations to Tess Garrett. She was free – and that meant she wouldn't be going back to see Dr Dana Shapiro again. She had other plans.

The line from Damascus was faint and crackly.

'Hey, how are you?'

Brooke paused the *Sex and the City* DVD she was watching from bed, glad to hear David's voice, even though it sounded so remote and tinny it was like talking to a stranger.

'Hey. You're there.' David had flown out to Syria almost twenty-four hours earlier to do a report on its political importance in the Middle East.

'Just about. It was the journey from hell.'

'Get some sleep. You'll feel better.'

'Sleep, yeah right. It's nearly six a.m. here. I've got meetings and filming all day. So how are you? How's work? Didn't you have a meeting with that agent?'

'All cancelled. I didn't even make it into work.'

'Really? Why not?'

'Just a bit of an accident.'

'Accident? Brooke, what happened?'

'I was out running. A pap was following me and I fell and sprained my ankle.' She tried to say it as casually as she could, but David was obviously concerned.

'Shit, baby. Are you okay?'

She looked down at her swollen, purple-tinged foot, which was balanced on a cushion. 'Nothing some very effective painkillers didn't sort out.'

She heard a low decisive snort down the phone. 'We need to get you security.'

She squirmed at the thought of herself flanked by burly men, Paris Hilton-style, and groaned. 'Oh come on, David, that's not necessary.'

'Honey, I think it's very necessary.'

The television was freeze-framed on a bare-breasted Samantha. She grabbed the remote control and switched it off. 'I don't want a bodyguard. It just looks ridiculous.'

'Baby, you need one. Today it's a pap guy and a swollen ankle, tomorrow it could be . . . well, anything.'

Brooke heard the disapproval in his voice but she was determined to stand her ground. It wasn't the actual bodyguard she objected to – in the last few months she'd met lots of bodyguards, and most of them were just like drivers with extra kung-fu skills. What bothered Brooke was what getting a bodyguard represented.

'David, the second I get a bodyguard,' she said firmly, 'is the second I admit I'm living in a prison. I don't want to live my life like that.'

'Robert told me recently about a really great guy who's worked with a lot of female celebrities. Ex-Israeli army. He's very good. Very discreet.'

Was he even listening to her?

'David . . .'

'So, the ankle. Is it all strapped up properly?'

Despite Tess Garrett's reaction, she wanted to tell him the truth. 'Yes. Matt Palmer had a look at it. I didn't want to go to Cedar Sinai.'

'Matt Palmer strapped your ankle,' he said. There was a long pause. Brooke felt sure it wasn't the poor telephone connection. 'What were you doing at Columbia-Presbyterian?'

She hesitated. 'I wasn't. I went to his apartment. It's not too far from where I fell.'

'Well, that was convenient.'

'Oh David, don't be like that. He's just a friend. Barely even that.'

'You can do without friends like him.'

Brooke felt her hackles rise. 'Do you want to tell me who I can and can't have as friends now?'

'I didn't mean that,' he snapped.

'Well what *did* you mean?'

There was a long, crackling pause.

'I've got to go,' he said finally. 'I've got a meeting at the Baath Party headquarters in an hour.'

'Fine,' she said quietly. 'You go off and play.' Then she hung up the phone, her hands shaking with anger.

For a few seconds she just stared at the television screen in front of her, eyes not focusing, just seeing shapes and colour. Then she began to move, as if on autopilot, sliding off the bed and hobbling to the kitchen. The fridge contained nothing of interest – carrot juice, a bottle of Skin Plus prebiotics ('Look after your skin from the inside out!' screamed the bottle), an artichoke, and a carton of egg whites to make the breakfast omelettes her personal trainer had recommended but she had never cooked. Moving to the cupboard, her heart gave a little flip of pleasure when she saw a large box of chocolates sent by a publicist a few weeks earlier, hidden behind her coffee grinder.

She ripped open the tasteful brown paper and orange ribbons, took a pink truffle from the box and popped it into her mouth, closing her eyes as it melted on her tongue.

It felt good. Brooke didn't consider herself a diet Nazi like half of the fashionistas and society girls in the city. But all the clothes she had sent to her were sample sizes, small and unforgiving, and paparazzi camera angles could be very unflattering, even with just a few surplus pounds on her tall, slim frame. Giving up chocolate had seemed a small price to pay.

She returned to her bed, lay back on the plump pillows and rifled through the box to find another pink truffle. She felt naughty and defiant, as if she were playing hookey from school, not that Brooke could remember ever playing hookey from school.

When her phone rang again she was tempted not to answer it. She hated leaving things awkward with David, but she felt so angry at his high-handed attitude, she really didn't want to speak to him.

Reluctantly she picked it up.

'How's the patient?' She recognized Matt's voice immediately.

'A box of truffles is dulling the pain,' she said, suddenly thinking about her foot again. 'I particularly recommend the pomegranate champagne truffle.'

'The medicinal powers of chocolate. I thought you society girls didn't touch the stuff.'

'I'm rebelling,' she said.

'That's not like you, Little Miss Perfect.'

She sat up, bristling again. 'I'll have you know I have a very rebellious streak.'

He chuckled down the phone. 'Brooke. You're hardly Che Guevara.'

'Meaning what?'

'You. A rebel. You think double parking is a felony.'

Her back stiffened. 'I do not.'

'Remember the first time we met at that party on Prospect Avenue? You told me the next day you went back to the house and took them a bag of bananas to replace the ones I'd taken for your hangover cure.'

'It was somebody else's food!'

'We were students!'

They both laughed at the memory.

'Well, I was just checking in,' said Matt after a pause. 'Making sure your ankle was okay. I'd better go.'

'Me too,' said Brooke quickly. 'I have a night to myself . . .

The week actually. David's away so I thought I'd make the most of it by indulging in the *Sex and the City* box set.'

'Where's he gone?'

'Syria.'

'Holiday?'

She laughed. 'No. He's signed up to do a series of six special reports for *Dispatches* on CTV. He's trying to sort out an interview with the President as we speak.'

'He's a busy guy.'

'David or the President?'

'Both, I dare say.'

'Well, thanks again for this morning. Those painkillers have had me walking on air.'

There was another pause. 'Listen, what are you doing this weekend?' she said suddenly.

'Not much. I'm not at the hospital.'

Well, let's do something. You always had the best ideas for days out as I remember.'

'There's a challenge, Asgill. You can hardly walk. And I'm not being seen out dead with you if you have to wear those awful cycling goggles.'

She laughed. 'I'll leave it in your hands,' she said. 'And I promise, no more glasses.'

22

'This place is fucking amazing,' said Jemma with a shriek of pleasure, bouncing up and down on the small double bed in the spare room of Tess's apartment. 'Can we go down to the Magnolia bakery and get cup cakes? No. Century 21! I'm desperate for some new clothes. No, that restaurant in Central Park that overlooks the lake.'

'The Boathouse?' chipped in Tess.

'That's the one. God, I just *love* New York, don't you?'

Tess smiled at the genuine glee on her friend's face as she looked around the West Village apartment. She had to admit it was impressive. The slim galley kitchen with the sleek, white fittings and granite surfaces. The bijou Philippe Starck bathroom, the living room painted in delicate creams with white shutters at the window that overlooked shady Perry Street.

'I can't believe you did this for me,' said Jemma, running to the window and looking out.

'Hey, I did it for me,' grinned Tess. 'I need you.'

'And how much is the rent on this place again?'

'It's rent-free.'

Jemma just laughed.

'I have a friend who moved here about a year ago – she's paying three thousand dollars a month for some dive in Brooklyn. And we thought London was a rip-off! New York, I am so ready for you,' she laughed, clapping her hands together.

Tess brought through two mugs of tea and they sat down on the sofa.

'So how's the *Globe*?'

Jemma pulled a face. 'I haven't sold one set of pictures to them

194

since you left, not even a fifty-quid red-carpet shot. I suppose you know they made thirty people redundant?'

Tess had heard. It was on days like this that she felt as if she had made the right move.

'Well, it's going to be no picnic here either,' she warned. 'What do they say about the rich? They're not like you and me? Well, it's true. They get up to ten times more trouble.'

'We can handle it,' said Jemma. There was such a look of resolve on her face, it made Tess smile – it was if she was preparing to do battle. It was amazing the difference the last two years had made, she thought. Back then, Jemma had been a graduate from Wimbledon School of Art and about to start on a career in fashion photography. They weren't close at first; in fact it had been Jemma's sister Cat who was Tess's good friend – she would only see Jemma popping in to say a glamorous hello at drinks parties or dinner. At that time, Jemma had struck her as a bit prissy and precious about her work. She had just landed a job in Paris as second assistant to French fashion photographer François Mitaud, and was full of her own creativity and fabulousness. Twelve months later, Tess had got a call. Jemma was in trouble and needed her help. Working late in Mitaud's studio, the photographer had tried to seduce her, Jemma had said no. François wouldn't accept it and had raped her. Tess had got on the Eurostar the next morning. Jemma's sister Cat was now working in Canada and her parents had emigrated to New Zealand many years before, so Tess was the closest thing she had to family.

Tess had persuaded Jemma to go to the police, but they were unsympathetic and aggressive, insinuating that anyone who worked in the fashion industry only had themselves to blame. The same day, she had received a phone call from François, threatening that she would never work in the fashion industry again. Against Tess's advice, Jemma had withdrawn her accusation, but the damage had already been done. Word was passed through the world of fashion that Jemma Davies was a troublemaker and she had returned to London broke and wounded. Tess looked at her friend, feeling terribly guilty. Despite knowing everything Jemma had been through, Tess hadn't shied away from exploiting her either, and she knew she couldn't keep it a secret any longer.

'Listen, Jem, I need to make a confession,' she said. 'It's been weighing on my mind since I got here. Those photos of Sean Asgill at the Venus party that we didn't use? I wasn't quite straight with you about why they disappeared.'

Jemma cocked her head to one side. 'I thought you said it was a legal situation.'

'It was. Sort of. But the truth is I spiked the story because Meredith Asgill asked me to. I wanted this job, so I gave them the photographs.'

Jemma frowned. 'So what are you sorry for? I thought you said those photos technically belonged to the *Globe*, didn't they?'

Tess nodded.

'Well then, you stitched the newspaper up, not me. And good for you; the *Globe* management stitched you up by not giving you the editor's position when you were clearly the best person for the job. So I figure we're all about even.'

'Well, that would be true, but you don't know the whole story,' said Tess. 'The Asgills offered me one hundred thousand pounds for the photographs at first. I turned that down.'

Jemma gave a low whistle. 'That's a lot of money.'

'I know, but it didn't feel right. Taking a job with them was easier to accept and I've always wanted to work in New York. But I feel bad about denying you that money.'

Jemma shrugged. 'It wasn't as if I'd snapped Madonna in bed with the Queen, was it? Then I'd have been really pissed off if you'd swiped the pictures!'

She gave Tess a long searching look. 'Look, so I might have been able to make a little bit of money, but Tess, without you, I'd probably be in some grotty bedsit in Camberwell on benefits. You have been a good friend to me, that's all that matters.'

Tess closed her eyes and felt the relief flood through her. She'd only done what she could. After the Paris incident, Tess had persuaded the photo editor at the *Globe* to give Jemma a few shifts on the picture desk. Through that she had begun to talk to the paparazzi and discovered how much money they could make. Jemma still took her camera everywhere and, one night, shopping for Christmas presents just off Oxford Street, she had seen a little group of shoppers laden with parcels standing around a car. As she pushed to the front, she saw the driver was rock star James Meller – he had hit someone crossing the road. Jemma sold the pictures for ten thousand pounds. In one sense it was the easiest money she'd ever made. In another, the hardest. Jemma had later told Tess how guilty, how dirty she had felt taking pictures of the scene. But with Tess's encouragement, she hit the streets as a freelance paparazzo, and the second picture she took was easier, and the third and the fourth. She set herself ground rules – she would never take a photo that hurt anyone. At least, no one who wasn't fair game. Tess smiled inwardly; it was funny how those goalposts quickly changed.

'Listen, Tess, don't feel badly about any of this,' said Jemma, gesturing towards the skyline. 'Look, I'm here in New York, what could be better than that? I do this job because I love the buzz. Maybe it's a different buzz than seeing my pictures in *Vogue*,' she added with a wry smile. 'But it's a buzz all the same.'

Tess nodded slowly. She'd heard Jemma's stories – three months earlier she'd been run off the road when she'd followed an A-lister's 4x4 on her moped. The bodyguard driving the car had deliberately smashed into her, leaving Jemma and her bike mashed up on a lonely grassy verge. On another occasion, Jemma had been hit over the head with a bicycle pump by one of London's most famous theatre actors. Some people might say that the paparazzi deserved it, but no one deserved to be killed or injured.

Jemma jumped up and went over to the window, gazing down with undisguised excitement at the yellow cabs in the street.

'So, do you think you are going to be in my spare room for evermore?' smiled Tess.

'Given half a chance,' grinned Jemma. 'Now, are we going to paint this town red, white, and blue?'

Matt picked up Brooke the following Saturday at seven thirty a.m. It seemed ridiculously early to go for breakfast, let alone lunch, but then Brooke reminded herself that he was an ER doctor, who had his days and hours out of synch. It must be like having permanent jet lag.

Walking out of her building, she glanced left and right. There were no paparazzi she could see, but nevertheless she had taken precautions. She'd dressed down in dark indigo jeans, her favourite Stella McCartney T-shirt and white pumps, because her ankle was not yet completely healed. Her hair was tied up and covered with a knitted cap. She had also covered her eyes with a pair of wide black sunglasses; it was a bright sunny morning so plenty of people were doing the same. The night before she had almost cancelled today's day out, feeling unsettled and guilty meeting Matt with David out of the country. But she'd shaken herself out of it. There was nothing to feel guilty about. Matt was just a friend and she was not going to let David, Tess Garrett, or the paparazzi dictate who she was going to be friends with. Was she supposed to go through life avoiding all men just because she was engaged and famous? Somehow going out with Matt felt like regaining control of her life.

'Now that's better,' smiled Matt, pointing to her sunglasses as she got into his car, discreetly hidden in a side street.

'I thought so,' she grinned. 'More Audrey Hepburn than Lance Armstrong. I have my Peggy Guggenheim in my bag too,' she said, pulling out a large pair of cream-framed sunglasses. 'But I try to match my glasses to my disguises.'

'Ah, it must be exhausting being a style icon,' he said, turning the key and setting off. 'Although where we're going, you won't need them.'

She looked at him suspiciously. Matt had been vague about their destination on the phone, only saying that no paparazzi would think to go there.

Brooke felt a little thrill of excitement as they left the metropolis behind.

'I'm surprised you ended up in book publishing,' said Matt as they drove along.

'Funny you should say that. I was interviewed for *Vogue* the other week. They asked me why I got into children's book publishing.'

'What did you tell them?'

'Because I have an English degree and I'm not sure you can do a great deal else with it. Plus the books that have had the most impact in my life are supposedly for children: *Charlotte's Web*, *The Giving Tree*, even Tolkien.'

'It's a good answer, but is it true?'

She smiled. 'The truth is I fell into it. After I graduated, my friend's mother fixed me up with work experience at Yellow Door. I took it mainly because it seemed like a nice way to make a living without working for the family company and being constantly compared to my workaholic sister Liz. Then I found out I loved publishing, so when they offered me an editorial assistant's position after my work experience stint, I jumped at it.'

'I bet your mother didn't like that.'

'The strange thing is, I really don't think she cared. Maybe because she already had William, Sean, and Liz working for the company. Maybe because she thought publishing would be better for me.'

'I can't imagine she just shrugged, though.'

'She said "Brooke, publishing is a very nice career for a girl looking for a suitable husband." And ever since I got together with David, she keeps reminding me that Jackie Onassis was an editor at Doubleday. If it's good enough for Jackie . . .'

Matt laughed.

'Well, if David does get to be president and you're his first lady, think of all the secrets you'll find out, like who really killed Kennedy.'

'Jack or Bobby?'

'Both. And find out about Roswell too.'

'Alien autopsies?' She grinned. 'I could tell you but then I'd have to kill you.'

'Let's hope it doesn't come to that.'

The roads out of New York were quiet. Conversation was casual and untaxing – gossip about mutual friends at Brown, her upcoming wedding, and life at Yellow Door.

Glancing at the clock on the dashboard, she realized they had been driving for over two hours. Towns had thinned out to open farmland and a sign shot past announcing they were in Pennsylvania.

'Where *are* you taking me?' she asked.

Seeing she wasn't going to get an answer, she opened the window to let in the crisp country air. They passed through small towns with funny names: 'Intercourse' and 'Bird-in-the-Hand' zipped by, their solitary high streets crowded with soda fountains and blacksmith's shops. Soon they were overtaking quaint farmers driving horse and buggies. If it were not for the constant presence of SUVs and pick-up trucks with tinted windows, she could almost convince herself that they had gone back in time. The penny finally dropped.

'We're in Amish country,' said Brooke, turning towards Matt.

'Is it a really stupid idea?' he asked. 'You said you hate getting hassled when you go out in public, so I thought we should go where people didn't have the slightest clue who you were.'

They looked at each other and burst out laughing. While Brooke could see that there were men with the trademark Amish spade beards and women in bonnets and pinafores, the towns still had fast-food joints and garish gift shops bristling with tourists. Brooke slipped her glasses back on.

'I never said my idea was foolproof,' smiled Matt.

They drove on into a valley. He pulled a piece of paper out of his pocket and glanced at it, keeping one eye on the road.

'Well, I think we're here.'

'It's incredible that communities like this can still exist in the twenty-first century,' said Brooke quietly.

'Actually the Amish are one of the fastest-growing communities in the world,' said Matt. 'They marry within other Amish communities and have lots of children.'

'That's so . . . so old-fashioned,' said Brooke.

Matt smiled. 'Not really. People tend to marry their own kind. Look at you and David. In fact all the way through college you had boyfriends like that.'

'Like what?'

'Boys with trust funds and sports cars.'

She blinked at him for a moment, then decided silence would be the best response. She wanted to disagree with him but her ex-boyfriends *were* of a type. No bad boys or losers. Just a string of Mr Rights. The one time she strayed off the path of nice boys from good families – with Dr Jeff Daniels, her former tutor who had bowled her over with his suave intelligence – it had ended quickly and badly. Looking back, that relationship had started when she had been in the throes of grief after her father's death, and he had been in the throes of a mid-life crisis. After that she'd reverted to type. And now she was getting married to David Billington – the prototype rich, successful, all-American male.

They took a right down a quiet dusty road. Finally they passed through a picket-fenced field and into the grounds of a small farm.

'Matt, we can't just drive into here,' Brooke hissed. 'This isn't Disneyland, it's someone's home!'

'Relax,' he said. 'A friend of mine from Brown, Tom Chance, knows this family. He's a doctor at a local hospital with an outreach programme for the Amish.'

As they got out of the car, a woman came out to greet them. She was dressed in a blue dress with a long full skirt, white apron, and a bonnet. Brooke thought she looked like Kelly McGillis in the film *Witness* – it was her only reference point for the Amish community.

'Welcome, Matthew,' she said with a smile. There was a faint inflection to her accent. *German?* thought Brooke. *Dutch perhaps?*

'Good to see you, Ruth. How's your little girl?'

'She's fine now. Tom is a good doctor. Now who is this?' she asked, turning her attention to Brooke.

'Ruth, may I introduce Brooke Asgill? She is an old friend from college.'

'Friends?' she said mischievously.

'Yes, Ruth,' Matthew said seriously.

'A man should not be without a wife, Matthew,' she said. 'It has been too long for you.'

Brooke watched his cheeks redden and smiled to herself.

'Okay, okay. Now how about this buggy ride we were talking about?'

The horse and buggy was standing outside a red barn. Ruth climbed into the front seat of the buggy, taking hold of the reins. Brooke and Matt clambered into the seat behind her.

'Our journey is going to be about three miles,' said Ruth as she geed the horse into a trot. She turned and gave them a mischievous smile.

As they jogged along, Ruth told them all about her life, using the various landmarks in the valley to illustrate her story. She showed them the simple wood-framed houses of their neighbours, where they worshipped on Sundays, and the one-roomed Amish schoolhouses.

Brooke closed her eyes and let the warm spring breeze stroke her face. It was the most pleasant sensation she'd felt in weeks. Simplicity. Anonymity. No one in this valley had any idea who Brooke Asgill was; they had no interest in where she bought her clothes or where she went out to eat. When they pulled up back in front of the farm, Ruth invited them into her large white house. It was simply decorated but the furniture – the long wooden table and dresser – were beautiful. It was scrupulously clean and there was a delicious smell in the air. She gave them a plate of pretzels that were thick, warm, and spicy. Brooke had not tasted pastry this good since she had been skiing in St Moritz a few years ago. She didn't mention it as she didn't know if Ruth would approve of a place like St-Moritz.

'Do you work, Brooke?' asked Ruth after a pause.

She nodded. 'I edit children's books.'

'Well, that's wonderful,' she smiled. 'That is a true calling.'

Ruth asked a few questions about life in New York, which seemed to both fascinate and repel her in equal measure, and then Matt gestured that it was time to go.

'That was great,' said Brooke as they climbed into the car. 'I might bring David. *You* should bring a date. Ruth wants to see you paired off again.'

He shook his head. 'Nah.'

'Have you dated since Elizabeth?' Brooke asked after a pause.

'A couple of dates,' he shrugged. 'It didn't feel right.'

'You still miss her,' said Brooke quietly.

'You know, almost every day I have to tell someone that their loved ones didn't make it. You give them coffee, you touch their arm, you direct them to a quiet room. Some of them scream and collapse, of course, but most of the time they are brave and solid. Before Katie died, that's how I thought you were supposed to behave, but now I wonder how they do it. How they can be so strong when every part of you feels crushed and helpless and keeps on feeling like that to the point where you wonder if it will *ever* feel better.'

'It will get better,' said Brooke simply, touching his arm.

'I know,' he shrugged. 'In fact I've applied to do a year on a voluntary scheme in Africa in the New Year. They're desperate for doctors out there. And I think it will be good for me. Stop me drinking too much and moping around.'

She was beginning to understand him. He blamed himself for not saving Elizabeth and now he wanted to get away. Brooke knew she could not persuade him otherwise; sometimes people needed to do these things to work them through.

'I'm impressed.'

'Didn't have me down as a do-gooder, huh?' said Matt with a wry grin. 'It was that or bum around the world for six months, and I thought I might get even more depressed, surrounded by backpackers ten years younger than me.'

'Maybe a hippy chick would do you good, Matt.'

He was quiet for a moment, concentrating on the road.

'If you could go anywhere in the world, where would it be?' he asked.

'David and I have been talking about that. You know, planning the honeymoon and so on. The problem is that David's been everywhere.

I have this romantic ideal that we will discover new places together.' She crunched up her nose thinking of David's latest suggestion: the Galapagos Islands. Admittedly, it would be a new passport stamp for both of them, but from what Brooke had seen on the Internet, it looked a bit cold, and nothing against the wildlife, just not very romantic.

'Well, here's mine,' said Matt, matter-of-factly. 'An Australian odyssey. Up the Hawkesbury River where they have freshwater crocodiles like three metres long, then into the red country, Ayers Rock – Uluru, Alice Springs, and the opal mines, and over to the Whitsunday Islands for snorkelling and sailing. Maybe with that hippy chick you mentioned.'

'That sounds a wonderful trip,' said Brooke dreamily. 'Can I steal it? Apart from the hippy chick, of course.'

When they stopped in town for gas, Brooke spotted a shop advertising 'Genuine Amish Clothes'.

Pointing to one of the plain dresses in the window, Matt joked: 'What about that for your Costume Gala next week?'

Inside, the shop was a classic tourist trap, with racks selling black trousers and bonnets next to Amish fridge magnets. Towards the back of the shop, almost hidden away, was a display of wooden furniture. Brooke reached for a pair of beautifully carved book ends and stroked the smooth wood.

'These are lovely, aren't they?'

'I'm going to buy them for you,' said Matt, taking them from her. Brooke pulled him back. 'Please. I want to buy them myself.'

Matt looked at her, puzzled. 'Why?'

Brooke paused before she spoke. 'Shall I tell you the difference between being rich and being famous?'

'I didn't know there was one,' said Matt, amused.

'When I was just rich, I always felt as if I had to pick up the cheque because my friends knew I had money. But now I'm famous, I go to a bar and there's always someone to buy me a drink, no matter how wealthy I am.'

Matt's expression clouded, his voice nipped with anger. 'So you think I want to buy you these book ends so I can tell all my friends?'

'No. I didn't mean that at all,' said Brooke, regretting her honesty.

'So let me buy you the book ends.'

He took them and walked back up to the cashier. Brooke stared after him, wondering how she had made him so angry.

Brooke slept for most of the rest of the journey back to the city.

'Can you drop me a block away from my apartment?' she said, uncoiling her body and stretching out her arms. They were back in the canyons of Manhattan and already she could feel anxiety creep back in as she looked around for paparazzi. Matt pulled up outside a convenience store on Lexington.

'Thanks Matt, I had a really good time,' smiled Brooke, putting her sunglasses back on.

'Me too,' said Matt. 'Although it was a long way to go for a buggy ride.'

'It's never too far for an experience like that, Matt. I could do with more friends like you who take me places like that. Nice, normal friends outside my crazy new world.'

'Hey, you love your world,' he laughed. 'Next time I see you you're going to be holding one of those rat-like little dogs under your arm.'

'Flanked by big burly bodyguards,' she laughed. As she waved him off and walked back along Lex, she suddenly realized that a much less light-hearted discussion about bodyguards with David was exactly what had made her call Matt in the first place, and would be the first thing they talked – or rowed – about as soon as he got back from Damascus. *Back to reality*, she thought with a twisted smile and strode towards home.

23

The first time Tess came back to London, it was for work, not pleasure. Neither she nor Dom were particularly surprised; as time went on it was becoming obvious that their original vision of a jet-set transatlantic relationship, with each visiting the other once a month, was almost impossible. Tess had to attend events at weekends, and Dom was often flying out to exotic resorts to report on them for the *Chronicle*. Even this visit was fraught; Tess was in England to attend the Annual UK Asgill Cosmetics sales conference at a luxury hotel in Windsor – it was a flying visit, only staying overnight at the hotel, then heading back across the pond in the morning. Meredith had suggested it would be a good idea for Tess to attend the conference, firstly to get a feel for the international side of the business, but it would also be a suitable opportunity to meet Sean, who was hosting a party in London to launch the latest Asgill fragrance, Lupin. Tess had spent the day with scores of Asgill sales consultants, brand managers, and sales teams from the UK offices. Not her favourite way to pass the day, but at least it hadn't been completely alien to her; she had been to countless focus groups when they had been trying to reposition the *Globe* and was fluent in marketing bullshit: the phrases 'dynamic multi-platform dissemination' and 'blue-sky viral paradigms' did not faze her. She had, however, been glad to escape for a drink with Leonard Carter, Meredith's brother and head of Asgill's international development.

'I'm amazed this is your first trip back to London since you joined us,' said Leonard when they had settled into a corner table of the hotel's bar. He was wearing a light-grey three-piece Prince of Wales check suit, which complemented his white hair and alert blue eyes.

'Well, I actually only left six weeks ago,' said Tess, gazing out at the view of the formal gardens. Everything seemed so much more spacious and airy after New York that even her breathing felt deeper and fuller. 'So much has happened, it seems so much longer.'

'I can imagine it feels even longer given that your boyfriend is still here,' said Leonard kindly. Tess smiled at him; he had the easy-going manner of a wealthy old man who had been around the block and seen everything that life could throw at you. She was starting to think of him as 'Uncle Leonard', like the rest of the Asgill children. Still, she didn't yet know him well enough to tell him that relations with Dom had seemed strained over the last few weeks, their conversations snappy and distant. She knew Dom wanted to be in New York too, but she was upset that he seemed to take his career frustrations out on her.

'Well, I'm back for five days at the end of this month,' said Tess vaguely. 'We can catch up then. Thanks for getting him an invitation to the party tonight, by the way.'

'The least I could do. How long have you been together?'

'Since we were twenty-one. It struck me the other day that it's been a third of my life.'

'And will you marry him?'

Tess smiled. 'I'm not a big believer in marriage.'

'Why not?'

'My parents had a difficult relationship. They were two people who shouldn't have got married and I think they only did because I came along. When I was twelve I found their marriage certificate stuffed in a book and I did the maths; they were married four months before I was born. It kind of made sense why they argued so much.'

Leonard took a drink of his Scotch, the ice cubes tinkling.

'Well, with all due respect to your parents, I've never been convinced by the argument that having failed once in love, you shouldn't have another stab at it. Isn't that what love's all about? Going into life's adventure with hope in your heart?'

'Would you remarry?'

'Perhaps,' he smiled sadly. 'My wife Marie died three years ago now. I doubt I'll ever meet anyone to match her, but I'm not too old to try.'

'Tell that to Meredith. Maybe it's time she found someone new.'

Leonard laughed at the idea. 'Oh, she'll never marry again.

They had a wonderful marriage. She told me once that the day she married Howard was the day she committed one hundred per cent to him. I don't think that's changed because he's not with us any more.'

Tess suddenly thought back to a story that Charles Devine had told her at Brooke's engagement party. A story that had been nagging at her since her arrival, a story she had since researched, although the press cuttings she had ordered had thrown up nothing beyond what Charles had told her back in March. She'd been waiting for a convenient opportunity to quiz the family on it further, but there had barely been the chance to do so. Until now.

'Was Howard faithful to Meredith?' asked Tess, unable to contain her curiosity.

'Probably not,' said Leonard with a gentle shrug. 'But it doesn't mean he had a bad marriage. Why do you ask?'

'I heard about the Olivia Martin story. People suspected Howard of murdering her, didn't they, because he was having an affair with Olivia?'

Leonard smiled and shook his head. 'Howard was a lot of things, but I don't think anyone really believed he was a murderer. In fact, personally I don't believe anyone murdered Olivia.'

She nodded. That appeared to be the general view throughout the media in 1964. Even the more scurrilous tabloid magazines like the *National Enquirer* only hinted at murder.

'Why don't people think she was murdered?'

'If you'd ever been to Riverview, where Olivia was last seen, you'd believe that too. The Mississippi is a powerful beast. We had dogs, horses go missing from the estate. The river just took them. And if Olivia had gone walking down there in the dark . . . Guests were told to stay away from the river, but she was not the sort to listen.'

'So you don't even think Howard and Olivia were having an affair?' she pressed.

'I don't think so, although Olivia was an *outrageous* flirt,' he added disapprovingly. 'The night of the wedding I saw her stroking a waiter's ass! In public. And she was there as an Asgill's ambassador, for heaven's sake.'

At that moment Asgill's UK marketing director appeared at the doorway and beckoned them to the lobby. 'Our car awaits,'

Leonard smiled. 'Let's get you into your carriage and off to meet Prince Charming. Speaking of which, have we looked into a visa for him yet?'

'Not as such, no.'

'Would you like me to?'

'It sounds an expensive process.'

Leonard smiled. 'We have money for essential projects such as bringing two hearts together.'

'I'll drink to that,' she replied slowly, still thinking about Olivia Martin.

The party was being held in a huge white house on the outskirts of Regent's Park. As Tess and Leonard pulled up alongside the Doric pillars in their black town car, there was already a parade of people in cocktail dresses and sharp suits walking in under a banner advertising Lupin. It looked great – a pretty purple bottle against a sparkling white background.

'This place is incredible,' said Tess. 'What is it?'

'An old embassy, I can't remember which one,' said Leonard. 'Sean organized it; pulled in some contacts to hire it.'

Tess was impressed. She was looking forward to meeting Sean, in fact couldn't quite believe she hadn't yet met him, considering he was without question the loose cannon in the family. The cuttings file on Sean was two inches thick. Working at the *Globe*, she had never particularly noticed his name, but once she had started looking, he was everywhere. Sean on P. Diddy's yacht in St Tropez. Sean at the winter polo in Gstaad. Sean with his arm around Sting and Trudie at a fundraiser in Monaco. He was connected, wealthy, and decadent, the dictionary definition of 'playboy'. How could he fail to be interesting, at the very least?

They left the car at the kerb and walked through the walnut double doors. Tess scanned the crowd anxiously for Dom. She was nervous that an unsuccessful reunion might deal a fatal blow to their transatlantic relationship.

For a split second she felt on edge – maybe he hadn't even come? – but then she saw him, patting his invite against the palm of his hand. She had run over this moment in her head a hundred times, knowing it would be a litmus test for whether their relationship was really in trouble or whether it was just a blip caused by pressure and distance. Tess was relieved to feel her heart give a little flutter of pleasure and she was equally pleased to see him grin as he spotted her. *Oh, he looks fantastic*, she thought.

'Here she is at last,' said Dom, hugging her. He looked her up and down: the tight curves of her Hervé Léger dress, the hint of tanned cleavage courtesy of her regular visits to the Portofino Sun Center, and seemed to approve. 'I've missed you, you know,' he added in a whisper as he slipped his hand in hers. It felt comfortable and familiar, two things that fitted together perfectly.

'Dom, meet Leonard Carter,' said Tess. 'You'll be pleased to hear that Leonard has said he'll sponsor your visa.'

'Wow!' said Dom, pumping Leonard's hand. 'Well, I can sincerely say pleased to meet you, Mr Carter.'

Leonard laughed. 'Well, I think that's enough of a reason to call for champagne all round,' he said, motioning to a waiter. He handed Tess a glass of bubbly.

'Just a few sips,' she said happily.

Amber light glowed around the room and shone off the circular zinc-topped bar at the centre. Against one wall was a huge avant-garde sculpture formed from mirrored cubes five feet wide. Lined up along each surface and lit from above were the purple Lupin bottles in random patterns. *Nice touch*, thought Tess, looking around the party with professional appreciation. It was a difficult thing to do a launch well – after all, she had attended enough in her time – and this one was very good. A great balance of beautiful people and industry players teamed with a smattering of hip celebrities, mixed together with interesting food and drink – the bar was serving something that appeared to have holly sprouting from the top – in an intriguing and unusual setting. If Sean had arranged this, she was becoming more and more intrigued.

And then she saw him. He had a square dimpled chin just like his sister Liz, and eyes that seemed to sparkle with mischievousness. Sean Asgill was walking across the room, shaking hands and exchanging whispered jokes, pressing the flesh like a pro. As he got closer, Tess could see his bespoke suit, his craggy smile and tanned skin, which surprised Tess considering he was supposed to have spent the last month in a rehab facility. Confidence oozed from every pore. No, not confidence, she corrected herself, *cockiness*. It was amazing how a few million dollars could made a guy think he was God's gift. Excusing herself from Leonard and Dom, she walked over to him, extending her hand.

'Sean Asgill?' she asked.

'That's me,' he said, switching his glass to his left hand. As they shook hands, Tess could see him checking her out.

'I'm Tess Garrett,' she said.

He started laughing, slowly at first, working up to a deep, throaty chuckle. 'You have my deepest sympathies,' he said.

'Sorry?' she asked, feeling her cheeks flush with annoyance.

'I wouldn't wish the job of taking my family in hand on anyone.'

'Well, they've got you to blame,' she smiled quietly.

'Yes,' he smirked, his pale-green eyes flashing. 'I guess I should thank you for that.'

'Well, you're welcome.'

'Although you weren't being entirely altruistic, were you? I mean, it did all work out for you too, didn't it?'

She took a deep breath. Working in newspapers for a decade had taught Tess not to suffer fools gladly, but Sean Asgill was the boss's son.

'Sean, I really don't think . . . Ugh!'

Suddenly Tess jerked backwards, coughing. A girl in a long lilac sequined dress had appeared, spraying her with the bottle of scent she was carrying on a silver platter.

'Tess, Tess,' said Sean, slapping her on the back, 'it's not acid, it's Lupin.'

She coughed a little more, then took a long drink of her champagne.

'Well, perhaps it's aimed at a younger market than you,' said Sean, with more than a hint of amusement in his voice.

'Or perhaps if she hadn't aimed it straight into my mouth,' snapped Tess.

'So you don't like it. Millions will,' he chided.

Tess tossed her hair back and cleared her throat in a vain attempt to regain a little composure.

'So, I thought you'd be at the sales conference today,' she said, trying to change the subject.

'Hey, parties like this don't magically happen,' he protested. 'I've been up since seven talking to the events planners.'

'Seven? I hope it wasn't a late night then,' she said with a hint of sarcasm.

'No later than usual,' he replied, his attention beginning to wander towards a group of giggling blondes.

'By the way, did you get my email about the charity dinners? Are you going to any of them?'

'Are we talking about the one in honour of the UN Secretary-General?' he asked, rolling his eyes.

'Okay, so it won't be very rock 'n' roll, but I still think you should go. Obama will be there. The French President, too. In fact, give me a few days' notice and I can fly over to accompany you.'

He looked back at her. 'You actually want to come to a party and hold my hand?'

'Simply to make sure we get the right photo opportunities.'

He was shaking his head and smiling. 'Come on, Tess. This is bullshit,' he said, lowering his voice.

'Bullshit?' she replied coldly.

'This ridiculous attempt at rehabilitation.'

He lowered his voice. 'Look. I had an overdose, yes. And thanks to you and your fearsome ambition, no one knows about it. So well done, Tess Garrett, and I'm sure my mother is very pleased.'

'What are you saying?' asked Tess, bristling.

'I'm saying, what if people did know that I'm not perfect? Would anyone really care? I know my mother is trying to protect Brooke and her precious fiancé, but let's be real here – who really cares what I get up to? I know the Billington family are conservative, but is David really going to dump my sister just because I'm not best friends with the President? Because I've taken drugs and inhaled.'

'Snorted and collapsed more like it.'

'Tess, it's all bullshit. Whatever I do isn't going to harm the wedding and you know it.'

'You might think it's acceptable behaviour to go to an orgy and almost flat-line on a ketamine and heroin cocktail, but I doubt Wendell Billington does. Or the American public,' Tess hissed, incensed at his lack of gratitude to both her and his own mother.

'That party was a one-off,' he said gruffly. 'I didn't know it was going to be so hardcore.'

'Well, I doubt that you just bowled up. I heard there was a ten-thousand pound-membership fee.'

Sean looked at her with a cruel smile. 'Not for people like me, honey.'

'Of course not,' she said. Tess knew that her first impression of Sean Asgill had been exactly right. He was a spoilt, condescending prick who thought that the world revolved around him and that, given the cushion of money around him, he could behave any way he chose.

'Listen, Sean, lightning can strike twice, believe me,' said Tess, the contempt in her voice barely concealed. 'There are only so many times I can bail you out. In fact, I think you've had your quota.'

His eyes narrowed. 'Sweetheart, I don't need a lecture, I don't need a baby sitter, and I certainly don't need a half-assed publicist telling me how to live my life. Do we understand one another?'

'Perfectly,' said Tess, turning on her heel and stalking towards the bar.

Arrogant, self-centred pig! she thought furiously. The nerve of the man! *'I don't need a publicist'!* Well, that's exactly what Liz had said and that's exactly what Brooke had said. Well, she was quickly learning that everyone in this damned family had a secret. *Just you wait until someone digs up yours, Sean Asgill,* she thought. *I won't be there to break your fall.*

She pushed her way to the vodka bar, snatched up a shot, and downed it in one.

'He gets under your skin, doesn't he?'

Tess looked up to see Leonard standing behind her. She shook her head, trying desperately to think of something diplomatic to say. Then she caught the smile on Leonard's face and she burst out laughing.

'He's . . . well, he's . . .'

'He's an asshole.'

'Well, I wouldn't go that far . . .'

'Perhaps you should, my dear,' said Leonard. 'He's part of your job, after all, and you need to know exactly who you're dealing with. Of course I love my nephew, he's my family and there's nothing I won't do for him, but he can be a bit of a *scoundrel*.'

Tess laughed out loud.

'The trouble is, I can see myself in Sean,' said Leonard, his wise eyes watching Sean across the room. 'When I was his age, I was just as irresponsible, just as vain.'

He chuckled as Tess looked at him.

'I had too much money, not enough focus, and I was surrounded by people who indulged me. That, I'm afraid, is Sean's problem, although I doubt he's aware of it. Underneath all that flash, Tess, is actually a very caring, sensitive man.'

Tess raised her eyebrows sceptically.

'Hard to believe, but he is.' He smiled. 'He just needs someone to knock a little sense into him. I'd love to do it myself – give him a more responsible job in the company, perhaps, because I actually think he'd thrive. But Meredith won't hear of it and, well, you can see her point,' he added, nodding towards Sean, who now had his arm around the most attractive woman in the room. Annabel, she assumed: glossy, expensively dressed, not especially beautiful up close, but the overall impression was striking. Tess was not surprised he was so shallow. 'On the other hand, *he* seems more of a catch . . .'

'Who?' asked Tess, her mind still on Sean.

Leonard pointed across the room. 'Him.' She followed his gaze. He was looking at Dom, who was deep in conversation with a man in a three-piece suit. Tess instantly felt a pang of affection. Compared to Sean Asgill, Russ Ford, and most of the men she had encountered in the past few weeks, Dom certainly was a catch. After nine years together, their relationship was not perfect, but whose was? She had met Dom just three years after her father's death and her mother's new marriage. Before Dom came along, Tess had simply thrown herself into her career, but now she supposed he provided a safe harbour for her, someone to lean and depend on. And he *was* cute. He looked up and she walked over.

'Ah, there you are,' he said. 'I thought you might have run off with Sean Asgill.'

'Ha! Not likely,' she replied, still fuming. 'He is an absolute prick.'

He laughed and pulled her into a hug. 'Come on, that's our meal ticket you're talking about there,' he smiled. 'You know your problem? You get too angry with people. Sean Asgill's only some pampered rich bloke, he's not Hitler.'

'It's just people like that make my blood boil.'

'Hey, I thought your plan was to become fabulously rich some day?' he teased.

'Yeah, so?' she asked.

'So why do you want to be rich if you can't stand rich people?'

Grabbing two glasses of champagne, Dom steered her towards

the side door, which led out onto a terrace and the walled gardens beyond. Tess felt happy and relaxed for once – tonight she was officially off duty. 'This is a great party. That was Sir Martin Sorrell I was talking to back there. We've swapped cards. Thought I might be able to swing an interview for the business section. That should earn me a few brownie points.'

Tess was only half listening. 'It smells good out here,' she said, breathing in the wet floral, dewy fragrance. It smelt of England.

Dom turned and planted a gentle kiss on her lips. 'It looks a bit like that place in Maryland we stayed at once,' he said.

'Oh yeah, that place George Washington stayed in. It seemed as if George had stayed in every house in the state.'

She remembered that hotel very fondly. They had barely left their room all weekend. In fact, the only time they had left the bed was to open the windows to let a little lazy light into the room or to collect the room service they'd asked to be left outside the door.

'Here, you've got some lipstick on your teeth,' said Dom. He took his finger and rubbed it under her lips, the gesture familiar yet intimate. She took his hand and bit his finger softly.

'Ooh,' he laughed. 'Saucy.'

'You know I've really missed you,' said Tess, meaning it this time.

He bent and brushed his lips against her neck. 'Come on, let's go.'

'I can't go,' she laughed slowly. 'I have to get back to Windsor tonight.'

'We won't be long,' he whispered, taking her hand and leading her away from the glowing lights, tinkle of glasses and laughter at the party. They disappeared out of the embassy's gates and hailed a black cab that was dropping guests off at the party.

Leaning into the driver's window, he said with a grin, 'Take us to the nearest hotel.'

Three minutes later, the nonplussed driver dropped the giggling couple at the Park House Hotel on the outer ring road. The room was shoebox-sized, with a small double bed, trouser press, and sink in the corner. Dom didn't even bother to switch on the lights as he peeled off Tess's dress and let it slide to the floor. They were both breathing heavily in their excitement as they kissed, both pulling at the buttons on Dom's shirt. Just then, Tess pulled away and sat on the edge of the bed, spreading her knees and pulling him between them. He remained standing as she unbuckled his trousers. His cock reared out in front of him and she took it in both hands. It was long and thick and she kept eye contact with him as she licked along his length, her saliva glistening in the street-lights. Still looking into his eyes, she took him into her mouth and unhooked her bra. He reached down and stroked her full breast, squeezing and rolling her nipples between his finger and thumb.

Both gasping with desire now, he pushed her back onto the bed. Taking off her high heels he started kissing her toes, the curve of her ankle, working his way up her leg with feathery kisses. His warm hands spread her legs as he flicked his tongue up the inside of her thigh, then nuzzled into her closed, secret lips with his nose and his tongue.

'Oh God, yes, yes,' she moaned, rubbing her own breasts now.

Dom inched aside her thong and pushed his tongue into her, taking long languid laps of her juices, circling her hard clitoris and up and down her slit.

'Now, now,' she panted. 'I want you, I want you.'

Grinning, he guided his cock into her slowly, slowly, feeding it inch by inch until he was buried deep inside. Impatiently, she thrust her hips up towards him and they fell back, their bodies together in rhythm and motion. His nose and chin were damp and musky from her juices as she took his face in both hands and kissed him, sucking on his tongue.

His lips moved down over her swollen nipples, biting and sucking, her arms splayed out behind her, grabbing at the pillows. The pleasure was intense now, her passion heightened by weeks of suppressed emotions: the anger from her confrontation with Sean, the longing and frustration of her separation from Dom, all building to a crescendo.

'Oh Jesus, oh Christ!' she cried out as she came in wave after wave. She clenched herself as tight as she could around his cock, her hips bucking upwards, her nails digging into Dom's taut buttocks. He fell down on top of her, spent and exhausted. They had not had sex like that in a long time. Ever. She felt a rush of excitement, as if she was falling in love all over again. She rolled over and folded herself into the curve of his body, wondering if it took being apart to bring some people back together. Lying there, she felt that their relationship wasn't just fixed, but infinitely better. He turned to her and smiled.

'I hope these walls aren't paper-thin.'

'Who cares?' she grinned, nestling into him.

'I can't wait to come to New York.'

'In which case, let's get back to the party and talk about that visa.'

24

Jewel Cay was even more beautiful than Brooke remembered. She hadn't visited Leonard Carter's colonial-style home, perched on a tiny private island in the Florida Keys, for years – before college, in fact. In the interim, Jewel Cay's grounds had grown more lush with foliage and, somehow, the water surrounding it had taken on an even brighter sparkle. Thankfully, David also loved the estate on sight, although in Brooke's mind it would be hard to dislike the proud white house with its long decked porch, the hammocks swinging between shady banana trees and manicured lawns sloping down to the turquoise Caribbean. No wonder Leonard had cut down his workload at Asgill's in the past few years, thought Brooke. During the winter months, he only worked two weeks out of every four, allowing him to come down and stay here. Since the death of his wife three years earlier, Leonard had begun to refer to Jewel Cay as 'The Sanctuary'. Brooke was honoured that he would allow her and David to share its tranquil atmosphere.

'This is just *glorious*,' said Alessandro Franchetti, watching a pod of dolphins leap across the bay through the wide French windows. Behind him it was getting dark, the sun setting in banners of vivid red, lavender, and bronze across the sky. Alessandro had arrived two hours earlier in order to see Jewel Cay at night – Brooke and David's wedding was to be at sunset. Alessandro was wearing a white linen suit, presumably in deference to his surroundings, although Brooke giggled to herself that he looked more like an up-market pimp. In Alessandro's flamboyant entourage were two representatives from Miami's leading wedding caterers, his handsome PA, who looked as if he belonged on the Versace runway, and two other assistants, whom he mysteriously referred to as the 'setup team'. Clicking his fingers, Alessandro beckoned them to follow him to the front of the house. Brooke gasped as she stepped outside. Somehow, since his arrival, candles had been placed all around the fountain on the front lawn, while strings of fairy lights seemed to drip from the mahogany trees.

'Alessandro, this is magical,' said Brooke, her hands to her mouth. 'Is this what your assistants have been doing?'

He gave a casual shrug.

'I just wanted to get us in the mood.'

'What for? I thought he was getting us to sample canapé options,' whispered David as Alessandro sat them at a small linen-draped table under a tree.

Alessandro clapped his hands. Soft jazz floated from inside the house and two white-coated waiters came out holding trays of tiny, delicate food.

'Imagine it's December the twenty-ninth, your wedding day. Close your eyes, David. Come on.'

Brooke took a small ball of choux pastry off the silver platter. As she bit the delicate crust, soft mousse dissolved onto her tongue. It was exquisite.

'Wow. David, try one of these.'

David gingerly picked one up and popped it into his mouth.

'Umm,' he nodded, 'that's really good.'

'Of course it's good,' said Alessandro, his eyes wide open. 'The guy who made it used to be Alain Ducasse's pastry chef. That mousse is truffle-scented.'

Each canapé seemed more delicious than the one preceding it: caviar on rye and pumpkin brittle, topped with crème fraîche and chives from England, spoons of Finnish cloudberry sorbet, the softest beef carpaccio, tartlets filled with rare cheese and asparagus.

Finally Alessandro clapped his hands and the waiters disappeared.

'These are my favourite caterers,' said Alessandro, sotto voce. 'I want to go with them, but the choice is entirely yours. They've signed a confidentiality agreement – but you never know. I dated a chef once: terrible gossip. He had to go of course, gossip is toxic in my professional life as you can imagine.'

David covered his mouth with a napkin to hide his laugh. 'I think they're amazing, Alessandro,' said Brooke. 'I love the food,

I love the lights, and I also love your idea to have the ceremony around the pool.'

'Well, I haven't quite worked out how we're going to build an aisle over the water, but leave it with me. In the meantime I've auditioned five Cuban jazz bands already. Miami-based but from Havana originally. One of them is especially cute.'

'We want to know what they sound like, not look like,' smiled David.

'I like a nice all-round package,' said Alessandro briskly.

'So I heard,' quipped Brooke. She had found Alessandro hard work at first but, having spent many hours with him, both in person and on the phone, she was beginning to enjoy his company. It was hard not to be dragged along in the slipstream of his seemingly endless enthusiasm.

'You are a very naughty young lady,' said Alessandro, swatting her on the arm.

Together the three of them walked through the grounds, talking through Alessandro's 'vision'. There would be jugglers and fire-eaters, a champagne bar by the ocean and an extravagant firework display at midnight. David was quiet throughout Alessandro's walk-through. Brooke watched him carefully as Alessandro explained how he planned to fly a DJ in from Paris for the dance floor they would build by the pool. In the ten days since he'd been back from Syria, he'd been spending long days in the studio, plus there had been a couple of big benefits including the Costume Institute Gala at the Met. No wonder he looked tired.

'Are we both okay for the second canapé-tasting at ten tomorrow?' asked Alessandro. 'It's with Starlight caterers. They're based in South Beach and they've done fabulous parties for Madonna and Julio Iglesias.'

Brooke nodded, her eyes still on David. Her fingers moved up to touch the scarf around her neck. It was a beautiful piece of copper silk, shot through with gold thread, which David had brought back from Syria. They'd made up on the telephone after their quarrel about the bodyguards, but Brooke had still been relieved to receive it.

'Wonderful, we'll see you then,' said Alessandro, summoning his PA and assistants, jumping into a waiting boat to take them back to the mainland. When the boat's engine had died away, all was quiet again, just the occasional rustle of the palm trees in the breeze.

Brooke walked back inside the house and poured them both a drink of iced tea from a pitcher.

'Do we have to do all that again tomorrow?' said David after a few moments.

'Do what?'

'Food theatre,' he said with a half-grin.

'This is really important, David,' said Brooke, trying to control her annoyance. 'And he's not being theatrical, he's just putting the food in context.'

David laughed lightly and shook his head. 'Honey, I think you need to reassess your definition of "important".'

'So you don't think our wedding is important?'

'Of course it's important. Jewel Cay is important. I needed to see it and I love it; I couldn't think of a more magical place to marry you in. But I'm being honest here: do I care if we have tea-smoked duck blinis or mini foie-gras mousses? Frankly, I don't.'

She recoiled, piqued at his flippancy.

I'm beginning to wonder how much you actually care about the wedding, period,' she snapped. 'If it's relative to how much you've done for it, then I'm beginning to think you don't care a great deal.'

She knew she was being a little unfair. David's workload was twice hers, but it annoyed her that he seemed quite content to leave every last detail and decision to her. She wondered suddenly if he would be like this if he was marrying Alicia Wintrop, and then stopped herself.

All she wanted was for David to hug her and reassure her that he wanted to marry her more than anything in the world, but instead he ran his hand through his hair irritably.

'Brooke, I have had a really tough week,' he said. 'I was just hoping this could be a break for us too. I mean, how often do we get away together these days?'

'And how often do we get married?'

David looked at her. 'I didn't come all this way to get into a fight.'

'Well, I didn't start it.'

'Neither did I.'

There was a tense pause and Brooke turned away, frowning more in puzzlement than anger. One of the reasons she'd been so sure that David was the right man for her was because they didn't row and always felt so easy and natural in each other's company. But recently, they'd had arguments about David's ex, Alicia Wintrop, and her involvement in the *Oracle* story, a spat about the bodyguard, plus dozens of other little cross words and disagreements. Each of them had been patched up by flowers or sex, but it all left an anxious feeling hovering over her like a black cloud.

'So why are we arguing, David?' she asked. 'Ever since we became engaged that's all we seem to have been doing.'

His voice was cold. 'That's a slight exaggeration.'

'Well, shall I be a little more specific then?' she continued. 'We argue whenever you're around, which hasn't been a great deal, has it?'

'So this is what it's *really* about? My job? Because I'm not in New York twenty-four/seven? Is that why you've been running around having lunch dates with Matt Palmer.'

'I met up with Matt once.' Brooke wished she'd never told him and was certainly glad she hadn't mentioned it was a six-hour round trip into Pennsylvania. 'It was just to say thanks for him looking at my foot.'

'Of course, his tender loving care,' he said sarcastically.

She looked at him as if observing a stranger. She'd never thought he'd be capable of jealousy, it just wasn't part of his personality; he had too much old-money self-confidence for that.

'David, when have I ever complained to you about seeing female friends?' It was true, she didn't complain, but it sometimes bothered her. She was glad David wasn't like his father and brother, traditional old-money alpha males who frequented private 'men-only' clubs like the Racquet and Tennis Club, and huddled together after dinner to talk about sports and stocks and shares. But David had an uncommon amount of female friends, especially at work, who were always calling him up to ask him to lunch or just to 'catch up'. It certainly bothered her, even if she didn't show it.

David looked over at her and his eyes softened. 'What's really wrong here, Brooke? You would tell me if something was wrong, wouldn't you?'

His expression was grave and earnest; Brooke called it his 'big story' face, the face he pulled when reporting from war zones or disaster areas. *God, is that what he's thinking about our relationship?* she wondered.

221

'You know there's something wrong, David,' she said quietly. 'Remember how good things were before we decided to get married?'

A deep frown appeared between his brows. 'Are you saying you don't want to get married?'

He sounded like David Frost quizzing Richard Nixon.

'No,' she said, honestly. 'But don't you miss the time when we could go to the movies, or eat hot dogs in Central Park without it being a circus?'

She had thought a lot lately about what point it had all become so crazy. The press attention had sneaked up on her. At first it was the odd photograph in *US Weekly* or *People* of them coming from a party, the occasional chase down the street by an enthusiastic pap. That had actually been quite exciting the first few times. Brooke supposed that before they had gone public as a couple there was no reason to suppose David's relationship with her was any more serious than it had been with any of his other girlfriends. But their engagement in February had caught the media by surprise. The day the story broke there had been at least fifty reporters outside her apartment.

'Yes, I loved that time,' said David. 'But I love the time we spend together now too. I know I'm busy, but it won't be forever, honey, I promise.'

He reached out for her and pulled her into his arms. 'That scarf looks really pretty on you.'

She grinned, remembering all the little gifts and trinkets he'd brought back from his travels. He kissed her bare shoulder, his lips moving up to her neck, to the soft curve of her cheek.

'Hmm. That's lovely,' she smiled, her anxiety melting away.

As their kisses became deeper, he used both hands to lift off her slip dress.

'Maybe we *should* argue more often,' she smiled, letting him push her down onto one of the soft cream sofas.

'Maybe we should,' he growled, taking off his T-shirt and unsnapping her bra. He lowered his mouth back onto hers, his taste warm and sweet, and as his dark chest hair brushed over her tight, erect nipples, she groaned with arousal and spread her thighs. Suddenly David pulled up on his elbows, his head cocked.

'Shit, my work phone.'

'Leave it, leave it, leave it,' she begged, linking her arms around his neck. He began to kiss her again, but the insistent ringing continued.

'Honey, I have to get it,' said David, pulling away.

'You were the one who said we were on holiday.'

'It could be important,' he said, getting up and reaching for the phone.

She watched his face cloud with concern, her ardour cooling. Brooke had a love-hate relationship with David's job. She smiled when her friends called him 'Action Man', and she enjoyed the fact that he was involved in important world events, even having some influence over them, however small. But it also bothered her every time he was sent away. David was not a war correspondent and rarely reported from the line of fire – David suspected his father had spies inside the newsroom making sure he never went anywhere near a mortar or landmine – but still, he was reporting from hot spots such as Palestine and Sudan and there always seemed to be some element of danger.

'What's wrong?' she asked, pulling her dress back on.

'It's the studio,' he said, covering the phone's mouthpiece. 'A boat is on fire just off Islamorada.'

Brooke's eyes widened. 'But that's in the Keys, isn't it?' she asked. 'Is it national news?'

He nodded. 'The boat was full of people. Women and kids. A fishing trawler is trying to get people out of the water now. Search and rescue are on the way there.'

David pulled his T-shirt back on awkwardly, trying to keep the phone to his ear.

'I'm on hold,' he said, 'they're trying to get hold of a local cameraman.'

'They want you to do a broadcast?'

David perched on the edge of the sofa. 'This is immigrant smuggling gone horribly wrong.'

'Immigrant smuggling?'

He held up a finger. He was back on the phone.

'Great,' he said into the receiver, his voice clipped and business-like. 'No, thirty minutes isn't fast enough. Okay, just get there as soon as you can.'

She watched him, mesmerized, as he shifted into full gear, gathering his things, dialling numbers, barking orders. She found it strangely erotic. Finally he reached for his jacket.

'So what's happening?' asked Brooke.

'I'm going down there. I can be there quicker than a news team coming down from Miami.'

'I'm coming with you,' she said suddenly, jumping to her feet.

'Honey, no,' said David, 'you stay here.'

Brooke shook her head adamantly. 'I'm not staying here thinking about canapés when there's kids drowning in the sea ten miles away.'

He gave her a grateful smile and took her hand. They ran out of the house took the boat back to the mainland and then jumped into Leonard's awaiting Jeep.

'So tell me about immigrant smuggling,' said Brooke. As they bumped along, her heart was racing at the drama of it all and, given her worried thoughts only minutes ago, she was excited to be involved with David's other life for once. She reached over and squeezed his hand. One of the many things she loved about David was that he seemed to know everything. He was not intellectual in the way those foul people at Estella Winston's party had been, but his head was like a dusty old library, packed with endless facts.

'Well, it's been going on for years,' said David, not taking his eyes from the road. 'Everyone thinks it's all about smuggling drugs in Florida, but human trafficking is, if anything, even bigger business. Every day of the week, you can almost guarantee there's some boat sliding up to some deserted beach along the Keys, dropping off people from Cuba, Puerto Rico, even Mexico. Smugglers can get up to ten thousand dollars a head, so if you're ferrying over thirty people, that's three hundred thousand a trip. It's illegal, of course, but the penalties for transporting heroin and cocaine and those for carrying a handful of farm workers just don't compare.'

'And what happens to the people?' asked Brooke, fascinated now.

'Ah, well, that's where it gets controversial,' said David. 'Generally, if they make it to land they can stay, but if they are found at sea they are sent back home. Although that only applies to Cubans. People from Haiti are usually sent straight back.'

'That doesn't seem fair.'

'Life's not fair, honey,' said David, pulling the car to a stop and pointing out to sea.

They had turned off the main road onto a beach track with what looked like a landing jetty, surrounded by vehicles, their lights still on. On either side, the beach looked grey in the moonlight, but out in the inky distance, possibly less than a thousand metres offshore, was a fireball. Above it, she could see a helicopter training its spotlight onto the choppy blackness of the sea. A pick-up truck was parked by the jetty and a tall man jumped out. David climbed out to meet him.

'Charlie, hi,' he said. 'You made good time.'

'We're the first media to get here,' said the cameraman, already unloading his equipment.

'Have you spoken to the police yet?'

Brooke could see the man's teeth flash in the Jeep's headlights. 'I thought I'd save that treat for you.'

Brooke saw her fiancé run over towards a police cruiser, its red and blue lights swirling.

'Sir, you're going to have to move back,' said the officer. He shone his flashlight into David's face and his tone immediately changed. 'Sorry, Mr Billington,' he said more politely. 'But you're still going to have to move.'

'How bad is it?'

'Can't say,' said the officer vaguely. 'I do know they're pulling bodies from the sea.'

'Alive or dead?' asked David without emotion.

'I don't know,' said the officer grimly. David quickly asked him a few more questions, memorizing the facts and figures.

'Please, sir,' said the officer, holding up his hands. 'You're going to have to move further down the beach. I'll speak to my captain, and see if someone will come talk to you later.'

They jumped in Charlie's pick-up and moved a hundred metres down the beach to the edge of the police cordon.

'Okay, we're not going to wait for the official version,' said David decisively. 'Let's roll from here, Charlie, with the fire in the background.'

He looked back at Brooke. 'Charlie can feed this straight back to the studio in New York from that little satellite dish in the back of his pick-up.'

Charlie grabbed some lights and set them up on the sand, running power cables from the truck. David stood in front of them and winked at Brooke.

'Well, this is going to be basic,' he said under his breath. She could see his sheer professionalism, his passion for what he was doing. She ran over to him and straightened his collar and smoothed down his hair, then ducked out of sight of the camera. He looked straight ahead, paused, then launched into an eloquent monologue about the events unfolding before them.

He's good, thought Brooke, unable to take her eyes from her fiancé. He had no speechwriter, no script, and few hard facts available, yet he spoke with knowledge and authority. He wasn't just good, he was brilliant. She felt a rush of pleasure, which turned into a curl of lust. She stopped herself, thinking how completely inappropriate it was to be thinking about sex when there was a search and rescue effort going on behind her.

Brooke's eyes drifted out behind David. The glow from the fire was illuminating the tops of the waves, like the last rays of a sunset. If it wasn't for the horror of what was happening out there, she thought, you might even think it was pretty. Suddenly she stopped, narrowing her eyes. There was something at the water line. Was it seaweed? Debris from the boat? Then she realized it was a body. Before she could think, she was running towards the sea.

'David!' she shouted. She turned and saw him drop his microphone and begin sprinting across the sand towards her.

Brooke splashed into the water, freezing cold against her bare legs, but David got there first. He hauled the body out and, with Brooke's help, dragged it onto the sand. David glanced up at Brooke and said simply: 'Get help.' Then he bent over the woman and began to pump her chest.

Brooke ran across the beach, towards the police cordon, waving her arms.

'Quick!' she screamed to a paramedic beyond the barrier. 'We have a woman over here.'

When she got back, David was bent low over the woman, his hand under her chin as he blew air into her lungs. Finally, a small plume of water exited her mouth, her whole body shaking as she turned onto her side, coughing violently. An ambulance roared up to them, the noise of the siren surrounding them.

David jumped out of the way as the paramedics got to work. Brooke threw her arms around him he squeezed her back as tightly as he could, kissing her neck. She didn't mind the cold wetness of his T-shirt sticking to her, she didn't mind the camera pointed at her tear-stained face. She felt safe and proud, in the embrace of the man she was going to marry.

'I love you, David. I love you so much,' she said, not wanting to let him go. And for the first time in months, she was more sure of those words than anything else in her life.

25

Two weeks after her trip to London for the Lupin launch, Tess was bustling around her apartment, getting ready for a day out in the Big Apple with Dom. After their glorious reunion in the low-rent hotel, she could barely remember a time she had felt so excited to see him. He had arrived late the previous night, but today Tess had a packed itinerary planned for him as she was keen to share all her newly discovered favourite places with him: the Conservatory Garden in Central Park, high up on One Hundred and Third Street which, at this time of year, was a riot of colour, or the Morgan Library in midtown, which housed everything from a Gutenberg Bible to Bob Dylan's original handwritten lyrics to 'Blowin' In The Wind'. Later, they would share freshwater crab at the Oyster Bar at Grand Central Station and hot chocolate at the Tea & Sympathy café, a slice of old England in the midst of the Manhattan exotica. Tess was beginning to think of New York as her home – at least for now – and she wanted to show it off like a prize.

It was nine a.m. by the time Tess walked into the living room. She had already taken a shower and put on her carefully chosen outfit for the day: a white skinny-rib T-shirt and dark J Brand jeans that made her legs look especially long and lean. After the shock of putting on five pounds in her first three weeks in the city, she had been on a ruthless eight-hundred-calorie-a-day grapefruit-and-egg diet given to her by one of the girls at work, which had miraculously shifted almost a stone. Feeling sexy, happy, and ready for anything, she ran through to the kitchen, which was flooded by New York sun.

'Hey, sexy,' she called through to the lounge, 'you ready for the Grand Tour?'

His body clock shocked by the jet lag, Dom had been up for hours and was lounging on the sofa, reading the *New York Post*. His hair was dishevelled and he was still in his boxer shorts and an old Ramones T-shirt, bought one Christmas from Harvey Nicks and now relegated to sleepwear.

He ignored the question, pointed and held up the paper. 'Is this your doing?'

'What?'

'How David saved my life,' he read in a faux theatrical voice. 'The survivors speak. See inside for an eight-page special.'

Tess stuck out her tongue at him. 'It's been one of the biggest stories of the year,' she said. 'It must have even reached that little backwater of London.'

Dom snorted. 'What? A bunch of boat people capsizing in the Carribean? That's hardly going to make the London *Times*.'

Tess brought two mugs of tea through. 'Actually, the BBC News reported it quite extensively. So did your paper. And it was also a lot more serious than your little summary. Thirty people died, Dom. It was horrific.'

Dom shrugged. 'But David really saved someone's life?' he asked. 'You sure it's not just his family positioning him on the political launch pad?'

She swiped him on the arm. 'You're a cynic, Dom Barton.'

'Speaks the professional PR.'

Although the incident in Florida had happened five days ago, the papers were still running stories with a host of 'new' photographs and first-hand accounts from survivors. Unsurprisingly, David had come out of it a hero. The Billingtons' PR machine had arranged a two-page interview with him in the *Washington Post*, and his opinions on immigration controls had kicked off the topic as a hot debate on talk shows on TV and radio across the country. Although her phone had been ringing off the hook, Tess couldn't take credit for this particular PR blitz. The cameraman on the beach had caught the whole drama in Technicolor and it had been beamed live across the world; David had created his own spin. Brooke, too, was now seen as the Florence Nightingale of society for her part in the rescue. *Us* magazine had run a front cover with the words 'Saviour of the

Sand'. Tess couldn't have created more positive press if she had tried for years. Dom handed her a plate with a cream cheese and lox bagel on it, and she took a delicate bite; she didn't want to mess up her lipstick.

'So where's Jemma?' asked Dom.

'Left early this morning. She's gone to see Cat in Toronto,' she said, reaching out to squeeze his bare knee. 'So we're all alone.'

Dom shook his head. 'Which is how it would be all the time if you hadn't invited her to live with you. Honestly, Tess, I can't believe you've come four thousand miles across the Atlantic Ocean to have Jemma back in the spare room.'

Tess had to stop herself frowning, upset that his good mood in London had evaporated. She put his crabbiness down to jet lag and didn't want to make it a bigger deal than it was. 'Dom, I like having her around,' she said softly. 'It's pretty lonely out here, you know – and besides, the Asgills only agreed to hire her if they didn't have to pay her accommodation as well. By the time you move over she'll have found somewhere else.'

Dom stood up and paced over to the window. 'Speaking of the apartment, I'm just not sure there's going to be enough room for the two of us.'

'It's not huge, but we'll manage.'

'*Not huge?* I've seen saunas bigger than this place. I mean, where are my golf clubs going to go?'

'Golf? In Manhattan?' laughed Tess.

'Hey, I read that David is a keen player,' said Dom defensively. 'He must be a member of some nice club.'

She smiled as she took a long slurp of tea. 'David and Brooke are lovely, but I'm not exactly best friends with them. It's not like they're always inviting me to come round for dinner or play golf.'

Dom looked disapproving. 'That attitude, baby, is exactly what's holding you back. Why do you think you never got one of the really big jobs at the papers?'

'Because they never came up?'

'No, networking,' said Dom. 'I mean, you were features editor of a national newspaper at twenty-three, so it's not for lack of talent, but that's not enough on its own. You need to get close to the people who can help you up the ladder.'

Tess briefly thought of her one-night stand with the *Globe*'s chief exec's son, the break that had really got her career moving, and turned away, feeling herself flush.

'Tess, come on,' insisted Dom, not unkindly. 'You've got to start being a player if we're going to get on over here.'

And there it was again – 'we'. The truth was that Dom wasn't concerned about Tess's career or how much she enjoyed her job; he was talking about his own position in the media world, what Tess could do for him. It was a side of Dom she had always tried to ignore in the past, hoping it was just youthful insecurity, but over the years his bitterness at his own advancement seemed to have increased. She bit her lip, for a moment remembering their night in London at the launch. How handsome Dom had looked; how charming and attentive he had been. How mind-blowingly fantastic the sex had been. And how excited she had been over the last two weeks at the thought of him getting a visa. There was no question that she loved him. But at times like this she wondered if she actually *liked* him.

Suddenly her thoughts were disturbed by the doorbell.

'Expecting someone?' asked Dom.

'No,' said Tess, shaking her head. There was a sudden unpleasant note in his voice. What was he implying? That she was constantly on call, or that she was used to having 'gentleman callers'? Either way, it wasn't nice.

'Oh hang on . . .' she said with a slight groan.

Tess ran down the four flights to the front door and, as she had expected, she found Jack Donovan, her eleven-year-old admirer, standing there slurping on a 7 Up. The kid had been 'popping round' with alarming frequency over the past few weeks. Tess did actually enjoy his company, he was funny and opinionated and actually very bright, but she already had a flatmate, she didn't need another lodger.

'Hi,' said Jack, taking the straw out of his mouth. 'Can I come in?'

She winced. 'Actually, my boyfriend's here. I told you he was coming last week, remember?'

'Cool, I can meet him?' said Jack, ignoring the hint and pushing past her.

She followed him up the stairs and just reached the lounge as Dom looked up, startled. 'Er, hello . . .' he said.

'Hiya,' said Jack confidently, offering his hand to Dom. 'I'm Jack, Tess has told me all about you. I'm not disturbing anything, am I? My mum was supposed to be coming but she phoned to say she's gonna be a couple of hours late. My dad is painting my bedroom and the place stinks.'

'Jack,' smiled Tess quickly. 'Go grab yourself something from the kitchen.'

'Cool. Just gonna use the bathroom first.'

Dom's face was a mixture of horror and outrage. 'Who the *hell* is that?'

'Just some kid that lives down the street,' said Tess, blushing.

'*And?* What's he doing here?'

'His dad is single parent,' said Tessa keeping her voice low. 'He pops round every now and then when it gets a bit much at home.'

'So you're telling me you have a little kid coming round to your house all the time?' he said incredulously. Tess found herself bristling, feeling strangely protective of the boy. Okay, so Jack's unannounced visits could be a little irritating when she had so few spare hours in the week to herself; last week he had appeared seconds before she was about to step out of the door to get a pedicure. But he was just a kid. A smartarse with a little too much lip, sure, but he was still a kid who had problems at home and needed sanctuary from them every now and then.

'He's funny,' said Tess, 'and I feel sorry for him. His dad's struggling to keep him at home, I think. He's a handyman and works a few shifts in a gym. I don't think they have much money.'

'Oh yes? And how much do you see of his dad?' said Dom sulkily.

'Oh for goodness' sake, Dom,' said Tess. 'Stop being so stupid. I've met his dad twice – in the street.'

Dom snorted. 'It just seems a bit weird.'

'What's *weird* about it?' she asked, beginning to lose patience.

'Tess, you've come to New York to mix with people like the Billingtons, even the Asgills, not single-parent labourers and their tearaway sons.'

Tess gaped at him with disbelief. 'Dom, you are the most frightful snob sometimes.'

'Snob?' laughed Dom. 'You're a fine one to talk, setting up dinner at Per Se tomorrow.'

Tess actually gasped. It felt as if she'd been slapped in the face.

She had been so excited about getting them a table at Per Se, widely believed to be the best restaurant in a city awash with amazing eating places, that she had told Dom about it as soon as he had arrived the night before. Per Se had a seventeen-course menu and a two-month waiting list, but Tess had used Brooke's name to jump the queue. It was a huge coup – there were people on the Upper East Side who would kill for a table and she was simply stunned that Dom would twist something she had lovingly arranged as a special romantic treat into a negative.

Jack came back through the door, polishing an apple on his shirt, then taking a bite.

'Hey, I like your T-shirt,' he said to Dom. 'What do they sing?'

'The Ramones?' he stuttered, momentarily floored. 'Oh, you know. Just stuff.'

Jack started laughing. 'Why are you wearing their T-shirt if you don't know any of their songs?'

Tess spurted out her tea.

'Tess says you're moving to New York,' Jack went on chattily.

'Probably, yes,' said Dom, clearly uncomfortable.

'Cool. Maybe we could go and see a band or something.'

'But you're about ten,' sneered Dom.

'Twelve next week.'

Just then, a muffled hip-hop tune came from Jack's jeans. He scrabbled to pull a bright-orange cell phone from his pocket. Looking at the screen, he tutted.

'Shit, it's mom. She's there already.'

'Jack,' said Tess. 'Don't swear.'

'Guess I shouldn't be surprised,' he said. 'Mom's new boyfriend has this super-fast car. An Aston Martin DB9. James Bond's car.'

Dom looked over. 'Actually James Bond drives the DB7,' he said, a superior note in his voice. 'What does he do, your mum's boyfriend?'

'Banker.'

'Aren't they all,' said Dom, climbing off the sofa. 'I'm going for a shower. We're going out very soon,' he added pointedly.

When he was gone, Jack grabbed Tess's arm and whispered in her ear. 'Can you walk me back to the apartment?' he hissed, looking warily towards the bathroom. 'Just you.'

'I'm kind of busy, Jack,' said Tess. 'Dom and I have a really busy day. I don't see him too often, you know.'

'Please?' he said, his eyes wide. 'My mum and her boyfriend are collecting me and I want my mum to think . . .' He tailed off.

'What?'

'I want her to think that my dad has girlfriends too,' he said, colouring a little. 'Especially pretty ones with smart clothes like you.'

Shaking her head, Tess grabbed her coat. 'Come on then, be quick. I want to be back before Dom gets out of the shower.'

When they were on the street, Jack cast a sidelong glance up at Tess.

'He doesn't like kids, does he?' he said.

'No, not really,' smiled Tess, playfully snatching Jack's apple and taking a bite.

She thought back to a holiday they had taken two years earlier to Antigua, a press trip where Dom was supposed to be checking out a new five-star boutique hotel. Tess had missed her period and, convinced she was pregnant, blurted it out to Dom as they had been about to leave the hotel. Dom had been silent on the nine-hour journey home, his eyes fixed on the seat-back in front of him even when he wasn't watching the movies.

His first words when they landed at Heathrow were, 'You'd better buy a pregnancy test, then.' It wasn't until they were back in the relative safety of the Battersea Park flat, Tess nervously clutching her little paper Boots bag in front of her, that they had talked about it.

'So what if I'm pregnant?' she had asked. She was scared and excited at the same time. She'd been twenty-seven, hardly a teen mother.

'Do you really want kids?' asked Dom.

'I don't know,' said Tess honestly. 'Not now. But, I suppose. What about you?'

Dom had paused for a long while before he answered. 'I'm not sure I do,' he had said quietly. 'In fact, I'm not sure I ever do. Our lives are just too good. Why should we have children just because people expect us to?'

Dom was never one for baring his soul, but this time she knew he was being truthful. In all their years together they had never had 'the children conversation', she supposed because neither of them wanted to admit to their own feelings. As it happened, Tess wasn't pregnant. Her period finally came along a week late.

Probably stress. She would be lying if she said she wasn't relieved, but there was still a part of her that had been disappointed.

'Don't mind Dom,' said Tess as they turned into Jack's street. 'He's just a little jet-lagged and grumpy. I'm sure he will take you to see a band when he comes over.'

Jack shrugged, as if he didn't care much one way or the other. Tess guessed he was used to adults making promises that might not come true.

'My mum wants another baby,' said Jack frankly. 'I hear her talking on the phone when she thinks I'm asleep. But she has to marry Steven first.'

'Steven? I assume that's her boyfriend? How long has she been seeing him?'

'About six months. Mom says that's long enough and that she isn't going to wait around if he isn't serious.'

They walked in silence to Jack's apartment building. Jack's dad Kevin was standing on the street with a black overnight bag, which he handed to Jack as they walked up.

'Hi Tess,' he nodded. Tess could see that his hands and face were flecked with blue paint. A petite woman with long black hair and an impatient expression was standing at the bottom of the stoop. Jack's mother Melissa, presumably. Standing a couple of feet away, Tess could smell her make-up, thick and floral.

'We said ten thirty, Jack,' said the woman sharply.

'You said you were going to be late,' he replied quietly.

Tess watched how Jack seemed to instantly withdraw into himself, the confident boy she knew shrinking before her eyes. She wanted to reach out and hug him. Instead, she looked over at the gunmetal-grey sports car parked next to them. It was a DB9, all right. A silver-haired man in chinos and a patterned golf shirt got out of the car and pulled his seat forward.

'Hop in, sport,' he said with forced cheerfulness. Reluctantly, Jack walked over and got into the car's cramped rear seat. When the door had slammed shut, Melissa turned to Kevin.

'And what's he wearing?' she demanded. Jack had on his usual uniform of super-baggy trousers and chunky trainers. All the kids around the Village wore them; he told Tess he got them in an ultra-cool skate shop on Broadway.

'What? Jesus, Melissa, it's just what he usually wears,' replied Kevin with resigned annoyance.

'One of Steven's business colleagues is having a party in Greenwich,' she snapped. 'It's going to be full of very nice kids.'

'Well, *Jack* is a nice kid.'

Melissa was shaking her head. Tess glanced over to Jack, sitting in the back seat, and wondered if he could hear the bickering. Tess knew very well what that was like; in fact, Melissa's expressions and tone of voice vividly reminded her of her own mother's hectoring manner. There were rarely any raised voices and certainly no violence in the Garrett household, but the atmosphere was still always stiff and hostile, and somehow that was worse, like a constant cloud of disapproval smothering everything. Over the years Tess had seen up close how marital disappointment had affected both her parents. Her father Graham had become more timid and eager to please, while her mother Sally became more cross and impatient, her voice developing a permanent arch inflection, as if she could distance herself from life's constant letdowns if she never enjoyed anything. That might have been tolerable when the Garretts lived in London and Sally had a wide circle of friends and a part-time job in a boutique, which itself was a substitute for the career in fashion she had always wanted. But when Graham bought the pub in Suffolk as a way of trying to make a fresh start, her mother had seemed to retreat from them completely. At first, her dissatisfaction at being 'dragged out to the sticks', as she put it, had manifested itself as tiredness. Sally complained that she could never work a late night in the pub because she was 'exhausted', 'headachy', or 'depressed'. After a while, she stopped coming down to the pub at all. In the end, it was no great surprise when she left them altogether for a life back in London.

Tess was shaken from her memories when she heard Kevin speak. 'So what time will he be back tomorrow?'

'Around six,' she replied, looking suspiciously at Tess. 'So maybe you can be ready this time, huh?'

Tess watched as Melissa stalked down to the gunmetal grey car, which shot off down the street as soon as she closed her door. She saw Jack's face in the rear window; he was giving her an okay sign. Kevin sighed and rubbed his paint-splattered face.

'He's a rich guy,' he said, almost to himself. 'All she's ever wanted, really. But she's still as uptight as she ever was.'

Tess simply nodded. 'Well, I'd better get back to my apartment,' she said. She didn't want to get sucked into the internal workings of another bad relationship. She'd had enough of that to last her a lifetime.

26

Paula Asgill only had to wait five weeks and three days before her daughter was invited to Princess Katrina's East Seventy-Second Street town house. Strictly speaking, Casey hadn't been singled out for the play-date. By happy accident, Carlotta's sixth birthday was in May and, in an effort to get her fully integrated with her new classmates, her mother had decided to throw a party at her house. Even so, Paula felt a sense of triumph when the stiff, pale-pink invitation bearing Carlotta's family crest arrived by courier at the house. She had immediately gone down to FAO Schwarz, the toy store where Carlotta's birthday list was held, to ensure that Casey could be assigned one of the best gifts on the list. Paula had then spent hours in Bonpoint on Madison Avenue selecting a new outfit for her daughter. But if Paula had put careful consideration into her daughter's appearance, it was nothing compared to the agony of deciding what to wear herself. Standing in her walk-in closet in just her Hanro underwear, her hair already cut and blow-dried by Paul Podlucky that morning, Paula silently bemoaned the fact that she had not one piece of couture to wear. She flipped through the racks dismissively. To her left were rows of white bags that contained her evening gowns. Above them, in see-through boxes, were other dresses that had been worn more than a handful of times; clearly they could not be seen out in public again until she handed them down to Casey and Amelia at sixteen, when they would be sufficiently vintage. Skirts in an assortment of neutral shades were to her right, colour coordinated cashmere tops were behind her. Her shoes were lined up in perfect symmetry, six pairs per row, like soldiers on parade, not one even slightly scuffed or dirty. Finally she picked up a cap-sleeved dress made by a small but promising French designer she had found through an obscure British fashion magazine. She put on a pair of high Zanotti heels, being careful not to touch the soles, which had been in contact with dirty streets, and examined herself in the mirror. The kingfisher-blue colour suited her; every time her photograph had appeared in *Vogue* she had been wearing this striking shade. She definitely wanted to stand out today.

Finally ready, Paula gripped her daughter's hand as she stood outside Princess Katrina's Upper East Side town house. She knew the six-storeyed building well, although she had never been inside. Double-fronted in dove-grey stone, with an ornate iron gate, it had originally belonged to a billionaire hedge-funder who had been jailed after a fraud scandal a year ago. Katrina's husband Arlo Savoy had bought it before it had even gone on the open market, for a sum rumoured to be in excess of eighty million dollars.

'Is Carlotta's daddy really a king?' whispered Casey as Paula rang the heavy doorbell.

'Almost,' replied Paula. She had researched the Savoy family obsessively and knew that, were it not for the revolution, Arlo would have been a prince of Italy. In his youth, the royal line had made Arlo one of Europe's finest catches, but then Katrina had been pretty eligible in her own right; her German father had made billions from steel and industry in Europe. Such a combination of wealth and class had catapulted them into the top strata of New York society the second they had arrived to follow Arlo's career at an Italian bank.

As a butler opened the door, Paula handed over the invitation and waited as their names were read out under the gaze of an unblinking security camera. Paula could barely suppress her delighted smile. She rarely thought about the old days any more. She had spent so long blocking out the memories, creating a newer, vaguer, more palatable past for those people who cared enough to ask, that it was as if her time growing up in North Carolina never really happened. But every now and then, she silently congratulated herself on how far she had come; and this moment, stepping inside one of the Upper East Side's finest homes, this was one of those times. Paula tried not to register any emotion as she walked into the grand living room, but it was undeniably impressive. Original Rothkos hung on the high walls above priceless furniture, modern pieces mixed with precious antiques in such an artful, studied way that it must surely have been the work of one of the city's most accomplished interior designers.

Instead, Paula examined the people, feeling a rush of anxiety as she examined the faces; there were some serious heavy-hitters from the social circuit already here, women from the golden circle of wives, the partners of some of the most wealthy and influential men in the city. These exquisitely groomed women sat on the most prestigious charity committees and could usually barely bring themselves to acknowledge Paula, other than to enquire after Brooke, despite the fact she had met them several times. A waiter approached and respectfully offered her a drink from his silver tray. She took a Bellini – she usually avoided alcohol in the daytime, but today she felt she needed it. She could feel her neck flush prickly and red, as it sometimes did when she was stressed or worried. *Calm down, pretend you do this every day*, she told herself sternly. To her dismay, Paula didn't see any friends; Casey was new to her class and, consequently, Paula did not know the parents. She took a sip of her drink and steeled herself. *Remember Carolina, honey*, she said to herself. It was true: she had been in far worse situations than this.

She turned to a tall, Latin-skinned brunette dressed in skinny jeans and white Hermès shirt and smiled. 'Do you know where the birthday girl is?'

The brunette simply looked through her and raised a finger in the air to summon the waiter. Paula turned away, trying to smother the anger she felt. *The bitch!* Of course, Paula knew she had never been one of the Queen Bees on Manhattan's social scene; she knew many of the women considered the Asgill family gauche. They secretly sniggered at Meredith's Rolls-Royce and the family's cheap range of cosmetics, but she had expected that Brooke's engagement would have given her a greater standing. She had obviously been wrong.

Suddenly she felt a tugging at her dress. 'Mummy, Carlotta wants me to come and see her bedroom. Can I go?'

She felt a new affection as she saw Princess Carlotta of Savoy standing in the doorway beckoning her new friend over. *Her new friend Casey Asgill*, thought Paula, looking at the tall woman who had snubbed her with glee.

'Of course, darling. Off you go,' smiled Paula, touching Casey's head.

'I don't believe we've met?'

Paula turned to see Princess Katrina standing next to her. She was petite and slim, wearing a navy Chanel Couture dress, and had hair the colour of roasted hazelnuts pushed back off her face. She radiated star quality in a way that Paula knew only a small number of celebrities did. Every inch of her looked expensively groomed; her skin was so smooth it looked polished, and whoever had done the Botox around her forehead and mouth had done a fantastic job, thought Paula. Unlined, sculpted, yet completely natural. *I must find out where she goes*, thought Paula absently.

'Paula Asgill,' said Paula, offering her hand.

Katrina's smile was warm and genuine and it caught Paula off guard. In her experience, there were two standard society smiles: the tight, false variety usually sported by someone looking over your shoulder, or the bright paparazzi-friendly smile which was, if anything, even more insincere. In New York, real smiles like the Princess's were as rare as hens' teeth.

'Lovely to meet you,' replied Katrina. 'I think your daughter joined Transition at the same time as Carlotta.'

Feeling flattered, but completely wrong-footed, Paula took an exuberant sip of Bellini.

'It's a shame they'll be breaking up for summer before we know it,' she said. 'Still, Casey can't wait to get to Bermuda.'

Katrina's smile shone even brighter and she touched Paula on the arm. 'Really? That's great news; perhaps see you there. We have a house in Tucker's Town. My family have had it forever.'

'No! What a coincidence,' smiled Paula. 'It'd be wonderful if the girls could get together while we're over.'

In actual fact, Paula wasn't going to Bermuda at all – not yet, anyway. She, William, and the girls were due to fly to Maine as soon as school had finished. It was William's favourite place and, as Paula had already decided on the rest of their holiday destinations for the year – St Barts, Careyes, Aspen, and Maui – she had been in no position to argue. But when Google had turned up a British *Vogue* interview wherein Katrina had described her Tucker's Town home as one of her favourite places, Paula knew she would have to shoehorn in a trip to the Atlantic island as well. It was just a matter of twisting William's arm the right way.

'We've been thinking of buying in Bermuda ourselves,' said Paula. 'Maybe you can point us in the right direction?'

'Of course,' said Katrina. 'We must get a play-date arranged for the girls, then we can talk more.'

Paula smiled, pleased that her well-placed white lies had worked. Not that she liked to view her words as lies, simply a stretch of the truth, a wishful thinking of things that would be correct given half the chance. It was something Paula was very good at, and over the years it had been a useful tool in her arsenal. To become an Upper East Side player, you needed wealth, contacts, and a talent for putting designer clothes together, but most of all, you needed a Machiavellian ability to spin the facts in your favour.

Katrina clasped Paula's hand. 'Well, I'd better mingle,' she smiled. 'We have the most amazing ballet on at three; we've flown over some girls from the Royal Ballet School to perform this crazy little version of *Angelina Ballerina*. Carlotta just loved those stories when we lived in London.' Katrina began to move away, but then turned back and grabbed Paula's hand again.

'Paula, you must meet Lucia De Santos,' she said, leading her over towards the rude brunette in the Hermès shirt. Paula instantly recognized the name: she was a Colombian heiress whose father owned half of Bogotá.

'Lucia, meet Paula. Paula, Lucia has just moved to New York so you must be nice to her.'

Lucia smiled broadly at Paula and then kissed her on both cheeks.

'How wonderful to meet you,' she said, making Paula instantly forget her snub just minutes earlier.

'I think we're going to be great friends,' said Paula.

27

In the late spring months, the twenty minutes before dawn was one of Liz's favourite times of the day. She loved sitting at her window that overlooked the park, watching the sky lighten from the horizon in gentle stripes of colour, bringing the city to life. It was not a time to work, but a time to think and collect those thoughts in a way that she could use to her advantage.

Draining the last of her freshly pressed mandarin juice, she bent down and slipped on her running shoes. She had already showered, put on her white tracksuit, and was now ready to go. Her tennis lesson, aimed at brushing up her second serve, was at six thirty and she liked to get there early. But before she could leave the apartment, there was one thing she needed to do first.

Standing up, she noticed someone hovering in the doorway.

'Hey. I was just about to wake you,' she said in a polite but not too friendly way.

Liz had met Rav Singh, a thirty-three-year-old investment banker at Merrill Lynch at a drinks party at the Downtown Association, a private members' club on Pine Street, the night before. He was half-Indian, half-Swedish, with latte-coloured skin, long almond-shaped eyes and an interesting perspective on global capitalism, having spent eighteen months in Mumbai. She had already gleaned that his father was a well-off Indian businessman living in London, although she had no idea if he was simply one of Mumbai's newly wealthy middle class, or whether he was one of those Asian billionaires, with interests in steel and manufacturing that marked them out as the new titans of the business world, who lived in London for tax purposes.

They had caught a cab together uptown, had a late supper and too many caipirinha in a Brazilian restaurant on Broadway and ended up at her apartment drinking a good Château Mouton Rothschild until midnight. When Liz had kissed Rav, and she had made the move first, she had almost laughed out loud at how *proper* her seduction had been. The sex had lacked the raw, drug-like excitement of her usual encounters with men she met in bars, but there had still been an urgency, a need to feel a man inside her. Regardless of the disdain she felt towards Dana's Shapiro's therapy, Liz had still avoided any more random one-night stands since Russ Ford. The restraint had made her irritable and easily distracted, even at work. It had driven her back to smoking, which she had quit after business school, and her alcohol consumption during her sexual abstinence had been high.

'I'd like to see you again.'

'I'm not the relationship kind,' she replied in an amused, detached way. She had no doubt given Rav the fuck of his life; no wonder he wanted to come back for more.

'Because of the divorce?'

'You've been swotting up on me,' she said, raising an eyebrow.

'Just something I heard. It was a while ago, Liz. You know, it might be time to move on . . .'

She found herself nodding slowly. Maybe it was time for a new strategy. This much she knew; she wanted sex. The incident with Russ Ford had frightened her. No-strings sex was now simply out of the question. And she could hardly pay for it for exactly the same reasons, although she heard about one Chinese masseur who offered 'extras'. But, try as she might, (the urban myth was that he had brought one Park Avenue Princess to orgasm half a dozen times in a one-hour session), Liz could not track him down, not knowing whether she had been too discreet in her investigations, or whether he simply did not exist. A relationship was beginning to look like an appealing option, if she could control it in the right way.

'I have to go,' she said quickly. 'I have to lock up.'

'You going running?' asked Rav, fastening the buttons on his shirt.

She pointed at her racket bag in the corner of the room.

'Tennis.'

'Where are you playing?'

'Sutton East.'

He nodded. 'Do you want company?'

'Why? Do you play?'

'A little. But mainly squash and court tennis down at the Racquet and Tennis Club.'

Her interest in Rav suddenly moved up a notch. Liz longed to play at the prestigious Park Avenue club, one of the few social-sporting establishments yet to extend their membership policy to admitting women. It gave Rav immediate social clout.

'Okay. You're on.'

'Let me swing by my apartment and pick up my stuff. I'll see you there.'

She smiled sweetly and watched him go. He would do. He would do for now.

'Tess Garrett?'

Tess leant over her desk to peer at the caller ID window. 'Unknown number,' it read. She didn't recognize the voice, either, but after Brooke and David's Key West coup, her phone had been ringing off the hook.

'It's Sean Asgill.'

'Oh,' she said, instantly pulling a face, aware that her voice had betrayed her disapproval.

'Hey, great to speak to you too,' he said sarcastically.

'Sorry, it wasn't you,' she said, trying to back-pedal. 'Someone was just waving at me at my office door.'

'Well, I hope you didn't ask them to get you coffee,' said Sean, more good-humouredly. 'Because it sounds as if you expect them to poison you.'

Save your charm for someone who gives a damn, she thought.

'What can I do for you, Sean?'

Sean laughed. 'I seem to remember that the last time we met, you told me you wouldn't do a damn thing for me.'

'Well, things change,' said Tess, reminding herself that – whatever she might think of him – looking after Sean Asgill was actually part of her job description. 'How can I help?'

There was a pause before Sean spoke.

'I need an escort,' he said, 'Thursday night.'

This time it was Tess's turn to laugh. 'And that escort is supposed to be me? Or are you asking me to flip through the Yellow Pages to find you a professional?'

'Come on, Tess, it can't be that bad spending time with me, can it? And you did say you wanted to vet my dates.'

For a moment, Tess began to consider the idea, but then remembered that Sean was based on the other side of the Atlantic.

'Hang on, you're asking me to fly to *London* for this?'

'You like London,' said Sean. 'They have red buses and fish and chips.'

Tess was smiling, despite herself.

'Well, I would have loved to go with you, Sean, but I can't,' she said, trying to suppress the grin. 'I'm already flying out to London on Friday.'

'Excellent,' said Sean smoothly. 'I'll change your flight.'

'You can't,' insisted Tess. 'It was one of those cheap fares.'

'Well, I'll buy you a new one, first class. It will be a treat for you.'

'Actually I've travelled first class before,' she lied, annoyed at the suggestion that she was a cattle-class girl.

'And I'll throw in a couple of nights at Claridge's.'

Despite herself, she felt a rush of excitement. It felt as if she were being whisked off her feet by a rich suitor who could brush all her objections aside with a wave of his chequebook. She tried to remind herself that it was Sean Asgill – effectively her boss – and that he'd probably used this routine on hundreds of girls in the past. Not that she was interested in *that way*, of course, but it still felt nice to be pampered.

'Sean, I don't mean to be rude, but are you sure you want to do this? I mean, you're a popular guy. You can get a million girls to go to some dinner with you.'

There was another pause down the line and, for a moment, Tess thought they'd been cut off.

'My mother suggested you,' said Sean.

'Your mum?' said Tess incredulously.

'Actually, she said I needed someone who will just sit there and look pretty.'

'Well, I'm flattered . . .' began Tess, 'but . . .'

'No, that's not why I asked you, actually.'

'Oh.'

'I need someone with brains. This is actually a very important dinner. It's with Sir Raymond Greig, who's opening a new retail paradise; we need to sweet-talk them to get Lupin into prime display space.'

'Ah, I see,' said Tess, 'and you're worried that your usual kind of date might not reflect well on you in the intelligence department?'

She could hear the smile in his voice as he said: 'They might not necessarily say the right things.'

She laughed.

'Come on, Tess, you'd be doing me a massive favour.'

Tess shrugged. It never did any harm to have someone like Sean owing her favours, especially since her primary function as Asgill's PR was to keep him under control. Plus, she was going to London anyway. She thought about it for a moment, then smiled.

'First class, you say?'

28

'Please, Brooke, you've got to do something!'

Debs Asquith was standing in the doorway of Brooke's office, her hands clasped together in front of her. Brooke's friend and fellow commissioning editor looked so anxious, it was making her feel even more edgy.

'Okay, so how long is he going to be in with Mimi?' asked Brooke, drumming her manicured nails on the desk nervously.

'He's only here until twelve,' said Debs, glancing at her watch. 'He's meeting Mimi, then he's leaving. You can't let him out of the building without this.'

She picked up a proof copy of *Portico* and waved it in front of Brooke's face. Brooke chewed her lip. She was glad Debs was on her side. The two women had started at Yellow Door at the same time and they had quickly bonded over their mutual dislike of Mimi Hall and their frustrations with the way the rest of the company looked down on the children's division. Even so, it wasn't Debs who had to risk the wrath of Mimi Hall by trying to get to her contact. Mimi was currently meeting with Hollywood movie executive P. J. Abrams about any Yellow Door books that might be suitable film vehicles.

She looked at Debs anxiously. 'Do you think she'll give him *Portico*?'

'Of course not,' said Debs, her hands now on her hips. 'She's not called Me-Me for nothing. That woman is totally self-seeking. Mimi might be publisher of this division, but the only time she wants a film made from a Yellow Door book is if it's one of hers.'

Debs popped her head out into the corridor and then jumped back into the room.

'Quick! Quick!' she hissed, flapping her hands. 'Go! He's just leaving Mimi's office.'

Debs grabbed the proof and thrust it into Brooke's hands. 'Ambush him!'

The lift doors were just closing when Brooke's hand shot through the gap, allowing her to jump inside. Suddenly she felt stupid and tongue-tied. *What the hell am I doing?* she asked herself. *Mimi's going to kill me.*

'Mr Abrams,' said Brooke, her voice faltering. 'You don't know me, but I was wondering if you had a minute?'

The man favoured her with a hawkish smile. He was short and wiry and was wearing a sharp three-piece suit.

'Of course I know you,' he said pleasantly, 'you're Brooke Asgill. I was hoping I might bump into you, but Mimi said you were tied up in meetings.'

Brooke offered up a prayer of thanks to Page Six. She knew this situation had been made easier by being well known.

'I'll be quick, Mr Abrams, I'm sure you're very busy,' she said. 'I have a book I think you might be interested in.'

'What is it? Your life story?'

The lift pinged open and they crossed the lobby. For a short man, Abrams walked incredibly quickly, and Brooke struggled to keep up with him.

'I guess I just missed my elevator pitch,' she smiled.

He stopped and glanced at his watch. 'Listen, I have lunch at the Cip in twenty-five. Want to join me for a drink at the bar?'

Brooke's smile turned to a grin. 'That sounds wonderful.'

P. J. Abrams was one of the most respected Hollywood scouts in the business. He was renowned for his knack of picking up 'properties' – magazine articles, books, even TV shows – that went onto become big box-office films. Once a year or so he came to Yellow Door to see if any editors had any new material and, obviously, every editor wanted their books to be made into a film. One recent Yellow Door book, an adult sci-fi thriller, had been made into a box-office-friendly Will Smith action movie, which had pushed the sales of the book over two million copies and had precipitated a run on the author's otherwise unknown and unloved backlist. But Brooke knew it was a long shot. In her time working at Yellow

Door, a handful of books had been optioned, but just one had ever made it onto the big screen and, therefore, it had limited impact on book sales.

Sitting at the bar, she could see a few people looking at her, no doubt wondering what she was doing in one of Manhattan's sexiest restaurants with a man who clearly wasn't her fiancé. *If I ever thought of cheating,* thought Brooke with amusement, *the New York public would soon put a stop to it.*

'So you missed the elevator,' smiled Abrams, 'why don't you give me the bar pitch?' He must only have been about thirty, thought Brooke, but he had the shiny armour-plated confidence of someone ten years older.

Brooke took a deep breath. 'Here's the short version. A teenage girl works for her father's magic show. She wakes up one morning to find that she has real magical powers and uses them to help solve mysteries and the dark forces behind them. Think *Harry Potter* meets *Medium,*' she said quickly, pulling the description from the air.

'Supernatural rather than fantasy?' 'Abrams pouted thoughtfully. 'Yes.'

'Good.'

'Why good?'

'Fantasy equals expensive,' he smiled. 'Loads of CGI, flying about on wires, building models, and so on. Let's just say teenage witches are cheaper, less risky.'

'It's such a gorgeous book,' gushed Brooke, 'so well written, with this beautiful romance spinning through it – and it's genuinely really scary.'

Watching him grin at her enthusiasm, she took a breath and tried to focus herself into a Liz mind-set. Cool, measured, impossible not to take seriously. She thought for a moment, realizing that Hollywood wouldn't care about how well written something was.

'It's a book that will appeal to both teenage girls and their mothers,' Brooke said firmly. 'It's got very widespread appeal, and Yellow Door are going to market it as such. This book is going to be an international best-seller. This time next year, Eileen Dunne is going to be a brand. Option now before the price skyrockets,' she said slowly.

That last line seemed to have impact.

'In which case I'd better give it a read.'

He'd already asked for the bill and was waving to a tall blonde woman who had walked through the door.

'My lunch appointment is here. Good luck with the wedding.'

'Thanks for making time for me.' She slid off her stool and grabbed her bag.

Mimi Hall was going to kill her.

29

Tess dropped her holdall in the living room of her Prince of Wales Drive mansion flat and flopped onto the sofa. It all looked so different, so tidy without her heels and clothes littering the floor and her *Vogue*s and nail polishes scattered across the table. Dom had always been more pernickety than she was about the smartness of the flat, and now it had all the clean lines and organization of a bachelor flat: CDs organized and filed alphabetically, magazines in a rack, pans gleaming on the hob, quite possibly untouched since she left. Tess had only been away for six weeks, but it even smelt different, of aftershave and burnt toast. Feeling tired and grubby, she went to shower, hoping the warm water and the zingy tangerine body polish she'd bought at JFK might provide a temporary pep-up from the six-hour flight. As she scrubbed, she ran over the two options she had brought with her to wear. One, a scarlet silk dress with a halterneck she had bought in a fit of excitement when she had first shopped along Madison Avenue a few weeks earlier. Too sexy, too dressy, *too much*, she thought, wondering why she had packed it in the first place.

But then the other outfit – black trousers and a black silk T-shirt – didn't seem appropriate to the occasion either. As she wrapped herself in a fluffy white towel – there had never been clean towels when she and Jemma had shared the bathroom either – she silently cursed Sean Asgill for changing her plans so abruptly, causing her to rush her packing the previous night. She also realized that she was still angry at Dom. As soon as she had hung up on Sean, she had emailed Dom about her new plans.

Coming to London Thursday! X

He had replied almost immediately.

In Dublin Thursday night. New hotel launch. Doing story on it. Want to come?

After his rudeness towards Jack, the weekend he had visited her in NY had gone from bad to worse. Despite her carefully planned itinerary, he always had somewhere else he wanted to go – somewhere better, somewhere more cool. It didn't matter that Tess wanted to show him places she had found, it all seemed to be a competition for Dom. *He'll fit right into New York life*, Tess could remember thinking. Tess's big treat of a table at Per Se hadn't gone down much better, as he'd been disappointed there were no celebrities to ogle and he bitched that the tasting menu was 'too fiddly'. So Tess hadn't been too upset that she'd had to reply to his email:

Can't come to Dublin. Asgill work do till late on Thurs. Hot date Friday? X

Despite her anger, a part of her was hoping that, back on English soil, they might regain the spark and spice of her previous visit. She parked the thought, realizing she was running late. Striding over to her bedroom she rifled through her wardrobe. Now full of suits and men's sweaters, her own clothes had all been squashed into a corner. She immediately recognized them as impulse, unflattering purchases that she'd not had the heart to throw away: a puffball skirt, a rip-off Lanvin cocktail dress made from a cheap turquoise satin, a beaded top that made her breasts look too big. There was nothing for it but one of the original two options. Over the top or underdressed. Which one should it be? Just then the intercom began buzzing fiercely. Still in her bra and pants, she ran over and pressed the button.

'Who is it?'

'Hi, it's Sean.'

Flustered, she stuttered, 'You're early.'

'Yeah. Can I come up?'

'I'm not dressed.'

There was a low laugh. 'I didn't realize it was that sort of a date.'

'Just stay in the car, Sean,' she snapped. 'I don't want neighbours thinking I'm bringing strange men up to my apartment. I'll be down in a sec.'

She released the button before Sean could say more and ran back to the bedroom, grabbing the red dress. As it slid down over her skin she felt a strange sort of illicit thrill.

Holding her coat and clutch she ran down onto the street. Sean was sitting in a sleek silver car.

'Whoo,' he said admiringly, as she slid into the seat. 'You look fantastic.'

She looked away from him to fasten her seat belt. Two months in New York had not yet taught her how to accept a compliment. New Yorkers did it extremely well, with a casual nonchalance – as if the praise was appreciated, but also expected.

'I feel a bit overdressed. I wasn't sure how smart it was going to be.'

'It's perfect,' he smiled, gunning the engine. 'You look the perfect date.'

His compliment both thrilled and annoyed her. 'This isn't a date, Sean,' she said, a little too harshly. 'It's a business meeting.'

'Of course,' he smirked as the car leapt forward, leaving S-shaped marks on the road behind them.

The dinner was being held at the restaurant on top of one of the City's smartest tower blocks, The Overlook, a shard of glass that stretched three hundred metres into the air. The host for the night was Sir Raymond Greig, a retail tycoon who was quietly gobbling up Britain's high street. His latest venture, a vast, multi-level store on Oxford Street called Pop, was one of the biggest retail sensations of the last five years. Aimed at young women, Pop was expanding into the provinces and America, while the London store was about to have its fifteen-thousand-square-foot ground floor converted into a beauty boutique: every mid-market cosmetics label wanted to be stocked in it. Sean wanted to use the launch of the department to increase the profile of the new Lupin fragrance, but Asgill's had its eye on a bigger prize – creating and manufacturing a range of Pop-branded cosmetics.

Tess had to admit, Sean was a natural at this. Seated next to Sir Raymond– in itself an impressive start – he had the billionaire in fits of laughter, regaling him with tales of debauchery and ill-doing after dark, but he also managed to skilfully drop in the odd boast about Asgill's prowess as a manufacturer and mid-market sales force, plus a couple of allusions to the family's influential position in the States. He was never explicit with promises or figures, but he was persuasive and charming, the sort of man you'd want to offer your business to. Tess was also able to hold her own, flirting and joking with Sir Raymond, teasing him with stories she'd picked up at the *Globe* about badly behaved celebrities. She did have the uncomfortable feeling, however, that Sean had told his host that Tess was his date, rather than his publicist.

'Well, I have to say, that was a very enjoyable meal,' said Sir Raymond, leaning over to Sean as the poached pear dessert was served. 'How about a sticky?'

Sean shook his head.

'Well, I wouldn't mind something in a Tokay style, especially if it's a Chambers Rosewood,' said Tess casually. 'The Aussies really do love their desserts, don't they?'

Sir Raymond smiled appreciatively. 'It's rare you find a beautiful young lady who appreciates such things.'

Tess murmured modestly; dessert wines had been her father's love, and he'd told her all about them once he'd opened his pub. Sir Raymond raised his hand for the sommelier, but Tess felt Sean's foot knock against her leg under the table.

'Actually, Sir Raymond,' said Tess quickly, 'on second thoughts, it's probably not wise on top of the jet lag.'

Sir Raymond nodded his agreement.

'Well, perhaps we can all have a supper at Scott's in the next couple of weeks,' he said. 'I'm sure Sean and I will have plenty to discuss by then.'

Outside, in the foyer, Tess and Sean had a fantastic view of London spread out below them like a carpet of lights.

'You know, you weren't nearly as bad in there as I thought you'd be,' said Sean as they stepped into the lift.

'Thanks,' said Tess sarcastically. 'There's a compliment in there somewhere. I just can't see it for the massive character slur.'

'I dated a journalist once,' he continued. 'Magazine editor. Neurotic, very snappy. Only ate bean sprouts.'

'I'll pretend that last statement is nothing to do with me and move on,' said Tess.

The lift slid down to the ground floor. As they walked outside, the early May air was balmy, offering a hint of the summer to come.

'So how's Dom?'

Tess was surprised that Sean even remembered Dom's name.

'Good,' she said warily. 'Actually, he's in Dublin tonight, so I won't be seeing him until tomorrow.'

'Ah, that's a shame.'

She shrugged. 'He's away a lot for work. He's a travel editor.'

'Yeah, I know,' he said distractedly, feeling in his pockets for his car keys. 'We spoke at the Lupin launch a few weeks ago.'

He unlocked the car and they slid into the buttery leather seats. 'So do you want me to drop you home or . . . ?'

She felt her heart jump; she hoped he wasn't going to try it on.

'Don't panic, I'm not about to seduce you,' he smiled wolfishly. 'Come on, Miss Garrett. It's just that it's not even ten. It's still afternoon on New York time.'

It was true – Tess didn't really feel tired; in fact she was quite energized after putting in an Oscar-winning performance as 'Sean's intelligent girlfriend'. Of course, it hadn't hurt that she had flown from New York first class. She had promised herself that she would stay awake as long as possible in order to get the most out of the experience, but the welcome cocktail and lie-flat bed had been too much. She had slept most of the way across the Atlantic, only waking for a light lunch of poached salmon and champagne. Besides, she didn't really want to go back to her empty flat.

'Okay then,' said Tess, 'as long as you're not dragging me to any of those horrible Eurotrash nightclubs or lap-dancing establishments.'

'Why have you got such a low opinion of me?' he asked, with mock outrage.

'I think you can guess, Sean,' she replied, a little too cattily, but Sean merely shrugged and pulled his mobile out of his pocket. 'It's me,' he said into the phone. 'Yeah, can you get me on the list for Nina's party tonight? I'm with a friend.'

Snapping the mobile shut, he twisted the key in the ignition and Tess's neck snapped back as they shot off into traffic.

'I thought you knew everyone,' said Tess.

'I do.'

'Not well enough to get your own invite?'

'Nina Cheskov is a friend of a friend,' he said with a thin smile, her barb clearly hitting its mark.

'So who is she? An old conquest?'

Sean laughed. 'Not this time. She's a Kazakhstan oligarchess, if that's the right term for the female of the species; one of the richest women to come out of Russia since Perestroika. She has one of the smartest places in Notting Hill – and yes, I have been – but she has just bought some ex-royal pad in Surrey, which is where she is having the party tonight.'

'Surrey? That's miles away!'

Sean turned to look at her, a twinkle in his eye. 'Where's your sense of adventure?'

Tess laughed.

'Seriously,' he said, putting his foot down and shooting through an orange light. 'It's just down the A3. I'm told the house is a case study in how billions of dollars can't buy you good taste. That's got to be worth a look, hasn't it?'

The silver sports car slid across the City streets, down through the gritty postcodes, and out where the houses grew larger and more suburban, exchanging London cool for trees and wide-open spaces. Sean reached over and pressed a button on the dashboard. A CD player blared into life: Gary Numan's greatest hits. Sean sang along, loudly and out of tune, his faux-English accent making Tess snigger.

'Hey, what's so funny?' he asked.

'Your confidence.'

'That's exclusive East Coast prep schools for you.'

Tess was quiet for a moment.

'Sean, you were so good at that meeting tonight – great, even. But then you have this terrible reputation that undermines it all. Don't you ever get sick of partying?'

Sean nodded. 'I'm over all that.'

Tess raised a sceptical eyebrow. 'Really?'

'Really. Listen, I'm thirty-five years old. I figure it's about time I stopped pretending I'm nineteen. So the man you see here is really, truly free of drink and drugs. Think of me as the brand-new Sean. I've reinvented myself.'

'So how's it going?'

'Pretty good,' he smiled.

'Spoken with confidence.'

'You think I'm an asshole.'

'I never said that.'

'Well, I apologize for the Lupin party. I was a little rude.'

'A little?' she smiled.

'I was being defensive, projecting my problems onto you.'

'Of course.'

'My mom has employed you to watch over me, but I'm determined to get it right on my own. I've made my own mistakes, now it's my responsibility to put it right. I guess I wanted to vent my frustrations with my mother and you got in the way.'

'But why do you have problems with your mum?' asked Tess.

Sean looked up to the roof and laughed. 'Hey, where do I start?'

Tess frowned. 'I was under the impression you were the apple of her eye.'

Sean nodded slowly. 'I can see why you might think that. I've certainly always been indulged by my mom. I could steal the crown jewels and she would just pat me on the head and say "Oh Sean".'

Tess was beginning to understand. Sean didn't want indulgence, he didn't want to be tolerated, he wanted to be valued and loved – noticed even. She could certainly understand that.

'So I get shunted off to London. Mom won't let me near anything important like marketing, but she thinks I might just be able to handle corporate entertaining. Well, she's right about that; in fact I'm pretty good, even if I do say so myself. Asgill Cosmetics might not make the most exclusive fragrances in the world, but we throw the best parties. They get all over the papers, which produces hundreds of free column-inches for us. On top of that, I've brought retailers into the fold, brokered distribution deals, and persuaded all the top fashion magazines over here to take our advertising. Sure, I was at all the hottest parties, on the yachts, but that's where the deals are done.'

Tess flashed him a crooked smile. 'So you're telling me you're not a playboy?'

Sean laughed. 'Hey, I'm not saying I don't enjoy it, I just wish—'

'You just wish Meredith had noticed what your huge bar bills were buying her.'

He smiled, then glanced at the GPS on his dashboard. 'One more right turn and I think we're here.'

They were now driving down country roads crowded with oak trees and big houses set back from the road. Sean swung the car into a driveway and Tess was surprised at what she saw. It was not a beautiful house like Belcourt, more like an overgrown Barratt show-home made from modern red brick with ugly concrete mock-classical pillars either side of the entrance. More impressive was the field to one side, where Tess could see at least four helicopters.

'Why drive when you can fly?' she said, wide-eyed.

Sean pulled to a stop and handed the keys to a uniformed valet. They walked towards the house, skirting around a dazzling collection of parked cars, from Bentleys to Lamborghinis. Serious-looking security guards, dressed from head to foot in black, stood by the door, presumably listening to the chatter in their high-tech earpieces.

'Hi Sean,' said the pretty girl with the guest-list clipboard, tottering over on her six-inch heels to kiss him on both cheeks.

'Hey Rachel, looking as lovely as ever,' said Sean.

'Go right in, sweetie,' she said, giving Tess the once-over as she passed. *I wonder what names Rachel is calling me under her breath*, thought Tess, before her first glimpse of the interior wiped all other thoughts from her head. Sean hadn't been joking when he said that expensive bad taste had run riot in Nina's mansion: it was a sensory overload.

The floor was white marble inlaid with gold, and the giant staircase that dominated the centre of the entrance hall was draped in velvet and garish silk tapestries. Behind the staircase was a huge stained-glass window depicting a naked couple, but the pièce de résistance was in the centre of the hall: a sculpture-cum-fountain featuring two rampant golden unicorns with purple water gushing from their engorged members.

'Good God,' said Tess.

'I couldn't have put it better myself,' said Sean. 'Worth the journey into darkest Surrey?'

'Absolutely,' she grinned.

He touched her arm and led her through the crowd. There must have been six hundred people packed into the grand entrance hall, each groomed to within an inch of their lives. Tess was suddenly glad she had worn the red dress.

'No! Tell me that's not who I think it is?' she gasped. She was staring through an open archway into what looked like a grand ballroom. On a stage at one end, just about to begin playing, were Duran Duran.

'I thought I'd better not mention that,' smiled Sean. 'You might not have come.'

'You're joking, aren't you?' protested Tess. 'I *love* Duran Duran!'

'Ah-ha! The daahrling Sean Asgill,' shrieked a voice, making them both turn. Sean was bear-hugged by a tall woman with blonde hair dropping down her back. She had wide feline eyes and around her waist was a sparkling band of diamonds that Tess felt sure were real.

'Nina,' said Sean, 'what a wonderful party.'

'Why wouldn't it be, dahrling? I'm forty and fabulous,' she purred. 'I thought "you can't stay thirty-seven forever", so why not flaunt it?'

Tess laughed. 'Happy birthday. I'm Tess.'

Nina looked at Tess, then gave Sean a slow wink. 'What are you doing bringing gorgeous girls to my party?' she teased. 'I thought I was the only one for you.'

'I didn't think you were available, Nina,' smiled Sean.

'When you look this good,' she said, striking a dramatic pose, 'I think it's cruel to keep it to one man.'

Wiggling her fingers in the air, Nina drifted off on the arm of a male model.

'Thirty-seven,' whispered Sean when she had gone, 'she's nearer fifty-seven.'

Tess laughed. 'Well, I don't know about you,' she said, 'but after that, I need a drink.'

He looked in the direction of the crowded vodka bar. 'Actually, I'd better go,' he smiled. 'I think we need someone with broad shoulders to get to the front – it'll be good to test my resolve too.'

'Okay, I'm going to see if there's anywhere to get rid of my coat.'

Sean touched her shoulder. 'Don't go far.'

She glanced back at him and, in the low light, she noticed what a sexy smile he had and just how pale green his eyes were. Tess hoped that it wasn't sexual tension she was feeling in the air. Whatever it was, it was glorious and nerve-tingling. *This is what happens when your boyfriend lives four thousand miles away and you don't get enough sex*, she told herself firmly.

She looked away as in the distance she could hear Simon Le Bon's gravelly voice telling the crowd that this was no 'Ordinary Day', followed by the familiar chiming melody of a song she had played a thousand times over on the stereo.

For a split second, she was so wrapped up in the music, she did not recognize the good-looking man standing a little way off to her left. Wearing a sharply tailored suit, he was turned away from her, but he was obviously having the time of his life talking to a slim blonde to his left. Tess gaped at him. It couldn't be, it *shouldn't* be. But it was. *Dom.*

Her shock and pleasure at seeing him curdled into a sense of dread and foreboding as she watched his hand sliding casually up and down the blonde's bare back. The girl leaned in and whispered something into Dom's ear, and he laughed – a flirtatious, happy, relaxed laugh that seemed so different from how he behaved with her. She stood fixed to the spot, unable to move or speak, when another couple came over to Dom and his new friend. Deeply tanned and rich-looking, Tess didn't recognize either of them, but Dom spoke to them as if they had been close for years. Strangely, it was that tiny observation that shocked Tess the most. Somehow, that felt like a bigger betrayal to her; somehow it made their life together an even bigger lie.

She was still standing there staring at Dom, when Sean arrived with a glass of champagne.

'You'll never believe the bar over there, it's covered with . . .' He trailed off as he followed the direction of her stare.

She barely turned to look at him, and just handed him her coat.

'Excuse me for one moment,' she said flatly as she walked straight over to Dom. The moment he turned and saw her, the relaxed confidence she had observed from a distance crumpled.

'Tess,' he spluttered. 'What the hell are you doing here?'

'I was just going to ask you the same thing,' she said evenly.

The blonde put her hand on Dom's. 'Is everything all right?' she asked in a clipped Home Counties accent. Tess noticed the way her fingers lingered on his just a second too long, and she instinctively knew that they had slept together.

'I was just talking to my boyfriend,' snapped Tess. 'Is that okay?'

The blonde looked at Dom and he shook his head slightly. She moved away quickly.

For several seconds, Tess simply couldn't think what to say. Her fingers gripped the silk of her dress.

'I didn't want you to find out like this,' said Dom, nervously glancing around.

'Of course you didn't,' said Tess. 'You didn't want me to find out at all.'

She inhaled sharply, psyching herself to stay strong. 'Who is she?' she asked as calmly as she could.

'She's called Tamara. Tess, I just—'

'Where did the two of you meet?' she interrupted.

'Oh you know, around town.'

261

'Where?' she demanded. '*Where?*' Suddenly Tess felt she needed to know everything. Tess looked over at the girl who had retreated to the bar, and instantly Tess *knew* where they had met. Tamara had been one of the London society blondes at the Lupin launch.

'It was the Asgill's party,' she said quietly, almost detached. 'Wasn't it?'

Dom took a deep breath. 'Briefly, yes. Then we bumped into each other again at Nobu.'

'*Nobu?*' she snorted. 'Your local fucking canteen now, no doubt.'

Tess thought of that amazing lovemaking session they had had in the seedy hotel straight afterwards and felt her face flush with stupidity. *Lovemaking!* All the time she thought it had been an indication of how much he really felt for her, a vindication of the strength of their relationship after all these years, but no. He had just been feeling horny.

Dom looked at Tess sheepishly. 'I'm so sorry.'

'Sorry,' she choked. 'You're "sorry"? After ten fucking years together, this is what I deserve: flaunting some posh bitch like a trophy in front of me? Did you really think I wouldn't find out about it eventually?'

'I was going to tell you,' he said lamely. 'But I didn't want to do it over the phone.'

She thought of all the things she'd planned for her trip in London that weekend. The cheesy double-decker bus tour, the meal at Chez Bruce, then cuddling up in bed afterwards, in *their* bed. But Dom had had other plans. He was going to finish with her.

She swallowed hard.

'Tess, come on,' said Dom. 'Our relationship has been dying on its feet for ages.'

She turned on him furiously. 'Oh, and that's enough to justify sleeping with that slut, is it? You're not happy, so you just jump into bed with the first tart who comes along?'

'No,' he sighed. 'But we both deserve to be happy.'

'This is what you've always wanted, isn't it? A rich girlfriend, rich and beautiful. Not smart of course – certainly not smart if she's interested in you.'

Dom glanced around and bent in closer to Tess. 'Keep your voice down, Tess.'

'Why? Frightened your fancy new friends won't approve of your old girlfriend? No, I was never rich or successful enough, was I?

You wanted a Chelsea flat, you wanted the *Tatler* party pages, didn't you, you shallow wanker? Well, I hope you're finally happy.'

He stopped and looked at her more coolly, his public-school confidence allowing him to step up and take the high ground.

'You can't criticize me for wanting this, Tess,' he said evenly. 'You were the one who high-tailed it to New York. You were the one who wanted the fat salary and the West Village apartment. And what am I supposed to do? You've been back once in two months – and that was for work.'

'Because I'm committed to my job – what's so wrong with that? I thought we were committed to each other too. I thought we would cope with the distance because we loved each other.'

Tess was dimly aware that she was shouting now. She would not cry. She absolutely would not allow herself, but her lips prickled, her breathing had quickened, and her cheeks flushed anxiously hot.

'This is not my fault alone, Tess,' said Dom cruelly. 'You forced me into this.'

'Fuck YOU!' shrieked Tess, turning and running for the door, crashing against a waiter and sending a pile of canapés flying.

She fled through the front door and down the steps, out into the stinging cold air. Wanting, needing to get away, she ran along the side of the house, her high heels scuffing against the gravel. *What have I done to deserve this?* she asked herself. *Did I really force him into cheating? If I had stayed here, would we still be together?*

'No, that's such crap,' she whispered, wrapping her arms around herself and sitting down on a stone step. 'That selfish wanker.'

She sat there, shivering, staring at the ground as her eyes blurred. Her body felt numb and hollow. *Was this really happening?* she asked herself. Everything seemed so surreal – being in Surrey, in Nina's mansion, seeing Dom with another woman – that she squeezed her eyes shut, hoping that when she opened them she'd be back in New York.

After a few moments she heard footsteps running in her direction and her heart gave a tiny lurch. Was he coming for her, to take her back?

'There you are.'

She looked up in misery. It was Sean, not Dom. He put her coat around her shoulders.

'Come on,' he said, pulling her up gently. 'I'll take you back home.'

Tess allowed herself to be led back to Sean's car and sat in silence as he drove off down Nina's long winding drive. Staring at her reflection in the window, she began to wonder if she was being truthful with herself. Did she really want Dom anyway? All that time she'd spent in New York, she hadn't really missed him, hadn't really longed for him to come and be with her. She had assumed it was because she had been too busy, of course, but was that really the reason? When she and Dom had discussed the Asgill job, they had smiled and talked about paying off the mortgage and the golden opportunities to be had in America. Never once had he said, 'Don't go, I'll miss you too much.' And neither had she.

Sean leant over and handed her a handkerchief. 'I can't blow my nose on this,' she said with a wan smile, 'it's silk.'

'Don't worry. I can afford it.'

'Thanks,' she said gruffly.

He paused for a moment before saying, 'Don't thank me.'

She looked at him and he would not catch her gaze.

The penny dropped.

'You knew about this, didn't you?' she said quietly.

More silence.

'You *knew*? You brought me out here especially? In fact, you *flew* me out here – to end my relationship?'

'Of course not,' said Sean defensively. 'I wanted you to come to the dinner.'

'But you knew Dom was going to be at this party.'

She looked at him, hoping it would not be true, hoping it would be a dreadful coincidence. He kept his eyes fixed on the drive and exhaled heavily.

'Yes,' he said flatly. Without thinking, Tess slapped him across the cheek. The car swerved dangerously across the gravel, the outside tyre bumping against the embankment.

'What the fuck?' shouted Sean as he struggled to gain control.

'You sadistic bastard!' she yelled. 'What have I ever done to you? Why would you want to hurt me like this? What was it, some sort of cabaret? A little bit of entertainment to amuse your friends?'

'No!' he shouted back. 'I was trying to help you!'

'That's what you call help?' she spat. 'Well, next time, don't bloody bother.'

Sean paused, then said quietly, 'It's a small social circuit, Tess. I saw Dom and Tamara out together at a restaurant in Chelsea a week after the Lupin party. I didn't want to tell you then, because it could have been a business meeting for all I knew. I wasn't sure what was happening. But then I heard Tamara had been boasting she was going to Nina's party with her new man.'

'And you wanted me to see,' said Tess, nodding. 'So you brought me to the most public place you could find so you could humiliate me.'

'Of course I didn't want you to be humiliated,' said Sean as evenly as he could. 'But when you told me earlier that Dom was in Dublin, it made me angry. I didn't want to hurt you, but I wanted you to see what he was like. If you hadn't seen it for yourself, he could have denied it, lied to you for months.'

'Right, so you have to be cruel to be kind,' she said, her voice wavering.

'He's just not worth it, Tess.'

'What do you know of worth, Sean?' she said, closing her eyes. 'You are a spoilt little rich boy. You use women how you please; you're no different to Dom.'

'Maybe not,' said Sean. 'But I tried, Tess—'

'Stop the car,' she said suddenly.

'Tess, don't be stupid.'

'I said stop the fucking car.'

Reluctantly, Sean slowed the car to a stop. As she reached for the door handle, he leant over to stop her. 'Tess, please . . .'

'Just leave me alone,' she said, climbing out of the car. They were not even out of the grounds of Nina's estate. Sean opened his door and made to follow her. 'Tess, come on, you can't just walk home!' he shouted.

Just then the bright headlights of a black cab came up behind them. She held her hand out to stop it.

'Please, can I get in? Please take me back to London,' she said. The driver nodded.

She slammed the door and avoided Sean's gaze as they drove past.

Tess looked into her bag to check she still had her passport – carrying it everywhere was a habit she had got into in the States, where bartenders still asked for ID; and she was glad of it now. She glanced at her watch, then tapped the driver on the shoulder. 'Forget London,' she said. 'Take me straight to Heathrow.'

She didn't want to see the inside of her flat, not even to collect her bag. She wanted to get back to New York.

30

Newport is one of the most exclusive seaside towns in America, and Cliffpoint – the Billingtons' summer residence – one of its most exclusive mansions. Located just off Bellevue Avenue, on a nine-acre site that sloped down to the Atlantic coast, it was a beautiful Beaux Arts building – not as big as the famous Vanderbilt mansion, The Breakers, nearby, but certainly prettier, with its white pillars and arched windows and manicured grounds studded with exotic trees and flowers.

Brooke had travelled up the night before with David, taking the Billington private jet from Teterboro to Providence. The rest of David's family – aunts, uncles, cousins, at least twenty in number – had been arriving throughout the day for a dinner in celebration of David's brother Robert's birthday. With all the activity in the great house, the appearance of guests, and the influx of additional staff, Brooke had spent the afternoon on a long walk along Newport's coastal path that ran directly in front of Cliffpoint. She had gone alone, while David had spent the day sailing around Narragansett Bay with his father and brother; although Brooke had been invited, she suffered terribly from seasickness and, anyway, disliked David's metamorphosis into a more macho creature in the presence of Wendell and Robert.

Instead she'd had a fabulous time walking the three-mile trail, which was sometimes a straight path, at other times more difficult terrain, where she had to scramble over slippy rocks. She loved the taste of the warm, salty air on her tongue, the noise of waves crashing against the shore, the sight of the ocean – almost turquoise in colour in some places. She had done the walk several times before; not just since she had dated David, but when she had been

267

at Brown University a short drive away in Providence. She had come up after exams with her girlfriends and they had peered over the hedges towards the grand mansion houses and other novelties on the trail, such as the Chinese Tea House pagoda, made especially for Mrs Cornelius Vanderbilt so she could enjoy the sight of the sea. Although Brooke and her friends were all from wealthy families, used to driving sports cars at college, holidaying in the best resorts around the world, wearing the finest designer clothes that Madison Avenue had to offer, they had all been stunned by the elegant, almost royal show of wealth that Newport offered up. It had ignited much discussion on the way home among Brooke's more socially ambitious friends about how to gain permanent entry into these gilded-age palaces. How many of these mansions were now national museums? How many still belonged to great families, and in those families how many young, single sons were there? She smiled at the memory of David's name being mentioned all those years ago by her friend Jenny, who had a particularly comprehensive database of America's most eligible men. She wondered how Jenny, with whom she had now lost contact, would react to the news of Brooke's engagement to him.

There was a gate along the back lawns that was an exit from the track back up to Cliffpoint. As Brooke neared the house after her walk, David's mother Rose approached. Despite the usual heat of the day, she looked cool, elegant, and composed in off–white, light wool slacks and a cream chiffon shirt with a large pussy bow at her neck.

Rose hooked her arm through Brooke's as they walked back in the house. Brooke found her a domineering woman, in a quiet but forceful way that older patrician women seemed to have, but thought life would definitely be easier if she made a friend out of her. Not just because she was close to her son and could no doubt make life difficult for Brooke should she take a sudden dislike to her. Not just because she had offered to take Brooke to the Chanel Couture show the following month to order her trousseau, which she insisted was an early wedding gift. But also because Brooke wanted Rose to like her. Accept her, approve of her in a way she no doubt did of Alicia Wintrop or any other of David's ex-girlfriends who came from old, established American families.

'The boys are back from sailing,' Rose smiled, accepting a gin and tonic from their English butler, Mr Steven.

'And what time is dinner?' asked Brooke. She was desperate for a lie-down after the long walk, but, looking at the sun already sloping low in the sky, knew there was little time.

'Seven thirty. Drinks at seven in the library – although it appears I've already started,' Rose said, raising her glass slightly. 'How's the house hunting coming along?'

'We've hardly had time,' Brooke told her. It was true; with all the wedding planning it just seemed another job that needed doing. David had suggested they didn't start looking until after the wedding, and in many ways it made the best sense. David's loft in TriBeCa was fabulous. Bright and spacious, with a fantastic roof terrace and close to all her favourite shops in SoHo and the bustle of Chinatown and Little Italy. But, despite Brooke's busy-ness and the wedding, she wanted to start their married life together in a place that was theirs rather than his.

Rose shook her head ever so slightly. 'I've never known the attraction of that loft, although I know it was a wise financial investment. I do know of a couple of excellent co-ops coming up in two very good buildings on Park. One is a triplex. Belongs to Janice Dupont who is on her last legs, God bless her. Her family will definitely want to get rid of her apartment, and my dear friend Aggy chairs the committee. And while they might be a little concerned about the press attention you two garner, I'm sure I can get Aggy to give you the nod.'

Brooke attempted a smile. She knew the building. Old and prestigious; a power building, full of the sort of people Brooke liked to avoid. And with Rose's dear friend Aggy in the building, it would be like being watched. Brooke had to think carefully about how to get out of this one. With a bit of luck, Janice Dupont would hang on until Brooke and David had found somewhere else to live.

She walked up the sweeping staircase to David's room at the front of the house. The long windows were open and the balmy evening air breezed through the space that had clearly changed little from when David was much younger. Fifties posters advertising the America's Cup held in Newport hung on the wall. There was a shelf full of trophies from her fiancé's school and college days, which always seemed to throw up more of David's secret talents every time she looked: trophies for rowing, chess, sailing, soccer, cross-country running. The room was a perfect reflection of him: sporty, adventurous, successful.

'How was the walk?' asked David, emerging from the en-suite bathroom towelling his hair.

'Hot,' she smiled, pulling off her T-shirt and exposing her firm breasts. 'I need to get a shower.'

'Tease,' he grinned, walking over and kissing the back of her neck.

Smiling, she shut the bathroom door behind her. At home he would have joined her in the wet room, but at Cliffpoint she felt strange about sex.

She emerged in her beige lace bra and Cosabella thong feeling clean and fresh. David was already in dress trousers and a white shirt that brought out the tan he had acquired sailing. Slipping into her cream Thakoon shift dress and five-inch heels, she caught sight of them both in the long Shaker-style mirror and felt a flood of contentment at how good they looked together.

David went to his bag and pulled out a slim black velvet case.

'I was going to wait until tomorrow to give you this, but that dress calls for a change of plan. Happy anniversary, honey,' he said, giving her a soft, tender kiss.

A year ago today they had met. Just a year. She thought back to that day in Biarritz. Meeting David on the beach when she had been standing on the shoreline in her wetsuit, boogie-board under her arm, a little afraid to step out into the cold Atlantic Ocean. Naturally he had been an adept surfer and he had spent the afternoon teaching her how to get the best rush from the waves. Afterwards, they'd gone for moules frites and lots of red wine, and, as the restaurant emptied out, they still kept talking, then on to a tacky tourist nightclub, desperate to extend the night until at three a.m. they had taken a walk along the beach and he had kissed her.

Her finger prised open the stiff box and she gasped when she saw a pair of exquisite emerald chandelier earrings lying on a bed of crinkled snow-white silk.

Brooke touched them gingerly. 'Can I put them on?'

'It's what they're there for,' he grinned. 'They'll look great with that dress.'

They did. She scooped her hair up, fastening it expertly into a chignon. Her neck felt longer and leaner.

'Wow. This is my Audrey Hepburn moment.'

'You can wear them at the Republican dinner in Houston, too. Maybe with that long green dress Galliano gave you.'

She looked down towards the floor. 'Yes,' she said finally, but it was too late – he had spotted the hesitation in her voice.

'What's wrong?'

'Nothing.'

'Brooke. You're a bad liar.'

The earrings weighed as heavy on her as the guilt. 'About that,' she said slowly. 'I'm not sure I'm going to be able to go.'

David looked puzzled. 'You were fine about it a week ago.'

The last thing she wanted to do was put a dampener on the evening ahead, but if she lied now it would be more difficult to get out of later. 'Remember the Hollywood scout that came to see me?' she asked. 'Well, he loved Eileen's book.'

'That's good news, isn't it?'

Of course it was good news. Such good news that when P. J. Abrams had phoned her up two days earlier, she'd actually burst into tears when she'd got off the phone.

'He wants to set up a meeting with the VP of development and a few other executives. Eileen wants me to come.' She paused. 'It's the same day as the Houston dinner.'

A vertical frown line appeared above his nose. 'Why does Eileen want you with her? She's got an agent, hasn't she? That's what they are there for – to hand-hold and do deals.'

'This feels like my project too, David.'

'So change the date of the meeting.'

'Come on, David. We were given that date. If we start trying to change it, you know how these things can suddenly go cold.'

'So this is more important than the Houston dinner,' he said flatly.

'It's just a dinner, David. If it was the Republican convention, or if you had started on the campaign trail yourself or something, then fair enough.'

'Just a dinner,' he said sarcastically.

'Well it is, honey. It's not as if you and your family don't know these people already. It's not as if *you* are turning down the invitation.'

Brooke took hold of his arm. It felt tense in her hand. 'Please don't be like this. I know the dinner is important to you, but this is important to me too. Eileen's my author and she needs me. You have your family to be there and back you up every step of the way, but Eileen has no one. She's twenty-six, bringing up three

271

kids, trying to make life better for those children. I really feel I can help someone.'

'Fine,' he said, walking towards the door.

'Where are you going?'

'For a walk.'

'David, you're obviously upset, let's talk about it some more.'

He didn't even turn to look at her. 'I'll see you downstairs at seven,' he said, closing the door.

If Brooke could have left Cliffpoint right then, she would have. Instead she had to walk alone into the throng of Billingtons, all congregated in the drawing room. At least David's cousin Lily was there; her co-opted bridesmaid was not her favourite person in the world, but when she saw Lily's lean form at the bottom of the stairs, Brooke almost leapt with joy. Conversation about Lily's Zac Posen bridesmaid dress easily took up the time until dinner was announced. Brooke was only faintly aware of David glowering at her from across the room and, when they sat next to each other at the enormous formal dinner table, no one seemed to notice that Brooke and David were speaking to everybody except each other.

The meal was exquisite; a starter of rare roast beef salad served with green beans and horseradish cream, and then cold lobster and aspic, served with the finest wines Brooke had ever tasted.

'So. How is the speech coming along for the Houston fundraiser?' asked Wendell, sticking his fork into a delicate walnut tart. 'There's a couple of good guys we can draft in to help with that; Ted is particularly good. Used to work with Condoleezza.'

'It's under control,' smiled David, taking a sip of Château Pétrus.

Rose was sitting opposite her future daughter-in-law. 'Brooke, I've got a few events planned in Houston for us both. I have a wonderful girlfriend who has invited us for lunch. There will be no finer guide to Houston. The shopping there is surprisingly good.'

Brooke took a breath and put her goblet of wine down on the table. 'I'm probably not going to be able to make the dinner,' she said, not meeting Rose's eye directly.

Wendell looked across the table at her. 'Really?' he said, trying to mask his disapproval with surprise.

'A business meeting in LA has come up. It's very important and can't be rescheduled.'

'I can't recall hearing of a meeting that can't be rescheduled,' he said with an overly enthusiastic smile. 'Some of the party's biggest donors are going to be at the dinner. Men who got both Bushes into the White House. Regardless of this family, they are going to be sizing David up. Checking him out, particularly with all those Florida Keys heroics still being talked about.' He wiped the edge of his mouth with a napkin. 'And of course everyone wants to meet you, Brooke. David, I think you should persuade her to attend,' he said, moving his gaze from Brooke to his son.

Brooke didn't dare look at her fiancé.

'Brooke's meeting is very important, and while she is going to try and move it, you know what these Hollywood lot are like,' David told him. 'Look like you aren't interested and you've missed your window of opportunity. Her career is important too.'

Wendell returned silently to his walnut tart, his mouth in a firm, tight line, and Brooke dropped her arm to her side, reaching over to touch David's leg gratefully.

'Coffee in the library,' announced Rose.

As David was caught talking to his two cousins from Boston, Brooke went outside to get some fresh air. It was a relief to be alone; the tension in the dining room had almost choked her.

Walking to the edge of the terrace, she stood at the top of the stairs that led to the lawns, listening to the distant roar of angry waves on the rocks and the rustle of a breeze in the trees.

Hearing footsteps behind her, she turned to see Robert Billington standing there, backlit by the glow coming from the house.

'Brandy?' He handed her a crystal balloon glass a third full of amber liquid.

Brooke observed him suspiciously. He was wearing a navy blazer with gold buttons that made him look about ten years older than thirty-three, and an arrogant half-smile. Brooke had never liked Robert. As a student at Yale, he had been in a terrible car accident when his vehicle had exploded in a fireball. Robert had been lucky to escape alive, but he still had burns all over his torso which crept up above the neck of his shirt like snake tongues. People whispered that his accident was why Robert worked for his father, instead of pursuing a political career, but in Brooke's opinion he was simply an unpleasant character devoid of the charm and smarts needed for Capitol Hill.

'How are the wedding plans coming along? Florida Keys was an unusual choice.'

'Not really, for a winter wedding. Plus we really wanted something with a family connection. Jewel Cay is my uncle's house. It will be private. I know security has been a bit of a concern for you.'

'Among other things,' he said casually, taking a sip of his drink. 'I take it David has already broached the matter of a prenuptial agreement with you.'

She shrugged. He hadn't, although she had been expecting it.

'It's obviously not the time or the place to talk about it here, but perhaps our lawyer and yours can speak next week to discuss the preliminaries.'

'I'll tell her to expect the call.'

Robert rested his glass on the wall and dipped his hand into his pocket.

'I overheard the conversation about the Houston dinner. It's very disappointing.'

'As David said, I have an important meeting.'

'Who with?' He laughed patronizingly. 'Some jumped-up twenty-five-year-old development exec?'

Brooke felt her cheeks run hot.

Robert walked closer to her. 'Brooke. I know you want to be good at something. It's human nature. My wife, she likes to *place*. She seats the best dinner-party tables of anyone in New York City. She doesn't have to be good at anything, of course. She has a chef to make our food, maids and decorators to look after the house, but her placements are very important to her and they do serve a very important role in our household. Our dinner parties are excellent. What she is good at serves us *both*.'

'What are you trying to say, Robert?'

'David doesn't need a career girl, Brooke. Look pretty. Be on as many best-dressed lists as you like. But know what your place is in the partnership.'

'I thought I was entering into a marriage, not a partnership.'

'David needs the right kind of wife, Brooke.'

'In case you hadn't noticed, it's the twenty-first century. People marry for love not usefulness,' she said, trying to keep her tone light.

'I think that's a little naive when the stakes are so high.' Robert sighed, his thin lips almost disappearing as he looked thoughtfully at a row of trees.

'David and I are happy, Robert.'

His face remained impassive. Brooke doubted that Robert cared at all for David's happiness. Looking at him, his poor complexion, the scars coiling up his neck, the features that on the surface looked like David's, but were in fact bigger or smaller – larger nose, narrower eyes and lips – making the construction of his face look out of kilter somehow, must surely make it impossible for Robert not to be jealous of his younger, more blessed brother.

'The secret of success is to know your strengths and your limitations. To have the wisdom and resolve to bide your time,' said Robert finally. 'Our family has produced six senators, four governors, two secretaries of state and a vice-president. But we haven't had a senior-level politician in the family for two generations now. My father sacrificed the chance to make serious money, and now he wants to convert that into real power. David is this family's golden opportunity. He is our time. We have been waiting for decades for someone with the brains and the charm to go all the way. In politics today, image is everything. David has that. Since he was a little boy he has been able to charm the birds out of the trees. He has looks, contacts, credibility, money. He has style and substance. He even has the common touch. And, after that Islamorada episode, the heroics. He might well have served in 'Nam.'

He paused and looked at Brooke more closely. 'David has all these things, and more. But what he also needs is the right spouse. A woman who knows that her own greatest ambition is to help propel her husband as high as she can.'

Brooke looked at him, shaking her head, a knot of anger in her stomach that felt ready to explode. Despite her earlier argument with David, she felt fiercely protective of him and of their future.

'Whose dreams are these, Robert – yours? Your father's? David's? Because, as far as I was aware, as his fiancé, David is very happy in television. Certainly for the short term. If he chooses to go into politics, then I will support him all the way. My career isn't getting in the way of anything important at the moment.'

'Of course you would say that,' he said sneeringly. 'You're not a woman who understands family destiny. Responsibility. Obligations. Which is why you are a children's book editor at a second-tier publishing house, rather than contributing to the somewhat diminishing fortunes of Asgill Cosmetics.'

She could feel tears welling behind her eyes, but she wouldn't let them fall, not for that little shit.

'Why do you think David chose you when he could have had anyone?' Robert continued, taking a step towards her in the dark.

'He loves me,' she said quietly, her breath becoming ragged. She had an ominous sense that Robert was about to deliver a brutal blow.

'He chose you because you are good wife material. Compliant. Not particularly driven. Prepared to give up the day job. He has known what sort of woman he has to marry since he was a boy.'

A stab of fear penetrated her chest so fiercely that she could not breathe. She inhaled as if she was surfacing from deep water.

Good wife material. What did he mean? That David was not truly in love with her? That she was just the right *type* of woman rather than the right woman. Frantically she searched her mind for clues that David's feelings for her were contrived or forced. Feeling her skin get cold with fear, the tears dangerously close to falling, she tried to block it out of her mind, at least until she was alone.

'Every woman in New York wants to get married into the Billington family. Of course that privilege is reserved for a very few. Don't blow your opportunity.'

He took another step towards her, so close that she could see their breath meet in the space between them.

'You're a very beautiful woman. I can see what caught David's attention. But personally I think you'd make a better mistress than a wife.' Robert lifted his hand and stroked her cheek. It was only the slightest gesture, but loaded with sexuality.

She jerked back as he smiled at her, his white teeth almost glowing in the dark.

'Don't worry, I prefer a less uptight fuck,' he laughed, looking at her with hard, unflinching eyes.

Without thinking, she slapped him across the cheek. Robert touched the pink skin on his face and narrowed his eyes. 'Be careful, Brooke. I can cause a lot of trouble.'

He walked off towards the house.

Yeah? Well, so can I, thought Brooke. *So can I.*

31

Parklands, the Asgills' country estate in Bedford, an elite pocket of New York State, always looked glorious; but today, on the fourth of July, it looked particularly magnificent. In preparation for the family's Independence Day festivities, the grounds-staff had manicured the lawns to perfection. The sky was the bright blue of a robin's egg, against which the ordered line of forest-green trees along the drive looked hyper-real. Liz walked across from the stables, back towards the neogothic house and smiled to herself. She was wearing jodhpurs and a fitted hacking jacket, having just returned from a bracing five-mile ride on her horse Dancer. Her mother's white Rolls-Royce was parked ahead of her on the gravel drive, and there were staff bustling around the grounds. *It's like being in a scene from The Great Gatsby*, she thought.

She walked around the side of the house and up a short flight of marble steps, her good mood putting a bounce in her step. Lunch was about to be served on the terrace, the table decorations suitably and stylishly patriotic. Jugs of red punch stood on the white tablecloths, along with little bunches of poppies, white roses, and delphiniums. From this position, Liz could see down into the gardens, where Greg, Parklands' young gardener, was bending over to prune a hibiscus bush. She smiled a little wider.

The French windows were open and Liz walked into the library to find Meredith sitting at the mahogany desk, leafing through a sheaf of papers.

'Ah, Liz, there you are,' she said, peering over the top of her half-moon glasses. 'I was just looking through these press cuttings that Tess Garrett gave me yesterday. I have to say she's doing a very impressive job.'

'Do you think?' said Liz sceptically, sitting in an armchair and stretching her long legs in front of her. Thinking of Tess made her uncomfortable, recalling as it did that sordid Russ Ford episode, but Liz was confident that Tess had kept it from her mother; otherwise she'd have heard about it long before now.

Meredith held up the cuttings file. 'Yes, we had the lovely *Vogue* cover for Brooke, plus some excellent news stories: Brooke and David at a soup kitchen in Central Park, looking so in love. You know, I had my doubts about this photographer friend of Tess's taking covert photographs of them, but it seems to be working. Then there's a *Forbes* magazine article about William, and even something in the *Wall Street Journal* describing Sean as a *philanthropist*,' she laughed. 'Can you believe it?'

Her mother's delight at Tess's work annoyed Liz, but she waited patiently: surely Meredith would comment on the volumes of positive press that Skin Plus had received? She looked expectantly at her mother, her eyebrows raised. Meredith said nothing.

'Are you going to get ready for lunch?' she said finally. 'I'm so glad you've brought Rav. He seems a very smart young man. Where in the world did you say he was from again?'

'He's American, Mum.'

'Hmm . . .'

Meredith averted her eyes. Liz didn't like to guess what she was alluding to. Was there a hint of casual racism in her enquiries? Did Rav's Indian heritage not fit in with her WASP ideal or the narrow-minded attitudes of her ageing Upper East Side friends?

I'm not seeking your approval, thought Liz. She was actually glad that her invitation of Rav to their fourth of July luncheon had provoked a reaction. She liked Rav. He was sociable, generous, well connected, and a good fuck. What more did anyone need from a man?

'So did you see that *Time* put me in the Top Forty under Forty?' asked Liz casually, wondering if Tess had managed to include that feature in the file of cuttings.

'Yes, I heard,' smiled Meredith, lifting a blonde brow. 'I'm not surprised, of course. The Skin Plus launch is one of the most exciting I've seen in all my time in the industry.'

Was that a compliment? thought Liz, narrowing her eyes to view her mother. *Good God.* She almost believed it was.

The library door creaked open and in walked William in chinos and a white shirt, holding a glass of red punch.

'Just wondered if you were coming through for lunch?' he asked, catching Liz's frown. 'I wasn't interrupting anything, was I?'

'No, no, we're coming,' said Meredith, rising to her feet. 'We were just discussing Skin Plus.'

William looked at his mother and then Liz. 'So you've told her?'

Meredith looked momentarily flustered and reached for the door-handle. 'Let's eat first, shall we?'

Liz stepped forward and put her hand on the door. 'Have I been told what, exactly?' she asked.

'Not now, darling,' said Meredith quickly. 'We're wanted on the terrace. I can smell the ham from here and you know Dolly cooks such a wonderful fourth of July ham.'

Liz pushed the door closed and turned to face them, her mouth set. 'What do you two have to tell me?' she asked more forcefully, a sensation of fear punching her in the chest.

'Liz, please. It's a holiday.'

Liz turned to William, who seemed to shrink as she looked at him. 'Well, then?' she asked her brother. 'Perhaps you'll tell me.'

William ran his hand through his hair.

'We thought you should know ahead of the next board meeting that we've decided to discontinue Natural Glow.'

Although Liz had been prepared for the announcement, she was still shocked and surprised.

'All those suggestions I made to salvage NG from the marketing idiots,' said Liz, 'I assume they have not been actioned?'

'Mother and I think it's best for the company if we cut our losses.'

'This is a board decision, William,' replied Liz. She knew of course that between them William and Meredith owned the bulk of the shares and could effectively do anything they liked.

'Liz, the decision has been made,' said Meredith. 'We made mistakes and we have to accept them.'

Liz snorted. 'Natural Glow was a one-hundred-million-dollar launch. That's an expensive mistake. In most companies, that would raise questions over leadership,' she added, looking directly at William.

'Come on, Liz,' said Meredith. 'We need to look forward now, not back. We have to take a long view about where the company is going, how the industry is changing, and our place within it.'

Liz caught her looking over at William again. 'Meaning . . .?'

William went and sat on the chaise longue by the window. 'Liz, we have tried to turn the company around and we've had some successes. But the fact of the matter is that five years ago we had sales of almost a billion dollars. Today it is four hundred million dollars.'

'I know the figures,' she snapped.

William stood up again and began pacing around the room as Meredith began to speak. Liz felt as if they were trying to assault her on both sides.

'In which case, you don't need me to remind you that the company is saddled with debt,' said Meredith. 'Skin Plus has cost us a fortune to launch. For longer-term growth we need liquidity. And the best way to obtain that is to sell a share in the company.'

'How much of a share?' said Liz, the sinking feeling growing in her stomach. 'How *much*?' she shouted.

William and Meredith kept silent, but they didn't need to speak. Liz knew exactly how much. *A majority share.* These idiots were going to lose control of the family company rather than admit their failures. Rather than hand the reins to her, let her turn the company around, they preferred to roll over and die.

'Bruno Harris has been sniffing around for a long time,' said William. 'I think we should talk to him.' Bruno Harris was a prominent Manhattan corporate raider. His investment vehicle, Canopus Capital, was known for buying up ailing companies, breaking them up, then selling them on for profit.

'Harris knows Asgill's is a strong brand name and that the perfume division is doing well. He told me he thinks The Balm can be converted into a multi-billion-dollar brand like Olay Beauty Fluid. I am going to propose at the board meeting that we enter into negotiations for a majority sale.'

Liz did a quick calculation in her head. Traditionally, sales of cosmetics companies were one to two times the amount of sales turnover. Liz estimated it would be nearer one than two, as Asgill's was a fading, debt-laden company and someone like Harris would take advantage of that. If the family sold a fifty-one per cent share, it would realize around two hundred million dollars, putting her

280

share at only ten million dollars. She could barely buy a Hamptons beach house with that! Struggling to contain her anger, Liz turned to her mother.

'We are a family company,' she said in a low voice, 'and it should stay in the family, growing for the next generation. There are ways to do that.'

Meredith shook her head sadly. 'Of course it's a family company, Liz, and no one is more ambitious for this family,' she said. 'When William says majority sale, what we are talking about is more of a *regroup.*'

Liz felt unnerved by that use of the word *we*. What had she and William been cooking up?

'A regroup?'

'We both feel that Skin Plus has enormous potential.'

Liz's eyes widened. She looked at them both disbelievingly. This wasn't happening. They couldn't be serious? Were they really talking about hijacking her business?

'We want to spin off the Skin Plus business,' explained William, avoiding her furious gaze. 'Harris doesn't particularly want it anyway, and if it's included in the deal, it will push the price too high. So our plan is to sell him the rest of the business and use the capital to expand Skin Plus aggressively. We're talking international growth within twelve months; it can be our platform for a more modern, more up-market family company.'

Liz was so shocked by the turn of events that she couldn't speak. Her mouth opened, but no sound came out. Undetered, William ploughed on.

'The cosmetics industry is not a one-size-fits-all business any more, Liz. Properly targeted niche brands are the future,' he said, as if she might actually believe this had been his plan all along. His cowardice and weakness made Liz want to vomit.

'Just think of it,' he said with excitement. 'We could go on a shopping spree to acquire more niche, up-market brands. Brands that would be a strategic fit with our new identity. We could do licensing deals with fashion houses and really reach out to the Chinese and Indian markets.'

But Skin Plus is mine, Liz felt like yelling. *I created this and now you're claiming it for your own, to save your ass.*

'It's the perfect time to be repositioning ourselves as a more up-market proposition,' said Meredith, looking brighter now their plot was out. 'Brooke's wedding is millions of dollars' worth of free advertising for the company.'

Liz looked out of the window, her mind reeling. Greg the gardener had now taken his shirt off, but his bare chest didn't even register on her consciousness.

'What's wrong, Elizabeth?' asked Meredith, unnerved by her daughter's silence. 'Don't you agree?'

Finally Liz could hold it in no more. 'Of course I agree!' she spat. 'This is *my* strategy; I am the one who created the Asgill luxury brand. I built Skin Plus up from nothing and now you are proposing to take it away from me to cover up *his* screw-ups?' she yelled, gesturing contemptuously at William.

'Elizabeth, this is a family company,' said Meredith.

'And I am the only one in this family with a successful track record,' shouted Liz. 'I have spent the last ten years using my talents to prop up this company and now I am the one made to suffer!'

Meredith flashed her a warning glance. 'Be careful, Liz,' she said. 'I wouldn't do or say anything foolish.'

Liz glared at her mother. *Oh, I haven't even started*, she thought. *You will pay for this; you will both pay.*

Her fury hadn't blunted her instincts, however, and she was a shrewd enough businesswoman to know that confrontation was not the best option when dealing with a stubborn, short-sighted enemy. And without a doubt, her family had just become her enemy. As she saw it, she was left with no choice, for one simple reason. Meredith and William's plan had completely failed to address the true problem: *them.* The strategy of selling off the outdated part of the company and using the proceeds to create a more modern, forward-looking business was actually quite sound. But the reason Skin Plus had worked was not because it was a niche brand or a luxury label: it had succeeded because of her, Liz Asgill; her vision, her hard work and her talent. Her mother clearly intended to create a brand-new, repositioned Asgill company, with the old management still in place. That was her mother's fatal flaw. She simply didn't know her children. Despite his repeated failures and ineffectual leadership, she still thought William was capable of running the company. *And me? You really have no idea what I am capable of, do you?* thought Liz, staring at her mother. *You really have no idea.*

'So what do you think?' asked William nervously, glancing across at Meredith for support. 'Do you agree to the plan? Because, if you do, I'll get a meeting in the diary with Bruno Harris as soon as we're back in the office.'

Liz didn't say anything for a moment; it was as if she hadn't heard him. William and Meredith exchanged worried looks.

'Liz?'

She glanced back at William, then simply nodded and walked towards the window. In her direct line of vision she could see an old oak tree on a stretch of grass that ran down to the river. It was where she used to go to sit and think. She would go there this afternoon. It was time to make a plan of her own.

32

Since Tess's arrival in New York, it had become a tradition that once a week she would have a catch-up with Brooke. Although their first meeting had been more like a council of war, Brooke had slowly come to enjoy their meetings, which were now more usually held at a lunch or at her flat over drinks. As much as Brooke had wanted to dislike Tess Garrett, assuming she would be pushy and sleazy like every other tabloid hack she'd ever met, to her surprise she had found the pretty English girl to be smart and refreshingly straightforward. On the face of it, their meetings were about work – which press had been offered or turned down, which stories had been deflected or buried, which events Tess thought Brooke should attend – but they often quickly descended into long girlie gossip sessions that were great fun.

Her intercom buzzed just as she had finished showering and changing into her favourite cashmere jogging pants. Tess was early, she thought, worrying that she had no time to blow-dry her hair, then laughing out loud at herself. *It's only Tess*, she reminded herself. *Those best-dressed lists have gone to my head.* She buzzed her in and poured a chilled Sauvignon from the fridge. It felt cold and fresh as it slipped down her throat.

'Hi. Sorry, I'm a bit early,' said Tess breathlessly as she bustled into the apartment laden down with bags and folders, dumping the lot on the B&B Italia dining table.

'Don't worry,' smiled Brooke, handing her a glass of wine. *She probably needs it*, she thought. Brooke had heard through the grapevine that Tess had just split up with that handsome English boyfriend of hers. Tess took a long sip of the drink.

'Cheap wine. Yuck,' she said. Brooke looked up with alarm before she saw a smile break out on her publicist's face.

'I'm joking,' smiled Tess. 'Sorry, English sense of humour. That is the most delicious Sauvignon I have ever tasted. Brooke, you have the best wine, the best clothes, the best men. I hate you.'

Brooke thought that this so-called English sense of humour seemed to comprise of sarcasm, half-truths, and irony, but she was too polite to say so.

'I shouldn't really be drinking,' said Brooke, taking a seat at the table. 'I've just had a very punishing session with my new personal trainer. Apparently I'll have a muffin top over my strapless wedding dress if I don't lose another one per cent of body fat.'

'Do you trust him?' asked Tess.

'My trainer? He has good results with other girls . . .'

'I don't mean that,' said Tess seriously. 'Can you trust him to keep quiet? I mean, if you're giving him details about your wedding gown being strapless, that sort of information can get out.'

Brooke felt herself blush. Obviously she hadn't thought about that when she'd told him.

'Sorry, I didn't think.'

Tess smiled. 'Don't be silly, I'm probably just being cynical and paranoid, but then that's my job, I'm afraid.'

'Well, we should probably talk about my trip to LA next week,' said Brooke, a little disappointed to be talking about PR matters so soon. 'I know the paps are pretty vicious out there, although really it's just an in-and-out trip to see the studio and then home.'

Tess was already reaching into her leather document case.

'First I think you should look at this.'

Brooke glanced up at Tess; she recognized the 'calm before the storm' coolness in her voice.

'A contact at one of the tabloids sent me this. It's a pap picture sent to her from Splash Pictures, one of the big photo agencies. My contact just wanted to check the designer of the jacket you're wearing because they plan to run the picture on the fashion pages.'

Brooke frowned. She couldn't see any reason for her publicist's concern, unless she had made some unforeseen fashion faux pas. Then Tess handed her the print and Brooke's heart leapt into her mouth. The picture was of herself and Matt Palmer. Since their day out to Amish country, Matt had called several times suggesting they meet for drinks or the movies. Most of the time she'd refused – there didn't seem to be enough hours in the day for anything non-crucial like *friends* these days – but last week Matt had called just as someone had cancelled on her for lunch. Matt had stepped into the breach and they'd met for pasta in Luigi's restaurant, back in the booth where they'd reconnected months ago. He'd told her a funny story about a young man who'd been brought into ER with a foreign body inside him which turned out to be a Barbie doll, while she'd told him about her difficult time in Newport and her forthcoming trip to LA. All very relaxed, just two friends catching up, yet Brooke looked down at the photograph with a sense of shame. It was certainly a poor picture, grainy and blurred, but it was obvious where they were, just emerging from the restaurant. Matt had been wearing sunglasses and on this shot his head was down. From that angle it looked like David, which surprised her because the similarity had never struck her before. Brooke kept quiet, waiting for Tess to speak first.

'Luckily, this isn't a big thing, Brooke,' she said, 'because the press clearly think it's David.'

Brooke had been so busy staring at the picture and worrying about the implications that she hadn't read the caption below the shot – a standard paparazzi agency practice – which read, 'Brooke Asgill and David Billington go shopping'.

'But it isn't David, is it?' said Tess. Her voice wasn't accusatory, but there was a definite note of concern. 'Similar build, but the angle of the cheekbones is different, as is the shape of his chin. And this guy looks about six foot two, but David is only six foot.'

Brooke could feel her cheeks redden. 'It's Matt Palmer,' she said as casually as she could.

'Really?' said Tess, tapping the photo. 'You must have forgotten to mention how good-looking he was.'

Momentarily Brooke stopped to marvel at how good her publicist was. Astute and accurate and detail-obsessed, like a good detective. In fact, she was exactly the sort of woman you wanted on your team – except when they were about to catch you out. But Brooke bristled at the implication; she had nothing to hide.

'He's just a friend, Tess.'

'Are you sure, Brooke?' asked Tess. 'Because I need you to be honest with me here. Are you both pretending you're just good friends when really you want to jump each other's bones?'

'Of course we don't want to jump each other's bones.'

An uncomfortable memory shifted to the front of her mind. It was so vague she half wondered if she'd dreamt it. She was in a club with Matt, some time after her final examinations, and she'd been drunk. Really drunk. The music had been loud; they'd been dancing together face to face, laughing, beer bottles clinking, when he'd leant forward and said to her, 'I think we should go home together.' Or at least that's what she thought he'd said over the pumping bass line. She'd ignored him, pretending not to hear, and he'd got the message.

She felt hot with embarrassment.

'We've known each other a long time and he's a really good listener.'

Tess rolled her eyes. 'Shit, Brooke. A shrink would be less bother.'

'When this picture was taken we'd met for lunch. It was in a public place, we weren't hiding, and I haven't mentioned him to you before because, well, it doesn't matter. There's no point whipping up trouble where there is no scandal, is there?'

Tess looked at her searchingly. 'Are you sure, Brooke?'

'Yes, I'm sure,' she replied, her skin prickling.

'Okay, fine,' she said, 'I know this is hard for you, having to monitor friendships, having to be careful who you're seen with – and I'm sorry to give you the third degree. But at least you know I'm watching out for you, and at least you know it's not forever.'

'But it is, isn't it?' said Brooke softly. 'This is what I've signed up to. A lifetime of being watched.'

Tess couldn't really disagree. Brooke drained her wine glass.

'I like the fact no one knows about Matt,' she said. 'I like the fact it's a little part of my life that's closed off, just mine.'

Her publicist was shaking her head. 'I wish I could tell you it was okay to have friends like that, but there are different rules for people like you. Just be careful, okay?'

'So, what do we do about this?'

'Well, you were smart to take Matt to a public place,' said Tess. 'I think you should do it again, somewhere really high profile, somewhere where he can be photographed with you and David so it looks as if you are all friends. In fact, make sure he gets to know David.'

Tess looked at Brooke.

'And Brooke, if Matt really *is* just a good friend,' she said, 'then that's what you should be doing anyway.'

Tess stared out of the cab window, watching Manhattan slip by in a blur. For a smart, decent girl, Brooke Asgill could be incredibly stupid, she thought. Okay, so maybe it was all above board and innocent, but that doctor was gorgeous! Some girls have all the luck, she smiled, making a mental note to get Jemma to keep an eye on Matt Palmer. The cab pulled up on Perry Street. Inside her apartment, Tess went straight to the fridge to see what she could cobble together. It was true what they said about New Yorkers living off takeouts, but tonight she couldn't wait. She found half a jar of pesto and stirred it into a bowl of piping hot penne and took it outside onto the deck with a glass of wine and a big stack of magazines. It was a balmy night, the faint sound of hip-hop in the distance, plus occasional honking cabs and police sirens: it was pure New York.

'Hey, I didn't know you were getting back so early.'

Tess was not annoyed to see Jemma coming through from the flat. She had been enjoying the rare solitude, but, despite sharing the flat, she rarely saw her friend. Jemma worked even longer hours than she did, stalking the hippest bars and restaurants in town for pap shots that she could sell back in England.

'It is eight o'clock,' said Tess. 'You're the one who works until three a.m.'

'Well, no one's out today,' said Jemma, perching on the little wooden chair opposite Tess. 'It's a quiet night, no parties, no openings – quite a relief, to be honest. So how was your day?' she asked, reaching over to pick a chunk of pasta from Tess's bowl.

'Oh, the usual,' sighed Tess. 'Exhausting. Do you know Dom had the cheek to phone me again today?'

'What did he say?'

'I never pick it up. But he's left four messages this week saying we need to talk.'

Tess stabbed at her penne, then put the fork down. Suddenly she wasn't feeling hungry any more. In the week after their split, she'd received a long email from him that started off apologetically but finished off by coldly suggesting that they should put their Battersea flat on the market. *Well, he could go and screw himself.* She didn't need the money and she had no need for the flat either, not now. Neither did he, she thought with a pang of jealousy, imagining him shacked up in some luxurious Holland Park mansion with 'Tamara'. She assumed he wanted the proceeds from the flat's sale so he could keep up with his new rich, fabulous friends: trips to Mustique and dinners at the Cipriani were not easily afforded by mid-ranking members of the press. *Well, I'm not going to help you with your little upper-class adventure. I'd rather burn that flat to the ground*, she thought, a little surprised at her own anger.

'So do you think he wants to get back with you?' asked Jemma, playing with a string of fairy lights that were wrapped around the terrace's railings.

'Huh,' snorted Tess, 'in his dreams.'

'That's the spirit,' grinned Jemma. 'Chuck me a magazine.'

Both girls began flicking through the big pile of publications that Tess had brought out. Most of them were British editions she read for work purposes, but somehow, she also found their familiarity comforting, like a little glimpse of home.

'Have you seen this picture of Sean with some dolly blonde?' asked Jemma, showing her the party section of *Tatler*.

'Hmm, yes. His new girlfriend, Annabel Calthorpe.'

'You know I think he's cute,' said Jemma casually. 'Cuter than David Billington, anyway. I know David is classically good-looking, but Sean looks as if he'd be very naughty in bed.'

'Urgh. You wouldn't say that if you'd met him.'

'So which one would you do?'

Tess flicked over another page, ignoring the question. She really didn't want to be asked questions about whether she found Sean Asgill attractive. She hadn't even spoken to him since the episode in London where he had humiliated her for what seemed like his own entertainment. She glanced up and saw that Jemma was still waiting for an answer.

'What?' she sighed. 'What was the question?'

'Which one would you shag? If you had to, I mean.'

'Jem, I work for them.'

'So what?' giggled Jemma. 'That would only make it more exciting. I think I'd shag Sean.'

Tess fell silent.

'What's wrong?' asked Jemma suddenly. 'Oh God! Have the Asgills got the flat bugged? Have I just got us both fired?'

But Tess wasn't listening. All her attention was focused on the

Hello she had just opened. Right in the centre of the news page was a large picture of Dom and Tamara next to the headline 'Society Beauty to Wed'. She tried to gulp in air but the oxygen failed to reach her lungs. She felt as if she was drowning.

'Tess? What's the matter?'

Tess finally took in a long, ragged breath. 'So that's why he's been trying to get in touch with me,' she whispered, her throat feeling dry.

Tess's hands were trembling as she passed the magazine over to Jemma. 'Look.'

Jemma's mouth slowly opened in an expression of shock, which swiftly turned to anger.

'The fucking snake,' she hissed. 'This magazine must have gone to the printers over a week ago. He must have proposed to her just after you two had finished.'

Tess nodded numbly. 'I can do the maths,' she replied flatly.

She fumbled for her glass and drained it. As Jemma came over and put a reassuring arm around her, Tess's shoulders began to shake.

'I'm an idiot,' she whispered. 'I'm a fucking idiot.'

'No, you're not,' said Jemma softly. '*He* is.'

Taking deep, heavy breaths, Tess rubbed her eyes with the palms of her hands. She did not cry. She never cried. She wasn't going to start now.

'You know what pisses me off the most? We were together for nine years. That's nearly a third of my life I've wasted on him.'

'It wasn't a waste, honey,' said Jemma. 'It's just life – you fall in love and things end.'

Tess banged her fist onto the table. 'But it's so unfair, Jem! I've worked my arse off for ten years and where does it get me? Yet *he* just strolls along to party – a party I had to beg to get him invited to – and walks off with a millionaire fiancée, while I'm stuck here in someone else's flat with no one but a twelve-year-old boy for company at the weekend.'

'Oh, thanks!' said Jemma with mock outrage. 'Jack gets top billing over me?'

But Tess was in no mood to laugh.

'I actually don't know why I'm so angry,' she went on. 'Is it because he's such a shallow, social-climbing rat and I didn't realize quite how much? Or because he seemed to fall in love with someone else so bloody quickly? Or . . .'

'What, honey?'

'. . . because he didn't want to marry *me*.'

She felt her lip quiver as she said the final word, the anger giving way to self-pity. Tess remembered how she had reacted to her father's death and how she had discovered that grief could be a selfish emotion. The distress for the loss of a loved one was often mixed up with a feeling of universal injustice: *Why did it happen to me? How could I have made things different? Why didn't I say all those things I wanted to?* In the end, it was all wasted emotion. What was done was done and no one could turn back time. The end of a relationship was no different. She looked at Jemma sadly.

'You know, through the first year of our relationship I used to have a photo of Dom as my screensaver? Pathetic, isn't it? I think it was to remind me that he was real. I couldn't believe that someone like me was going out with someone as good-looking as him.'

'Oh Tess, now you're just being silly,' said Jemma. 'You know you're gorgeous. And I'll be honest, Dom's never done it for me.'

Tess wondered for a moment whether Dom had really been doing it for her. She supposed he hadn't, not really, not for a long time. For the past year, Tess had found that the slightest thing irritated her about Dom. His endless grooming before leaving the house, his know-it-all pontificating about the world's 'best places', his terrible name-dropping about work: everything about him seemed to set her teeth on edge. Maybe they really had been growing apart, falling out of love. But it wasn't that truth which hurt, the knowledge that she should really have done something about their relationship sooner. No, what really hurt was that someone she loved had preferred someone else. Seeing him grinning happily from the pages of the magazine had simply compounded every feeling of insecurity and inadequacy she had ever felt. Underneath all the career bravado and ambition were old wounds, and this had just torn them open.

'If I hadn't taken this job, we would never have gone to that Asgill Cosmetics launch and he would never have met Tamara . . .' began Tess.

'Okay, stop that!' said Jemma sharply. 'You're not a victim, Tess. You are a strong, beautiful, kick-ass bitch and you're not going to sit here wallowing.'

She pulled Tess's arm, dragging her into the flat.

'Right, get in that bedroom and doll yourself up,' she said sternly.

'There's a great salsa bar in the East Village. We're going to go and drink loads of margaritas and find ourselves two chilli-hot men, then dance until they throw us out.'

Despite herself, Tess laughed. 'Okay,' she smiled. 'But, if you don't mind, I think I'll give the men a miss and stick with the margaritas.'

33

The penthouse bar of the Clifton Hotel had taken over from the Gansevoort as the hottest rooftop watering hole in Manhattan and, despite her bad, distracted mood, Liz could not fail to be impressed by the views. In front of her the Empire State Building was lit up blue, red, and silver, like a giant platinum rocket, while the lights of Manhattan twinkled and shimmered like an oasis in the desert. Inside the bar, the faces of the crowded party-goers were given a golden cast by the hurricane lanterns placed on the bar and the walls. It was cosy, yet exclusive – an apt location for tonight's event, a Wall Street networking event-cum-drinks party hosted by the financial magazine, *The Fund*. Liz was here at Rav's invitation and, as she looked around, she was amazed how few women went to these things. Perhaps that was accounted for by the fact that there were so few very senior women on Wall Street. If you weren't in the boys' club, you didn't get on. Rav approached carrying two drinks with an apologetic half-smile.

'Sorry,' he said, kissing her on the lips as he handed her a stemmed martini glass.

'Whatever for?' she asked.

'For leaving you alone for so long.'

Liz was almost touched by his protectiveness, although suspected that his alpha-male routine was for the benefit of his fellow party-goers, most of whom Liz had noticed checking her out. No wonder, she smiled to herself: she did look sensational in a chocolate-brown, form-fitting Gucci dress that accentuated her slim waist and pert breasts.

'Don't worry, I can look after myself,' she said with just the right balance of censure and flirtation. Rav's dark eyes danced across Liz's before he spoke.

'I've just been speaking to some of the guys from Petersen's,' he said, name-checking the boutique investment bank and jerking his thumb towards a group of suits standing by the bar. She glanced at her watch, already bored, already having dismissed Rav's banking friends as being too far down the pecking order to be of any importance. In fact, in the ten minutes she had been sitting on her own, she had worked out there was no one here worth meeting that she didn't already know and, as she had a hair appointment at seven a.m. with Enrique at Skin Plus, she wanted an early night.

'A group of them have rented a chalet in Aspen for Christmas,' continued Rav. 'They wanted to know if I wanted in.'

'Sounds fun,' shrugged Liz. 'What's the problem?'

'It's over Christmas and New Year.'

Liz smiled at Rav's ham-fisted transparency. 'Is that a roundabout way of asking me if you're invited to Brooke and David's wedding?' she asked archly.

'Well, I didn't know if it was going to happen over the holidays,' he stammered.

'You're a bad liar, darling,' she smiled, touching his chin. 'The tabloids all seem to think it's on New Year's Eve, and I know you read those awful rags because I've seen you.'

Watching him smile like a child with his hand caught in the cookie jar, Liz realized that she did not entirely object to Rav being at Brooke's wedding with her. He made her laugh, sometimes, and while he had not introduced her to anyone important, he *had* provided a distraction this summer. At weekends he took her to parties in the Hamptons; he was a more than competent tennis partner and he was generous with his money. Although Liz generally preferred older men, the beauty of a younger man – particularly one in clear awe of Liz's sexuality – was his *eagerness*.

Her eyes wandered across the crowd and met a familiar stare. 'I don't believe it,' she said. 'Leonard's here.'

She strode over, but instead of an embrace, she met her uncle with a challenging stare. 'What on earth are you doing here?' she demanded.

'You're not the only one with friends on Wall Street,' replied Leonard with a half-smile. 'Not that I'm fitting in here, by any means. The banking profession gets younger every time I look.'

He accepted a cocktail from a passing waiter and looked at the purple concoction curiously while Liz watched him. This was the first time Liz had spoken to Leonard since the Asgill's board meeting the day before, when William and Meredith's plan to put Asgill Cosmetics up for sale had been officially ratified. While she was still angry, she knew she had to step carefully: Leonard was no fool, and had many friends and allies both inside the company and out.

'Liz, I just want you to know that I respect your judgement and I know how much the family business means to you,' said Leonard, addressing the unspoken.

'Which is why you sold me down the river in the board meeting?' asked Liz, her tone light, but the point deliberate. Liz had spent the previous week considering her options, even discreetly consulting an attorney to discuss suing her family. It had been disappointing; the lawyer had advised that direct legal action was possibly not the best course of action until she had explored every other avenue, first trying to persuade the board not to sell. Unanimous board approval was needed for a company sale, and so immediately she had picked off the three board members she thought might listen to what she had to say, taking them to the city's best restaurants and giving them her impassioned plea not to approve the sale. Even as she was doing it, Liz knew it wasn't going to be enough. She knew that even the board members who were prepared to listen to her didn't exactly like her. It was obvious why: time and time again, Liz had showed up their shortcomings. To Liz's mind, it was deeply unfair that she was being penalized for being the only voice on the board willing to speak out and make brave suggestions, even if it meant disrupting the status quo. They thought she was a bitch; she thought they were pussies.

In the event, only Leonard had raised any objections to the proposed sale. Liz was pleased; she had always had a much closer relationship with her uncle than with her mother and, while he had an annoying tendency to sit on the fence, at least he seemed to respect Liz's capabilities. She had been outraged therefore when he had capitulated under the full force of Meredith's disapproving gaze and had voted for a sale. Left without allies, Liz had also been forced into a 'yes' vote, knowing that if she were the sole dissenter her mother, with her majority shareholding, would simply vote her off the board.

God, I hate my family, she thought suddenly, closing her hands into tight fists.

'Anger isn't going to achieve anything, Liz,' said Leonard, catching the gesture.

'I'm not angry. Just disappointed,' she said as evenly as she could. 'Although I knew you would all just stick together like sheep, following Mother's lead as always.'

'My decision was for the long-term good of the company, not your career,' said Leonard. 'Your time will come.'

'And when will that be?' she asked tartly.

He paused to look at her, the light from the lamps making his face ghostly pale.

'Meredith won't stay chairman of the board forever, Liz.'

She rolled her eyes. *Yeah, right.* Her mother was not yet seventy, and strong as a horse. She could keep going for another ten years at least, just popping in for meetings, being wheeled out for events. Estée Lauder had been a figurehead for their company until her *nineties*. Besides which, with Meredith and William in charge, Asgill's might be finished in three years, let alone thirty. It was a fear that had kept Liz up at night. Without her work, her business, what did she have left? Staring down the barrel of forty with no business, no relationship, no family – where did that leave her in the world? She could start again, of course, but if her family drove the Asgill brand into the ground, they would take her reputation with it; she would find it difficult to find any backers.

Anger isn't going to achieve anything, Liz; that's what Leonard had said. Well, anger was all she had. She could not tolerate the thought of little doe-eyed Brooke ending up with everything, while she ended up with nothing, living off the reflected glory of her sister's charmed life. Not that Liz wanted Brooke's life – in fact that looked like hell to her: following a man around, simpering and smiling, pleasing. No, Liz was not jealous, she was simply meritocratic: she wanted a chance to prove how good she was. But right now, Liz saw that it was pointless to give Leonard a hard time. She had tried reason and it had failed, she would have to come up with something more effective.

'When this deal goes through, Liz,' said Leonard, 'I will speak to Meredith about stepping up your role at Asgill's. I would recommend you be made Chief Operating Officer. You'd be practically co-chief executive, although I suspect you wouldn't like to be "co" anything.'

Liz didn't dignify the idea with a reply.

'So when does due diligence begin?' she asked, referring to the process whereby a potential purchaser investigated a company before sale. They would examine the company accounts, assess stock and contracts, look for ways they could make cutbacks or maximize productivity.

'It starts on Monday, I believe,' said Leonard, sipping his cocktail. 'Bruno Harris has instructed Petersen's and they are very efficient. I know everyone concerned is keen to get this deal through quickly.'

Liz looked over at Rav, laughing with his banker pals.

'Me too, Uncle Leonard,' she said, a plan beginning to form in her head. 'Me too.'

34

Tess licked the last of the Frozen Hot Chocolate off her spoon and pulled a face at Jack.

'Now I feel totally fat,' she said. She glanced down at the huge serendipity menu, wondering if they offered Alka-Seltzer as a digestif.

'Come on, it was worth it,' smiled Jack, still struggling through his giant banana split.

Tess did have to admit she was enjoying the famous Upper East Side eatery enormously. When she had promised to spend the afternoon with Jack and he insisted they go to Serendipity, Tess had groaned. Too many children, too much noise, much too *much*, she had thought. But once she had got there, she had discovered the restaurant was like a tiny *Alice in Wonderland* cavern full of sweet ice-creamy confections and happy people. She had also discovered that Frozen Hot Chocolate dessert was the perfect way to cool down on a stiflingly humid late August afternoon in the city.

'I'm going to be really sad when I don't live in New York any more,' said Jack, taking a long slurp of cola.

Tess pointed her spoon at him. 'Hey, I thought you were embarrassed to be seen out with me,' she teased. 'Don't tell me you're actually enjoying yourself?'

Jack shook his head and looked serious. 'I think I might be moving to Connecticut,' he said.

Tess sat back, momentarily thrown. Over the past few months, Jack had almost become part of the furniture, turning up at inopportune moments, raiding the fridge, hogging the cushions when they were watching reruns of *Seinfeld*. Jemma thought he was hilarious and would get into deep conversations with him about space and time travel, two of Jack's favourite subjects. He had become part of their little impromptu family. But Tess had suspected this was on the cards, especially as his mother had been visiting more and more frequently.

'My mom has come back for me,' said Jack. 'I heard them talking a couple of nights ago.'

'But I thought you liked it with your dad,' frowned Tess.

'I do.'

He looked down at his plate, drawing patterns in the chocolate sauce. 'I don't want to go, Tess, but I feel bad about saying that because it's my mom and I love her.'

He looked up at her, his eyes flat and sad. 'Will you come and visit me?'

Throwing a fifty-dollar bill onto the table, she heard a nagging voice inside her head telling her not to get too involved.

'Come on, I'd better get you home,' she said.

Tess had never been inside Jack's apartment before and was pleasantly surprised by what she saw. From the outside, the building was scruffy and run-down, but inside it was very nice; actually better than her own apartment in many ways, not least in terms of space. It had four large rooms with high ceilings and a bright living room/kitchen painted pale grey with bold prints on the walls. As they walked in, Kevin was sitting at the computer, a concentrated frown on his face.

'Hey,' he said, standing up as he saw Tess, running a flustered hand through his hair. 'I didn't expect you so soon.'

'Sorry,' said Tess, 'I hope I'm not disturbing anything.'

'No, no, come in. Let me get you some coffee,' he said.

Tess sat down on the bright-yellow sofa with Jack. Immediately, the boy began whispering in her ear.

'Hmm, why do I get the feeling you're about to gang up on me about something?' said Kevin, putting a mug of coffee on a coaster in front of Tess.

'Jack told me about his mother.'

Kevin nodded and looked at Jack. He pulled a crumpled five-dollar bill from his pocket and handed it over. 'We need bread. Go get some.'

'Oh I get it,' said Jack, grinning as he got up. 'Adult talk.'

Tess waited until she heard the door close, then looked at Kevin seriously. 'Listen, I know none of this is my business,' said Tess, cradling her coffee, 'but Jack told me he wants to stay with you, so I was wondering why does Melissa want him back all of a sudden?'

'You met Steven,' sighed Kevin. 'Apparently it's serious, and what I hear is he can't have kids and wants a family. QED, Melissa wants Jack in her life full time again.'

Kevin was trying to be matter-of-fact, but Tess could tell that this was troubling him deeply. 'Steven's a rich guy,' he said. 'And rich guys always get what they want, don't they?'

'Not necessarily,' said Tess. Once again her inner voice told her to butt out, but she couldn't help feeling sympathy for Kevin's plight. Tess had always got the feeling that Melissa only liked spending time with her son when it suited her. In the short time Tess had known the family, there had been at least three weekends when Melissa had stood Jack up. She always called after the fact to offer some unavoidable crisis as explanation, but Tess saw the effect it was having on Jack. He tried to brush it off, but he was just a kid and he took each missed visit as a rejection.

'I don't know a great deal about family law in New York,' said Tess, 'but I do know you're the primary carer. Surely they can't just take him away?'

'Problem is, I haven't officially got custody of Jack,' said Kevin. 'Melissa and I never married. Never saw the point, to be honest. And, as it turned out, I was right about that.'

'Ah, let me guess,' said Tess. 'She was having an affair.'

Kevin snorted. 'Yes, with a so-called friend of mine from Buffalo while I was in Iraq. She left me a few weeks after I'd got home, which was real nice. I said I wanted Jack to stay with me; after all, I came back from Iraq to find I'd lost Melissa. I didn't want to lose my son as well.'

'And she agreed to that?'

'It was the one thing we didn't really argue over. Can you believe not fighting to keep your child? Man, I cut that woman a lot of slack in my time, but I could never understand that one. Anyway, when his mother moved downstate, I moved too. Not too close to her, of course, but close enough so we could still keep the agreement.'

'So have you seen a lawyer?'

'Well, I got legal advice,' he said slowly, not quite meeting her eye.

'Which is what?'

Kevin looked sheepish.

'I've been on the Internet looking up the law. There's this really good site where people reply to your legal problems. Eric from New Jersey says my position would be stronger if Melissa and I had been married.'

Tess was shaking her head. 'Eric from New Jersey?' she said incredulously. 'And you *trust* Eric from New Jersey?'

She walked over to the computer. There was a large pile of books on the windowsill behind it and she could see that most were legal texts from the library and, on the desk, pages and pages of notes. She turned back to him.

'Kevin, you can't do this on your own. Their lawyers will crucify you.'

Kevin looked defensive.

'So I guess you know how much lawyers cost in America?' he said. 'It's two thousand dollars just for the initial consultation.'

'But he's your son!'

'Hey, I would walk into hell for that boy,' he said angrily, 'but, but . . .' His voice cracked and he sank down onto the sofa. '. . . I just don't have the money.'

His hands went to his face and, when he looked back up, Tess saw tears glistening in his eyes.

'Ah shit, maybe Jack is better off with his mom,' he said, pinching his eyes with his fingertips. 'Their relationship is okay, I guess. Now she can give him a good home, you know? A big house and the best schools.'

'That's bullshit,' said Tess fiercely. 'This has nothing to do with a big house.'

'But what life can I provide for him?' he asked miserably. 'I work shifts, Tess, ninety-hour weeks sometimes. I do the best I can, but for two hours every day Jack is looked after by our fifteen-year-old neighbour when he comes home after school. I'm barely managing this thing.'

'It doesn't matter,' said Tess. 'You provide Jack with a life he loves and a home he's loved in. That's far more important.'

Her depth of feeling and sense of injustice surprised her. She dimly remembered seeing flashes of fighting spirit in her father shortly after her mother left them. But it was temporary, a precursor to his slide into the depression that left him a broken man.

'Listen to me, Kevin,' she said firmly, 'we will not let Melissa get custody of Jack.'

Kevin shook his head. 'I know you want to help, Tess, but Melissa knows that Jack is looked after by our neighbour and she's going to use it against me to show I am not a good father.'

'Well, I'm not going to let that happen.'

'You? Are you a lawyer?'

'No,' said Tess, 'but I know someone who is.'

They both turned as they heard the front door open, to see Jack standing in the doorway holding a loaf of bread.

'Is everything okay?' he said hopefully.

'It's going to be,' nodded Tess. 'It's going to be just fine.'

35

'You're working late.'

Liz looked up, startled. She was standing at her assistant's desk by the clutter of office equipment – fax, binding machine, shredder – waiting for a document to come off the printer.

'Late? Not especially,' she said. It was eleven p.m. and frankly she was amazed to see William. All the lights on this floor were off and there was little sign of life, except for the low buzz of a vacuum cleaner. Most days her brother left the office by six thirty, and at drinks, launches, or networking events he stayed less than an hour. Benefit dinners and parties were even worse; if you wanted to find him, he would be standing by the door holding Paula's coat, waiting for his wife to finish socializing so he could go home. Which is why Liz was on full alert now: if he was in the office so late, there must be a very good reason for it.

William perched on the desk and began drumming his fingers on the edge nervously.

'I've been upstairs with marketing since eight this morning,' he said. 'There's a lot of due diligence questions to sort out.'

He nodded to where she was shuffling papers in the binding machine. 'Shouldn't you get your assistant to do all that?'

Liz hated having been caught off guard, but hid her annoyance by pushing hard down on the lever. 'I'm saving you money,' she said.

William folded his arms in front of him and looked at his sister intently.

'Liz, I have to know if you are happy with all this.'

'All what?' she asked flatly, putting down her document.

'Selling Asgill's. Spinning off Skin Plus. I know you expressed doubts in the board meeting and I know how important Skin Plus is to you, but it's a good offer from Canopus. You have a sharp, clever brain, Liz: you must know this is the right thing to do.'

Sharp, clever brain indeed, she thought. How she could run circles around him. How she was *going* to.

'Yes, I'm upset, William, I won't deny it, but not for the reasons you think. I'm not upset for greed or hurt pride.'

'I don't think that,' frowned William. 'So why are you upset?'

She paused, tried to look as solemn as possible.

'I just don't think Dad would have wanted us to sell out,' she said quietly.

A half-smile curled up on his face. 'Come on, Liz, you of all people wouldn't make decisions based on sentimentality. Anyway, we're not closing down by any means – we're simply offloading the weakest parts of the business and starting again, debt-free, with a brand that has much more potential.'

She had to turn her face away from him, pretending to fiddle with her documents, so he would not see the anger in her eyes.

'It's too late to talk about all this,' she said.

'Well, you're right about that,' he said, misunderstanding her. 'Paula will be in bed by the time I get home and she's off to Bermuda tomorrow, so I'm hardly going to see her in the next week.'

Liz had no idea what Paula could be doing in Bermuda but, whatever it was, the thought riled her. Yet more squandering of money, no doubt. William stood up, stretching.

'Well, I'm glad we've talked, Liz,' he said, touching her arm. 'I'll see you tomorrow.'

'Goodbye,' she said softly as she watched him disappear down the dark corridor.

And I mean that in every way possible, she added to herself.

She picked up the document she had been holding minutes earlier and smiled. She had quite enjoyed the illicit thrill of almost being caught. Walking back to her desk, she flipped it open and began to read by the thin cone of light from her desk lamp. *Is there enough here?* she wondered, thumbing through the pages. *Yes, there's plenty.*

She slipped the file into a brown envelope and addressed it – with a label from the printer, naturally; she couldn't have her handwriting on it – to Hugh Montague, an analyst at Petersen's. Rav had been delighted when Liz had shown so much interest in his friends at the financial institution. After Rav's gossipy break-down of their relative strengths and weaknesses, she had chosen Hugh Montague instantly. He was perfect – just moved over from London and keen to make his mark. Rav had even hinted that Hugh might be involved with some slightly shady offshore deals. Oh yes, he sounded perfect, thought Liz, picking up her coat and heading for the blue postbox on the corner of Fifth. I think Hugh Montague and I are going to be very good friends indeed.

36

'You are going to love it here,' said Katrina Savoy, pressing her foot down on the gas pedal of her Jeep.

Paula turned and smiled, watching her new friend's hair blow back in the Bermudan breeze. Frankly, Paula couldn't believe how well they were getting along – it was far beyond what she had hoped for. If she didn't know better, she would have said the princess was treating her like a genuine friend. Already that morning they'd had a game of tennis at the Coral Beach and Tennis Club, the prestigious and virtually impossible-to-access private members' club. The following day they had lunch pencilled in with some of Katrina's Bermudan friends at the famous Tom Moore's Tavern and, in between, she had promised to help Paula buy a place on this delightful island where she already felt at home. The Jeep stopped outside Paula's hotel and Katrina stretched over to kiss her on both cheeks.

'I'm so glad you love the island as much as we do,' said Katrina, waving goodbye. 'See you tomorrow!'

Paula waved back, her cheeks flushed with excitement. Even though this trip had started out as a throwaway conversational titbit at Carlotta's birthday party, Paula was genuinely impressed with Bermuda and its bright sunshine, glorious-coloured beaches, and refined Englishness. If she was honest, however, the beauty of the island was simply a bonus. The primary objective of coming here was to further her relationship with the royal family and, even if Bermuda had been a mosquito-infested swamp, she would still have considered buying here if it meant she could boast Katrina as a friend. She had worked on her plan like a military campaign,

using Casey's play-date with Carlotta a week after Carlotta's
birthday party to casually extract from Katrina the dates she would
be in Bermuda, then had rushed home to book a suite at the exclusive Pink Beach Club hotel the same week. As it had turned out,
the timing could not have been more perfect. Paula had been
absolutely delighted to hear about the proposed sale of a majority
shareholding in Asgill Cosmetics to Canopus Capital. She had never
been particularly interested in the business, but William seemed
incredibly excited about the deal, and a part-realization of his
shareholding would give them lots of liquid cash to play with.
Incredibly, William had even been receptive to the idea of looking
for a place to buy in Bermuda. She had raved about Bermuda's
proximity to Manhattan; only a two-hour flight away from New
York – less door-to-door if she invited Brooke and David, when
they would no doubt fly private out of Teterboro. She pointed out
its position as an understated playground for Manhattan's most
wealthy, including its fabulous championship golf courses. But most
of all, Paula had emphasized how a second home on the island
might make her more relaxed and receptive.

On the night before she'd left for the island, she'd initiated sex
and, afterwards, curled into his arms to weave a fantasy of a
future life for them together. 'Just think,' she'd said as she stroked
the hair on his chest. 'In five, ten years' time, you can take early
retirement from Asgill's and we can move to Bermuda full time.
Me, you, and the kids. Lots of them, all running around in the
sun. I'd like that.'

William had seemed to like the idea too.

The Pink Beach Club was in the exclusive Bermudan enclave of
Tucker's Town. Paula was standing on the patio of her cottage,
sipping a freshly pressed orange juice, when she heard a knock at
the door. She answered it, to find a handsome, confident-looking
man of about thirty-five standing there. His skin was lightly tanned,
he had short dark hair; his suit, thankfully, was of the regular
variety, rather than worn with Bermuda shorts as was the custom
here. Paula just couldn't get used to that.

'Mrs Asgill?' he said with a bright smile. 'Are you ready?'

'Oh, you're Tom?'

'That's right, shall I lead the way?'

She had spoken to real-estate agent Tom Hawsley at length over the phone, but had never met him until now. Their discussions had been long and detailed, as Paula had very definite requirements for a property: something of size, something suitable for high-level entertaining. Sea views were essential, of course, as were at least four guest bedrooms and staff quarters, which did not have to be attached to the main house. A tennis court was also a must, along with at least five acres of grounds and an infinity pool. She was also very particular about the type of architecture of the property: ideally something with an English colonial flavour to it. Something of an Anglophile, Paula had always fancied herself as a Henry James-type heroine after once seeing Nicole Kidman in some period adaptation, and she made it clear she would not settle for any billionaire-funded eco-homes or anything with an eccentric Japanese-Mexican fusion theme.

Tom led her towards a silver car and gallantly opened the door for her. 'We have several very nice properties lined up for you today,' he smiled as they set off.

As they wound around the narrow, fragrant lanes, he pointed out Michael Bloomberg's house and a number of other dwellings owned by celebrities. They spent three hours driving round the island; the more Paula saw of Bermuda, the more she loved it. It was incredible to think it was less than seven hundred miles away from the coast of North Carolina. The sand was the pale pink of a ballet slipper; even the air, surrounded by thousands of miles of Atlantic Ocean, smelt fresher and sweeter. The houses, however, were less than satisfactory.

'I'm not interested in anything that looks like a Fort Lauderdale retirement home,' she said after the third house had been rejected. 'I want old-school Bermuda. I want class and elegance.'

Tom Hawsley smiled politely. He had gently tried to tell her that the eight-million-dollar price ceiling she had given him was unrealistic given her long list of requirements, but he was sure his objections had fallen on deaf ears.

'Well, I've saved the best till last,' he said, as they headed back towards Tucker's Town. 'This one is a little more than you wanted to pay, but it's one of the most outstanding properties to come on the market in a long time.'

'In that case, I'm definitely interested,' said Paula briskly as she watched the lush countryside give way to a more built-up area.

'How do you like Tucker's Town?' asked Tom, glancing across at her.

'I love it,' she smiled. She had been particularly impressed that you had to pass a uniformed guard just to get into the most exclusive pocket of the island.

'Yes, I think you're probably best suited to this area,' he said smoothly, the compliment not wasted on his companion.

'It's where my friends live. Do you know Katrina Savoy's place?'

Tom raised an eyebrow and his interest in Paula seemed to click up a notch. 'Oh yes, I do,' he said. 'A beautiful house.'

Swinging left, the car passed through iron gates, down a long drive, and pulled up outside a white detached residence with a large veranda that snaked around its whole perimeter. 'Now this is more like it,' smiled Paula, climbing out. The setting was spectacular, with views out to the Atlantic Ocean lying in turquoise and cobalt blue stripes in front of her.

The house was not huge, but big enough, with seven bed- and bathrooms. The interior design was a little too chintzy, but already Paula was making mental notes on what improvements she could make, and imagining taking afternoon tea with Katrina and her new friends on the veranda.

'There are beautiful fireplaces in every room,' said Tom, handing her a colour sales brochure. 'Bermudan winters can get a little fresh, although nothing like the temperatures in New York, of course. The grounds are wonderful, too. Orange, lemon, and avocado trees grow just over there by the infinity pool.'

Paula watched him pace around the room and just for a moment saw a little of herself in Tom Hawsley. He was not of this world, just play-acting, pretending he was comfortable in this environment. It was something she could relate to. During her final two summers at high school, Paula had worked as a maid at the local hotel in Greenboro, a beautiful stately house where she could imagine herself living as the rich, beautiful chatelaine. Back then, she realized, she might even have found Tom Hawsley attractive. She hadn't missed how lovely his eyes were, a pale grey, with long spidery black lashes.

As Paula had been lost in thought, Tom had walked up behind her. 'I take it you like it,' he said, touching her bare arm.

Paula flinched, feeling uneasy with the thoughts now running through her head. She had learnt, long ago, to block anything inappropriate out of her life, and she stepped away from him, flustered.

Her mother had taught her that one slip could ruin your life and she wasn't going to let anything spoil her perfect moment.

'I think I just need a few moments alone,' said Paula quickly, taking her cell phone out of her Birkin. 'I need to speak to my husband about the house.'

She retreated to the veranda, her gaze lost on the blue horizon. She'd always wanted a house with an ocean view. When she had been in Greenboro, surrounded by trailers and broken cars, she swore to herself that, one day, she would live in the light where she could see for miles. People in her hometown used to say that money didn't matter. Well, whoever had said it hadn't been here, where the air tasted cleaner and the sun seemed to shine through the haze like liquid silk. Excited now, she scrolled down to William's number and pressed 'call'.

'Darling, it's me.'

'Oh, hi. How's Bermuda?'

Suddenly she felt a rush of warmth for her husband. 'Oh darling, you're going to absolutely love it. The golf here is fantastic. The house I'm standing in front of at the minute is going to blow your mind. I mean, it's Price on Application, so I don't even know how much it is yet but—'

'Paula, the Bermuda house will have to wait.'

Despite the heat, her skin felt icy cold. 'Sorry? I don't understand. But we agreed . . .'

'Honey, the deal is off.'

William's voice sounded tired and weary down the line.

'Canopus have pulled their offer,' he continued. 'Or rather, they've revalued the company and are now offering half the value per share.'

'*Half?*' she almost shrieked. 'Why the hell have they done that? *Can* they do that? A deal's a deal.'

'Not exactly, honey,' he said patiently. 'They have to do due diligence first, investigate the company, look at the accounts, and work out if the company is worth what they've offered.'

Paula looked around at the house. Suddenly it seemed even more beautiful than before, now that it was slipping from her grasp. 'So what's wrong with the company?'

William sighed. 'It's too complicated to go into right now. We are trying to answer Bruno Harris's concerns, but if they won't back down, the bottom line is that we can't sell Asgill's.'

'I . . .' she stuttered, 'I just don't believe it.'

'I know it's disappointing, honey.'

'But this house is in Tucker's Town,' she said, her voice almost pleading. 'It's so beautiful. Do you know how rarely properties like this come on the market?'

'Honey, a house in Bermuda wasn't really a priority anyway.'

She fell silent, unable to speak. Her heart was racing, her breath fluttery. *Not a priority? How dare he! After all she'd done to position them in high society!* She flipped her mobile shut angrily.

Tom Hawsley walked out onto the veranda.

'Is everything all right, Mrs Asgill?'

'It will be,' she said coolly, opening her phone again and scrolling through her numbers.

Who shall I call, she wondered. Buffy Meyers, perhaps? Jasmine Pilcher? Someone in her social database would be able to help. Because, for the first time ever, Paula Asgill was looking for a good divorce lawyer.

37

Tess was on a mission. As soon as she got into the office on Monday morning, she headed straight for Patty Shackleton's.

'Pats, I need a favour,' she said, popping her head around the door.

It was seven a.m. and Patty Shackleton already looked hard at work.

'I'm not sure I can handle another sex scandal,' she said wearily. 'Everyone seems to be getting it except me.'

Sliding into the chair opposite the lawyer, Tess launched into her story of Kevin's custody fight with Melissa. When she had finished, Patty sat back in her chair and steepled her fingers in front of her mouth and chuckled, 'And when did you become the patron saint of lost causes?'

'Hey, don't be like that,' said Tess. 'Jack is my friend and he needs my help.'

'And the father, this Kevin? He wouldn't be the strong handsome type by any chance, would he?'

'I've had enough of men,' Tess smiled cynically.

For a moment, Patty sat there, thinking. Even though they were friends, Patty's calm unnerved Tess. She wasn't used to dealing with someone so composed, not after a decade of working in newspapers, where anger was regularly vented in outbursts of expletives and desk-thumping. Finally Patty said, 'I'm not a family lawyer.'

'But you are a lawyer,' insisted Tess, 'a good one.'

'I'm a lawyer who works fifteen hours a day for the Asgills. I have no life, let alone spare time to go on a crusade. I just don't have the time for taking on board Kramer versus Kramer.'

It was exactly the way Tess had expected her to respond. After all, Tess would have said the same thing six months ago. Back then she had practically been allergic to children, but now, having got to know and care for Jack and his father, she couldn't stand by and watch their family broken up.

'That little boy means the world to Kevin,' she said. 'I don't know how he'd react if his wife took Jack away.'

'Then why can't he get a lawyer?'

'Because he just hasn't got that type of money. As we speak, he's probably on the Internet trying to do it himself, taking advice from amateur Judge Judys.'

Patty raised a hand, 'Okay, okay. I get the picture.'

'He's single—'

'And that's supposed to make a difference?'

'He's cute too . . .'

Tess could see the crack of a smile on her friend's lips.

'All right, what do you want me to do?' said Patty with a note of slight exasperation.

'Meet Kevin. Give him some advice. In fact, let's make a night of it. Come to mine for supper tomorrow and I'll invite Kevin. I'll get Jemma in too and we can all put our thinking caps on.'

Patty looked wary. 'I'll be working late all week,' she said.

'Friday night then,' said Tess, refusing to give up. 'No one works late on a Friday night.'

Patty let out a long breath. 'Okay, as long as you make one of those English roasts with those funny little potatoes.'

'It's a deal!' said Tess. 'I might even do bread sauce.'

'Eweugh!'

Tess got up and backed out through the door before Patty could change her mind.

'Eight p.m.,' she said, 'and maybe you should think about dressing up?'

'Out!' shouted Patty, throwing a paper clip at the space where Tess had been.

Tess's apartment was more crowded than it had been since she had arrived in New York.

Four people in the little flat was enough to make it feel like a party, especially as Kevin and Jemma were already halfway through a bottle of Chablis by the time Patty rang the doorbell.

313

'So where's the roast?' she asked as she handed Tess her Armani coat.

Tess held up a carton of noodles. 'Well . . . I thought I'd call in Chinese instead. Didn't want anyone to die of food poisoning.'

Patty rolled her eyes, then extended her hand to Kevin and Jemma. Kevin stood up, almost jumping to attention as he shook her hand. Tess could see why Kevin was looking intimidated, especially as Patty wasted no time in sitting down and opening her notebook.

'The situation is this,' she said finally, pausing for a sip of wine. 'New York State doesn't recognize one parent as being *better* than the other. However, the fact that you and Melissa never married puts a slightly different complexion on things.'

Kevin face, which minutes before had looked hopeful, now seemed to fall. 'So the court will rule in Melissa's favour?'

'No, not exactly. The fact that Jack currently lives with you helps enormously. What we need to do is prove to the court that this is a stable home for Jack.'

Tess looked at Kevin. 'Well, that will be easy – it is, isn't it?'

Patty shook her head. 'I'm afraid it is a claim that Melissa will try and sabotage.'

Kevin nodded. 'I thought of that, so I've already asked about getting school reports to show that Jack is happy and settled and doing well.'

'Good start,' said Patty. 'We need more of that. People in the community who can attest to your stability as a family unit – perhaps a priest or a doctor? We just need to gather as much evidence in our favour as possible and try and anticipate where Melissa's people will try to trip you up.'

She paused and smiled. 'And on top of that, there are a few tricks I've learned in corporate law. Winning is not just about firefighting, it's about going on the attack.'

'You mean you need to prove Melissa is a crappy mother?' said Jemma.

Patty smiled. 'That would certainly help.'

'Well, you've come to the right place. I can do some snooping around,' said Jemma, snapping a prawn cracker. 'She lives in Greenwich right? That's not too far. I bet you fifty quid she's no Mother Teresa.'

'It's dollars now, Jem,' smiled Tess. They continued the discussion as they picked at the takeaway and opened more wine, laughing and joking, although Tess thought that Kevin was still looking cautious. As Jemma cleared away the plates, he began playing nervously with the cuff of his smart pale blue shirt.

'I just want to say how grateful I am to all you ladies,' he said haltingly. 'But I want you to know I've got money. I got a five-thousand-buck loan from a friend, so I want to pay everyone for what they're doing.'

A quiet, uncomfortable hush descended around the table.

'That won't be necessary, Kevin,' said Patty gently. 'I'm happy to look after this for the moment, and if it starts getting too time-consuming, then I'll hand it over to a friend of mine who has a great family law practice in Brooklyn.'

'I don't know what to say,' said Kevin.

'My pleasure,' she said, waving his thanks away, then glanced down at her Cartier watch. If Tess didn't know better, she'd say she was a little embarrassed.

'I'd better go,' she said, closing her notebook. 'I have to be in work at six.'

'It's Saturday tomorrow, Pats,' smiled Tess, walking her to the door. 'I thought it was only me who was on duty twenty-four/seven.'

'Thanks,' said Tess simply when they were out of earshot of Kevin and Jemma.

Patty hooked her Bottega Veneta bag over her shoulder and opened the front door. 'You know what?' she said, her face shining, 'it felt good tonight. I've definitely been working in the corporate jungle too long – sometimes you need to come up for fresh air.'

Silently Tess agreed with her.

When she had gone, Tess walked back into the living room.

'Well, I'm going to bed,' said Jemma, stretching her arms out. 'I was out until four a.m. last night.'

'Good luck in Greenwich,' said Kevin.

'She's a wily old fox. She'll get results,' grinned Tess.

'Less of the old, more of the foxy,' said Jemma playfully. Yawning, she waved at them. 'G'night.'

Tess poured herself another glass of Chablis and sank onto the sofa next to Kevin.

'Remind me not to get on your bad side,' he said as they heard Jemma's bedroom door click shut.

Tess frowned. 'My bad side? What do you mean? It's Patty Shackleton you have to worry about.'

'Oh yes, she's great too,' said Kevin. 'But you got this whole ball rolling, getting things fixed and arranged. I'm impressed.'

Tess shrugged modestly. 'Is that a compliment?' she smiled, the wine's warm fuzziness making her a little flirtatious.

'Sure,' he grinned.

'Well, thank you,' said Tess. 'A lot of men seem to think that strong women are intimidating.'

'Hey, I didn't say I wasn't intimidated,' he teased.

Suddenly Tess was very aware of just how close they were sitting on the sofa, his warm thigh against hers. Four glasses of wine had made her feel light-headed and unusually calm, and she found she was enjoying Kevin's company. Maybe she was projecting an image of the strong, sensitive type onto Kevin after all the crap with Dom and his shallowness, but Kevin seemed different, and not in a bad way. Plus, she couldn't help noticing what blue eyes he had.

'Listen,' he began, leaning over to put his wine glass on the coffee table. In almost slow motion, Tess saw it overbalance and tip sideways in a perfect arc onto the floor.

'Oh shit, damn!' he said, jumping up. 'Sorry, sorry,' he muttered, stretching to pick it up.

Tess grabbed his arm, which felt strong to the touch.

'It's only wine. Forget it,' she said, and without thinking she leant forward and touched her lips against his, her eyes closing as she opened her mouth gently for a sweet featherlight kiss. But it never came. Kevin was moving back, his lips pulling away until there was nothing between them but three feet of air prickling with awkwardness.

'Oh, uh, that's probably not a good idea,' he said, looking at the floor.

Tess felt her cheeks flare. 'Yeah, I'm sorry . . . Kevin, sorry,' she said, cursing. She felt stupid and ashamed, suddenly realizing how it must look to him: that the whole night had been cooked up with the sole intention of seducing him.

She closed her eyes, wishing that she could be magically transported out of the room.

Kevin smiled and pointed to the wine. 'Don't worry, I blame the devil's soda.'

'Absolutely,' said Tess firmly. 'I think my alcohol tolerance is way down from what it was in London. I'm just so drunk, I . . .' She shook her head. 'I'll just stop babbling now.'

'Shit, and I thought it was my movie-star good looks,' said Kevin kindly.

They both laughed weakly.

'I think I should go,' said Kevin, grabbing his jacket. 'I told the babysitter I wouldn't be late.'

She waved him out of the room. 'Yes, go. Go pick up Jack. Go.'

When he was gone, Tess sank down into a chair and put her head in her hands. 'Nooo . . .' she whispered to herself. 'Someone tell me that didn't just happen.'

But it did and it had, and it didn't look like the ground was going to open up and swallow her. So, groaning, Tess got up, grabbed the empty bottle of Chablis, and threw it into the bin with a thud.

38

Debs Asquith marched into Brooke's apartment and handed her a takeaway coffee. 'Are you ready?'

'Not quite,' said Brooke, hunting around her bedroom for a missing Jimmy Choo flip-flop. They were due to set off for a girlie afternoon of pampering at Skin Plus, Brooke's treat to Debs for all the extra *Portico*-related work she'd had to pile onto her friend recently.

'So, how good are these therapists at your sister's spa exactly?' asked Debs, sipping her Frappuccino. 'Can they get me looking as good as you by this evening? I could do with it because, believe it or not, I have a date.'

'A date!' smiled Brooke, looking up from her closet. 'You didn't tell me.'

'Well, you've been in La La Land for the last three days, haven't you? Speaking of which, how was the City of Angels?'

'Fantastic,' grinned Brooke, still on a high. 'Do you know what? I think I could live in LA.'

'You? The die-hard New York City girl?'

Brooke had surprised herself by how much she had enjoyed herself on the West Coast, despite the scariness of the meetings at the Hollywood studios. At one point she and Eileen had been round a conference table with seven executives, one of whom actually had four flashing telephones in front of him, and there was still no word about whether they wanted to option *Portico*. But what Brooke had loved was the LA life. For a huge metropolis, teeming with freeways, cars, and beautiful people, she'd had an unusually relaxed time. She'd stayed at the home of one of

Sean's ex-girlfriends, an actress currently out of the country filming, which was high up and secluded in the Hollywood Hills, surrounded by oleander bushes and covered with a wraparound sky that seemed so close Brooke could almost touch it. Even better had been when she and Eileen had ventured out to dinner at a Japanese restaurant recommended by one of the studio execs. The paparazzi's flashbulbs had started popping on the streets as soon as she stepped out of her car but, to her astonishment, she saw that the fuss and excitement was actually over the arrival of Hayley Milano, an eighteen-year-old singer caught in the middle of a sex-tape scandal. Brooke realized with a flutter that outside New York she just wasn't that famous, and it felt *wonderful*.

The missing flip-flop, inexplicably, was in her swimwear drawer.

'Finally,' sighed Debs, 'let's *go*!'

Brooke held up one finger. 'Just a minute,' she said, beckoning Debs towards her spare room. 'What size feet are you again?'

'Eight,' replied Debs, following her friend with a puzzled look.

'Shit,' she gasped. The room was crammed with boxes and bags full of clothes, handbags, shoes, jewellery, and cosmetics, piled in heaps and spilling onto the floor. Debs ran a finger along a rail full of designer clothes.

'Look at this stuff.'

'Take what you want,' smiled Brooke. 'You have got a date tonight, after all.'

'But . . . but there's thousands of dollars' worth of stuff in here,' Debs protested.

'Don't worry, I didn't pay for any of it,' said Brooke. 'As soon as I got engaged, whoosh, all this free stuff started appearing. Apparently celebrities get given free stuff by publicists and designers so they can wear it, get photographed in it, endorse it, so that thousands of women around the world run out and buy it. Cheap advertising for them, I guess.'

Debs clapped her hands together. 'I love having a friend getting married to a famous billionaire.'

Brooke smiled with pleasure as she watched Debs dance around the room like a child in a sweet shop. Debs was her most down-to-earth friend, openly disdainful of the society world and the fashion circus that Brooke was obliged to involve herself in, but every girl loved shoes and handbags, didn't they? Putting down her drink, she joined in, opening bags and foraging in boxes. Debs slipped on a pair of zebra-print high heels, then unzipped a white linen garment bag, peeking inside. 'Oh, now this is fucking amazing,' she said, pulling out a long, quartz-coloured gown and holding it against her. She posed in front of the full-length mirror, then pulled a face.

'Nah, one for you, I think,' she said. 'For a start, I wouldn't get the zip halfway up, and I'm not quite sure where the hell I'd wear it in Brooklyn.'

But Brooke was only half listening. She couldn't take her eyes off the dress that she had just removed from a black garment bag. It was incredible. Long, lean, and so fluid it shimmered. An elegant V-shaped neckline curved into a finely beaded bodice, the slim column of the dress sweeping out into a fishtail. She couldn't believe she hadn't even bothered to open it before now.

She quickly stripped off her jeans and top.

'Having a hot flush or something?' smiled Debs, raising an eyebrow.

Ignoring her, Brooke slid into the dress. Looking in the mirror, her heart leapt. It was perfect, her dream dress. In fact it was exactly the dress she had imagined she would get married in. Not the colour, or even the fabric, but the shape – it was exquisite, both relaxed and romantic yet elegant and dramatic. It was exactly what she had been trying to describe to Guillaume Riche before he had steam-rollered her into an elaborate corseted gown she knew in her heart of hearts was wrong.

'Now that's . . . wow!' was all Debs could say.

Feeling a little shudder of excitement, she went over to the bag to examine the label. Nicholas Diaz. She'd never heard of him. But he was going to hear from her, and soon.

Of Meredith's many skills, one of her most impressive was entertaining. More precisely, she was a seasoned expert in commanding and coordinating a vast team of people – chefs, maids, butlers, waiters, and barmen – who together would create a dinner that looked, to its guests, effortless. In another life, Meredith would have made a great general. Every one of her talents was required for this night, however, as it would be the first time all of the Billingtons and Asgills would meet. The arranging of their respective diaries had been a military campaign in itself, but Meredith would not – could not – let a single detail slip on this important night. By three in the afternoon, Meredith's house was chaos, with caterers, delivery men, and flower arrangers all jostling for space. Liz was used to the pomp and circumstance of her mother's parties, but she had never seen so much intense activity before a 'casual supper'.

'I don't remember you making all this effort for a meet-the-family supper when I was getting married,' said Liz, watching from the doorway of the formal dining room as her mother supervised three Filipino maids in the delicate task of arranging the Smythson place cards according to her intricate table plan.

'We had a brunch,' said Meredith distractedly, before turning her attention back to the maids. 'No, no, Sunita. Wendell must go to my right, David to my left. Can we please do it as per the plan?'

Liz smiled as her mother flapped and clucked like a hen. Party arrangements were the only time she saw Meredith lose her seamless elegance. Then again, she was probably still upset about the sale of Asgill Cosmetics falling through. Well, it was swings and roundabouts; the very reason for her mother's disappointment was Liz's cause to celebrate tonight.

'Correction, Mother. We had a brunch the day before the ceremony as part of the festivities,' said Liz, pointedly.

'So let me get this straight,' said Meredith, picking a crystal goblet off the table and examining it in the light. 'You are objecting to getting to know the Billingtons better on the basis of *wedding envy?*'

'I never said that,' snapped Liz, annoyed at the insinuation that she might be jealous of Brooke and her fairy-tale wedding. She narrowed her eyes as Meredith fussed over the china. She was almost pitiful, thought Liz. Meredith was like a downtrodden girl-friend running after a badly behaved boyfriend, knowing you are never going to get treated with the respect you deserve but still desperate for whatever scraps of attention you can get. She had no intention of behaving like a fawning schoolgirl that evening. The only way to get respect from people like the Billingtons was to behave as if you were on level pegging with them. In fact, she was quite looking forward to that.

'Is this getting serious?' asked Brooke in a low conspiratorial voice as she followed Liz into the dining room. Liz followed her gaze to Rav, who she had to admit looked utterly handsome in a navy-blue suit and pale-pink shirt.

'Not all of us are obsessed with wanting a lifetime commitment,' she whispered back.

Brooke frowned. 'I don't know why you are so wedding-phobic. Not when you've been down that road yourself.'

'*Especially* as I've been down that road myself,' said Liz, looking around the table with interest to see who had been seated next to whom. Wendell Billington, she smiled, picking up the place card. Thank goodness it wasn't David, she thought, taking a few moments to observe her future brother-in-law. He was so clean-cut, she wondered if he squeaked between the sheets. Liz did admire his success and potential, however, although he still had that slightly useless look about him that Liz despised. Good-looking and charming, he was the perfect puppet. Success was easy when you'd been spoon-fed from the cradle; with the right schools and contacts, anyone with a modicum of drive would do well.

Conversation flowed steadily and politely over dinner. Paula talked about the decline of couture with Rose Billington with such authority that the older woman assumed she was a long-standing couture client. William, Leonard, Robert, and Rav kept to the safe confines of sport, while Sean, who had been forced to make the journey from London, discussed David's chances of an Emmy and Peabody award for his report on human trafficking between Cuba and the Florida Keys.

Meredith monopolized Wendell, while Liz, quietly enjoyed the selection of fine wines – the very best that Meredith's wine cellar had to offer.

After a dessert of rose-infused pannacotta, Meredith suggested they adjourn to the library for port.

'I hear you are a cigar man,' said Liz, leaning over to Wendell.

'Say that quietly. Rose has me on a health kick.'

'We have an excellent selection,' she whispered.

Everyone filed out of the room except Wendell, who loitered in his seat while Liz made a phone call to Sunita in the basement staff quarters. A few minutes later, one of Meredith's hired waiters came through holding a heavy walnut humidor.

'After you,' said Liz.

'You surprise me,' said Wendell, arching an eyebrow.

'Why?'

'I don't meet many female cigar smokers.'

'Well, I have made it a rule never to smoke more than one cigar at a time,' said Liz, smiling flirtatiously.

'Mark Twain.'

'Very good.' Liz shrugged and went on, 'I just like it. The rituals. The smell. It relaxes me. It's a little like creating a fragrance.'

She watched him as he browsed through the humidor. Meredith had stocked it especially, largely from a cigar auction in Zurich; there were even some pre-Castro Montecristos, which must have cost her upwards of thirty thousand dollars. He looked up and saw her smiling.

'I was just trying to guess what kind of cigar man you were.'

'Then why don't you guess?'

'Experienced, robust . . .'

Actually, she knew a great deal about Wendell Billington. His official age was fifty-eight, although Liz had worked out he was nearer sixty.

'Ah, you flatter me.'

'A Cohiba number five?'

Wendell laughed. 'Good choice,' he said, taking one from the box.

He paused for a moment, then said, 'I hear Bruno Harris has re-evaluated his offer for Asgill's.'

Liz nodded as she snipped the end off her cigar with a pair of gold scissors.

'Yes, it caused the deal to fall through,' she said, not wanting to give away her own feelings.

She looked at Wendell. She wished she could tell him all about her business dealings over the past fortnight, feeling sure he would approve of her ruthlessness and single-mindedness. In fact, her idea to derail the sale of the family company to Bruno Harris's Canopus Capital had been so simple it was almost laughable. Through a network of contacts, carefully hiding her trail as she went, Liz had leaked a number of damaging documents about the company to Bruno Harris's advisers; most notably, the flurry of legal threats Asgill's had suffered recently over a self-tanning product which, on certain types of skin, caused an extreme reaction, in some cases actually leading to scarring. Even more damaging were the potentially explosive revelations about Asgill's iconic

323

cleanser The Balm, which had been sent directly to Hugh Montague, who was in charge of the due diligence. According to her sources, the main reason Harris was so interested in purchasing Asgill Cosmetics was that he felt he could market it to the East, particularly the rapidly expanding Indian beauty market, thereby doubling its value as a brand. But Liz had correctly predicted that someone had not done their homework properly. One of the key ingredients of The Balm was beef tallow and enzymes derived from pigs, ingredients not welcome in either Hindu or Muslim markets. Five years earlier, anticipating a boom in the global beauty markets, the Asgill Research and Development lab had tried, unsuccessfully, to replicate The Balm using a beef tallow substitute, but the product just wasn't as good and, anyway, it had pushed the price up considerably.

Given this information, it was no wonder Bruno Harris had wanted to rethink the price he would pay for the company. For her part, Liz had no regrets about pointing out what thorough due diligence would have thrown up anyway. And why should she? William and Meredith hadn't considered *her* feelings when they attempted to blind-side her with the sale; they hadn't worried when they had tried to piggyback on her years of toil on Skin Plus.

'So you think the family are right to sell Asgill's?'

Wendell had the most confident, languid way about him that Liz found very attractive. Someone as sure of his own abilities as she was.

'Some of the multinationals will be interested in us now Skin Plus is taking off,' shrugged Liz. 'But personally I don't want to let the company go.'

'I assume you've thought about floating a minority share like Estée Lauder?'

'I've thought about every option,' she said, walking over to the lacquered drinks cabinet and pulling out a bottle of Richard Hennessy, her favourite cognac.

Wendell nodded approvingly.

'New York is becoming so healthy. I've friends – smokers of forty years – on macrobiotic diets. I need a partner in crime. You must come to my club on Wall Street. Excellent cigar bar.'

'You know where to find me,' smiled Liz, pouring the golden nectar into two glasses.

Robert appeared at the door looking concerned.

'Is everything all right? Mother was wondering where you'd got to.'

Wendell glanced over at Liz, his look loaded with meaning.

'Don't worry,' he smiled. 'We were just coming.'

39

Liz hadn't been surprised when Wendell had called three days after Meredith's dinner suggesting lunch at his club. They spent the better part of five minutes on the phone competitively comparing diaries, refusing dates as if to prove how busy and important they both were. Eventually they found a mutually convenient window in November, at which point Wendell buckled, suggesting that he could clear Friday afternoon if she could too. What did surprise Liz was that when a Billington executive car came to pick her up at one p.m. as arranged, the black Mercedes did not have Wendell in it. She was not particularly alarmed until she realized they were heading for the heliport at East Thirty-Fourth Street. As she was ushered through the terminal towards a helicopter in the Billington corporate colours, she picked up her phone and dialled Wendell's number.

'I assume we're not going to your club,' she said, amusement in her voice.

'What? And have one hundred bankers gawk at us?'

'So where are we meeting? I assume we *are* meeting?'

She heard Wendell chuckle, then the phone went dead. Rolling her eyes, she switched off her phone and the pilot started the engine. The helicopter hovered into the air, bobbing gently until it gathered speed and began its journey across the East River towards Long Island. Liz turned her face into the sunshine. The fact that she was heading to destinations unknown sent a sexual thrill through her. Most of the time she was in charge and she liked it that way, but a little chaos, a little mystery every now and then shook things up and gave life an edge.

Smiling, she watched the billowing clouds scud across a watery blue sky and she actually felt herself relax for once. After a short flight the helicopter spiralled down onto a large H in the grounds of one of the big ocean-front palaces on Southampton's Gin Lane. Liz recognized the area even from the air, having often been to parties on this exclusive stretch. She'd heard the whispers around New York about how much these properties went for: sixty, seventy million dollars. She wondered who the house belonged to, knowing from Brooke that the Billingtons did not own a property in the Hamptons, and whether this was how really rich men operated – lending each other their exclusive homes for under-the-radar 'entertaining'. She smiled to herself. At her mother's dinner for the Billington family, Liz had decided that she wanted Wendell, and now she was going to have him. Another executive car was waiting for her at the helipad and it took her down a long gravel drive, stopping outside the white stucco house. It was impressive in size but not in architectural style, thought Liz; but then size mattered when it came to a statement of wealth. Liz stepped out of the car, annoyed that in her five-inch Manolo heels and severe Martin Margiela shift dress, she was not dressed for the beach.

The double doors to the house were open and Liz entered and proceeded down an eerily quiet hallway, at the end of which she could see a stretch of shimmering blue sea. It was the sort of property that usually had lots of staff, but today it was ghostly quiet.

She walked out onto the veranda and found Wendell sitting on an Adirondack chair, dressed in a fitted shirt and cream chinos, saluting her with a tumbler of gin.

'So what happened to lunch?' she said playfully.

He laughed. 'I had the chef go. I thought there were more important things to do this afternoon.'

'Like what?'

'Talk.'

A bottle of Pouilly-Fumé was chilling in a silver bucket on a table beside him.

'A drink before lunch?' he asked, pouring her a glass. 'Then how about we take a walk?'

Liz took off her shoes and followed him down a flight of wooden steps to the beach. She could tell that summer was winding to a close by the way the sand underfoot was losing its heat.

'Can I ask you something?' he said.

'Of course.'

They had reached the shore and paused for a moment to listen to the crashing sound of the Atlantic waves.

'Is Brooke committed to David?'

As much as it annoyed Liz to see her sister as America's crown princess, she could see how it might have its advantages.

'Absolutely,' replied Liz. 'Why do you ask?'

'You heard she refused to go to a fundraiser dinner with him the other week? Some meeting in LA for one of her books was apparently more important.'

Liz smiled inwardly, feeling a rush of pleasure at the power she had in her hands right now. What if she told him that no, Brooke would not make a committed wife for his son, then what would Wendell Billington do? Would that bring the whole thing crashing down?

'I shouldn't worry,' smiled Liz. 'Brooke is just playing at publishing. Of course David has to let her run with it for now, but she will soon tire of it. She loved the social scene when she left Brown and now she complains about attending fundraisers?' Liz laughed. 'Give her time. Every young girl these days wants to feel as if she has a career. But that will change when she's married, trust me.'

'Well, of course I don't object to her having a career,' replied Wendell quickly. 'Nothing wrong with that, but we don't want her becoming a ball-breaker on us all of a sudden. David wouldn't like it. He doesn't like clever girls, never has. And, on the other hand, I don't want him to appear a lightweight. A wife with a career, a small, successful career is fine, up to a point.'

'Wendell, it would be hard to find anyone less controversial than Brooke – you must know that. She is *perfect* for David.'

Wendell was nodding his head. 'Good. Because from now on we don't need any more distractions.'

'Why?'

He touched her arm and motioned for her to walk back up the sand to the house. She looked at him sideways, with a pique of annoyance. What was with the politics lesson? She had come here for a purpose, an agenda she thought was clear the minute he had phoned her private line. Liz began to wonder if she had misread the signals. Was he mocking her, bringing her out all this way, only for an innocent 'getting to know you' session? What would he think of her? Gullible, egocentric, a *slut?* Anger flashed inside her. She had rarely met a man who did not find her sexually attractive, it was one of her gifts, like a photographic memory and great posture; and while she conceded that Wendell was her future brother-in-law's father, it was hardly incest. Besides, Wendell Billington was one of the most ruthless businessmen in the country: he'd been known to completely destroy people who stood in his way. He was certainly not above fucking someone he shouldn't.

'It looks like a Congressional seat in Connecticut will be coming available shortly,' continued Wendell.

Liz tried to compose herself. It wasn't over yet. 'But it's mid-term, surely?'

'It would be a special election. The Congresswoman for the sixth district is going to announce her retirement in the New Year on the grounds of ill health. The district leans Republican, and David would be perfect for it, although with his profile at the moment I think he'd win it even if the district were Democrat.'

Liz looked at him with increased respect, wondering how he'd got this information, even wondering whether Wendell in some way had influenced the Congresswoman's decision to retire. With his reputation, she would not put it past him.

'I thought David wanted to wait until the Congressional general election in a couple of years' time?' said Liz, as they approached the steps up to the house.

Wendell shrugged. 'Yes, that was the original plan. My advisers have been eyeing up open or vulnerable seats in New York and Connecticut, states he can claim residency in through his own home or family properties, but it will certainly be easier this way. After all, David is still a political rookie, so he's by no means a sure thing. But if David can win the special election, and we'll put every resource behind him to make sure that happens, he'll be an incumbent Congressman at the general election. He'll certainly win that. That will give him three years in the House, then we can move him up to Senate. I've already had meetings with some GOP seniors and a very well-respected campaign consultant. Everyone is agreed that David should make the move now.'

'So, president by forty-five?' she asked playfully.

'Why not?' said Wendell candidly. 'We don't just want the presidency, we want a notable presidency. As good as Lincoln, as dynamic as Kennedy.'

Liz nodded, pondering how ambition was such a limitless beast. No matter how successful you were, there was always more to be done; it was something she understood very well. She also understood why David's political future was so important to Wendell. The Billingtons were rich beyond most people's imagination, but having all the money they needed or wanted, they now desired power. More power equals more money, and so the cycle continues.

Wendell stopped at the bottom of the stairs and looked at Liz.

'You know you could have a future in politics, Liz,' he said with a smile. 'Although I'm not sure our families can cope with two rising stars.'

'Me?' she laughed, thinking instantly of Russ Ford. It would take an army of PRs to keep her secrets under wraps if she wanted political office.

'The only thing I plan on running for is the New York marathon,' she laughed, turning away and climbing the steps. As she reached the veranda, she turned, her hands on her hips. 'Don't look at me like that,' she said flatly.

'Like what?'

'Like you're eyeing me up as some filly you could run in the Derby.'

'I was just thinking how capable you were,' he said. His delivery was slow, deliberate, loaded with suggestion, and she felt the warmth of his half-smile.

'Capable?' said Liz seductively, feeling a change in the atmosphere between them. 'If by that you mean I'm good at lots of things, then I guess I am.'

Wendell moved forward and touched her cheek. Liz shut her eyes, feeling his warm hand on her skin, smiling with anticipation, her sexual magnetism still intact. *This is the real prize*, she thought. If Brooke had the Billington prince then she wanted the king.

Silently he took her hand and led her into the house, up the grand staircase, and into a bedroom overlooking the ocean. By the window was a dressing table arranged with pomade and perfume, the chair draped with a robe in stripes of silken colour. Being surrounded by a stranger's things was turning her on even more: the forbidden, the untouchable was hers for the taking. She turned, kissing him fiercely. Liz began to undo the buttons on his Charvet custom-made shirt, pushing back the cotton to expose a tanned, firm chest, only a circle of dark grey hair betraying his age.

Unzipping his trousers, she sank down onto her knees, cupping and stroking his balls before taking his erect billion-dollar cock entirely into her mouth. His wiry, dark pubic hair tickled her cheeks as he pushed into her, holding her head firmly in his hands. Liz didn't need any encouragement to stay down there, she knew how to suck cock, and from the thick, hard mouthful she could feel throbbing between her lips, she knew he was enjoying it as much as she was.

'Now,' he gasped, 'on the bed.'

Turning her around, he unzipped her dress, which slipped to the floor; he began to plant soft kisses down her spine. Impatient, she unfastened her own bra, then pulled him down onto the huge bed. Rolling over, she straddled him and leant forward to brush her breasts against his chest, dipping her nipples towards his mouth, then playfully retreating as his tongue gave the briefest sweep of her aureole.

'God, this is good,' he moaned, grabbing hold of her wrists and rolling her over, pushing her thighs wider and wider. Finally, he reared forward and sank his cock into her. She flung her arms back, gripping the silk sheets as he bent down to kiss her mouth, her neck, the curve of her armpit and across to her hard, budded nipples, his appetite ruthless, unyielding, and urgent. Tasting her sweat on his tongue, she spread her legs so he could push further into her wetness. Thrust by thrust their pace quickened, powered by desire and need, two expert lovers, each as driven and focused as the other, each taking turns to dominate, be in control. Arching her back, she squeezed herself tighter around his cock, knowing he was about to come. Her concentration was so fierce that she screamed, but she knew she could delay the fierce sweet pulse of pleasure around her own body no longer. Wendell pulled out of her and slid down to put his face between her thighs, finishing her off with long, luxurious laps of her clitoris until she came so hard her entire body was trembling.

He rolled over and sank back onto the pillow, propping his hand casually under his head.

'I might have to revisit my assessment of you as *capable*,' he said finally with a note of amusement.

For a moment Liz was speechless. Sex was not something that

ever threw her, but what had just happened had shaken her. It had been incredible. She turned to kiss him again, but, as she moved, he slipped out of the other side of the bed.

'I'm staying here for the evening,' he said, picking up his silk boxer shorts and pulling them back on. 'I'm due to meet a friend for dinner at seven.'

There was a detachment in his voice that had not been present before they had sex. Liz knew the code: she was being given the brush-off. She felt a flare of annoyance, but to show it would be to show weakness.

'Yes, I should get back to work,' she said, standing up and stretching her long, naked body, knowing that his eyes were on her, knowing that he already wanted more in spite of himself. She bent down at the dressing table, showing him her perfectly shaped ass, and quickly checked her make-up.

'Could you have the helicopter take me back?' she asked casually.

'Of course.'

Their eyes met, and for the first time in her life, Liz Asgill knew she had found her personal, professional, and sexual equal.

40

'So sweet pea, are you anywhere nearer making a decision about the guest books?' Alessandro Franchetti's voice on the telephone was impatient. 'If you need a steer, I just love the hand-bound midnight-blue calfskin or the taupe ostrich. Two hundred gsm paperweight, ivory rather than white. The paper is handmade in Italy, by the way. I just love it.'

Brooke sighed. For some reason she just couldn't seem to muster much enthusiasm for the guest books. After all, it was just a large bound book left at the wedding for people to write their messages of goodwill in. She looked at the huge pile of them that Alessandro had sent over. It wasn't just the guest books, of course. Her apartment was littered with swatches, folders, boxes, and endless samples of envelopes, cards, fabric, and even cutlery. There were so many choices to be made, she felt overwhelmed.

'Okay, yes to the heavy ivory paper and I like the midnight blue,' she said, 'but I'm just not comfortable with the idea of calfskin.'

'What are you suggesting, baby?' he asked. 'Fish skin? Tofu? Never mind, never mind. I'll sort something out. Now, are you totally happy with that?'

'Absolutely,' said Brooke, propping the receiver under her chin and flicking idly through a copy of *Elle*. She wondered when the shift had happened, when choosing every last detail for the wedding had become, well, a bit of a chore. It hadn't been so long ago that she had bought every single bridal magazine – US and international – poring over them night and day. She wanted her day to be perfect, of course. Of *course* she did, but Jewel Cay was so gorgeous, she knew that just the sound of the sea and the tropical breeze washing

333

over them as they said their vows would give the day all the stardust it needed. If she was honest, she really didn't care what sort of card the place settings were made from. Brooke was well aware of the irony; she and David had quarrelled over this very thing only weeks ago, but now meetings, phone calls, and emails from Alessandro took up at least an hour of her time a day. It was starting to get too much.

'We can still do lunch on Friday, sweetness?' asked Alessandro. 'I haven't quite worked out the details for the ceremony departure yet.'

'What's that?'

There was the smallest of sighs down the phone. 'When you leave the chapel, darling. Well, in this instance, the ceremonial platform.'

'Oh, you mean the "confetti bit",' said Brooke.

He coughed meaningfully. 'Alessandro Franchetti doesn't do confetti, sweet thing. I was thinking hundreds of butterflies released from an aviary. Maybe red admirals, as red is traditionally good luck at Chinese weddings?' he mused aloud. 'Although blue is the lucky colour in the West, isn't it?'

'What do they say about working with children and animals?' said Brooke, smiling to herself, but Alessandro didn't seem to be listening.

'Maybe I'll give Princess Olga of Greece a call,' he said. 'You must know her, right? She's a butterfly catcher. I'll call her right now. Get her view on it and call you straight back.'

Gratefully, Brooke put down the phone and threw herself back on the sofa, gazing out at the greying Manhattan sky. It was funny how quickly the dark nights came in, she thought. She grabbed the controls for her TiVo, and decided to watch *Dispatches*, which she had recorded earlier in the week. It featured the thirty-minute documentary segment David had recorded in Iraq. He had a presence and substance you didn't often see in TV presenters. The critics seemed to agree with her and were already calling it one of the documentaries of the year, while at the network there were rumours about a promotion for David to lead anchor, or even his own show. Brooke hoped he got it; to her mind, that was a better fit than politics.

When her phone rang, she debated not answering it, but while she'd definitely had enough of Alessandro Franchetti for one evening, it was better to get this guest book and butterfly business sorted out sooner rather than later.

'I was just thinking,' she said, snatching up the phone, 'maybe we should go for red butterflies. I think David's dad is inviting lots of prominent Republicans, so I think he'll prefer the party colours.'

'Butterflies? What are you talking about, Brooke?'

'Matt, is that you?' she said, pleased to hear his voice.

'The same.'

She giggled. 'God, save me from wedding madness. I've just been debating whether I should have five hundred red or blue butterflies released after my wedding.'

'What happened to the plain old shower of confetti?'

'Too plain and old, apparently.'

There was an awkward pause.

'I haven't seen you for ages,' she said. 'Where did you get to?'

'Just busy,' said Matt vaguely.

'Well, how about doing something this weekend?' She ran through her diary in her head. David was away again and although Tess *had* said she and David should meet Matt together, what harm could a coffee or a pizza do?

'I think I'm busy this weekend.'

'Long shift?'

There was a long pause.

She knew instinctively what he was doing that weekend.

'You have a date!' she said, chiding him.

'I guess.'

'I thought we were friends, Matthew Palmer,' she said over-brightly. 'But you tell me nothing.'

Matt laughed. 'There's nothing much to tell. We've only been out a few times.'

'You've been out a few times and there's nothing to tell? You have a *girlfriend*!'

'She's not my girlfriend,' said Matt. 'She's called Susie, she's fun, she's an aromatherapist.'

'Ooh, just think of all those sexy, oily massages.'

'Brooke—'

'So where did you meet her?'

'At a party. She's a friend of a friend.'

Brooke was suddenly aware that Matt had a life that she knew nothing about. Somehow she had this romantic notion of him toiling in ER for twenty hours at a time, then returning home only to sleep and eat pizza before doing it all again, but clearly he was out at parties with attractive bohemian aromatherapists.

'So when am I going to meet her?' asked Brooke.

'Well, that's why I'm calling. It's my birthday in a couple of weeks, I thought I'd better do the decent thing and celebrate.'

'Great. I'll bring David. My publicist has been telling me forever that you two should meet . . .' She paused, realizing that sounded wrong somehow. 'Well, you know, just in case anyone thinks there might be something funny going on between us. Ridiculous, but you know how people talk.'

'No, no, she's right,' said Matt. 'That's a good idea.'

There was another long pause.

'Well, I'll text you the details of the meal when I've decided what to cook.'

'Fine. Great. See you then.'

She snapped her mobile shut and marched straight over to the towering pile of guest books, taking them down and examining them with total concentration. Suddenly choosing between the blue book and the taupe one was the most important decision in the world.

41

Tess never wanted to see another envelope in her entire life. Her desk and floor were covered with a rainbow of different-coloured paper, along with endless Jiffy bags and packages. She had just spent the last hour laboriously going through them and her fingers – not to mention her head – were starting to ache. It was one of the chores she hated. Every morning she received an enormous volume of post that took hours to sift through, so she invariably left it until last thing. The vast majority of the envelopes contained party invitations for Brooke, everything from red-carpet events to fundraisers to shop openings. Brooke had to be seen at some of them, of course, the ones Tess would cherry-pick as the most high profile or 'on brand', but the majority went straight into the over-sized recycling bin.

It wasn't as if she didn't have other things to do. As September slipped into October, media speculation about Brooke and David's wedding had already cranked up several notches, meaning that Tess was constantly fielding phone calls and emails from press and television stations wanting everything from confirmation of location and dates to actual access to the wedding.

Today had been a particularly arduous day, and Tess was looking forward to going home. She had just pulled her coat off the back of her chair when she heard footsteps in the corridor outside her door.

'Meredith,' said Tess looking up. 'I didn't think you were in today.'

'My secretary called me so I've just dropped by.'

'Well, that's good luck, because I wanted to speak to you. Could you come in? Sorry about the mess.'

Meredith walked into the room and took the seat opposite Tess, folding her pale, stocking-clad legs elegantly under the chair as she waited for Tess to continue.

'I want to take a holiday,' said Tess, trying keep her voice even. She was unsure why she thought the request might be interpreted as unreasonable – perhaps because of the 'in at six, home at ten' mentality of the New York worker; perhaps because they were getting closer to the 'big day'; but either way she had been delaying asking Meredith. In the event she merely nodded.

'Very well,' she said. 'When were you thinking, and for how long?'

'This weekend actually. I'm sorry for the late notice but I've only just found out about the trip. It's just a Friday night until Tuesday trip, so it would involve very little time out of the office and I would have my BlackBerry on all the time . . .'

Meredith was already shaking her head. 'I'm afraid it's not convenient.'

Tess felt a sinking disappointment, but knew she couldn't object. Her job came first – it had to, the amount they were paying her – but when Jemma had told her about a trip she was taking to Lake Tahoe with some new friends, Tess had been keen to go along. She barely knew Jemma's new social circle, but to Tess that was a bonus. What she really wanted to do was interact with people who weren't anything to do with work. A look in the mirror told her she was tired. The nagging pains between her shoulder blades said she was stressed. She just wanted to have some fun.

'Really?' she said, flipping a few pages of her diary with a frown. She couldn't see any pressing events written there. 'Anything I should know about?'

'Every year we have a Miss Asgill Hawaiian Glo pageant in Hawaii,' said Meredith. She was trying to be matter-of-fact, but she clearly found the idea a little distasteful. Didn't fit in with her new vision of Asgill's as a luxury brand, perhaps, thought Tess.

'We usually have a representative from the company on the judging panel. This year I was keen for Leonard to go along, but he's had to schedule a hospital appointment.'

Tess nodded sympathetically, recalling that she hadn't seen Leonard around the office all week.

'As it happens, Sean is in New York this week,' continued Meredith. 'He heard that Leonard can't make the pageant and suggested he should attend in his place.'

'I bet he did,' said Tess. 'But Meredith, I'm not at all sure—'

Meredith raised her hand to silence Tess's objections.

'I am aware this goes somewhat against the grain of the wonderful work you have been doing to reposition Sean in the public mind, but he has done it before without incident, and it is a very good photo opportunity. It raises the profile of the pageant and hence the sun cream and, at the moment, that has to take precedence over any concerns about putting Sean, shall we say, in "harm's way"?'

'I appreciate that, Meredith,' said Tess. 'And I hear he has managed to stay sober since rehab, which is brilliant; but, even so, he's too much of a loose cannon in the company of beautiful girls in bikinis.'

'Which is why I want you to go.'

Tess's mouth opened. 'You want me to *baby-sit* him?' She looked away, lest her anger show on her face. She could not believe Sean Asgill was once again interfering with her life, ruining her plans. As if unveiling Dom as an unfaithful bastard purely for his own entertainment wasn't bad enough, now he was putting the kibosh on a much-needed trip to Lake Tahoe.

'Not baby-sit, no,' said Meredith. 'I simply want you to make sure he doesn't get into any trouble. Young girls and rich men don't mix.'

Tess blew out her cheeks in frustration and Meredith looked at her with a more kindly countenance.

'It won't be so bad, Tess,' she smiled. 'Hawaii is a beautiful island and I understand the hotel where the pageant is being held is, well, fun. If you like, the company will pay for you to stay on a couple of nights afterwards; that way you still get your break. Take an airplane flight over Mauna Loa at night – it's something you will never forget in your life. Invoice everything to me.'

Tess nodded numbly. She knew she was in no position to argue. 'I'll make all the arrangements tomorrow,' she said.

'No need,' smiled Meredith. 'I had my secretary book you on Saturday's flight to Hilo. She has all the details.'

Meredith stood up and walked towards the door on her Ferragamo heels. 'I do appreciate everything you're doing for the family, Tess. I know your contract with us was until David and

Brooke's wedding, but I really hope you'll stay on with us after that. Perhaps we can talk about it a little nearer the time?'

Tess wondered if now would be a good time to remind her employer of the quarter-of-a-million-dollar bonus she had been promised if the wedding went ahead. It had been mentioned at her first conversation with Meredith at the Connaught, and Tess had insisted it was put into her contract, but with rumours of financial trouble at the Asgill company beginning to surface, Tess made a mental note to double-check her contract to make sure there was no way they could wiggle out of it.

'Oh, before I forget,' said Meredith, slipping her slim hand into her Chanel quilt bag. 'I received this today.' She pulled out an envelope and handed it to Tess. It was addressed to Meredith at the Asgill's office. Inside the envelope was a letter on blue airmail paper, the likes of which Tess hadn't seen in a decade. She unfolded it and read the short message.

Your family has a secret.

Flipping over the envelope, she examined it.

'Well, it's a South Carolina postmark. I'm assuming you don't know who it's from?'

Meredith gave the smallest of shrugs. 'I have no idea.'

Tess wasn't unduly worried. One thing she had learned from her time in the tabloids was that the world was full of crackpots. At the *Globe*, they had regularly received letters from one of Britain's most notorious criminals, sent from Broadmoor Hospital (the institution that in less enlightened times had been known as Broadmoor Asylum for the Criminally Insane); here, barely a week at the Asgill's office went past without some email or letter from someone claiming to be Brooke's best friend wanting her cell-phone number, or a long-lost relative claiming a slice of the annual profits. New York seemed to be particularly full of crazies. Tess tapped the letter against the palm of her hand thoughtfully.

'Well, it's not a demand or an accusation. It's probably just another attention-seeker.'

'Perhaps,' said Meredith quietly. 'But I'd like it taken care of.'

'Don't worry. I'll handle it,' said Tess with as much reassurance as she could muster. 'And get any post like this diverted to me as soon as it arrives.'

'Thank you, Tess,' said Meredith. 'This is exactly the reason I hired you.'

She watched Meredith leave the room and her face creased into a frown. *What the hell does she want from me?* she thought, annoyed. *First a PR, then a babysitter, now they want me to be a private bloody detective!*

She grabbed her coat and switched off the light, throwing the letter into the back of her drawer.

42

'What do you *mean*, you can't make it?' asked Brooke, cradling her phone to her ear as she pushed through the revolving door of her office building and out onto the cold street.

David's voice sounded apologetic but firm. 'I'm sorry, honey, but it's impossible. The producer wants to follow up a story that has just broken on the Huffington Post. We're going to do an extended segment about it on the show tomorrow, so it's all hands on deck. Meetings with the researchers, you know the drill. I think it's going to be a late one.'

'But we're supposed to be there in an hour,' said Brooke, exasperated. She heard a long sigh into the phone.

'Brooke, this is my job, whereas tonight's supper is for a guy I don't even know; in fact it's for someone I'm not actually that happy you're seeing, if I'm honest.'

Brooke felt angry and defensive. When she had finally plucked up the courage to invite David to Matt's birthday dinner, it had raised all sorts of difficult questions. Why had Matt invited Brooke when they weren't even close friends? *Who wouldn't invite New York's premier couple to their birthday party if they knew them?* she'd answered. How many times exactly had she seen him? *She could count them on one hand,* she'd said. Was she regularly in touch with him on text and email? *Yes! But wasn't that how everybody maintained friendships in the twenty-first century?*

'If you had a problem with me going, you should have said so earlier,' said Brooke with irritation. 'Then I wouldn't have accepted his invitation. I can't exactly get out of it now when we're supposed to be there in an hour.'

'Listen why don't you just go?' he said after a pause. 'But come and stay at mine tonight? At least that way I'll get to see you.'

'Well, I'll just have to see how busy I am,' she said curtly and hung up. As she stepped into the waiting car, she ran over David's words. Why had he made a point of asking her over to his place? she wondered. Was it a test or did he really want to see her? She shook her head angrily and resolved not to think about it for the rest of the night.

Brooke stood outside Matt's apartment, holding a bottle of Château Pétrus, feeling such nerves that she wanted to open the claret there and then. The endless parties and fundraisers she'd attended with David over the past year had made Brooke much more confident in social situations, but she still felt anxious. It hadn't helped that she had told Tess Garrett that she was going to Matt's dinner party – Tess hadn't been pleased. How had she put it? *Beware new friends*, that was it. Brooke kept the advice in mind as she pressed the bell. A pretty blonde about her own age opened the door with a broad smile.

'Hi, I'm Brooke.'

'Of course you are,' said the girl, moving out of the way to let Brooke inside. 'I'm Susie, I'm Matt's girlfriend.'

Her wheat-coloured hair was piled up on her head, slim jeans showed off her long legs, and a tie-dyed Indian smock top made Brooke irrationally wonder if she was into tantric sex. The thing she noticed most, however, was how wide her eyes were, giving her a slightly manic look. Brooke had met this type of girl at college. She'd heard men refer to them as 'mad chicks'.

'Hey.' Matt came forward and awkwardly air-kissed her.

'Oh, you shouldn't have,' said Susie, as Brooke handed her the wine.

Matt peered at the label on the bottle. 'Wow, you really *should* have,' he said.

Matt led her down a short hallway and into the living room; as she stepped through the door, everyone turned towards her and conversation hushed to a silence. Brooke could feel herself blushing. On the New York social circuit, no one ever acted in a self-conscious way around her because to do so would be tantamount to admitting Brooke was somehow more important than they were. Instead, they adopted an over-friendly and familiar tone, whether they had

343

met her before or not. All of which made Brooke feel even more awkward, even more of a circus freak, standing in Matt's small living room.

'Please Brooke, come and meet Greg,' said Matt, ushering Brooke over to a rangy blond man on the sofa. 'Greg's a friend from school,' said Matt, 'and this is his girlfriend Courtney.'

Courtney was the youngest in the room, perhaps early twenties, and had obviously dressed up for the occasion in a sequined emerald cocktail dress. She seemed to be completely star-struck and could only offer an open-mouthed smile when Brooke said hello. Matt then introduced Peter and Ed, doctors from the hospital and their wives, Sally and Grace. While Matt went to get Brooke a drink, she glanced around the room, noting the changes since her last visit when she had twisted her ankle in the park. It had definitely had a woman's touch: the boomerang and baseball had gone from the bookshelf to be replaced by a line of scented candles. She made a mental note to check the bathroom for signs of Susie's permanency: another toothbrush by the sink, perhaps, or bath oil in the cabinet. Brooke took a glass of white wine and sidled up to Sally.

'Great tan. Have you been anywhere nice?' Brooke asked politely.

'Actually we've spent the year in Ghana,' said Sally. 'We've been on a medical exchange programme. Grace is a nurse, too. We all went out together.'

'Wow, that's amazing,' said Brooke. 'Is that the programme Matt is interested in?'

She said it without thinking, realizing too late that Matt might not have made his plan public just yet. Future politicians' wives have to learn to be more diplomatic, she reminded herself.

Ed seemed to pep up noticeably at the question. 'Oh yes. I emailed him for months while I was out there, telling him what a life-changing experience it was. The poverty we saw out there was depressing, but it's humbling to go out there and try and make a difference.'

Susie pulled a face to communicate that she had been rather less enamoured by the idea; Brooke noticed the atmosphere and dropped the subject. There was another lull in the conversation. Brooke was just about to remark on the change in the weather when Courtney piped up, 'So, when's the wedding?'

Brooke laughed out loud and everyone else followed suit. She felt a sense of relief that someone had pointed out the obvious and broken the ice.

'She's been dying to ask ever since Matt told her you were coming,' said Grace in a stage whisper. 'Poor girl's been beside herself.'

'Oh please,' said Courtney to Brooke eagerly. 'Can't you tell us? I read in *US Weekly* it was going to be in May at some grand lodge upstate. But people are now whispering that it's going to be over Christmas at Belcourt.'

Brooke flashed her a smile. 'You don't expect me to tell you that, do you?' she teased.

'Yes, Courtney, the Secret Service will have you killed,' said Susie, her smile not quite reaching her eyes.

'I doubt Brooke has any dealings with the Secret Service,' replied Ed, not unkindly. 'Not yet, anyway,' he added with a wink.

'But I bet you will, one day,' said Courtney, pushing her olive around her glass. 'Matt says David is going to be president in fifteen, twenty years' time. Imagine that life, it'd be so glamorous! Not being able to eat, sleep, shop without some man with an earpiece and a gun in his pocket guarding you. Do you think they monitor the President having sex?' She dissolved into giggles.

'Doctor, can you get this woman a coffee to sober her up?' said Greg to Matt only half jokingly.

'Speaking of the wedding, you must let me make you an essential oil for the big day,' said Susie. 'Lavender and neroli oil would be just dreamy.'

'Actually, that reminds me,' added Brooke, picking up her clutch, 'I must just go and deliver something to the birthday boy.' She crossed the corridor and went into the kitchen. It had a wooden swinging door like a Wild West saloon. The windows were steamed up and Matt was bent over the stove, tasting something that looked like bubbling stew from a wooden spoon. The scene reminded her of his attempts at cooking when they were in college, and she found it comforting that some things hadn't changed all that much. He looked up from his pots with a start.

'Hey, what are you doing in here?' he said, taking a long swig of his claret. 'Go and get back to your adoring audience.'

He gave her a big, wide smile. He seemed happier, more relaxed than usual. Then again, he'd clearly had quite a bit to drink. Matt had always liked his liquor.

'Don't be silly,' she said with a playful tap. 'They're here for your birthday, remember?'

'Don't kid yourself,' smiled Matt. 'I can't believe how everyone has dressed up in your honour. You should see what they look like on a normal day, it's like Halloween. Honestly, when Courtney knocked on the door, I wasn't sure if it was my guests arriving or the early delivery of my Christmas tree.'

Her gaze tracked across the room to where a large chocolate gateau was defrosting on a shelf above the radiator. 'You should have said you were doing food. I know a couple of really great chefs that do private catering.'

'Like I'm a private chef kinda guy,' he laughed.

'Sorry, I didn't mean it like that,' said Brooke, a little embarrassed.

'Money isn't the issue, Brooke,' he said, holding her gaze. 'Anyway, shame David couldn't make it.'

'Yeah, well. He's working late. Again. I counted up the nights I see him per month and I'm lucky if I get to double digits.'

'Maybe it was just as well he didn't come. He'd have made us men feel inferior.'

'I'm not marrying Bruce Wayne,' she said, nudging his arm playfully.

He grinned and lifted the wooden spoon to her lips. 'How does that taste?'

She licked her lips. It wasn't half bad. 'And a good cook too,' she said. 'You *are* a catch. Oh, I think I'd better warn you,' she said, changing the subject. 'I think I put my foot in it. I asked if Ed and Peter's medical exchange programme was the one you wanted to do. Susie seemed a bit surprised.'

He shrugged, turning back to the stove. 'Oh, she knows about it. I haven't made my mind up yet, but she isn't going to influence that decision anyway.'

Brooke found herself feeling oddly relieved. 'Oh, I forgot,' she said, producing a small package wrapped in shiny red paper. 'Your birthday present.'

'I thought that was the Château Pétrus you brought. I am a lucky boy.' He wiped his hands on a tea towel and tore the paper off. Inside was a slim box. He opened it and his eyes widened with pleasure.

'Tickets for the Guns N' Roses reunion gig?' he cried. 'No way! Shit, these are impossible to get hold of. I can't believe you remembered I like them.'

'How could I forget all that posing in front of the mirror?' she grinned.

He wrapped his arms around her and gave her a kiss on the cheek. A stillness descended between them. Brooke stepped back, brushing a trace of sauce from her cheek just as Susie burst through the Wild West doors.

'We're already out of red wine,' she announced, squeezing into the small space. 'You should have reminded me what big drinkers you doctors are.'

She paused and then examined Matt and Brooke, who both carried slightly guilty faces.

'Is everything okay?'

'More than okay,' said Matt enthusiastically, showing her the tickets. 'Look what Brooke gave me. Guns N' Roses, man!'

'Great,' said Susie flatly. 'I didn't know you were into rock.'

'Ah, you should have seen him in college,' smiled Brooke. 'He wanted to grow his hair like Slash, but it just hung there like two curtains.'

'Hey!' he protested. 'And you call me indiscreet!'

Susie eyed them warily. She pushed past Matt and began to stir the stew furiously.

'Go on, get back in there,' she said. 'I'll take over. Dinner will be just a couple of minutes.'

Sitting down at the dinner table, wedged in between Ed and Courtney, Brooke quickly found herself much more at ease. Matt's friends were fun and intelligent and conversation bounced between the serious, such as universal health-care schemes, to the more frivolous, such as the latest exposés in the *New York Post*. The casserole was actually excellent, although the gateau was still semi-frozen – but by then Brooke didn't care; she was relaxed and having fun. It was so unlike the birthday celebrations she usually went to these days: they were more like exercises in social competitiveness. They were held in restaurants that hadn't yet officially opened or had the guest list managed by the hottest PR agencies in town. When they *were* held at people's homes they were grand affairs: dinner-parties catered by Joël Robuchon or cocktail parties for one hundred to demonstrate the size of their duplex. Brooke had also found that once she started talking about David, in particular recounting the Florida drama for the benefit of an open-mouthed Courtney, Susie relaxed a little and seemed actually quite sweet.

She was clearly besotted with Matthew, at any rate. *And isn't that a good thing?* she asked herself. Of course it was.

'So, Brooke, will you be having frozen gateau at your wedding?' asked Greg, crunching his fork into icy chocolate. Matt threw a napkin at his friend.

'Hey, you're a guest,' he laughed, 'but any more cheek from you and you'll be washing up.'

Ed and Peter cheered raucously at the suggestion, drumming their hands on the table.

Courtney leant forward, resting her small breasts on top of the table. 'Is it all right if Matt tells us every detail of the wedding after it's happened?'

Matt looked up. Although Courtney was at the other end of the table, his ears seemed to be tuned into any conversation directed at Brooke.

'Oh I'm not going,' he said quickly.

'Why not?' asked Courtney.

'Nah, quite right, I wouldn't invite this reprobate either,' said Greg, winking over to Brooke.

'No, no, of course you're invited,' said Brooke, fixing her gaze on the birthday boy.

Matt smiled and then looked down at his empty plate. 'So who's for coffee?' he said, quickly getting to his feet. 'I think we need something to defrost that cake.'

Brooke glanced her watch. It was gone eleven and she was feeling more drunk than she had done in ages. 'No, I think I have to run,' she said, beginning to rise, then sitting down again. 'Actually, stagger is more like it. I think I've had one too many of Greg's cocktails.'

'If you need any help with the bar at your wedding, you know where to find me,' smiled Greg. Susie went to get Brooke's cashmere coat from the bedroom and helped her on with it.

'Good luck with everything,' said Courtney, grabbing Brooke and clasping her to her sequined bosom. 'I wish I was you.'

'I'll come out and get a taxi with you,' said Matt, guiding her out into the dark hallway. He pressed the button and they waited for the elevator.

'That was fun,' smiled Brooke, buttoning up her coat. 'And Susie is so lovely.'

'Brooke. Don't make this bigger than it is,' he replied. He was standing so close to her that she could smell the alcohol on his breath.

'Listen, Matt. I know you're still thinking about Katie, and that's really sweet, but you don't have to feel guilty for dating again.'

They both turned as they heard Matt's front door creak open. 'Matt. Do you want me to make the coffee?'

Susie had a slightly hopeless, insecure look on her face that made Brooke's heart go out to her. She was just an ordinary girl doing her best to defend her new man – a doctor no less, a real catch in most circles – from a threat she saw as impossibly glamorous. Brooke felt awful for all the uncharitable things she had thought about Susie throughout the night. *In the end, like all of us*, she thought, *she's just looking for someone to love*. Brooke tapped Matt's arm in the most platonic way she could.

'Oh, I forgot,' she said, looking over at Susie, 'it's the launch party for one of my books on Friday. It would be great if you could both come along.'

Susie's worried face broke out into a relieved smile. 'That would be great,' she beamed, walking over to Matt and hooking her arm through his. The lift arrived and the doors swished open.

'Well, goodnight,' said Brooke, hurriedly air-kissing them both like the good politician's wife, then jumped inside, watching the floors click past, suddenly glad to be out of there.

43

'Mr Billington,' she gasped. 'That was . . . absolutely . . . spectacular.'

Liz slid off Wendell's cock and collapsed onto the mattress, her flushed face mashing into the pillow. Liz and Wendell had been meeting three times a week since their first encounter in the Hamptons, and the sex just seemed to get better and better every time. The convenience of Wendell's permanent suite at The Pierre certainly helped. They had been known to slip out of their respective offices for lunch and be back, invigorated and alert, for a meeting an hour later. Far from interfering with work, Liz felt there was nothing like a quick, hard lunchtime fuck to sharpen you up for the day ahead.

Wendell got out of bed, put on a bathrobe and moved to the table by the window where lunch had been set out on starched white table linen. He stabbed his fork into his swordfish and picked up the *Financial Times*, neatly folded by his china side plate.

Liz looked over with interest. As one of the world's most important investors she felt sure that Wendell read every piece of global financial journalism, but the question was: what was he reading about? With his insider knowledge and contacts, she might be able to sniff out some valuable information; in fact Liz had heard a rumour that Wendell was about to buy Vue, a huge British vision-care business, for an estimated billion dollars.

'Have they reported about Vue yet?' she asked innocently.

Wendell looked at her with surprise. 'And how would you know about that?'

She walked over to him and stroked the back of his neck. 'Knowledge is power, darling,' she smiled coquettishly.

350

His eyes trailed across to her bare breasts as he reached out for her, but she nimbly stepped out of his reach, scooping up her knickers and sliding into her dress. She did not want him distracted when they were talking business. She sat opposite Wendell, pouring herself a glass of water and feeling the autumn sun on her face.

'I want to buy Skin Plus from the family,' she said without preamble.

A small smile crept onto her lover's lips. 'And do Meredith and William know this?' he asked.

'Not yet,' she replied, shaking her freshly highlighted bob.

'Be careful, Liz. This is family now.'

'No, Wendell, this is *business*,' she said firmly. She looked at him, waiting for a reaction. 'So what do you think?'

Wendell wiped his mouth with a napkin.

'I think that you should be CEO of Asgill's because I think that you could turn the company around. And I think you probably will be one day. So I don't think you should try and buy Skin Plus out of spite simply because your family aren't giving you the recognition you deserve.'

Liz smiled. 'Oh, I'm past spite. I'm talking to you as a business-woman who sees something with enormous potential, who wants to be in total charge of realizing that potential.'

Wendell gave a low, slow laugh. 'You are very sexy when you're angry.'

Under the table, Liz curled her hand into a fist. 'Why don't you try taking this conversation fucking seriously?'

There was a long, stagnant pause.

'Why are you mentioning this to me?' said Wendell finally.

'Because you are an investor and you know I am a good bet,' said Liz. 'Plus you have no interests in the cosmetic industry, but you do have complementary businesses: airport outlets, media, pharmaceuticals. Diversification is always a good idea in tough times.'

Wendell viewed her sceptically. 'I don't need to remind you that Meredith and William will soon be my family too. It might not be such a good idea to upset them quite so soon.'

Liz waved a hand dismissively. 'It won't be a problem, not if I handle it in the right way. And if you didn't want to disclose your involvement, I'm sure you have plenty of covert investment vehicles you could use.'

Wendell shook his head, chuckling. 'You're persuasive, you know that? And I should know, I hear seventy per cent bullshit most of the day.'

'So. Are you interested?'

'Get a business plan over to me by Monday,' he said coolly. 'Maybe we'll talk. No promises.'

'I'll courier it round to your office first thing tomorrow morning.'

'You're good,' he said, smiling.

'I know.'

'Come here.'

She walked to the other side of the table and pulled back his chair. Slipping open his white towelling robe, she ran her hands across his chest hair, sank to her knees, and got to work.

44

Book launch parties are traditionally quite low-key affairs – usually a few drinks in a bookstore followed by a short speech to the assembled sales team about 'distribution channels' and 'retail footfall'. The launch for *Portico*, however, was the literary equivalent of a red-carpet premiere. It was held at a private club on Fifty-Third Street and Yellow Door had converted the entire top floor into a Victorian magician's den, complete with scarlet drapes, strange oriental cabinets, and an ornate cage of flapping doves. Outside, photographers swamped the street, desperate for shots of Brooke and David together, not to mention the high-profile guest list the party had managed to attract. Half of New York's A-list seemed to be here with their children for the hottest kids' book since *Harry Potter*. The atmosphere inside the club room was just as electric. Even the most hard-to-please critics had been lining up to congratulate Brooke and her MD, Edward Walker, on this 'startling debut'.

Everything had come together like a dream, thought Brooke, unable to wipe the broad grin off her face. Two days earlier she had received a phone call from Janice Douglas, the head of development for Unicorn Studios, whom Brooke and Eileen had met in LA three weeks earlier. Unicorn had duly bought the options to *Portico* for a high six-figure sum, but Brooke didn't expect much more, as studios were notorious for purchasing options and then sitting on them. So she had nearly fallen off her chair when she'd heard that the head of the studio had almost immediately green-lighted the project, with principal photography due to commence in the spring. Eileen had burst into tears when Brooke had called her with the news.

Yellow Door's faith in *Portico* seemed to be paying off at grass-roots level too. Three hundred thousand copies had been printed to satisfy orders from bookstores all across America, and it seemed certain that a second print run would soon be necessary. As Brooke and David watched from the back of the room, Edward clambered onto a podium to give a speech to the assembled staff, journalists, and industry bigwigs, most of it praising Brooke Asgill and her vision.

Brooke blushed furiously, her cheeks clashing with her forest-green Prada cocktail dress. 'I wish he'd hurry up and finish,' she whispered to David, but he was looking down at his BlackBerry, an agitated expression on his face.

'What's wrong, honey?' asked Brooke, smoothing down the lapel of his Tom Ford jacket.

'Nothing,' he said vaguely. 'Just waiting to see if someone is going to turn up or not.'

Mildly irritated, Brooke watched him leave, glad-handing the crowd as he passed through. *You're not on the campaign trail yet,* thought Brooke, frowning.

'What's his problem?' whispered Debs.

Brooke shrugged. 'Another crisis, no doubt. He's due in the studio in a couple of hours as it is.'

The crowd broke into applause for the end of the speech and Brooke saw Eileen make her way over.

'Hey, Eileen,' she smiled. 'I lost sight of you, you were surrounded by so many journalists.'

Brooke found it hard to stay annoyed with David with Eileen around. Just looking at the young woman's transformation from downtrodden mother struggling on the breadline to feted literary sensation was enough to fill you with faith, hope, and vigour. The awkward yet resilient woman Brooke had met in the restaurant at The London all those months ago had certainly emerged from her shell. Her hair was blonder, her clothes more chic; even her posture was different, making her look taller and more confident. Brooke felt a warm glow, not just from the knowledge that she had had something to do with Eileen's change of fortune, but from the idea that, in a heartbeat, life could alter its path and take you off on a thrilling and unexpected journey.

'Someone from *Publishers Weekly* was asking me if I thought *Portico* was going to get in the *New York Times'* best-seller list,' said Eileen with a trace of anxiety. 'I just wondered how many copies we need to sell for that.'

'No one knows,' replied Debs, taking a long slurp of a bright-red cocktail called Magician's Brew. 'It's compiled from a variety of bookselling sources and it's not always the biggest-selling books – which can either work for or against you. Very confusing; not entirely sure I understand it myself.'

Over Eileen's shoulder, Brooke could see David approaching, and she stiffened when she saw he was accompanied by an attractive brunette.

'Brooke, I'd like you to meet Charlotte Field,' he said.

'Hello,' smiled Brooke, offering her hand, trying to work out from where she recognized the name.

'Charlotte is a booker for Oprah's show.'

Brooke nearly spluttered out her Bellini. When she looked up, Charlotte was already introducing herself to Eileen.

'David was telling me about your incredible story, Eileen,' she said, pumping her hand. 'I'm going to run it past my producer, but I don't think there will be any problem at all getting you a slot with Oprah.'

Eileen and Charlotte had fallen into deep conversation. Brooke turned to David and squeezed his fingers.

'Is she going to get Eileen on the show?' she said, trying to whisper, but her words coming out in a squeak.

'I think she's going to try,' said David.

Brooke clutched his arm, not wanting to let go. Wanting to kiss him. 'I know you can do anything, David,' she hissed, 'but how, why is she here?'

David put his BlackBerry back in his pocket.

'I met her through a friend at the network. I know how import-ant it is to get books on shows like *Oprah* and *Regis and Kelly*, and I know how important this book is to you,' he said, smiling. Brooke thought that when David Billington smiled, he was the most handsome man in the world.

'Well, it was a very good thing that you did,' she said, taking a deep breath to recover a little of her composure. 'You know you are going to change that woman's life?' she said, pointing at Eileen.'

'One person at a time,' smiled David, kissing the side of her head.

'Hey Brooke.'

She spun round towards the voice. It was Matt. He was standing there, looking very uncomfortable in a suit and tie, Susie at his side, hopping from one foot to the other. To her amazement, Brooke realized that she was wearing a sort of ethnic skirt and a Greenpeace T-shirt. She hoped it was Susie's attempt at a fashion statement.

'Matt, Susie. You came.'

She felt David's grip on her hand tighten. There was a frosty silence as they eyed each other.

'Please, may I take one of these?' asked Susie, waving a copy of *Portico* in the air. She sounded so polite, so nervous, that both Brooke and David smiled. It was enough to break the ice.

'And I'd get Eileen to sign it if I were you,' said Brooke. 'It might be worth something one day.'

David stepped over to Matt. 'I'm David,' he said, extending a hand. 'Pleased to meet you.'

'Really?' replied Matt with a little knowing smile. 'After the *Oracle* thing?'

'Brooke explained. It's all forgotten,' said David after a moment, smiling at Susie. 'Brooke tells me you're invited to the wedding. Both of you, of course.'

'Wow, me?' gasped Susie, holding her hand to her mouth. 'That's so kind. I can't wait.'

'Yeah, thanks, David,' said Matt, obviously quite taken aback. Brooke stood back and watched them chat, seeing Matt wilt ever so slightly under David's star power.

She felt David's hand around her waist, firm and strong. She enjoyed the sensation of him being there, of people watching them together. She turned to Susie and said, 'I'm so glad we've all finally met.'

And it was true. The sense of relief was palpable, almost like a physical release of pressure. But there was something more: a feeling of righteousness that, despite the thoughts and desires, she had not betrayed David's trust. And now everything was out in the open and in its place. She had an overwhelming sense that things were as they should be.

'Who on earth is that terribly unkempt woman talking to Brooke?'

Meredith had been watching the scene from a distance and did not like the look she had seen pass between her youngest daughter and the man she recognized as Matthew Palmer. She had met him once before, at Parklands many years earlier, and had predicted back then he would be trouble. The sort of sullen, long-haired boy with no real drive to do anything with his good looks and brains. Although she had been reassured by Tess Garrett that his quote to the *Daily Oracle* had been taken out of context, Meredith did not like to see him back in her daughter's life. Well, at least he had a girlfriend with him. Or at least she thought it was a girlfriend, though she looked more like a crazed nuclear disarmament peace protestor who had walked in off the street.

'I assume we're talking about Miss Greenpeace,' said Liz with a sly half-smile. 'Perhaps it's a friend. I mean, who knows who Brooke is running around with these days. I met Jessica Johnston the other day; she says the old Spence crowd don't see anything of Brooke any more.'

Meredith clasped her Hermès Kelly bag close to her body and vowed to quiz Brooke on it later.

'I think it's time to go,' she said, glancing around the room with distaste. 'Are we having supper? Wasn't there something you wanted to discuss?'

'Yes,' said Liz, smiling with anticipation. 'I thought perhaps we could go to Daniel?'

'Daniel sounds fine.'

A red velvet throne sat invitingly at the back of the room. Tess knew it was a prop, but it looked so wide and soft, like a bed in a department store during a hard afternoon's shopping, that she couldn't resist sitting in it just for one moment. She took off her shoe and rubbed the arch of her foot as she looked around at the party. Across the room she could see Brooke and David laughing with Matt Palmer. It really was quite uncanny how the two men looked alike. The same height and build; the same dark, good-looking features. Matt Palmer's eyes were narrower than David's, his face looked more tired, his clothes not as sharp or expensive were-looking. In fact, Matt Palmer could be David's naughtier, cooler big brother.

'Tess Garrett. How wonderful to see you again.'

She looked up to see an elegant elderly gentleman smiling at her. 'Charles Devine?' she smiled.

'The very same, how could you forget me, darling?' he said, stooping to kiss her cheek.

It had been six months since Tess had last seen Charles Devine, the eccentric English gossip who had charmed her at Brooke and David's engagement party. Despite Meredith's description of him as a silly social butterfly, Tess had barely seen him at any of the recent society functions in New York, leading her to suspect that Charles's place in the Upper East Side firmament was on the wane.

'What on earth are you doing here?' she asked, rising to her feet.

'I adore books and I adore parties,' said Charles. 'Why shouldn't I be here?'

She couldn't disagree, but she had a feeling Charles had another reason for coming.

'Is it pleasure or business tonight?' she asked.

'Well, I was actually hoping I might bump into you, darling,' he said conspiratorially.

Tess couldn't help smiling. 'Ah, so how can I help you, Charles?'

From the corner of her eye she saw Meredith being helped into her mink coat.

'You could start with a wedding invitation,' he winked, nodding towards Meredith.

'I'm not sure I can help out in that department,' she shrugged. 'Close friends and family only, I hear.'

'Well, in that case, perhaps you could help me out with another small matter.'

Meredith was beckoning Tess, an impatient look on her face.

'Sorry Charles, I have to go . . .'

'So how about tea?'

Tess winced. Charles was fun, but she simply didn't have time for social calls this close to the wedding.

'Maybe in the New Year?' she said distractedly.

'I can't wait that long,' he said, a little irritation entering his voice.

'Okay, maybe tea,' she replied, prepared to say anything just to escape.

'Oh goodie,' said Charles, brightening instantly. 'I'll be in touch. And give my love to she who must be obeyed.'

Daniel was one of Meredith's favourite restaurants in New York. French, old school, and elegant, it appealed to the part of Meredith that fancied herself as a European aristocrat. Liz had never seen her mother dine here and not leave in a good mood. And tonight, Liz needed all the help she could get.

'So. Are you going to tell me?' asked Meredith, dipping her spoon into the terracotta depths of her lobster bisque.

Liz nodded and placed her hands on her lap.

'It's about the direction of the company,' she said.

Meredith gestured impatiently with her spoon. 'There's a board meeting next Friday to discuss that.'

'Yes, but I wanted to talk mother to daughter.'

Meredith looked up curiously. 'Oh?'

Liz took a deep breath. She was glad to have secured a discreet table in the corner of the room.

'I know William is trying to sound out a couple of the multi-nationals to see if they are interested in the Asgill sale, but you and I both know they are only going to be interested if Skin Plus is part of the deal.'

'And do you foresee a problem there?'

'The problem is, Mother, that if we sell the entire company, then we are left with nothing.'

'We're left with a very large cheque, darling,' said Meredith tartly.

'Not that large,' countered Liz. 'The multinationals will play hardball and we're not offering them anything particularly unique. Most of them have successful cosmeceutical ranges of their own and they'll undervalue the rest of the business.'

Meredith put her spoon down. 'Darling, you needn't worry about your position. Whoever buys Skin Plus will bring in a first-rate management team to support you in taking it to the next level.'

Liz shook her head slowly but firmly. 'I have no intention of staying with Skin Plus if it becomes an appendage of some conglomerate.'

Meredith's face paled. Liz knew she recognized that having Liz Asgill on board would be a vital, even non-negotiable part of any deal. When she spoke, her mother's voice was quiet and measured, her eyes icy blue.

'You would be deliberately sabotaging any negotiations by withdrawing your involvement.'

Liz was glad they were in the rarefied surroundings of the restaurant. Meredith could be fiery when roused. Nothing that was a match for Liz, of course, but Liz preferred to do her business dealings in a setting where she could control the heat and tempo of the situation.

'There are other options, Mother,' she said calmly. 'I'm sure, if given the choice, you would rather not sell Asgill's in a cut-price deal. Father would turn in his grave, for one thing.'

'Elizabeth . . .' began Meredith, her voice low and full of warning.

'Hear me out,' said Liz. 'As I say, there is another way, a way in which you get to keep the company, William can keep control, and I will keep doing what I do best.'

Meredith sipped her wine. 'Carry on.'

'It's very simple: I will buy Skin Plus and I will pay a good price. You can pay off the debts and it's an ideal opportunity to stream-line the company, kill off some of the lines that are long past their sell-by date, and pump cash into the areas that have potential: The Balm, the fragrances, and so on.'

'You're cutting off your own family,' said Meredith, her elegant nostrils flaring.

'This is not a hostile act, Mother,' said Liz smoothly. 'This is win-win. I'll even keep my position on the Asgill board if you think you can benefit from my skill-set.'

She had to use every ounce of restraint to stop the latter part of that sentence dissolving into sarcasm. If her mother thought for one minute that this approach was rooted in her daughter's bitter-ness – or in truth, hatred – she would dismiss it without a moment's thought. Liz knew that she had definitely got her ruthlessness from her mother's side of the family. Meredith stared at Liz and she could almost see the thought process going on inside her head.

'And where do you propose getting that sort of money?'

Liz popped a sliver of foie gras into her mouth and let it melt on her tongue before she replied. 'This is an *in principle* conver-sation, Mother,' she smiled. 'But I think I may have some interest.'

Meredith shook her head slowly, never taking her eyes from Liz. 'Let me discuss it with your brother.'

Liz nodded and signalled to the waiter to clear their plates. But inside, she was jumping for joy.

45

Tess leant forward in her seat and waved a hundred-dollar bill at her Hawaiian taxi driver.

'Here's your tip if you can go any faster,' she said. For the first time in her life, she had missed her flight and had to wait around JFK for eight hours to get on the next one to Hawaii's Big Island. And now she was late – very, very late. So late, in fact, she would barely have time to change out of the jeans and T-shirt she had worn on the plane, let alone have a pre-pageant meeting with Sean Asgill.

In the rear-view mirror she saw the driver smile, then nod, while making no apparent effort to hurry up.

We're not in New York any more, she sighed, consoling herself with the thought that this was a baby-sitting gig, not a life-or-death business appointment. Suddenly, the driver swung right into a palm-tree-lined drive and under an archway reading 'Welcome to the Aloha Grand Hotel'.

'Oh. We're here?' said Tess, quickly putting the hundred-dollar bill back into her purse. She stepped outside into the balmy, sweet-scented evening air, took her wheelie-case off the driver, ignoring his upturned hand, and bolted for her suite.

Already it was dark, and from the noise of Hawaiian drums and cheers coming from the beach, the pageant was clearly reaching some sort of crescendo. Throwing on an olive-silk wrap dress and some silver Jimmy Choo sandals, Tess raced downstairs and out to the long lawns by the beach where the pageant stage had been erected. Either side of the stage were bleachers full of cheering frat-house boys and, in the centre, at least fifty tables of sponsors,

361

press, and Hawaiian dignitaries. Tess was amazed at the scale of the event. The pageant was clearly big business, much more than some lame publicity stunt for Asgill's Hawaiian Glo suntan lotion. She flashed her pass at security and slipped into a table at the back. The event was part Hawaiian luau, part beauty contest, and while the final girls in the competition slipped into their evening wear, the stage was filled with a fire-eating and hula dancing display. Finally, after much whooping from the drunken frat boys, five girls paraded back on stage in jewelled gowns cut low in the front and high on the thigh.

The master of ceremonies, a rotund Hawaiian in an electric-blue blazer, lifted his microphone.

'Ladies and gentlemen,' he chimed. 'Please welcome, from Asgill's Hawaiian Glo, Mr Sean Asgill!'

Sean bounded on stage, his white teeth flashing in the Polynesian darkness.

'The moment of truth, ladies and gentlemen,' he said, his voice popping in the PA. 'What we've all been waiting for . . .'

'He's so cute, don't you think?' whispered a blonde to her left.

Tess smiled weakly. 'Too many teeth for my liking.'

There was a drum roll and Sean ripped open a silver envelope with a flourish.

'And the winner is . . .' He paused for effect, then looked down at the card, feigned surprise, then pleasure. *Yeah right,* thought Tess. *As if you didn't have her all picked out from the start.*

'Candy Cooper!' he cried, as the crowd went wild and an incredibly curvaceous brunette wearing a sash reading 'Miss Asgill Hawaiian Glo Oregon' stepped up to be crowned Miss Asgill Hawaiian Glo.

It took Tess ten minutes to push through the sea of people heading for the free bar once the official ceremony was over. *Where is he?* seethed Tess. *After I rushed all this bloody way . . .*

Finally she saw a poolside gazebo that seemed to be doubling as the VIP bar. As she turned the corner, she saw Sean engrossed in conversation with Candy Cooper.

He glanced up and his face fell.

'Yeah, aloha to you too,' said Tess, sitting down next to him and Candy.

'So the nanny's finally arrived,' Sean deadpanned.

'Finally?' said Tess as casually as she could.

'My mother phoned about three hours ago. Apparently you and I were supposed to have a meeting before the pageant to discuss press coverage.'

Tess didn't speak, determined not to show her discomfort.

'I said you hadn't checked in and I presumed you weren't coming.'

'You said *what?*' she replied, her cool cracking.

Sean's face creased up and he started to chuckle. 'I could have said that, but I didn't,' he laughed. 'I said we'd just touched base and how you had everything under control.'

Tess was grateful but didn't want to show it too much. 'Well, my flight was delayed,' she said crisply.

Candy Cooper flicked her long bouncy beauty-queen hair over one shoulder. 'I hate flying, don't you?' she said, oblivious to the conversation. 'It's so bad for the skin.'

Tess nodded politely, trying to assess Candy's age – sixteen? Eighteen? – when she saw Candy's hand casually slide up Sean's thigh.

'Okaayyy,' said Tess quickly, standing up and taking Candy's arm. 'I think it's about your bedtime.'

Candy pulled her arm away, pouting. 'Says who?'

'Says me,' replied Tess. 'I'm the personal representative of Meredith Asgill, the woman who has the final say on whether your face ends up on a thousand Hawaii Sun posters or whether winning this pageant is the highlight of your career.'

'Tess,' said Sean angrily.

She glared at him, then turned back to Candy.

'Beauty sleep time,' she said, pointing towards the hotel.

Sulkily, Candy did as she was told. Sean stood up and stormed out of the gazebo. Tess followed, matching him stride for stride. As he reached the beach, he stopped and turned to face her.

'What the fuck was that all about, exactly?'

'*That* was about Candy Cooper being a statutory rape allegation waiting to happen.'

'Well, if you'd been there at the beginning of the pageant you'd have heard that Candy is nineteen,' said Sean sarcastically.

'Which makes it okay to fuck her?' asked Tess, her hands on her hips. 'And anyway, what about that supermodel, what's her name? Annabel something? Aren't you supposed to be dating her?'

'Like you care about Annabel,' snapped Sean.

'Sean, I care about doing my job.'

'Well, do it without being such a bitch then!' he shouted.

'I'm not being a bitch,' she said as coolly as she could. 'I'm doing what you pay me for.'

'You really are a piece of work,' he said under his breath, and stalked back towards the hotel. This time, Tess let him go. She took off her shoes and wandered along the beach, feeling the still-warm sand between her toes. It was so tranquil, so relaxing; she felt a wave of tiredness consuming her. *I need a shower and a sleep*, she thought wearily. Glancing at her watch, Tess realized it was getting late.

'Ah bugger, the volcano!' she said suddenly, pulling up the hem of her dress and running towards the hotel lobby.

'Can I help you, madam?' asked the girl behind the 'Guest Relations' desk.

'Can you book me onto the volcano flight on Sunday?' panted Tess. 'And what about this swimming with dolphins package? Is that any good?'

The girl was nodding. 'It's a once-in-a-lifetime experience. Three hundred dollars, but the best stress reliever you'll find anywhere.'

'Stress reliever sounds perfect,' replied Tess gratefully.

Just then she heard laughing behind her.

'I hope the dolphins know what they're getting into. I should think they'll come out needing a holiday.' Sean Asgill was standing six feet away, leaning against a pillar with a cynical smile.

'What do you want?' Tess scowled at him, but Sean held up his hands.

'Listen, sorry, I felt bad about shouting at you,' he said. 'I just felt a little frustrated to be denied female company. You were probably right.'

Tess nodded graciously.

'Fine, apology accepted, now if you'll excuse me . . .'

'Hey, I thought I wasn't to be left alone,' said Sean. 'I thought that's what Mommy wanted.'

'Just during the pageant,' said Tess. 'Tomorrow I am officially on holiday and, as I haven't had a day's break in six months, I'd like to plan my day without you scoffing in the background.'

Sean winked at the girl behind the desk.

'Charge all that to my room. And can you confirm my taxi for seven a.m.?'

'Certainly, Mr Asgill.'

'Come on,' he said, taking Tess by the arm and leading her towards the bar. 'If you're really that stressed, then I have the perfect solution. The Asgill Zombie, it's a cocktail I invented back in my darker days.'

Tess flashed a look at him.

'Don't worry, not me . . . I think you could do with a couple. Think of it as a peace offering.'

'Sean, we're not at war . . .' began Tess, looking up towards the bar.

And it was then that she saw him, walking out of the bar. He was older, more tanned, but it was definitely him. Her heart leapt into her mouth. She couldn't believe she had come halfway across the world only to bump into the one person she never wanted to see again. Grabbing Sean, she swung him around in front of her.

'Please,' she hissed. 'Just stay there.'

She felt Sean's grip tighten protectively around her.

'What's wrong?' he asked, looking around.

'Shhh . . .' whispered Tess, 'he'll hear. He's walking over to the lobby.'

Tess peeked around Sean's shoulder, watching the man enter the lift. Her shoulders sagged with relief as she saw the doors close.

'What was all that about?' asked Sean with concern.

'Can we go back outside?' said Tess. 'He might come back to the bar.'

'Do you want to come to my cottage?' said Sean. 'It's away from the main drag, by the beach.'

She nodded and rushed out of the hotel.

'I'm sorry, you must think I'm stupid,' she said when they were safely away from the building.

Sean shrugged. 'No. I think you've just seen something that's upset you or bothered you.'

They walked towards a row of four cottages by the shore.

'Thanks,' she said simply, walking into the living space, which opened out to secluded decking and, beyond that, a private pool. Sean threw his keycard on the side and picked up the telephone.

'I asked for the minibar to be cleared before I came so I'll have to order you something from the hotel.'

'I thought you were drinking cocktails earlier?'

'Cream and pineapple. Totally nonalcoholic but very sickly. I wouldn't recommend it.'

Tess went and sat on a lounger by the small pool, shining like a sheet of sparkling tourmaline, while Sean made the call to room service. He walked out and sat next to Tess. 'Am I allowed to ask what happened back there?'

Tess looked up, grateful that the cool Pacific breeze was cooling her red cheeks.

'I saw my mother's husband,' she said simply.

'Which isn't your father . . . ?' he said, brows creasing.

'My dad's dead. My mother remarried this guy, Anthony, who was one of my dad's friends. That's who I saw in the lobby.'

'So why did you want to avoid him?'

'Because it probably means my mother is here.'

'And you don't want to see her?' he said, looking increasingly baffled.

Tess shook her head, looking down at the pool. 'I haven't spoken to her in ten years.'

She saw the confusion on his face. Total estrangement from a parent was an alien concept to most people, especially to someone like Sean, brought up in the tightly knit Asgill clan, where life and business overlapped and every part of your life was planned, watched, and discussed. Tess sighed.

'My mum and dad were never a match made in heaven,' she began. 'I think she always felt that she hadn't fulfilled her potential with him. My dad, on the other hand, was crazy about her. You know some women have that effect on men.'

Sean nodded.

'So my dad bought a pub in Suffolk – Constable country, a gorgeous place. We moved up there from North London.'

She smiled to herself. She could appreciate the county's beauty now, but back then as a teenager, she'd been as negative about it as her mother. Back in Edgware, Tess was cool and popular, going to gigs in London, getting served in the local pubs. At the Suffolk sixth-form college, suddenly she was no one, an outsider surrounded by people who had known each other since primary school. These people thought she was showing off when she mentioned that she'd been to the Astoria or Hammersmith Apollo. London to them was somehow corrupt and unsavoury, and Tess was tarred with the same brush. Still, she made every attempt she could to fit in because she knew her father had made the move to save their family, which was why she had taken refuge at the college newspaper, where her own back story wasn't important as long as she could deliver her copy on time.

The bell to the cottage rang and Sean got up and returned with two bottles of beer on a tray.

'I didn't think one was enough,' he smiled.

Tess took a long, grateful swallow before continuing. 'My mum hated Suffolk. Instead of saving the marriage, it drove them further apart. She would go and spend half the week in London visiting friends while Dad would be putting in fifteen-hour days in the pub. He still stuck by her, though,' said Tess, shaking her head in wonder. 'But it wasn't enough, and finally she walked out on us. Turns out she'd been having an affair with Anthony, one of Dad's so-called friends, and she moved back to London to be with him. I stayed with Dad, of course. I'd just finished my A-levels and I had a place to do English at Bristol University, but I deferred it to help Dad in the pub. Dad had overstretched himself to buy it in the first place and he couldn't cope alone. He tried, God knows he tried, but two weeks before Christmas, the pub got repossessed. My dad died of a heart attack a month later.'

It had been a long time since Tess had told that story, and all the years in between had not made it any easier. She could still remember vividly the day they moved from the pub into a rented flat in the village, and she could still hear the sympathetic whispers of the locals. But most of all, burned indelibly into her mind, was the memory of finding her father dead, slumped on the gaudy living-room carpet, when she had returned from a supermarket run one evening. Ten years hadn't been able to wipe away that. At night she could sometimes hear the ambulance, the blue light flashing through the window and casting a ghoulish glow around the room. To this day she did not know what had caused his heart to give up. A genetic weakness, his expanding waistline – working in a pub serving 'good solid English food' certainly hadn't helped – or perhaps it really was a broken heart, having lost his wife, his business, and his dream in the space of a few weeks.

'I'm so sorry,' said Sean, awkwardly putting a hand on her shoulder.

'So I never got to uni,' said Tess with a small smile. 'You can probably tell.' For a second she thought of Dom's friends talking about their time at Oxford or Durham and looking down on Tess with her A-levels and on-the-job experience.

'I got a very junior, very badly paid job on the local paper; the editor had been a regular at the pub and I think he took pity on me. That's the path that led me here,' she said, gesturing towards the sea. She brushed a hand against her cheek and it came away wet – she hadn't even noticed the tears falling. At the funeral, her mother wept openly in the front pew of the church while Tess sat as far away from her as possible. She had not cried once that day, her grief crushed by a tight ball of anger deep inside her. When she walked away from the grave, it was the last time she had seen or spoken to her mother.

She wiped her red eyes and inhaled loudly to catch her breath. *How ridiculous to be crying after so long*, she thought angrily, hoping Sean wouldn't tell his mother; her career had meant everything to her. For ten years she had worked so hard she would never feel lonely or insecure again. Money couldn't bring her father back but it could give her a safety net from the world. She couldn't allow herself to lose that; she had seen what it had done to her father.

She blew her nose and looked at her watch. It was now almost midnight.

'Thanks for the beer. I should get back,' she said, standing up, feeling suddenly embarrassed at her outpouring to someone she barely knew.

'Are you sure you don't want to talk about this some more?'

'I'm sure,' she said, laughing. 'I just want to go to my room and pack.'

'You're leaving? I thought this was your holiday. What about the volcanoes and the dolphins?'

She shook her head vigorously. 'And bump into Mother and Anthony on their romantic holiday? No way.'

'But if you haven't spoken to her for ten years, maybe your mother isn't even with Anthony any more?' said Sean. 'Maybe she's not in Hawaii.'

She could be dead for all I care, thought Tess, instantly feeling bad for having had the notion. She shook her head; surely she would have heard. And she would definitely have heard if her mother had left Anthony. Every now and then she heard snippets about their life through friends such as Jemma's sister Cat, so she knew about their big house in Edgware, their life of happy retirement enjoying cruises and holidays, just like the one they were on now.

'I have another idea,' said Sean, looking thoughtful. 'I was going to head to Maui tomorrow, it's the next island over. My friend has a great house in Hana, a really quiet, fantastic spot. Why don't you come?'

He looked completely serious.

'No, they're your friends . . .' she said, jangling the silver bracelets around her wrist. 'I don't want to intrude.'

Sean shook his head. 'No, it's just going to be me, if you can stomach that,' he smiled. 'Chris is away in Europe. I'm just staying there for a couple of nights before I head back to London.'

'Sean, I can't.'

'Yes you can. You told me you've got a couple of days off yourself, and my mom is in Paris with Brooke doing wedding dress stuff, so she won't be needing you. And really, I don't bite.'

He smiled, his eyes crinkling up. Tess couldn't believe she was actually tempted by his suggestion. But then she badly needed a break from New York. And she couldn't stay here.

'When are you leaving?'

'Seven tomorrow morning, before anybody else is up and around, even for breakfast.'

'I must be crazy.'

Sean laughed. 'Hey, I could have told you that the day I met you.'

It was only a short hop over to Maui on a twelve-seater plane that Sean had chartered for the day. Maui looked more green than the Big Island, but its volcanic past was still evident from the huge, lunar-like crater she could see in the middle of the island. From the air, they could also see the perfect, crescent-shaped beaches all along the coast, some black, some white, some even a dark red. She loved it already. They landed at Hana airport, little more than an airstrip on the lush eastern side of the island, and climbed into an open-topped Jeep waiting for them by the tiny office building.

This was a different Hawaii from the one she had experienced on the Big Island, which was built up and touristy with skyscrapers in the business districts and cruise ships on the horizon, every shop seemingly packed with plastic surfboards, fluoro towels, and crazily patterned shirts. Hana, by contrast, had a unique calm that was almost spiritual. Tess loved the smell of the frangipani-and rain-scented breeze as they took a ten-minute trip around narrow, mango-strewn lanes into the small town.

They pulled up in front of a one-storey oriental-styled house with emerald-green lawns that sloped down to the ocean. Inside it was like a Thai boutique hotel, with maple floors, ceiling fans, and grey, cream, and charcoal minimalist furnishings. She walked out onto the *lanai* – the terrace at the back – and saw a black marble infinity pool stretching out in front of her. In New York she was sometimes intimidated by the luxury: the museum-quality splendour of Belcourt, or Meredith's chilly Upper East Side WASP palace. But here, she felt as if she could lie down on one of the ivory sofas by the pool, drink in the views, and feel entirely at home.

'Who *owns* this place?' she asked Sean, who had already changed into khaki shorts and a white T-shirt. He grinned.

'Chris Kennedy.'

'The rock star?'

Sean nodded. 'I've known Chris for years – well, before the band got really famous. Lots of musicians live around here actually. George Harrison used to have an estate down the road.'

'Blimey,' said Tess, looking at the house in a different light now she knew it was owned by a celebrity. Still, there was no harm in enjoying the luxury while she was here, was there?

'Mind if I take a dip in the pool?' she asked.

'Oh no,' said Sean. 'Grab your bikini, I can think of somewhere better to swim than here.'

'Better than *here*?' she said suspiciously.

'Trust me.'

They got back in the Jeep and drove back towards the tiny village, turning off down a bumpy road behind the one-room schoolhouse, finally coming to a dusty dead end where Sean parked and jumped out.

'Come on!' he grinned, heading for a hole in a barbed-wire fence.

'Where exactly are we going?' said Tess.

'Off-piste,' called Sean as he disappeared through the hole. She followed him through and down a trail heading towards the jagged cliffs. They were surrounded by lush forest on all sides. Flowers on the trees were the bold red of traffic lights, the ripe mangos were as shiny as topaz; it was a picture-book Garden of Eden – apart from the fact that Tess felt the loose earth of the path might fall away into the sea at any moment. They slowly edged along a dusty and treacherous path that clung to the side of a cliff-face, at one point even having to double back where the trail disappeared into the sea from a landslide.

As they walked, Sean began to open up to Tess, and she learnt the real stories behind some of the things she had read or heard about him. Yes, he had been expelled from his exclusive prep school, but he had been dyslexic. 'Couldn't make sense of all those jumbled letters,' he smiled. Relegated to the bottom stream, he became frustrated, which led to 'high jinks' to keep himself amused. 'They didn't really go for high jinks at my school,' said Sean. 'They suggested I might be happier elsewhere.'

Tess laughed. 'And to think I thought you were just a troublemaker. It just goes to show that behind every story is another more interesting story. My first editor always used to tell me that.'

'Well, he was right about that,' said Sean, 'certainly when it comes to my life.'

Just then, Tess slipped on a loose rock and fell sideways. Sean's hand shot out to grab her and they both sat down on the path with a bump. They exchanged a look of alarm, then both cracked up laughing. 'Come on,' said Tess, as she dusted herself off and sat down on a large rock.

'What exactly am I risking my neck for?'

'We're going to the Secret Beach,' said Sean as he sat down next to her.

'Secret beach?' she repeated with wonder. 'How come you know this island so well?'

Sean sighed. 'Ah well, that's another of your "hidden stories". Do you remember after the Venus party, my mother checked me into a rehab facility in Minnesota?'

She nodded. Meredith had told her.

'Well, I lasted ten days. There were some seriously fucked up people there and it made me feel worse. It wasn't that I didn't agree with what they were saying at the clinic, I just didn't like the way they went about it,' said Sean. 'All that public confession, it's not what I was brought up to do. The Asgills deal with their problems within the family – I'm sure you're up to speed on that?'

Tess smiled and nodded.

'Anyway, the overdose had scared the hell out of me and I knew I had to do something. So I came out to Chris's place. Believe it or not, they have NA meetings in a place as little as this – all those rock stars, perhaps. Anyway, I went to a few sessions but I found I didn't really need it. Not here. Not when you're surrounded by all this.' He paused and looked around at the forest and the sea beyond.

'I guess what happened just scared me shitless.'

'At least you met Annabel in Minnesota,' said Tess good-naturedly. She figured it was about time she brought up Sean's girlfriend in conversation.

'Annabel and I aren't together any more,' said Sean after a moment.

'Really?' she said, trying to sound casual. 'I didn't know.'

'It only happened last week. I didn't think it was serious enough to make an official statement,' he replied, eyeing her cynically.

'Well, you need to tell me these things.'

'Do you ever stop thinking about work?' he smiled, helping her up and setting off up the steep track once more.

'Only today,' she said, realizing that it was actually true. She hadn't thought about work once since she had stood outside the Aloha Grand at seven a.m. that morning, waiting for the taxi, when she had pondered whether going on a two-day vacation with Sean Asgill was a sackable offence. More importantly, Tess realized she hadn't even thought about her mother's husband – *my evil stepfather*, she corrected herself – all morning.

'Are you sure this is the way?' puffed Tess as she followed Sean up a steep incline, the crumbling rock sliding away behind her feet. Sean pointed around the next corner and grinned. 'I'm sure.'

As she turned the corner, Tess gasped out loud. They were high up on a rocky outcrop, looking down into the most glorious cove she had ever seen. It was as if a giant had scooped out the side of a mountain, leaving the rainbow layers of sheer rock exposed, plunging down to a perfect crescent of beach protected from the pounding water by a line of rocks jutting from the sea two hundred yards out. It was completely deserted apart from a pair of pelicans perching on a boulder.

'Bloody hell,' she whispered.

'Exactly,' said Sean.

They scrambled down the narrow ledge to the beach. The sand was bright red and the water like a flat piece of jade, the natural lagoon making it calm and clear. Tess could see a shoal of tiny fish darting about in the shimmering brine, like a translucent cloud. Whooping, they ran down the sand and splashed out into the sea. They swam to a tall wall of black volcanic rock forming the edge of the lagoon, where Sean hoisted himself out and onto the rock, while Tess floated lazily on her back, gazing up at the blue sky.

For some reason she began to think about the holidays she'd had as a child. Her mother Sally had always insisted on going to the chic resorts that her posh friends were visiting: Marbella or Nice; except the Garretts could only afford to stay in the cheapest places. They'd buy things from the supermarket and eat a picnic on the beach while Sally griped about the injustice of not being able to lunch in the beach cafés only yards away.

'Hey, you looked deep in thought back there,' said Sean as they swam back to shore.

'I was just thinking how much I loved travelling.'

'Just as well, with the job Dom did, I guess.'

'That was different,' she said, smiling ruefully. 'It wasn't really about having fun.'

From this distance she could see how travel had bound Dom and her together like some sort of artificial glue, and how the mini-breaks, luxury hotels, and Caribbean beaches were just mood enhancers to disguise the fact that they didn't really have that much in common. Tess flopped down on her towel and drank the bottled water greedily as Sean towelled his face.

'So do you forgive me?' he asked.

'For what?'

'What happened in London with Dom,' he said quietly. 'I was only trying to protect you, Tess, but you know that's an uphill battle.'

She squinted up at him, shielding her eyes. 'What do you mean?'

'Well, you have this "leave me alone, I can handle it myself" vibe going on, don't you?'

'I do not!'

'Okay, but it was fairly obvious you hated me from the second you met me.'

'That's not true,' she protested.

'It is.'

She smiled, taking in a deep breath of sea air.

'I have this theory that how you feel about someone stems from the time you first meet them – that "first impressions last" thing, you know?' said Tess. 'I remember at sixth-form college there was this girl called Big Marie. She was cuddly and lovely, but she was very big. Last year I went to a college reunion and Big Marie was there, except she wasn't big any more. She was slim and beautiful and had just got married to Greg Butler who was the heart-throb of college. No one could believe it; they were all sniping about how this fat girl had landed the hunk; it was as if they couldn't see what was in front of them. Their view of Marie was fixed – to them she would always be big and awkward and unattractive.'

Sean looked at her. 'Am I Big Marie in this scenario?'

Tess giggled.

'When I first met you, or should I say when I first *knew of* you, you were the guy at the orgy full of drugs, remember?'

'Hmm . . . I can't deny that. But, you know, some people do think I'm an okay guy.' He looked at her. 'Hey, what's that look for?' he asked.

'You. Today. You're being such a gent.'

'D'you think I'm trying to seduce you?' he grinned.

Her cheeks flushed red and she avoided his eyes.

'Do you want me to seduce you?' he said more softly.

'It doesn't matter, does it?' said Tess, finally looking at him. 'It's not going to happen.'

Leaning towards her, he took her face in his hands and his lips came down on hers. With minimal resistance she pushed him away. 'No Sean, I'm serious, we can't.'

'Yes, we can,' he said with a chocolaty laugh.

She groaned as he kissed her damp neck, his hand sliding across her stomach, gently pushing her back onto the hot sand. She felt his lips over her sun-kissed skin; her shoulders, fingertips, stomach. He slid off her bikini top and sucked her dark, cherry-like nipples as his fingers peeled off her briefs.

'Not here,' she gasped. 'Someone might come.'

'Hopefully you,' he chuckled as he dipped two fingers through her damp, dark triangle of hair and deep into her, stroking her hard, throbbing clit with his thumb.

'Oh Jesus,' she whispered, digging her toes into the sand as he pulled down his swimming shorts in one impatient movement. She no longer cared who might come and see them. Here, with Sean in this secret cove, it seemed the most natural and perfect thing to do.

'Please, now,' she gasped, knowing she was already on the edge of climax. Pulling his hard, muscular body towards her, she could think of nothing but how she needed his cock, beading with dew, inside her. And as she moved in unison with his body, his cock filling her completely, every sensation she had felt over the past twenty-four hours: the annoyance, panic, sadness, the pleasure, they all crystallized into one hot, burning climax so intense that she saw spots of light bursting on her vision.

Afterwards, they lay together, their damp bodies caked in the red sand, Sean stroking her hair, Tess enjoying the feel of his strong arms around her. They went back to Chris Kennedy's house and, after a long cool shower together, made love again, this time on the crisp white sheets of an emperor-sized bed, more slowly, less urgently, but with just as much desire. Stepping onto the *lanai*, watching the streak of peppery starlight across the inky-black sky, she smiled to herself. Now she could see that Sean's actions in London were only designed to show her how little Dom cared for her feelings. But did that mean Sean cared for her? She didn't want to think about that too thoroughly right now.

He walked out and handed her a glass of pink lemonade and they both sat on the swinging love-seat, watching the fireflies come out to dance around a bush.

'What are you doing after the wedding?' asked Sean after a long pause.

'You mean, am I staying in New York?'

He nodded.

'I'd like to,' she said slowly, unsure if that was the right answer – whether it was true and whether it was what he wanted to hear. She was enjoying this moment and didn't want to break the spell. Did he expect her to want to run back to London because he was there, just because they had had sex? Is that what she wanted to do? Tess just didn't know anything any more.

'So what about you? How long are you staying in London?' she asked cautiously.

He rocked the seat back and forth with his foot. 'Initially it was a year, then it became two; now I consider it home. You probably don't know this, but I want to start my own PR and events management agency next year.'

'Really? And not work for Asgill's?'

'No, I'd still work for Asgill's, they'd just be one of my accounts,' said Sean. 'Over the years, a lot of blue-chip companies have approached me to do events and PR for them, and it seems a waste to let those opportunities pass, especially when I can still do my bit for the family company.'

She glanced at him; here was yet another side of him she hadn't noticed. She'd been so quick to write him off as a waster and a dilettante that she hadn't recognized his ambition and passion for what he did. 'Anyway, how can I leave England,' he said with a cheeky twinkle, 'when my latest addiction is English girls?'

She punched him on the arm.

'Hey! Let me finish!' he cried. '. . . Although it's just a shame that the one I like lives in New York.'

'Well, if you . . . oh dammit!' Tess said, annoyed, her thought cut off by the chirping of her mobile phone.

'Sorry,' she said, jumping up, 'I'd better get that.'

'Leave it.'

'You know I can't do that,' she said, dashing into the house. 'I've had two missed calls from Jemma already.'

'But you're with the boss,' he shouted after her.

'Boss's son,' she yelled back.

Snatching up the phone, Tess was surprised and flustered to hear Meredith.

'Tess. How was the pageant?'

Tess closed the patio door behind her and moved into the bedroom.

'Great. Wonderful,' she said breathlessly. 'Lovely winner.'

'And where are you now?'

Despite the thousands of miles of distance between them, she felt her cheeks redden with embarrassment.

'Still Hawaii, although I took a plane over to Maui, extending my trip as you suggested.'

'Oh, not at the Aloha Grand?' she replied with evident disapproval.

'Well, it was quite busy, and someone said Maui was the place to really chill out,' said Tess, trying to sound as casual as possible.

'Yes, Sean loves it there. I assume he tipped you off?'

'He did, yes.'

'And how is my youngest son? I hope he behaved himself. Although, knowing Sean, he probably even tried it on with you.'

Tess laughed nervously.

'Between you and me, I think he is calming down,' continued Meredith conspiratorially. 'When he was here, he asked me for one of my old rings. I think he's going to propose to Annabel.'

Tess felt her heart lurch. 'Are you sure?'

'Well, you can never tell, can you, with Sean?' said Meredith. 'But I met her last month in London. Wonderful girl.'

Tess's throat was feeling more constricted by the second. 'I wasn't aware it was serious.'

'Neither was I,' laughed Meredith. 'I told him at the time not to even think about doing anything until after Brooke's wedding. I don't want anything stealing her thunder.'

Feeling weak, Tess sank down on the bed and tried to take two deep breaths. Through the slatted window she could just make out Sean's silhouette, and a cold shiver passed over her.

'What were you calling for again, Meredith?'

'Oh, just to check when you're going to be back in New York. Brooke and I return tomorrow. The dress is just exquisite, by the way . . .'

They made polite small talk for a few minutes, then Tess closed her phone, dropping it onto the crumpled sheets. She bit her lip in anger and humiliation, thumping her fist against her thigh. *I'm such an idiot.* What on earth did she expect, having sex with Sean Asgill? Did she expect this was going to be converted into a relationship? Did she really think Sean Asgill was going to want anything more? For him, this was just a dalliance with the hired help, an amusing trip below stairs to ravish the servants. *Behind every story there's another*, she thought to herself, *of course there is.* How could she have been so stupid?

She went back outside, trying to keep as natural and calm as possible.

'Who was that?' asked Sean.

'Brooke,' she lied.

He held out his hand to touch her fingers. 'What's so important? It must be seven o'clock in the morning in Paris.'

She wondered angrily if she should confront him, accuse him of lying to her about Annabel, or whether she should wait until she had more proof. A snake like Sean Asgill would only deny it unless she could fling it in his face. That thought led to another: Sean had come to Hawaii directly from New York and was going straight onto London. It made sense that he would have Meredith's ring with him. That would be all the proof she needed.

'Something's come up,' said Tess quickly, moving back towards the house. 'She wants me back in New York as soon as possible. I need to look into flights back to JFK tomorrow.'

He groaned. 'Duty calls,' he said flatly. 'How about we head back to bed and worry about Brooke in the morning?'

Tess felt her body stiffen. 'No, I want to get on the Net and see if I can sort the flights.'

She sat down at the desk and opened her laptop, but he crept up behind her, peeled off the strap of her slip dress and kissed her shoulder. She flinched.

'Don't you ever stop?' she said, swatting his hand away as playfully as she could.

'Is everything all right?' he asked.

She turned to face him. 'I was just wondering if this is such a good idea?' she said slowly. 'I'm mean you're just out of a relationship . . .'

She met his gaze directly, wanting to test him.

'Listen, Tess, I know what you're thinking, but you're wrong. This is very simple. I like you, I hope you like me. And if that's the case, then I think this is a very good idea.'

'Okay,' she nodded. 'Why don't you let me get on and I'll meet you in bed.'

Tess stared at the screen, not knowing what to do, not knowing what to think. Had Sean deliberately misled her? Or did Meredith suspect something – perhaps she was trying to throw a spanner in the works? No, that was just wishful thinking, wasn't it? She crept back into bed, hoping Sean was already asleep. He wasn't.

'Are you sure you're that tired?' he smiled, nuzzling his lips into her neck.

'Let's pick this up again tomorrow morning, huh?'

Sean seemed content at that response and rolled away. Lying back into the soft mountain of pillows, Tess waited, watching the dark ceiling until Sean's breathing became a soft snore and she was certain that he was fast asleep. Carefully, she removed his arm from around her and slid off the mattress, creeping into the dressing room. Sean's bag was unzipped but still packed. She stuck her hand in and rifled through, pulling out shorts and sweaters and shoes, silently praying that she would not find what she was looking for. Finally, her searching fingers felt a zip compartment at the bottom of the case. Opening it, her heart sinking, she pulled out a navy velvet box. Holding her breath, she opened it to see an enormous sapphire ringed by twinkling diamonds. It was a little old-fashioned, yes, but it was a big, bold expression of something. *Love? Devotion? Commitment?* she thought with a sickening feeling. Angrily, she snapped the box shut, then froze, the sound cold and hard in the still air. There was no sign of movement from the bedroom, so she sank back to the floor, holding her head in her hands. *What a fucking idiot.* What made her think for a second that she could turn Sean Asgill's head, let alone tame him? She made a quick decision.

Creeping through the bedroom, checking Sean was still asleep, she padded to the other side of the house and picked up the phone. By the time her taxi arrived, she was already packed and dressed. She returned to the bedroom and, for a moment, watched Sean sleeping, the white sheet rising lightly with each breath. He looked so peaceful. *Dammit! What am I doing?* she scolded herself angrily. *That man betrayed you, cheated you!* What she really should do was slap him awake, throw the ring in his face, and tell him exactly what she thought of him. But then, what would that achieve? She could picture his apologetic yet slightly smug face as he explained that his relationship with Annabel wasn't *exactly* over.

Well, she had no intention of letting him have that little satisfaction. She was going to keep her dignity. She tore a page out of a notebook by the phone and scribbled a message.

Sorry. This is a bad idea. See you at the wedding.

Leaving it on the bedside table, she tiptoed out into the waiting taxi, closed the door quietly, and turned to the driver.

'Airport,' she said. 'And step on it.'

46

Brooke jumped into David's car and kissed him wildly on the lips.
'Hey, hey!' he laughed, gently pushing her back. 'What's all this
about?'

'*Portico* is number seven, David!' she said breathlessly. 'It's
number *seven* on the *New York Times* best-seller list!'

'Honey, that's amazing. Does Eileen know?' he said with genuine
delight, giving her another kiss before gunning the engine and setting
off along Lexington.

'Yes, of course. She screamed down the phone for about three
minutes and then begged me to come shopping with her for a
Chanel handbag.'

David chuckled. 'What is it with women and handbags?'

Brooke reached over and squeezed his knee. 'Please, you'll have
to understand that before you even think about marrying me,' she
teased him.

While David called his assistant on his hands-free phone to
make a reservation for dinner at Raoul's that evening, Brooke
gazed out of the window, thinking about the excitement of the
last hour. Yellow Door's managing director Edward had come
into her office to tell her the news privately, and had to quickly
shush her when Brooke had squealed. That had been swiftly
followed by an impromptu champagne toast in the boardroom
when everyone had told her what a visionary she had been to
rescue *Portico* from the slush pile. For once, Brooke hadn't
contradicted them; everyone needed a few moments of glory,
didn't they? In truth, Brooke hadn't exactly been surprised about
Portico's high chart position – not after Eileen's brilliant, modest,

380

and funny appearance on *Oprah* the previous week. The next day Brooke had spent her lunchtime loitering in the big Borders at Columbus Circle, just watching as the books disappeared before her eyes.

And now, as a perfect end to a perfect day, she and David were off to see an apartment that Brooke had been dreaming about all week. She had been aware of the building on Riverside Drive long before the realtor had called her to say 'a very special apartment' was coming on the market. She had once been to a party in the building many years ago and had always fantasized about one day being able to live there.

'Hang a left and go across the park,' said Brooke excitedly.

'*West* side?' said her fiancé, raising a brow.

'Just trust me, okay?' she smiled.

The car traversed Manhattan and wound up Riverside Drive, the most westerly point of the island.

'Pull up just over there,' she pointed. David looked increasingly uncertain as they walked towards a grey stone Beaux Arts apartment block, but she linked her arm through his and pulled him in tight. She had anticipated that he'd be surprised about where she'd brought him, especially as so far they'd been looking in the 'best buildings' on Fifth Avenue and Sutton Place South and at houses around West Tenth and Eleventh Streets. The west side of the island was a part of town that they rarely came to, but something about it had become more appealing of late. Perhaps it was the disconnection from where they worked and where their friends and family lived. Perhaps it was the views over the river, a reminder that they were on an island, and the fact that there was a whole wide world beyond it. Perhaps because fewer celebrities lived here than in the smart streets of the West Village – not to mention fewer paparazzi. Or maybe it was because the air smelled slightly less of overt social snobbery. Whatever it was, Brooke felt more at home here than any of the areas they'd looked at so far, and she was hoping David would feel the same.

The agent was waiting for them at the elevator and they rode up to the triplex on the top floor in silence. The apartment's front door opened into a hallway, then a sunken living room surrounded by a wraparound balcony, the lights of New Jersey twinkling beyond the dark river ahead.

'I think this place speaks for itself,' smiled the realtor, clearly giddy with anticipation of a fat commission cheque. 'I'll leave you two alone to explore.'

'I love it,' whispered Brooke, squeezing David's hand as they walked up a wide staircase into the master bedroom.

'Yeah, it's a find.'

He was trying to please her, but Brooke could detect the forced enthusiasm in his voice.

'What's wrong?'

'Nothing,' said David, not looking her in the eye.

'David, what's wrong? You've been acting weird all week when I've mentioned stepping up the apartment search.'

'I just don't think we're going to be needing another apartment in New York,' he said, opening a closet door with little interest.

'Honey, I know you love the loft, but you know I want to start afresh.'

'Maybe we should talk about this over dinner?' he said, walking back to her. 'In fact, maybe we shouldn't. Tonight we're supposed to be celebrating *Portico*, aren't we?'

'Well, I was rather hoping to end the biggest day of my working life finding our new home as well,' she replied, turning towards the window, her arms folded.

'Let's not be greedy.'

She couldn't understand his attitude. 'David, what *is* the problem? I thought you'd love this place too.'

He paused, then looked at her seriously.

'I've kinda had a big day at work too.'

She suddenly felt guilty; she'd been so excited by her own news she hadn't bothered asking about his day. And, from his expression, this was serious.

'Oh wow, I'm sorry,' she said, stepping forward and touching his hand. 'What's happened?'

'I've been offered my own talk show,' he said simply.

'What? Like David Letterman?'

'Kind of,' he smiled. 'A little more political.'

Brooke threw her arms around him and squealed. 'Honey that's amazing! Why didn't you tell me? Oh that's brilliant – and of course you deserve it, you're so good.'

'The problem is . . .' he said slowly, 'it's based in Washington.'

'DC?' said Brooke.

'A five-night-a-week gig, ten p.m. slot on NBS, very serious,' he said excitedly. 'It's a brand-new show replacing that tired old political debate format. They're really getting behind it and the exposure will be incredible.'

Brooke wanted to share David's excitement, but instead she felt cold. Of course she'd been to Washington before, and each time she'd tried to make herself enjoy its European majesty, see it was the centre of the nation, feel the energy of change all around her. But she couldn't. She found it a sterile, pompous, one-industry town where people seemed to grow old and cynical before their time.

'Are you sure this is the right thing for you?' she asked.

'How could it not be right?' said David, holding out his hands.

Brooke lifted her shoulders. 'I mean, you certainly don't need the exposure. You have media requests coming out of your ears and you turn ninety-nine per cent of them down. And anyway, won't your father think that sort of exposure is vulgar?'

'My father has mixed feelings,' said David. 'He knows it would be a heavyweight show interviewing heads of state and so on – that he likes. What he doesn't like is the fact that it would mean putting the Congress run on the back burner.'

'You spoke to your father about this before me?' said Brooke, unable to hide her disappointment.

'I was with him when I got the call, Brooke,' he replied impatiently. 'I wanted to wait until I saw you in person to tell you.'

The agent was hovering at the door. David flashed her a look and then closed the oak door behind her with a thump. He looked back at Brooke and his expression softened.

'Honey, I don't want to be doing the news forever. And this is a move away from it, a new avenue to explore.'

Brooke was aware that her arms were crossed again. 'I thought you loved doing news,' she said.

'Hey, I thought you said you hated me running off to Beirut at the drop of a hat.'

'I do.'

'Well then. This is an honour, Brooke, can't you see?' he said, his dark-blue eyes pleading with her. 'Ever since that human trafficking report I did, they've been lining me up for something really big. You say I'm travelling all the time; well, here's my opportunity to stay in one place.'

'A different place from our home, our friends, our family – and, let's not forget, *my* job.'

'Well, that's something we've got to talk about . . .'

'You're damn right we do,' she said hotly. 'Last time I looked there were no major children's publishing houses in Washington.'

'Come on, Brooke, you could easily do something else. In fact, you don't have to do *anything*.'

She curled her hands into fists. 'And that's exactly what you want, isn't it?'

She thought of Robert Billington in the gardens of Cliffpoint, telling her how David just wanted a good wife. Well, screw them, she thought angrily.

'Brooke, calm down . . .'

She looked at him, feeling her bottom lip tremble.

'I have a career, David,' she said. 'I have a book at number seven on the *New York Times* best-seller list, destined for number one. Do you know how rare that is for a children's author? Do you know how good that made me feel?'

She shook her head at his silence. 'You know my achievements to date have been unremarkable. People thought I was another rich girl playing at a career until I got married off. Sure, I'm the company golden girl, but not because they take me seriously. Because I'm Brooke Asgill, engaged to David Billington, not because I'm Brooke Asgill, talented commissioning editor. Until today, that is. Today, I published a great book, a fantastic book that everyone is talking about – everyone is reading all over the country. That's why I couldn't "easily do something else", because – and I'm sorry if it's inconvenient for you – I think I've found something I'm good at.'

She looked at his face. He was looking down, his eyes seemingly focused on a small point on the expensive walnut floors.

'A marriage is about two people, Brooke.'

'Exactly,' she said bitterly, and suddenly she realized what Washington represented to her: second place. If they went there now, she would be a TV host's wife. In a few years, a congressman's wife; somewhere down the line, maybe even first lady. And that was the irony of it: there was nothing *first* about life with a man like David Billington. She was always expected to come second.

'You sound resentful,' said David quietly, his eyes still on the floor.

'Do you blame me?'

'Brooke, my career is the most important thing in my family's life.'

'Of course,' she said tartly. 'Your family. Not me, not even you. Your family.'

'But you knew—'

'Yes, I knew that was the deal when I agreed to marry you,' said Brooke. 'I've always known the deal.'

Finally he looked up. His eyes were sad.

'Sounds like you don't want the deal, any more.'

Brooke didn't say anything. She blinked as fat tears began to roll down her cheeks.

'I'm sorry, baby,' said David. 'I want this opportunity. I really want to do it.' She could see how much this meant to him and it broke her heart.

'I thought you wanted Congress,' she said. 'The Connecticut seat.'

His handsome face looked awkward, confused. 'I'm thinking I could do this and then go straight for Senate, or maybe a governorship somewhere.'

Brooke bit her lip until she tasted blood. She could barely believe that, only an hour ago, she had been thinking this was the happiest day of her life. She covered her face and gulped at the air.

Slowly, she realized that David's arms were around her.

'I want to take this job, but I *do* want you to be happy too,' he said urgently into her ear. 'If it means that much to you, I can turn it down. I *will* turn it down.'

Gently, she pulled away from him. 'I never said I wanted you to do that,' she said softly, wiping her face.

The agent knocked on the door and entered cautiously.

'So what do you think?' she smiled.

'I think we've got a lot of thinking to do,' said David, looking at Brooke.

Brooke nodded. 'Yes, we have.'

47

'I thought you were supposed to be on holiday.'

Tess closed her eyes and cursed. She had been trying to sneak past Patty Shackleton's door unnoticed. Most mornings it was her first port of call on her way to her own office, but today she didn't feel like seeing anyone, least of all shrewd, intuitive Patty, who had an uncanny ability to read people's moods.

'Sorry, Pats,' said Tess, standing in the doorway awkwardly. 'Just in a bit of a rush. I've got a few urgent calls coming in—'

'So how was the trip?' interrupted Patty.

'Great. Nice. Not much of a holiday, really.' She thumbed towards the door. 'I'd better get on.'

'So everything went okay with Sean?' said Patty, not letting her go. 'He didn't screw the new Miss Asgill Hawaiian Glo?'

'Yes, everything went well. No, he didn't have sex with Candy Cooper.'

Patty lowered her chin and raised her brow. 'Tess? I know that expression.'

'What expression?' said Tess, feeling her cheeks prickle. *Don't blush*, she scolded herself, *don't blush*.

Patty pointed at Tess's face. 'That expression. In the legal profession, we call it guilt.'

Flustered now, Tess touched her face, as if she could feel her own expression.

Patty's eyes opened wide. 'Shit, Tess, no!' she gasped. 'Tell me nothing happened.'

'What are you talking about?' said Tess, stepping into Patty's office and casually shutting the door.

'You and Sean Asgill, in Hawaii.'

Tess frowned. 'Don't be ridiculous,' she said, trying to bluff it out. 'The man's an ape. An under-evolved, cocksure, brain-dead primate.'

Patty clapped her hands together gleefully. 'You dark horse. You had sex with him!' Patty broke down into helpless giggles.

'As *if!*' snorted Tess. 'My opinion of him as a self-centred prick has not changed since before the trip,' she said. 'Anyway. Did you want something?'

Patty covered her mouth to stifle her sniggers.

'What I wanted to discuss before this revelation,' she said, once she had regained control, 'is the *great* news about Kevin and Jack.'

'What news?' asked Tess eagerly, taking a seat opposite her.

'I take it you haven't spoken to Jemma? I know she tried to call you in Hawaii.'

Ah, those must have been the missed calls she had seen on the phone when Meredith called in Hana, thought Tess, suddenly furious that Sean bloody Asgill's seduction had got in the way of something this important. Tess hadn't had time to speak to her flatmate yet, having only got back to New York late the night before.

'Well, Jemma took a trip up to Greenwich and did some digging around,' said Patty, a pleased look on her face. 'She followed Jack's mum, Melissa, to some swanky dinner party and crawled around the back with her long lens. She got some lovely shots of Melissa taking cocaine through the conservatory window. Turns out Mel and Steven the boyfriend have a real taste for the white stuff.'

'*What?*' said Tess, with amazement. 'That's incredible.'

Patty was nodding. 'When Jemma couldn't get hold of you, she called me. I faxed the photographs over to Melissa's house, then called her up and asked her what Steven's very conservative bank would think of his coke habit.'

'What did she say?' asked Tess, thinking that Patty would have made a very good tabloid journalist.

'She slammed the phone down,' smiled Patty. 'But she obviously called her own lawyer soon afterwards, because, a few hours later, she was back on the phone, and suddenly they are happy with the existing custody arrangement.'

'So Jack stays with Kevin?'

'Yes!' squealed Patty, drumming her hands on the table, her usual cool, composed façade completely gone.

'Kevin must be overjoyed,' said Tess.

'I've never seen a man down a bottle of champagne so quickly.'

'You had champagne?' She didn't want her voice to come out all brittle, but it did. Her first rush of happiness was now replaced by a hollow sense of somehow missing out.

'We just had a little celebratory supper at Ryan's on Bleeker Street,' replied Patty.

'The four of you? Kevin, Jem, and Jack.'

Patty looked embarrassed. 'Jack was staying at a friend's and Jemma was working. I think Kevin just wanted someone to celebrate with.'

'Of course,' said Tess. 'I'll call him right now. It's brilliant news.'

Her secretary Annie popped her head around the door.

'Sean Asgill is on the line for you.'

'I'm busy,' said Tess, not looking up.

'He says it's important.'

Patty had a playful smile on her lips. 'So take the call . . .'

'I'm busy,' said Tess firmly. She had no desire to speak to Sean Asgill ever again if she could help it.

'Well, I've got some emails to send,' she said, heading for the door. 'Thanks so much for everything with Kevin and Jack, Patty. It's way beyond the call of duty.'

'My pleasure,' said Patty, and Tess knew she meant it.

Back in her office, she sank back into her chair and switched on her computer.

There were dozens of emails since she'd last checked her BlackBerry.

Distractedly, she clicked on the most recent. With a lurch, she spotted the address it had come from: Sean@Asgills.com. She sat up and quickly read it.

It's not that complicated. Let's at least talk about it. Back in NYC in two weeks.

Tess angrily clicked the 'delete' button. 'In your dreams,' she whispered.

'What dreams would these be?' said a voice.

She looked up and saw Meredith standing there.

'Meredith,' said Tess, a little flustered, wondering how long she had been there. It was a company joke that Meredith was so thin and dainty she could enter the room like a ghost.

'Is everything all right?' she asked, her eyes searching Tess's.

'Of course,' said Tess, thinking that, when her son was involved, nothing was ever all right.

'In which case,' said Meredith smoothly, 'can we talk?' She closed the door and moved across to sit elegantly on the chair opposite Tess's desk. She opened her handbag and pulled out a blue letter.

'Because I've just received another one of these.'

48

The Sundowner Hotel in Charleston was the sort of plantation house that was once exceptionally grand, a proud symbol of the wealth and power generated by cotton in the eighteenth century before the Civil War. Now the Sundowner seemed to live up to its name, having become part of a big mid-market corporate hotel chain, and seemed to have lost a little of its charisma and charm in doing so. But the location of the hotel, in the historic district of the city, more than made up for it, thought Tess. The pastel-coloured town houses, gas-lamp streetlights, and grand clapboard houses with Juliet balconies and shutters – they all had a romance and a certain faux-English grace that was somehow appropriate for a city named after King Charles II.

The air-con hit Tess as she walked into the Sundowner's grand but slightly peeling lobby and she was glad of the cool. The weather was beginning to turn rather cold in New York, so the balmy warmth of South Carolina had been most welcome, *but a Southern lady never perspires*, she thought with an inward smile. In these surroundings, Tess could actually imagine herself as a character in *Gone with the Wind*, especially when the concierge with a thick Deep South accent directed her to the Mistral Bar; this was the fictitious hometown of Rhett Butler, after all.

Her good mood evaporated as she spotted the man she was meeting. Ted Kessler was in his late fifties, with a grey moustache. He was dressed in dark trousers and an open-necked blue shirt. A crumpled jacket hung over the back of his chair. He didn't rise when he saw her, simply put down his paper, and nodded.

'I thought I'd get a table by the window,' he said. 'Don't suppose you'll be in town long, but you can see everything worth seeing from this spot right here.'

'How kind,' said Tess thinly, taking a seat opposite him and holding his gaze.

'What do you want, Mr Kessler?'

When Meredith had given her the blue letter three days earlier, Tess had been surprised that the anonymous sender had decided to reveal himself, signing off his simple message with a scrawled telephone number. Tess had wasted no time in arranging a meeting; there wasn't long to go until the wedding and she wanted nothing and no one to spoil her clean slate and jeopardize her bonus. Ted Kessler had to be dealt with as swiftly and ruthlessly as possible.

'Can't we start with a little old-fashioned Southern hospitality?' He called over a white-coated waiter and ordered two bourbons.

'I wish I had the time,' said Tess coolly, shaking her head at the waiter. 'As I said, what do you want? I feel certain you do want something.'

She pulled out the first letter Ted had sent and put it on the table.

Your family has a secret, it had said. *Which secret, exactly?* wondered Tess. *They've got plenty.*

The bourbon arrived on a silver platter and Ted took it, settling back in his chair, a smug expression on his face.

'How about I tell you a little story?' he smiled.

Tess rested her hands in her lap and tilted her head. 'Please do.'

'I'm from North Carolina and for five years I was with a marvellous woman. She died recently.'

'I'm sorry,' said Tess, not feeling too much sympathy for this obvious opportunist.

'The lady's name was Marion Quinn,' said Kessler, leaning forward and handing Tess a photograph. In it a smiling lady of about forty was flanked by a little boy and a very young girl aged about four who was in a wheelchair. The girl in the wheelchair was obviously severely disabled. Her long hair was shiny and golden as corn, but her head flopped to one side of her body, her small shoulders were hunched. It was the sort of photograph that made you instantly sad.

'The lady in the picture, that's Marion,' continued Kessler. 'She was as sweet as she was pretty. She lived hereabouts and she used to take in foster kids – all the ones no one else wanted. Sick kids, handicapped kids. She had the patience of a saint.'

Tess pointed at the handicapped girl in the picture. 'Was this little girl one of her foster children?'

Her words had a shot of both curiosity and wonder. Professionally she was trying to work out the connection to the Asgills, but privately she was marvelling at this remarkable woman who would take on a child who was not her own flesh and blood, a child that must take enormous time and personal strength to look after. Most of all, she wondered what a woman like Marion Quinn was doing with Ted Kessler, a man clearly on the make.

'That's an old photo,' said Kessler, sipping his whiskey. 'Marion took in those kids nearly ten years ago, before I was with her. A few months after this photo was taken she got sick, Crohn's disease. It was pretty bad and she couldn't do the foster thing no more. Those two kids went back to their natural parents.'

Tess looked at him, wondering where this was leading, but suspecting this was just the beginning of the story.

'The little girl was called Violet,' he said, pointing to the young child in the wheelchair. 'Marion heard rumours that Violet's mother didn't want her no more and, well, you can imagine how that made Marion feel; made her feel as if she let poor little Violet down. Then she heard the child had been put up for adoption. As it happened, Marion had met Violet's mother a few times before and she tried to get back in touch with her, maybe persuade her to keep Violet, but it was too late, the mother had moved out of town. She didn't care nothing for the kid. Anyways, before she knew it, child had gone to new parents.'

'Mr Kessler, I'm a busy woman, can we get to the point? How does this involve my clients?' asked Tess. She was trying to brazen it out, but suspicions were already forming in her mind. Kessler waved away her protestations; he was clearly going to tell the story at his own pace.

'I met Marion five years ago when she moved down to Charleston. She wasn't as sick as she had been then, so we got married.'

'And when did she die?'

'Beginning of summer.'

He paused and drained off his bourbon.

'Of course, I had to go through all her stuff, sort things out. She used to keep this file full of letters and pictures from the kids she'd looked after, real sweet. But then I found something interesting.' He pulled out a toothpick and began to clear something from his teeth. 'I found an old *New York Times* newspaper clipping that she'd kept. A story 'bout eight or nine years old, a story about a New York model called Paula Abbott who was marrying some super-rich heir to a cosmetic empire.'

Tess and Ted looked at each other across the table. Ted put the toothpick down on the table and smiled.

'The little girl Violet, the handicapped foster kid? She was called Violet Abbott.'

Tess instantly recalled that Paula's maiden name was Abbott, one of the bits of trivia she'd picked up when she'd researched the family before she began working with them.

'Paula is Violet's mother?'

'You didn't know that?' he laughed sarcastically. 'I don't suppose she would have told many people. Probably not the sort of thing you boast about in polite society, that you dumped your kid because they weren't perfect.'

Tess pursed her lips. 'It's speculation at best, Mr Kessler. Abbott is not exactly an unusual name.'

Kessler laughed. 'Oh, give me a break.'

He reached into his jacket and pulled out another creased photo and slid it across the table. 'As I said, Marion kept everything, she was quite a hoarder.'

The photo was old and grainy, but it was clear enough. Paula couldn't have been more than twenty. She was kneeling down next to the girl who, heartbreakingly, appeared to be smiling at her mother.

'Same girl as in the *New York Times* wedding story, right?' said Kessler, a note of triumph in his voice.

Tess couldn't deny it. Impossible though it seemed, Paula Asgill had another daughter. *Focus, Tess, focus*, she told herself. Okay, was this really such a big deal? After all, John Kennedy had a sister closeted away in a mental home and it didn't do *his* political career any harm. But a nagging voice in her head told her that things were different back then; in the Sixties the mainstream press didn't pick over a public figure's private life and use it as fuel to burn them at the stake.

Still, this might be a scandal, but it wasn't an overdose at a sex party. Tess could certainly spin this in a more positive way – frightened young girl forced into adoption by circumstance and poverty, society is to blame, the child was well cared for – but there was one big stumbling block to that approach. Meredith. She wouldn't like this at all. Tess had no idea how badly a scandal about Paula's past would upset the Billington family, but she knew for sure that Meredith had been firm about one thing: no controversy before the wedding. None at all.

'Is it money you're after, Mr Kessler?' said Tess.

'Smart girl. Money for my old age,' he said matter-of-factly. 'Marion looked after that kid good. She never told no one.'

'Which is more than can be said for you.'

Kessler ignored the jibe. 'This Paula's a wealthy woman now,' he said. 'She got the life she wanted at the expense of her child. Well, now she can afford to pay me to keep her little secret.'

There was a tiny part of Tess that agreed with him. She wondered how Paula could have given her child away? She had seen how hard Kevin Donovan was prepared to fight for Jack and what the thought of living without him had done to him. Tess felt sure that if she were a parent she wouldn't – *she couldn't*. She paused, realizing it was the first time she had thought about motherhood in a very long time.

'It isn't going to look very good, is it, Miss Garrett?' continued Kessler, wiping his palms on his trouser legs. 'Even down here we've heard of the Billington family. I don't reckon a grand family like that is gonna like seeing Paula Asgill disowning her handicapped kiddie like that.'

'I didn't come here to be blackmailed, Mr Kessler,' said Tess.

Kessler appeared unmoved. 'Do you know how much Marion got for looking after Violet?' he said. 'Two hundred dollars a month. She paid for the medical bills out of her own pocket. She wasn't a rich woman, just a decent one.'

'More than can be said for her taste in men.'

His expression soured. 'Take the photograph Miss Garrett,' he said, standing up. 'I got copies. Unless you wire me two hundred thousand bucks, I'll be sending it to the media.'

'Two hundred thousand . . .' Tess tried to keep her cool.

Kessler buttoned his jacket and nodded to the waitress. 'I'll let you pick up the cheque. And I expect an answer by Friday.'

49

Nine o'clock at night and Brooke was still in the office. Over the past few weeks, this had become a routine, especially since the office had been closed for Thanksgiving. With the wedding practically on top of her and most of January blocked off for the honeymoon – a fifteen-day tour of Australia with a week at the Wakaya Club, the super-exclusive private resort in Fiji – she was desperate to get ahead of herself with work. Besides which, she liked to edit at night when it was completely quiet, with just the desk lamp and soft blue glow from the computer illuminating the pages of the manuscript. The dark seemed to insulate her from everything: the stress and expectation of the wedding and the vague, unsettled feeling that had been nagging at her since David's new job offer.

At least this was one less worry, thought Brooke, turning another page. It had only taken a week to edit Eileen Dunne's second novel; it was incredible how little work it needed doing to it. After the adulation that had greeted *Portico*, Eileen's writing seemed to have grown in confidence, and this novel was even more accomplished than the first. Brooke had loved the way the story had grabbed her and transported her to another land, another world. It would be another runaway best-seller, she felt sure of it, and if it sold like *Portico*, it would make the 'outrageous' advance of three hundred thousand dollars look like a bargain. She looked up from the page as her mobile phone vibrated. Reluctantly, Brooke flipped it open.

Rocking Portico *window display in Barnes and Noble. Matt*

She put it down, smiling, wishing that David was not so busy and important that he couldn't send her more impromptu, random texts. Suddenly she looked up again as she heard a chuckle. Mimi Hall was standing in the open doorway, sipping a cup of coffee.

'God, Mimi!' said Brooke, clasping her hand to her chest. 'You scared the life out of me.'

'Who was that? Matthew?' asked Mimi, smiling in the dark.

'Matthew?' repeated Brooke dumbly.

'Palmer,' said Mimi, stepping forward. 'Matthew Palmer, your friend from Eileen's launch party.'

Brooke examined Mimi's knowing expression. She was not going to lie to her, although she had no right whatsoever asking about her personal phone calls made out of work hours.

'Actually yes. Why do you ask?'

'You speak to him a lot, don't you? He must be a very good friend.'

'He's an old friend, yes,' said Brooke, struggling to keep her voice calm. 'But no, we don't speak that often actually. He's an ER doctor, they tend to be busy people.'

'Funny you're so close after that Jeff Daniels story earlier this year,' said Mimi with deliberate vagueness.

'Is there a problem here, Mimi?'

The older woman shrugged and took another sip of her drink. There was a long pause.

'You owe me, you know that.' There was levity in her voice but her eyes were still jealous and nasty.

'And what exactly do I owe you for?' replied Brooke, sounding defiant but feeling a sense of dread. Mimi had always had the ability to frighten her.

Mimi took a step nearer Brooke's desk. She seemed to tower over Brooke, who found herself sitting up straighter in her chair.

'Do you know how many reporters I've had calling me up, emailing me, even following me? All of them want to know information about you. Dirt.'

'I hope you told them there's nothing to tell. I think I'm what the tabloids call boring.'

'I wouldn't call you boring,' said Mimi with a hard little laugh. 'The papers would have a field day with this Matthew Palmer business. I think it's what the tabloids call "dynamite".'

'Mimi, Matthew is a friend. David knows him too.'

'Funny,' said Mimi sarcastically. 'I thought Eileen's launch party was the first time they met.'

Brooke knew why Mimi was confronting her. Not because Brooke was suddenly a threat to Mimi's position – it would take more than one success to be promoted even one rung up the ladder – no, Mimi was coming after Brooke simply because she was being *talked about*. For the last two years, Brooke had been the star of Yellow Door. The only person worth talking about at the tables at Michael's, or the various book industry awards that littered the year. Mimi might have an editor-of-the-year trophy and a fearsome reputation in the industry but, since Brooke's involvement with David Billington and the 'new Jackie O' headlines, Mimi had retreated into the shadows. Brooke had always sensed that Mimi disliked her, but it was only now that she appreciated exactly how much.

Mimi placed her cup on a shelf and picked up a little snow globe that Brooke had bought in Paris on the trip when David had proposed.

'You must know the emails are monitored at Yellow Door,' said Mimi casually. 'Someone told me there have been over fifty emails in the last two months between you and Matthew Palmer. *Fifty*. That's quite a lot, especially for someone who apparently works as hard as you do. I guess if they checked out the phone records, you've been calling him a lot too.'

How dare she! *Someone told me there have been fifty emails.* More like Mimi had been rooting around her office, checking her computer.

'I am not having an affair with Matthew Palmer, if that's what you're implying, Mimi. If it's any business of yours – which it most certainly is not – he is a friend. If you hadn't heard, I am getting married to David, and I am in love with my fiancé.' She stopped, aware that her voice was becoming louder as she spoke.

'Congratulations by the way,' said Mimi, 'on David's new show, I mean.'

The change in tack took Brooke completely by surprise. 'What show?'

'I know it's not officially been announced yet,' said Mimi, 'but I have friends at the network and I hear that David's been offered a prime-time Washington show.'

Brooke gaped at her. Both the Billington family publicity machine and the network had wanted to hold back on announcing David's new show until the inevitable media frenzy surrounding the wedding reached its peak – that way they were guaranteed maximum advance coverage for the show. The only people who knew about it were David's family and the executives at the television station, so Mimi's contacts and information were impressive.

'As it's Washington-based, I assume both of you will be moving to DC?'

'No decisions have been made yet,' said Brooke, flustered. 'That's why I haven't discussed it yet with Edward.'

'I think it would be a good idea if you did go,' said Mimi.

Brooke snorted. She was not easily angered, but Mimi was pushing her near boiling point. Trust Mimi to find my Achilles heel, thought Brooke furiously. The issue of their imminent move away from New York remained raw and unresolved between herself and David.

'What are you really saying, Mimi? That you'll go to the press with details of an imaginary affair if I don't hand in my notice?'

'My, my,' smiled Mimi. 'All this press attention *has* made you paranoid.' She folded her arms carefully in front of her. 'What I am saying is that, while some people might think that having you at Yellow Door is good for business, I'm not so convinced. How do you think your fellow editors feel about you being invited to the executive board meetings when they are not? There are other, more senior editors with longer track records who don't tell slush-pile authors to get the most fearsome agent in town. And they get pushed out for someone in the supermarket gossip magazines.'

'Well, thanks for the vote of confidence,' said Brooke calmly, wondering how much of what she was saying was spite and how much was true.

'Do yourself a favour, Brooke – do us all a favour,' said Mimi with a twisted smile. 'Be the wife everyone wants you to be. Stop playing at being something you're not.'

'Speaks the ball-breaking feminist.'

'Speaks someone who knows what's best for everyone,' she added with syrupy condescension.

'Good for everyone? Or good for you, Mimi?' spat Brooke, finally losing her temper. 'The truth is, Mimi, that I probably will go to Washington. My husband's life is going to be there, in the short term at least, and I want to support him one hundred per cent. Plus, it does have the added bonus that I won't have to see your bitter face every day.'

'Is that your four weeks' notice?'

'No!' she said fiercely.

Mimi smiled slowly and the coffee on her lip glistened. 'Not yet, anyway.'

She paused at the door. 'He's very good-looking, isn't he? Matthew Palmer, I mean? I love those dark, brooding sorts.' She winked. 'But don't worry. The next time the reporters ring, I'll be in a meeting.'

Turning on her spiked heel, she left the room silently. Brooke watched her go, not entirely sure whether the tight knot in her stomach was there because Mimi Hall was a scheming bitch, or because Mimi Hall was right about everything she had said.

50

In a state of deep anxiety, Paula was examining gift bags. There were twelve in total, one for each guest, all lined up at ninety-degree angles to the edge of the walnut dining table.

'I'm just not happy about the candle,' she said, her face creased with worry. She turned to Karl Lee, her three-hundred-dollar-an-hour 'entertainment consultant' and waved a fat Jo Malone candle at him.

'Lime, Basil and Mandarin, Karl? Isn't that a little obvious? What about the Pomegranate Noir, like I suggested?'

The slim man, dressed head to toe in black, shook his head adamantly.

'No, no, the Lime is definitely a safer option; it's one of Jo's most popular scents. Plus I know Pomegranate Noir candles were used at a lot of important Thanksgiving dinners last week. Dinners your friends might have attended.'

Paula sighed, remembering that Karl *had* been recommended by Rose Billington, and therefore should be the best in the party business. And Paula was fairly happy about everything else in the bags: the tan Smythson 'Travel & Experiences' notebooks, handmade chocolates from the by-appointment-only chocolatier Au Lait on Madison, and Loro Piana scarves so fine that they folded up into nothing. Each party bag had cost her over five hundred dollars, but it was worth it, because everything had to be just right: Saturday night's dinner was perhaps the most important night of her entire social life. She'd spent two months engineering the guest list and it was A-list only. Socially competitive friends like Gigi Miller and Samantha Donahue certainly did not make the cut and, anyway, those girls didn't really fit her lifestyle these days. When she had seen them at fundraisers, Paula had noted they were now occupying tables that bordered on Social Siberia. She had heard a whisper that such had been the downturn on Wall Street, Samantha had even had to suffer the indignity of moving out to Brooklyn Heights. It almost made Paula shudder to think they had once been such good friends.

No, Saturday's dinner guests were of a much higher calibre; in fact the seating plan was a dream come true: Princess Katrina and her husband Arlo, Brooke and David, Lucia De Santos, who, after the rocky start at Carlotta's birthday party, had turned out to be just *delightful*, and two friends of Katrina's from the Bermuda circuit whose husbands were something terribly important in the media. After all, she had not given up on the Tucker's Town dream quite yet.

As soon as she had arrived back from Bermuda, Paula had consulted with Charles Nicholls, the society divorce lawyer nicknamed 'the Scythe' both for his ability to cut down his opponents in court, and also for his skill in maximizing the financial harvest. Charles had been extremely supportive and had made very positive noises about Paula's possible settlement, given the presence of children and the length of their marriage, but he had also encouraged Paula to choose her moment carefully to file papers. He had heard about the stalling of the Asgill's sale and cautioned Paula that her husband's fortune was almost entirely linked to the fortunes of the company; if the company slumped any further, it would impact on her potential 'dividend' from the divorce.

Paula had thought about filing divorce papers there and then, but when news reached her that Liz was trying to raise the money to buy Skin Plus, she knew she had to put her plans on hold. In just a few months' time, the Asgills – and, by extension, William – would be more flush with cash. She had no idea of the figures involved, but surely it would be enough to buy a modest little second home? And if William refused to make life more comfortable for her . . . well, there was more money in the pot for a divorce settlement.

Karl was collecting his table plans and files together and looked ready to leave. 'Let's talk tomorrow, darling,' he said.

Paula touched her heavily perfumed cheek against his, quickly ushering him towards the door. She had a Shiatsu massage at Skin Plus in forty minutes and it couldn't come a moment too soon.

'Mrs Asgill, you have another visitor.' Paula rounded angrily on Maia, her maid, who stood nervously at the bedroom door.

'Who on earth is it?' She tapped her gold Cartier watch. 'I'm late for my Shiatsu.'

'Sorry, madam,' Maia said, 'but it's Tess Garrett from Asgill's. She says it's urgent.'

Cursing, Paula walked through to the hallway to see Tess Garrett taking off her beige Burberry mackintosh. Rather presumptuous, thought Paula with irritation: did these Brits have no manners?

'I'm afraid I'm on my way out,' said Paula briskly, gesturing towards the door.

'Sorry, Paula,' said Tess, not moving. 'I need to speak to you. Urgently.'

There was a sobriety to the publicist's voice that put Paula immediately on edge. Surely nothing had happened to William or the family? No, Tess Garrett wouldn't be delivering that sort of news. Had she heard about Paula's visit to Charles Nicholls? She pushed that thought from her head; the Scythe's whole business demanded discretion.

Paula pointed towards the living room, glancing down at her watch again. 'I can spare a few moments,' she sighed.

Tess settled on the sofa and waited until Paula was sitting opposite her. 'I've just come back from South Carolina,' she began.

'How nice,' smiled Paula thinly.

'I was there to meet someone called Ted Kessler. You wouldn't know him, but you do know his ex-wife. Her name was Marion Quinn.'

At the mention of those two words, Paula felt as if she'd stepped off a cliff. She sat motionless, unable to breathe. Tess saw her reaction and nodded.

'Yes, I know everything, Paula,' she said quietly. 'He told me everything.'

Paula closed her eyes. This had to be a dream. A *nightmare*. It couldn't be happening, not after all this time.

'Have you seen Violet?' she whispered. It was obvious there was no point in lying to Tess. Even if she was bluffing – and why would she be? – she was working for the family. She was on their side, wasn't she?

'No, I haven't seen Violet,' replied Tess. She opened her bag and pulled out a photograph, handing it to Paula. 'I don't know where she is. But this is what that man Kessler gave me.'

Paula took the photograph of Violet and Marion, her hands trembling so violently that she had to put it down. She covered her mouth with her hand. Her fingers smelt of candles and chocolate, of her new life, the life she was meant to have. Feeling warm tears trickle down her cheeks, she began to breathe deeply, distant memories she dearly wished to leave in the past floating to the surface.

'Violet is in a nursing home in North Carolina,' said Paula, licking her dry lips. 'Her new parents wrote to me and told me that she needed constant care a few years ago. I guess she'll still be there. She'll be fifteen now.'

She saw Tess Garrett's disapproving expression. *Goddamn limey bitch*, she thought, *what gives her the right to judge me? She has no idea what my life was like.* And all this because Marion Quinn's husband had crawled out of the woodwork.

'How bad was Violet's condition?' asked Tess.

'She has severe microcephaly,' said Paula grandly, like someone comparing the models of their Gulfstream jets. 'It is a life-threatening disease.'

A chill suddenly ran through Paula as it occurred to her that she didn't actually know whether Violet was alive or dead. It had been a long time since Violet's adoptive parents – a professional couple called Kate and Don something, Richards perhaps? – had written her a short, polite letter assuring her that they were getting the best care for their new daughter. Violet's had been an open adoption, meaning that Paula could keep in touch with her daughter, although, as the years passed, Paula had felt increasingly uncomfortable with the arrangement. Given the choice, she would have closed that particular chapter of her life forever.

'I never wanted this to happen,' whispered Paula, pressing her fingertips into her cheeks. 'I was nineteen years old when I had Violet. I was called Pauline then; I bet you didn't know that either,' she said, her voice hard and brittle.

'Violet's dad was a summer fling I had after high school, a construction worker on some development job in Nowheresville. He had left town long before I even found out I was pregnant. I knew something was wrong the second I held Violet in my arms.' She looked up at Tess, her eyes pleading. 'I had only just left school,' she said. 'I wasn't ready for a child, let alone one that was severely disabled.'

'So Violet was put in foster care?' prompted Tess.

'I couldn't cope,' said Paula bitterly, her anger at the situation bubbling to the surface. 'My mum was dying so Violet went in to the system and, thank God, she went to Marion Quinn, a woman in Greensboro who took in a lot of difficult children. I went over to see her and she seemed to really care. But then Marion got sick and by then I was in New York, modelling, so Violet was formally put up for adoption. I mean, who would make a better parent? Me? A twenty year old, or adoptive parents who were desperate for kids? It was a better life for her.'

'And a better life for you,' said Tess, unable to stop herself.

Paula's face twisted into a scowl. 'How dare you sit there and judge me?' she spat bitterly. 'You have no idea what I had to go through, how I felt. Do you have the slightest idea what it's like looking after a child that can't even hold its head up? Who will never be able to run or read or even talk? Of course not, you haven't got a clue.'

'Violet's not just a child,' said Tess defensively. 'She's *your* child.'

'Yes, she is,' said Paula. She had no desire to justify her actions to Tess Garrett, but telling her the story had actually reassured Paula that she had done the right thing.

'Violet is my child, and I did what I thought was best for her.'

The two women glared at each other. Finally Tess looked away and her expression softened.

'Do you think about her?'

Paula was silent. Thick gulps caught in her throat and then she couldn't hold back the tide of sadness, anger, and frustration any longer. She covered her face and sobbed, her shoulders shuddering, tears running between her fingers. When she had recovered a little, she accepted the tissue Tess passed to her and wiped her face.

'It was an open adoption because I thought that way I could still hear what Violet was doing,' said Paula. 'Maybe one day see her again. But when I met William, I knew that could never happen.'

'Why not?'

'For all their smiles, manners, and smart clothes, society people are *vicious*,' she whispered. 'The WASP ideal is perfection. Comply or die.'

'Well then, we have a problem,' said Tess. 'This man Ted Kessler wants two hundred thousand dollars to keep quiet.'

Paula felt icy cold.

'Have you told Meredith?'

Tess shook her head.

'Not yet. I thought you might like to tell her before me.'

Paula was shaking her head and her hands were trembling. 'Can't you make it go away?' Her voice rose with desperation. 'I thought that's what we were paying you to do.'

Tess folded her top lip over her bottom one. 'The easiest thing to do is run away or bury it as deep as you can, but in my experience it's not always the best thing to do.'

'Let me find the money,' said Paula quickly. 'It might take a couple of days . . .'

'No, Paula,' said Tess firmly. 'You have *got* to tell Meredith. We have to deal with this. For one thing, blackmailers are rarely satisfied with one pay-off and, even if we could shut Kessler up, secrets like this have a habit of getting out.'

Tess examined Paula's face. 'Does William know?'

'Of course he doesn't know,' she moaned, feeling the tears begin to fall again. She closed her eyes, remembering the one moment she had almost told William. It had been six months into their relationship and Paula had begun to realize that, as well as being rich and halfway good-looking, William Asgill was a decent man, a rarity in such circles. She and William had been sitting under a tree with a picnic, when he had told her that he loved her. It had been the first time he had said it and, looking into his eyes, Paula knew that he meant it. She knew in that moment that she could tell him anything and it wouldn't change how he felt about her. But still she couldn't tell him because she wanted to be part of his safe, perfect world. She'd worked so damn hard to get to that place, to become a successful model with a rich, clever guy doting on her. She couldn't let anything screw that up. Most of all, she didn't want to give his bitch of a mother the opportunity to say, 'I told you so. A gold-digger with a dirty secret.'

Paula shook her head again. 'He doesn't know and the moment has passed to tell him,' said Paula softly. 'So I've just tried to forget about it, about her. I try to pretend that was a part of my life that never happened.'

She looked up as Tess picked up her mobile phone.

'What are you doing?' said Paula, panic in her voice.

'Arranging a meeting with Meredith,' said Tess. 'Then we need to go to Charleston and meet Ted Kessler. We should fly down tomorrow.'

'I can't fly anywhere tomorrow,' said Paula, her eyes wide. 'I have people coming. Everything is arranged, it's important.'

'And this is important,' said Tess sternly. 'We need to sort this all out and we can't leave it another day.'

51

In the weeks following the *Portico* launch, Charles Devine had phoned Tess at the Asgill offices at least half a dozen times. Convinced he was angling for a wedding invitation, she successfully managed to field his calls. But when a handwritten dove-grey Mrs John L. Strong notelet arrived requesting her company for afternoon tea, Tess knew the only way to put a stop to it all was to take him up on his invitation and, secretly, Tess was looking forward to it. She was desperate to escape the Asgill universe, which was becoming increasingly fraught and all-consuming as the wedding approached, and suspected that a spot of Lapsang Souchong and a good old natter might be just what she needed right now.

Tess pulled up in a cab outside Charles's apartment on East Seventy-First Street, the first floor of a brownstone on one of the best streets in the Upper East Side 'grid'. Tess pressed the doorbell, smoothing down her blue Marc Jacobs tea dress. It was a few seasons old – which she felt sure Charles would notice – but it was the most appropriate thing she had in her wardrobe.

'Oh, just delightful, darling,' smiled Charles as he took her coat, hanging it on a pair of antlers in the narrow hallway. 'It dismays me how woefully eroded the art of dressing for tea has become, but you and I obviously sing from the same hymn sheet.'

Charles had certainly made the effort himself for their little tête-à-tête. A starched white shirt, crisp navy suit, an extravagant crimson cravat, and patent shoes, while his grey hair had been combed into submission, carefully parted and brushed severely over to one side.

407

He looked as if he was heading out for martinis with Dorothy Parker at the Algonquin.

Even by Manhattan standards, Charles's apartment was tiny, but it was perfectly formed. He ushered her through to his bijou duck-egg-blue living room.

'Sit sit,' he said, shooing her towards an elegant chair upholstered in grey damask.

'Would you like tea?'

'That would be lovely,' said Tess, trying to make herself comfortable on the exquisite yet spindly furniture. Charles put a finger up against his smooth cheek – Tess was convinced he'd had a face-lift since Brooke and David's engagement party – and pouted dramatically.

'Now, let me see,' he said, surveying Tess like an art dealer eyeing a potential acquisition. 'I have fifty-three varieties of tea. For you, my dear, I am going to suggest a Ceylon Silver Leaf. Subtle yet strong. May I suggest you take it with the tiniest twist of lemon?'

Tess could only grin. Charles disappeared into a tiny galley kitchen and returned with a rattling silver tray laden with two miniature teapots. A small round antique table had already been beautifully set with polished cutlery and a cake-stand stacked with perfect triangles of cucumber sandwiches and sugar-dusted madeleines.

'Darling, I hope you don't mind me saying how much you have bloomed since you first arrived in New York,' gushed Charles, pouring the tea. 'Look at you! You could pass for a Park Lane Princess. That's what they call the young girls around here, apparently. I find it rather vulgar myself; most of them are as near to being a princess as I am to being a Chinaman. Still, they are beautifully groomed, which you can't often say about English girls. I never think as a breed you quite make the best of yourselves. But you, my dear, have truly risen to the challenge. You do our diminishing empire proud.'

Tess giggled behind a hand. Charles was an eccentric, a one-off, like Quentin Crisp or a quirky character in a Jane Austen novel. He had the plummiest accent Tess had ever heard, although, if the rumours were true, he had not a drop of blue blood in him, having come across to America in the Fifties and milked the life out of his minor English public-school background. Tess thought he was wonderful, and wished she'd come to see him sooner.

'I have to say this is a bit of a surprise, Charles,' said Tess, taking a sip of the delicate tea.

'Yes, I know I've been a little low-key of late,' he nodded. 'I imagine you've been wondering why I've not been at any of the dinners and parties all year. Well, I can now reveal my secret,' he said dramatically, dabbing his lips with a napkin and rising. 'And, as you'll see, I've been very busy.'

He walked over to the bookcase, pulled out a thick volume and put it in front of Tess.

It had a shiny navy jacket that said 'Simply Divine' in huge pink Art Deco lettering. Underneath, in smaller type, were the words *Charles Devine – the whole story*.

'My memoir, darling. It's been exhausting.'

'I can imagine,' said Tess, picking it up. It was like a brick.

Charles sighed. 'I always thought that writing my memoir would be easy, but when you've led a life as rich and full as I have, the sheer volume of material becomes both a blessing and a curse. I've had to be so selective. Do I put in the wonderful little anecdote about choosing emeralds with Babe Paley, or having dinner with the Shah? How *does* one choose?'

'It looks as if you've written about both,' said Tess, noting that the book was seven hundred pages long. 'I can't wait to read it. Who's publishing it?'

Her host's lips moved into a tight, unsmiling line. 'Bloody agents and publishers. These days it appears that they are only interested in autobiographies written – and I use that word loosely – by nineteen-year-old pop stars with nothing to document except one hit record and a drug habit. Entirely indicative of what's wrong with society today, if you ask me: a world run by teeny-boppers for teeny-boppers.'

'I'm sorry,' said Tess sympathetically. Charles nodded sadly.

'*Entre nous*, I've been very disappointed, but you can't let these things defeat you, can you?' he asked, brightening. 'So, as you can see, I've self-published. Come this way, darling.'

He led her into the bedroom that contained one single bed, exquisitely dressed in white linens, a wardrobe, and a bedside table. Every other inch of floor space was taken up by piles of *Simply Divine*, stacked floor to ceiling. There must have been at least five hundred copies, reckoned Tess, perhaps a thousand.

'How can I help, Charles?' she asked as they returned to the sitting room. He wagged his finger at her and smiled.

'Sharp as a tack, as they say over here,' he said. 'I knew we would be friends. Yes, you can help poor old Charles in his hour of need. I feel sure there's a huge market for my memoirs, but first I have to create a buzz. If I can make this book hot, then the big publishers will come knocking. Do you know that John Grisham self-published originally? He sold his books from the boot of his car. Not that I would ever compare myself to John Grisham,' he said tartly. 'Plus I never travel by car.'

'And I suppose this is where I come in,' observed Tess, taking a cucumber sandwich.

'Darling, you've acquired a glorious reputation as a top-notch publicist – nothing like these brash harridans you see around New York. You have class, my dear. You'd be perfect.'

Tess nodded thoughtfully. She didn't doubt that his memoirs would be fascinating, not to say scurrilous and possibly libellous. And she had not forgotten Brooke and David's engagement party, when Charles had been one of the few people who had spoken to her as an equal. On top of that, she liked him a lot and would love to see him succeed. But right now, she simply didn't have the time.

'Charles, you know I would love to help and I can try and give you some advice, but I do have my work cut out with the Asgills. The wedding and everything . . .'

Charles arched an eyebrow. 'Darling, I thought you'd like to do something a little more constructive with your time than hiding the dirty secrets of the Asgill family.'

Charles looked so downcast and – frankly – lonely, that Tess couldn't help herself.

'Perhaps I can look at it in the new year?' she sighed.

'Marvellous,' he beamed, clapping his manicured hands together. 'I knew you would be the woman for the job. You're just going to adore it, I promise you. All the stories I have, the parties, the pictures. I have plenty of pictures, look!'

He flipped through the book to the bound-in photographs in the centre.

'Here I am at Truman's black-and-white ball,' he said, pointing at one snapshot. 'And this is me at Studio 54 with Warhol,' he said, jabbing at another. 'Now, wherever did I put that wonderful dogtooth suit?'

He snapped *Simply Divine* shut and handed it to Tess. 'Go away and read it and then we can talk again.'

'I will,' she said as enthusiastically as she could.

'You really are a darling,' he smiled and picked up the teapot. 'More tea?'

52

Mayflower House, a sprawling red-brick residence in a quiet suburban area of Wilmington, North Carolina, didn't look particularly scary. In fact, the house was remarkable only in its ordinariness, just another large building in a neighbourhood full of similarly over-sized relics from a grander age, yet still Paula found herself shaking as she walked towards it. Of course, it wasn't the building itself that frightened Paula, but what was inside. Her past and, possibly, her future, both repelling her and drawing her in at the same time. It seemed impossible to believe that only twenty-four hours earlier, the most pressing thing in her life was deciding whether to use the black or white Limoges china at her dinner for Savoy. Now her life was unravelling so fast she dared not even think about where it might all end.

Tess Garrett had flown down with her to give moral support, but also to deal with Ted Kessler. Meredith had insisted that 'all loose ends were tied off' in person. Paula winced at the vivid memory of facing her mother-in-law after Tess had filled her in on the blackmail threat. Sitting behind the mahogany desk, Meredith had been economical with her words.

'Pay him,' she had said firmly.

Tess had objected. 'There must be another way. You can't start paying people like Kessler; the demands for money will never stop.'

'We'll cross that bridge after the wedding,' replied Meredith. 'The wedding is only six weeks away. We need to keep him quiet until then, after which his information will be less valuable.'

Then Meredith had turned the full force of her stare on Paula.

'Now we have to consider your position, Paula,' she had said coolly. 'In some strange way, the Billington family might *welcome* a disabled child in the family, given their plan to push David to the highest levels of politics. Tragedy and heroics are tools commonly used to court media and public sympathy, and I doubt the Billingtons would be above it. *Perhaps* you might even weather the fact that you put Violet up for adoption. But to have hidden it for so long? To have abandoned your child then to have lied about your past for social acceptance and material gain? That would not be palatable to most people.'

Meredith had been careful to talk about the impact her revelation would have on the Billington family and their standing in society. She had never once referred to the Asgills, but Paula did not miss the implication. Her place in the family was now under threat.

Paula had left the meeting humiliated, feeling cheap and guilty. But most of all she left knowing that Meredith was right. For years, Paula had managed to justify her actions to herself, using her mother's downward spiral and their slide into poverty to rationalize clawing her own way to the top, no matter the cost. But deep, deep down, Paula felt ashamed of what she had done.

She turned and looked back to the street where Tess was waiting in the car. Tess had offered to come inside, but Paula had refused. It was too private, too raw. She looked back at the entrance and took a deep breath. *Just do it*, she told herself. She followed the signs through the main doors and down a long corridor towards a huge conservatory filled with people and noise. It was the nursing home's Winter Fair, and dotted around the room were stalls selling Christmas decorations, bags of taffy, and mugs of hot, spiced apple juice. Double doors led to a walled garden. Somehow, it seemed to be sunnier here than on the street outside, and the sky was as blue as a robin's egg. There must have been at least a hundred people out here – parents, children, and nurses all wandering between the willow trees, smelling the cinnamon and honey and the cool freshness of the Cape Fear river close by. Paula felt a nervous rush of expectation, although she had taken two little yellow pills to calm herself when they'd left the hotel.

Her eyes kept straying towards the children; some walking around, others confined to their wheelchairs, although most looked severely disabled. For a second Paula had to close her eyes and

413

take in a long breath, the weight of her feelings making her chest feel tight.

'Are you okay?' asked a voice, and Paula turned to see a middle-aged woman with a concerned expression.

'I'm looking for, umm, Violet?' stammered Paula. She was going to say 'Violet Abbott', but remembered that she would now have changed her name. *We're no longer connected*, thought Paula, with a strange lurch of pain.

'Are you family?' asked the woman. 'I don't think we've met? I'm Etta, the admin assistant here. I know Violet's mum and dad are on vacation this week so they couldn't come down for this.'

Paula nodded feebly. 'Family, yes. Although I haven't seen her in a very long time.'

'She's over there,' said the woman, pointing to the far side of the grounds, where a uniformed nurse was pushing a wheelchair.

Thanking her, Paula moved towards them. Just one step, then another, she told herself. Just one foot in front of the other. Closer and closer to the wheelchair, everything else became blocked out and meaningless as Paula stopped in front of her little girl. Although she wasn't such a little girl any more; she was almost an adult. But her long limbs were thin and twisted, her shoulders hunched, head lolling to one side. Nodding to the nurse, Paula crouched down in front of the wheelchair, her knees trembling.

'You're such a big girl now,' she said, her voice only a whisper, barely registering the tears that ran in hot streams down her cheeks. She reached out and touched Violet's gnarled fingers. To Paula's surprise, Violet's eyes looked up, meeting her gaze. For a moment she seemed more alert. *Does she recognize me?* thought Paula wildly, covering her mouth to choke back a sob. *No, how could she?*

But they had the same eyes, thought Paula. She had tried to forget that detail, but now she could see it; the same big, grey eyes that looked back at her from the mirror every morning. And such beautiful, thick golden hair. Although she had let Violet go, although they were no longer connected by the same name, they were linked by genetics forever. Somehow, that gave Paula comfort. There were so many things she wanted to say as she stared at her daughter's face, but she knew she couldn't. Violet's understanding was limited, but even a childlike mind would understand if she told her she was her mother. But it just wasn't fair. *The truth usually isn't*, thought Paula.

'I think your friend is here,' said the nurse, nodding behind Paula. She turned, expecting to see Tess, but her jaw dropped.

It was William.

How could he be here? she thought, gripped with panic. *How could he know?*

William had left for London the morning Tess had come to the apartment to tell her about Ted Kessler, and although she had spoken to him on the phone, Paula had not breathed a word of what was going on. Meredith? Tess? She was too emotionally drained for anger, she simply stood there, her shoulders sagging as he approached.

'You're here,' she said, fighting to keep composed. 'How did you know where to find us?'

William gave a half-smile. 'I've been here before.'

'I don't understand.'

William touched her arm gently and led her slightly away from Violet and the nurse.

'Paula, I knew.'

'You *knew*?' she whispered incredulously.

'About six months ago, I bought you that dress for the Met gala dinner, remember?'

Paula nodded dumbly. It had been a beautiful vintage Valentino evening dress. He was always giving her little surprises, she thought, her mind wandering off on a tangent. *About time I gave him one back*, she added to herself.

'Well, I had gone into your closet to find out your dress size and I . . . well, I found an old letter that Marion Quinn had sent you,' he said, his cheeks colouring a little. 'It mentioned your daughter Violet.'

Paula remembered that letter. Marion Quinn had sent it to her modelling agency when she was in her early twenties and she thought it had been well hidden. *Obviously not.* Paula knew all along she should have destroyed that letter, but she had never been able to, and now it was too late. Her throat felt so thick she could barely swallow. He was going to divorce her. She almost laughed out loud at the irony: now she was getting what she wanted, she found she didn't want it at all.

'I hired a private investigator and eventually he found Violet,' said William. 'I wanted to meet her so I came down here on my own.'

415

'Why didn't you tell me you knew?' asked Paula, her voice hoarse. William shook his head sadly. 'Honey, I tried so many times.' She nodded. 'I know how that feels.'

'Mother told me yesterday about Ted Kessler,' continued William, 'and that you were coming down here with Tess. So I got a flight straight here from London.'

With an effort, Paula looked up at his face, trying to read his expression.

'I'm sorry,' she said, 'I'm so, so sorry.'

The nurse, who had been hovering, came over and took hold of the wheelchair handles. 'I have to take Violet inside now,' she smiled apologetically.

'Just another minute, please,' asked Paula. Hesitantly, the woman retreated and Paula reached out to gently stroke Violet's hair.

'I understand what you did. Why you did it,' said William quietly. Paula looked up sharply. 'But you don't approve,' she said.

William ran a hand over his chin. 'No, but . . . but she's still your daughter, Paula. There's no need to hide her any more. Violet has a new family now, but we don't have to pretend she doesn't exist.'

For a moment, Paula looked at him with hope. Was he suggesting that they could move on from this? No, that was too much to hope.

'Your mother hates me,' she said. 'And the Billingtons will go crazy.' For a moment she thought about her friends in New York, about her newly elevated social circle and how they would freeze her out, but suddenly their disapproval seemed immaterial compared to what her husband was thinking.

'William, I . . .' she began, but he stepped forward and took her in his arms.

'Shhh . . .' he said softly as she burst into tears, sobbing into his shoulder.

'What's so bad?' he whispered into her hair. 'What's so bad? We've still got each other; we'll always have each other.'

She shut her eyes, feeling the warm afternoon sunshine on her neck and enjoying the sensation of William's arms wrapped tightly around her. At that moment, she realized how completely she loved him. Perhaps it was a different sort of love from the one she had read about as a teenager. This love was not breathless, thrilling, and sensual, but was protective, deep and, above all, forgiving. How could she ask for more than that?

The nurse walked over.

'I'm sorry,' she said, 'Violet really needs to go inside now.'

Paula nodded sadly and she bent to kiss her daughter on the cheek. As she did so, her eyes met Violet's, and she could have sworn they shone with happiness.

'See you soon, darling,' whispered Paula as she watched the nurse pushing her back into the building. William wrapped his arms around her from behind and squeezed.

'She knows,' he said simply.

Paula nodded sadly. 'Let's go home.'

53

David Billington was waiting for Tess when she got back to the apartment. She silently cursed when she saw him sitting in the living room. She had spent the last forty-eight hours flying from New York to Charleston to Wilmington and back to New York again. In that time she'd paid off a blackmailer, seen Paula's long-lost daughter, and was frankly so emotionally and physically exhausted she felt quite sure she could sleep for a week, not that there was any hope of that. She gave David a bright smile, trying to hide her annoyance. After all, this was not what she had signed up to do. She was a *publicist*, for God's sake! She was supposed to firefight any negative stories, massage the press, maybe set up a few interviews. Right now she felt like a cross between Henry Kissinger and Bruce Willis in *Die Hard*. But her irritation gave way to worry as she saw his grave expression. Besides which, he had never been to her flat before, and thus she had to assume he had good reason. She sat on the armchair and peeled off her coat.

'Been waiting long?' she asked. 'Sorry, I've just been out of town on business.'

If only he knew where she'd been and why. Another mission impossible, covering up the tracks of the Asgill family. And what was it all for? The career of the handsome, if tired-looking, man sitting opposite her. He shook his head.

'Just twenty minutes or so. Jemma was in but she just popped out to get cigarettes.'

He was fiddling with the cuffs of his white shirt and it unnerved her. Tess had never seen David look anything less than immaculate and composed. There was a pot of coffee on the table in front of him. Tess leant over and poured herself a mug. It was thick, hot, and black and it sent an instant jolt around her body. No wonder New Yorkers loved the stuff. Tea just didn't pep you up like this.

'So is everything okay?' Now she was more awake she could sense his troubled vibe.

David reached into the inside pocket of his cashmere overcoat and pulled out a magazine. 'Ever heard of the *Washington Spy*?'

Tess was vaguely aware of it, although it was outside her usual frame of reference. A satirical Washington magazine printed on grey recycled paper, it had a small circulation but was a popular guilty pleasure for the younger Washington movers and shakers, who loved its irreverent and scurrilous take on political events and life on Capitol Hill. She took the magazine from David and examined the cover. It was a line drawing of David Billington opening a wardrobe full of skeletons.

'What have they got?' she asked, flipping to the story anxiously.

'The Olivia Martin story. I assume you know all about that saga?'

Tess nodded as she scanned the pages. It was a rehash of the Olivia Martin story, except this piece was bolder than the cuttings Tess had previously read. It stated that Howard Asgill had been having an affair with Olivia, insinuated that Howard had something to do with the drama of her disappearance, and asked the question as to whether David Billington could weather the scandal if he ran for Congress next year. Tess felt her heart sink. The *Washington Spy* might be a small-time magazine but it still had influence, particularly where it mattered, in the corridors of power and, by extension, the news media. And while Tess had warned Brooke on several occasions that she couldn't control tabloid gossip, she felt sure Brooke's mother held her personally responsible for every nasty blind story or unflattering paparazzi shot of her daughter. *Well, the shit is really going to hit the fan this time*, thought Tess. And this time she felt sure that the Billingtons were going to take exception to the story too.

'This is an early subscribers' edition, so the story won't have broken in any of the papers yet,' said David. 'I don't think my father knows about it yet, but I have my lawyer on it already seeing what we can do.'

Despite her misgivings, Tess shifted into reassurance mode.

'This is old news, David. It's just tittle-tattle, nothing more.'

'Come on, Tess. We all know about this story, but this is the first time Howard Asgill's name has been publicly linked to Olivia's disappearance.'

Tess knew he was right. This story had always unsettled her, but when it was just a missing actress at a wedding, even a semi-famous actress who had supposedly drowned in a drugged-up stupor, Tess knew it would not have any direct impact on David's popularity and electability.

But the *Washington Spy* story was exactly the kind of 'no smoke without fire' story that could easily smear someone's name, and Tess knew how these things could easily run out of control. And, worst of all, the tabloids could say what they liked about Howard, using the press's favourite get-out clause: 'You can't libel the dead.' From the look on David's face, he didn't find any comfort in Tess's reassuring words either.

'It may all have happened over forty years ago, Tess,' he said, 'but for many people, especially for the younger politicos in Washington, this story would be a fresh scandal. And scandal is the last thing we need right now.'

He lowered his head and rubbed his chin.

'You know, three months after I started dating Brooke, my father came to me to talk about Olivia Martin,' said David, looking down at his hands. 'He told me it might cause "problems". He had an investigator snoop around the story, but it threw up nothing.'

He looked up at Tess with genuine sadness. 'I love Brooke, Tess, and I want to marry her. I don't care about what her father might or might not have done because, whatever it is, it's nothing to do with us. But my father *does* care, and if any more stories start coming out of the woodwork—'

'Well, we can't let that happen,' said Tess quickly. 'Besides, I'm sure there's nothing more to say on the subject. No one knows *what* happened to Olivia Martin.'

His dark-blue eyes grew softer. 'I was hoping you'd say that.'

Tess rubbed her cheeks to shake off her tiredness. 'Look, I doubt we can injunct the magazine, seeing as they are simply rehashing an old story, but see what your lawyers say. Either way, I'd say it's better to try to get the magazine on our side rather than against us. Do we know who owns it?'

'Ben Foley. I know him vaguely. Rich parents. The magazine is a very successful little hobby for him.'

'Well, see if you can speak to him,' said Tess. 'We don't want this Olivia Martin story to run and run. In the meantime, the best way of killing it off once and for all is to find out what really happened.'

Just then Jemma burst through the door with a cigarette in her mouth and a brown bag under her arm.

'I got wine,' she said, looking hopefully from Tess back to David.

'Great,' said Tess. 'Get three glasses, because we have to talk.'

54

Liz had arrived first. She let herself into the hotel suite at The Carlyle with her own key. It was a welcome change to meet here instead of Wendell's place at The Pierre, as Liz never felt truly in control unless she was on her own or neutral territory. She took off her clothes and had just slid naked under the crisp white sheets when Wendell appeared at the bedroom door.

'You're late,' she smiled, stretching her arms out languorously on the pillows.

Instead of his usual smile, Wendell frowned and threw a copy of the *Washington Spy* on the bed.

'Have you seen this?' he asked.

Liz bent forward, clutching the sheet around her body.

'What is it?'

'Take a look and then you might understand why you're not the person I most want to see this afternoon.'

Confused, she flicked through the magazine.

'Not this bullshit story again,' she said with irritation. Wendell slipped off his Brioni jacket and unfastened his tie. His mouth was set in a firm, fixed line. She knew the expression well – she called it 'the death-mask'. It only hinted at the ruthlessness he was prepared to bring to a problem.

'You would say it was bullshit,' he said, sitting on the edge of the bed. His implication annoyed her. She was not her mother, or Brooke, or Tess Garrett, all of whom would be scared stiff of this story derailing their precious wedding. Liz couldn't care less whether they got married or not, none of that fairy-tale shit bothered her. What did bother her, however, was the idea that Wendell – and every other gossip down the years – was accusing her father of being somehow involved in Olivia Martin's disappearance. It was a foul slur Liz would not tolerate.

'Screw you, Wendell,' she spat, pulling the sheet further up her body. 'Olivia Martin was a crazy bitch who killed herself, end of story. It's nothing to do with my father or my family, and the idea that you believe in this groundless crap pisses me off.'

There was a long silence as they glared at each other, then Wendell slowly shook his head. He looked up sceptically. 'I hope you're right about it having nothing to do with the Asgill family, because I'm not in the mood to take any chances.'

Liz took a deep breath to calm herself. She was still mad as hell, but tearing into Wendell wasn't going to solve anything. She especially didn't want to rock the boat with the Skin Plus buyout so imminent. It had been like extracting teeth to get Wendell to agree to finance the deal; he was a bitch about negotiating even the finest details of the contract. If Liz had been expecting any special favours because she was sleeping with him, she was very much mistaken. Instead Wendell had demanded 80 per cent of the equity in return for the purchase price from Asgill, although Liz had worked out some share clawback provisions if certain optimistic sales targets were reached. She was confident they would be and she was also confident she and Wendell would be a sensational partnership out of bed, as well as in it. The man was a pit bull: a huge asset if he was on your side, but you really didn't want him snapping at your heels.

'Come here,' he said gruffly.

She paused and then crawled across the mattress, sitting behind him with her long, smooth legs either side of him. Pressing her naked breasts into his back, she planted feather-light kisses on the back of his neck and unbuttoned his shirt, caressing his chest.

'Between us,' she whispered, 'we can sort out anything.'

Sliding her hands down the front of his body, her nimble fingers undid his trousers and eased out his hardening cock.

'David and Brooke should do a pre-wedding interview,' she said, coiling her fingers around his thick pink shaft, moving her hand expertly up and down as she felt him grow bigger and harder in her grip.

'We'll manage the story,' she whispered, feeling herself moisten. 'Control it, tell our side. Look at Obama, he came clean about taking drugs before he came to office and everyone forgave him. But Clinton with that whole "I didn't inhale" bullshit? They crucified him.'

'That was a joint,' growled Wendell. 'This is murder.'

Her hand stopped moving and her fingers tightened on his cock just a fraction.

'It was suicide,' she said firmly, 'or an accident. Fuck, maybe Olivia is still alive, who knows. There was never a body.'

Suddenly Wendell stood up and, facing away from her, zipped himself back up. 'I don't think this is a good idea today.'

She looked at him fiercely. 'I guess not.'

Sliding out of bed, she strode into the bathroom, still smarting, her tingling damp cunt denied its pleasure. Putting her black trouser suit back on, she splashed water onto her face and stared at her pale reflection in the mirror. *Calm down, Liz, remember the big picture*, she told herself. *Control your story. Manage him.*

When she reappeared, to Liz's surprise, Wendell had a sheepish look on his face.

'Liz, I'm sorry. I just have a lot on my mind,' he said, holding out his hand. She allowed him to pull her in.

'I'm sorry too,' she said, not used to hearing Wendell apologizing. 'It's just that this is my father.'

'And this is my son.'

He kissed the soft fold of her ear lobe and it felt good. She stroked his neck, feeling his body become less tense.

'I'm busy with work all week, but how about we come back to this next Tuesday or Wednesday?' she asked, caressing his cheek. 'There are lots of Christmas parties you could pretend to be at.'

'Let's do that,' he said softly. He took her hand and put her fingertips in his mouth, kissing them.

Smiling, Liz gently pulled away. 'Now, I think I should get back to the office. I'll check out.'

Picking up her clutch bag and the room key, she stepped out into the ghostly quiet corridor and pushed the elevator button. They rarely met anywhere other than Wendell's suite but, when they did, they made sure to take precautions, especially when it came to leaving and entering hotels separately. Once, they had spent the whole afternoon at Belcourt, fucking in the stables, by the boat-house and, most thrillingly, in the bed he shared with Rose, such abandon made possible by Wendell's generous instruction to the staff to take the whole day off.

Liz pulled out her Black American Express card and paid her bill as quickly as she could. She was just striding across the lobby when she felt a tap on the shoulder.

'Liz. What a nice surprise.'

She turned to see Robert Billington, buttoning his overcoat and smiling thinly at her. 'What are you doing here?' he asked with his usual sly smile.

Her heart started fluttering wildly, wondering if he had seen her at reception.

'I've been staying here the last few days. My bathroom is being renovated.'

Robert nodded. 'Not moved in with that Indian? I heard it was all hot and heavy with you two.'

You are just horrible, thought Liz, narrowing her eyes.

'I'm the independent sort,' she said as mildly as she could. 'I thought you knew that about me, Robert.'

She heard the elevator behind her ping. Instinctively she turned and saw Wendell walking past them. *Shit.*

'Father?'

Liz glanced at Robert and could see a look of confusion turn to gleeful triumph as he realized he had caught his father out. Wendell, however, did not even flinch, walking over to them with open arms.

'Robert. Liz. What are you two doing here?' He tapped Robert on the arm jokily. 'You two aren't arriving together, are you?' he said with mock suspicion. Liz almost laughed out loud at his brazen performance. He was so consummate and slick it made her feel amateur by comparison.

'Where did you just come from?' asked Robert, looking momentarily thrown.

'I'm having a late lunch with Ty Connor. Did you see him in there?' he said, nodding towards the restaurant. 'Only just got here and needed the bathroom.'

Robert examined his father cautiously. 'No, I didn't see him . . .'

Wendell smoothed down his blazer and nodded more soberly. 'Have you seen the *Washington Spy*?' he asked his son, neatly changing the direction of the conversation.

Robert glanced at Liz, his expression turning guarded. 'Yes. Let's talk later.'

Wendell reached over to kiss Liz on the cheek. It was still flushed from the warmth of their hotel room.

'Well, goodbye Wendell, Robert. I'll guess I'll see you both at the wedding.'

She walked out of the plush lobby, eyes staring directly in front of her until she was on the street. Stepping out into the road, a yellow cab beeped at her and swerved, the driver yelling from his window. *Another near miss*, she thought, a smirk on her lips.

55

Jemma may have been small, but she certainly had a big voice. Every face in the dining room turned towards her as she stood to raise a birthday toast to her friend.

'Thirty today, Tess Garrett may be on the shelf,' she began to laugh, 'but with Tess, you can be sure she built the damn thing herself: sawed the wood, drilled the holes, and everything. This woman is capable, resourceful, she is brilliant, and she knows how to use a hammer, so watch out.'

Everyone laughed and clapped. Jemma shushed them down.

'Seriously, though, Tess Garrett has helped a lot of people round this table and many of us owe her a great deal. She is the best friend anyone could hope to have. Raise your glasses please to say "Happy Birthday, Tess"!'

Tess groaned, everyone cheered, and a happy ripple of applause went round the private dining room Brooke had hired to celebrate Tess's birthday. Upstairs from San Carlos, a lively Italian restaurant in SoHo, Tess felt happy and relaxed. She was certainly glad Brooke hadn't picked one of the super-fashionable places that peppered this part of town. Candlelit with low ceilings, there was a splendid earthiness about San Carlos that reminded her of her favourite pubs back home. Carafes of red wine littered the table and the remnants of a delicious gooey tiramisu scented the air. She didn't have a big collection of friends here, just Patty, Kevin and Jack, Brooke and David, Jemma, of course, who was accompanied by her new friend, a photographer called Phil she had met on the trip to Lake Tahoe, plus her old friend 'Bonkers' Becky from the *Oracle*, here with her latest boyfriend, a pashmina-wearing banker called Ronaldo. But it was enough for Tess. Everyone seemed to be in very good spirits, the benefit – Tess always felt – of having a birthday only a few days before Christmas. She'd hated it as a child, of course, but as she grew older, when parties rather than presents were the hallmark of a great celebration, her birthday was double the fun. She sighed happily, trying to remember what she was doing this time last year. Right now, it escaped her.

'You do know we can't be friends any more?' said Jack gravely.

Tess looked up, alarmed. 'Really? How come?'

'Twenty-somethings are cool. Thirty-somethings are old,' he laughed, grabbing her glass of red wine and taking a cheeky sip.

'Hey! Put that down,' she scolded.

Jack just laughed and gave her a hug. 'Don't worry, we're going,' he said. 'Dad says it's past my bedtime, but what does he know? Will we see you next week? Just thought I ought to remind you that Christmas is coming and in this country we give each other presents.'

'Presents?' she grinned. 'I had no idea!'

As Jack returned to his father, Patty came over and kissed Tess on the cheek.

'I'm off, honey. It's been such a great night and Jemma's little speech said it all.'

'That I'm on the shelf?' she smiled.

'What a good friend you've been. Look at Kevin. He'd have lost Jack without you.'

Tess looked over to where the father and son were putting on their thick ski jackets.

'Maybe, who knows?' she shrugged. 'I somehow doubt Kevin would have given up where Jack was concerned.'

'But how many people can afford a paparazzo or a PI?' Her eyes flicked around the table, to Jemma, Brooke, David. 'You sort everyone's life out, don't you?'

'Except my own,' she replied with a twisted, almost self-pitying smile. 'Anyway, what do you mean, *you're off*?' she asked. 'At exactly the same time as Kevin and Jack?'

For a moment, Patty looked ruffled.

'He's a great guy,' she blushed.

Tess clapped her hands together. 'What's going on?' she whispered. 'Tell me! You're so secretive.'

Patty lowered her voice. 'We had supper together the other night. Nothing happened.'

'And what's tonight. Dessert?'

Patty tried to look serious, but Tess could see she was bursting with joy.

'He's walking out to find a taxi with me. Although I've been invited back for coffee. Just coffee.'

'Just coffee my arse.'

'Tess, he's a client,' scolded Patty.

'*Was* a client,' corrected Tess. 'I think the tables are about to turn and he's going to be providing you with a very special service.'

Patty rolled her eyes with a smile. 'Naughty girl. You're not working for the London tabloids now.'

'Well, the ice queen melteth,' said Tess, rubbing her friend's arm. 'The ice queen needs some fun, you were right.'

Tess watched Patty cross the room where Kevin helped her with her coat. He put his big hand on her shoulder, the other behind Jake's head as he guided them out of the door. Suddenly Tess cringed, remembering her own drunken attempts to kiss Kevin and the way he had looked at her with such awkwardness and embarrassment. Tonight, with Patty, his face was shining with hope and happiness. What a curious beast sexual chemistry was, she smiled to herself – something you could not predict or force. Who knew what made two people completely wrong for each other, while other people fitted together like a jigsaw puzzle? On the face of it, she would not have put Patty, the sophisticated career woman, and Kevin, the down-to-earth handyman, together in a month of Sundays. And yet she had a strong feeling that, together, they'd found their Happy Ever After.

'What do you think of Phil?' whispered a voice at her elbow. She turned to see Jemma, an anxious look on her face. Tess smiled and patted her hand.

'He's cute. I knew I should have gone to Tahoe instead of Hawaii.'

'Hey, hands off!' grinned Jemma. 'Oh, talking of which, I've got a present for you.'

'Fantastic,' said Tess. 'Is Brad Pitt going to jump out of my birthday cake?'

'Not even Brooke can swing that one,' said Jemma, taking a piece of paper from her jeans pocket. Tess unfolded it. It was the printout of a photograph. In the picture, a glamorous brunette was leaning forward kissing a balding, thirty-something man wearing a long black overcoat. Glancing around the table, Tess pulled Jemma into a corner.

'Who are they?' she asked, sensing that this was important.

'The brunette is Alicia Wintrop.'

Tess frowned. 'Why do I know that name?'

'She's David Billington's ex-girlfriend.'

Tess glanced over at David, who was laughing and feeding tiramisu to a protesting Brooke.

'Guess why the *Washington Spy* ran the Olivia Martin story?' said Jemma. 'Alicia Wintrop is sleeping with this guy,' she said, tapping the picture of the balding man. 'The very married but easily distracted Benjamin Foley, CEO of Spy media. Which owns the *Washington Spy*.'

'Shit! How do you find these things out?'

'Elementary, my dear Tess,' said Jemma. 'I wondered who would have the balls to sanction a story like that, when they knew that they would be pissing off someone as powerful as the Billingtons? Only the proprietor, which made me wonder why he'd do such a crazy thing. So I followed Foley for a couple of days. He's spent at least two afternoons at Alicia's house in the Village in the last week alone.'

'So you have Alicia's address?'

'She's within spitting distance of our apartment.'

Tess grabbed Jemma's face and kissed her. 'Jem, you're a genius!'

'Steady on,' laughed Jemma, 'I'm saving myself for Phil.'

Tess heard a polite cough to her left.

'Miss Garrett?' said the waiter, hovering apologetically. 'There is someone outside for you. I've told him your party is almost finished, but he asks if you can step out to speak to him for a moment?'

Tess glanced in bemusement at Jemma.

'It better not be Sean,' whispered Jemma, waving a cake knife. 'I could take his head off with this.'

Sean Asgill, thought Tess with an involuntary flutter. *That man's a bastard.* But why did she find herself hoping it was him? She walked through the noisy restaurant and out onto the street, where she crossed her arms against the winter cold.

'Hey Tess.'

A familiar figure was standing on the sidewalk, his face lit by the soft glow of a streetlamp.

'Dom?'

'Surprise,' he said awkwardly, taking a nervous step towards her.

'What the hell are you doing here?' she asked, stepping back towards the safety of the restaurant.

'I was in the area.'

'No, you weren't.'

Dom shrugged. 'I just wanted to say Happy Birthday, Tess.'

'Thanks. You've just disturbed my party.' She shook her head. 'How did you know I was here?'

'I'm a journalist.'

She snorted. 'Is that what you call it?'

Dom moved forward and touched her bare arm.

'Tess, I've been travelling for ten hours just to see you.'

'What? Do you want a fucking medal?' she snapped, wondering vaguely why she was being quite so mean to him. Okay, so he'd been a snake, but the truth was she hadn't thought of him for weeks. She'd moved on.

'I just want five minutes of your time,' said Dom, 'to tell you how sorry I am. To say how stupid I've been and that I miss you so much I didn't want to be anywhere in the world on your birthday except right here, with you.'

Tess glared at him. 'Well, perhaps you should have thought about that before you married someone else.'

Dom looked down at the floor. 'It didn't work out with Tamara,' he said. 'You were right about that.'

She laughed bitterly. 'Married and separated in six months? I don't believe it! Jesus, Dom, it must be some sort of record, especially for someone who claims he never wanted to get married.'

Dom exhaled, his breath puffing in the air.

'I was blinded by it all, Tess. The money, the glamour, the red carpets, and the parties. I thought it would make me feel special, but when you don't really belong there, it makes you feel worthless.'

Tess stopped and looked at him and for the first time she saw how tired and miserable he looked. She knew exactly what he was talking about, of course. She remembered the first time she'd stepped out of a town car to arrive at a glamorous New York party. The paparazzi had lifted their cameras, and the murmur of 'who's that?' had rippled around the crowd.

'It's no one,' someone had said while all the cameras were set down, not bothering to waste their film. *I am not 'no one'*, she had thought fiercely, striding past them, but it was funny how the words stayed with you.

'What do you want, Dom?' she said, her voice almost lost in the noise from the restaurant.

'I want another chance,' he said, no trace of his usual blustering confidence in his words. 'I love you, Tess. I always did. I always will. I should have married you but I was scared. I was scared of what it meant. Scared of waking up one morning to find out I'm an old man; scared of settling for a life I thought should have turned out better.'

His honesty and hopefulness began to melt a little of the ice around Tess's heart. Gentle spots of rain began falling from the moonlit sky, sparkling as they hit his thick dark lashes. On the quiet cobbled SoHo street, framed by the shadows of million-dollar lofts and designer boutiques, he really did look like a movie star. Examining him, she noticed the beginnings of lines around his eyes, but even that suited him. Just a few months ago his looks had been pretty and frivolous; tonight he looked more serious, more grown up.

'What do you say?' he asked, moving closer. The darkness seemed to close around them until it was as if it was just him and her, alone together, back to what she knew.

'No,' she said simply.

Dom stepped back as if he had been slapped.

'There's someone else, isn't there?' he said, looking around her towards the door of the restaurant. 'Is he in there?'

She kept deliberately silent, wanting to make him suffer.

'Who is it?' he asked, his wide mouth sneering. 'Let me guess. Sean Asgill? I bet he comforted you after Nina's party, didn't he?'

She couldn't help flushing and he picked up on her guilt instantly.

'I can't say I'm surprised,' he scoffed. 'After all, you're obsessed with the Asgills, aren't you? You want their rich, glossy life because it's the life you've always wanted for yourself.'

'How dare you,' she spat defensively.

He took a step closer towards her. At this distance he looked more wounded. 'I didn't think you'd be that gullible, to be seduced by him,' he replied more evenly. 'Asgill likes you because you helped him, that's all. But let me tell you this, his friends won't accept you, and his family won't accept you, not as an equal. I don't want you to feel like I've felt for the last three months. At first they think you're funny, a novelty. Fresh blood for their group, perhaps, or some other motive. Tamara just used me to piss off her father,

432

did you know that? She wanted to show him he couldn't control her, so she married beneath her. And for a while that's all fine, but then they tire of you. Then they close ranks and then you're finished.'

Tess felt her lips dry. She didn't like seeing Dom's pain, but she hated the way he was saying she was the same as him, just some pawn for the upper classes.

'I'm not *with* Sean,' she said defiantly. 'I'm not with anyone. I don't need anybody, Dom. And especially not you.'

He looked at her for a moment, then nodded.

'Everybody needs somebody, Tess,' he said quietly, then he turned to leave. 'I'm staying at the Mercer if you work that one out.'

She watched him walk down the street, disappearing into the shadows of SoHo. *What did I come here for?* she asked herself. The truth was she had come to New York to find the magic and romance that only this wonderful city could provide. So why did it feel like it was the loneliest place in the world?

56

Alicia Wintrop lived in a red-brick town house on West Eleventh Street, so close to Tess's own apartment that, if she stood on her roof terrace, they could probably have a conversation.

'Can I help you?' said Alicia, appearing in the open doorway. Even at nine thirty in the morning, she was perfectly dressed in West Village chic with her dark-blue designer jeans, white, long-sleeve T-shirt, and vertiginous heels that looked more like bondage gear than casual footwear. Tess stood on the top step of the stoop, breathing the cold air deeply, desperately trying to shrug off the hangover from the night before's drinking. 'I'm Tess Garrett, a friend of Brooke Asgill and David Billington's,' said Tess, handing her an Asgill business card. 'I wanted to talk to you about a private matter. Can I come in?'

Alicia frowned at the card then reluctantly beckoned her into the house.

'Are you going to the wedding?' asked Alicia, leading Tess into a sleek kitchen that smelt of flowers and fresh bread. Tess looked around enviously, doing a quick inventory of the ground floor. Painted in muted, elegant colours and dotted with impressive-looking modern art, the house had to be a ten-million-dollar property and yet Alicia Wintrop could be no more than thirty. How do these people do it? wondered Tess.

Alicia opened the fridge and poured two glasses of fresh juice.

'Yes, I'll be at the wedding,' said Tess, taking her glass, 'although I'm sort of working.'

'So you work for Brooke?'

'I'm her publicist.'

434

'Ah. You must be busy,' smiled Alicia, taking a sip of her juice. Tess suppressed a sigh. There was no time for small talk.

'Maybe my job has made me a cynic,' she said, 'but I don't really believe in coincidences. Do you, Alicia?'

Alicia leaned against the granite worktop and shrugged.

'I've never really thought about it,' she replied guardedly.

'Let me explain,' said Tess evenly. 'Brooke and David are extremely distressed about a story that appeared in the *Washington Spy* this week. A story that makes all sort of insinuations about Brooke's family. A story that, to be frank, can cause a lot of damage.'

'Really? I don't read the *Washington Spy*,' said Alicia, averting her green eyes.

'That's strange,' said Tess. 'Pillow talk obviously isn't what it used to be. You see, I heard you're sleeping with Benjamin Foley, the *Spy*'s proprietor, and I think you asked him to run the Olivia Martin story.'

Alicia's cheeks coloured but her expression was defiant.

'And *I* think you have horribly bad manners coming into my home and accusing me of such things. David Billington is my friend.'

'Exactly,' replied Tess.

Alicia stared down at the floor and Tess took her silence as her cue to continue.

'A contact at the *Oracle* told me that the story about Brooke and her college tutor was leaked by an ex-girlfriend of David's. I think that girlfriend was you, Alicia. I also think you persuaded Ben Foley to run the story. The Billingtons are very influential in Washington, and not many people would want to piss them off by running a story like this, not even a satirical magazine. This is a little rich even for their blood. But then, maybe a good fuck persuaded Foley, eh?'

Alicia dipped her chin and glowered. 'This is outrageous!' she spat. 'Complete speculation.'

Tess didn't move or speak. It was one of the tactics she had picked up from her old editor at the *Globe*, who used it to great effect with publicists and lawyers. It gave nothing away and yet hinted at power and knowledge.

'You don't want David to marry Brooke, do you?' said Tess finally.

'No, I *don't!*' yelled Alicia finally, her nostrils flaring angrily.

Tess breathed a silent sigh of relief. She was right after all.

'I have known David for fifteen years,' said Alicia, her voice trembling. 'I was in a relationship with him for two of those years. I know his family well and I know the plans they have for him. I *loved* David Billington, do you understand that? I believe in him. It may be your job to protect the Asgills, but at what cost? You know David's political aspirations. You'd be a fool not to recognize that he'd be a great politician. But if his wife's father murdered someone and it's been covered up for all these years by her family, how is that going to look to the American public? They deserve more; they deserve the truth. Can you live with yourself trying to cover that up? Can you live with having denied this country a great leader – and for what? A salary?'

Tess looked at Alicia contemptuously. She did not believe for one second that Alicia's motives had been so altruistic, that she cared so much about the American public. This was a woman who only cared about herself and was prepared to use any tactic to get her own way.

'Don't give me all this morality,' said Tess. 'This is about you still wanting David. It's about you being jealous of Brooke Asgill and wanting to split them up.'

'I had my whole life, *our life*, planned out before he met her.'

'Your relationship was over by the time David met Brooke.'

'Yes, and I ended it. Foolishly playing hard to get,' she said. 'I wanted him back, but by that point, he had already met her. It wasn't supposed to happen like this.'

Tess examined her face, seeing that her eyes were glossy with tears and, for a moment, felt sympathy. She remembered the sharp pain when she saw the sapphire ring in Sean's bag in Maui. A ring for someone else. Yes, she knew what it was to want someone and discover that they wanted someone else. But that didn't justify Alicia's actions. She wasn't just damaging Brooke; she could bring down a whole family, perhaps two.

'The story about Howard Asgill and Olivia Martin is over forty years old,' said Tess steadily. 'It's dead, forgotten. More to the point, it's not even true. Don't sabotage David's relationship because of it.'

Alicia stared directly at her. 'And you are sure about that, Tess? Absolutely sure about it?' said Alicia with contempt. 'Why don't you speak to Olivia's sister and then tell me you're so sure. She certainly doesn't believe Olivia just disappeared.'

'Oh, and now you care about Olivia Martin's family too?' scoffed Tess.

'At least I care about someone,' said Alicia.

Tess put down her glass and picked up her bag.

'Goodbye Alicia,' said Tess, turning towards the door. 'I'll see myself out.'

Out on the street, it was cold. Tess pulled her coat up around her ears and hurried back towards Perry Street. With every step, Alicia's words grumbled uncomfortably around her mind. *At least I care about someone.* Maybe she was right. Would she be doing this if she wasn't being so well paid? No, absolutely not. But she had come to think of Brooke as a friend and, for all Meredith's frostiness and Sean's cavalier way with her feelings, she did care about the Asgill family. What annoyed Tess more was Alicia's claim to care for David and his career. *It may be your job to protect the Asgills*, she had said, *but at what cost?* It reminded her of a conversation she'd once had with a barrister friend of Dom's. He was renowned for getting violent criminals off their charge and Tess had asked him, 'How can you? How can you do it when you know they are guilty?'

His response had been simple; that if his client told him he was innocent, then that's what he believed. Tess remembered mocking him for his self-seeking blindness, and he'd reminded her that journalists were not such moral creatures themselves. Maybe he was right, too. But that wasn't why she had got into journalism: what she'd loved back in the days of the *Colchester Observer* was breaking stories and digging up the truth. Tess had to admit that, somewhere along the line, that ideal had become pushed to one side. The *Sunday Globe* had been as much about the fancy job title and the fat pay-cheque as about chasing down the truth. But was she still that way? she wondered. Was she still so blinded by ambition that the truth no longer mattered? She shivered as she opened the door to the apartment. Jemma was coming out of the kitchen holding a glass jug filled with something thick and creamy.

'Oreo Cookie Jello,' she smiled, holding it up. 'Want some?'

'Jello? At eleven o'clock in the morning?'

'Jello is good any time,' winked Jemma, plunging a spoon into the gloop with a satisfying slurp. Tess sighed and flopped down on the sofa.

'Am I a bad person?' she asked Jemma.

'Why?' said Jemma, sitting on the armchair. 'Am I to assume you've just attacked Alicia Wintrop and left her for dead?'

Tess smiled weakly. 'No, not that, it's just this job . . . Ah, sod it,' she said, and reached for the Jello. She ate in silence for a moment.

'What if Howard Asgill killed Olivia Martin?' she asked quietly.

'I thought you and David Billington were working diligently to make that story go away.'

'But what if it's *true*, Jem?'

'I'm not sure it's that important these days,' she shrugged. 'Bill Clinton's brother was a coke dealer and it didn't harm his career, did it?'

'It was his half-brother and Bill was already a governor,' replied Tess quickly.

Jemma curled her feet under her and looked at her friend directly. 'Why do you think this Olivia woman was murdered all of a sudden?'

Tess rubbed her lips thoughtfully. 'I don't know what happened to her. Certainly nobody has openly talked about Howard's involvement before now, unless you count Charles Devine.'

'Who's a terrible old gossip.'

'But I've just got a feeling that something's not . . . not right here, Jem. We're both news-hounds, aren't we? That's what we'd have been called in the old days. We sense stories like dogs sense blood. I've just got that tingle.'

'So what's your theory, Sherlock?'

'Charles Devine said that Howard was rumoured to be having an affair with Olivia. We know from press cuttings from the time that Olivia's career was on the skids, plus she had a drug habit. What if she needed money and went to Howard demanding some kiss-off from him once he got married? He kills her. Gets rid of the body.'

'Maybe, but Tess, maybe she got abducted by aliens who'd come to see the Beatles at Madison Square Garden.'

Tess wasn't listening. She stood there thinking for a moment.

'Pass me the phone,' she said quickly.

'Who are you calling?'

'Dom.'

'*Dom?*' shrieked Jemma. 'I thought you said you never wanted to see him again after he turned up last night to fuck with your mind . . .'

'He can get free hotels,' said Tess, determined to be practical.

'Is now the right time to be going on holiday?'

'I'm not going on holiday,' said Tess, putting the receiver to her ear. 'I'm going to Louisiana. To Meredith's family home.'

'When?'

'As soon as I can get on a plane.'

Jemma shook her head and slammed the jug of Jello on the coffee table.

'Tess. For as long as we have known each other, you have always wanted to work in New York. You've wanted the life, the excitement, the buzz, and the Asgills have handed you that opportunity on a plate. Shit, if it wasn't for the Asgills, I'd be back snapping celebrity cellulite as they get out of taxis. We owe them, Tess. We're here to make sure this wedding happens, not to dredge up the past and point the finger. We're supposed to be protecting them, not running around the country trying to stitch them up.'

'I'm not stitching them up. I'm doing my job, Jemma,' cried Tess angrily. 'This story has been rumbling around for decades, but if I don't try and find out what really happened to Olivia Martin, it's a story that is never going to go away.'

'I just don't want you chasing after ghosts,' said Jemma. 'You've been doing it for the last ten years. You don't have anything to prove to anyone. Not any more.'

'That's not true,' said Tess, her voice barely a whisper. 'I do have something to prove. I have something to prove to myself. And no matter how much you think we owe the Asgills, if that family were involved in Olivia's disappearance somehow, then I'm not going to turn a blind eye to murder.'

57

Brooke bit her lip and looked at her wedding dress. It had just arrived at her apartment, having flown across the Atlantic in its own first-class seat. It was magnificent, there was no denying that. The silk was exquisite, the construction intricate; everything about it was sumptuous and grand. She should have been pleased, delighted, delirious with excitement even. But she wasn't.

It's not what I wanted, she thought miserably, sliding to the floor of her closet and holding her head in her hands. *It's just not what I wanted*, she thought over and over again as fat tears began to plop onto her knees. At the final fitting in Guillaume Riche's atelier, she'd felt exactly the same way, but she hadn't dared breathe a word to Liz and her mother. She knew how much was resting on it, especially now the company looked to be in trouble. Brooke wiped her eyes and looked up at it again. It wasn't that it was an ugly dress by any means. It was beautiful, a work of art even. The beading, the work of French embroidery house Lesage, was jaw-dropping, hundreds of thousands of tiny crystals and baroque pearls hand-sewn into the shape of feathers with fine silver thread, while the vast dress coat was made of ninety-five metres of silk tulle. But hanging on its own gold rail in her closet, it just looked like a museum piece. Rich and voluminous, it would have suited an ancient queen like Catherine the Great or Marie Antoinette. And Brooke knew she was no queen, however hard she tried.

Getting to her feet, Brooke went into the kitchen to get herself a glass of wine, and then walked through to the living room carrying the bottle and a corkscrew. The dining table was still piled high with gifts from her bridal shower three days earlier at a suite at The Plaza. Bags of beauty products in brown and white candy-striped Henri Bendel bags, duck-egg-blue Tiffany boxes, Smythson notelets branded with the name Brooke Billington, gold Louboutin thongs for her honeymoon, and scores of other bits of girlie paraphernalia. She was the luckiest girl in the world. So why did she feel so anxious, so empty? She picked up the phone and dialled David, who was on his bachelor party weekend in Vegas.

'Honey, it's me.'

'Sweetheart, we're just heading out,' he said. In the background, she could hear laughter and jeering. 'Is there something wrong?' he asked.

'I hate my wedding dress,' said Brooke.

David chuckled. 'Shouldn't you be keeping those details from me?' he asked. 'Look, Robert's shouting for me and we should have left the hotel an hour ago, although God knows why. I shudder to think what he's got planned for me.'

'You go,' said Brooke, feeling selfish and silly. 'Have a great time, I'm fine. Really.'

'You're sure?'

'Sure.'

She put down the phone and paced around the room.

Knowing she had to get it off her chest, she returned to the phone, meaning to call Debs Asquith; but as her finger hit the digits, she dialled another New York number.

'Matt, is that you?'

In the three weeks since her office confrontation with Mimi, she had tried to keep her distance from Matthew, citing work or hectic wedding preparations, although she hardly needed the excuse, she had been flat out. There had been hairstyling sessions, facials, meetings with photographers, florists, and caterers, not to mention the endless summits with Alessandro Franchetti over the tiniest details. But suddenly, out of nowhere, Matthew Palmer was the one person she wanted to talk to.

'Hey,' he said warily. 'What's up?'

'My wedding dress looks like a snow storm.'

'I thought it cost two hundred thousand bucks.'

Now she felt really sick. 'It did. And that buys a lot of fabric.'

'Bummer.'

His voice was distant and strange.

441

'Are you okay?' she asked.

'Fine,' he muttered.

'You don't sound fine. In fact, you sound as lousy as I feel.'

There was an awkward silence. Brooke listened to the faint static on the line, trying to sense something of his mood.

'Matt, what's up? You're worrying me.'

He sighed. 'Oh, it's no big deal. Susie and I split up.'

'Oh no. When did it happen?'

'A couple of nights ago,' he said. 'Look, Brooke, it's nothing, seriously. I'm a big boy. I'm just a little tired. I've just got pizza and I need a sleep.'

'Oh I'm sorry,' she said, 'I forget what you do sometimes. You go and get some rest, I'll speak to you later.'

She put down the phone and slumped back on the sofa. Then, seized with a sudden impulse, she picked up her bag and the unopened bottle of wine. *Forget Mimi trying to make me feel guilty*, she huffed, snatching up her keys. In twenty minutes she was at his apartment.

'Brooke?' His eyes widened in surprise as he opened the door.

Matt looked dreadful. His face was pale and she could smell the alcohol on his breath.

'Surprise,' she said weakly, as she realized that he was not pleased to see her. Brooke was not generally a spontaneous person, and it was for reasons like this that she was usually more considerate. It was, however, too late to turn back, so she walked into the apartment, flushing with embarrassment. The living room smelt stale and sour. Beer bottles were littered all over the table, and the pizza lay barely eaten in its brown box, as if he had been unable to stomach it.

'Sorry,' he said, trying to scoop up some of the mess.

His movements were clumsy and slow, and Brooke could tell he was drunk. She was surprised to find that this annoyed her. For weeks he had been dismissing Susie as nothing serious, and yet here he was, drunk, depressed, self-pitying. She felt a prick of anger that he had lied to her.

'No, don't be sorry,' said Brooke, lending a hand in the cleanup. 'You're allowed to wallow. When relationships end, it's sad. Do you want to tell me what happened?'

He shrugged. 'You know what it's like. You disagree about something dumb and it escalates into an argument. Thirty minutes later you've said things you shouldn't have and she's slamming the door. Then, well,' he gestured at the pile of bottles. 'You wallow.'

She put the wine down on the side with an apologetic expression.

'I guess we'd better not open this.'

'I guess not.'

He looked up and managed a smile. 'So how bad is the wedding dress?'

She pulled a face and suddenly they were both laughing.

'You know what we need?' she said.

He looked sceptical.

'A good night out.'

'Aren't you knee-deep in wedding stuff? I mean, it's your bachelorette night on Thursday. Then it's Christmas. Then . . .'

'Well, what are you doing tomorrow night?'

'I'm off. I'm down for a shift on Christmas Day instead.'

'I want you to come with me somewhere,' she said. 'Don't worry, you're not pulling me away from wedding stuff. In fact I'll be multitasking.'

'What, you want me to choose the bouquet?' he asked.

'Something like that.'

Matt rubbed his stubble thoughtfully, then smiled. 'Well, in that case, count me in.'

58

Liz caught sight of herself in the reflective surface of her oven door and realized she couldn't remember the last time she had cooked dinner. After all, she'd had macrobiotic meal packs delivered to her door every day for the last two years, which had left her body enviously lean and her gadget-packed designer kitchen remarkably untouched. She smiled to herself as she pulled the rack of honey-and-balsamic-glazed lamb out of the oven to add a few sprigs of rosemary before triumphantly removing her new beige Williams-Sonoma apron. Not quite Thomas Keller, but good enough. She was mildly freaked out by this rush of domesticity, although she had managed to convince herself – somewhere in between buying the rack of lamb and roasting it – that there was nothing wrong with showing the occasional glimpse of her feminine side. Wendell always said he liked to be surprised. Not that she was cooking for Wendell, she told herself firmly, merely expanding her portfolio of skills.

Outside, snow was falling, smudging her windows with wintry flakes that looked like sprays of diamonds on the glass. She loved how definite New York's seasons were. The arctic chill of winter, the blistering humidity of summer, the freshness of spring and fall. The changes and precise cycles kept you feeling alive, as if things were constantly moving forward. It was the same reason she did not regret the emotional turbulence she had felt this year. The buyout of Skin Plus was now a matter of weeks rather than months away. It was taking a little while to get the intricate financing sorted out, as Wendell kept insisting there be no financial paper trail direct to him, while on top of that was all the other corporate paperwork. Her new company was going to be called Vincita, Italian for win. And that win had been all the sweeter for the difficulty of the journey.

The concierge buzzed her intercom to announce her visitor. Liz went to the bedroom, squirted bespoke scent between her breasts, applied a fresh layer of plum gloss, and smoothed her hands over her ink-black Balmain dress, so tight that it was just as well she was wearing no underwear. She surprised herself by how nervous she was feeling. They had scheduled a supper a week ago, and this was the first time Wendell had come to her apartment. Liz was sick of their low-key dinners in hotel suites or restaurants, whose only recommendation was that they were so far off the radar of fashionability that no one knew who they were. In the past Wendell had complained that her building, 15 Central Park West, was too high profile, too full of people he might bump into, but tonight he had agreed to come. Tonight could be the turning point in the relationship that she had been hoping for since that first fuck in the Hamptons. She was realistic enough to know that Wendell would not leave his wife for her, but she could name half a dozen rich, powerful men who had such long-term, stable relationships with their mistresses that the situation was a whisper away from bigamy. Was that what she wanted? Did Liz Asgill really want to tie herself to one man? She barely dared think of it, but what she did know with absolute certainty was that when she was with Wendell Billington, she was happy. That was the thought that scared her.

'You cook?' said Wendell, taking off his coat and putting it on the back of a chair. 'I didn't think you were the cooking kind.'

'I can turn my hand to anything, darling,' she smiled.

Liz lowered the lights, until the room just glowed with the candle-light from the expensive arrangement in the middle of the table. Taking the lamb from the oven, she put it on the table alongside china dishes of zucchini flowers, dauphinoise potatoes, and chestnut gravy. 'Sit down and let me enjoy my Martha Stewart moment,' she said. 'It doesn't come out on show very often.'

Wendell settled into one of the high-backed dining chairs, picking up a fork and rolling it around in his fingers.

'So, how was Switzerland?' she asked, leaning across and putting a perfect slice of meat onto his Wedgwood plate.

'Cold and dull,' he said, taking a sip of the Château Margaux she had poured.

'At least David will be having a good time,' said Liz. 'Brooke says he left for Vegas this morning. I thought you'd be going, although I didn't quite think bachelor parties were your thing.'

'Look, Liz, we need to talk,' he said, looking at her directly.

'That's one of the reasons you're here,' she smiled crisply. 'There're several Skin Plus matters that need discussing. I wanted to talk to you rather than the lawyers. I particularly want to run my first choice of CFO past you. Then, when we've agreed that, I'm going to give you the best sex you've had in your life.'

Cooking for Wendell was really just the window dressing for Liz. Really she was looking forward to the luxury of sex with him in her own bed. Momentarily she thought of Rav. She was still seeing him, although the only excuse she now had for keeping that relationship going was the smoke screen it provided for her affair with Wendell. As Rav had pointed out himself, *their* sex was becoming less frequent, less adventurous. But what did she need him for when she had Wendell, here, in her bed? She licked her lips with anticipation.

'I don't want to talk about business,' said Wendell, his voice low and steady. Liz looked up sharply. She had always prided herself on razor-sharp instincts, and right now they were telling her to go on guard. Something was wrong.

'So, what do you want to talk about?' she said casually.

'Us. I'm not sure it can continue.'

She sliced her knife through the tender lamb and did not look at him.

'Liz, are you listening to me?'

She put down the knife, hoping he didn't see her fingers tremble. 'Yes, I'm simply waiting for your explanation.'

His dark, serious eyes looked away from her. 'Robert spoke to me in private just before I left for Switzerland. He asked me straight out if we were seeing each other.'

She felt a jolt of illicit pleasure that their secret was out. 'You denied it, of course,' she said.

'Of course I denied it,' he said, his brows knitting together.

'Then what's the problem?'

'The problem is, Liz, that he's my son and he knew I was lying.'

'So fucking what? You know as well as I do that your sons, your wife, everyone knows what you get up to.'

'That's right,' he said, laying his hand flat on the expensive table linen. 'They do know my needs can't be satisfied by their mother. So I have sex with a bar girl or a shop assistant. So what? They turn a blind eye to it. But you are not some bar girl, Liz. You are about to be my son's sister-in-law.'

'That didn't seem to bother you in the Hamptons,' she said, taking a long, determined gulp of claret.

Wendell pushed his chair back and massaged his temples. 'I care about you, Liz. I enjoy spending time with you, but you know how it works. The press won't touch me for fucking a cocktail waitress; half the men in this city are banging someone they shouldn't. But this can be damaging.'

Their gaze locked. She could tell that he was still holding something back and it made her skin suddenly chill.

'What about Skin Plus?' she said, addressing the elephant in the room.

He was squirming now. 'What do you think,' he said. It was not a question.

'Think?' spat Liz. 'I think we've put hundreds of man-hours into this deal. I think it's the best investment you're going to make all year. I think it's far, far too good to pass up just because you're getting cold feet about our relationship,' said Liz, trying unsuccessfully to squash her panic.

Wendell's voice was weary now. 'I have enough good investments, Liz. What I don't need is aggravation.'

'*Aggravation*?' She curled her fingers into a fist. 'Is that what I am to you?'

'I didn't mean it like that,' said Wendell in a more placatory tone. 'I just think it's probably not a good idea if we're *connected* in this way any more. It's too much pressure, too much temptation.'

'You're pathetic,' she hissed.

'Liz, calm down. Don't be so childish.'

Liz stared at him, her eyes narrowing. 'Oh. I can do childish, Wendell,' she growled, lifting the gravy boat, walking over to him, and tipping the contents into the lap of his navy woollen Ralph Lauren trousers.

'You bitch!' he yelled. 'You've scalded me!'

He stood up, thick brown liquid collecting around his crotch as he grabbed his mobile phone and started barking orders to his driver into it.

'Rodney. Are you still outside? Get me some pants. I don't care where from. Your own if necessary.'

Gravy had dripped all over her cream carpets, but she hadn't even noticed.

'Get out,' she snarled, watching him grab his belongings and flee, the billionaire powerhouse reduced to a scampering tom cat.

'I never want to see your snivelling face again!'

She waited until the front door had slammed, then she sank down to the floor. Hugging her knees, she rocked to and fro, sobbing and wailing, her tears flowing not just for the loss of her business but for the green shoots of love and joy that had just been ground into mud. Liz Asgill's heart had finally been broken.

59

Tess almost gasped as her hire car swung off Louisiana's Great River Road. She could see Riverview, Meredith's childhood home, at the far end of the long, oak-lined drive, its full majesty becoming clearer as the car rolled closer. She had swotted up on Riverview's history on the three-hour flight to Baton Rouge: how it had once been one of the biggest sugar plantations in the Deep South, how Meredith's family had owned it from the mid-Fifties to the early Seventies, and how it had now been a luxury hotel for over thirty years. The main house, a restored 1808 colonial mansion, was white and imposing, with five long pillars at the entrance and tall windows. It was not dissimilar to Belcourt, if that house had been dipped in chalky paint. As she drove through the grounds, Tess caught a glimpse of a few of the twelve clapboard cottages dotted around the grounds, a grim reminder of the history of the house, although she doubted their present occupants had any clue as to their past. Today, the cottages were deluxe one-thousand-dollar-a-night bolt holes for well-heeled honeymooners and holiday-makers, but back in the nineteenth century, they were slave cabins.

She shuddered, wondering, not for the first time, whether she should be here. In fact, Tess had made the call to Dom before she had time to properly think about what she was doing. He was obviously excited to hear from her, and Tess had felt bad as the hope in his voice quickly died away when he realized Tess's call was not to arrange a reconciliation.

'I need you to do something for me,' she'd told him bluntly.

'I might have known you'd want something,' he said sarcastically. 'Well, what did you expect?'

There was a long pause.

'I need a couple of nights at Riverview Plantation,' said Tess. 'It's super-expensive, and I'm not sure I can write it off as expenses. Plus, I need an excuse to ask lots of questions.'

'Why do you need to go snooping around Riverview?'

'Don't ask.'

'Well, you'll have to write the story up for me,' he said.

Tess laughed. 'Does that mean I can send you an invoice?' she asked.

'Does this mean we can be friends?' he replied.

'Maybe. One day.'

Tess put the thought out of her mind as she stepped out of the car and pulled her overnight case from the boot. The balmy honeysuckle-scented air was soothing and warm. Checking in at the desk of the beautiful mahogany reception, she was effusively greeted by the manager who introduced himself as Sidney Garner.

'So you're from the London *Times*?' he said with a thick, deep Southern accent.

'*Chronicle*,' corrected Tess.

'Well, we're very pleased to welcome you here, Miss Garrett.' He motioned to a waiter, who ran over with a tray bearing a mint julep.

Tess shook her head politely. 'I have to drive again in a little while.'

'But you only just got here!' he protested. 'Riverview is all about relaxation.'

Tess smiled at the way he separated the word into four syllables: 're-lax-ay-shun'.

'Well, I'll try,' smiled Tess, 'but sadly it's not a holiday.'

Sidney shooed the waiter away. 'Well, why don't I show you to your room? You're in the Dovecote.'

Tess tried to hide her disappointment. She had asked Dom to try and secure bungalow twelve, the guesthouse nearest the river. The one Olivia Martin had stayed in.

They wound down a path that took them through manicured gardens bursting with roses and flowering trees.

'So, what can you tell me about the history of the house, Mr Garner?' asked Tess.

'Sidney, please,' he blustered. 'Well, the Portland hotel group bought Riverview from the previous owners three years ago. We've spent millions since then remodelling it, keeping the essence of the estate but bringing it into the twenty-first century.'

He led her up to a pretty grey outbuilding and handed Tess a key. 'The Dovecote is one of our best rooms. Very quiet. I thought you'd prefer that to the rooms in the main house if you wanted to work.'

Tess smiled. 'Do you mind if I have a look around?'

'Not at all. Any questions, just let me know.' He thrust a brochure into her hands. 'A CD of images, a factsheet on the hotel's history. It's all in there.'

'Is it possible to see bungalow twelve?'

He gave his head a half-shake. 'Unfortunately not. We're at eighty per cent capacity this weekend and twelve is occupied. Usually is. It's very popular with honeymooners doing the River Road trail. We've got honeymooners in there now.'

'See what you can do?' said Tess, pressing a flirtatious hand on his arm. 'I only need a few minutes to see the view and so on. I'd be very grateful.'

Sidney's eyes widened slightly. 'I'll try,' he said, attempting a coquettish look. 'I'll be in touch.'

He was just walking away when he turned back. 'You know, another journalist phoned up a few weeks ago asking the same question. I believe there's a history to number twelve. Some actress disappeared from a party here in the Sixties, but I'd prefer it if you didn't put that in the story. Some tourists get a bit spooked by things like that.'

'Of course,' smiled Tess. 'You can rely on my discretion.'

Tess wondered who had called. *Alicia? Someone from the* Washington Spy? *One of Wendell Billington's people?* It hardly mattered. No one had got any further with the story or she would certainly have heard about it by now.

There was a chirping sound and Sidney took his cell phone out of his pocket.

'Do you mind?' he said, reading his message. 'I'm wanted in the restaurant. New chef, I'm afraid,' he said with a lame wink.

'Well, I'll just go and settle into my room if that's okay. I have a meeting in Vacherie in less than an hour.'

'Better hurry,' said Sidney. 'It's pretty far out.'

You said it, thought Tess.

* * *

Dennis Carson had been a difficult man to track down. Given that Tess only had limited time, she had been forced to ask Becky at the *Oracle* to help in return for another Brooke and David wedding story, but there was no other way to find the policemen who had been responsible for investigating Olivia's disappearance. Vacherie was a small, pretty town set just back off the highway. It was mainly a cluster of creole cottages and clapboard buildings surrounding a small white church with a tall pointy steeple. The retired officer lived just behind the general store, and he was out in the garden digging in a rose bush when Tess walked up. Carson was around seventy, with military-short steel-grey hair, a heavy jaw, and dark, alert eyes.

'Thanks for seeing me,' said Tess, as Carson led her to a small cane sofa on the porch, sitting on a wooden chair opposite, wiping his brow with a spotted handkerchief.

'I wasn't too surprised,' said Carson. 'Someone called me up about this business a few weeks ago.'

'So I keep hearing,' replied Tess with a smile. 'Could I ask who it was?'

'Don't know. They left a message on my machine, but I've been in Oregon for the last few weeks visiting my son.'

Tess nodded, feeling a sense of relief. Perhaps no one else had got to the bottom of this story.

'So you work for the Asgills?' he asked.

'I work for Meredith Asgill, yes. I'm the family publicist. And, as I'm sure you'll have gathered, the Olivia Martin story has resurfaced.'

Carson shrugged. 'Bound to happen when her daughter's marrying that old-money guy. The one from the television?'

Carson smiled at Tess's surprised reaction. 'Hey, I'm retired,' he laughed, 'I ain't dead. We get the newspapers here too, you know.'

Tess blushed a little.

'So can you tell me what happened back then?'

'Well, I ain't too sure I'm gonna be able to tell you anything you ain't already read,' he shrugged. He rolled his neck and his eyes took on a faraway look. 'After the wedding dinner, there was a big party out at Riverview. This was the Saturday night. According to witnesses, Olivia Martin was drunk and a little high on something. About half a dozen guests said they saw her glassy-eyed and not too stable on her feet. She'd come to the party on her own and was staying in cottage twelve, I believe. The last people to see Olivia alive were Meredith's folks, at about eleven p.m., when Olivia came to say thank you for the evening. No one saw her leave or go into her cottage, she just disappeared.'

Tess nodded. That was the version of the story everyone knew. 'So when was she reported missing?'

'The Tuesday, almost three days later. The day after the wedding, the Sunday, Meredith's family threw a brunch for the guests that had stayed overnight at Riverview, in the main house or in those little shotgun cottages around the grounds. Olivia didn't arrive at the meal, but people assumed she was just sleeping off a hangover. It wasn't until that evening that one of the maids noticed that all Olivia's belongings were still in cottage twelve. She reported it to Meredith's mother, who did nothing about it until the next day.'

'Why not?'

Carson shrugged.

'A pretty actress doesn't come home after a party, I guess you don't panic immediately. You think maybe she met a guy, went back to his place. Plus, she's from that Hollywood world, maybe a little erratic – who cares if you've left all your stuff at your host's house? Actresses, models aren't known as the most reliable people. Anyways, Meredith's mother called Howard in Capri on the Monday and they decide to call the police if she's not turned up the next morning.'

'Which she didn't.'

Carson shook his head. 'So we didn't get to cottage twelve until eleven a.m. on Tuesday morning. Her bedside cabinet is covered with barbiturates and there's a half-drunk bottle of vodka in the bathroom. And have you seen the proximity of the river to cottage twelve? It's maybe a hundred yards. The Mississippi is almost a mile wide in this part of Louisiana and the currents are strong. A body has got a fifty-fifty chance of floating out into the Gulf of Mexico and never being recovered.'

'So you think she fell in?'

'Fell in, walked in, we'll never know. We do know Olivia had a history of depression. We know a television contract got cancelled shortly before she went missing. We also know there's been no activity on her bank accounts or social security number ever since, so it's unlikely she's alive.'

'You say fell or walked into the river. What about pushed? Or thrown in?'

Carson's eyes searched Tess's. After a couple of seconds he nodded. 'Of course that's possible, but there was no sign of a struggle in the cottage. No one saw or heard anything unusual and we interviewed maybe a hundred guests at the party. We even brought dogs into the grounds, but we got nothing.'

'What about the rumour that Howard was having an affair with her? He was getting married, Olivia might have started being difficult . . .'

Carson smiled slightly. 'Howard Asgill was with his wife all night. Anyway, not one person came to us to say that Howard was having an affair with Olivia. And even if he was, it doesn't mean to say he killed her.'

He wiped his hands on his handkerchief and Tess could tell that his patience was wearing thin.

'Miss Garrett,' he sighed, 'it's our job to find out the truth and to bring people to justice and I spent my whole career trying to do that. But sometimes we go looking for things and they just ain't there.'

Tess nodded. 'I appreciate that, Mr Carson,' she said, 'but it's also my job to find out the truth, too. I have to know. If you've read the papers, you'll understand just how much is at stake.'

Carson began to massage his neck. 'Sure, I got that. But you gotta understand that Olivia Martin was a high-profile woman and this case was investigated properly. She wasn't reported missing for over thirty-six hours, and missing people who aren't found in the first forty-eight hours are very rarely found at all.'

'So do you think she's alive?'

Carson turned up his hands. 'Some people do manage to drop out of society, but Olivia was well known and people were looking for her; I think she would have been spotted. I do know her sister down in Sacramento got an inquest, but it didn't go so far as to declare suicide. That's pretty much impossible when there's no body.'

'Did the sister get any money?' asked Tess.

He shrugged. 'I've heard of a few cases like these. A missing person can be declared dead after seven years. The sister was the only living relative and she would have got any life insurance.'

Tess could tell that she had exhausted her welcome. She could understand it: who wants to keep answering questions about something that happened forty-something years before, especially when there were no answers. Tess picked up her bag and stood up.

'Thank you for your time, Mr Carson,' she said, offering her hand. 'Before I go, can I just ask you what you think happened? Was it suicide? Murder?'

Carson rubbed his chin thoughtfully. 'Ever heard of Ockham's Razor?'

Tess shook her head.

'It's a principle used in medicine. In layman's terms, it means that when you have different conflicting theories, the simplest explanation is most likely to be the best, or most true explanation.'

Tess mulled it over as they walked down the steps and into the garden.

'So the theory that a depressed, drugged-up Olivia Martin takes a walk by the river and then falls in is more likely than the theory that her sister killed her for insurance money or Howard Asgill killed her so she'd keep quiet about an affair?'

Carson opened the garden gate for Tess.

'I do believe that, yes,' he said. 'Especially when witnesses put her sister in Sacramento on the evening of the wedding. And security at that wedding was tight; no one else could have got into that party.'

Tess paused on the sidewalk and looked back. 'But what about Howard Asgill?'

Carson closed the gate with a click.

'Miss Garrett, I interviewed Howard Asgill myself,' he said firmly. 'In my professional opinion, he wasn't involved in any way. If someone killed Olivia Martin, it wasn't him.'

Tess was thoughtful as she drove back to Riverview. She was honestly no wiser as to the truth of the Olivia Martin case, but she found that she was enjoying the process: asking questions, talking to people; it felt as if she was doing something constructive. If she was honest, her confrontation with Alicia Wintrop had upset her more than it should. Alicia's accusation that working for the Asgills and effectively covering up lies and transgressions – misleading people – was somehow morally suspect had hit a nerve. It was something Tess knew to be true, but had so far managed to ignore. But now, out here, away from the glitter of Manhattan, Tess could see that the truth was actually a little more complicated. Everyone had things in their past that they would rather stayed in the past; everyone made mistakes. The question was which of them should remain buried.

Tess felt a sense of real relief as she turned through the iron gates of Riverview. She hadn't changed her clothes since her flight down, and was beginning to feel a bit icky. Back in her room, she showered, changed into a long cool dress and headed down to the hotel restaurant. It was busy, but Tess found a quiet table in the corner and ordered a mint julep. She had been thinking about the one she had rejected a couple of hours earlier all the way back from Vacherie.

'Is everything all right, Miss Garrett?'

She looked up to see an elegant woman of around sixty, whose dove-grey linen slacks were exactly the same colour as her hair.

'Lori Adams,' she said, extending a hand. 'Assistant manager. I believe you're here from the *Chronicle*?'

Tess smiled politely. It was par for the course on press trips to be accosted by the management for a tour of the grounds or a detailed briefing on the latest improvements to the hotel. She knew it was the trade-off for getting free accommodation, but she wished she'd called room service.

'Everything's fine,' she smiled. 'Beautiful, actually. This is a really special place.'

'May I?' asked Lori, pointing at the chair opposite Tess.

'Please do.'

Lori signalled to the waiter to bring her another mint julep. 'Yes, it is special, isn't it?' she said. 'It's certainly going to be hard giving it up, I can tell you.'

'Giving it up?'

'I retire next week,' smiled the woman. 'There's a lot of memories here; Riverview has been my life. Although perhaps it's time; things are beginning to change now we're part of a big corporate business. It wasn't like that when I started working here forty years ago.'

'Forty years?' said Tess, sipping her drink thoughtfully. 'I didn't think Riverview was a hotel back then?'

'It wasn't,' said Lori wistfully. 'I worked for the family who used to own the house.'

'Meredith Asgill's family, the Carters?'

'You're well informed.'

'New York's a small place,' shrugged Tess. 'I know Brooke Asgill quite well.'

The older woman's face lit up. 'You do? Oh how wonderful. Do you know Meredith too?'

Tess nodded. She had a hunch Lori Adams might be more help to her than Sidney Garner.

'And how is she?' asked Lori as she took her cocktail from the waiter. 'How is Meredith?'

'A little stressed. Usual mother-of-the-bride stuff.'

Lori gave a little tinkling laugh. 'That doesn't surprise me. Meredith always was very particular, very exact. I remember her wedding day – everything had to be just so.'

'Really?' said Tess, trying to contain her excitement. 'You were at the wedding?'

'I was the Carters' maid back then,' said Lori. 'I worked my way up through housekeeping to a management position. As I said, I've been at Riverview all my working life.'

'So what happened at Meredith's wedding?'

Lori arched her brow. 'You mean the Olivia Martin business?'

Tess put down her drink. 'Oh, don't worry, this isn't for the story. I don't think any of our readers in England would know who Olivia Martin was. I just know that Brooke is curious; you must know there're still some pretty nasty rumours about her father?'

Lori nodded.

'Have you been out to see cottage twelve?' she asked, lowering her voice a little.

Tess shook her head. 'No, Sidney told me that there was someone in it.'

Lori pointed to a couple holding hands at a table on the far side of the restaurant.

'That's them having dinner over there,' she said with a wry smile. 'We can go and have a look quickly if you'd like?'

The grounds were quiet after the noise of the busy restaurant, the sky jet black and marbled with starlight. They skirted around the back of the house and followed the lantern-lit path, past a stone fountain and a small Japanese garden, until Tess could hear the low, rumbling sound of water.

'What's that?' asked Tess.

'The Mississippi,' said Lori. 'Folks are often surprised that she makes a little noise, but she's a grand old lady.'

Finally they saw the cottage, its windows glowing orange. It was certainly private. There were just two other cottages within view. Using her pass-key, Lori let them in. Tess felt a sudden rush of adrenaline, partly from doing something slightly underhand, but also because she felt she was getting closer to the truth. There wasn't much to the cottage, simply a living space, a bedroom, and a bathroom.

'It's all been changed since then, of course,' said Lori. 'But the layout is the same.'

Seeing the couple's clothes and personal items everywhere, Tess began to feel a little awkward.

'Shall we go back outside?' she said. They closed the door and stood on the small veranda, leaning against the rail.

'So what were you doing that night, Lori?' asked Tess, her voice hushed.

'Well, I was a drinks waitress. There were hundreds of people here, all very thirsty,' she laughed. 'The wedding was at four in the afternoon, then the wedding dinner lasted until about eight p.m., and then there was dancing. There was a wonderful jazz band and at midnight an incredible fireworks display that folks said you could even see in the next county.'

Tess tried to put herself there, tried to imagine it was 1964 and that the party was going on all around her.

'Where was the firework display?'

'Everyone crowded around the front of the house to watch it, right by the fountain.'

'So, when the fireworks went off, this area by the cottage would have been deserted. If Olivia did take a midnight walk by the river and fell in, no one would see it or hear her scream because nobody was around.'

Lori nodded. 'Yes, I always thought that too. Apparently there was a poker game going on from about one a.m. to four a.m. in cottage ten just there,' she said, pointing to the nearest neighbouring cottage to cottage twelve. 'The guests in cottage nine and eleven were also up until three a.m. There would have been far more chance of someone seeing or hearing something then.'

Lori caught Tess's enquiring look and laughed. 'You're wondering how I remember all these details? Because no one talked about anything else for weeks afterwards, months even. It was the biggest thing to happen in these parts for years. I guess we all became little detectives, trying to work out what had happened to poor Olivia.'

Tess felt her mobile vibrate in her pocket.

'Excuse me,' she said to Lori, and moved down the steps out of earshot.

'Tess? Why haven't you been answering your cell?'

Tess recognized Meredith's voice immediately. 'I'm out of the city.'

'*Out of the city?*' she hissed. 'I need to see you at once. I've just had Wendell Billington on the phone about this *Washington Spy* story. Where are you?'

Tess hadn't wanted to tell Meredith she had visited Riverview until she had found out more. After all, it could well have been a wild-goose chase. But there was another reason. For all she knew, Meredith could have given Howard his alibi and been covering up his involvement in Olivia's disappearance for decades. She didn't want to tell her employer that she was gathering evidence that might send her to jail. Still, there was no reason to pretend and, anyway, it was David who had asked her to get to the bottom of the story. If Meredith had been talking to his father, she might well find out anyway.

'I'm at Riverview,' said Tess.

There was silence at the other end of the phone.

'David asked me to come, Meredith,' she explained. 'We need to know what happened. It's the only way we can kill this story.'

When she spoke, Meredith's voice was icy. 'With respect, Tess,' she said, 'dozens of police officers couldn't find out what happened to Olivia and I doubt you'll have any more luck over forty years later. I would suggest your time would be better spent doing your real job, putting a more positive spin on the *Washington Spy* story before Wendell starts having serious conversations with David about his bride.'

She sounded furious. Tess could imagine her pacing up and down her Upper East Side drawing room, demanding her maid bring camomile tea and bourbon to calm her.

'The Billingtons are putting the thumbscrews on Ben Foley to run an apology in the next issue of the *Spy*. Plus I've set up an interview with the *New York Chronicle* magazine for David and Brooke to run just after the wedding. It will bring up the Olivia Martin case and say that the police have no reason to believe this was ever foul play.'

'I want you back in the city, Tess.'

'Just give me twenty-four hours on this,' pleaded Tess.

Meredith paused for a moment. 'Very well. I'll see you in the office on Thursday.'

'Thank you, Meredith,' said Tess, feeling a little thrill as she hung up. What was it? Fear? Excitement? And then she remembered: it was the story. It was what she had loved doing on newspapers and what she had missed working for the Asgills. The thrill of the chase. The story. The truth. Whatever *that* was.

60

Matt looked at Brooke incredulously. 'You're taking me for a night out in Brooklyn? I didn't think you ever crossed the river, uptown girl, or are we going to Peter Luger for steaks,' he said name-checking Manhattan's best steakhouse.

Brooke giggled.

'Strictly speaking, this is not a night out.'

The taxi stopped on a quiet cobbled street in Brooklyn Heights, in front of a small red-brick building that looked as if it might once have been a stables. Brooke walked to the door and pressed a buzzer.

'So where are we?'

'Nicholas Diaz's studio,' said Brooke. 'He is *the* most talented designer I've ever seen. He sent me a dress a few months ago and I loved it so much, I'm getting him to make me one for my rehearsal dinner.'

The studio was a small room at the top of the building.

'Brooke! Darling!' said Nicholas, as he threw open the door and air-kissed her. He was tall and thin, with a shaved head, goatee beard, and a big smile.

'Nicholas, this is my friend Matt.'

The two men shook hands, then Nicholas took Brooke's arm and led her into a corner.

'Tell me he's going to be at the wedding,' he whispered, fanning his face with the back of his hand.

'He's going to be at the wedding,' she smiled.

'Tell me he's gay,' he grinned mischievously.

'Sadly, he's not,' said Brooke. 'Sorry, honey.'

461

Nicholas threw his hands in the air. 'Huh!' he said in mock disgust. 'And here I was thinking you'd brought me a wedding present.' He glanced over at Matt, then back at Brooke. 'Or is he your own little gift to yourself?'

She slapped him gently on the arm. 'No, Nicholas. No,' she said, but the designer did not look convinced. Nicholas had only graduated from the Parsons Fashion School three years ago. He'd gone directly to work for YSL in Paris, subsequently starting his own label just over a year ago with a loan from his parents. His label was still little more than a cottage industry – when Brooke had first met him, he'd confided in her that he knew the best way to get his designs noticed was by sending them to the most beautiful, high-profile girls in the city, but he did not have the money to send $25,000 gowns out to socialites on the off chance. He'd chosen Brooke carefully and he had confessed to 'weeping buckets' when she had made her appointment to see him.

'Come here,' said Nicholas, waving Matt over to a table at the far end of the studio. 'I have champagne, I have chocolate, I have strawberries.'

Nicholas shook his finger at Brooke. 'No chocolate for you, sugar plum.'

He then went across to a garment rail and unzipped a dress bag. He pulled out a biscuit-coloured gown that fluttered through the air like a butterfly. Brooke clapped her hands together in glee.

'Oh Nicholas!' she exclaimed.

'I'm glad you like it,' said Nicholas, beaming.

'Like it? I *love* it,' she gasped, fingering the gossamer-light material.

'Shame it's just for the rehearsal dinner,' said Matt, taking a drink of champagne from a mini-bottle.

Both Brooke and Nicholas scowled at him, making him snort his drink down his nose.

'Speaking of which, I have something for you,' added Nicholas, looking a little embarrassed. She followed him into a white dressing room where he pulled back a curtain. 'Just in case,' he whispered.

Brooke gasped. It was a beautiful ivory sheath of satin, a wonderful dress she just knew she'd look amazing in.

Nicholas shrugged. 'Now, I know you have another dress, a much grander one than this. But I thought if you wanted to change into something a little simpler for the party?'

'Oh Nicholas, it's amazing.'

Nicholas smirked. 'So I take it you want to try it?'

Brooke nodded, then looked back at Matt.

'Hey, don't worry about me,' he said, pouring another glass of champagne, 'I'll be fine out here.'

Excited as a little girl, Brooke quickly slipped into the dress. Nicholas helped her onto a little footstool to elevate her off the ground and he darted around her, making fine adjustments with pins. Looking into the long gilt mirror in front of her, she scooped her hair up to show her long neck. She almost felt like crying. Brooke had never been the sort of girl to believe it when people told her she was beautiful, but the poised, sophisticated woman staring back at her from the mirror was as stunning as she had ever dared hope to be. The A-line skirt was grand yet modern, the neckline low and scooped, while the fitted bodice emphasized her long torso. It dipped down just past her shoulder blades at the back, enough to be proper but low enough for a suggestion of sensuality and daring. Not only did it look good, it felt good too. The ivory satin-faced organza felt light and luxurious on her skin, both fragile and strong, like a secret armour. As Matt walked to the entrance of the dressing room, Nicholas retreated. She felt a vague sense of disloyalty that Matt was seeing her dress before David, but reminded herself that this wasn't actually her wedding dress, so it didn't really count. Still, she held her breath as she awaited his response.

'Very nice,' he nodded. 'I thought you hated it.'

She held her skirt out, feeling a pang of disappointment at his polite reaction. Her heart started beating faster with the realization that she wanted him to think she looked beautiful. *Stop it*, she told herself. *Stop it*. Doesn't every woman just want a compliment from an attractive man? 'It's the other dress I have a problem with,' she said quickly, stepping down from the stool. 'The Disney princess dress. But this one just feels *right*. Shame I can't get married in it.'

'What do you mean?'

She saw his confused expression and waved a dismissive hand. 'Don't ask, family politics. Now if you'd just care to step out again . . . ?'

When Brooke had changed back into her own clothes, she thanked Nicholas and led Matt back out onto the street. They slowly walked back towards the Brooklyn Bridge, along a tree-fringed promenade, staring out at the glistening oily-black waters of the East River, not speaking. It was unusually quiet, no joggers or stumbling drunks, the bitter cold keeping people indoors or in bars and restaurants enjoying Christmas parties.

'Shouldn't we be with a bodyguard about now? Anyone could jump out at us around here.'

'I've got you,' she said, playfully nudging his shoulder.

They walked in silence for a while. 'Sorry for bringing you out here,' said Brooke finally. 'I thought it might be fun, but it's just made me depressed.'

'You don't have to wear that other dress, you know,' said Matt.

She sighed. 'I do. It cost such a lot of money, and Asgill's got the licence to manufacture the Guillaume Riche perfume because he was making the dress.'

'Does that appear in a contract anywhere?'

'I don't think so, but Liz would go crazy. She spent weeks negotiating with Guillaume's business partner.'

He smiled and rubbed the dark stubble on his chin. 'So you'd prefer to feel like a cream puff on your wedding day than piss off your sister? The sister you don't like very much, I should add?'

She smiled ruefully and they stopped at the iron railings, looking across to the magical Manhattan skyline sparkling against a Prussian-blue sky. Brooke sighed. It was one of her favourite views in the world, especially at night, when the Brooklyn Bridge was festooned with lights, its arches like two black bishops' mitres.

'Funny how the best view of the city isn't even in the city,' she said, suddenly feeling like Audrey Hepburn in *Roman Holiday*. 'Sometimes you need to get out of somewhere to get the best perspective on it.'

She glanced across at Matt and felt a strange illicit thrill being with him, seeing wedding dresses, taking romantic walks. Matt pulled up the collar of his long overcoat and thrust his hands in his pockets. He looked more brooding than usual tonight, his wide mouth in a long firm line, his eyes fixed at some vague point on the river. Brooke frowned, wondering if he was thinking about Susie. To her amazement she felt a sharp jolt of jealousy.

'I'm going to Africa in February,' he said, turning to face her. 'I've decided to do the programme and it looks like I'll be offered a place in Ghana.'

Although she had known about it for ages, she still felt disappointed he was leaving. 'That's great, Matt,' she said, forcing out her enthusiasm. 'Good job I brought this from the studio then, huh?'

She took a mini-bottle of champagne from her coat pocket and struggled with the cork until it eased off with a pop.

'To the future,' she said, offering him the bottle.

He took a long gulp and turned to look at her. 'I'm going to miss you,' he said simply.

She waved her hand to laugh off his comment. 'Hey, I'll expect postcards,' she said. 'And anyway, it's only for a year, isn't it?'

'It won't be the same though, will it?' he said. 'I've got a feeling that when you're married we might not see so much of each other.'

She knew he was right. In a week's time she would be married and she knew in her heart of hearts that, even if Matt stayed here, their friendship would not last long. She wasn't sure if that made their friendship false, it was just the dynamics of a marriage. She would have made a commitment to David that changed things. Still, she wasn't quite ready to say it out loud.

'Matt, you're my friend,' she said. 'David isn't some ogre, you know. Of course we'll see each other after the wedding.'

'Hey, don't worry,' said Matt, taking another drink. 'It's what happens. You get married, somehow all your friends of the opposite sex, particularly *unmarried* friends, just drop off. It happened to me.'

Brooke felt a sudden twist of jealousy. She often forgot that Matt had been married before.

'Don't be silly, we can still have lunch and drinks when we're not working,' she insisted. 'In fact, we should make a date for you to come to our house for dinner.'

'Well, if you do, make sure you fix me up with a Park Lane Princess so I never need to work again.'

'You'd hate that,' she smiled. *I'd hate that*, she thought, feeling a shift in mood between them.

Just then, specks of snow started falling, drifting down from the sky like stardust. Smiling, she began walking towards the bridge again.

'So what do you think?' she asked, trying to steer them back onto a more platonic footing. 'What am I going to do about my wedding dress? Guillaume's or Nicholas's?'

'It's very simple: do what makes you happy, Brooke,' said Matt. 'What feels right to you, not other people.'

'It doesn't work like that though, does it?' she asked searchingly.

'I thought you wanted to become a rebel,' he chided.

'I think I'm a very bad rebel,' she grinned back.

'You want to wear Nicholas's dress, so wear it. Fuck what everyone else thinks.'

'What do you think? You didn't like Nicholas's wedding dress, did you?' she asked, scanning his face. 'Don't lie to me. I saw it in your eyes.'

The snow was beginning to fall in thicker flakes, smearing the sidewalk in a glossy white sheen.

'You're beautiful, Brooke,' he said after a long searching pause. 'You know, the first moment I ever saw you, you looked so beautiful I never thought I would feel that way about somebody again,' he said softly. 'But it happened back there, seeing you in that dress, I felt my heart stop again.'

Thoughts raced frantically around her head. Was he admitting feelings for her, or acknowledging her beauty, like everyone did around her? Over the last few months she had got so used to reading her name prefaced by the word 'beautiful' that she had become numbed to the compliment. But hearing it from Matt was making her heart beat hard. She took a breath as the memory of their last night together in Providence began replaying itself in her head. She remembered wanting him that night. She remembered enjoying their closeness, his sexiness, as they danced. At the time she'd thought it was the unusually large amount of alcohol she had drunk, but was their quirky friendship, their easy intimacy that had survived all the way through college, actually something more? Suddenly she had to know.

'Do you remember our last night out at Brown? On the dance floor. Did you ask me to go home with you?'

He gave her a small, self-conscious smile. 'Yeah, I did.'

'I wasn't sure what you'd said.'

'*You weren't sure?*'

'I couldn't hear over the music . . . And I didn't want to spoil things.'

He looked confused and regretful. 'You didn't say anything. You just walked away. I thought you were just blowing me out in the most elegant way possible.'

In a way I did, thought Brooke sadly, scanning her eyes over every inch of his face. That night in the club, Brooke had been *almost* sure what he had said. But she had chosen to ignore it and, in doing so, had rejected him. If she'd kissed him that night, what would it have achieved? She knew she was not supposed to end up with someone like Matt Palmer – from the cradle Brooke had been brought up, *conditioned*, to believe that she was a princess, destined for her Lancelot. Her first summer at Brown she had taken Matt to Parklands and had registered her mother's silent disapproval. And for reasons she didn't even understand, Brooke had listened to it.

He gave a small smile before looking away in discomfort.

'It was crass, I know, but I was in love with you. For nearly three years I'd wanted to ask you to come home with me. I guess that last night I had to try. But I was right all along. I wasn't good enough.'

'Matt, it was never that. We were friends.' Her cheeks reddened as she thought of her snobbishness, buried so deep inside her she hadn't recognized it or chosen to rebel from it.

Time seemed to stand still as tension welled between them.

The snow was getting heavier. 'We should get back,' she said at last.

He nodded as they turned off the promenade. Matt flagged a cab down, and on the ride back to Manhattan Brooke was too embarrassed to talk. As the cab drew up at Matt's apartment building, he turned to her.

'Listen, I know you want to get back, but do you mind coming up for a moment? I just wanted to give you my wedding present.'

'You are still coming to the wedding?' she asked quickly, wondering if what had been said back in Brooklyn had changed anything.

'I plan to,' he smiled. 'I'd just rather I gave it to you now.'

She shrugged. 'Okay, but just for a moment. I really need to get back, and it's probably not a good idea for me to be seen here, either.'

The building's lobby was mercifully empty and they didn't speak in the elevator, both avoiding the other's eyes. He pushed the key in the door and, as it opened, Brooke knew it was a bad idea her being here.

There was just a single lamp casting low light around the room, and suddenly Brooke felt exposed and thrillingly vulnerable.

Standing in front of her, Matt took off his coat. His back was wide and muscular and his jumper had ridden up to show a tiny stripe of tanned flesh.

He turned round and they stood and faced one another.

'Matt, I . . .' She stopped herself. *I want you*, she said silently.

As if he had read her mind, he took a step nearer towards her, his green eyes lingering on hers until he brought his hand to her cheek.

The air charged magically as their faces drew towards one another in unison until his lips brushed against hers. A voice of resistance yelled from somewhere deep inside her. *Stop! Slow down!* her mind told her, wanting her mouth to protest. But this was what she wanted. This, and nothing else.

'Was that my present?' she gasped as he pulled momentarily away from her.

He gave a slow, sexy smile. 'No. It's a coffee machine, but hopefully you like this better . . .'

His strong arm circled her small waist as he pulled her closer. His lips crushed down on hers once more and she felt powerless to resist. His tongue searched inside her mouth and she closed her eyes, every nerve ending igniting in pure liquid desire, as she felt unable to process anything beyond the exquisite pleasure of his lips on her skin.

Still entangled in his arms, she shrugged off her coat and he pulled her into the bedroom. The door shut and he pushed her against it. She grabbed the nape of his neck and probed her fingers through his short thick hair, feeling his hard cock push towards her. Separating for an instant, his fingers unbuttoned her blouse, letting the fabric flutter to the floor, while she pulled his jumper over his head, stroking her hand across his dark, wiry scrub of chest hair. He gave a low moan, before his lips stroked her neck and shoulders. Pushing her onto the bed he straddled her, cupping and rolling her breast in his hand. Her nipple flinched and hardened as his flesh touched the tight dark-beige skin through the lace fabric of her bra. His hands pushed down her ribcage until his fingers could unbuttons her jeans. Involuntarily she parted her legs. He kissed the hollow of her neck, slowly moving his mouth down towards her tanned, taut belly, savouring every inch of skin until it descended into the deep V-shape of her unbuttoned denim. His lips sent a ribbon of fire to her hot, wet core. She felt drugged with desire. She wanted him inside her; she wanted him to taste her. She wanted to feel her hard, tight nipples between his soft lips, his tongue to stroke and suck her secret slit. His hands began to pull down her jeans. Her eyes half closed in lust, she looked at him, the strong familiar jaw line, the long lashes framing green intelligent eyes, his handsome features, and saw . . . *David.*

'*No,*' she screamed suddenly, as a wave of guilt crashed over her, sucking her desire away like the ocean pulling sand away from the shore.

'No, Matt, I'm sorry, we can't,' she gasped, rolling away from him and shaking.

'I'm engaged, I'm getting married next week, this is *wrong,*' she said with an emphasis she did not feel.

He rubbed his hands disappointedly across his lips. 'Is it?' he asked bitterly.

She swung off the bed and pulled on her blouse hurriedly.

Silence rang around the room. Matt was unsmiling. 'Do you love him?' he said finally.

She hesitated, not wanting to hurt him, but not wanting to lie to him either.

'So the answer is yes,' he pre-empted regretfully. 'And are you going to marry him?'

Thinking of the wedding, she felt a hollowness and detachment. She didn't know what she wanted at the moment. *A few moments ago, all you wanted was Matt,* she told herself, shutting her eyes in grim helplessness. *What a mess.*

'How can I not?' she said, her voice cracking with regret. 'It's a big oil tanker careering towards its final destination. How do you stop that?' she asked, daring to wonder if she *wanted* to stop it.

'You could come with me to Ghana.'

She gave a low, slow laugh.

'Now *there's* a solution,' she said, looking at him. 'Running away to Africa.'

She saw hurt flicker in his dark green eyes and she understood why he was going to Africa: he was running away too. She didn't know if he was tired of New York and the endless stress of the ER, or whether the truth was that he had never got over the death of his wife. She felt almost certain it had nothing to do with Susie, but maybe, just maybe, it had something to do with her.

'Okay, if not Africa,' said Matt, 'how about Paris or London or LA? You said you loved it in LA.'

She zipped her jeans, not daring to look at him. 'Matt, stop it please. I *do* love David.'

He stood up and took her hand, spinning her round to face him.

'And I love you, Brooke, I always have. You never gave me the chance to show you how great we could be together, but it's not too late.'

'I'm getting married in six days' time, Matt.'

'So?' he said, gripping her arms tightly with his fingers. 'Call it off. Do what *you* want to do. Not what everyone wants you to. Break the fucking cycle, Brooke.'

She shrugged him off, suddenly flinching at his touch. Pulling open the bedroom door, she grabbed her coat and bag, feeling the walls of Matt's small apartment close in on her.

'I have to go,' she mumbled.

'Think about it, Brooke. Think about it.'

But she was already out of the door.

61

Mary-Ann Henner was a drunk. You could see it and you could smell it. Her sixty-something face, obviously once very pretty, was now puffy and lined, her complexion rough and uncared for. She smelt of booze and bars and cigarettes, and so did her little home in Queens.

'Come in, come in,' she said, leading Jemma into her small living room. It was chintzy and neat and there were pictures of two children everywhere – on the walls, in silver frames lined along the shelves, even on the top of a kitsch trinket box on the sideboard, the sort of thing you could have made up at funfairs.

'My two kids, Lauren and Jerry,' said Mary-Ann. 'They've long since flown the nest. Same can be said for their father,' she added with a hard smile, directing Jemma to the red velveteen sofa. Mary-Ann used the remote to flick the television off, and Jemma noted that it had been showing *It's a Wonderful Life*. *Ain't it just*, she thought. There was a bottle of nail polish and a tumbler of clear liquid on the coffee table. It looked like water, but Jemma knew it wasn't.

'So you work for Meredith Asgill?' said Mary-Ann, picking up the tumbler. 'I have to say Brooke's done well for herself. Then again, she was always such a pretty girl.'

Mary-Ann Henner had been Howard Asgill's PA for almost forty years, 'retiring' just before his death when her drinking was beginning to interfere with her ability to do her job. However, she was the obvious first point of contact when Jemma had agreed to join in Tess's investigation: secretaries often knew where the bodies were buried – perhaps literally in this case.

471

Jemma had meant what she had said when she and Tess had quarrelled at the apartment. Her friend seemed to be chasing her tail in some futile search for the truth, and she feared that her life would come crashing down if she found it. So it was with mixed emotions that Jemma had volunteered to help when Tess had called her from Louisiana with the latest information she had found.

'You worked for Howard for a long time, didn't you?' said Jemma.

Mary-Ann wiggled her scarlet painted toes and looked out of the window as if doing mental arithmetic. 'Started when I was sixteen. I was the assistant to Howard's PA back then, the assistant's assistant,' she laughed.

'And did you go to his wedding?'

''Course I did,' said Mary-Ann. 'The most glamorous thing I'd ever been to. I've *ever* been to. Cary Grant was there, ferchrissakes!'

Jemma shifted uncomfortably in her seat. This was awkward, but Mary-Ann with her world-weariness and her vodka looked ready to talk.

'Did Howard Asgill have an affair with Olivia Martin?' she asked flatly.

Mary-Ann offered a weak smile. 'Has that story raised its head again? Thought it might with all this wedding business. Papers, they can't seem to write enough about Brooke and David, can they?'

She took a cigarette out of its packet and lit it, blowing out a smoke ring. 'Police interviewed me about this at the time.'

'I know, Mary-Ann, but it would help if you could remember anything about those days.'

'As I said back in Sixty-four, I never saw anything that made me think Howard was doing the dirty,' said Mary-Ann. 'I sent flowers to Olivia from Howard – tiger lilies mostly, she really loved tiger lilies – and they met for lunch in New York, but she was an Asgill's ambassador, so there was nothing that made me think it was anything other than work.'

'Was Howard ever unfaithful to Meredith?'

After a few moments, she nodded. 'Couldn't keep his pecker in his trousers, if that's what you mean. But then, aren't most rich, powerful men like that? Most men, come to that,' she added, casting a glance at a framed picture of her children.

'Do you remember anything strange about the night of the wedding? Anything unusual? Did you see Howard with Olivia, for instance?'

'Sure. They even had a dance. Howard danced with all the Asgill's ambassadors, showed them off in front of the crowd. He always did mix work with pleasure, even on his wedding day. I'm not sure Meredith liked it much, though. I saw her having quite a ding-dong with Olivia.'

'Did you tell the police this?'

Mary-Ann looked sheepish and shook her head.

'I was seventeen years old, honey,' she shrugged. 'It was my first job and I didn't want to rock the boat. They asked me if Howard was running around with Olivia. I said no and that was the truth, but I wasn't going to go digging up any more trouble. Still, he's dead now,' she said, blowing out a long stream of smoke. 'I can say what I like.'

'Where did Meredith and Olivia have this conversation exactly?'

'Just across from the big fountain in front of the house. It was about eleven p.m.'

'You've got a good memory,' said Jemma.

Mary-Ann snorted. 'Big night for me, baby, it was the night I lost my cherry. You remember nights like that.'

'Ah, I see,' said Jemma awkwardly.

'Should have been the most romantic night of my life,' said Mary-Ann, looking wistful. 'All that beautiful jazz music, the smell of the flowers in the rose garden – that's where we did it,' she whispered. 'First night a man let me down, but not the last. Said he'd meet me at midnight for the fireworks. Son of a bitch never showed.'

'Do you remember seeing Howard Asgill around midnight? Maybe after the fireworks?'

Mary-Ann nodded. 'I remember that one because by then I was crying. Howard saw me and gave me his handkerchief. Must have been about twelve thirty, I guess.' She reached for the tumbler and drained the last of the liquid. She waggled the glass at Jemma.

'Drink?'

'No, I must be going,' she said, standing up. 'But thank you so much for your time.'

'No problem, honey,' said Mary-Ann, showing her to the door. 'Always happy to talk about the good old days.'

She opened the door and Jemma stepped out.

'Never get involved with a man, honey,' said Mary-Ann as a parting shot. 'They all let you down in the end.'

Amen to that, thought Jemma as she heard the door close behind her.

62

Brooke had been dreading her bachelorette party, given that her sister Liz was in charge of the arrangements. She had been expecting some humiliating stripper bar involving baby oil and beefcake, so she was therefore astonished to find Liz had booked the private room of the Buddha Bar, the hottest club-restaurant in the Meatpacking District, and had filled it with pink champagne and exquisite canapés. She had also invited at least forty of Brooke's closest friends: people from school and college, colleagues from Yellow Door, and girls from the society circuit. Brooke reminded herself what her sister was like: whatever Liz did was always the best it could be. On the other hand, Brooke was mildly cynical about this show of good nature – there just *had* to be some motive behind it, didn't there? – although standing at the bar, strewn with gardenia petals, surrounded by friends, it was hard to think what it might be.

'I just want to say thank you for all this,' said Brooke, touching Liz on the arm. 'It's just perfect. I can't believe you've got so many of the old crowd here.'

Liz gave a casual little shrug. 'I just thought it was a shame you don't see too many of the Spence and Brown lot any more,' she said quietly. 'It's important to stay connected.'

Tiny tea-lights dotted round the room gave Liz's face a soft golden glow, but her expression was unsmiling and melancholic. If Brooke hadn't known better, she would have said her sister actually looked, well, *sad*. She glanced at her again; it was rare you saw any emotion from Liz apart from anger. Brooke leant across the bar and ordered two champagnes, handing one to Liz, who drained it in one long gulp.

'Liz, are you okay, honey?' asked Brooke.

'Are you sure you're ready for the Billington family?' said Liz, ignoring the question. Her gaze was unsettlingly direct, her tone unmistakably heartfelt, and for one anxious moment Brooke wondered if Liz knew about last night, the night she had almost had sex with Matt Palmer, a memory that had been both thrilling and repelling Brooke in the twenty-four hours since it had happened. The irony was that Brooke was desperate to talk to her sister about her misgivings. While the two women were not close, Liz was the smartest, wiliest person she knew; no trouble ever seemed insurmountable to her, every problem was an opportunity, and she always seemed able to manoeuvre her way out of anything. Brooke would have loved her sage advice, but the truth was that Brooke just didn't trust her.

'Of course I'm ready for them,' said Brooke.

'Well, you'd better be,' Liz replied, her eyes flat and sad, 'because they don't care about anybody or anything except themselves.'

Brooke frowned. 'Liz, is there something—'

Her question was interrupted as a tall, slender blonde approached, wearing a skin-tight sequined mini-dress, the veil of a pillbox hat obscuring her face.

'Lily? Is that you?' asked Brooke, bending to peer under the veil. The hat nodded, a quiet sniffling coming from beneath.

'There's been an accident, Brooke,' whispered her bridesmaid-to-be. 'Something awful's happened.'

Her heart lurched – did Lily know? If his cousin knew, did *David* know? She felt completely paranoid.

'It's the Botox,' sniffed Lily as she lifted her veil. Her left eyelid was puffy and drooping badly, as if she'd been punched squarely in the eye.

'I was having a quarter-head especially for the wedding, and it's slipped.'

'Slipped?' replied Brooke incredulously, having had no experience of the cosmetic procedures that half the girls in the city were undergoing.

'What were you doing? Cartwheels after the procedure?' said Liz tartly.

Brooke glanced at her sister. It was insensitive, even for her, but Lily didn't seem to mind.

'Please, can you help me?' said Lily, clasping Liz's arm. 'There must be someone at Skin Plus who can help! How can I be a bridesmaid like this? I can't,' she said, beginning to sob.

Liz peered at her more closely. 'I'm not sure anything can be done,' she said. 'Don't worry, though. It will probably wear off in two to three weeks.'

Brooke and Lily watched her disappear through the crowd, open-mouthed.

'How can I come to the wedding looking and feeling so terrible?' whispered Lily.

Oh I know the feeling, thought Brooke sadly. Just then Brooke's mobile phone rang. Her throat tightened as she saw the name on the LCD display. David.

She had avoided his calls all day, but she couldn't carry on ignoring him forever. He was due back from Las Vegas any time and she had no idea what to do or say to him. She took a deep breath and picked it up.

'Hi honey,' he said. 'I've been trying you all day. Is everything okay?'

The sound of his voice churned up the guilt that had been staved off with champagne and old friends; his concern only made her feel worse.

'Fine, fine. I've just been rushed off my feet with the party and everything. Where are you?'

'We got into New Jersey ten minutes ago. I just wanted to say have fun this evening.'

'How was Vegas?'

'Robert lost a hundred thousand dollars on blackjack.'

'He can afford it. It's the strippers I'm worried about.'

He laughed. 'It's the strippers *I'm* worried about, Brooke. Bachelorette nights are always far worse than bachelor parties.'

'Hmm, I doubt that,' she said, over-playfully.

'I guess you don't want me to come round tonight?'

'I think it's going to be a late one.'

'But I'm driving up to Belcourt in the morning. Are you sure you don't want to come with me?'

She inhaled to steady her voice. 'Honey, this will be my last Christmas with my family. I thought that's what you wanted too.'

Part of her was desperate to see him at that very moment, as if his presence would somehow erase what had happened the night before. On the other hand, she was grateful for the three days of Christmas that were conspiring to keep them apart.

'I know, I know. I just miss you, Mrs Billington.'

Mrs Billington. Suddenly she started feeling hot. 'Not yet,' she replied weakly, feeling her skin flush.

'I love you.'

'I love you too.'

She snapped the phone shut, tugging at the high funnel neck on her black jersey cocktail dress. There didn't seem to be much air in the room. She pushed through the crowd, heading for the outside. On the dark cobbled street she bent down, hands on her knees, blonde hair falling forward. She was sure she was going to be sick. She had spent the last twenty-four hours in a state of complete anxiety, constantly bouncing from one conflicting emotion to the next: fear, love, guilt, shame – and right now she felt so consumed by it she could barely breathe.

'Hey Brooke. What's wrong?'

She looked up to see that Tess had followed her into the little side street.

'I'm okay, I just felt a little sick in there.'

Tess looked down at her, those searching eyes examining Brooke's face.

'Brooke. What's wrong?'

She uncurled her body, feeling the knot of claustrophobic panic subside a little. But she couldn't go on like this; she had to tell someone. It might as well be the person paid to sort out her troubles.

'I'm not sure I can go through with it, Tess,' said Brooke, tears welling up. 'I don't know if I can marry David.'

She watched Tess's eyes widen in amazement. 'I don't understand.'

Neither do I, thought Brooke, closing her eyes. *Neither do I.* She had no idea whether it was because she loved David too little or cared for Matt too much. It had been something she had been raking over again and again in her mind since she had left Matt Palmer's apartment. As she had stepped out of his building, darkness and calm had still shrouded the city, the late-night Christmas revellers were still partying and the shoppers had gone home. In a taxi, watching Manhattan slide by, she had asked the driver to keep on driving, hoping that the right answer would present itself somewhere out there in the panorama of New York. The thought of having to drive to Belcourt over Christmas and call off her wedding made her feel physically ill, but the idea of never seeing Matt again made her heart thud with pain. It was in that lonely journey that Brooke had realized that, no matter how selfish and greedy it may seem, the truth was that maybe the human heart was big enough to love more than one person.

Tess walked over to Brooke, high heels clacking on the cobbles. 'You're drunk, it's just nerves,' she said, rubbing Brooke's shoulders. 'It's only natural. Why don't I call you a cab? I'll take you back home and we can talk this over.'

Brooke looked up at her. 'I slept with Matt Palmer.'

Tess's hand covered her mouth. 'Oh Brooke, you didn't.'

Brooke dipped her head in shame. 'Well, no, I almost slept with him. I was about to. It was the best sex I never had.'

Her publicist's brows arched hopefully. 'So you didn't actually have sex with him?'

'That's not the point,' she said fiercely, thinking about Matt's mouth on her skin and how much she'd enjoyed it. Brooke supposed that everyone's definition of unfaithful was different, but the fact that she had kept her jeans on throughout the interlude still made her – by most people's standards, including her own – guilty of infidelity.

'You don't think you're in love with him, do you?' said Tess incredulously.

Thump, thump. Was it the music from the club or the pounding in her head?

'I don't know,' Brooke croaked, thinking back to the night in the Providence club and what would have happened if she had gone home with Matt Palmer. Life was full of small decisions that had monumental consequences. Like going up to Matt's apartment last night to collect her wedding present, which had thrown everything she thought she wanted into question.

'I know that when I'm with him I feel happy. Somehow lighter.'

'Go on a diet,' said Tess scornfully.

Brooke turned to her angrily. 'Tess, I'm serious. Matt is leaving New York and he wants me to go with him.' Tears that tasted of salt and cosmetics dripped into her mouth.

Tess glared at her. 'Are you out of your *mind*?' she said, her hands on her hips.

'Maybe,' said Brooke fiercely, 'or maybe this is the first time in years I am actually using my own mind.'

Tess was shaking her head slowly. Brooke did not need her to say the words to tell what she was thinking. *I told you so.* She had warned her about playing with fire.

Suddenly Brooke shook her fists and kicked out angrily at the wall.

'Do you think I want to be going through this, Tess? I don't even *recognize* myself, doing something as awful as this,' she cried. 'David's a good man. I love him, I really do. I owe it to him – to myself – to go into this marriage being one hundred per cent committed to him. Call me old-fashioned, call me a romantic, but when I marry someone I want the whole of my heart to belong to them. I don't want to be fresh out of another man's bed.'

Tess suddenly grabbed Brooke's shoulder and pushed her back towards the club.

'What on earth . . . ?' she protested.

'Look,' said Tess urgently, pointing towards the other end of the alley. A dark figure was moving towards them holding the unmistakable shape of a long-lens camera.

'Bloody paparazzi,' hissed Tess, 'get back inside.'

'I can't!'

'You have to,' said Tess, her voice firm but tough. 'Go back in there, have a drink and try and act as normal as possible.'

'Tess . . .' she pleaded, but Tess's grip was strong.

'Do you want David to read about this in tomorrow's papers?' she asked. 'If you leave now, they will know something is wrong. Just get through tonight, pretend you're having a brilliant time. We'll talk this through first thing tomorrow.'

Brooke looked at Tess, her expression one of abject misery. 'You wouldn't marry someone if you were happy with somebody else, would you?' she asked, her voice almost lost on the cold wintry air.

'I don't ever want to get married,' said Tess, turning away.

'Hey, look, the bride is getting all teary and loved up,' giggled Debs Asquith as Brooke re-entered the party.

'I'm allowed to get a little sentimental aren't I?' she smiled weakly, taking a plastic tiara from her friend's head and wedging it onto her own. 'Now, hand me that bottle, I need a drink.'

For the next hour she drifted from group to group, barely

registering the conversations she was having, trying to lose herself in a fug of champagne.

'Brookey, I can't believe we haven't spoken to you yet!'

Evelyn Roche and Grace Elliot were two friends from Brown that Brooke had not seen or heard from in over two years as they had moved to Chicago and Boston respectively.

'It's so great to see you,' said Brooke, hugging them tightly. She was glad to see her old friends, but she just wished it was somewhere else, some other time, when this bad dream was all over.

'We were just remembering that time when we drove up to Newport the week after our exams had finished,' said Evelyn. 'Do you remember? We saw Cliffpoint, and Jenny Sanders identified David Billington as the second most eligible man in America. She said she was going to make it her mission to track him down.'

'Gosh yes,' said Brooke listlessly. 'Whatever happened to Jenny?'

'Married the most eligible man in Europe, I think,' said Grace. 'You know she always had focus.'

Brooke smiled weakly, desperate to leave.

'Speaking of those happy days at Brown,' continued Grace, 'I read what Matt Palmer said about you in the *Oracle*.'

Brooke drew a sharp breath and avoided their eyes, trying not to register any emotion.

Grace leant in and dipped her chin conspiratorially. 'Well, I met Sandy Steele the other week in Boston, I don't think you knew her. She married her med-school boyfriend from Brown and it turns out he knows Matt Palmer. Apparently there were some pretty racy rumours going around about him a couple of years ago. Didn't surprise me in the slightest when I heard what a rat he'd been with you and the gossip columns.'

'Rumours?' asked Brooke with a flicker of panic.

Grace grimaced. 'Apparently he beat up his wife,' she whispered.

Completely stunned and bewildered, Brooke felt her pulse start racing wildly.

'I knew a doctor who did the same,' said Evelyn, nodding. 'Big drinkers.'

Brooke felt her fingers tremble. Her throat felt so thick with bile she could barely draw breath. 'No,' she said a little too loudly. 'I can't believe that.'

Grace shrugged. 'That's what Sandy's husband said. Apparently Matt's always been the sort of guy you avoid when he's drunk, but there's never any excuse for it, is there? Anyway, Matt and his wife separated and then she died. It was all pretty grim.'

'Yes, that's really bad,' nodded Brooke dumbly. *And you have no idea just how bad*, she thought. *No idea at all.*

63

Despite the champagne, Brooke had found it impossible to sleep. She had spent the night tossing and turning, unable to believe what Grace had said about Matt. No, that wasn't true: she could certainly believe he had a drink problem; she'd smelt the sour whiff of alcohol in his apartment, and seen him bleary and hung-over after his break-up with Susie. But believing that he'd hit his wife? It was impossible, wasn't it?

Sitting in a Brooklyn coffee shop, she rubbed her eyes and downed her espresso in one.

Glancing anxiously at the clock on the wall, Brooke saw it was eight thirty-five a.m. She was five minutes late, and every second Brooke felt more confused and stupid. At eight forty a.m. precisely, Susie walked through the door. At first Brooke didn't recognize her; her strawberry-blonde hair had been cut into a bob that swung around her face. She looked better, thought Brooke.

'Well, this is a nice surprise,' said Susie nervously, ordering some camomile tea from the waitress. 'But I can't stay long, I'm getting the train to my parents' house in Albany in a couple of hours. Christmas Eve is a big deal in our household, so I'd be in the worst trouble if I miss a second of it.'

When Brooke had finally given up trying to sleep, she had gone into the bathroom and had a scalding hot shower. She didn't know if it was the reviving power of the water giving her clarity, or her sheer desperation, but she had suddenly been seized with an idea. Scrabbling around in her bag, she had found the business card Susie had given to her at Eileen's launch party and sent a carefully worded text asking if they could meet.

Sitting opposite her now, Susie looked decidedly uneasy, and Brooke could understand it entirely: why would Brooke Asgill call her up on Christmas Eve morning?

'Well, Happy Christmas anyway,' said Susie, fishing around in her leather satchel and pulling out a small brown medicine bottle with a bright red bow tied around the neck.

'It's the oil I promised you. Sweet almond, lavender, and neroli. It's a wonderful de-stresser. I thought you might need it, what with the wedding and all.'

Brooke smiled sadly and wrapped her fingers around the bottle, rubbing her thumb up and down the glass.

'Susie,' she said quietly, 'why did you break up with Matt?'

Susie paused as the waitress brought her tea. She sipped it, holding the cup in both hands. 'It just didn't work out, I guess,' she said. 'Busy doctor. Kooky aromatherapist. It was never going to work.'

She smiled broadly. A little too broadly.

'I saw a friend last night,' said Brooke slowly. 'She said that Matthew used to hit his wife.'

A deep furrow appeared between Susie's brows. 'Really?' she said, her eyes flickering to the table.

'Yes, really.'

There was a long, clumsy silence.

'Tell me, Susie. Did he hit you?'

Brooke could see that Susie was clasping her cup so hard, her fingers were trembling. 'It was just a couple of times.'

Brooke felt her skin turn hot, then cold.

'The first time it happened I thought it was my fault,' said Susie softly. 'It was the night of the dinner party and he was pretty drunk. Everyone had gone home and I was a little upset about the way I saw Matt behave when he was around you – stupid, isn't it?' she said, trying to laugh. 'I said a few things I shouldn't and he hit me. Not hard – I wasn't hurt, just shocked. I even blamed myself for annoying him and accusing him of being in love with you.'

Her pale cheeks flushed. 'I tried to forget about it, but it kept bothering me, so a week or so later I told a friend of mine who's a therapist in the healing centre where I work. She said it was a pattern and that if Matt hit me once it would happen again.'

Susie was shaking her head. 'I didn't want to believe it. You imagine men who hit women are monsters, don't you? But Matt is a great guy in so many ways and, I know this sounds silly . . .

but I really thought I could marry him. So I had to know if it was true.'

Susie trailed off, carefully placing her cup back on its saucer.

'So I went to see his wife's sister,' she said, her voice sounding almost apologetic. 'I went snooping around Matt's apartment and found her contact details in an address book. Well, when I turned up at her doorstep and told her I was Matt's girlfriend, she knew why I had come. She said Katie, his wife, was about to divorce him just before she died.'

Finally she looked up at Brooke. 'And that's why you're here, isn't it?' she asked. 'You had to know too, didn't you?'

Brooke looked into Susie's eyes and she saw trust, solidarity, sadness. She nodded, anger and disappointment making her body feel hollow.

'He hit me again when I told him I knew about Katie.'

'I'm sorry,' said Brooke desperately, putting her hand over Susie's.

'People come into our lives and disappoint us, but at least we both found out in time,' said Susie quietly. 'And at least you didn't make a mistake. Your David looks like one of the good guys.'

'I know,' whispered Brooke sadly. 'I know.'

Leaving the diner, Brooke walked across to Prospect Park and sat down. No one noticed New York's most famous woman, her hood pulled tight around her head, her eyes fixed in front of her, staring at the tall, bare trees. The bench was cold beneath her coat and snowflakes had begun to fall from the sky. She watched them drift down from the grey sky, so tiny, so perfectly formed, each one dissolving on the wet path as they landed. Her stomach knotted with anger and disappointment. She felt empty, sad, foolish, betrayed, and so very, very sorry.

Finally Brooke pulled out her phone and called Tess Garrett.

'Don't panic,' she said with as much certainty as she could muster. 'The wedding's going ahead.'

64

'Who wants Irish coffee?' asked Kevin.

Tess flopped back on his bright-yellow sofa and rubbed her stomach.

'I don't think another thing is going to fit in there,' she said. 'I think that was the biggest Christmas dinner I have ever eaten.'

'I'll have some!' said Jack eagerly.

'I don't think so,' smiled Patty, pouring cream into long glass mugs and handing to Kevin. Tess saw him smile and wrap a hand round Patty's slim waist. They had been discreet with their shows of affection all day, but they obviously couldn't keep their hands off each other.

'Ah, young love,' sighed Jack, rolling his eyes dramatically. 'Come on, Tess, let's leave them to it. I've got something to show you.'

Groaning at her bloated tummy, she stood up. It was time she was going anyway; it had been so kind of Patty to invite her, especially when she was clearly looking forward to a quiet intimate Christmas with her new boyfriend, and she didn't want to outstay her welcome. She followed Jack into his room where he presented her with a box gift-wrapped in brightly coloured paper and ribbon.

'Ooh, what's this?' she said, eagerly tearing it open. Inside were half a dozen DVDs.

'Just a few recommendations. I thought you could do with some help if you're sneaking into horror movies all the time.'

'Wow, Jack, these are great,' she said, hugging him. 'I haven't seen any of these.'

'I'm not surprised,' he said wryly. 'You're always working.' Jack looked at her with a frown. 'Why *do* you work so hard?'

She screwed up a ball of gift-wrap and threw it at him. 'Because I have to.'

'No, you don't,' he said simply. 'You think it makes your life better but it doesn't, it makes it worse. I mean, if you didn't work so hard, you could have gone back to England for Christmas.'

Tess shrugged. 'I don't think going back to London for Christmas would make my life better. It's not like there's anyone I really care about over there any more.'

'That's sad, isn't it?' said Jack, and Tess felt herself squirm. There was no accusation in his words, just good nature and concern, but he was right. It *was* sad. Where had she gone so wrong? she wondered; what bad decisions had she made that had brought her here? Thousands of miles from home. Yes, she was rich, yes, she was successful, but she was alone, despite all the friends around her.

'Couldn't you go and see your mum?' asked Jack.

Tess shook her head. 'She's not a very nice person. She hurt me very badly and I guess I blame her for how a lot of things in my life turned out.'

'But she's still your mum.'

Out of the mouths of babes . . . thought Tess. With Jack's childish simplicity, it almost made sense.

'So why don't you call her?' he said, warming to his idea. 'You know, after my mum tried to take me away from Dad, I didn't want to talk to her for a few weeks. But I forgave her. Isn't that what we're supposed to do at Christmas?'

Tess sprang forward and pulled him into a bear hug. 'You know, if I ever have a son, I hope he's just like you.'

'I thought you didn't want kids?'

She laughed. 'D'you know, I'm not sure what I want any more.'

Scooping her DVDs into her bag, she went back into the living room. 'I'm off,' she said, more brightly than she felt.

'Not back to work I hope?' said Patty sternly.

'Just a few emails,' smiled Tess. 'Can you believe I've had ten calls from the photo agencies today? Apparently word's out that the wedding is going to be at Leonard's house over the holidays. I have to get back and arrange a photo-call. I thought we could release one picture of the happy couple and the proceeds can go to charity.'

'Do it tomorrow,' smiled Patty lazily from Kevin's arms. 'It's Christmas.'

Tess almost laughed out loud. What had turned this ball-breaking career girl to mush? *Love,* she decided, realizing with an uncomfortable afterthought that it had made Patty a stronger, richer person. Tess had always thought of love in negative terms: vulnerability, loss of independence, the possibility – no, the inevitability – of heartbreak. After what had happened to her father, Tess had convinced herself that she didn't want a family, deciding instead that it was money and position that made you safe. But looking at Kevin and Patty, it dawned on her that maybe she'd got it upside down. Perhaps Jack was right; instead of rejecting the idea of family entirely, perhaps she just needed to approach it in a different way.

She waved goodbye and went out onto the cold street, where an inch-thick layer of snow was already covering the sidewalk. She trudged back to the apartment, breaking the virgin snow with her lonely footprints. The flat was silent and cold. Jemma had gone to Toronto to see her sister and the small Christmas tree in the corner of the room looked rather forlorn without its lights on. *Join the club,* thought Tess.

She uncorked a bottle of wine, turned on the stereo, and flopped down on the sofa. Letting the red liquid slip down her throat, she closed her eyes and listened to Nick Drake and his lilting melancholic song. In three days' time the wedding would be over and her contract with it. Then what? Where exactly did she fit in the world now? She would have no job and – she realized suddenly – nowhere to live. The flat came as part of the package with the Asgills; if she was no longer in their employ, she'd have to ship out. But where to? Could she go back to London? What was there? Who was there? Dom. Sean. Her *mother?*

Tess looked over to the mantelpiece where she and Jemma had lined up their Christmas cards. This was the first year she hadn't had a card from her mother, she realized. In the years after her father's death, her mother had kept sending her birthday and Christmas cards, usually to Tess's work address. She wasn't sure how her mother kept tabs on where she worked, but for years the cards kept coming, always containing her mother's contact details. *You could call her,* said a little voice in Tess's head. *What a stupid idea,* she scolded herself, grabbing a copy of the nearest book to distract herself. *Simply Divine: Charles Devine – the whole story.* Stretching out on the sofa, she began flicking through the pages of Charles's memoirs. She had to admit he had a wonderful narrative voice, camp and witty, and couldn't understand why a publisher hadn't picked up his manuscript. Perhaps that's what happened when you were out of favour. Too tired to read any more, she turned to the photographs in the middle of the book. Charles as a toddler, running around a country garden. Charles as a teenager. How handsome he was! Charles with Truman Capote, Pamela Harriman, Babe Paley, Gregory Peck. Just as he said, they were all there. Charles looked so glamorous and chic in every one. *What a life he's led,* marvelled Tess. Suddenly she stopped, one particular face catching her eye. Yes, it was definitely her: much younger; much happier, it seemed. Tess read the caption: 'On the high seas with Olivia Martin and Meredith Carter. Catalina Island. July 1963'. She examined the picture more carefully. The three of them were on a yacht, Olivia and Meredith were dressed in bathing suits, laughing and clinking two flutes of champagne together. It was a happy, relaxed photograph, but something about the image just didn't fit. She reread the caption: Catalina Island, July 1963. Tess frowned. She remembered back to one of her first conversations with Meredith, at Brooke and David's engagement party at Belcourt. Yes, that was it! She distinctly remembered Meredith saying that she barely knew Olivia. Tess grabbed her mobile and phoned Charles.

'Darling Tess! Yuletide greetings to you,' said Charles with evident pleasure. 'How are you? I thought I was never going to hear from you again.'

'I was just reading your memoirs.'

'Aren't they splendid?'

'Yes, yes, they're wonderful.'

She paused. 'Charles, are you at home? I need to talk to you.'

She could hear him clapping his hands.

'I knew it! You smell best-seller, don't you?' he trilled.

'Just put the tea on,' said Tess. 'I'll be there as soon as I can find a cab.'

Charles answered the door in a blue velvet smoking jacket and matching slippers, his initials embroidered in gold on both.

'Single malt,' he smiled, pushing a tumbler of amber liquid into her hand. 'It is Christmas, after all.'

One delicate silver star propped up on the fireplace was the only sign of Christmas.

'I find holiday decorations so vulgar,' he said airily.

'I have to say I've hardly bothered myself this year,' said Tess, sitting on the chair opposite Charles.

'Well, you do have the wedding,' he sighed. 'My invitation never did show.'

'It's a fairly small affair, Charles,' said Tess sympathetically.

He snorted. 'More likely the Asgills have got too big for their own boots.'

Tess smiled politely. 'Actually, it was the Asgills I wanted to talk to you about.'

'What about my memoirs?' he said, frowning.

'That too.'

Tess took the book out of her bag and turned to the photograph of Meredith.

'What was this event?' asked Tess, moving over to sit next to him on the sofa.

Charles's face softened. 'Ah, Bunny Bartlett's twenty-first,' he said warmly. 'The yacht belonged to her father, somebody terribly important in Hollywood, I believe. New money, but a wonderful party nevertheless. A six-tier coconut birthday cake, and Daddy had parked a brand-new Porsche for her at the harbour when we docked. Ah, happy days,' he smiled, sipping his Scotch.

'So were Meredith and Olivia Martin friends?'

'I assume so, although I only met them both for the first time that day. Talking of Meredith . . .'

Charles put down his glass and looked at Tess mischievously. 'You know I heard a delicious little rumour the other day about your employer.'

Tess felt a twitch of anticipation.

'I shouldn't really be telling you this,' he continued, 'but since I haven't been invited to the wedding, I don't see why it's my place to be discreet any longer.'

'What was it?'

'I was talking to Tony Scalino, a fabulous chef who does private catering for Gillian Pope.'

Tess looked at him blankly. 'You must know Gillian. Filthy-rich Upper East Side *grande dame*, excellent face-lift, friends with Meredith. Anyway, apparently Meredith and Gillian aren't just friends. They're *companions*.' Charles framed the last word with bunny-ear quotation marks, his voice a theatrical whisper.

'Companions?' asked Tess.

'*Lovers*,' said Charles.

'*Lovers?*' coughed Tess, choking on her whisky. 'Meredith has a lover? A *female* lover?'

Charles laughed, clapping his hands with glee. 'Darling, you'd be amazed how many people in New York society swing both ways, although it's the women who always keep it the most secret, particularly the very rich, powerful ones. The *clitorati*, as I like to call them.'

Tess thought back to what Leonard had told her many months before, how Meredith had never taken another lover after Howard. If Charles's rumour was correct, it seemed that she had, but she had chosen to keep it secret.

'It actually makes sense,' smiled Charles languorously. 'Howard had so many damn affairs you have to assume he wasn't getting too much action at home. I'm amazed Meredith's little secret hasn't got out before now, though. According to Tony, a grubby journalist was sniffing around at one point. Asked him a few questions about Meredith and Gillian but he never heard any more about it. Reckoned Meredith must have paid them off to stop digging.'

Brooke's eyes stared back to the photograph of Meredith and Olivia. One thing she had learned working with the paparazzi was that it was very difficult to fake intimacy. Certain things could not be staged convincingly. Those carefully stage-managed long-lens photographs of TV starlets 'working out' on a beach in very little looked real enough, but those 'fake' Hollywood couples, put together by their agents to promote a film or hide their sexuality, they never looked convincing. But Meredith and Olivia, now that looked real. Tess realized that that was what had jumped out at her when she had first seen the photograph. Intimacy; the way Meredith's head was resting on her friend's shoulder as Olivia laughed with carefree abandon.

'You don't think Meredith and Olivia were together?' said Tess.

Charles shrugged and glanced at the picture. 'I suppose it's possible. Everybody was jumping in and out of bed with everyone that summer. Now tell me, what did you think about chapter seven?'

Although the bed in her old room had been turned down and fresh flowers left on the nightstand in a Chinese vase, Brooke just couldn't face sleeping at her mother's. She couldn't put her finger on why, it just didn't feel right. She had managed to get through the day there, trying her best to enjoy all the traditional Christmas cele-brations with the rest of the family, but now she felt hemmed in, trapped. She waited until Meredith went up to her bedroom and followed her up, leaving William, Sean, Liz, and Leonard in the cinema room watching *Casablanca*.

'I have to go,' said Brooke, standing at the doorway of her mother's pale-blue bedroom.

'It's Christmas Day,' said Meredith, putting down the lipstick she had freshly applied. 'You can't be alone on Christmas Day.'

'Mother, we're leaving for Florida in thirty-six hours,' said Brooke. 'There's so much to do and I've still not properly packed.'

Not bothering to hide her displeasure, Meredith sighed. 'Very well. Is David coming round?'

'No, he's still at Belcourt. I won't see him until we get to the Keys.'

Meredith's shrewd eyes narrowed. 'Everything is all right, isn't it?' she asked, walking over to Brooke.

'Of course. Why shouldn't it be?'

Meredith's watery-blue eyes searched hers. 'You know you had a lucky escape.'

Brooke froze. *Did her mother know about Matt?* She had a sudden sick feeling that someone had taken a photograph of them together on Brooklyn Promenade.

'Lucky?' she stammered.

Her mother nodded gravely. 'Once that story about Olivia Martin was published in the *Spy* I thought Wendell might put pressure on David to *reconsider*.'

Relief washed over Brooke. 'Wendell knows as well as we do that there's no hidden scandal behind that story,' she said, looking away. Meredith put a hand up to Brooke's face.

'You do know you can tell me anything, don't you?' she asked, searching Brooke's face.

Brooke forced a smile. 'I know, I just have such a lot on my mind at the moment.'

Meredith looked at her for a moment, then leant forward and kissed her. 'Well, Happy Christmas, darling.'

'Happy Christmas,' said Brooke. *Happy*, she thought. *If only that were true.*

She was home for nine p.m., changing into her cream silk dressing gown before phoning David. Mostly she just let him talk; he was telling her about the Christmas gifts he had given and received, and snippets of Billington family gossip; horses they had recently bought; the new sailing boat Robert had on order; the pregnancy of his cousin Laura. The ordinariness of their conversation soothed her, and helped her blank out the turmoil that she had gone through over the past few days. When they had hung up, Brooke laid out her silk ivory shoes and Sabbia Rose underwear next to her Louis Vuitton cases, then put Guillaume's wedding gown on the bed.

'I'm going to wear it,' she whispered to herself. She turned to look at Nicholas's beautiful white gown, then quickly zipped it back in its dress bag, putting it away in the furthest part of her closet, trying to block out any memories she associated with it. She squashed the remaining items into her cases and snapped them shut. Just then her cell phone rang.

'Have you made a decision?'

Her mouth went dry as she recognized Matt's voice. 'Decision?' she croaked, feeling sick.

'Are you at home?' he asked, his voice sounding anxious.

'Yes,' she said, closing her eyes. *Not now*, she thought. *Not now.*

'I've just finished my shift. Can I see you?' said Matt. 'I can't stand not to see you on Christmas Day, not when I've been thinking about you for every minute since I last saw you.'

Brooke's heart felt as if it were tearing apart. He sounded so sincere, so loving.

'I don't think it's a good idea, Matt,' she said.

'Oh.'

The silence was like a siren.

'Matt, I'm getting married in a matter of days.'

'But what about the other night?' His voice was hurt, pleading.

'Matt, don't. It's better this way.'

'NO!' he shouted. 'Listen, I'm coming round. We should at least talk about it.'

'No,' she said, feeling irrational butterflies of fear.

'Please. Just give me five minutes.'

He is not a monster, she told herself. *You at least owe him that.*

'Five minutes,' she said.

He walked into her apartment silently, his eyes heavy and sad. Brooke stood in the centre of her living room, arms folded defensively in front of her.

493

'What changed, Brooke?' he said quietly. 'I thought we had something that night. I *know* we did.'

She forced herself to look at him. She had spent the last twenty-four hours demonizing him, convincing herself that he was a violent, snarling beast, but she didn't see any of that in the man standing in front of her. He was just a flawed man, perhaps a weak one, a man who had made mistakes like everyone else, and the fact that she could see him suffering – the red rings of tiredness around his handsome eyes, the furrowed brow – only made her more sad. She had never wanted to lie to Matt; for the last nine months he had been a good friend, her little oasis of sanity. Okay, so perhaps he was not the man she thought he once was, but she still felt she owed him the truth.

'You hit Katie,' she said, struggling to keep her voice flat and composed. 'You hit Susie too.'

He looked at her sharply. 'Who said that to you?'

'It doesn't matter. All that matters is that I know.'

'It's not true,' he said, his voice rising, trembling.

Brooke realized that she still wanted to believe him, she still wanted to believe that Susie and Grace had been lying, but the look in his eyes gave him away. Guilt.

'That's why you're going to Africa,' she added, suddenly seeing it clearly. 'You don't just want to get away from work, from New York, you want to escape from who you've become.'

She looked up and was shocked to see that he was crying.

'Do you know how bad it gets in the hospital?' he said quietly. 'When you try to save a child and you can't? When a twelve-year-old kid dies of a gunshot wound? When a man who has just got engaged and has his whole life ahead of him gets stabbed in the heart by some crazy homeless guy and dies on a table in front of you?'

'No, no, I don't and I'm sure it's hard. But it's no excuse to drink and take out your frustrations on other people. To *hurt* other people,' she said, her voice raised and trembling.

Matt looked at her, then glanced away, walking over to the window.

'Katie forgave me, you know,' he said, staring out. 'We'd separated but I convinced her I'd changed. We went on a holiday to patch things up, but . . . well, that's when she died.'

'And Susie?'

He slammed his fist against the wall. 'I lost my wife, Brooke!' he shouted. 'Forgive me if things haven't been too easy for me.'

He turned and stepped towards her. She could see the muscles in his jaw flex as he tried to contain his emotion. He took a deep breath.

'Brooke, I love you.'

He raised his hand to touch her cheek. His knuckles were grazed. She flinched and moved away.

'Just go, Matt,' she said calmly.

She walked over to the door and held it open. 'Please, just go.'

He walked past her, his face bleached with emotion, then paused in the doorway.

'But what about us, Brooke?' he asked.

'There is no us, there never was,' said Brooke sadly, and closed the door. And in that moment, Brooke realized she was right. And she knew exactly what she had to do.

65

Sitting at the back of Wendell Billington's Gulfstream, Liz waved away the stewardess offering her a cold glass of Dom Perignon, wishing this whole damned wedding would just hurry up and finish. It didn't help that she had always imagined she would be flying on this jet alone with him, side by side as business partners and as lovers, yet instead Wendell had graciously lent the G-5 to the Asgill family to fly from New York to Key Biscayne. She looked out through the small porthole window at the carpet of clouds below and curled her fingers into a fist. In four days' time it would be New Year and, frankly, Liz couldn't wait. This year had been ghastly and she needed to move on, leave it all behind her. Okay, so Wendell might have pulled out of financing the Skin Plus spin-off but she would find somebody else, she could meet the challenge – she would *enjoy* the challenge – and as soon as this dreadful wedding pantomime was over she would start looking for backers. She might even meet that investor at the wedding.

Glancing down the aisle, she saw Brooke engrossed in a magazine and Leonard asleep in a cream leather chair. She was sleepy herself, although the small bed behind her was occupied by a mountainous linen dress bag that contained her sister's gown. She groaned silently as Meredith stood up and approached her. *Just* what she needed.

'You're quiet,' said Meredith, taking a seat opposite Liz.

Liz smiled thinly. 'Well, the party hasn't started yet.'

'Are you sure it's not because of Rav?'

Liz almost laughed out loud. She had finally killed off that

romantic charade a week ago and her mother seemed to think it
mattered.

'Rav's and my relationship had run its course,' she said politely.

'Well, it was good of Wendell to let us use the jet, wasn't it?'
said Meredith, changing the conversation.

It stung just to hear his name. She had spent the whole Christmas
period feeling numb, emotionally exhausted. If she was honest, Liz
had been deeply hurt by Wendell's rejection. Somehow he had got
under her skin and made her drop her guard, then when she was
just softening – hell, even considering a relationship, for Christ's
sake – he had delivered his knockout punch. Liz Asgill wasn't used
to being on the canvas, her first instinct was always to go on the
offensive; but this time . . . well, this time she wasn't sure she knew
how to strike back.

'Wendell's just asserting his power and financial position by giving
us the jet,' said Liz caustically. 'He's reminding us who's boss.'

Meredith touched her hand to her daughter's knee. 'That's what
I wanted to talk to you about.'

Liz felt her back stiffen. 'If it's about the financing for Skin Plus,
I have two meetings lined up in the new year,' she said quickly.

'What I have to tell you may make you reconsider,' said Meredith.
She sat back in her chair and paused.

'I want you to be CEO of Asgill's.'

Liz looked at her mother, unblinking, not willing to let one trace
of emotion show.

'What about William?' she said. Her brother had not taken the
jet with them. Liz had thought it strange at the time, but now it
was beginning to make sense.

'He is stepping down. I spoke to him yesterday. It's a very long
story, but suffice to say William wants to spend more time with
his family.'

Liz wasn't sure if she had remembered to breathe. 'What
happened?' she asked.

'I can't go into that now. Problems with Paula, shall we say?
And he wants to make his marriage his priority from now on.'

She looked at her mother archly. 'Ah, for one moment I thought
it might have something to do with me being better suited for
the job.'

'Don't be like that, Liz,' said Meredith impatiently. 'I thought
this was what you've always wanted.'

'Yes. It is what I always wanted, but I've never wanted anything by default.'

'It's not default, Liz. You've always been good enough – the best, in fact – but the company was your brother's birthright. Maybe he isn't as ruthless as you, Liz, but as a family, I've always hoped we'd be able to work together, using all our skills and talents to make the company as great as it can be. But you've never wanted that. It's always been like a competition for you.'

'You *made* it a competition, Mother,' she replied harshly.

Meredith's cool face showed a flash of hurt and surprise. 'Is that really how you feel?'

Liz nodded, feeling a dull ache in her chest. 'It's always been about the others,' said Liz, her voice thick, tears welling behind her eyes. 'It's always been about Brooke's beauty, Sean's charm, William's so-called birthright. *What about me?*' she said, thumping her chest with her fist.

She looked away, angry that she'd revealed the burning sense of injustice she'd been carrying around with her for so long, ashamed that her mother had brought her to the edge of tears.

'You are my most capable child, Elizabeth,' said Meredith softly.

Liz turned on her. 'Then why do you reject me?' she hissed.

'Because you don't need me,' said Meredith quietly.

Liz turned towards the window, closing her eyes, trying to make sense of all these unfamiliar emotions. It was true that Liz had never needed anyone in order to succeed in the world, but didn't everyone need to be wanted? She suddenly felt cold and lonely.

Her mother had rejected her because she felt that Liz didn't need her. Wendell had wanted her, but discarded her because he didn't need her.

Liz took a deep breath and turned back to Meredith. 'I'd want to increase my shareholding,' she said. 'Build stock options and bonuses into my contract.'

Meredith nodded. 'As I'd expect.'

Her mother moved back down the plane to speak to the pilot, and Liz sat back in her seat. She should have felt on top of the world, but she just felt empty. Here she was, being handed what she'd always wanted, and yet somehow the victory felt hollow. *Come on, Liz*, she scolded herself. The business was hers, and the business had always meant everything to her. Just for a moment, she thought of Wendell, and a solitary tear escaped down her cheek. She brushed it away angrily. Yes, business meant everything to her. Because it had to.

66

Jewel Cay wasn't just a house, it was a private island off the Florida coast, one of the dozens of sandy dots of land that made up the beautiful Keys. In denim shorts and a T-shirt, Tess walked round the island's perimeter, watching the small ferry that linked Jewel Cay to the mainland shuttle back and forth to transport crates and boxes of food and champagne. On the tennis courts, workmen were erecting a huge marquee, while an army of gardeners were manicuring the lush grounds to perfection. As she walked, Tess could also see Wendell's security team sweeping the area to make sure it was locked-down in preparation for the arrival of VIP guests tomorrow. She thought of Jemma and the way she had infiltrated the security team at the Venus party with a smile, but that inevitably led her onto think of Sean Asgill, and she shook her head to clear the image.

Tess took off her flip-flops and went to sit on an outcrop of rock that jutted into the jade green ocean. It was late afternoon, and the sun was a soft saffron ball sinking low in the pastel sky. She relaxed her shoulders, trying to empty her mind, but it was impossible to unwind. Tess knew she should be happy – the last few months had been a bumpy ride, but she had made it: the wedding would go ahead the day after tomorrow and her job would be done. A barrage of threats from the Billington legal machine had put the lid on the Olivia Martin story being reported further, and Ted Kessler, having received his two-hundred-thousand-dollar cheque, had crawled quietly back under his rock. Even better, Meredith had made noises about giving Tess her bonus and – should she want it – a full-time role on staff once the wedding was over. She'd been a success. So why did she feel such a failure?

She watched a pelican swoop down from the sky, marvelling that it ever got off the ground with that fat body and ridiculous beak. Tess kept trying to think of other things, but of all the thousands of thoughts churning around her mind, she kept returning to one question. *How did Olivia Martin die?*

Hearing a scrabbling sound on the rock behind her, she turned. Her heart lurched as she saw it was Sean Asgill. *Him*. It was inevitable their paths would cross at the wedding, of course, and Tess had been preparing herself for this moment, rehearsing what she'd say to him, convincing herself that she was a professional and that she could deal with it. But right now, she wasn't so sure.

'Hey,' he said, sitting down next to her and sweeping his hand through his dirty-blonde hair.

'Hello.' She managed a weak smile, although her heart was thumping so hard she felt sure he could hear it. *Be normal*, she said to herself. *Make small talk.*

'So when did you get here?'

'About an hour ago,' said Sean. 'I'm staying here. Are you at the hotel?'

Tess nodded, pointing to the exclusive resort a few hundred metres away on the mainland where tomorrow's rehearsal dinner was being held. They both watched the pelican land on the water with a splash.

'Marriage, huh?' said Sean. 'It's a big old scary thing.'

Tess said nothing, biting her tongue.

'Although I guess maybe not if you're marrying the right person,' added Sean casually. She looked at him sideways, wanting to scream at his insensitivity, but then reminded herself that he didn't know she'd found the engagement ring in his bag. Tess wasn't supposed to know, so she couldn't complain. Trying to calm herself, she wondered when he was going to propose to Annabel. Maybe he would fly them both down to St Barts after the wedding and do it on New Year's Eve. Perhaps he'd even do it on the night of the wedding, during the fireworks display, possibly on this very secluded stretch of white beach. *Stop it, Tess*, she thought angrily. *Stop!*

'So how are you anyway?' he asked.

'Busy. It looks like I'll be staying on in New York after the wedding. Not sure what I'll do yet, though.'

A trace of a frown appeared between his brows. 'Oh. Well, good luck with it all,' he said lamely.

She turned away. The lapping ocean reminded her of their time in Maui and yet here they were, only weeks later, talking like virtual strangers.

'You'd better get back to Annabel,' she said, throwing a pebble into the water.

'What?'

His surprised tone made her turn back.

'Annabel, your girlfriend. Maybe we can all have a drink later. It would be nice to finally meet her properly.'

The look on his face was one of genuine puzzlement. 'I haven't seen Annabel in a month, Tess.'

It was her turn to feel confused. 'What are you talking about? She's your fiancée, isn't she? Or about to be.'

'What are *you* talking about, Tess?'

She laughed lightly. 'I know you have to keep it quiet until after Brooke and David's wedding, but your mother told me that you were going to propose to Annabel. Although you probably should have told me yourself. I do need to know about things like that. It is my job,' she added a touch sarcastically.

But Sean was shaking his head. 'I don't understand,' he said. 'Why would she say something like that?'

Tess stood up and clambered off the rock back onto the pale sand. It was just typical of him to keep up this ridiculous pretence.

'Sean, don't be so stupid,' she said with irritation. 'Meredith called me in Maui and told me that when you came to New York you picked up a ring of hers that you were going to give to Annabel. At first I didn't believe her, but it was in your bag. A big sapphire and diamond ring.'

His cheeks had turned pink in anger but she didn't care if he hated her for snooping through his stuff.

'*That* ring?' he said incredulously. 'Kinda old-fashioned looking?' He stopped and shook his head. 'That ring was supposed to be a surprise gift from the family to Brooke for her wedding. "Something blue", you know? Mom gave me the ring to use the stones. I have an amazing jeweller friend in London who has reset the stones into a necklace. I had it with me in Maui because I was going to take it straight home to London.'

Tess shuddered as adrenaline rushed through her body. Was he telling the truth? She looked into his eyes and saw nothing but confusion.

'Why would Mom say that?' he said, his expression clouding with disapproval. 'She knew Annabel and I weren't together any more.'

Tess frowned, recalling Meredith's cool words on the phone that night.

You're in Maui? Sean loves it there. I assume he tipped you off? Knowing Sean he probably tried it on with you.

Meredith had guessed! She had guessed that something had happened between them and had acted quickly to halt it in its tracks. She looked at Sean, his eyes outraged yet anxious, and she knew she believed him about the ring.

'Well, I suppose she doesn't approve of me and you,' said Tess, trying to contain her fury at the betrayal. 'And your mother always gets her way.'

Sean stepped towards her on the sand and Tess shivered. The sun had dipped below the horizon and it had suddenly become cool.

'Has she got her way, Tess?'

'Well, has it really finished with Annabel? I saw some red-carpet photograph of you with her a week after Maui.'

He nodded and took hold of her fingers. 'I didn't lie to you in Maui, Tess. I *had* finished with Annabel and yes, that photograph was taken at the premiere of her new film after Maui, but Annabel begged me to go with her. The press didn't know our relationship had finished and I agreed to keep up the pretence just until the publicity for her new film was over. But you left Maui so quickly and made it pretty clear you didn't want anything to happen between us, I thought you wouldn't care. I also didn't want you to know you'd hurt me.'

'I hurt *you*?' she gasped, barely daring to believe him.

He squeezed her fingers more tightly. 'I know you think I'm incapable of committing to anything, but it's not true. When we were in Maui, all I was thinking about was how you could come back to London and we could be happy together. Stupid, isn't it?'

Tess searched his face, wanting to believe him, but still too scared to. She could see that the usual mischievous twinkle in his eyes had dimmed into a softer sparkle of hope.

'Is it true?' she croaked.

He nodded, then pulled her closer and kissed her, soft lips brushing tenderly against hers, and at that moment, moulding herself to his body, surrounded by the glory of nature, she knew just how well they fitted.

'Don't leave me again,' he smiled, stroking her hair. 'Promise me.'

She inhaled, her breath shuddering, then laughed. She had spent so long in the wrong relationship, surrounding herself with things she didn't need – the smart apartments, the high-flying job, the exotic holidays – desperately trying to convince herself it was right; suddenly now, being here with Sean, just felt an enormous, joyous relief.

'I won't,' she whispered. 'Believe me, I won't.'

Tess knocked on the door of Meredith's suite at Jewel Cay. Sean had gone to the airport to pick up William and Paula, and Tess knew there was only a small window of opportunity to confront her. The older woman was standing on the balcony of the grand old house in a long billowing linen dress, white hair swept into a chignon. She moved back into the room, closing the French doors behind her.

'I was expecting you to come,' she said flatly.

'Really?' said Tess, determined to keep her cool.

'I saw you on the beach talking to Sean.' Meredith's face did not show one trace of guilt or discomfort. Tess knew that her employer was glacial at the best of times, but she wondered if ice really did run through her veins. She must have guessed that Tess would find out the truth about her attempt to derail her relationship with Sean, and yet it did not seem to bother her one jot. *And why would it?* thought Tess bitterly. *I obviously mean nothing to her.* She was disposable, just another employee like the gardeners and the maids. As for Sean, she supposed Meredith would think she had acted absolutely and unfailingly in his best interests.

'Yes, we were talking,' said Tess evenly. 'And he told me that his proposal to Annabel was complete fabricated nonsense.'

'Ah, the business about the ring,' said Meredith coolly, gazing back out of the window. 'I believe I made an understandable mistake.'

'Mistake?' spat Tess. 'You knew exactly what the ring was for but you just lied to me, Meredith. You just didn't want Sean and me to be together.'

'A mother has to do what she has to do, Tess,' she said simply. 'I did what I thought was right.'

A well of fury grew in Tess's stomach, as she thought about the hours of hard work and dedication she had put into protecting Meredith's plans and ambitions. It hadn't just been a nine-to-five job – Tess had actually cared about the wellbeing and status of the Asgill family. Well, she was not going to protect her another moment.

'It's not the only thing you've lied to me about, is it?' said Tess.

This time the old woman looked back at her. 'I don't understand you.'

Tess steadied herself. She knew she was taking a risk in proceeding; the last thing she wanted to do was jeopardize her relationship with Sean again, and she knew he wouldn't take too kindly to threats and accusations about his mother, but Tess felt so close to the truth she could not stop herself.

'You and Olivia Martin were having an affair, weren't you?' she said in a low, controlled voice.

Meredith looked at Tess with genuine surprise, then threw her head back and laughed, her tight, white face pinching up into a jigsaw of lines.

'Oh my dear,' she cried. 'How ridiculous you are.'

'Am I?' said Tess. 'You've had discreet "companions" since Howard died; in fact you had them throughout your marriage. But you were in love with Olivia.'

'This is nonsense,' hissed Meredith, waving her hand dismissively. 'You know nothing about me.'

It was at that moment that Tess knew she was right. It was the sort of intuitive bullishness that had got her to the very top of journalism, a charge and passion for her career that she knew she sorely missed.

'I know that you and Olivia were together on Bunny Bartlett's yacht in Catalina,' said Tess, ticking off the points on her fingers. 'I know you were still close just before your wedding. I know you and Olivia were seen arguing at Riverview an hour before she vanished.'

She paused and looked at Meredith, whose face was now pale and unsmiling. 'But what I *don't* know is if you were involved in Olivia's disappearance,' said Tess. 'If you were, I suggest you tell me right now. You can't escape the truth forever, Meredith, I think we both know that.'

Meredith sat down in a wicker chair. Tess could see that her hands on the armrests were trembling as she realized she had been caught out.

It was a full minute before she spoke.

'I loved Howard, I truly loved him,' she said, her eyes sparkling with tears. 'Love isn't about passion, Tess, whatever you might think. Love is about understanding, and Howard and I *understood* one another. He was driven and dynamic, everyone who met him knew how successful he was going to be, but we did it together, we were a good team. In Howard I got what I had been taught to want and need. A companion, a wonderful provider, a friend. We had four beautiful children together.'

'But you were never in love with him.'

She gave the slightest shrug. Her mouth turned down sadly. 'I never felt those feelings for him. Passion, desire. Things I felt for Olivia,' she said quietly. Tess felt a rush of conflicting emotions: relief, validation, fear. As much as she wanted to hate Meredith right now for jeopardizing her relationship with Sean, she still didn't want her to be a murderer. But she had to know.

'Did you kill Olivia Martin?' said Tess.

'NO!' shouted Meredith, slamming her hand against the chair. She glared at Tess for a moment, then looked away. 'But you're right, Tess, as you always are. I was in love with Olivia.'

She stood up and walked to the window, eyes searching the darkening horizon.

'I first met Olivia on Bunny's yacht. She was so beautiful and exciting, so alive. It was a year before Howard and I were married. Olivia and I could only make time to see each other about once a month, but we spoke all the time, wrote letters. And yes, we were still together until the night of her disappearance.'

Tess moved a little closer.

'Tell me about the night of your wedding – the truth, Meredith. Everything. I need to know what you were quarrelling about.'

When she turned back, the old woman's expression was fearful and pained.

'Olivia was drunk. High. It always made her aggressive. She cornered me by the fountain and said we needed to talk. I told her it was my wedding day and begged her to wait, but she wouldn't, so we agreed to meet in the rose garden a few minutes later.'

'What time was this?' asked Tess.

'Maybe eleven fifteen,' she sighed. 'When we did meet, she looked so hard-faced. She told me she wanted money. Ten thousand dollars a month to keep quiet about *us*.'

'Did you agree?'

'It's such a lot of money,' she said with a small, hard laugh. 'But still, I didn't want it to come out. I knew very well why Howard married me: *respectability*. Times were different back then, Tess. A story about Olivia and me would have been a scandal, but it would have been a *disaster* for a family cosmetics company selling lipsticks and blusher to wholesome Middle America. It seems ridiculous today, but that's just the way it was.'

Tess frowned. 'Surely she was just bluffing, though?' she asked. 'She had just as much to lose. Why would Olivia allow a story like that to come about herself?'

She shrugged her thin shoulders. 'Olivia's career was over. She was twenty seven and there were younger, prettier girls on the scene. Her TV career had failed to launch and she couldn't have stayed as an Asgill's girl for much longer. Besides, I was scared. I was young and it was my wedding day. Forgive me if I didn't think as rationally as you would have liked.'

Tears glistening on her cheeks, Meredith took a sip of water from a glass standing on the dresser, her hand shaking as she picked it up.

'I told Olivia we'd talk about it after my honeymoon, then she turned around and left while I went back to the party to watch the fireworks. That was the last time I ever saw her . . .' Finally Meredith's voice cracked and she covered her face, sobbing at the memory of a love lost but never forgotten.

'I believe you,' said Tess quietly, suddenly feeling as if she was intruding on someone's grief. Meredith looked up as Tess walked to the door.

'Forgive me about Sean, Tess,' she said. 'I was wrong, I know that now.'

Tess forced a smile. 'Yes, you were,' she said. 'But I'm still going to find out what happened to Olivia.'

If only she knew how.

67

Brooke was still half asleep when she felt the bed move. She turned her head, squinting at the sun creeping through the long white shutters, and saw David sitting there, smiling at her.

'Are you a sight for sore eyes,' he said softly, touching her cheek.

'You're here?' she said groggily, struggling back on the pillows. It was the 28th of December. David should have arrived the previous night, but he had phoned to tell her he had to fly to Washington en route to attend some urgent meeting about his new show.

'Flew straight back from DC,' he said. 'I'm sorry I haven't seen you all week, baby, but I figured it was better to get all the meetings out of the way so they won't be disturbing us on honeymoon.'

'Which they will . . .' she said with a slow smile.

'Which they will *not*,' he said firmly, sliding over to lie next to her.

'They'd better not,' she grinned, putting her arms around his neck. 'I want you all to myself.

'Well here I am,' he said, kissing her neck and bare shoulders. Brooke giggled, feeling herself relax with the touch of his lips against her skin. After the emotional roller-coaster of the last few days, she had been frantic about how she would feel about David when they finally came face to face. Would her guilt overtake her? Would she baulk at his touch? But as soon as her eyes met his, she felt such an enormous surge of relief and love that the memory of what had happened with Matt just melted away. She pulled him closer and beamed into their kiss. When she finally let him go, David sat up and pulled a piece of paper from the back of his trouser pocket.

'Alessandro's countdown,' he said, smiling. 'Have you got one of these?'

She nodded, rolling her eyes. David dramatically cleared his throat and began reading aloud.

'Meet pastor three p.m. Return to hotel to change four twenty p.m. Final debrief five thirty-five p.m. Rehearsal dinner seven thirty p.m.'

'Well, he's nothing if not organized,' said Brooke. 'He was having pink kittens you weren't here yesterday.'

'Well, there's something he missed out from the list.'

Brooke looked puzzled. 'I don't think we're going to squeeze much else into today,' she said.

'One last date,' said David, looking more serious.

'A last date?' said Brooke, her heart beating too fast. *Last date as in he is going to finish with me?*

'I was hoping we could slip off after the dinner,' said David. 'Just me and you. I want one last date with my girlfriend before she becomes my wife.'

She started laughing, taking in big gulps of air.

'One last date,' she said. 'Yes, that sounds lovely.' And she threw back the sheet and pulled him into the bed.

In an emperor-sized bed in an executive suite at the Pelicano hotel, Sean Asgill rolled over, panting. Finally, he turned back towards Tess and grinned.

'Come back with me,' he said.

Tess laughed and propped her arm behind her head. 'Can we talk about it after the wedding?' she asked, avoiding his eyes.

'So you mean you want to take things slow?' said Sean, resting his head up on his elbow.

'Maybe.'

He bent over and took her nipple between his lips, gently pulling on it, then running his tongue around it in lazy swirls.

'You mean slow like this?'

'Oh God,' gasped Tess.

On her bedside cabinet, her mobile suddenly began to buzz.

'Leave it,' came Sean's muffled voice.

'Can't,' she said, pulling away and planting a kiss on the top of his head. 'We've got guests arriving from three continents, and hundreds of media outlets baying.'

She swung her legs out of bed and snatched up the phone.

'Ouch,' said Sean with mock hurt. 'I never had you pegged as the love 'em and leave 'em sort.'

509

'Only when I've got important things to do,' she laughed, sliding out of bed. She ran into the bathroom and jumped under the shower, still smiling as she enjoyed the cool water running all over her sticky body.

'Only when I've got important things to do . . .' she repeated softly to herself. There was something about that phrase that was ringing a bell in the back of her mind, something she had heard in the last few days that had been nagging at her, something which didn't quite . . .

'Oh my God!' she whispered. Suddenly she knew why. The last piece of the puzzle slipped into place with a flash of such clarity that Tess cursed herself for not seeing it before. Shutting off the water, she jumped out of the cubicle, and rubbed a towel across her body vigorously.

Scrambling into a white T-shirt dress and flip-flops, she grabbed her mobile.

'Hey, sexy,' called Sean from the bed, 'see you here for lunch?'

'Yeah, sure,' she said distractedly, hurrying out of the room as she called Jemma. She glanced at the time on the phone's screen, hoping that Jemma had arrived in Florida from Toronto.

'Are you here yet?' she asked anxiously as soon as her friend picked up.

'Yeah, I'm at the hotel. I called you ten minutes ago, didn't you get my message?' said Jemma. 'I got in really late last night but didn't want to disturb you.'

'What room are you in?'

'One of the cottages by the pool. The blue one at the end of the row.'

Tess ran down the stairwell, her flip-flops clattering against the marble floor. The door to the cottage was open and inside she could see Jemma sitting on the patio having breakfast under a gently fluttering palm tree.

'Hey there you,' said Jemma, clearly enjoying herself, 'come and try these croissants, they're amazing.'

Putting her finger to her lips, Tess glanced up and down the beach, then beckoned to Jemma to come back inside the cottage.

Frowning, Jemma pulled the patio door closed and followed Tess over to a white sofa under the ceiling fan.

'You've found something out, haven't you?' said Jemma quietly, and Tess nodded.

'What I've found out is that Meredith was having an affair with Olivia Martin.'

Jemma looked wide-eyed. 'You're kidding!'

'It seems Olivia was trying to blackmail Meredith to keep quiet about their affair, which is why Mary-Ann Henner saw them arguing before the fireworks display.'

Jemma mulled it over. 'How much was she blackmailing her for?'

'Ten thousand dollars a month,' replied Tess.

'Shit . . . Well, so much for the broke, depressed Olivia theory, then. That certainly doesn't sound like the mind-set of someone who was going to commit suicide a couple of hours later.'

Tess nodded. 'Exactly what I thought, especially as Meredith didn't cough up immediately. She says she asked her to wait and discuss it after she got back from her honeymoon, so all the more reason for Olivia to hang around.'

'It could still have been an accident,' said Jemma, distractedly brushing flakes of almond croissant from her shirt. 'She was a boozer and a pill-popper, wasn't she?'

Tess stared down at her fingers, deep in thought.

'Have you got Mary-Ann Henner's phone number?' asked Tess.

'Sure.'

Jemma was already scrolling through her BlackBerry. 'What do you want me to ask her?'

'Ask her who she had sex with in the rose garden on the night of Meredith and Howard's wedding.'

Jemma winced in disbelief. 'Come on, Tess. That's a bit hard-core, even for someone as shameless as me.'

Tess had a firm look on her face.

'You said Mary-Ann told you that she had sex with someone in the rose garden some time around eleven fifteen, right? Well, that's just around the time Olivia tried to blackmail Meredith, also in the rose garden,' said Tess. She thought back to her visit to Riverview, how she and Lori, the assistant manager, had walked past the secluded garden around that time of night; how still and clear it had been; how she could hear every noise, from the crickets in the trees to a couple walking across the lawns to their room.

'It was all go in the rose bushes that night,' said Jemma, raising a shaped brow.

Tess didn't smile. 'Mary-Ann also said the guy she was with

didn't show up for the fireworks, which is when Lori Adams thought something might have happened to Olivia.'

Jemma was hesitating, her thumb over the 'call' button of her BlackBerry.

'Just make the call, Jem,' said Tess. 'And put it on loudspeaker so I can hear.'

'But what do you think she's going to tell us?'

'I think I know who was with Mary-Ann that evening,' said Tess with conviction. 'I think he heard Olivia's threats and decided to shut her up.'

Jemma pulled a face, then made the call. 'Wish me luck,' she said.

Tess walked onto the balcony, leaving Jemma to speak to Mary-Ann, although she could hear both sides of the conversation.

'Mary-Ann?' said Jemma.

'Yes?'

'Er. Hi. Happy Christmas. It's Jemma Davies, I came round a few days ago.'

'Of course. How are you?'

She sounded buoyant, full of festive spirit.

'Uh, Mary-Ann, I have to ask you a very personal question,' said Jemma quickly.

'Shoot,' chuckled Mary-Ann, 'you know me.'

'It's about the night of Howard Asgill's wedding.'

'Found out anything interesting?'

Jemma looked up at Tess.

'I think we're getting there.'

She paused and took a breath. 'I need to know who it was you had sex with that night in the rose garden at Riverview.'

Mary-Ann chuckled again. 'My, my. That *is* personal.'

'Please, Mary-Ann.'

Mary-Ann paused and both Tess and Jemma could hear the sound of ice cubes clinking in a glass.

'If you must know, it was Leonard Carter. Meredith's brother.'

Tess and Jemma exchanged a look.

'Yeah, I know what you're thinking,' continued Mary-Ann. 'Should have lost my cherry to my high-school sweetheart rather than a one-night stand at a wedding? But hormones don't work like that, do they, darling? I'd been at Riverview for a couple of days before the wedding. Sorting things out for Howard, you know how it is. We'd gotten pretty friendly, me and Leonard, and gosh, he was so good-looking. A real charmer.'

'And did you leave the rose garden together?' said Jemma, looking over to an anxious Tess.

'No. I ran off when I heard someone coming into the garden,' she laughed bitterly. 'I didn't want to get caught with the bride's brother, for crying out loud. I was supposed to be working, not fucking.'

'Thanks Mary-Ann,' said Jemma awkwardly. 'I didn't mean to drag up old memories.'

Mary-Ann laughed again. 'Memories are all I got left, sweetheart. You take care now.'

Jemma put down the receiver and looked at Tess, her mouth open.

'Leonard,' she whispered. 'It was Leonard.'

Tess nodded. 'I knew.'

The rehearsal dinner at the Pelicano hotel was beautiful. Alessandro had worked his magic, transforming the hotel's orangery into a sophisticated yet intimate space. The eight round tables were simply covered with French brocade linens, and each had a centrepiece of pale yellow and white blooms cascading from a large cream vase. It was as understated as you could get considering the occasion. The seventy-five guests – family and close friends plus a smattering of celebrities and political dignitaries – had been served the finest wines from cut-glass crystal, and the menu offered the state's finest produce: braised artichokes with fennel and lemon, fresh lobster and miniature key lime pies from Joe's Stone Crab. When the coffee had been served, Wendell Billington stood to give a surprisingly heartfelt speech welcoming Brooke to the family, then Sean brought the house down with a story about the time Brooke, aged seven, had written a letter to Prince Charles proposing marriage. Ignoring his sister's blushes, Sean revealed that the palace had been good enough to write back to politely decline on the grounds that HRH was already married to Princess Diana.

After the speeches, the French windows were opened and the party spilled out onto the hotel's terrace and down into the tropical gardens. Excusing herself from Rose Billington, Brooke quietly slipped down the stairs and into the tropical gardens, finding a hidden nook surrounded by mango trees. She sat down on a cold stone bench and breathed in the warm evening air, enjoying a little time out, and pretending for just one minute she was plain old Brooke Asgill again. All evening she had enjoyed having people tell her she looked beautiful, fielding the wide-eyed enquiries about Nicholas's long biscuit silk dress, but right now she needed a moment to sit and be still, to listen to the sea, smell the blossoms, to think for herself. Her heart sank a little as she heard footsteps on the path. She looked up, expecting to see David; he had been so wonderful all day, so solicitous, so kind, as if he understood that the wedding, however perfect, would be difficult for her, and she wouldn't have been surprised if he had come to check she was okay. But it wasn't David, it was Tess.

'Oh, hi Tess,' she said, forcing a smile as Tess came to sit beside her.

'Was everything okay in there?' she asked.

Brooke sighed, knowing she couldn't lie to her friend. Besides, she was the only one who knew the whole story about her and Matt. Well, most of it, anyway.

'I'm just trying to convince myself certain things didn't happen,' said Brooke quietly. 'So far it's working.'

'So the thing with Matt—'

'It's definitely all over,' said Brooke quietly.

Tess nodded. 'You made the right decision.'

Brooke looked down at her hands. She hadn't told Tess why she had no plans to see Matt Palmer ever again. Why not let her assume it had been a decision based on her love of David? Hell, it might even be true.

'The right decision . . . yes,' said Brooke. 'In fact, I'm off on a date with my fiancé right now. David should be here any minute to take me for a last romantic interlude as a single person.'

'Ah, well in that case I'd better go.'

'Back to Sean?' said Brooke, looking up with a smile.

'I don't know what you're talking about,' said Tess wryly.

'I saw that kiss by the rest rooms after Sean's speech.'

'You did?' Tess shook her head, laughing. 'I suppose I should have told you earlier – not that there was anything to tell. We had a little thing in Hawaii but I thought he was trouble.'

Brooke raised her brow.

Tess shrugged. 'But, even if he is, I like him a lot. One thing this year has taught me is that you can be with someone for the longest time, the person who you think is right for you, but it can still be wrong. And that person that you think is wrong for you can be so, so right.' Tess giggled. 'If any of that gibberish made any sense?'

Brooke nodded. 'Perfect sense.'

Just then, David appeared from the darkness. In a midnight-blue suit, his hair cropped close to his head, Tess thought he looked like James Bond.

'Well, I think I'll leave you two lovebirds to it,' said Tess, heading back towards the hotel as David took Brooke's hand. He led her down into the gardens, down a torchlit path, until they reached a dock, where a small boat was waiting for them.

'Oh honey,' said Brooke, her eyes sparkling, 'it's perfect.'

David climbed on board, helping Brooke in her long dress across the rickety gangplank.

He started the engine and the boat carved through the water, which was still and black with ribbons of silver dancing across its surface. In just a few minutes they had arrived at another small island, just a circle of sand and scrub barely two hundred metres wide. David pulled a torch and a small rucksack bag from behind the wheel and threw them onto the beach then, with an 'allez-oop!', he hoisted a laughing Brooke over his shoulder and splashed to the shore. It was deliciously deserted and romantic on the beach, the sand cold beneath their bare feet, the full moon and stars providing a shimmering light. David spread a blanket on the sand, popped a bottle of fizzing champagne and poured out two paper cups.

'To tomorrow,' he said, tapping his cup against hers. In the distance they could hear music and laughter drifting from the hotel, and Brooke laughed, hiking up her dress and crossing her legs, thinking that – despite the million dollars' worth of jewels she was wearing: long chandelier Harry Winston earrings and a rope of diamonds borrowed from Rose Billington – she still felt like Robinson Crusoe.

'Oh, why don't we do this more often, honey?' she asked happily.

'Trespass on a deserted key with a rucksack full of alcohol?' he smiled.

She leant across and kissed him and thought how much she liked this David. Relaxed, playful. It was how he had been the first time she met him all those months ago in Biarritz: that was the man she fell in love with. It was never about the money, the position in New York society, or the guaranteed lifetime of luxury and privilege. It was about a man who cared for her deeply and who she cared for back. But they didn't live on a deserted island where they could pretend they were castaways – they lived in New York, where their lives were public property and where they could never truly relax, always knowing that someone was watching or snapping or even simply gossiping about them. She was sure this life wouldn't get any easier when they moved to Washington, and when David embarked on his political career, the chances were it would only get worse.

Sitting in the silence, surrounded by just sky and sea, a note of sadness invaded her happy mood. Brooke knew of course it was this situation, the feeling of being funnelled into a restricted, narrow life, which had led her to Matt. Yes, he was good-looking, yes they had been friends, and yes, there was the lure and nostalgia of a less complicated past. But above all, Matt was a liferaft. She hadn't really wanted to run away to Africa with him, but part of her *did* want to run away. Lying here, away from the circus, she could see that clearly now.

'I've got you a present,' said David.

She looked up at him with surprise and alarm. 'I thought we weren't bothering.'

David smiled. 'Well, this present will make me happy if it makes you happy.'

He pulled out a small suede pouch and handed it to her. She tipped the contents into the palm of her hand and looked down to see a set of keys.

'What are these for?' she asked, thinking back to a few weeks earlier when she had seen a cherry-red vintage Mercedes parked on a street in SoHo and had drooled over it.

'Look David, it's a *Hart to Hart* car,' she had laughed, reminded of the cheesy Eighties detective series she loved watching on cable. It would be typical of David's thoughtful extravagance to track down the owner and buy it.

'Is it a car?' she asked.

David chuckled. 'No, the apartment on Riverside Drive, that triplex you loved.'

Brooke gasped out loud. 'But how can we . . . ?' she began, but he put up a hand to silence her.

'Honey, I know you've never been keen on a permanent move to Washington, so I've been thinking over and over how we can work this out,' he said. 'I've spoken to Edward at Yellow Door and he says you can work three days a week. I could fly back from Washington to New York on Fridays and stay until Tuesday. My meeting yesterday was about taping the show one day a week from the studio in Manhattan, and the producer isn't totally against the idea, so splitting our time between DC and New York shouldn't be that difficult.'

She closed her eyes, clasping her fist around the cold metal. *He was so sweet. He was so lovely. Surely love didn't have to be this complicated.*

The words came tumbling from her mouth before she could stop them. 'Something happened between me and Matt Palmer,' she said, unable to keep the truth from her loving, honourable man any longer.

He stared at her for a few moments, his expression one of incomprehension, then cold, bitter knowing. 'What happened exactly?' he said with such icy composure it frightened her.

She nodded, the shame filling her up, sitting on her heart like marble. 'We kissed. We fooled around . . .'

'You had sex with him,' he stated coolly.

'No. I stopped. I couldn't do it.'

'How loyal of you,' he spat bitterly. 'When was this?'

'When you were in Vegas,' she said, not daring to breathe.

David stood up, grabbed the bottle of champagne and hurled it into the sea.

'Fuck!' he roared. Brooke reflected that it was the only time she'd ever heard him swear.

'David, I'm so sorry,' she said, scrambling to her feet, her hand outstretched, but he moved away from her.

'What a laugh you two must have been having behind my back,' he said, his mouth turned sourly downward. '"Oh David, come to Matt's dinner party,"' he mimicked, '"he's such a good friend."'

'We *were* friends,' pleaded Brooke. 'It was only once. I was scared about the wedding and confused about our future.'

'Well, I'm sorry that a future with me is so disturbing,' he deadpanned.

She tried to hold his arms, but he shook her off and turned his face away.

'David, you know I love you.'

He looked at her and all she could see in his eyes was pain. 'Do I?'

He was right. What could he possibly know about her feelings when, here she was, hours away from their wedding, completely unsure of what she felt, of what she really wanted? Thousands of happy memories flashed through her mind: those first dates, their trips to the Hamptons, the Bahamas, even just sharing breakfast in bed on a Saturday, lazily swapping snippets from the morning papers. But was he the one? Her one true love? Was it unrealistic to think that – out of all the billions of people in the world – you could find the one person that was a perfect fit?

Brooke certainly knew that she had compromised with David. He was handsome, clever, kind, and she *adored* him, there was no question about that; but neither was there any question that signing up to a life with David was a life of standing two steps behind him, a curious mixture of living both in the public eye and yet in the shadows. Maybe that was what she might have wanted once, when she and her Brown friends went walking along the cliff-path below David's home, but now it felt as if she were cheating herself, cheating herself out of a happier life. Brooke knew she could lie to him, she could back-pedal, fudge the facts, tell him it all meant nothing. But it did, it had. Whatever and whoever Matt had turned out to be, it had been more than a silly fling; it had been her own heart telling her something.

'This isn't about you, David,' she said finally. 'I love you. I know it doesn't sound like it right now, but I do, I honestly do. This is about our lives, it's about the life we would have together.'

'But if you're unhappy with the way I—' he began, but she cut him off.

'No,' she said firmly. 'It's not that I'm unhappy with you, honey. Don't ever think that. I'm just unhappy with our lives.'

The relief she felt in finally admitting it out loud was almost physical. Her back straightened and her ears sang. It was as if she was finally taking a step towards freedom, but she realized with a terrible sinking feeling that that freedom could mean giving up David.

'What's *happened* to you, Brooke?' he asked, unable to disguise his pain. 'There's a million girls who'd want to swap places with you.'

'Maybe,' she said slowly, 'maybe you're right.'

Her stomach clenched with fear, but then out of nowhere she thought of Eileen Dunne and their first lunch together at The London.

'Someone told me once that marriage isn't just about love,' said Brooke, finding strength and courage in the words. 'It's about wanting to go on life's adventure with your chosen partner.'

'So you don't want to do that with me?' His tone was desperate and woeful.

She reached up and touched his face tenderly. 'More than anything, David. But I just don't think we want to go on the same adventure.'

He blinked at her, as if she had said something unfathomable.

'So that's it,' he said flatly.

Suddenly Brooke felt overcome with an unfamiliar emotion: anger. Anger at the situation, anger at him, anger for him. He had been bred for this life; he had never chosen it himself. This kind, sensitive man was being pushed into something he'd never asked for.

'Is this really the life *you* want, David?' she asked. 'The politics, the ambition? Is this really all you've ever wanted?'

'Of course, I . . .'

'Okay, so if you wanted to be president one day so badly, why aren't you running for Congress next year? Why are you putting it off for the Washington show? I know you love working in television, but that's not just it, is it?'

'You know this, Brooke,' he said with irritation. 'The Washington show is a positioning tool; it raises my profile and sets me up as a serious political player.'

'Oh bullshit!' spat Brooke, surprised at herself. 'You're just postponing the inevitable.'

'And what's that?'

'Taking up a life someone else chose for you.'

Indecision flickered across his face and then it was gone. 'This life might have been chosen for me, Brooke, but it's what I want.'

'It's not,' she said, grabbing both his shoulders. 'You're too honest; you're too decent for the life they want for you. Why are you doing it? Why?'

'It's what I want,' he repeated, but he wouldn't meet her eye.

'Well, it's *you* I want, David. Not your life, not your family – you.

If you still want me, then maybe it doesn't have to end like this,' she said desperately, tears beginning to roll down her face. 'We can have another life, David. We can start again somewhere else. London, LA; anywhere where you're not being crushed by the weight of expectation.'

'I have ambitions too, Brooke,' he said softly. 'It's not just my family; I want to succeed for myself. Yes, they have certain expectations of me, I'm aware of that – no, I *respect* that, because I happen to think family is important. But I'm not a robot, I can make my own choices.'

Brooke listened to the slow laps of water rolling towards them and thought about the cruel irony of the setting. This was how their relationship had begun eighteen months ago, a first kiss on a beach in bright moonlight. Now their relationship seemed destined to finish in exactly the same way. Perhaps it was the pressure his family had brought to bear on him over a lifetime of conditioning, or perhaps it was genuinely David's own choice to pursue politics. Either way, he was unwilling to compromise those ambitions for her. And, for her part, she was unwilling to compromise herself. She was unwilling to become part of the Billington machine, but, more than that, she was unwilling to become a part of David. And that was the saddest thing of all. Finally, Brooke began to sob.

'I'm sorry,' she whispered, 'I never meant to hurt you. I do love you.'

Slowly, sadly, he took a step towards her and took her into his arms.

'I'm sorry too,' he whispered. 'I really am.'

68

By the time Tess got back to the party, most guests had left the tables. Some were laughing and drinking champagne in the garden, others had begun to drift back to their hotel rooms. Looking around for Sean, she saw a glint of rich red hair. Paula Asgill was sitting alone at a side table, staring down into her coffee.

'Paula,' she smiled, walking over. 'I haven't seen you in two weeks.'

Paula looked up and smiled. 'No, there's been lots to do. Lots to think about,' she said with unexpected warmth.

Tess was pleasantly surprised; Paula's demeanour had always been so prim and icy, but there was a softness around the eyes that hadn't been there a few weeks ago. Perhaps not every crisis was a bad thing, she thought.

'Did you get my interview with *Metropolitan* magazine arranged?' asked Paula.

Tess nodded. 'Next week, it's all set. Full copy approval.'

Alongside everything else she'd had to do over the last few weeks, Tess had set up an interview for Paula with *Metropolitan*, a smart society read that ran puff-pieces alongside glossy photo-shoots of all the Park Avenue Princesses who mattered. Tess had struck a bargain with Shelley Vine, the editor; she would get a scoop that would reverberate all around Manhattan, as long as she promised to treat Paula and her family in the most sympathetic manner possible. Tess could tell that Paula just wanted to get her story out there, to finally be free of the burden, but, having talked to Shelley, Tess genuinely believed that Paula could come out of it unscathed.

'Well, thanks for everything, Tess.'

'I was just doing my job.'

Paula shook her head, meeting Tess's gaze. 'No, it was more than that.'

'So what happens now?' said Tess, a little embarrassed. 'I hear that William is stepping down from the company.'

'Yes, from the CEO job at least. Leonard wants to retire in the new year, so William might take on his international development role, but we'll see,' she smiled again. 'The emphasis is on our own little family for the moment. We're buying a house in North Carolina, maybe somewhere near the mountains. I think it will be good for both of us to spend more time out of the city. I'm not sure that fierce competition and stress is particularly good for you, especially when we want to try for another baby.'

Tess was amazed to see Paula's face glow at the thought of it. Tess had always thought of Paula as a particularly hard creature but, in the end, it turned out she was just running away from her demons. It wasn't difficult to see what the trauma of having to deal with a disabled daughter would do to a young girl with no support network, but the endless acidic guilt of having abandoned her must have eaten away at her year after year. Perhaps Paula was harder than she had given her credit for, thought Tess as she excused herself and went to the bar for a martini. She took out the olives and knocked the drink back in one, steeling herself for what she had to do next.

'Ah, there you are.'

Turning, she saw Sean. 'What's up?' he said, his big green eyes searching hers.

Dammit, am I that transparent? Tess thought.

'Oh, nothing,' she replied dismissively. 'I just needed to speak to Leonard. Have you seen him?'

'He went back to Jewel Cay on the boat with my mom about ten minutes ago,' said Sean. 'Honey, are you okay?'

No, I'm not okay, she thought, averting her eyes. She had been unable to settle all day, debating over and over in her head whether to act on the information she had pieced together about Olivia Martin's disappearance. Her first instinct was to tell Meredith and let her sort it out; after all, that was her job, wasn't it? But then how would Meredith feel about her publicist accusing her brother of killing Olivia? And, assuming it was true, would she really want to know after all these years? More importantly, how would Sean feel about it? At best

522

it would create a family rift, at worst . . . well, she didn't want to think about that. Anyway, it wasn't as if Tess had any real proof about what happened on the night of Meredith and Howard's wedding and, even if she did, what real purpose would it serve to dredge up old secrets that would cause the family so much pain? Certainly it would not help Brooke and David, whose private lives she was being paid to protect. But – and this was what Tess kept coming back to again and again – what if this was *murder*? If Leonard had killed Olivia, how could she keep that secret to herself: just file it away under 'unpleasant truths'? She didn't know Olivia or her family, but she did know that if she had been in a similar situation, she would want to know the truth about her loved ones, even if it was difficult to bear. And that was the final twist, of course: Meredith had married Howard for social convention and companionship, but her heart had belonged to Olivia. Surely she would want to know what had really happened? But at what cost?

Tess forced a smile onto her face. 'Don't worry, I won't be long.'

She leant forward and kissed him on the lips. For one second, she wanted to wrap herself in his arms, tell him everything, let him help her. But that was a cop-out. This was something she had to do herself.

'Can I come to your room later?' he smiled lazily.

'I'll be waiting,' she said, hoping against hope that, by then, things would not have changed irrevocably.

Tess was the only person on the small boat ferrying guests to and from Jewel Cay. Sitting in the darkness, she watched the lights strung from the masts of the million-dollar yachts moored at the hotel's dock get smaller and smaller. The short journey across smooth waters still made her stomach churn; *maybe that martini was not such a good idea after all*, she thought, hopping onto the jetty. The house in front of her looked like a huge ghostly face – the glowing windows its eyes and nose, the double-fronted oak doors a gaping mouth, and suddenly Tess thought about taking the boat straight back to the hotel and climbing into bed with Sean.

Be brave, she scolded herself. *You're almost there.* A maid smiled as she opened the front door and pointed towards the east wing of the house. Tess could hear gentle classical music coming from the drawing room and, through the open doorway, could see Meredith and Rose and Robert Billington laughing over champagne. She moved away before anyone saw her: Leonard wasn't with them. Over the past twenty-four hours she had got to know the layout of Jewel Cay well, so she walked across to the other wing of the house. The corridors were dark, but light was spilling from the far room that Tess knew was Leonard's study. Quietly approaching, she peered around the door of the room, a hexagonal space with long windows and wood-panelled walls decorated with maps and nautical paintings. Her pulse jumped as she saw Leonard sitting behind a huge sea-captain's desk.

'Good heavens Tess,' he laughed. 'You did give me a fright!' He stood up to beckon her in. 'Come in, come in. Shouldn't you still be at the party? I thought we'd leave you youngsters to it.'

Tess smiled weakly, suddenly finding that she couldn't swallow as she looked at him. What made this worse was that she *liked* Leonard Carter.

'I have to ask you something, Leonard,' she said with more resolve than she felt. She moved a few feet further into the room but remained standing, still not wanting to get too close.

'I have to know what happened on the night of Meredith's wedding. I have to know what happened to Olivia Martin.'

His smile was rigid, but his tone remained light.

'Surely that's all water under the bridge,' he said. 'We all read the *Washington Spy* story, but it didn't have any impact – old news. Certainly the wedding is still going ahead tomorrow, which it wouldn't be if Wendell Billington believed a word of what was being alleged.'

'I know what happened, Leonard,' she said softly, forcing herself to meet his gaze.

His smile relaxed until his mouth was a thin line. 'No one knows, Tess,' he said. 'No one will ever know.'

'No one except you.'

'I don't know what you're talking about,' he replied airily.

'I think you do, Leonard,' insisted Tess. 'You'd do anything for family, isn't that what you told me once? Support them, protect them? Does that extend to killing for them?'

He put down his pen. The genial smile had now completely left his face.

'*Do what?*' he said, his eyes narrowing. 'How can you say such a thing, Tess? After everything this family has done for you.'

Tess could feel her fingernails pressing into her palms. Her resolve was wavering, but she had to go on.

'You were in the rose garden the night of Meredith's wedding, weren't you, Leonard?' she persisted. 'You had just had sex with Mary-Ann Henner and, when she left, you saw your sister and Olivia come into the rose garden. You overheard Olivia blackmailing Meredith.'

'This is nonsense!' he said, his voice angry and raised.

Tess heard a noise behind her and turned to see Meredith standing in the doorway, her face still. For a long moment, her eyes locked with Leonard's, then he looked away.

'Well, Leonard?' she said. 'Is she correct?' Meredith's voice was taut yet even, her eyes hard as flint.

'Of course she's not right. This is fantasy, supposition.'

Meredith closed the door to the study, the satin of her Valentino couture rustling as she walked slowly into the room. 'I want the truth, Leonard.'

Leonard sank back into his chair. 'It is the truth.'

His sister walked up to the desk and placed both hands on the dark wood.

'Tell me!' she hissed. 'Tell me now.'

For several long, painful moments, he just stared back at her. Finally he gave a tiny shrug and nodded.

'Yes, Mary-Ann and I were in the rose garden. She returned to the party but I stayed back to have a cigarette. You and Olivia came in, but I was sitting on the ground so you didn't see me. I heard you talking, and I heard how much money she wanted.'

His expression darkened. It was a few seconds before he continued.

'Olivia was a slut, Meredith,' he whispered. 'A few weeks earlier I found out that she had been sleeping with Howard. I tried to warn her off, but she just laughed at me. Then I saw her chatting up everything that moved at the wedding.'

'What happened, Leonard?'

He stood up and paced to the window, staring out at the blackness.

'I went to her cottage to talk to her, maybe even threaten her a little. I'd tried the softly, softly approach and where did that get me? So I told her she was a two-bit whore and she wouldn't get a penny out of us. But she was as high as a kite – she patted the bed and told me she wouldn't mind fucking me too.' He turned to look at Meredith. 'She said it turned her onto keep it in the family.'

'What did you do to her?' breathed Meredith heavily.

Leonard turned back to the window, staring at his own reflection in the black glass.

'I grabbed her. It was easy; I was so much bigger than her. Bitch tried to scratch me with her nails, so I held her down on the bed, my hands on her shoulders. Before I knew it they were around her neck. My two hands could wrap all the way around her neck. I kept squeezing, telling her to leave my sister alone. She was nodding or struggling, I couldn't tell which. Then she stopped.'

He turned back and looked from Meredith to Tess and back again. 'I only meant to scare her,' he said blankly.

Meredith's body was rigid as she leant on the desk. 'I loved her, Leonard,' she whispered.

Leonard spun round angrily. 'You loved her?' he sneered. 'You loved a slut who was blackmailing you?'

'Don't you dare!' screamed Meredith, sweeping a glass off the desk. 'Don't you dare try to justify this. You killed the woman I loved!'

Leonard looked his sister in the eye. 'I didn't want you to be . . . like that. You'd never have stopped paying her. With your money and with your heart, I was saving you from that. I was looking after you.'

'Looking after me?' said Meredith incredulously. 'When have I ever needed that?'

Leonard laughed mockingly. 'Oh, and you're always so careful, always so in control? Well, what about all those grubby little relationships you've had since, all those companions? Why do you think they have never come out? The inherent decency of dykes?' he spat. 'No, Meredith, I paid them all off.'

She glared at him and a single tear trickled down Meredith's cheek.

'Where did you put her body?' she asked, her fury and bitterness barely concealed. '*Where?*'

Leonard sat down heavily in his chair.

'I took her down to the river,' he said in a low, controlled voice. 'I threw her in. I did it for you, Meredith. I was *protecting* you.'

'You *murdered* her!' she howled, slamming her fist onto the leather top of the desk.

'I'm your brother. I just wanted to fix it.'

'Fix it? You ruined everything!'

Tess was frozen to the spot, wishing more than anything she was back in the safe, secure newsroom of the *Globe*, writing up this story, not witnessing it. She had come here to confront Leonard, to get the truth, but now she was intruding on some horrendous private tragedy. Just then Leonard pitched forward and she saw his hand grip the desk. Instantly she knew something was wrong. Even in the soft light of the study, Tess could see that the colour had bleached completely out of his face. He let out a strangled cry, his right-hand side shuddered, and his features contorted in agony. His body was beginning to slide down the leather of the chair. Tess jumped forward, trying to help him back up.

'Meredith, help me,' she grunted, but the older woman simply turned and walked out of the room, leaving Tess to pull Leonard's heavy body back into the chair as best she could. Leonard's mouth had drooped open, his limbs dangling at the sides of the chair, but his eyes looked alive and frightened. He tried to cry out but his voice sounded as if it had been filtered through a muffler.

Tess ran to the door. 'Help!' she screamed. 'Someone, please!'

Then she snatched up the desk phone and called 911, praying it was not too late.

Throughout the night, word spread quickly through the hotels and houses around Jewel Cay that the wedding between Brooke Asgill and David Billington had been called off. The area was packed with media who were there to cover the nuptials and, although the Billington security team had managed to cordon off the area opposite the Cay, few of the press missed the medical helicopter swooping down to the Carter house at around eleven p.m.

When news reports started circulating that Brooke Asgill had been taken seriously ill, Tess hastily arranged a press conference for seven a.m. the next morning to clear up the error.

By six thirty, there were at least one hundred and fifty journalists in the gardens of the Pelicano hotel, gathered around a hastily erected podium.

Tess rubbed her eyes and threw a petrol-strong espresso down her throat. After everything that had happened over the last eight hours, she should have been running off pure adrenaline, especially as she had uncovered the biggest story of her life; but sadness and concern for the family were weighing her down.

She watched the ripple of activity as Liz Asgill stepped up to the podium and pulled out a single sheet of paper from her pocket. She was so calm and composed, it was as if she was unaware of the scores of jostling, shouting reporters and film crews in front of her. With everyone in the family rattled, Liz was the perfect choice for reading the statement. *An earthquake couldn't unsettle her*, Tess thought. She'd heard the rumour that Liz was taking over from William as CEO of Asgill's and that seemed eminently fitting. Wasn't it John Donne who had written that 'No man is an island'? But not everyone needed someone, mused Tess, watching her. Some men – or women – just needed some*thing*, and Liz had the business. *I hope you'll both be very happy together*, she thought with a smile.

'Thank you all for coming, ladies and gentlemen,' began Liz, with the sincere tone of a seasoned politician. 'As you all probably know by now, the wedding between Brooke Asgill and David Billington has been postponed. I will now read a short statement from my sister and her fiancé: "Due to the hospitalization of Brooke's uncle, Leonard Carter, a few hours ago, we have decided that it is not appropriate for the wedding to proceed as scheduled. We thank you for your good wishes and wish Leonard a speedy recovery."'

Liz looked out at the sea of expectant faces. 'Questions?' she said.

A pushy blonde with a microphone stood up. 'Is the wedding postponed or off altogether?'

Liz shot her a withering look. 'Postponed.'

A tall man in a loud tie waved a notebook. 'Is the rumour true that Leonard Carter was attacked by a member of his family?'

Tess laughed quietly.

'Absolutely not,' said Liz with the right note of surprise and disapproval. 'Unfortunately my uncle has not been in the best of health lately. I can't say anything more at the present, but his condition is stable.'

Suddenly a dozen questions were being shouted out at once. Liz calmly raised a hand. 'No more questions, please. Both the Asgill and Billington families would be grateful if you'd respect their privacy at this time.'

Tess slipped off as quietly as she could. There was little point staying at the Pelicano, where journalists would persist in asking questions she could not answer. She caught the ferry back across to Jewel Cay and was shown up to the master bedroom. There Tess found Brooke on the balcony, gazing out onto the azure ocean.

When she heard Tess approach, she turned, and Tess could see that her eyes were red-rimmed from crying. She walked back into the bedroom and began packing her beautiful clothes into brown Louis Vuitton trunks.

'Is it done?'

Tess nodded, then looked around. 'Where's David?'

'He's at the house where his brother is staying,' she said, not looking up.

Tess examined Brooke's face. 'The wedding's not postponed, is it?' she said quietly.

Brooke shook her head, then glanced up at Tess. 'I told him. About Matt.'

'Oh Brooke . . .'

'It's over,' she continued, 'but we'll let people know that when the dust settles.'

'I'm sorry. Sorry about David. Sorry that Matt didn't turn out to be the person you thought he was.'

Brooke finally met Tess's gaze. 'I didn't break up with David because of Matt,' she said. 'I broke up because of me.'

Tess frowned. 'Hang on, *you* broke up with *him*?'

'I suddenly realized that I'm not going to be happy with David, or Matt, or anyone, before I'm happy with myself,' she said, sitting down on the bed. 'With David, I was smothered, forced into a role I didn't want to play. Everyone expected so much from David, but no one expected anything from me – except to be the wife, seen and not heard.'

'Thousands of girls would swap with you, Brooke,' said Tess with a wry smile.

'Why does everyone keep telling me that?' she laughed. 'And maybe in the past I would have been happy with that too. But things have changed this year; *I've* changed this year. Discovering Eileen Dunne's book, seeing it at the top of the *New York Times* best-seller list, flying to Hollywood: Tess, I think this is just the start of things. I'm not ready to be a part of someone else, I'm just beginning to be me.'

'But I really thought you loved each other,' said Tess sadly.

Brooke smiled at the thought. 'I think what I had with David was like winning the lottery and finding out your numbers had been for the wrong week. Love isn't enough to make the relationship work – there're too many other factors. Family, ambition—'

'Lust . . .'

They both laughed. Brooke reached over and took Tess's hands. 'You've been a good friend to me, Tess, so thank you, thanks for everything,' she said, her eyes sparkling with tears.

'It'll all work out,' said Tess quietly, realizing how much she was going to miss her.

Brooke nodded. 'I know. I feel free, Tess. I feel free. And that's all the happy ending I need.'

Tess walked out barefoot onto the beach, passing the empty marquee, the canvas flapping disconsolately in the gentle breeze. As she walked, she let her mind run back over the last ten months; all that excitement, all that drama and glamour – and it had all come to this. She had no job, no secure home, and – as the wedding hadn't happened – no bonus. Meredith had merely whispered 'thank you' before retreating back to her room before the press conference that morning. Tess hadn't been sure if it was heartfelt or loaded with irony. Either way, it didn't really matter. She couldn't stay working for the Asgills. And the reason for that was right in front of her, sitting on the sand near where the waves lapped onto the shore. Sean. Her heart leapt just a little when she saw him and she thought of his words just twenty-four hours earlier: 'Come back with me.'

She doubted the offer still stood. She wondered whether he would hate her for the damage she had caused to his family. Well, she would return to London anyway, she decided suddenly. If Sean Asgill was one of the pieces of her life that had been missing, then she knew that her home – and maybe even her own family, her mother – was part of the rest. She walked slowly over to where he was sitting, holding a drink that looked suspiciously alcoholic.

'Hi, how was the hospital?' she asked nervously.

He squinted up at her. 'I think they categorized Leonard's stroke as massive.'

Tess's heart sank. 'What does that mean?' she asked.

'I think it will be a few hours before the doctors work out how extensive the damage is. They're doing tests to see if there is permanent brain damage. He's certainly paralysed down his right-hand side, but there's some signs of speech and they think there's a chance he may walk again.'

'Oh God, Sean, I'm so sorry.'

Sean nodded, his eyes fixed on the horizon. 'Yeah, my mom told me what happened in the study.'

He took a slug of his drink and looked at her. 'My mother is going to tell the Louisiana police what he said, but who knows what will happen then. I guess it depends whether Leonard wants to confess again – whether he *can* confess again. I expect the police will want to speak to you about that, anyway.'

Tess rubbed her eyes. 'Perhaps he's had punishment enough.'

Sean looked into her eyes. 'You know, back in the hospital, there were some moments when I hated you.'

Tess held her breath. She could feel the sun burning her skin, but she dared not move. Sean picked up a pebble and threw it towards the waves.

'I kept asking myself what I would have done if I'd been in your shoes.'

Her heart was pounding now.

'And the truth is, I would have done the same,' said Sean slowly. 'As much as I care for my uncle, however much you wish something wasn't true, Leonard killed someone. Sure, it was all those years ago and I think I can understand his motivation – wanting to protect Mom, I guess – but it was still wrong. And whatever has happened, you're not to blame for any of it.'

He took a sip of his drink, which Tess took out of his hand. 'You don't need that,' she whispered.

'No, I need you,' he said, pulling her close and stroking her lips with a kiss.

Tess squeezed him as tightly as she could, happiness mixed with relief. He stroked her neck and she winced.

'Shit, you're as red as a lobster,' he said, looking at her burning skin. 'Come on, let's get you in the shade. I'm not sure you limeys are built for this climate.'

They walked slowly along the shore. 'Talking of which, are you going to stay in New York? I mean, I guess your job is done, isn't it?'

Tess smiled. 'Well, when I thought you were going to dump me, I had decided I was going home, but I think I'm officially homeless,' she said with a slow grin. 'I've no job. I've got two journalists on a year-long tenancy in my Battersea apartment and no family to speak of . . . well, not yet, anyway.'

'It just so happens there's a hot new PR consultancy starting in

London very shortly,' said Sean. 'I think you know the CEO. I hear he needs an assistant.'

'*Assistant*,' she scoffed with a laugh. 'We'll be talking director of PR at the very least. Although have you seen my CV lately? Disaster follows me wherever I go.'

'I know,' he sighed dramatically, 'but you've got to start somewhere in the big, bad city. The pay's awful but there's a rent-free flat thrown in. You'll have a roommate, but I hear he's a devilishly handsome young fellow.'

The peach morning sun emerged from behind a bubble of brilliant white cloud, and suddenly Tess felt the warmth and light wash over her. 'In that case, I'll think about it,' she smiled, and they walked hand in hand back towards the house.